'Rankin weaves his plot with a menacing ease . . . His prose is understated, yet his canvas of Scotland's criminal underclass has a panoramic breadth. His ear for dialogue is as sharp as a switchblade. This is, quite simply, crime writing of the highest order'
Daily Telegraph

'A series that shows no signs of flagging . . . Assured, sympathetic to contemporary foibles, humanistic, this is more than just a police procedural as the character of Rebus grows in moral stature . . . Rankin is the head capo of the MacMafia' *Time Out*

'Rankin has followed one success with another. Sardonic and assured, the novel has a powerful and well-paced narrative. What is striking is the way Rankin uses his laconic prose as a literary paint stripper, scouring away pretensions to reveal the unwholesome reality beneath' *Independent*

'Rankin strips Edinburgh's polite façade to its gritty skeleton' *The Times*

'A teeming Ellroy-esque evocation of life at the sharp end in modern Scotland . . . Rankin is the finest Scottish crime writer to emerge since William McIIvanney' *GQ*

'Rebus resurgent . . . a brilliantly meshed plot which delivers on every count on its way to a conclusion as unexpected as it is inevitable. Eleventh in the series. Still making waves' *Literary Review*

'His fiction buzzes with energy . . . Essentially, he is a romantic storyteller in the tradition of Robert Louis Stevenson . . . His prose is as vivid and terse as the next man's yet its flexibility and rhythm give it potential for lyrical expression which is distinctly Rankin's own' *Scotland on Sunday*

'Top notch . . . the bleakness is unrelenting, but it quite suits Mr Rankin who does his best work in the dark' *New York Times*

'The internal police politics and corruption in high places are both portrayed with bone-freezing accuracy. This novel should come with a wind-chill factor warning' *Daily Telegraph*

'Detective Inspector Rebus makes the old-style detectives with their gentle or bookish backgrounds, Alleyn, Morse, Dalgliesh, look like wimps . . . Rankin is brilliant at conveying the genuine stench of seedy places on the dark side of Scotland' *Sunday Telegraph*

'It's the banter and energy, the immense carnival of scenes and charaters, voices and moods that set Rankin apart. His stories are like a transmission forever in the red zone, at the edge of burnout. This is crime fiction at its best' *Washington Post*

Born in the Kingdom of Fife in 1960, Ian Rankin graduated from the University of Edinburgh in 1982, and then spent three years writing novels when he was supposed to be working towards a PhD in Scottish Literature. His first Rebus novel, *Knots & Crosses*, was published in 1987, and the Rebus books are now translated into over thirty languages and are bestsellers worldwide.

Ian Rankin has been elected a Hawthornden Fellow, and is also a past winner of the Chandler-Fulbright Award. He is the recipient of four Crime Writers' Association Dagger Awards including the prestigious Diamond Dagger in 2005 and in 2009 was inducted into the CWA Hall of Fame. In 2004, Ian won America's celebrated Edgar award for *Resurrection Men*. He has also been shortlisted for the Anthony Awards in the USA, and won Denmark's *Palle Rosenkrantz* Prize, the French *Grand Prix du Roman Noir* and the *Deutscher Krimipreis*. Ian Rankin is also the recipient of honorary degrees from the universities of Abertay, St Andrews, Edinburgh, Hull and the Open University.

A contributor to BBC2's *Newsnight Review*, he also presented his own TV series, *Ian Rankin's Evil Thoughts*. He has received the OBE for services to literature, opting to receive the prize in his home city of Edinburgh. He has also recently been appointed to the rank of Deputy Lieutenant of Edinburgh, where he lives with his partner and two sons. Visit his website at www.ianrankin.net.

By Ian Rankin

All Ian Rankin's titles are available on audio.
Also available: *Jackie Leven Said* by Ian Rankin and Jackie Leven.

IAN RANKIN

Tooth & Nail

StripJack

Tooth & Nail
First published in Great Britain by Century
under the title *Wolfman* in 1992

Strip Jack
First published in Great Britain by Orion in 1992

This omnibus edition published in 2010
by Orion Books Ltd
Orion House, 5 Upper St Martin's Lane
London WC2H 9EA

An Hachette UK company

A CIP catalogue record for this book is available
from the British Library.

2

ISBN 9781407230191

Printed in Great Britain by Clays Ltd, St Ives plc

www.orionbooks.co.uk

Tooth & Nail

'How many wolves do we feel on our heels,
while our real enemies go in sheepskin'

Malcolm Lowry, *Under the Volcano*

Prologue

She drives home the knife.

The moment, she knows from past experience, is a very intimate one. Her hand is gripped around the knife's cool handle and the thrust takes the blade into the throat up to the hilt until her hand meets the throat itself. Flesh upon flesh. Jacket first, or woollen jersey, cotton shirt or T-shirt, then flesh. Now rent. The knife is writhing, like an animal sniffing. Warm blood covering hilt and hand. (The other hand covers the mouth, stifling screams.) The moment is complete. A meeting. Touching. The body is hot, gaping, warm with blood. Seething inside, as insides become outsides. Boiling. The moment is coming to an end all too soon.

And still she feels hungry. It isn't right, isn't usual, but she does. She removes some of the clothing; in fact, removes quite a lot of it, removes more, perhaps, than is necessary. And she does what she must do, the knife squirming again. She keeps her eyes screwed tightly shut. She does not like this part. She has never liked this part, not then, not now. But especially not *then*.

Finally, she brings out her teeth and sinks them into the white stomach, until they grind together in a satisfying bite, and whispers, as she always does, the same four words.

'It's only a game.'

* * *

It is evening when George Flight gets the call. Sunday evening. Sunday should be his blessed relief, beef and Yorkshires, feet up in front of the television, papers falling from his lap. But he's had a feeling all day. In the pub at lunchtime he'd felt it, a wriggling in his gut like there were worms in there, tiny blind white worms, hungry worms, worms he could not hope to satisfy. He knew what they were and they knew what they were. And then he'd won third prize in the pub raffle: a three-foot high orange and white teddy bear. Even the worms had laughed at him then and he'd known the day would end badly.

As it was doing now, the phone as insistent as last orders. Ringing with whatever bad news couldn't wait until the morning shift. He knew what it meant of course. Hadn't he been expecting it these past weeks? But still he was reluctant to pick up the receiver. At last he did.

'Flight speaking.'

'There's been another one, sir. The Wolfman. He's done another.'

Flight stared at the silent television. Highlights of the previous day's rugby match. Grown men running after a funny-shaped ball as though their lives depended on it. It was only a bloody game after all. And propped up against the side of the TV that smirking prize, the teddy bear. What the hell could he do with a teddy bear?

'Okay,' he said, 'just tell me where ...'

'After all, it *is* only a game.'

Rebus smiled and nodded at the Englishman across the table. Then he stared out of the window, pretending once more to be interested in the blur of dark scenery. If the Englishman had said it once, he had said it a dozen times. And during the trip, he had said little else. He also kept stealing precious legroom from Rebus, while his collection of empty beer cans was creeping across the table, invading

2

Rebus's space, pushing against the neatly folded stack of newspapers and magazines.

'Tickets, please!' yelled the guard from the other end of the carriage.

So, with a sigh, and for the third time since leaving Edinburgh, Rebus sought out his ticket. It was never where he thought it was. At Berwick, he'd thought it was in his shirt pocket. It was in the outer top pocket of his Harris tweed jacket. Then at Durham he'd looked for it in his jacket, only to find it beneath one of the magazines on the table. Now, ten minutes out of Peterborough, it had moved to the back pocket of his trousers. He retrieved it, and waited for the guard to make his way forward.

The Englishman's ticket was where it had always been: half-hidden beneath a beer can. Rebus, although he knew every word almost by heart, glanced again at the back page of one of his Sunday papers. He had kept it to the top of the pile for no reason other than a sense of devilment, enjoying the thick black letters of the headline – SCOTS WHA HAE! – beneath which was printed the story of the previous day's Calcutta Cup clash at Murrayfield. And a clash it had been: no day for weak stomachs, but a day for stout hearts and determination. The Scots had triumphed by thirteen points to ten, and now here Rebus was on a late evening Sunday train packed with disappointed English rugby supporters, heading towards London.

London. Never one of Rebus's favourite places. Not that he was a frequent visitor. But this was not pleasure. This was strictly business, and as a representative of the Lothian and Borders Police, he was to be on best behaviour. Or, as his boss had put it so succinctly, 'No fuck-ups, John.'

Well, he would do his best. Not that he reckoned there was much he *could* do, right or wrong. But he would do what he could. And if that meant wearing a clean shirt and tie, polished shoes and a respectable jacket, then so be it.

3

'All tickets, please.'

Rebus handed over his ticket. Somewhere in the corridor up ahead, in the no-man's-land of the buffet car between first and second class, a few voices were raised in a verse of Blake's *Jerusalem*. The Englishman across from Rebus smiled.

'Only a game,' he said to the tins in front of him. 'Only a game.'

The train pulled in to King's Cross five minutes late. It was a quarter past eleven. Rebus was in no hurry. A hotel room had been booked for him in central London, courtesy of the Metropolitan Police. He carried a typed list of notes and directions in his jacket pocket, again sent up from London. He had not brought much luggage with him, feeling that the courtesy of the Met would extend only so far. He expected the trip to last two or three days at most, after which time even they would realise, surely, that he was not going to be of much help to them in their investigations. So: one small suitcase, one sports bag and one briefcase. The suitcase contained two suits, a change of shoes, several pairs of socks and underpants and two shirts (with matching ties). In the sports bag were a small washbag, towel, two paperback novels (one partly read), a travel alarm clock, a thirty-five millimetre camera with flashgun and film, a T-shirt, retractable umbrella, sunglasses, transistor radio, diary, Bible, a bottle containing ninety-seven paracetamol tablets and another bottle (protected by the T-shirt) containing best Islay malt whisky.

The bare essentials, in other words. The briefcase contained notepad, pens, a personal tape recorder, some blank tapes and prerecorded tapes and a thick manila file filled with photocopied sheets of Metropolitan Police paper, ten-by-eight inch colour photographs held together in a small ring-binder affair and newspaper clippings. On the

4

front of this file was a white sticky label with one word typed upon it. The word was WOLFMAN.

Rebus was in no hurry. The night – what was left of it – was his. He had to attend a meeting at ten on Monday morning, but his first night in the capital city could be spent however he chose. He thought he would probably choose to spend it in his hotel room. He waited in his seat until the other passengers had left the train, then slid his bag and briefcase from the luggage rack and made for the sliding door to the carriage, beside which, in another luggage rack, sat his suitcase. Manoeuvring these out of the train door and onto the platform, he paused for a moment and breathed in. The smell was not quite like any other railway station. Certainly it was not like Waverley Station in Edinburgh. The air wasn't quite foetid, but it did seem to Rebus somehow overused and tired. He felt suddenly fatigued. And there was something else in his nostrils, something sweet and revolting at the same time. He couldn't quite think what it reminded him of.

On the concourse, instead of making directly for the Underground, he wandered over to a bookstall. There he purchased an A–Z of London, slipping it into his briefcase. The next morning's editions were just arriving, but he ignored them. This was Sunday, not Monday. Sunday was the Lord's day, which was perhaps why he had packed a Bible along with his other possessions. He hadn't been to a church service in weeks … maybe even months. Not since he'd tried the Cathedral on Palmerston Place in fact. It had been a nice place, light and bright, but too far from his home to make for a viable proposition. And besides, it was still organised religion and he had not lost his mistrust of organised religion. If anything, he was warier these days than ever before. He was also hungry. Perhaps he would grab a bite on the way to the hotel….

He passed two women having an animated discussion.

5

'I heard it on the radio just twenty minutes ago.'

'Done another, has he?'

'That's what they're saying.'

The woman shivered. 'Don't bear thinking about. Did they say it was definitely him?'

'Not definitely, but you just know, don't you?'

There was a truth in that. So, Rebus had arrived in time for another small piece of the drama to unfold around him. Another murder, making four in all. Four in the space of three months. He was a busy little man, this killer they had named the Wolfman. They had named him the Wolfman and then they had sent word to Rebus's boss. Lend us your man, they had said. Let's see what he can do. Rebus's boss, Chief Superintendent Watson, had handed the letter over to him.

'Better take some silver bullets with you, John,' he had said. 'It looks like you're their only hope.' And then he had chuckled, knowing as well as Rebus knew himself that he could be of little help in the case. But Rebus had gnawed on his bottom lip, silent in front of his desk-bound superior. He would do what he could. He would do *everything* he could. Until they saw through him and sent him back home.

Besides, perhaps he needed the break. Watson seemed glad to be rid of him, too.

'If nothing else, it'll keep us out of one another's hair for a while.'

The Chief Superintendent, an Aberdonian, had earned the nickname 'Farmer Watson', a nickname every police officer beneath him in Edinburgh understood. But then one day Rebus, a nip of malt too many beneath his belt, had blurted out the nickname in front of Watson himself, since when he had found himself assigned to more than his fair share of tedious details, desk jobs, lookouts and training courses.

Training courses! At least Watson had a sense of humour. The most recent had been termed 'Management for Senior Officers' and had been a minor disaster – all psychology and how to be nice to junior officers. How to *involve* them, how to *motivate* them, how to *relate* to them. Rebus had returned to his station and tried it for one day, a day of involving, of motivating, of relating. At the end of the day, a DC had slapped a hand onto Rebus's back, smiling.

'Bloody hard work today, John. But I've enjoyed it.'

'Take your hand off my fucking back,' Rebus had snarled. 'And don't call me John.'

The DC's mouth fell open. 'But you said …' he began, but didn't bother finishing. The brief holiday was over. Rebus had tried being a manager. Tried it and loathed it.

He was halfway down the steps to the Underground when he stopped, put down his suitcase and briefcase, pulled open the zip on his sports bag and found the transistor radio. Switching it on, he held it to his ear with one hand while the other turned the tuning dial. Eventually, he found a news bulletin, listening as the other travellers passed him, a few of them staring, but mostly ignoring him. At last he heard what he had been waiting for, then switched off the radio and threw it back into the sports bag. Now, he released the two catches on his briefcase and brought out the A-Z. Flipping through the pages of street names at the back, he remembered just how large London really was. Large and populous. Something like ten million, was it? Wasn't that twice the population of Scotland? It didn't bear thinking about. Ten million souls.

'Ten million and one,' Rebus whispered to himself, finding the name he had been looking for.

The Chamber of Horrors

'Not a pretty sight.'

Looking around him, Detective Inspector George Flight wondered whether the sergeant had been referring to the body or to the surrounding area. You could say what you liked about the Wolfman, he wasn't choosy about his turf. This time it was a riverside path. Not that Flight had ever really thought of the Lea as a 'river'. It was a place where supermarket trolleys came to die, a dank stretch of water bordered on one side by marshland and on the other by industrial sites and lo-rise housing. Apparently you could walk the course of the Lea from the Thames to up past Edmonton. The narrow river ran like a mottled black vein from east central London to the most northerly reaches of the capital and beyond. The vast majority of Londoners didn't even know it existed.

George Flight knew about it though. He had been brought up in Tottenham Hale, not far from the Lea. His father had fished on the Navigation section, between Stonebridge and Tottenham Locks. When he was young he had played football on the marshes, smoked illicit cigarettes in the long grass with his gang, fumbled with a blouse or a brassiere on the wasteland just across the river from where he now stood.

He had walked along this path. It was popular on warm Sunday afternoons. There were riverside pubs where you could stand outside supping a pint and watching the Sunday sailors plying their crafts, but at night, only the drunk, the reckless and the brave would use the quiet and ill-lit path. The drunk, the reckless, the brave ... and the locals. Jean Cooper was a local. Ever since the separation from her husband, she had lived with her sister in a small, recently-built estate just off the towpath. She worked in an off-licence on Lea Bridge Road, and finished work at seven. The riverside path was a quick route home.

Her body had been found at nine forty-five by a couple of young lads on their way to one of the pubs. They had run back to Lea Bridge Road and flagged down a passing police car. The operation thereafter had about it a fluid, easy movement. The police doctor arrived, to be met by detectives from Stoke Newington police station, who, recognising the *modus operandi*, contacted Flight.

By the time he arrived, the scene was organised but busy. The body had been identified, questions asked of nearby residents, the sister found. Scene of Crime Officers were in discussion with a couple of people from Forensics. The area around the body had been cordoned off and nobody crossed the tape without first of all donning polythene cover-alls for their feet and hair. Two photographers were busy taking flash photographs under portable lighting powered by a nearby generator. And next to the generator stood an operations van, where another photographer was trying to fix his jammed video camera.

'It's these cheap tapes,' he complained. 'They look like a bargain when you buy them, but then halfway through you find there's a twist or a snag in them.'

'So don't buy cheap tapes,' Flight had advised.

'Thank you, Sherlock,' had been the cameraman's ill-meant response, before once again cursing the tapes, the seller of the tapes and the seller's market stall in Brick Lane. He'd only bought the tapes that day.

Meantime, having discussed their plan of attack, the forensic scientists moved in towards the body armed with sticky tape, scissors and a pile of large polythene bags. Then, with extraordinary care, they began to 'tape' the body in the hope of lifting hairs and fibres from the clothing. Flight watched them from a distance. The portable lights cast a garish white glow over the scene, so that, standing further back in unlit gloom, Flight felt a bit like someone in a theatre, watching a distant play unfold. By God, you had to have patience for a job like this. Everything had to be done by the book and had to be done in meticulous detail. He hadn't gone near the body yet himself. His chance would come later. Perhaps much later.

The wailing started again. It was coming from a police Ford Sierra parked on Lea Bridge Road. Jean Cooper's sister, being comforted in the back of the car by a WPC, being told to drink the hot sweet tea, knowing she would never see her sister alive again. But this was not the worst. Flight knew the worst was still to come, when the sister would formally identify Jean's body in the mortuary.

Jean Cooper had been easy enough to identify. Her handbag lay beside her on the path apparently untouched. In it were letters and house keys with an address tag attached. Flight couldn't help thinking about those house keys. It wasn't very clever to put your address on your keys, was it? A bit late for that now though. A bit late for crime prevention. The crying started again, a long plaintive howl, reaching into the orange glow of the sky above the River Lea and its marshes.

Flight looked towards the body, then retraced the route Jean had taken from Lea Bridge Road. She had walked less than fifty yards before being attacked. Fifty yards from a well-lit and busy main thoroughfare, less than twenty from the back of a row of flats. But this section of path depended for light upon a street lamp which was broken (the council would probably get round to fixing it now) and from whatever illumination was given from the windows of the

10

flats. It was dark enough for the purpose all right. Dark enough for murder most foul.

He couldn't be sure that the Wolfman was responsible, not completely and utterly sure at this early stage. But he could feel it, like a numbing injection in his bones. The terrain was right. The stab wounds reported to him seemed right. And the Wolfman had been quiet for just under three weeks. Three weeks during which the trail had gone stone cold, as cold as a canal path. The Wolfman had taken a risk this time however, striking in late evening instead of at the dead of night. Someone might have seen him. The need for a rapid escape might have led him to leave a clue. Please, God, let him have left a clue. Flight rubbed at his stomach. The worms were gone, consumed by acid. He felt calm, utterly calm, for the first time in days.

'Excuse me.' The voice was muffled, and Flight half-turned to let the diver past him. This diver was followed by another, both of them holding powerful torches. Flight did not envy the police frogmen their job. The river was dark and poisonous, chilled and most probably the consistency of soup. But it had to be searched now. If the killer had dropped something into the Lea by mistake, or had thrown his knife into the river, it had to be recovered as soon as possible. Silt or shifting rubbish might cover it before daybreak. Simply, they couldn't afford the time. And so he had ordered a search just after hearing the news, before he had even left his warm and comfortable home to hurry to the scene. His wife had patted him on the arm. 'Try not to be late.' Both knew the words were meaningless.

He watched the first frogman slip into the water and stared entranced as the water began to glow from the torchlight. The second diver followed the first into the water and disappeared from view. Flight checked the sky. A thick layer of cloud lay still and silent above him. The weather report was for early morning rain. It would dissolve footprints and wash fibres, bloodstains and hair into the hard-packed soil of the path. With any luck, they would complete the initial scene of crime work without the need for plastic tents.

'George!'

Flight turned to greet the newcomer. The man was in his mid-fifties, tall with cadaverous features lit up by a wide grin, or as wide as the long and narrow face would allow. He carried a large black bag in his left hand, and stretched out his right for Flight to shake. By his side walked a handsome woman of Flight's own age. In fact, as far as he could recall she was exactly one month and a day younger than him. Her name was Isobel Penny, and she was, in a euphemistic phrase, the cadaverous man's 'assistant' and 'secretary'. That they had been sleeping together these past eight or nine years was something nobody really discussed, though Isobel had told Flight all about it, for no other reason than that they had been in the same class together at school and had kept in touch with one another ever since.

'Hello, Philip,' said Flight, shaking the pathologist's hand.

Philip Cousins was not just a Home Office pathologist: he was by far the *best* Home Office pathologist, with a reputation resulting from twenty-five years' worth of work, twenty-five years during which, to Flight's knowledge, the man had never once 'got it wrong'. Cousins's eye for detail and his sheer bloody doggedness had seen him crack, or help crack, several dozen murder investigations, ranging from stranglings in Streatham to the poisoning of a government official in the West Indies. People who did not know him said that he looked the part, with his dark blue suits and cold grey features. They could not know about his quick and ready humour, his kindness, or the way he thrilled student doctors at his packed lectures. Flight had attended one of those lectures, something to do with arterial sclerosis and hadn't laughed so much in years.

'I thought you two were in Africa,' he said now, pecking Isobel on the cheek by way of greeting.

Cousins sighed. 'We were, but Penny got homesick.' He always called her by her surname. She gave him a playful thump on his forearm.

'You liar!' Then she turned her pale blue eyes to Flight. 'It was Philip,' she said. 'He couldn't bear to be away from his corpses. The first decent holiday we've had in years and he says he's *bored*. Can you believe that, George?'

Flight smiled and shook his head. 'Well, I'm glad you were able to make it. Looks like another victim of the Wolfman.'

Cousins looked over Flight's shoulder towards where the photographers were still photographing, the crouched scientists still sticky-taping, like so many flies about to settle on the corpse. He had examined the first three Wolfman victims, and that sort of continuity helped in a case. It wasn't just that he would know what to look for, what marks were indicative of the Wolfman; he would also spot anything not in keeping with the other killings, anything that might hint at a change of *modus operandi*: a different weapon, say, or a new angle of attack. Flight's mental picture of the Wolfman was coming together piece by tiny piece, but Cousins was the man who could show him where those pieces fitted.

'Inspector Flight?'

'Yes?' A man in a tweed jacket was approaching, carrying several cases and trailing a uniformed constable behind him. He placed the bags on the ground and introduced himself.

'John Rebus.' Flight's face remained blank. 'Inspector John Rebus.' The hand shot out, and Flight accepted it, feeling his grip strongly returned.

'Ah yes,' he said. 'Just arrived, have you?' He glanced meaningfully towards the bags. 'We weren't expecting you until tomorrow, Inspector.'

'Well, I got into King's Cross and heard about …' Rebus nodded towards the illuminated towpath. 'So I thought I'd come straight over.'

Flight nodded, trying to appear preoccupied. In fact, he was playing for time while he tried to come to grips with the Scotsman's thick accent. One of the forensic scientists had risen from his squatting position and was coming towards the group.

'Hello, Dr Cousins,' he said, before turning to Flight. 'We're pretty much finished if Dr Cousins wants to take a look.' Flight turned to Philip Cousins, who nodded gravely.

'Come on, Penny.'

Flight was about to follow them, when he remembered the new arrival. He turned back to John Rebus, his eyes immediately drifting down from Rebus's face to his loud and rustic jacket. He looked like something out of *Dr Finlay's Casebook*. Certainly, he looked out of place on this urban towpath at the dead of night.

'Do you want to take a look?' Flight asked generously. He watched as Rebus nodded without enthusiasm. 'Okay, leave your bags where they are then.'

The two men started forward together, Cousins and Isobel a couple of yards in front. Flight pointed towards them. 'Dr Philip Cousins,' he said. 'You've probably heard of him.' But Rebus shook his head slowly. Flight stared at him as though Rebus had just failed to pick out the Queen from a row of postage stamps. 'Oh,' he said coldly. Then, pointing again: 'And that's Isobel Penny, Dr Cousins's assistant.'

Hearing her name, Isobel turned her head back and smiled. She had an attractive face, round and girl-like with a shiny glow to her cheeks. Physically, she was the antithesis of her companion. Though tall, she was well-built – what Rebus's father might have called big boned – and she boasted a healthy complexion to balance Cousins's sickly colour. Rebus couldn't recall ever having seen a really healthy looking pathologist. He put it down to all the time they spent standing under artificial light.

They had reached the body. The first thing Rebus saw was someone aiming a video camera towards him. But the camera moved away again to focus on the corpse. Flight was in conversation with one of the forensics team. Neither looked at the other's face, but concentrated instead on the strips of tape which had been carefully lifted from the corpse and which the scientist now held.

'Yes,' said Flight, 'no need to send them to the lab yet. We'll do another taping at the mortuary.' The man nodded and moved away. There was a noise from the river and Rebus turned to watch as a frogman broke the surface, looked around him, and then dived again. He knew a place like this in Edinburgh, a canal running through the west of the city, between parks and breweries and stretches of nothingness. He'd had to investigate a murder there once, the battered body of a tramp found beneath a road bridge, one foot in the canal. The killer had been easy to find: another tramp, an argument over a can of cider. The court had settled for manslaughter, but it hadn't been manslaughter. It had been murder. Rebus would never forget that.

'I think we should wrap those hands up right away,' Dr Cousins was saying in a rich Home Counties voice. 'I'll have a good look at them at the mortuary.'

'Right you are,' said Flight, going off to fetch some more polythene bags. Rebus watched the pathologist at work. He held a small tape recorder in one hand and talked into it from time to time. Isobel Penny meantime had produced a sketch-pad, and was drawing a picture of the body.

'Poor woman was probably dead before she hit the

15

ground,' Cousins was saying. 'Little signs of bruising. Hypostasis seems consistent with the terrain. I'd say she certainly died on this spot.'

By the time Flight returned with some bags, Cousins, watched intermittently by Rebus, had taken readings of the air temperature and of internal temperature. The path on which they all stood was long and reasonably straight. The killer would have had ample visual warning of any approach. At the same time, there were homes and a main road nearby, so any screams would surely have been heard. Tomorrow there would be house-to-house enquiries. The path near the body was littered with rubbish: rusting drinks cans, crisp packets, sweet wrappers, torn and faded sheets of newsprint. In the river itself floated more rubbish and the red handle of a supermarket shopping-trolley broke the surface. Another diver had appeared, head and shoulders bobbing above the water. Where the main road crossed over the river, a crowd had gathered on the bridge, looking down towards the murder scene. Uniformed officers were doing their best to move the sightseers on, cordoning off as much of the area as they could.

'From the marks on the legs, dirt, some grazing and bruising,' continued the voice, 'I would say the victim fell to the ground or was pushed or lowered to the ground on her front. Only later was she turned over.' Dr Cousins's voice was level, disinterested. Rebus took in a few deep breaths and decided he had postponed the inevitable long enough. He had only come here to show willing, to show that he wasn't in London on a joyride. But now that he was here he supposed he should take a good close look at the body for himself. He turned away from the canal, the frogmen, the sightseers, and all the police officers standing behind the cordon. He turned away from the sight of his baggage standing all alone at the end of the path and gazed down on the corpse.

She was lying on her back, arms by her sides, legs together. Her tights and knickers had been pulled down to knee level, but her skirt was covering her, though he could see it was rucked up at the back. Her bright ski-style jacket was unzipped and her blouse had been ripped open, though her bra was intact. She had long straight black hair and wore large circlet earrings. Her face might have been pretty a few years ago, but life had ravaged it, leaving its marks. The killer had left marks, too. There was blood smeared across the face and matting the hair. The source of the blood was a gaping hole in the woman's throat. But there was also blood lying beneath her, spreading out from under the skirt.

'Turning her over,' said Dr Cousins to his tape recorder. He did so, with Flight's help, and then lifted the woman's hair away from the nape of her neck. 'Puncture wound,' he said into his tape recorder, 'consistent with larger wound to the throat. An exit wound, I'd say.'

But Rebus wasn't really listening to the doctor any longer. He was staring in horror at where the woman's skirt was rucked up. There was blood on the body, a lot of blood, staining the small of the back, the buttocks, the tops of the thighs. From the reports in his briefcase, he knew the cause of all this blood, but that didn't make it any easier to face the reality of it, the cold clear horror of it all. He took in more deep breaths. He had never yet vomited at a murder scene and he wasn't about to start now.

'No fuck-ups,' his boss had told him. It was a matter of pride. But Rebus knew now that the purpose of his trip to London was very serious indeed. It wasn't to do with 'pride' or 'putting up a good show' or 'doing his best'. It was to do with catching a pervert, a horrifically brutal sadist, and doing so before he could strike again. And if it took silver bullets, by God silver bullets there would be.

* * *

17

Rebus was still shaking when, at the operations van, someone handed him a plastic beaker of tea.

'Thanks.'

He could always blame his gooseflesh on the cold. Not that it was cold, not really. The cloud cover helped and there was no wind. Of course, London was usually a few degrees warmer than Edinburgh at any time of year and there wasn't the same wind, that bitter and biting wind which whipped across the streets of Edinburgh in summer as well as winter. In fact, if Rebus were asked to describe the weather on this night, the word he would use would be balmy.

He closed his eyes for a moment, not tired, just trying to shut out the sight of Jean Cooper's cooling body. But she seemed etched onto his eyelids in all her grim glory. Rebus had been relieved to note that even Inspector George Flight was not unmoved. His actions, movements and speech had become somehow damped or more muted, as though he were consciously holding back some emotion, the urge to scream or kick out. The divers were coming up from the river, having found nothing. They would look again in the morning, but their voices betrayed a lack of hope. Flight listened to their report and nodded, all the time watched, from behind his beaker of tea, by Rebus.

George Flight was in his late forties, a few years older than Rebus. He wasn't short, yet he had an appearance best described as stocky. There was the hint of a paunch, but a much greater hint of muscle. Rebus didn't rate his own chances against him in a clinch. Flight's wiry brown hair was thin at the crown, but thick elsewhere. He was dressed in a leather bomber jacket and denims. Most men in their forties looked stupid in denims, but not Flight. They fitted his attitude and his brisk, businesslike walk.

A long time before, Rebus had graded CID men into three sartorial groups: the leather-and-denim brigade, who

18

wanted to look as tough as they felt; the suit-and-tie dapper merchants, who were looking for promotion and respect (not necessarily in that order); and the nondescripts, men who wore anything that came to hand of a morning, their year's fashions usually the result of an hour's shopping in a big-name department store.

Most CID men were nondescripts. Rebus reckoned he himself fell into that group. Yet catching a glimpse of himself in a wing-mirror, he noticed that he had a dapper look. Suit-and-ties never got on with leather-and-denims.

Now Flight was shaking hands with an important looking man, who other than for the handshake, kept his hands in his pockets and listened to Flight with head angled downwards, nodding occasionally as though deep in thought. He wore a suit and a black woollen coat. He couldn't have been more crisply dressed if it had been the middle of the day. Most people were beginning to look fatigued, their clothes and faces crumpled. There were only two exceptions: this man and Philip Cousins.

The man was shaking hands with Dr Cousins now and even extended a greeting to Dr Cousins's assistant. And then Flight gestured towards the van ... no, towards *Rebus*! They were coming towards him. Rebus brought the beaker away from his face, and swapped it from his right to his left hand, just in case a handshake was in the offing.

'This is Inspector Rebus,' Flight said.

'Ah, our man from north of the border,' said the important looking man with a wry, rather superior smile. Rebus returned the smile but looked to Flight.

'Inspector Rebus, this is Chief Inspector Howard Laine.'

'How do you do.' The handshake. Howard Laine: it sounded like a street-name.

'So,' said Chief Inspector Laine, 'you're here to help us with our little problem?'

'Well,' said Rebus, 'I'm not sure what I can do, sir, but rest assured I'll do what I can.'

There was a pause, then Laine smiled but said nothing. The truth hit Rebus like lightning splitting a tree: *they couldn't understand him*! They were standing there smiling at him, but they couldn't understand his accent. Rebus cleared his throat and tried again.

'Whatever I can do to help, sir.'

Laine smiled again. 'Excellent, Inspector, excellent. Well, I'm sure Inspector Flight here will show you the ropes. Settled in all right, have you?'

'Well, actually –'

Flight himself interrupted. 'Inspector Rebus came straight here, sir, as soon as he heard about the murder. He's only just arrived in London.'

'Is that so?' Laine sounded impressed, but Rebus could see that the man was growing restless. This was smalltalk, and he did not like to think he had time for smalltalk. His eyes sought some escape. 'Well, Inspector,' he said, 'I'm sure we'll meet again.' And turning to Flight: 'I'd better be off, George. Everything under control?' Flight merely nodded. 'Good, fine, well ...' And with that the Chief Inspector started back towards his car, accompanied by Flight. Rebus exhaled noisily. He felt completely out of his territory here. He knew when he was not wanted and wondered just whose idea it had been to second him to the Wolfman case. Someone with a warped sense of humour, that was for sure. His boss had passed the letter over to him.

'It seems,' he had said, 'you've become an expert on serial killers, John, and they're a bit short on those in the Met just now. They'd like you to go down to London for a few days, see if you can come up with anything, maybe give them a few ideas.'

Rebus had read the letter through in growing disbelief. It

referred to a case from a few years before, the case of a child murderer, a case Rebus had cracked. But that had been personal, not really a serial killer at all.

'I don't know anything about serial killers,' Rebus had protested to his boss.

'Well then, it seems like you'll be in good company, doesn't it?'

And now look at him, standing on a stretch of ground in north-east London, a cup of unspeakably bad tea nursed in both hands, his stomach churning, nerves buzzing, his bags looking as lonely and out of place as he felt. Here to help solve the insoluble, *our man from north of the border*. Whose idea had it been to bring him here? No police force in the country liked to admit failure; yet by lugging Rebus down here the Met was doing precisely that.

Laine had gone and Flight seemed a little more relaxed. He even found time to smile reassuringly across to Rebus before giving orders to two men who, Rebus knew, would be from a funeral parlour. The men went back to their vehicle and returned with a large folded piece of plastic. They crossed the cordon and stopped at the body, laying the plastic out beside it. It was a translucent bag, over six feet long with a zip running from head to toe. Dr Cousins was in close attendance as the two men opened the bag and lifted the body into it, closing the zipper. One photographer had decided to shoot off a few more flash photographs of the spot where the body had lain, while the attendants carried the corpse back through the cordon and up to their vehicle.

Rebus noticed that the crowd of onlookers had disappeared, and only a few curious souls remained. One of them, a young man, was carrying a crash helmet and wore a shiny black leather jacket with shinier silver zips. A very tired constable was trying to move him on.

Rebus felt like an onlooker himself and thought of all the

TV dramas and films he'd seen, with detectives swarming over the murder site in minute one (destroying any forensic evidence in the process) and solving the murder by minute fifty-nine or eighty-nine. Laughable, really. Police work was just that: work. Relentless, routine, dull, frustrating, and above all time-consuming. He checked his watch. It was exactly 2 am. His hotel was back in central London, tucked somewhere behind Piccadilly Circus. It would take another thirty to forty minutes to get back there, always supposing a spare patrol car was available.

'Coming?'

It was Flight, standing a few yards in front of him.

'Might as well,' said Rebus, knowing exactly what Flight was talking about, or more accurately *where* he was talking about.

Flight smiled. 'I'll give you this, Inspector Rebus, you don't give up.'

'The famous tenacity of the Scots,' said Rebus, quoting from one of Sunday's newspaper rugby reports. Flight actually laughed. It didn't last long, but it made Rebus feel glad that he'd come here tonight. The ice hadn't been broken completely perhaps, but an important chunk had been chipped away from one corner of the berg.

'Come on then. I've got my car. I'll get one of the drivers to put your bags in his boot. The lock's stuck on mine. Somebody tried to crowbar it open a few weeks back.' He glanced towards Rebus, a rare moment of eye contact. 'Nowhere is safe these days,' he said. 'Nowhere.'

There was already a lot of commotion up at road level. Voices and the slamming shut of car doors. Some officers would stay behind, of course, guarding the site. And a few might be going back to the warmth of the station or – luxury hardly to be imagined! – their own beds. But a few of the cars would be following the funeral van, following it all the way to the mortuary.

Rebus travelled in the front of Flight's own car. Both men spent the journey in desperate pursuit of a conversational opening and as a result said very little until they were near their destination.

'Do we know who she was?' asked Rebus.

'Jean Cooper,' said Flight. 'We found ID in her handbag.'

'Any reason for her to be on that path?'

'She was going home from work. She worked in an off-licence nearby. Her sister tells us she finished work at seven.'

'When was the body found?'

'Quarter to ten.'

'That's a fair gap.'

'We've got witnesses who saw her in the Dog and Duck. That's a pub near where she works. She used to go in there for a drink some evenings. The barmaid reckons she left at nine or thereabouts.'

Rebus stared out of the windscreen. The roads were still fairly busy considering the time of night and they passed groups of youthful and raucous pedestrians.

'There's a club in Stokie,' Flight explained. 'Very popular, but the buses have stopped by the time it comes out so everyone walks home.'

Rebus nodded, then asked: 'Stokie?'

Flight smiled. 'Stoke Newington. You probably passed through it on your way from King's Cross.'

'God knows,' said Rebus. 'It all looked the same to me. I think my taxi driver had me down as a tourist. We took so long from King's Cross I think we might have come via the M25.' Rebus waited for Flight to laugh, but all he raised was a sliver of a smile. There was another pause. 'Was this Jean Cooper single?' Rebus asked at last.

'Married.'

'She wasn't wearing a wedding ring.'

Flight nodded. 'Separated. She lived with her sister. No kids.'

'And she went drinking by herself.'

Flight glanced towards Rebus. 'What are you saying?'

Rebus shrugged. 'Nothing. It's just that if she liked a good time, maybe that's how she met her killer.'

'It's possible.'

'At any rate, whether she knew him or not, the killer could have followed her from the pub.'

'We'll be talking to everybody who was there, don't worry.'

'Either that,' said Rebus, thinking aloud, 'or the killer was waiting by the river for anyone who happened along. Somebody might have seen him.'

'We'll be asking around,' said Flight. His voice had taken on a much harder edge.

'Sorry,' said Rebus. 'A severe case of teaching my granny to suck eggs.'

Flight turned to him again. They were about to take a left through some hospital gates. 'I am not your granny,' he said. 'And any comments you have to make are welcome. Maybe eventually you'll come up with something I haven't already thought of.'

'Of course,' said Rebus, 'this couldn't have happened in Scotland.'

'Oh?' Flight had a half-sneer on his face. 'Why's that then? Too civilised up there in the frozen north? I remember when you had the worst football hooligans in the world. Maybe you still do, only these days they look like butter wouldn't melt in their underpants.'

But Rebus was shaking his head. 'No, it wouldn't have happened to Jean Cooper, that's all I meant. Our off-licences don't open on Sunday.'

Rebus fell silent and stared fixedly at the windscreen, keeping his thoughts to himself, thoughts which ran along a very simple plane: fuck you, too, pal. Over the years, those four words had become his mantra. Fuck you, too, pal. FYTP. It had taken the Londoner only the length of a twenty-minute car ride to show what he really thought of the Scots.

As Rebus got out of the car, he glanced in through the rear window and saw, for the first time, the contents of the back seat. He opened his mouth to speak, but Flight raised a knowing hand.

'Don't even ask,' he growled, slamming shut the driver's-side door. 'And listen, I'm sorry about what I said …'

Rebus merely shrugged, but his eyebrows descended in a private and thoughtful frown. After all, there had to be *some* logical explanation as to why a Detective Inspector would have a huge stuffed teddy bear in the back of his car at the scene of a murder. It was just that Rebus was damned if he could think of one right this second …

Mortuaries were places where the dead stopped being people and turned instead into bags of meat, offal, blood and bone. Rebus had never been sick at the scene of a crime, but the first few times he had visited a mortuary the contents of his stomach had fairly quickly been rendered up for examination.

The mortuary technician was a gleeful little man with a livid birthmark covering a full quarter of his face. He seemed to know Dr Cousins well enough and had prepared everything for the arrival of the deceased and the usual retinue of police officers. Cousins checked the post-mortem room, while Jean Cooper's sister was taken quietly into an ante-room, there to make the formal identification. It took only a tearful few seconds, after which she was escorted well away from the scene by consoling officers. They would take her home, but Rebus doubted if she would get any sleep. In fact, knowing how long a scrupulous pathologist could take, he was beginning to doubt that any of them would get to bed before morning.

Eventually, the body bag was brought into the post-mortem room and the corpse of Jean Cooper placed on a slab, beneath the hum and glare of powerful strip lighting. The room was antiseptic but antique. Its tiled walls were cracking and there was a stinging aroma of chemicals. Voices were kept muffled, not so much out of respect but from a strange kind of fear. The mortuary, after all, was one vast memento mori, and what was about to happen to Jean Cooper's body would serve to remind each and every one of them that if the body were a temple, then it was possible to loot that temple, scattering its treasures, revealing its precious secrets.

A hand landed gently on Rebus's shoulder, and he turned, startled, towards the man who was standing there. 'Man' was by way of simplification. This tall and unsmiling individual had cropped fair hair and the acne-ridden face of an adolescent. He looked about fourteen, but Rebus placed him in his mid-twenties.

'You're the Jock, aren't you?' There was interest in the voice, but little emotion. Rebus said nothing. FYTP. 'Yeah, thought so. Cracked the case yet, have you?' The grin accompanying this question was three-quarters sneer and one-quarter scowl. 'We don't *need* any help.'

'Ah,' said George Flight, 'I see you've already met DC Lamb. I was just about to introduce you.'

'Delighted,' said Rebus, gazing stonily at the join-the-dots pattern of spots on Lamb's forehead. Lamb! No surname in history, Rebus felt, had ever been less deserved, less accurate. Over by the slab, Dr Cousins cleared his throat noisily.

'Gentlemen,' he said to the room at large. It was little more than an indication that he was about to start work.

The room fell quiet again. A microphone hung down from the ceiling to within a few feet of the slab. Cousins turned to the technician. 'Is this thing on now?' The technician nodded keenly from between arranging a row of clanging metallic instruments along a tray.

Rebus knew all the instruments, had seen them all in action. The cutters and the saws and the drills. Some of them were electrical, some needed a human force to drive them home. The sounds the electrical ones made were horrible, but at least the job was over quickly; the manual tools made similarly revolting sounds that seemed to last forever. Still, there would be an interval before that particular shop of horrors. First of all there was the slow and careful business of removing the clothing and bagging it up for Forensics.

As Rebus and the others watched, the two photographers clicked away, one taking black and white shots and the other colour, recording for posterity each stage of the process. The video cameraman had given up, however, his equipment having jammed irreparably on one of the bargain tapes. Or at least that was the story which kept him away from the mortuary.

Finally, when the corpse was naked, Cousins pointed to a few areas meriting particular close-up shots. Then the Forensics men moved in again, armed with more lengths of sticky tape. Now that the body was unclothed, the same process as was carried out on the tow-path had to be gone through again. Not for nothing were these people known as Sellotape Men.

Cousins wandered over towards the group where Rebus, Flight and Lamb stood.

'I'd kill for a cup of tea, George.'

'I'll see what I can do, Philip. What about Isobel?'

Cousins looked back towards where Isobel Penny stood, making another drawing of the corpse despite the welter of camera shots. 'Penny,' he called, 'care for a cuppa?' Her eyes opened a little and she nodded enthusiastically.

'Right,' said Flight, moving towards the door. Rebus thought the man seemed more than a little relieved to be leaving, albeit temporarily.

'Nasty little chap,' Cousins commented. Rebus wondered for a moment if he were talking about George Flight, but Cousins waved a hand towards the corpse. 'To do this sort of thing time after time, without motive, out of some need for ... well, pleasure, I suppose.'

'There's always a motive, sir,' said Rebus. 'You just said so yourself. Pleasure, that's his motive. But the way he kills. What he does. There's some other motive there. It's just that we can't see it yet.'

Cousins stared at him. Rebus could see a warm light in his deep eyes. 'Well, Inspector, let us hope *somebody* spots whatever it is before too long. Four deaths in as many months. The man's as constant as the moon.'

Rebus smiled. 'But we all know that werewolves are affected by the moon, don't we?'

Cousins laughed. It was deep and resonant and sounded extraordinarily out of place in this environment. Lamb wasn't laughing, wasn't even smiling. He was following little of this conversation, and the realisation pleased Rebus. But Lamb wasn't going to be left out.

'I reckon he's barking mad. Hee, get it?'

'Well,' said Cousins, as though this joke was too well-worn even to merit acknowledgment, 'must press on.' He turned towards the slab. 'If you've finished, gentlemen?' The Forensics men nodded in unison. 'Jewellery removed?' They nodded again. 'Good. Then if you are ready, I suggest we begin.'

The beginning was never too awful. Measurements, a physical description – five feet and seven inches tall, brown hair, that sort of thing. Fingernail scrapings and clippings

28

were deposited in yet more polythene bags. Rebus made a note to buy shares in whichever company manufactured these bags. He'd seen murder investigations go through hundreds of them.

Slowly but determinedly, things got worse. Swabs were taken from Jean Cooper's vagina, then Cousins got down to some serious work.

'Large puncture wound to the throat. From size of wound, I'd say the knife itself had been twisted in the wound. A small knife. From the extent of the exit wound I would say the blade was about five inches long, perhaps a little less, and about an inch deep, ending in a very fine point. The skin surrounding the entry wound shows some bruising, perhaps caused by the hilt-guard or handle. This would seem to indicate that the knife was driven in with a certain amount of force.

'The hands and arms show no signs of defence wounding, so the victim had no time in which to defend herself. The possibility exists that she was approached from behind. There is some colouring around the mouth and the victim's lipstick had been slightly smeared across her right cheek. If she was approached from behind, a possible scenario would be that the attacker's left hand closed over her mouth to stop her from screaming, thus smearing the lipstick while the attacker stabbed with the right hand. The wound to the throat shows a slight downward angle, which would indicate someone taller than the victim.'

Cousins cleared his throat again. Well, thought Rebus, so far they could strike the mortuary attendant and one of the photographers off the possible list of suspects: everyone else in the room was five feet eight or over.

The pause in proceedings gave the onlookers a chance to shuffle their feet, clear their own throats, and glance at each other, taking note of how pale this or that face was. Rebus was surprised at the pathologist's 'scenarios': that was supposed to be *their* job, not his. All the pathologists Rebus had ever worked with had given the bare facts, leaving the deductions to Rebus himself. But Cousins obviously did not work that way. Perhaps he was a frustrated detective. Rebus still found it hard to believe that people came to pathology through choice.

Tea appeared, carried in three beakers on a plastic tray by Inspector Flight. Cousins and Isobel Penny took a cup each, and Flight himself took the other. There were jealous stares from a few dry-mouthed officers. Rebus was among them.

'Now,' said Cousins between sips, 'I'm going to examine the anal wound.'

It just kept on getting worse. Rebus tried to concentrate on what Cousins was saying, but it wasn't easy. The same knife had been used to make several stabs to the anus. There were friction marks on the thighs from where the tights had been roughly pulled down. Rebus looked over to Isobel Penny, but, apart from some slight heightening of the colour in her cheeks, she seemed dispassionate. A cool customer and no mistake. But then she'd probably seen worse in her time. No, no, she couldn't possibly have seen worse than *this*. Could she?

'The stomach is interesting,' Cousins was saying. 'The blouse has been torn away to expose the stomach, and there are two lines of curved indentations in the skin, enough to have bruised and broken the skin, but there is little actual marking of the skin and no blood, from which I would say that this act was perpetrated only *after* the stabbings. After, in fact, the victim was dead. There are a few dried stains on the stomach near these bite marks. Without prejudging, past evidence from three very similar cases showed these stains to be saline in nature – teardrops or perhaps beads of sweat. I'm now going to take a deep body temperature.'

Rebus felt parched. He was hot, and the tiredness was

30

seeping into his bones, lack of sleep giving everything a hallucinatory quality. There were halos around the pathologist, his assistant, and the technician. The walls seemed to be moving, and Rebus dared not concentrate on them for fear that he would lose his balance. He happened to catch Lamb's eye and the Detective Constable gave him an ugly grin and an uglier wink.

The body was washed now, washed for the first time, freed from a staining of light brown and black, from the pale matt covering of blood. Cousins examined it again, finding nothing new, after which another set of fingerprints was taken. Then came the internal examination.

A deep incision was made down the front of the body. Blood samples were taken and handed to the forensics team, as were samples of urine, stomach contents, liver, body hair (eyebrows included) and tissue. The process used to make Rebus impatient. It was obvious how the victim had died, so why bother with everything else? But he had learned over the years that what you could *see*, the external injuries, often wasn't as important as what you couldn't see, the tiny secrets only a microscope or a chemical test could reveal. So he had learned patience and exercised it now, stifling a yawn every half minute or so.

'Not boring you am I?' Cousins's voice was a polite murmur. He looked up from his work and caught Rebus's eyes, then smiled.

'Not a bit,' said Rebus.

'That's all right then. I'm sure we'd all rather be at home tucked up in bed than in this place.' Only the birthmarked technician seemed doubtful as to the truth of this statement. Cousins was reaching a hand into the corpse's chest. 'I'll be out of here as soon as I can.'

It wasn't the sight of this examination, Rebus decided, that turned men pale. It was the accompanying sound effects. The tearing of flesh, as though a butcher were yanking meat from a flank. The bubbling of liquids and the soft rasping of the cutting tools. If he could somehow block up his ears, maybe everything would be bearable. But on the contrary, his ears seemed extraordinarily sensitive in this room. Next time, he'd bring plugs of cotton wool with him. Next time …

The chest and abdominal organs were removed and taken to a clean slab, where a hose was used to wash them clean before Cousins dissected them. The attendant meantime was called into action, removing the brain with the help of a tiny powered circular-saw. Rebus had his eyes shut now, but the room seemed to swirl all the same. Not long to go now though. Not long, thank God. But it wasn't just the sounds now, was it? It was the smell too, that unmistakable aroma of raw meat. It clung to the nostrils like perfume, filling the lungs, catching the back of the throat and clinging there, so that eventually it became a tang in the mouth and he found himself actually tasting it. His stomach moved momentarily, but he rubbed it gently, surreptitiously with a hand. Not surreptitiously enough.

'If you're going to throw up,' it was Lamb again, like a succubus over his shoulder, hissing, 'go outside.' And then the chuckle, throaty and slow like a stalled engine. Rebus half-turned his head and gave a dangerous smile.

Soon enough, the whole mess of matter was being put together again, and Rebus knew that by the time any grieving relatives viewed the mortal remains of Jean Cooper, the body would look quite natural.

As ever, by the end of the autopsy the room had been reduced to silent introspection. Each man and woman present was made of the same stuff as Jean Cooper, and now they stood, momentarily stripped of their individual personalities. They were all bodies, all animals, all collections of viscera. The only difference between them and Jean Cooper was that their hearts still pumped blood. But one

32

day soon enough each heart would stop, and that would be an end of it, save for the possibility of a visit to this butcher's shop, this abattoir.

Cousins removed his rubber gloves and washed his hands thoroughly, accepted from the attendant a proffered sheaf of paper towels. 'That's about it then, gentlemen, until Penny can type up the notes. Murdered between nine o'clock and nine-thirty I'd guess. Same *modus operandi* as our so-called Wolfman. I think I've just examined his fourth victim. I'll get in Anthony Morrison tomorrow, let him have a look at the teeth marks. See what he says.'

Since everyone seemed to know except Rebus, Rebus asked, 'Who's Anthony Morrison?'

Flight was first to answer. 'A dentist.'

'A dental pathologist,' corrected Cousins. 'And quite a good one. He's got details of the other three murders. His analyses of the bite marks have been quite useful.' Cousins turned to Flight for confirmation of this, but Flight's eyes were directed towards his shoes, as if to say *I wouldn't go that far*.

'Well,' said Cousins, seeming to take the silent hint, 'at any rate, you know my findings. It's down to your lab chaps now. There's precious little there …' Cousins nodded back towards the scooped-out husk of the corpse, 'to help with your investigation. That being so, I think I'll go home to bed.'

Flight seemed to realise that Cousins was displeased with him. 'Thank you, Philip.' And the detective lifted a hand to rest it against the pathologist's arm. Cousins looked at the hand, then at Flight, and smiled.

The performance at an end, the audience began to shuffle out into the cold, still darkness of an emerging day. By Rebus's watch, it was four thirty. He felt completely exhausted, could happily have lain down on the lawn in

33

front of the main building and taken a nap, but Flight was walking towards him, carrying his bags.

'Come on,' he said. 'I'll give you a lift.'

In his fragile state, Rebus felt this to be the nicest, kindest thing anyone had said to him in weeks. 'Are you sure you have room?' he said. 'I mean, with the teddy bear and all.'

Flight paused. 'Or if you'd prefer to walk, Inspector?'

Rebus threw up his hands in surrender, then, when the door was unlocked, slipped into the passenger seat of Flight's red Sierra. The seat seemed to wrap itself around him.

'Here,' said Flight, handing a hip flask to Rebus. Rebus unscrewed the top of the flask and sniffed. 'It won't kill you,' Flight called. This was probably true. The aroma was of whisky. Not great whisky, not a smoky island malt, but a decent enough proprietary brand. Well, it would help keep him awake perhaps until they reached the hotel. Rebus toasted the windscreen and let the liquid trickle into his mouth.

Flight got behind the steering-wheel and started the car, then, as the car idled, accepted the flask from Rebus and drank from it greedily.

'How far to the hotel from here?' Rebus asked.

'About twenty minutes at this time of night,' said Flight, screwing tight the stopper and replacing the flask in his pocket. 'That's if we stop for red lights.'

'You have my permission to run every red light you see.'

Flight laughed tiredly. Both men were wondering how to turn the conversation around to the autopsy.

'Best leave it until morning, eh?' said Rebus, speaking for them both. Flight merely nodded and moved off, waving to Cousins and Isobel Penny, who were about to get into their car. Rebus stared out of his side window to where DC Lamb stood beside his own car, a flash little sports model.

Typical, thought Rebus. Just typical. Lamb stared back at him, and then gave that three-quarters sneer again.

FYTP, Rebus mentally intoned. FYTP. Then he turned in his seat to examine the teddy bear behind him. Flight was resolutely refusing to take the hint, and Rebus, though curious, wasn't about to jeopardise whatever relationship he might be able to strike up with this man by asking the obvious question. Some things were always best left until morning.

The whisky had cleared his nostrils, lungs and throat. He breathed deeply, seeing in his mind the little mortuary attendant, that livid birthmark, and Isobel Penny, sketching like any amateur artist. She might have been in front of a museum exhibit for all the emotion she had shown. He wondered what her secret was, the secret of her absolute calmness, but thought he probably knew in any case. Her job had become merely that: a job. Maybe one day Rebus would feel the same way. But he hoped not.

If anything, Flight and Rebus said less during the drive to the hotel than they had done on the way to the mortuary. The whisky was working on Rebus's empty stomach and the interior of the car was oppressively hot. He tried opening his window a quarter of an inch, but the blast of chill air only made things worse.

The autopsy was being played out again before him. The cutting tools, the lifting of organs out of the body, the incisions and inspections, Cousins's face peering at spongy tissue from no more than an inch away. One twitch and his face would have been smothered in ... Isobel Penny watching all, recording all, the slice from throat to pubis ... London sped past him. Flight, true to his word, was cruising through some red lights and slowing merely for others. There were still cars on the streets. The city never slept. Nightclubs, parties, drifters, the homeless. Sleepless dog-walkers, all night bakeries and beigel shops. Some spelt 'beigel' and some spelt 'bagel'. What the hell was a beigel? Wasn't that what they were always eating in Woody Allen films?

Samples from her eyebrows, for Christ's sake. What use were samples from her eyebrows? They should be concentrating on the attacker, not the victim. Those teeth marks. What was the dentist's name again? Not a dentist, a dental *pathologist*. Morrison. Yes, that was it. Morrison, like the street in Edinburgh, Morrison Street, not too far from the brewery canal, where the swans lived, a single pair of swans. What happened when they died? Did the brewery replace them? So damned hot in this shiny red car. Rebus could feel his insides wanting to become his outsides. The knife twisted in the throat. A small knife. He could almost visualise it. Something like a kitchen knife. Sharp, sour taste in his mouth.

'Nearly there,' said Flight. 'Just along Shaftesbury Avenue. That's Soho on the right. By God, we've cleaned that den up this past few years. You wouldn't believe it. You know, I've been thinking, where the body was found, it's not so far from where the Krays used to live. Somewhere on Lea Bridge Road. I was just a young copper when they were on the go.'

'Please …' said Rebus.

'They did somebody in Stokie. Jack McVitie, I think it was. Jack the Hat, they called him.'

'Can you stop here?' Rebus blurted out. Flight looked at him.

'What's up?'

'I need some air. I'll walk the rest of the way. Just stop the car, please.'

Flight began to protest, but pulled over to the kerb. Stepping out of the car, Rebus immediately felt better. There was cold sweat on his forehead, neck and back. He breathed deeply. Flight deposited his bags on the pavement.

'Thanks again,' said Rebus. 'Sorry about this. Just point me in the general direction.'

'Just off the Circus,' Flight said.

Rebus nodded. 'I hope there's a night porter.' Yes, he was feeling much better.

'It's a quarter to five,' said Flight. 'You'll probably catch the day shift coming on.' He laughed, but the laugh died quickly and he gave Rebus a serious nod of his head. 'You made your point tonight, John. Okay?'

Rebus nodded back. *John*. Another chip from the iceberg, or just good management?

'Thanks,' he said. They shook hands. 'Are we still on for a meeting at ten?'

'Let's make it eleven, eh? I'll have someone pick you up from your hotel.'

Rebus nodded and picked up his bags. Then bent down again towards the car's back window. 'Good night, teddy,' he said.

'Watch you don't get lost!' Flight called to him from the car. Then the car moved off, making a screeching u-turn before roaring back the way they had come. Rebus looked around him. Shaftesbury Avenue. The buildings seemed about to swamp him. Theatres. Shops. Litter: the debris from a Sunday night out. A dull roar preceded the arrival, from one of the misty side streets, of a dustcart. The men were dressed in orange overalls. They paid no attention to Rebus as he trudged past them. How long was this street? It seemed to follow a vast curve, longer than he had expected.

Bloody London. Then he spotted Eros atop his fountain, but there was something wrong. The Circus was no longer a Circus. Eros had been paved in, so that traffic had to sweep past it rather than around it. Why the hell had anyone decided to do that? A car was slowing behind him,

37

coming parallel with him. White car with an orange stripe: a police car. The officer in the passenger seat had wound down his window and now called out to him.

'Excuse me, sir, do you mind telling me where you're going?'

'What?' The question stunned Rebus, stopped him in his tracks. The car had stopped too and both driver and passenger were emerging.

'Are those your bags, sir?'

Rebus felt it rise within him, a shining hard steel pole of anger. Then he happened to catch sight of himself in the window of the patrol car. A quarter to five on the streets of London. A dishevelled, unshaven man, a man obviously without sleep, carrying a suitcase, a bag and a briefcase. A *briefcase*? Who the hell would be carrying a briefcase around at this time of the morning? Rebus put down his luggage and rubbed at the bridge of his nose with one hand. And before he knew what was happening, his shoulders began moving, his body convulsing with laughter. The two uniformed officers were looking at one another. Rebus sniffed back the laughter and reached into his inside pocket. One of the officers stepped back a pace.

'Take it easy, son,' Rebus said. He produced his ID. 'I'm on your side.' The less cagey officer, the passenger, took the ID from Rebus, examined it, then handed it back.

'You're a long way off your patch, sir.'

'You don't have to tell me that,' said Rebus. 'What's your name, son?'

The constable was wary now. 'Bennett, sir. Joey Bennett. I mean, Joseph Bennett.'

'All right, Joey. Would you like to do me a favour?' The constable nodded. 'Do you know the Prince Royal Hotel?'

'Yes, sir.' Bennett began to point with his left hand. 'It's about fifty yards –'

'All right,' Rebus interrupted. 'Just show me, will you?'

The young man said nothing. 'Will you do that, Constable Bennett?'

'Yes, sir.'

Rebus nodded. Yes, he could handle London. He could take it on and win. 'Right,' he said, moving off towards the Prince Royal. 'Oh,' he said, turning back and taking in both men with his glance, 'and bring my bags, will you?' Rebus had his back to them again, but he could almost hear the sound of two jaws dropping open. 'Or,' he called back, 'shall I just inform Chief Inspector Laine that two of his officers harassed me on my first night as his guest in this fine city?'

Rebus kept on walking, hearing the two officers pick up his luggage and hurry after him. They were arguing as to whether or not they should leave the patrol car unlocked. He was smiling, despite everything. A small victory, a bit of a cheat, but what the hell. This was London, after all. This was Shaftesbury Avenue. And that was showbiz.

* * *

Home at last, she had a good wash, and after that she felt a little better. She had brought in a black bin-liner from the boot of her car. It contained the clothes she had been wearing, cheap flimsy things. Tomorrow evening she would tidy the back garden and light a bonfire.

She wasn't crying any more. She had calmed down. She always calmed down afterwards. From a polythene shopping bag she removed another polythene bag, from which she removed the bloodied knife. The kitchen sink was full of boiling, soapy water. The polythene bags went into the bin-liner with the clothes, the knife went into the sink. She washed it carefully, emptying and refilling the washing bowl, all the time humming to herself. It wasn't a recognisable song, nor even really a tune. But it calmed her, it soothed her, the way her mother's hummed lullabies always had.

There, all done. It was hard work, and she was pleased to be finished with it. Concentration was the key. A lapse in concentration, and you could make a slip, then fail to spot that slip. She rinsed the sink three times, sluicing away every last speckle of blood, and left the knife to dry on the draining-board. Then she walked out into the hallway and paused at one of the doors while she found the key.

This was her secret room, her picture gallery. Inside, one wall was all but covered by oil and watercolour paintings. Three of these paintings were damaged beyond repair. A pity, since all three had been favourites. Her favourite now was a small countryside stream. Simple, pale colours and a naive style. The stream was in the foreground and beside it sat a man and a boy, or it could have been a man and a girl. It was hard to tell, that was the problem with the naive style. It was not as though she could even ask the artist, for the artist had been dead for years.

She tried not to look at the other wall, the wall directly opposite. It was a horrid wall. She didn't like what she could see there from the corner of one eye. She decided that what she liked about her favourite painting was its size. It was about ten inches by eight, excluding the rather Baroque gilt frame (which did not suit it at all – her mother had never had much taste in frames). These petite dimensions, added to the washed colours, gave the whole a subtlety and a lack of vision, a humility, a gentleness, which pleased her. Of course, it depicted no great truth, this painting. In fact, it was a monstrous lie, the absolute opposite of the facts. There had been no stream, no touching scene of father and child. There had been only horror. That was why Velázquez was her favourite painter: shadowplay, rich shades of black, skulls and suspicion … the dark heart exposed.

'The dark heart.' She nodded to herself. She had seen things, felt things, which few were ever privileged to witness. This was her life. This was her existence. And the painting began to mock her, the stream turning into a cruel turquoise grin.

Calmly, humming to herself again she picked up a pair of scissors from a nearby chair and began to slash at the painting with regular vertical strokes, then horizontal strokes, then vertical again, tearing and tearing its heart out until the scene disappeared forever.

Underground

'And this,' said George Flight, 'is where the Wolfman was born.'

Rebus looked. It was a depressing location for a birth. A cobblestoned alley, a cul-de-sac, the buildings three storeys high, every window either boarded up or barred and grilled. The black bags of rubbish looked to have been languishing by the side of the road for weeks. A few had been impaled on the steel spiked fencing in front of the shut-up windows, and these bags leaked their rank contents the way a cracked sewage pipe would.

'Nice,' he said.

'The buildings are mainly disused. Local bands use the basement of one of them as a practice room, and make quite a racket while they're about it.' Flight pointed to a barred and grilled window. 'And I think that's a clothing manufacturer or distributor. Anyway, he hasn't been back since we started taking an interest in the street.'

'Oh?' Rebus sounded interested, but Flight shook his head.

'Nothing suspicious in that, believe me. These guys use slave labour, Bangladeshis, mostly illegal immigrants. The last thing they want is policemen sniffing around. They'll move the machines and set up again somewhere else.'

Rebus nodded. He was looking around the cul-de-sac, trying to remember, from the photographs he had been sent, just where the body had been found.

'It was there.' Flight was pointing to a gate in the iron

railings. Ah yes, Rebus remembered now. Not at street level, but down some stone steps leading to a basement. The victim had been found at the bottom of the steps, same *modus operandi* as last night, down to the bite marks on the stomach. Rebus opened his briefcase and brought out the manila folder, opening it at the sheet he needed.

'Maria Watkiss, age thirty-eight. Occupation: prostitute. Body found on Tuesday 16th January by council workmen. Estimated that victim had been murdered two to three days prior to being discovered. Rudimentary attempt had been made to conceal body.'

Flight nodded towards one of the impaled bin-liners. 'He emptied a bag of rubbish out over her. It pretty well covered the body. The rats alerted the workmen.'

'Rats?'

'Dozens of them, from all accounts. They'd had a bloody good feed, had those rats.'

Rebus was standing at the top of the steps. 'We reckon,' said Flight, 'the Wolfman must have paid her for a knee-trembler and brought her down here. Or maybe she brought him. She worked out of a pub on Old Street. It's a five minute walk. We interviewed the regulars, but nobody saw her leave with anyone.'

'Maybe he was in a car?'

'It's more than possible. Judging by the physical distance between the murder sites, he must be pretty mobile.'

'It says in the report that she was married.'

'That's right. Her old man, Tommy, he knew she was on the game. It didn't bother him, so long as she handed over the cash.'

'And he didn't report her missing?'

Flight wrinkled his nose. 'Not Tommy. He was on a bender at the time, practically comatose with drink when we went to see him. He said later that Maria often disappeared for a few days, told us she used to go off to the seaside with one or two of her regular johns.'

'I don't suppose you've been able to find these … clients?'

'Leave it out.' Flight laughed as though this were the best joke he'd heard all week. 'For the record, Tommy thought one of them might be called Bill or Will. Does that help?'

'It narrows things down,' Rebus said with a smile.

'In any event,' said Flight, 'I doubt Tommy would have come to us for help if she hadn't come back. He's got form as long as your inside leg. To tell you the truth, he was our first suspect.'

'It follows.' Every policeman knew it as a universal truth: most murders happen in the family.

'A couple of years back,' Flight was saying, 'Maria was beaten up pretty badly. A hospital case, in fact. Tommy's doing. She'd been seeing another man and he hadn't been paying for it, if you understand my meaning. And a couple of years before that, Tommy served time for aggravated assault. It would have been rape if we could have got the woman into the witness box, but she was scared seven colours shitless. There were witnesses, but we were never going to pin rape on him. So aggravated assault it was. He got eight months.'

'A violent man then.'

'You could say that.'

'With a record of particular violence against women.'

Flight nodded. 'It looked good at first. We thought we could pin Maria's murder on him and make it stick. But nothing added up. He had an alibi for openers. Then there were the bite marks: not his size, according to the dentist.'

'You mean Dr Morrison?'

'Yes, that's right. I call him the dentist to annoy Philip.' Flight scratched at his chin. The elbow of his leather jacket gave a creak. 'Anyway, nothing added up. And then when the second murder came along, well, we knew we were working in a different league from Tommy.'

'You're absolutely sure of that?'

'John, I'm not *absolutely* sure what colour of socks I've put on in the morning, I'm sometimes not even sure that I've put socks on at all. But I'm *fairly* sure this isn't Tommy Watkiss's work. He gets his kicks from watching Arsenal, not mutilating dead women.'

Rebus's eyes had not left Flight's. 'Your socks are blue,' he said. Flight looked down, saw that this was indeed the case, and smiled broadly.

'They're also different shades,' Rebus added.

'Bloody hell, so they are.'

'I'd still like to talk to Mr Watkiss,' Rebus continued. 'No hurry, and if it's all right with you.'

Flight shrugged. 'Whatever you say, Sherlock. Now, shall we get out of this shit-hole, or is there anything else you want to see?'

'No,' said Rebus. 'Let's get out of here.' They started back towards the mouth of the cul-de-sac, where Flight's car waited. 'What's this part of town called again?'

'Shoreditch. Remember your nursery rhymes? "When I am rich, say the bells of Shoreditch".'

Yes, Rebus had a vague memory. A memory of his mother, holding him on her knee, or maybe it was his father, singing him songs and bouncing the knee in time. It had never happened that way, but he had a memory of it all the same. They were at the end of the cul-de-sac now. A larger road flowed past, busy with daytime traffic. The buildings were black with grime, windows thick with the stuff. Offices of some kind, warehouses. No shops, save one selling professional kitchenware. No houses or even flats in the upper storeys by the look of it. No one to hear a muffled scream at the dead of night. No one to see, from an unwashed window, the killer slinking away, dappled with blood.

Rebus stared back into the cul-de-sac, then up at the corner of the first building, where a barely legible plaque bore the cul-de-sac's name: Wolf Street E1.

This was the reason why the police had come to call the killer Wolfman. Nothing to do with the savagery of his attacks, or the teeth marks he left at the scene, but simply because, as Flight had said, this was so far as they could know his place of birth, the place where he had defined himself for the very first time. He was the Wolfman. He could be anywhere, but that was relatively unimportant. What was more important was that he could be *anyone*, anyone at all in this city of ten million faces, ten million secret lairs.

'Where next?' he said, opening the passenger door.

'Kilmore Road,' said Flight. He exchanged a glance with Rebus, acknowledging the irony.

'Kilmore Road it is,' said Rebus, getting into the car.

The day had started early. Rebus, waking after three hours' sleep and unable to drop off again, switched on the radio in his room and listened to the morning news programme as he dressed. Not knowing exactly what the day would bring, he dressed casually: caramel cord trousers, light jacket, shirt. No tweeds or tie today. He wanted a bath, but the facilities on his floor of the hotel were locked. He would have to ask in reception. Near the stairs there stood an automatic shoeshine machine. He polished the toes of both well-worn black shoes before starting down to breakfast.

The restaurant area was busy, most of the customers looking like businessmen or tourists. The day's newspapers had been arranged across one vacant table and Rebus lifted a *Guardian* before being directed to a table laid for one by the harassed waitress.

Breakfast was mainly help-yourself, with juices, cereals and fruit crammed onto a large central display. A pot of coffee appeared, unasked for, on his table, as did a toastrack filled with cool half-slices of lightly tanned bread. Not so much toasted as wafted in front of a lightbulb, Rebus thought to himself as he smeared a portion of butter across one pitiful triangle.

The Full English Breakfast consisted of one slice of bacon, one warm tomato (from a tin), three small mushrooms, a sickly egg and a curious little sausage. Rebus wolfed down the lot. The coffee wasn't quite strong enough, but he finished the pot anyway and asked for a refill. All the time he was flicking through the paper, but only on a second examination did he find anything about the previous night's murder: a short, bare-bones paragraph near the foot of page four.

Bare bones. He looked around him. An embarrassed looking couple were trying to hush their two vociferous children. Don't, thought Rebus, don't stifle them, let them live. Who could know what might happen tomorrow? They might be killed. The parents might be killed. His own daughter was here in London somewhere, living in a flat with his ex-wife. He should get in touch. He *would* get in touch. A businessman at a corner table rustled his tabloid noisily, drawing Rebus's attention towards the front cover. WOLFMAN BITES AGAIN.

Ah, that was more like it. Rebus reached for a final half-slice of toast, only to find that he'd run out of butter. A hand landed heavily on his shoulder from behind, causing him to drop the toast. Startled, he turned to see George Flight standing there.

'Morning, John.'

'Hello, George. Sleep okay?'

Flight pulled out the chair across from Rebus and sat down heavily, hands in his lap.

'Not really. What about you?'

'I managed a few hours.' Rebus was about to turn his near-arrest on Shaftesbury Avenue into a morning anecdote, but decided to save it. There might come a time when they would need a funny story. 'Do you want some coffee?'

Flight shook his head. He examined the food on display. 'Some orange juice wouldn't go amiss though.' Rebus was about to rise, but Flight waved him down and rose himself to fetch a glassful, which he promptly downed. He squeezed his eyelids together. 'Tastes like powdered,' he said. 'Better give me some of that coffee after all.'

Rebus poured another cup. 'Seen that?' he said, nodding towards the corner table. Flight glanced at the tabloid and smiled.

'Well, it's their story now as much as ours. Only difference is, *we'll* keep things in perspective.'

'I'm not sure just what that perspective is.'

Flight stared at Rebus, but said nothing. He sipped at the coffee. 'There's a conference in the Murder Room at eleven o'clock. I didn't think we'd be able to make it, so I left Laine in charge. He likes being in charge.'

'And what are *we* going to be doing?'

'Well, we could go up to the Lea and check on the house-to-house. Or we could visit Mrs Cooper's place of employment.' Rebus didn't look enthusiastic. 'Or I could give you a tour of the other three murder scenes.' Rebus perked up. 'Okay,' said Flight, 'the scenic route it is. Drink up, Inspector. There's a long day ahead.'

'Just one thing,' said Rebus, lifting the cup halfway to his mouth. 'Why the nursemaid treatment? I'd have thought you'd have better things to do with your time than act as my chauffeur?'

Flight examined Rebus closely. Should he tell Rebus the real reason, or invent some story? He opted for invention and shrugged. 'Just easing you into the case, that's all.'

Rebus nodded slowly, but Flight knew he didn't wholly believe him.

Out at the car, Rebus glanced in through the back window, seeking the teddy bear.

'I killed it,' Flight said, unlocking the driver's door. 'The perfect murder.'

'So what's Edinburgh like?'

Rebus knew Flight wasn't talking about the tourist Edinburgh, home to the Festival and the Castle. He was talking about criminal Edinburgh, which was another city altogether.

'Well,' he replied, 'we've still got a drug problem, and loan sharks seem to be making a comeback, but other than that things are fairly quiet at the moment.'

'But,' Flight reminded him, 'you did have that child killer a few years back.'

Rebus nodded.

'And you solved it.' Rebus made no reply to this. They'd managed to keep out of the media the fact that it had been personal, had not exactly been 'serial'.

'Thousands of man hours solved it,' he said casually.

'That's not what the chiefs think,' said Flight. 'They think you're some kind of serial killer guru.'

'They're wrong,' said Rebus. 'I'm just a copper, the same as you are. So who exactly *are* the chiefs? Whose idea was it?'

But Flight shook his head. 'I'm not exactly sure. I mean, I know who the chiefs are – Laine, Chief Superintendent Pearson – but not which one of them is responsible for your being here.'

'It was Laine's name on the letter,' said Rebus, knowing this didn't really mean anything.

Then he watched the midday pedestrians scurrying along the pavements. The traffic was at a standstill. He and

Flight had come just over three miles in the best part of half an hour. Roadworks, double (and triple) parking, a succession of traffic lights and pedestrian crossings and some maddening tactics from selfish drivers had reduced their progress to a crawl. Flight seemed to read his mind.

'We'll be out of this in a couple of minutes,' he said. He was thinking over what Rebus had said, *just a copper, the same as you are.* But Rebus *had* caught the child killer, hadn't he? The files on the case credited him with the collar, a collar which had earned him the rank of Inspector. No, Rebus was just being modest, that was it. And you had to admire him for that.

A couple of minutes later, they had moved a further fifteen yards and were about to pass a narrow junction with a No Entry sign at its mouth. Flight glanced up this side-street. 'Time to take a few liberties,' he said, turning the steering-wheel hard. One side of the street was lined with market stalls. Rebus could hear the stall-holders sharpening their patter against the whetstone of passing trade. Nobody paid the slightest attention to a car travelling the wrong way down a one-way street, until a boy pulling a mobile stall from one side of the road to the other halted their progress. A meaty fist banged on the driver's side window. Flight rolled down the window, and a head appeared, extraordinarily pink and round and totally hairless.

'Oi, what's your fucking game then?' The words died in his throat. 'Oh, it's you Mister Flight. Didn't recognise the motor.'

'Hello, Arnold,' Flight said quietly, his eyes on the ponderous movement of the stall ahead. 'How's tricks?'

The man laughed nervously. 'Keeping me nose clean, Mister Flight.'

Only now did Flight deign to turn his head towards the man. 'That's good,' he said. Rebus had never heard those two words sound so threatening. Their road ahead was now clear. 'Keep it that way,' Flight said, moving off.

Rebus stared at him, waiting for an explanation.

'Sex offender,' Flight said. 'Two previous. Children. The psychiatrists say he's okay now, but I don't know. With that sort of thing, one hundred percent sure isn't quite sure enough. He's been working the market now for a few weeks, loading and unloading. Sometimes he gives me good gen. You know how it is.'

Rebus could imagine. Flight had this huge, strong-looking man in the palm of his hand. If Flight told the market-traders what he knew about Arnold, not only would Arnold lose his job, but he'd be in for a good kicking as well. Maybe the man *was* all right now, maybe he was, in psychiatric parlance, 'a fully integrated member of society'. He had paid for his crimes, and now was trying to go straight. And what happened? Policemen, men like Flight and like Rebus himself (if he was being honest), used his past against him to turn him into an informant.

'I've got a couple of dozen snitches,' Flight went on. 'Not all like Arnold. Some are in it for the cash, some simply because they can't keep their gobs shut. Telling what they know to somebody like me makes them feel important, makes them feel like they're in the know. A place this size, you'd be lost without a decent network of snitches.'

Rebus merely nodded, but Flight was warming to his subject.

'In some ways London is too big to take in. But in other ways it's tiny. Everyone knows everyone else. There's north and south of the river, of course, those are like two different countries. But the way the place divides, the loyalties, the same old faces, sometimes I feel like a village bobby on his bicycle.' Because Flight had turned towards him, Rebus nodded again. Inside he was thinking: here we

51

go, the same old story, London is bigger, better, rougher, tougher and more important than anywhere else. He had come across this attitude before, attending courses with Yard men or hearing about it from visitors to London. Flight hadn't seemed the type, but really everybody was the type. Rebus, too, in his time had exaggerated the problems the police faced in Edinburgh, so that he could look tougher and more important in somebody's eyes.

The facts still had to be faced. Police work was all about paperwork and computers and somebody stepping forward with the truth.

'Nearly there,' said Flight. 'Kilmore Road's the third on the left.'

Kilmore Road was part of an industrial estate and therefore would be deserted at night. It nestled in a maze of back streets about two hundred yards from a tube station. Rebus had always looked on tube stations as busy places, sited in populous areas, but this one stood on a narrow back street, well away from high road, bus route or railway station.

'I don't get it,' he said. Flight merely shrugged and shook his head.

Anyone coming out of the tube station at night found themselves with a lonely walk through the streets, past net-curtained windows where televisions blared. Flight showed him that a popular route was to cut into the industrial estate and across the parkland behind it. The park was flat and lifeless, boasting a single set of goalposts, two orange traffic cones substituting for the missing set. On the other side of the park three hi-rise blocks and some lo-rise housing sprang up. May Jessop had been making for one of those houses, where her parents lived. She was nineteen and had a good job, but it kept her late at her office, so it wasn't until ten o'clock that her parents started to worry. An hour later, there was a knock at the door. Her father rushed to answer, relieved, only to find a detective there, bearing the news that May's body had been found.

And so it went. There seemed no connection between the victims, no real geographical link other than that, as Flight pointed out, all the killings had been committed north of the river, by which he meant north of the Thames. What did a prostitute, an office manageress and the assistant in an off-licence have in common? Rebus was damned if he knew.

The third murder had taken place much further west in North Kensington. The body had been found beside a railway line and Transport Police had handled the investigation initially. The body was that of Shelley Richards, forty-one years old, unmarried and unemployed. She was the only coloured victim so far. As they drove through Notting Hill, Ladbroke Grove and North 'Ken' (as Flight termed it) Rebus was intrigued by the scheme of things. A street of extraordinarily grand houses would suddenly give way to a squalid, rubbish-strewn road with boarded-up windows and bench-bound tramps, the wealthy and the poor living almost cheek by jowl. It would never happen in Edinburgh; in Edinburgh, certain boundaries were observed. But this, this was incredible. As Flight put it, 'race riots one side, diplomats the other'.

The spot where Shelley Richards had died was the loneliest, the most pathetic so far. Rebus clambered down from the railway line, down the embankment, lowered himself over the brick wall and dropped to the ground. His trousers were smeared with green moss. He brushed them with his hands, but to little effect. To get to the car where Flight was waiting he had to walk under a railway bridge. His footsteps echoed as he tried to avoid the pools of water and the rubbish, and then he stopped, listening. There was a noise all around him, a sort of wheezing, as if the bridge itself were drawing its dying breath. He looked up and saw the dark outlines of pigeons, still against the supporting girders. Cooing softly. That was what he could hear, not wheezing at all. There was a sudden rumble of thunder as a train passed overhead and the pigeons took to the wing, flapping around his head. He shivered and walked back out into sunlight.

Then, finally, it was back to the Murder Room. This was, in fact, a series of rooms covering most of the top floor of the building. Rebus reckoned there to be about twenty men and women working flat out when Flight and he entered the largest of the rooms. There was little to differentiate the scene from that of any murder investigation anywhere in the country. Officers were busy on telephones or working at computer terminals. Clerical staff moved from desk to desk with seemingly endless sheafs of paper. A photocopier was spewing out more paper in a corner of the room and two delivery-men were wheeling a new five-drawer filing cabinet into position beside the three which already stood against one wall. On another wall was a detailed street map of London, with the murder sites pinpointed. Coloured tapes ran from these sites to spaces on the wall where pictures, details and notes had been pinned. A duty roster and progress chart took up what space was left. All very efficient, but the faces told Rebus their own story: everyone here, working hard as they were, was waiting for the Lucky Break.

Flight was immediately in tune with the glaze of efficiency in the office, firing off questions. How did the meeting go? Any word from Lambeth? (He explained to Rebus that the police lab was based there.) Any news on last night? What about house-to-house? Well, does anyone know *anything*?

There were shrugs and shakes of the head. They were simply going through the motions, waiting for that Lucky

Break. But what if it didn't come? Rebus had an answer to that: you made your own luck.

A smaller room off this main office was being used as a communications centre, keeping the Murder Room in touch with the investigation, and off this room were two smaller offices yet, each crammed with three desks. This was where the senior detectives worked. Both were empty.

'Sit down,' Flight said. He picked up the telephone on his desk, and dialled. While he waited for an answer, he surveyed with a frown the four-inch high pile of paper which had appeared in his in-tray during the morning. 'Hello, Gino?' he said into the mouthpiece. 'George Flight here. Can I order some sandwiches? Salami salad.' He looked to Rebus for confirmation that this would be acceptable. 'On brown bread, please, Gino. Better make it four rounds. Thanks.' He cut the connection and dialled again. Only two numbers this time: an internal call. 'Gino has a cafe round the corner,' he explained to Rebus. 'He makes great sandwiches, and he delivers.' Then: 'Oh, hello. Inspector Flight here. Can we have some tea? A decent-sized pot should do it. We're in the office. Is it wet milk today or that powdered crap? Great, thanks.' He dropped the receiver back into its cradle and spread his hands, as if some feat of magic had just been performed. 'This is your lucky day, John. We've got real milk for a change.'

'So what now?'

Flight shrugged, then slapped a hand on the bulging in-tray. 'You could always read through this little lot, keep yourself up-to-date with the investigation.'

'Reading about it isn't going to do any good.'

'On the contrary,' said Flight, 'it helps you answer any awkward questions that may be asked by those on high. How tall was the victim? What colour was her hair? Who found her? It's all in there.'

'She was five feet seven and her hair was brown. As to who found her, I don't give a tinker's cuss.'

Flight laughed, but Rebus was being serious. 'Murderers don't just appear,' he continued. 'They're created. To create a serial killer takes time. It's taken this guy years to make himself what he is. What's he been doing during that time? He may well be a loner, but he's probably got a job, maybe even a wife and kids. *Somebody* must know something. Maybe his wife wonders where he goes at night, or how blood got onto the tips of his shoes, or where her kitchen knife disappeared to.'

'All right, John.' Flight spread his hands again, this time in a gesture of peace-making. Rebus realised that his voice had been getting louder. 'Calm down a little. For a start, when you go on like that I can hardly make out a word you're saying, but I get your point. So what are we supposed to do?'

'Publicity. We need the public's help. We need anything they've got.'

'We already get dozens of calls a day. Anonymous tip-offs, nutters who want to confess, people snitching on their next door neighbour, people with grudges, maybe even a few with genuine suspicions. We check them all out. And we've got the media on our side. The Chief Super will be interviewed a dozen times today. Newspapers, magazines, radio, TV. We give them what we can, and we tell them to spread the word. We've got the best bloody Liaison Officer in the country working round the clock to make sure the public knows what we're dealing with here.'

There was a knock on the already open door and a WPC carried a tray into the room and left it on Flight's desk. 'I'll be mother, shall I?' he said, already starting to pour the tea into two plain white mugs.

'What's the Liaison Officer's name?' Rebus asked. He knew a Liaison Officer himself. She, too, was the best there was. But she wasn't in London; she was back in Edinburgh ...

'Cath Farraday,' said Flight. 'Detective Inspector Cath Farraday.' He sniffed the milk carton, before pouring a dollop into his tea. 'If you stick around long enough, you'll get to meet her. She's a bit of a cracker is our Cath. Mind you, if she heard me talking about her like that, she'd have my head on a plate.' Flight chuckled.

'And salad on the side,' came a voice from just outside the door. Flight, flinching, spilt tea down his shirt and jumped to his feet. The door was swinging open now, to reveal a platinum blonde woman leaning against the jamb, her arms folded, one leg casually crossed over the other. Rebus's gaze was drawn to her eyes, which were slanted like a cat's. They made her whole face seem narrower than it was. Her lips were thin, lined with a thin coat of bright red lipstick. Her hair had a hard, metallic look to it, reflecting the look of the woman herself. She was older than either of the men in the room by several years and if age hadn't withered her, the frequent use of cosmetics had. Her face was lined and puffy. Rebus didn't like a lot of make-up on a woman, but plenty of men did.

'Hello, Cath,' said Flight, trying to regain at least an outer shell of composure. 'We were just ...'

'... talking about me. I know.' She unfolded her arms and took a couple of steps into the room, extending a hand to Rebus. 'You must be Inspector Rebus,' she said. 'I've heard all about you.'

'Oh?' Rebus looked to Flight, whose attention, however, was fixed on Cath Farraday.

'I hope George here is giving you an easy ride.'

Rebus shrugged. 'I've had worse.'

Her eyes became more feline still. 'I'll bet,' she said. She lowered her voice. 'But watch your back, Inspector. Not everyone's as nice as George. How would you feel if

57

someone from London suddenly started to poke his nose into one of your cases, hmm?'

'Cath,' said Flight, 'there's no need for ...'

She raised a hand, silencing him. 'Just a friendly warning, George, one Inspector to another. We've got to look after our own, haven't we?' She glanced at her watch. 'Must be going. I've a meeting with Pearson in five minutes. Nice to have met you, Inspector. Bye, George.'

And then she was gone, the door left wide open, a strong perfume lingering in the room. Both men were silent for a moment. Rebus was the first to speak.

'I believe your description was "a cracker", George. Remind me never to let you arrange a blind date for me.'

It was late afternoon and Rebus sat in Flight's office alone, a pad of paper in front of him on the desk. He tapped his pen like a drumstick against the edge of the table and stared at the two names he had written so far.

Dr Anthony Morrison. Tommy Watkiss.

These were people he wanted to see. He drew a thick line beneath them and wrote two more names: Rhona. Samantha. These, too, were people he wanted to see, though for personal reasons.

Flight had gone off to see Chief Inspector Laine on another floor of the building. The invitation did not extend to Rebus. He picked up the last remaining quarter of his salami sandwich, but thought better of it and tossed it into the office's metal bin. Too salty. And what kind of meat was salami anyway? He now had a craving for more tea. He thought Flight had dialled 18 to order up the first pot, but decided against trying it. He didn't want to make a fool of himself, did he? It would be just his luck to get through to Chief Superintendent Pearson.

Just a friendly warning. The point was not lost on Rebus. He crumpled up his list and threw that in the bin too, then got up out of his chair and made for the main office. He knew he should be doing something, or should at least *seem* to be doing something. They had brought him four hundred miles to help them. But he couldn't for the life of him see any gaps in their investigation. They were doing everything they could, but to no avail. He was just another straw to be clutched at. Just another chance for that elusive Lucky Break.

He was studying the wall-map when the voice sounded behind him.

'Sir?'

He turned to see one of the Murder Room team standing there. 'Yes?'

'Someone to see you, sir.'

'Me?'

'Well, you're the most senior detective around at the moment, sir.'

Rebus considered this. 'Who is it?'

The officer checked the scrap of paper in his hand. 'A Dr Frazer, sir.'

Rebus considered a moment longer. 'All right,' he said, turning back towards the tiny office. 'Give me a minute and then send him in.' He stopped. 'Oh, and bring some tea, will you?'

'Yes, sir,' said the officer. He waited until Rebus had left the room, then turned to the others, seated at their desks and smiling at him. 'The cheek of these fucking jocks,' he said, loud enough for everyone to hear. 'Remind me to piss in the teapot before I take it in.'

Dr Frazer turned out to be a woman. What was more, as she entered the office, she was attractive enough to have Rebus half-rise from his desk in welcome.

'Inspector Rebus?'

'That's right. Dr Frazer, I presume?'

'Yes.' She showed a row of perfect teeth as Rebus invited her to take a seat. 'Though I'd better explain.' Rebus fixed his eyes on her own and nodded. He kept his eyes fixed on hers for fear that otherwise they would be drawn down to her slim tanned legs, to that point where, an inch above the knee, her cream skirt began, hugging her thighs. He had taken her body in with a single sweeping glance. She was tall, almost as tall as him. Her legs were bare and long, her body supple. She was wearing a jacket to match the skirt and a plain white blouse, set off by a single string of pearls. There was a slight, exquisite scar on her throat just above the pearls and her face was tanned and without make-up, her jaw square, her hair straight and black, tied back with a black band, so that a shock of it fell onto one shoulder. She had brought a soft black leather briefcase into the room, which she now held up in her lap, running her fingers around the handles as she spoke.

'I'm not a medical doctor.' Rebus registered slight surprise. 'I'm a doctor courtesy of my Ph.D. I teach psychology at University College.'

'And you're American,' said Rebus.

'Canadian actually.'

Yes, he should have known. There was a soft lilt to her accent, something few Americans possessed. And she wasn't quite as nasal as the tourists who stopped in Princes Street to get a picture of the Scott Monument.

'I'm sorry,' he said, 'so, what can I do for you, Dr Frazer?'

'Well, I did talk to someone on the telephone this morning and I told them of my interest in the Wolfman case.'

Rebus could see it all now. Another nutter with some crazy idea about the Wolfman, that's probably what the Murder Room had thought. So they'd decided to play a joke on him, arranged a meeting without letting him know, and then Flight, forewarned, had made himself scarce. Well, the joke was on them. Rebus could always find time for an attractive woman, crazy or not. After all, he had nothing better to do, had he?

'Go on,' he said.

'I'd like to try to put together a profile of the Wolfman.'

'A profile?'

'A psychological profile. Like an identikit, but building up a picture of the mind rather than the face. I've been doing some research on criminal profiling and I think I can use similar criteria to help you come to a clearer understanding of the killer.' She paused. 'What do you think?'

'I'm wondering what's in it for you, Dr Frazer.'

'Perhaps I'm just being public spirited.' She looked down into her lap and smiled. 'But really, what I'm looking for is validation of my methods. So far I've been experimenting with old police cases. Now I want to tackle something real.'

Rebus sat back in his chair and picked up the pen again, pretending to study it. When he looked up, he saw that she was studying him. She was a psychologist after all. He put down the pen. 'It isn't a game,' he said, 'and this isn't a lecture theatre. Four women are dead, a maniac is loose somewhere and right now we're quite busy enough following up all the leads and the false trails we've got. Why should we make time for you, Dr Frazer?'

She coloured, her cheekbones blushed a deep red. But she seemed to have no ready answer. Rebus hadn't much to add, so he too sat in silence. His mouth was sour and dry, his throat coated in a layer of resin. Where was the tea?

Eventually she spoke. 'All I want to do is read through the material on the case.'

Rebus found some spare sarcasm. 'That's *all*?' He tapped the mound of paperwork in the in-tray. 'No problem then, it'll only take you a couple of months.' She was ignoring him, fumbling with the briefcase. She produced a slim orange folder.

'Here,' she said stonily. 'Just read this. It'll only take you twenty minutes. It's one of the profiles I did of an American serial killer. If you think it has no validity in helping to identify the killer or target where he might have struck next, fair enough, I'll leave.'

Rebus took the file. Oh God, he thought, not more psychology! *Relating … involving … motivating*. He'd had his fill of psychology on the management training course. But then again, he didn't want her to leave. He didn't want to be left sitting here on his own with everyone in the Murder Room smirking at their little trick. He opened the folder, drew out a typed and bound thesis about twenty-five pages long and began to read. She sat watching him, waiting for a question perhaps. Rebus read with his chin held up, so that she wouldn't see the sagging folds of flesh on his neck, and with his shoulders back, making the best of his admittedly not very muscular chest. He cursed his parents for not feeding him up as a child. He had grown skinny, and when eventually he had started to put weight on, it had been to his gut and his backside, not his chest and arms.

Backside. Chest. Arms. He gazed hard at the words in front of him, but aware of her body resting in his line of peripheral vision, just above the top edge of the paper. He didn't even know her first name. Perhaps he never would. He frowned as though deep in thought and read through the opening page.

By page five he was interested and by page ten he felt there might be something in it after all. A lot of it was speculative. Be honest, John, it was almost all conjecture, but there were a few points where she made a telling deduction. He saw what it was: her mind worked in a different orbit from a detective's. They circled the same sun, however, and now and then the satellites touched. And what harm could come from letting her do a profile for the Wolfman? At worst, it would lead them up another dead end. At best, he might enjoy some female company during his stay in London. Yes, some pleasant female company. Which reminded him: he wanted to telephone his ex-wife and arrange a visit. He read through the final pages quickly.

'All right,' he said, closing the thesis, 'very interesting.'

She seemed pleased. 'And useful?'

He hesitated before replying. 'Perhaps.'

She wanted more from him than that. 'But worth letting me have a go on the Wolfman?'

He nodded slowly, ruminatively, and her face lit up. Rebus couldn't help returning her smile. There was a knock at the door. 'Come in,' he called.

It was Flight. He was carrying a tray, swimming with spilt tea. 'I believe you asked for some refreshment,' he said. Then he caught sight of Dr Frazer, and Rebus delighted in the stunned look on his face.

'Christ,' said Flight, looking from woman to Rebus to woman, before realising that he had somehow to justify his outburst. 'They told me you were with someone, John, but they didn't, I mean, I didn't know …' He tumbled to a halt, mouth still open, and placed the tray on the desk before turning towards her. 'I'm Inspector George Flight,' he said, reaching out a hand.

'Dr Frazer,' she replied, 'Lisa Frazer.'

As their hands met, Flight looked towards Rebus from the corner of his eye. Rebus, beginning to feel a little more at home in the metropolis, gave him a slow, cheerful wink.

'Christ.'

She left him a couple of books to read. One, *The Serial Mind*, was a series of essays by various academics. It included 'Sealing the Bargain: Modes of Motivation in the

Serial Killer' by Lisa Frazer, University of London. Lisa: nice name. No mention of her doctorate though. The other book was an altogether heavier affair, dense prose linked by charts and graphs and diagrams: *Patterns of Mass Murder* by Gerald Q MacNaughtie.

MacNaughtie? That had to be a joke of some kind. But on the dustjacket Rebus read that Professor MacNaughtie was Canadian by birth and taught at the University of Columbia. Nowhere could he find out what the Q stood for. He spent what was left of the office day working through the books, paying most attention to Lisa Frazer's essay (which he read twice) and to the chapter in MacNaughtie's book concentrating on 'Patterns of Mutilation'. He drank tea and coffee and two cans of fizzy orange, but the taste in his mouth was sour and as he read on he began to feel physically dirty, made grubby by tale after tale of casual horror. When he got up to visit the bathroom at a quarter to five, everyone in the outer office had already quit for the day, but Rebus hardly registered the fact. His mind was elsewhere.

Flight, who had left him to his own devices for most of the afternoon, came into the office at six. 'Fancy a jar?' Rebus shook his head. Flight sat down on the edge of the chair. 'What's the matter?'

Rebus waved a hand over the books. Flight examined the cover of one. 'Oh,' he said, 'not exactly bedtime reading, I take it?'

'Not exactly. It's just … evil.'

Flight nodded. 'Got to keep a perspective though, John, eh? Otherwise they'd go on getting away with it. If it's so horrible, we all shy away from the truth, then everybody gets away with murder. And worse than murder.'

Rebus looked up. 'What's worse than murder?'

'Lots of things. What about someone who tortures and

rapes a six-month old child and films the whole thing so he can show it to similarly minded individuals?'

Rebus's words were barely audible. 'You're kidding.' But he knew Flight was not.

'Happened three months ago,' Flight said. 'We haven't caught the bastard, but Scotland Yard have got the video – and a few more besides. Ever seen a thalidomide porn film?' Rebus shook his head wearily. Flight leaned down so that their heads were nearly touching. 'Don't go soft on me, John,' he said quietly, 'that's not going to solve anything. You're in London now, not the Highlands. The top deck of a midday bus isn't safe here, never mind a tow-path after dark. Nobody sees any of it. London gives you a thick skin and temporary blindness. You and I can't afford to be blind. But we can afford the occasional drink. Coming?'

He was on his feet now, rubbing his hands, lecture over. Rebus nodded and rose slowly to his feet. 'Only a quick one though,' he said. 'I've got an appointment this evening.'

An appointment reached by way of a packed tube train. He checked his watch: 7.30 pm. Did the rush hour never stop? The compartment smelt of vinegar and stale air, and three not-so-personal stereos battled it out above the roar of speeding and juddering. The faces around Rebus were blank. Temporary blindness: Flight was right. They shut it all out because to acknowledge what they were going through was to realise the monotony, the claustrophobia and the sheer agony of it all. Rebus was depressed. And tired. But he was also a tourist, so it had to be savoured. Thus the tube journey instead of a closeted taxi ride. Besides, he'd been warned about how expensive the black cabs were and he had checked in his A-Z, and found that his destination was only a quarter of an inch from an Underground station.

So Rebus travelled through the Underground and tried

hard not to look out of place, not to gawp at the buskers and the beggars, not to pause in a busy conduit the better to read this or that advertising poster. A tramp actually entered his carriage at one stop and as the doors closed and the train pulled away again he began to rave, but his audience were deaf and dumb as well as blind and they successfully ignored his existence until the next stop where, daunted, he slouched from the carriage onto the platform. As the engine pulled away, Rebus could hear his voice again, coming from the next carriage along. It had been an astonishing performance, not by the tramp but by the passengers. They had closed off their minds, refusing involvement. Would they do the same if they saw a fight taking place? Saw a thick-set man stealing a tourist's wallet? Yes, they probably would. This wasn't an environment of good and evil: it was a moral vacuum and that frightened Rebus more than anything else.

But there were compensations of a sort. Every beautiful woman he saw reminded him of Lisa Frazer. Squeezed into one compartment on the Central Line, he found himself pressed against a young blonde girl. Her blouse was undone to the cleft of her breasts, giving the taller Rebus an occasionally breathtaking view of slopes and swells. She glanced up from her paperback and caught him staring. He looked away quickly, but felt her cold gaze focusing on the side of his head.

Every man is a rapist: hadn't someone said that once? *Traces of salt … Bite marks on the …* The train slowed into another station: Mile End, his stop. The girl was getting out, too. He lingered on the platform until she was gone, without really knowing why, then headed up towards ground level and a taste of fresh air.

Taste of monoxide, more like. Three lanes of traffic were jammed in either direction, the result of an articulated lorry failing to reverse through the narrow gates of some building. Two exasperated constables were trying to untie this Gordian Knot and for the first time it struck Rebus how silly their tall rounded hats looked. The Scottish-issue flat caps were more sensible. They also made less of a target at football matches.

Rebus wished the constables a silent 'Good luck' and made for Gideon Park – not a park but a road – and for number 78, a three-storey house which, according to the front door's entry system, had been split somehow into four flats. He pressed the second-from-bottom buzzer and waited. The door was opened by a tall skinny teenage girl, her long straight hair dyed black, three earrings in each ear. She smiled and gave him an unexpected hug.

'Hello, Dad,' she said.

Samantha Rebus led her father up a narrow staircase to the first-floor flat she shared with her mother. If the change in his daughter was striking, then the change in Rebus's ex-wife was doubly so. He had never seen her looking so good. There were strands of grey in her hair, but it had been cut fashionably short and there was a healthy suntanned look to her face, a gleam to her eyes. They studied one another without words, then embraced quickly.

'John.'

'Rhona.'

She had been reading a book. He looked at its cover: *To the Lighthouse*, Virginia Woolf. 'Tom Wolfe's more my style,' he said. The living-room was small, cramped even, but a lot of clever work with shelves and wall-mirrors gave the impression of space. It was a strange sensation, seeing things he recognised, that chair, a cushion-cover, a lamp, things from his life with Rhona, now transported to this pokey flat. But he praised the interior decoration, the snug feel of the place and then they sat down to drink tea. Rebus had brought gifts: record tokens for Samantha, chocolates for Rhona – received with a knowing, coded look between the two women.

Two women. Samantha was no longer a child. Her figure might retain a child's suppleness, but her way of moving, her actions, her face were all fully formed and adult.

'You look good, Rhona.'

She paused, accepting the compliment. 'Thank you, John,' she said at last. He noted her inability to say the same of him. Mother and daughter shared another of their secret looks. It was as though their time together had led to a kind of telepathy between them, so that during the course of the evening Rebus was to do most of the talking, nervously filling the many silent gaps in the conversation.

None of it was very important anyway. He spoke of Edinburgh, without going into detail about his work. This wasn't easy, since work apart he did very little. Rhona asked about mutual friends and he had to admit that he saw none of the old crowd. She talked about her teaching, of property prices in London. (Rebus heard nothing in her tone to suggest that he should pay something towards a bigger place for his kin. After all, it had been her idea to leave him. No real grounds, except, as she'd put it, that she'd loved a man but married a job.) Then Samantha told him about her secretarial course.

'Secretarial?' said Rebus, trying to sound enthusiastic. Samantha's reply was cool.

'I told you about it in one of my letters.'

'Oh.' There was another break in the conversation. Rebus wanted to burst out: I read your letters, Sammy! I devour your letters! And I'm sorry I so seldom write back, but you know what a lousy letter-writer I am, how much effort it takes, how little time and energy I have. So many cases to solve, so many people depending on me.

But he said nothing. Of course he said nothing. Instead, they played out this little sham scenario. Polite chit-chat in a tiny living-room off Bow Road. Everything to say. Saying nothing. It was unbearable. Truly unbearable. Rebus moved his hands to his knees, spreading the fingers, ready to rise to his feet in the expected manner of one about to leave. Well, it's been nice seeing you, but there's a starched hotel bed waiting for me, and a machine to dispense ice, and another to shine shoes. He started to rise.

And the buzzer sounded. Two short, two long. Samantha fairly flew to the stairs. Rhona smiled.

'Kenny,' she explained.

'Oh?'

'Samantha's current gentleman.'

Rebus nodded slowly, the understanding father. Sammy was sixteen. She'd left school. A secretarial course at college. Not a boyfriend, a gentleman. 'What about you, Rhona?' he said.

She opened her mouth, forming a reply, when the thump of feet climbing the stairs closed it for her. Samantha's face was flushed as she led her gentleman by his hand into the room. Instinctively, Rebus stood up.

'Dad, this is Kenny.'

Kenny was clad in black leather zip-up jacket and black leather trousers, with boots reaching almost to his knees. He squeaked as he moved and in his free hand he carried an upturned crash-helmet, from which poked the fingers of a pair of black leather gloves. Two fingers were prominent, and appeared to be pointing directly at Rebus. Kenny removed his hand from Samantha's grip and held it out towards her father.

'Wotcher.'

The voice was abrupt, the tone deep and confident. He had lank black hair, almost parted at centre, some residual acne on cheeks and neck, a day's growth of stubble. Rebus shook the hot hand with little enthusiasm.

'Hello, Kenny,' Rhona said. Then, for Rebus's benefit: 'Kenny's a motorcycle messenger.'

'Oh,' said Rebus, taking his seat again.

'Yeah, that's right,' Kenny enthused, 'down the City.' He turned to Rhona. 'Made a fair old packet today, Rhona,' he said, winking. Rhona smiled warmly. This young gentleman, this lad of eighteen or so (so much older, so much more worldly than Samantha) had obviously charmed his way into mother's heart as well as daughter's. He turned now to Rebus with that same winning way. 'I make a hundred quid on a good day. Course, it used to be better, back at Big Bang. There were a lot of new companies then, all of them trying to show off how much dosh they had. Still, there's a killing to be made if you're fast and reliable. A lot of the customers ask for me by name now. That shows I'm getting somewhere.' He sat down on the sofa beside Samantha and waited, as did they all, for Rebus to say something.

He knew what was expected of him. Kenny had thrown down a gauntlet, and the message was, Just you dare disapprove of me now. What did the kid want? A pat on the ego? Rebus's permission to deflower his daughter? A few tips on how to avoid speed-traps? Whatever, Rebus wasn't about to knuckle under.

'Can't be good for your lungs,' he said instead. 'All those exhaust fumes.'

Kenny seemed perplexed by this turn in the conversation. 'I keep myself fit,' he said, sounding slightly piqued. Good, thought Rebus, I can nettle this little bastard. He knew Rhona was warning him to lay off, warning him with her piercing eyes, but Rebus kept his attention on Kenny.

'Must be a lot of prospects for a lad like you.'

Kenny cheered up immediately. 'Yeah,' he said, 'I might even set up my own fleet. All you need's –' He fell silent as he belatedly noticed that use of 'lad', as though he were dressed in shorts and school-cap. But it was too late to go back and correct it, way too late. He had to push on, but now it all sounded like pipe-dreams and playground fantasies. This rozzer might be from Jockland, but he was every bit as oily as an East End old-timer. He'd have to watch his step. And what was happening now? This Jock, this rough-looking tosser in the ill-fitting gear, the completely uncoordinated gear, this 'man at C&A' type, was reminiscing about a grocery shop from his youth. For a time, Rebus had been the grocer's 'message boy'. (He explained that in Scotland 'messages' meant 'groceries'.) He'd run about on a heavy-framed black bicycle, with a metal rectangle in front of the handlebars. The box of groceries would be held in this rectangle and off he would pedal to do his deliveries.

'I thought I was rich,' Rebus said, obviously coming to a punch line. 'But when I wanted more money, there wasn't any to be had. I had to wait till I was old enough to get a proper job, but I loved running around on that bike, doing errands and delivering messages to the old folk. Sometimes they'd even give me a tip, a piece of fruit or a jar of jam.'

There was silence in the room. A police siren sped past outside. Rebus sat back and folded his arms, a sentimental smile spread across his face. And then it dawned on Kenny: *Rebus was comparing the two of them!* His eyes widened. Everyone knew it. Rhona knew it. Sam knew it. For tuppence, he'd get up and stick the nut on the copper, Sam's dad or not. But he held back and the moment passed. Rhona got up to make more tea, and the big bastard got up and said he had to be going.

It had all happened so fast. Kenny was still trying to unravel Rebus's story and Rebus could see it. The poor half-educated runt was trying to work out just how far Rebus had put him down. Rebus could answer that: as far as was necessary. Rhona hated him for it, of course, and

Samantha looked embarrassed. Well to hell with them. He'd done his duty, he'd paid his respects. He wouldn't bother them any more. Let them live in their cramped flat, visited by this … gentleman, this mock adult. Rebus had more important things to do. Books to read. Notes to make. And another busy day ahead. It was ten o'clock. He could be back at his hotel by eleven. An early night, that's what was needed. Eight hours' sleep in the last two days. No wonder he was ratty, looking for a fight.

He began to feel a little bit ashamed. Kenny was too easy a target. He'd crushed a tiny fly beneath a tower-block of resentment. Resentment, John, or plain jealousy? That was not a question for a tired man. Not a question for a man like John Rebus. Tomorrow. Tomorrow, he might start getting some answers. He was determined to pay for his keep now that he had been brought to London. Tomorrow, the task began in earnest.

He shook Kenny's hand again and gave him a man-to-man half-wink before leaving the flat. Rhona offered to see him to the door. They went into the hall, leaving Samantha and Kenny in the living-room, behind a closed door.

'It's okay,' Rebus said quickly. 'I'll see myself out.' He started downstairs, aware that to linger was to invite an argument with Rhona. What was the point? 'Better go keep an eye on Lothario,' he called, unable to resist the parting shot.

Outside, he remembered that Rhona liked her lovers young, too. Perhaps she … but no, that thought was unworthy of him. 'Sorry, God,' he said, turning with a steady stride back towards the Underground.

* * *

Something is going wrong.

After the first killing, she had felt horror, remorse, guilt. She had begged forgiveness; she would not kill again.

After a month, a month of not being found, she grew more optimistic, and grew hungry too. So she killed again. This had satisfied for another month, and so it had gone on. But now, only twenty-four hours after the fourth time, she had felt the urge again. An urge more powerful and focused than ever. She would get away with it, too. But it would be dangerous. The police were still hunting. Time had not elapsed. The public was wary. If she killed now, she would break her patternless pattern, and perhaps that would give the police some clue that she could not predict.

There was only one solution. It was wrong; she knew it was wrong. This wasn't her flat, not really. But she did it anyway. She unlocked the door and entered the gallery. There, tied up on the floor, lay the latest body. She would store this one. Keep it out of sight of the police. Examining it, she realised that now she would have more time with it, more time in which to play. Yes, storage was the answer. This lair was the answer. No fear of being found. After all, this was a private place, not a public place. No fear. She walked around the body, enjoying its silence. Then she raised the camera to her eye.

'Smile please,' she says, snapping her way through the film. Then she has an idea. She loads another film cartridge and photographs one of the paintings, a landscape. This is the one she will carve, just as soon as she has finished playing with her new toy. But now she has a record of it, too. A permanent record. She watches the photograph develop but then starts to scratch across the plate, smearing the colours and the focus until the picture becomes a chemical swirl, seemingly without form. God, her mother would have hated that.

'Bitch,' she says, turning from the wall filled with paintings. Her face is creased with anger and resentment.

73

She picks up a pair of scissors and goes to her plaything again, kneels in front of it, takes a firm hold of the head and brings the scissors down towards the face until they hover a centimetre away from the nose. 'Bitch,' she says again, then carefully snips at the nostrils, her hand shaking. 'Long nosehairs,' she wails, 'are so unbecoming. So unbecoming.'

At last she rises again and crosses to the opposite wall, lifts an aerosol and shakes it noisily. This wall – she calls it her Dionysian wall – is covered in spray-painted black slogans: DEATH TO ART, KILLING IS AN ART, THE LAW IS AN ARSE, FUCK THE RICH, FEEL THE POOR. She thinks of something else to say, something worth the diminishing space. She sprays with a flourish.

'This is art,' she says, glancing over her shoulder towards the Apollonian wall with its framed paintings. 'This is fucking art. This is fuck art.' She sees that the doll's eyes are open and throws herself down to within an inch of those eyes, which suddenly screw themselves shut. Carefully, she uses both hands to prise apart the eyelids. Faces are close now, *so* intimate. The moment is always *so* intimate. Her breath is fast. So is the doll's. The doll's mouth struggles against the tape holding it shut. The nostrils flare.

'Fuck art,' she hisses to the doll. 'This is fuck art.' She has the scissors in her hand again now, and slides one blade into the doll's left nostril. 'Long nosehairs, Johnny, are so unbecoming in a man. So unbecoming in a man.' She pauses, as though listening to something, as though considering this statement. Then she nods. 'Good point,' she says, smiling now.

'Good point.'

Catching a Bite

The telephone woke Rebus. He could not locate it for a moment, then realised that it was mounted on the wall just to the right of his headboard. He sat up, fumbling with the receiver.

'Hello?'

'Inspector Rebus?' The voice was full of zest. He didn't recognise it. Took his Longines (his father's Longines actually) from the bedside table and peered through the badly scratched face to find that it was seven fifteen. 'Did I wake you up? Sorry. It's Lisa Frazer.'

Rebus came to life. Or rather his voice did. He still sat slumped and jangling on the edge of the bed, but heard himself say a bright, 'Hello, Dr Frazer. What can I do for you?'

'I've been studying the notes you gave me on the Wolfman case. Working through most of the night, to be honest. I just couldn't sleep, I was so excited by them. I've made some preliminary observations.'

Rebus touched the bed, feeling its residual warmth. How long since he'd slept with a woman? How long since he'd woken up the following day regretting nothing?

'I see,' he said.

Her laughter was like a clear jet of water. 'Oh, Inspector, I'm sorry, I've wakened you. I'll call back later.'

'No, no. I'm fine, honestly. A bit startled, but fine. Can we meet and talk about what you've found?'

'Of course.'

'But I'm a bit tied up today.' He was trying to sound vulnerable, and thought on the whole that it was probably working. So he played his big card. 'What about dinner?'

'That would be nice. Where?'

He rubbed at a shoulder-blade. 'I don't know. This is your town, not mine. I'm a tourist, remember.'

She laughed. 'I'm not exactly a local myself, but I take your point. Well in that case, dinner's on me.' She sounded set on this. 'And I think I know just the place. I'll come to your hotel. Seven thirty?'

'I look forward to it.'

What a very pleasant way to start the day, thought Rebus, lying down again and plumping up the pillow. He'd just closed his eyes when the telephone rang again.

'Yes?'

'I'm in reception and you're a lazy git. Come down here so I can put my breakfast on your tab.'

Cli-chick. Brrrr. Rebus slapped the receiver back into its cradle and got out of bed with a growl.

'What kept you?'

'I didn't think they'd appreciate a stark naked guest in the dining-room. You're early.'

Flight shrugged. 'Things to do.' Rebus noticed that Flight didn't look well. The dark rings around his eyes and his pale colouring were not due simply to lack of sleep. His flesh had a saggy quality, as though magnets on the floor were drawing it down. But then he wasn't feeling so great himself. He thought he'd probably picked up a bug on the tube. His throat was a little sore and his head throbbed. Could it be true that cities made you sick? In one of the essays Lisa Frazer had given him someone had made that very claim, stating that most serial killers were products of their environment. Rebus couldn't really comment on that, but he did know that there was more mucus in his nostrils

76

than usual. Had he brought enough handkerchiefs with him?

'Things to do,' Flight repeated.

They sat at a table for two. The dining-room was quiet, and the Spanish waitress took their order briskly, the day not yet having had enough time to wear her down.

'What do you want to do today?' Flight seemed to be asking this only in order to get the conversation rolling, but Rebus had specific plans for the day and told him so.

'First off I'd quite like to see Maria Watkiss's man, Tommy.' Flight smiled at this and looked down at the table. 'Just to satisfy my own curiosity,' Rebus continued. 'And I'd like to talk to the dental pathologist, Dr Morrison.'

'Well, I know where to find both of them,' said Flight. 'Go on.'

'That's about it. I'm seeing Dr Frazer this evening –' Flight looked up at this news, his eyes widening in appreciation '– to go over her findings on the killer's profile.'

'Uh huh.' Flight sounded unconvinced.

'I've been reading those books she lent me. I think there may be something in it, George.' Rebus used the Christian name carefully, but Flight seemed to have no objections.

The coffee had arrived. Flight poured and drank a cup of it, then smacked his lips. 'I don't,' he said.

'Don't what?'

'Don't think there's anything in all this psychology stuff. It's too much like guesswork and not enough like science. I like something tangible. A dental pathologist, now that's tangible. That's something you can get –'

'Your teeth into?' Rebus smiled. 'The pun's bad enough, but I don't agree anyway. When was the last time a pathologist gave you a precise time of death? They always hedge their bets.'

'But they deal in *facts*, in physical evidence, not in mumbo-jumbo.'

Rebus sat back. He was thinking of the character in a Dickens book he'd read a long time ago, a schoolteacher who wanted facts and nothing but. 'Come on, George,' he said, 'this is the twentieth century.'

'That's right,' said Flight. 'And we don't believe in soothsayers any more.' He looked up again. 'Or do we?'

Rebus paused to pour some coffee. He felt his cheeks tingling. Probably, they were turning red. Arguments did that to him; even casual disagreements like this were sometimes enough. He was careful to make his next utterance in a soft, reasonable voice.

'So what are you saying?'

'I'm saying policework is plodding, John.' (Still on first name terms, thought Rebus: that's good.) 'And shortcuts seldom work. I'm saying don't let your Hampton do your thinking for you.' Rebus thought about protesting, but realised he wasn't exactly sure what Flight meant. Flight smiled.

'Rhyming slang,' he explained. 'Hampton Wick, prick. Or maybe it's dick. Anyway, I'm just warning you not to let a good looking woman interfere with your professional judgment.'

Rebus was still about to protest, but saw that there was little point. Having voiced his thoughts, Flight seemed content. What's more, maybe he was right. Did Rebus want to see Lisa Frazer because of the case, or because she was Lisa Frazer? Still, he felt the need to defend her.

'Listen,' he said, 'like I say, I've been reading the books she gave me and there are some good things in them.' Flight looked unconvinced, goading Rebus into ploughing on. And as he fell for it, beginning to speak, he saw that Flight had played the same trick on him as he himself had played on the motorcycle messenger last night. Too late: he had to defend Lisa Frazer, and himself, even though everything he now said sounded stupid and half-baked to his own ears, never mind to Flight's.

'What we're dealing with is a man who hates women.' Flight looked at him in amazement, as though this were too obvious to need saying. '*Or*,' Rebus went on quickly, 'who has to take out his revenge on women because he's too weak, too scared to take it out on a man.' Flight admitted this possibility with a twitch of the head. 'A lot of so-called serial killers,' continued Rebus, his hand unconsciously grasping the butter-knife, 'are very conservative – small c – very ambitious, but thwarted. They feel rejected from the class immediately above them, and they target this group.'

'What? A prostitute, a shop assistant, an office worker? You're saying they're the same social group? You're saying the Wolfman's social group is lower than a tart's? Leave off, John.'

'It's just a general rule,' Rebus persisted, wishing he'd never started this conversation. He twisted the knife in his hand. 'Mind you, one of the earliest serial killers was a French nobleman.' His voice fell away. Flight was looking impatient. 'All I'm saying is what's in those books. Some of it may make sense, it's just that we don't have enough on the Wolfman yet to allow us to see what sense it's all making.'

Flight finished another cup of coffee. 'Go on,' he said, without enthusiasm. 'What else do the books say?'

'Some serial killers crave publicity,' said Rebus. He paused, thinking of the killer who had taunted him five years ago, who had led them all a merry chase. 'If the Wolfman gets in touch with us, we've a better chance of catching him.'

'Perhaps. So what are you saying?'

'I'm saying we should set some snares and dig some pits. Get Inspector Farraday to pass on a few tidbits to the press, all about how we suspect the Wolfman's gay, or a transvestite. It can be anything, so long as it jars his conservatism, and maybe it'll force him into the open.'

Rebus let go of the knife and waited for Flight's response. But Flight wasn't about to be rushed. He ran a finger around the rim of his cup. 'Not a bad idea that,' he said at last. 'But I'm willing to bet you didn't get it from your books.'

Rebus shrugged. 'Maybe not exactly.'

'I thought not. Well, let's see what Cath says to it.' Flight rose from his chair. 'Meantime, on a less lofty plane of existence, I think I can take you straight to Tommy Watkiss. Come on. And by the way, thanks for breakfast.'

'My pleasure,' said Rebus. He could see Flight was unconvinced by his defence, such as it had turned out to be, of psychology. But then was it Flight he was trying to convince, or himself? Was it Flight he was trying to impress, or Dr Lisa Frazer?

They were passing through the foyer now, Rebus carrying his briefcase. Flight turned to him.

'Do you,' he said, 'know why we're called the Old Bill?' Rebus shrugged, offering no answer. 'Some say it's because we're named after a certain London landmark. You can try guessing on the way there.' And with that Flight pushed hard at the rotating door which served as the hotel's entrance.

The Old Bailey was not quite what Rebus had expected. The famous dome was there, atop which blindfolded Justice held her scales, but a large part of the court complex was of much more modern design. Security was the keynote. X-ray machines, cubicle-style doors which allowed only one person at a time into the body of the building and security men everywhere. The windows were coated with adhesive tape so that any explosion would not send lethal shards of glass flying into the concourse. Inside, ushers (all of them women) dressed in flapping black cloaks ran around trying to gather up stray juries.

'Any jurors for court number four?'

'Jurors for court number twelve, please!'

All the time a PA system announced the names of missing single jurors. It was the busy beginning of another judicial day. Witnesses smoked cigarettes, worried-looking barristers, weighed down by documents, held whispered dialogues with dull-eyed clients, and police officers waited nervously to give evidence.

'This is where we win or lose, John,' said Flight. Rebus couldn't be sure whether he was referring to the courtrooms or to the concourse itself. On floors above them were administrative offices, robing rooms, restaurants. But this floor was where cases were held and decided. Through some doors to their left was the older, domed part of the Old Bailey, a darker, more forbidding place than this bright marbled gallery. The place echoed with the squealing of leather soled shoes, the clack-clack-clacking of heels on the solid floor and the constant murmur of conversation.

'Come on,' said Flight. He was leading them towards one of the courtrooms, where he had a word with the guard and one of the clerks before ushering Rebus into the court itself.

If stone and black leather predominated in the concourse, then the courtroom belonged to wood panelling and green leather. They sat on two chairs just inside the door, joining DC Lamb, already seated there, unsmiling, arms folded. He did not greet them, but leaned across to whisper, 'We're going to nail the cunt', before stiffening into his former position.

On the other side of the room sat the twelve jurors, looking bored already, faces numb and unthinking. To the back of the court stood the defendant, hands resting on the rail in front of him, a man of about forty with short, wiry

81

silver and black hair, his face like something hewn from stone, his open-necked shirt a sign of arrogance. He had the dock to himself, there being no police officer on guard.

Some distance in front of him, the lawyers sorted through their papers, watched by assistants and solicitors. The defence counsel was a thick-set and tired-looking man, his face grey (as was his hair), gnawing on a cheap ballpoint. The prosecutor, however, was much more confident looking, tall (if stout), dressed immaculately and with the glow of the righteous upon him. His pen was an intricate fountain affair and he wrote with a flourish, his mouth set as defiantly as any Churchill impersonator. He reminded Rebus of how television liked to think of QCs, Rumpole aside.

Directly overhead was the public gallery. He could hear the muffled shuffling of feet. It had always worried Rebus that those in the public gallery had a clear view of the jury. Here, the court had been designed in such a way that they stared directly down and onto the jurors, making intimidation and identification that much easier. He'd dealt with several cases of jurors being approached at day's end by some relative of the accused, ready with a wad of notes or a clenched fist.

The judge looked imperious as he pored over some papers in front of him, while just below him the Clerk of Court spoke in hushed tones into a telephone receiver. From the time it was taking to begin proceedings, Rebus realised two things. One was that the case was continuing, not beginning; the other was that some Point of Law had been placed before the judge, which the judge was now considering.

'Here, seen this?' Lamb was offering a tabloid to Flight. The newspaper had been folded to a quarter of its size and Lamb tapped one column as he passed it to his superior.

Flight read quickly, glancing up at Rebus once or twice, then handed the paper to Rebus with a hint of a smile.

'Here you go, expert.'

Rebus read through the unattributed piece. Basically, it concerned itself with the progress or lack of it on the Jean Cooper murder inquiry. But the closing paragraph was the killer: 'The team investigating what have come to be known as the "Wolfman Murders" are being assisted by an expert on serial killers, drafted in from another police force.'

Rebus stared at the newsprint without really seeing it. Surely Cath Farraday wouldn't have? But then how else had the newspaper got to know? He kept his eyes on the page, aware that both Flight and Lamb were looking at him. He couldn't believe it: *him*, an *expert*! Whether it was true or not – and it wasn't – didn't really matter now. What mattered was that results would be expected from him, results above the norm. Yet he knew he couldn't deliver and in not delivering he would be made to look a laughing stock. No wonder those two pairs of eyes burned into his head. No hard-working policeman liked to be usurped by 'experts'. Rebus didn't like it himself. He didn't like any of it!

Flight saw the pained expression on Rebus's face and felt sorry for the man. Lamb, however, was smirking, enjoying Rebus's agony. He accepted his newspaper from Rebus and stuffed it into his jacket pocket.

'Thought you'd be interested,' he said.

The judge finally looked up, his attention fixed on the jury. 'Members of the jury,' he began, 'it has been brought to my attention in the case of Crown versus Thomas Watkiss that the evidence of Police Constable Mills contained a passage which may have lodged in your minds, influencing your objectivity.'

So, the man in the dock was Tommy Watkiss, Maria's husband. Rebus studied him again, shaking his mind clear of the news story. Watkiss's face was a curious shape, the top half much wider than the cheekbones and jaw, which fell almost to a point. He had the look of an old boxer who had suffered one dislocated jaw too many. The judge was going on about some cock-up in the police case. The arresting constable had given evidence stating that his first words on reaching the accused had been 'Hello, Tommy, what's going on here?' By giving this in evidence, he had let the jury know that Watkiss was well known to the local constabulary, something which might well influence their judgment. The judge was therefore ordering the jury to be dismissed.

'Good on ya, Tommy!' came a cry from the public gallery, quickly silenced by a glare from the judge. Rebus wondered where he had heard the voice before.

As the court rose, Rebus stepped forward a few paces and turned to look up at the balcony. The spectators had risen, too, and in the front row Rebus could see a young man dressed in bike leathers and carrying a crash-helmet, grinning towards Watkiss. He raised his fist in a gesture of triumph, then turned and began to climb the steps to the gallery's exit. It was Kenny, Samantha's boyfriend. Rebus walked back to where Flight and Lamb were standing, watching him curiously, but Rebus directed his attention towards the dock. The look on Watkiss's face was one of pure relief. DC Lamb, on the other hand, seemed ready to kill.

'Luck of the fucking Irish,' he spat.

'Tommy's no more Irish than you are, Lamb,' Flight said phlegmatically.

'What was the charge?' Rebus asked, his mind still confused by the newspaper story, by Kenny's presence in this place and by his actions. The judge was leaving by a green padded-leather door to the side of the jury box.

'The usual,' said Lamb, calming quickly. 'Rape. When

his old woman snuffed it, he needed somebody else on the game. So he tried to "persuade" a girl on his street that she could make a few bob. When that didn't work, he lost his rag and had a go at her. Bastard. We'll get him at the retrial. I still think he did for his old woman.'

'Then find the evidence,' said Flight. 'Meantime, I can think of a certain Police Constable who needs a good kick up the arse.'

'Yeah,' said Lamb. He was grinning evilly at the thought, then took the hint and left the courtroom in search of the unfortunate PC Mills.

'Inspector Flight.' It was the prosecuting counsel, striding briskly towards them with documents and books cradled in his left arm, his right arm outstretched. Flight took the well-groomed hand and shook it.

'Hello, Mr Chambers. This is Inspector Rebus. He's come down from Scotland to help us on the Wolfman investigation.'

Chambers looked interested. 'Ah, yes, the Wolfman. I look forward to prosecuting that particular case.'

'I just hope we can give you the opportunity,' said Rebus.

'Well,' said Chambers, 'meanwhile it's tricky enough landing the little fish like our friend.' He glanced back in the direction of the dock, which now stood empty. 'But we try,' he said with a sigh, 'we try.' Then he paused, and added in an undertone, directed at Flight: 'Get this, George, I don't like being royally shafted by my own team. Okay?'

Flight blushed. Chambers had dressed him down in a way no Superintendent or Chief Constable could ever have done, and he knew it. 'Good day, gentlemen,' he said, moving away, 'and good luck, Inspector Rebus.'

'Thanks,' Rebus called to the retreating figure.

Flight watched as Chambers pushed open the doors of

the court, the tail of his wig flicking from side to side, robes flapping behind him. When the doors were closed, Flight chuckled.

'Arrogant prick. But he's the best there is.'

Rebus was beginning to wonder if anyone in London was second-rate. He'd been introduced to the 'top' pathologist, the 'best' prosecuting counsel, the 'crack' forensic team, the 'finest' police divers. Was it part of the city's own arrogance?

'I thought the best lawyers all went in for commercial work these days,' Rebus said.

'Not necessarily. It's only the really greedy bastards who go in for City work. Besides, this sort of stuff is like a drug to Chambers and his ilk. They're actors, bloody good ones at that.'

Yes, Rebus had known a few Oscar-winning advocates in his time, and had lost a few cases more to their technique than to the strength of their defence. They might earn a quarter of the riches earned by their brothers in the commercial sector, might take home a scant £50,000 each year, but they endured for the sake of their public.

Flight was moving towards the doors. 'What's more,' he said, 'Chambers studied for a time in the USA. They train them to be actors over there. They also train them to be hard-nosed bastards. I'm told he came out top of his class. That's why we like having him on our side.' Flight paused. 'Do you still want a word with Tommy?'

Rebus shrugged. 'Why not?'

Out in the concourse, Watkiss was standing by one of the large windows, relishing a cigarette and listening to his solicitor. Then the two men started to walk away.

'Tell you what,' said Rebus, 'I've changed my mind. Let's skip Watkiss for the moment.'

'Okay,' said Flight. 'You're the *expert* after all.' He saw the sour look on Rebus's face and laughed. 'Don't worry about it,' he said. 'I know you're no expert.'

'That's very reassuring, George,' Rebus said without conviction. He stared after Watkiss, thinking: And I'm not the only one leaving court without conviction.

Flight laughed again, but behind his smile he was still more than a little curious about Rebus's action in the courtroom, walking out into the court like that to peer up at the public gallery. But if Rebus didn't want to talk about it, then that was his privilege. Flight could bide his time. 'So what now?' he asked.

Rebus was rubbing his jaw. 'My dental appointment,' he said.

Anthony Morrison, who insisted that they call him Tony, was much younger than Rebus had been anticipating. No more than thirty-five, he had an underdeveloped body, so that his adult head seemed to have outgrown the rest of him. Rebus was aware that he was staring at Morrison with more than common interest. The scrubbed and shiny face, the tufts of bristle on chin and cheekbone where a razor had failed to fulfil its duties, the trimmed hair and keening eyes: in the street, he would have taken Morrison for a sixth-year pupil. Certainly, for a pathologist, albeit a dental pathologist, the man was in stark contrast to Philip Cousins.

On learning that Rebus was Scottish, Morrison had started on about the debt modern-day pathology owed to the Scots, 'men like Glaister and Littlejohn and Sir Sydney Smith' though the latter, Morrison had to admit, had been born in the Antipodes. He then said that his own father had been a Scotsman, a surgeon, and asked if Rebus knew that the earliest British Chair of Forensic Medicine had been founded in Edinburgh. Rebus, swept away by the welter of facts, said that this was news to him.

Morrison showed them into his office with an enthusiastic bounce to his walk. Once inside, however, the dentist's demeanour changed from social to professional.

'He's been busy again,' he said without preamble, leading them to the wall behind his desk, where several ten by eight colour and black and white photographs had been pinned. They showed precise close-ups of the bite marks left on Jean Cooper's stomach. Arrows had been drawn in, leading from particular spots on certain photographs out to where pinned notes gave Morrison's technical summary of his findings.

'I know what to look for now, of course,' he said, 'so it didn't take long to establish that these are probably the same teeth used in the previous attacks. A pattern is also emerging, however, perhaps a disturbing one.' He went to his desk and returned with more photographs. 'These are from victim number one. You'll notice that the indents left by the teeth are less marked. They grow a little more marked by victims two and three. And now –' he pointed to the current crop of pictures.

'They've got even deeper,' Rebus answered. Morrison beamed at him.

'Quite right.'

'So he's becoming more violent.'

'If you can term an attack made on someone who's already dead "violent", then yes, Inspector Rebus, he's getting more violent, or perhaps more unstable would be a better way of phrasing it.' Rebus and Flight exchanged a glance. 'Apart from the change in the relative depth of the bite marks, there's little I can add to my previous findings. The teeth are quite likely to be prosthetic –'

Rebus interrupted. 'You mean false?' Morrison nodded. 'How can you tell?'

Morrison beamed again. The prodigy who liked to show off in front of his teachers. 'How can I best explain this to a layman?' He seemed to consider his own question for a moment. 'Well, one's own teeth – your own, for example, Inspector Rebus – and by the way, you should get them seen to – they get a little ragged over time. The cutting edge gets chipped and worn. The edge on false teeth is more likely to be smoother, more rounded. Less of an edge to the front teeth especially, and less chips and cracks.'

Rebus, lips closed, was running his tongue over his teeth. It was true, they had the serrated feel of a workman's saw. He hadn't visited a dentist in ten years or more, had never felt the need. But now Morrison had commented on them. Did they really look so awful?

'So,' Morrison continued, 'for that reason, as well as for several others, I would say the killer has false teeth. But he also has very curious teeth indeed.'

'Oh?' Rebus tried to speak without showing Morrison any more of his own decaying mouth.

'I've already explained this to Inspector Flight,' Morrison paused so that Flight could nod agreement of this, 'but briefly, the upper set has a greater biting curve than the lower set. From my measurements, I conclude that the person in possession of these teeth must have quite a strangely shaped face. I did draw some sketches, but I've managed to come up with something better. I'm glad you've come this afternoon.' He walked over to a cupboard and opened it. Rebus looked to Flight, who merely shrugged. Morrison was turning towards them again, his right hand supporting a large object covered by an inverted brown-paper bag.

'Behold,' he said, lifting the bag from the object. 'I bring you the head of the Wolfman!'

There was silence in the room, so that the traffic noise from outside became conspicuous. Neither Rebus nor Flight could think of anything immediately to say. Instead, they walked across to meet with the chuckling Morrison, who was regarding his creation with a measure of glee. There was a squeal of suddenly braking tyres outside.

'The Wolfman,' Morrison repeated. He was holding the cast of a human head, constructed so far as Rebus could ascertain from pale pink plaster. 'You can ignore the idea from the nose upwards, if you prefer,' said Morrison. 'It's fairly speculative, based on mean measurements taking into account the jaw. But the jaw itself is, I believe, pretty accurate.'

And a strange jaw it was. The upper teeth jutted out from the mouth, so that the lips over them and the skin below the nose was stretched and bulging. The lower jaw seemed tucked in beneath in what seemed to Rebus a Neanderthal display, to the extent that it almost disappeared. The chin had a narrow, pinched look and the cheekbones were swollen in a line with the nose, but concave as the face extended downwards. It was an extraordinary face, the like of which Rebus could not recall having encountered in the real world. But then this was not the real world, was it? It was a reconstruction, depending upon a measure of averages and guesswork. Flight was staring at it in fascination, as though committing the face to memory. Rebus had the chilling notion that Flight would release a photograph to the papers and charge the first poor soul he came across possessing such a physiognomy.

'Would you call that deformed?' Rebus asked.

'Heavens, no,' said Morrison with a laugh. 'You haven't seen some of the medical cases I've had to deal with. No, this couldn't be termed deformed.'

'Looks like my idea of Mr Hyde,' commented Flight.

Don't mention Hyde to me, Rebus thought to himself.

'Perhaps,' said Morrison, laughing again. 'What about you, Inspector Rebus? What are your thoughts?'

Rebus examined the cast again. 'It looks prehistoric.'

'Ah! said Morrison enthusiastically. 'That was what I thought at first. The jutting upper jaw especially.'

'How do you know that is the upper jaw?' asked Rebus. 'Couldn't it be the other way round?'

'No, I'm pretty sure this is correct. The bites are fairly consistent. Apart from victim three, that is.'

'Oh?'

'Yes, victim three was a strange one. The lower set, that is the smaller set, seemed more extended than the upper set. As you can see from this cast, the killer would have had to make an extraordinary contortion of his face to produce such a bite.'

He mimed the bite for them, opening his mouth wide, lifting his head, and pushing out his lower jaw, then making a biting motion, the lower jaw doing most of the work.

'In the other bites, the killer has bitten more like this.' Again he put on a dumb show, this time drawing his lips back from his upper jaw and biting down sharply so that the upper teeth closed over the lower teeth, the teeth themselves snapping together.

Rebus shook his head. This wasn't making things clearer. If anything, he was growing more confused. He nodded towards the cast. 'You really believe the man we're looking for looks like this?'

'The man or woman, yes. Of course, I may have exaggerated a little with this cast, but I'm more or less convinced.'

Rebus had stopped listening after the first sentence. 'What do you mean, or woman?' he asked.

Morrison shrugged his shoulders theatrically. 'Again, this is something I've discussed with Inspector Flight. It just seemed to me that, purely on the dental evidence you understand, this head could as easily belong to a woman as to a man. The large upper set of teeth seems to me very male, judging from size and what have you, but the lower

91

set, just as equally, seems very female. A man with a woman's chin, or a woman with a masculine upper jaw?' He shrugged again. 'Take your pick.'

Rebus looked to Flight, who was shaking his head slowly. 'No,' Flight said, 'it's a man.'

Rebus had never considered the possibility that a woman might be behind the killings. It had never entered his head. Until now.

A woman? Improbable, but why impossible? Flight was dismissing it out of hand, but on what grounds? Rebus had read last night that a growing number of multiple murderers were women. But could a woman have stabbed like that? Could a woman so completely have overwhelmed victims of similar height, similar strength?

'I'd like to get some photographs of this,' Flight was saying. He had taken the cast from Morrison and was studying it again.

'Of course,' Morrison said, 'but remember, it's only my idea of the look of the killer's head.'

'We appreciate it, Tony. Thanks for all your work.'

Morrison shrugged modestly. He had fished for a compliment and had hooked one.

Rebus could see that Flight was convinced by this whole piece of theatre, the unveiling of the head and so on. To Rebus it was more showmanship than tangible truth, more the stuff of courtroom melodrama. He still felt that to trap the Wolfman they had to get inside his head, not play with plaster mock-ups of it.

His or her head.

'Would the bite marks be enough to identify the killer?'

Morrison considered this. Then nodded. 'I think so, yes. If you can bring me the suspect, I think I can show that he or she is the Wolfman.'

Rebus persisted, 'But would it stand up in court?'

Morrison folded his arms and smiled. 'I could blind the

jury with science.' His face became serious again. 'No, on its own I don't think my evidence would ever be enough to convict. But as part of a larger body of such evidence, we might be in with half a chance.'

'Always supposing the bastard makes it to trial,' Flight added grimly. 'Accidents have been known to happen in custody.'

'Always supposing,' Rebus corrected, 'we catch him in the first place.'

'That, gentlemen,' said Morrison, 'I leave entirely in your capable hands. Suffice to say, I look forward to introducing my friend here to the real thing.' And he tipped the plaster head backwards and forwards and backwards again, until it seemed to Rebus that the head was mocking them, laughing and rolling its sightless eyes.

As Morrison showed them out, he rested a hand on Rebus's forearm. 'I'm serious about your teeth,' he said, 'you should get them seen to. I could look at them myself if you like?'

When he returned to headquarters Rebus went straight to the wash-room and, in front of a soap-spattered mirror, examined his mouth. What was Morrison talking about? His teeth looked fine. Okay, one of them had a dark line running down it, a crack perhaps, and a few were badly stained from too many cigarettes and too much tea. But they looked strong enough, didn't they? No need for drills and piercing, grinding implements. No need for a dentist's chair, sharp needles, and a spitting out of blood.

Back at his designated desk he doodled on his notebook. Was Morrison just the nervous type, or was he hyperactive? Was he perhaps mad? Or was he merely dealing with the world in his own idiosyncratic way?

So few serial killers were women. Statistically, it was unlikely. Since when had he believed in statistics? Since he

93

had started to read psychology textbooks, last night in his hotel room after the disastrous visit to Rhona and Samantha. Kenny: what the hell was Kenny doing running around with Tommy Watkiss? His daughter's 'gentleman'. A smiling villain? Forget it, John. You don't control that part of your life any more. He had to smile at this: what part of his life did he control? His work gave his life what meaning it had. He should admit defeat, tell Flight he could be of no help and return to Edinburgh, where he could be sure of his villains and his crimes: drug pedlars, protection racketeers, domestic violence, fraud.

A murder each month, regular as the moon. It was only a saying, wasn't it, regular as the moon? He unhooked a calendar from the wall. Portraits of Italy, donated to the station by Gino's Sandwich Bar. Time of the month. Had there been a full moon around 16th January when Maria Watkiss was found? No, but then they reckoned she might have lain undiscovered for two or three days. Thursday 11th January had been the full moon. The full moon affected the Wolfman in the movies, didn't it? But they had named the killer Wolfman after Wolf Street, not because he, or she, killed by the light of the full moon. Rebus was more confused than ever. And weren't women supposedly affected by the moon, something to do with their time of the month?

May Jessop had died on Monday 5th February, four days *before* another full moon. Shelley Richards had died on Wednesday 28th February, nowhere near a full moon. Morrison had said her case was unusual, the bites had seemed different. And then Jean Cooper had died on the night of Sunday 18th March, two days before the vernal equinox.

He threw the calendar onto the desk. There was no pattern, no neat mathematical solution. Who was he trying to kid? This wasn't the movies. The hero didn't stumble upon the answer. There were no shortcuts. Maybe Flight was right. It was all plodding routine and forensic evidence. Psychology was no shortcut, barking at the moon was no shortcut. He couldn't know when the Wolfman would strike again. He knew so little.

Flight wandered exhaustedly into the room and fell onto a chair, causing it to creak in protest.

'I finally got through to Cath,' he said. 'I put your idea to her, and she's giving it some thought.'

'That's big of her.'

Flight gave him a warning look and Rebus raised his hands in apology. Flight nodded towards the calendar. 'What are you up to?'

'I don't know, nothing much. I thought there might be some pattern to the dates when the Wolfman struck.'

'You mean like the stages of the moon, the equinox, that sort of thing?' Flight was smiling. Rebus nodded slowly. 'Hell, John, I've been through all that and more.' He went to a particular manila folder and tossed it towards Rebus. 'Take a look: I've tried number patterns, distance between murder sites, possible means of transport – the Wolfman's pretty mobile, you know, I think he must have a car. I've tried linking the victims, checking which school they went to, which libraries they used, whether they liked sports or discos or classical bloody music. Know what? They don't have *anything* in common, not a single thing linking the four of them save the fact that they were women.'

Rebus flicked through the file. It was an impressive amount of slogging, all to no end save that of clarification. Flight hadn't climbed the ladder to his present rank by a fluke, or by keeping in with his superiors, or by signifying greatness. He had got there by sheer hard work.

'Point taken,' said Rebus. Then, because this didn't seem quite enough: 'I'm impressed. Have you shown this lot to anyone else?'

Flight shook his head. 'It's guesswork, John. Straw-clutching. That's all. It would just confuse the issue. Besides, do you remember the story of the boy who cried wolf? One day, there really was a wolf there, but by then no one believed him because he'd given them so much crap before.'

Rebus smiled. 'Still, it's a lot of work.'

'What did you expect?' Flight asked. 'A chimpanzee in a whistle? I'm a good copper, John. I may be no *expert*, but I'd never claim to be.'

Rebus was about to remonstrate, then frowned. 'What's a whistle?' he said.

Flight threw back his head and laughed. 'A suit, you plonker. Whistle and flute, suit. Rhyming slang. God sakes, John, we're going to have to educate you. Tell you what, why don't we go out for a meal ourselves tonight? I know a good Greek restaurant in Walthamstow.' Flight paused, a gleam in his eye. 'I know it's good,' he said, ''cos I've seen a lot of bubbles coming out of it.' His smile was inviting. Rebus thought quickly. Bubbles? Was the food gassy? Did they serve champagne? Rhyming slang. Bubbles.

'Bubble and squeak,' he said. Then a pause. 'Greeks, right?'

'Right!' said Flight. 'You're catching on fast. So what about it? Or Indian, Thai, Italian, you decide.'

But Rebus was shaking his head. 'Sorry, George, prior engagement.'

Flight pulled his head back. 'No,' he said, 'you're seeing *her*, aren't you? That bloody psychiatrist. I forgot you told me at breakfast. You bloody Jocks, you don't waste any time, do you? Coming down here, stealing our women.' Flight sounded in good humour, but Rebus thought he detected something a little deeper down, a genuine sadness that the two of them couldn't get together for a meal.

'Tomorrow night, eh, George?'

'Yeah,' said Flight. 'Tomorrow night sounds fine. One word of advice though?'

'What?'

'Don't let her get you on the couch.'

'No,' said Dr Lisa Frazer, shaking her head vigorously. 'That's psychiatrists. Psychiatrists have couches, not psychologists. We're like chalk and cheese.'

She looked stunning, yet there was no alchemy involved in the process. She was dressed simply and wore no make-up. Her hair had been brushed straight back and tied with a band. Still, casually, elegantly, simply, she was stunning. She had been dead on time at the hotel and had walked with him, her arm linked in his, along Shaftesbury Avenue, past the scene of his run-in with the patrol car. The early evening was warm, and Rebus felt good walking with her. Men were glancing towards them, okay, be honest, towards *her*. There might even have been a wolf whistle or two. It made Rebus feel good all the same. He was wearing his tweed jacket with an open-necked shirt and had the sudden fear that she would lead him to some fancy restaurant where men were not admitted without ties. That would be just his luck. The city teemed with nightlife, teenagers mostly, drinking from cans and calling to each other across the busy road. The pubs were doing good business and buses chugged grime into the air. Grime which would be falling unseen on Lisa Frazer. Rebus felt valiant. He felt like stopping all the traffic, confiscating all the keys so that she could walk unsullied through the streets.

Since when did he think like that? Where had this tiny unpolished stone of romance come from? What desperate corner of his soul? Self-conscious, John. You're becoming too self-conscious. And if a psychologist didn't spot it, nobody would. Be natural. Be calm. Be yourself.

She brought him into Chinatown, a few streets off

Shaftesbury Avenue, where the telephone boxes were shaped like oriental temples, supermarkets sold fifty-year-old eggs, gateways were decorated like relics from Hong Kong and the street names were given in Chinese as well as English. There were a few tourists about, but mainly the pedestrianised walkway was filled with scuttling Chinese, their voices shrill. It was a different world, like something you would expect to find in New York but never dream of finding in England. Yet he could look back along the street and still see the theatres on Shaftesbury Avenue, the red buses chug-chugging, the punks yelling obscenities at the tops of immature voices.

'Here we are,' she said, stopping outside a restaurant on the corner of the street. She pulled open the door, gesturing for him to precede her into the air-conditioned chill. A waiter was upon them at once, showing them to a dimly-lit booth. A waitress smiled with her eyes as she handed them each a menu. The waiter returned with a wine list, which he placed beside Rebus.

'Would you like a drink while you are deciding?'

Rebus looked to Lisa Frazer for guidance. 'Gin and tonic,' she said without hesitation.

'And the same for me,' said Rebus, then regretted it. He wasn't all that keen on gin's chemical smell.

'I'm very excited about this case, Inspector Rebus.'

'Please, call me John. We're not in the station now.'

She nodded. 'I'd like to thank you for giving me the chance to study the files. I think I'm already forming an interesting picture.' She reached into her clutch-purse and produced a collection of a dozen index cards held together with an outsize paper-clip. The cards were covered in lines of tiny, neat handwriting. She seemed ready to start reading them. 'Shouldn't we at least order first?' Rebus asked. She appeared not to understand, then grinned.

'Sorry,' she said. 'It's just that I'm ...'

'Very excited. Yes, you said.'

'Don't policemen get excited when they find what they think is a clue?'

'Almost never,' said Rebus, appearing to study the menu, 'we're born pessimists. We don't get excited until the guilty party has been sentenced and locked up.'

'That's curious.' She held her own menu still closed. The index cards had been relegated to the table-top. 'I'd have thought to enjoy police work you would need a level of optimism, otherwise you'd *never* think you were going to solve the case.'

Still studying the menu, Rebus decided that he'd let her order for both of them. He glanced up at her. 'I try not to think about solving or not solving,' he said. 'I just get on with the job, step by step.'

The waiter had returned with their drinks.

'You are ready to order?'

'Not really,' said Rebus, 'could we have a couple more minutes?'

Lisa Frazer was staring across the table at him. It wasn't a large table. Her right hand rested on the rim of her glass, barely an inch from his left hand. Rebus could sense the presence of her knees almost touching his own under the table. The other tables in the restaurant all seemed larger than this one, and the booths seemed better lit.

'Frazer's a Scottish name,' he said. It was as good a line as any.

'That's right,' she replied. 'My great grandfather came from a place called Kirkcaldy.'

Rebus smiled. She had pronounced the word the way it looked. He corrected her, then added, 'I was born and brought up not far from there. Five or six miles, to be precise.'

'Really? What a coincidence. I've never been there, but

my grandaddy used to tell me it was where Adam Smith was born.'

Rebus nodded. 'But don't hold that against it,' he said. 'It's still not a bad wee town.' He picked up his glass and swirled it, enjoying the sound of the ice chinking on the glass. Lisa was at last studying her menu. Without looking up, she spoke.

'Why are you here?' The question was sudden, catching Rebus off-balance. Did she mean here in the restaurant, here in London, here on this planet?

'I'm here to find answers.' He was pleased with this reply; it seemed to deal with all three possibilities at once. He lifted his glass. 'Here's to psychology.'

She raised her own glass, ice rattling like musical chimes. 'Here's to taking things one step at a time.' They both drank. She studied her menu again. 'Now,' she said, 'what shall we have?'

Rebus knew how to use a pair of chopsticks, but perhaps tonight had just been the wrong time to try. He suddenly found himself unable to pick up a noodle or a sliver of duck without the thing sliding out of his grasp and falling back to the table, splashing sauce across the tablecloth. The more it happened, the more frustrated he became and the more frustrated he became, the more it happened. Finally, he asked for a fork.

'My coordination's all gone,' he explained. She smiled in understanding (or was it sympathy?) and poured more tea into his tiny cup. He could see that she was impatient to tell him what she thought she had discovered about the Wolfman. Over a starter of crabmeat soup the talk had been safe, guarded, had been of pasts and futures, not the present. Rebus stabbed his fork into an unresisting slice of meat. 'So what have you found?'

She looked at him for confirmation that this was her cue.

When he nodded, she put down her chopsticks, then pushed aside the paper-clip from her index cards and cleared her throat, not so much reading from the cards, more using them as occasional prompts.

'Well,' she said, 'the first thing I found revealing was the evidence of salt on the bodies of the victims. I know some people think it may be sweat, but I'm of the opinion that these are tear stains. A lot can be learned from any killer's interpersonal relationship with his or her victim.' There it was again: his or her. *Her.* 'To me the tear stains indicate feelings of guilt in the attacker, guilt felt, moreover, not in reflection but at the actual time of the attack. This gives the Wolfman a moral dimension, showing that he is being driven almost against his will. There may well be signs of schizophrenia here, the Wolfman's dark side operating only at certain times.'

She was about to rush on, but already Rebus needed time to catch up. He interrupted. 'You're saying most of the time the Wolfman may seem as normal as you or me?'

She nodded briskly. 'Yes, exactly. In fact, I'm saying that between times the Wolfman doesn't just seem as normal as anyone else, he *is* as normal, which is why he's been hard to catch. He doesn't wander around the streets with the word "Wolfman" tattooed across his forehead.'

Rebus nodded slowly. He realised that by seeming to concentrate on her words, he had an excuse for staring at her face, consuming it with eyes more proficient than any cutlery. 'Go on,' he said.

She flipped one card over and moved to the next, taking a deep breath. 'That the victim is abused *after* death indicates that the Wolfman feels no need to control his victim. In some serial killers, this element of control is important. Killing is the only time when these people feel in any kind of control of their lives. This isn't the case with the Wolfman. The murder itself is relatively quick, occasioning little pain or suffering. Sadism, therefore, is not a feature. Rather, the Wolfman is playing out a scenario upon the corpse.'

Again the rush of words, her energy, her eagerness to share her findings, all swept past Rebus. How could he concentrate when she was so close to him, so close and so beautiful? 'What do you mean?'

'It'll become clearer.' She stopped to take a sip of tea. Her food was barely touched, the mound of rice in the bowl beside her hardly dented. In her own way, Rebus realised, she was every bit as nervous as he was, but not for the same reasons. The restaurant, though hectic, might have been empty. This booth was *their* territory. Rebus took a gulp of the still-scalding tea. Tea! He could kill for a glass of cold white wine.

'I thought it interesting,' she was saying now, 'that the pathologist, Dr Cousins, feels the initial attack comes from behind. This makes the attacks non-confrontational and the Wolfman is likely to be like this in his social and working life. There's also the possibility that he cannot look his victims in the eye, out of fear that their fear would destroy his scenario.'

Rebus shook his head. It was time to own up. 'You've lost me.'

She seemed surprised. 'Simply, he's taking out revenge and to him the victims represent the individual against whom he's taking his revenge. If he confronted them face to face, he'd realise they're not the person he bears the grudge against in the first place.'

Rebus still felt a little bit lost. 'Then these women are stand-ins?'

'Substitutes, yes.'

He nodded. This was getting interesting, interesting enough for him to turn his gaze from Lisa Frazer, the better to concentrate on her words. She was still only halfway through her cards.

'So much for the Wolfman,' she said, flipping to the next card. 'But the chosen location can also say a lot about the inner life of the attacker, as can age, sex, race and class of the victims. You'll have noticed that they are all women, that they are mostly older women, women approaching middle age, and that three out of four have been white. I'll admit that I can't make much out of these facts as they stand. In fact, it was just the failure of pattern that made me think a little harder about location. You see, just when a pattern looks to be emerging, an element arises that destroys the precision: the killer attacks a much younger woman, or strikes earlier in the evening, or chooses a black victim.'

Or, Rebus was thinking, kills outside the pattern of the full moon.

Lisa continued, 'I started to give some consideration to the spatial pattern of the attacks. These can determine where the killer may strike next, or even where he lives.' Rebus raised his eyebrows. 'It's true, John, it's been proved in several cases.'

'I don't doubt it. I was raising my eyebrows at that phrase "spatial pattern".' A phrase he'd heard before, on the loathed management course.

She smiled. 'Jargon, yes. There's a lot of it about. What I mean is the pattern of the murder sites. A canal path, a railway line, the vicinity of a tube station. Three out of four take place near travel systems, but again the fourth case defeats the pattern. All four take place north of the river. At least there's *some* evidence of a pattern there. But – and this is my point – the non-emergence of a pattern seems to me in itself a conscious act. The Wolfman is making sure you have as little as possible to go on. This would indicate a high level of psychological maturity.'

'Yes, he's as mature as a hatter all right.'

She laughed. 'I'm being serious.'

'I know you are.'

'There is one other possibility.'

'What's that?'

'The Wolfman knows how *not* to leave a trail because he is familiar with police work.'

'Familiar with it?'

She nodded. 'Especially the way you go about investigating a series of murders.'

'You're saying he's a copper?'

She laughed again, shaking her head. 'I'm saying he may have prior convictions.'

'Yes, well,' he thought of the file George Flight had shown him a few hours earlier, 'we've checked on over a hundred ex-offenders already. No luck there.'

'But you can't possibly have talked to every man who has ever been convicted of rape, violent assault or the like.'

'Agreed. But there's something you seem to have overlooked – the teeth marks. Those are very palpable clues. If the Wolfman is being so clever, why does he leave us a neat set of bite marks every time?'

She blew on her tea, cooling it. 'Maybe,' she said, 'the teeth are a – what do you call it – a red herring?'

Rebus thought about this. 'It's possible,' he conceded, 'but there's something else. I visited a dental pathologist today. From the marks made by the teeth, he said he couldn't rule out the possibility that the Wolfman is a woman.'

'Really?' Her eyes opened wide. 'That's very interesting. I'd never even considered it.'

'Neither had we.' He scooped more rice into his bowl. 'So tell me, why does he, or she, bite the victims?'

'I've given that a lot of thought.' She flipped to her final card. 'The bite is always on the stomach, the female stomach, carrier of life. Maybe the Wolfman has lost a child, or maybe he was abandoned and consequently adopted and resents the fact. I don't know. A lot of serial killers have fragmented upbringings.'

'Mmm. I read all about it in those books you gave me.'

'Really? You read them?'

'Last night.'

'And what did you think?'

'I thought they were clever, sometimes ingenious.'

'But do you think the theories are valid?'

Rebus shrugged. 'I'll tell you if and when we catch the Wolfman.'

She toyed with her food again, but ate nothing. The meat in her bowl had a cold, gelatinous look. 'What about the anal attacks, John. Do *you* have any theories there?'

Rebus considered this. 'No,' he said finally, 'but I know what a psychiatrist might say.'

'Yes, but you're not with a psychiatrist, remember. I'm a psychologist.'

'How can I forget? You said in your essay that there are thirty *known* serial killers active in the USA. Is that true?'

'I wrote that essay over a year ago. By now, there are probably more. Frightening, isn't it?'

He shrugged, the shrug disguising a shiver. 'How's the food?' he asked.

'What?' She looked at her bowl. 'Oh, I'm not really very hungry. To tell you the truth, I feel a little bit … deflated, I suppose. I was so excited at what I thought I'd managed to piece together, but in telling it all to you, I see that really there's not very much there at all.' She was thumbing through the index cards.

'There's plenty there,' said Rebus. 'I'm impressed, honest. Every little bit helps. And you stick to the known facts, I like that. I was expecting more jargon.' He remembered the terms from one of her books, the one by

MacNaughtie. 'Latent psychomania, Oedipal urgings, gobbledygook.'

'I could give you plenty of that stuff,' she said, 'but I doubt it would help.'

'Exactly.'

'Besides, that's more in line with psychiatry. Psychologists prefer drive theories, social learning theory, multiphasic personalities.' Rebus had clamped his hands over his ears.

She laughed again. He could make her laugh so easily. Once upon a time he'd made Rhona laugh too, and after Rhona a certain Liaison Officer back in Edinburgh. 'So what about policemen?' he asked, closing off the memory. 'What can psychologists tell about us?'

'Well,' she said, relaxing into her seat, 'you're extrovert, tough-minded, conservative.'

'Conservative?'

'With a small "c".'

'I read last night that serial killers are conservative, too.'

She nodded, still smiling. 'Oh yes,' she said, 'you're alike in a lot of ways. But by conservative I mean specifically that you don't like anything that changes the status quo. That's why you're reticent about the use of psychology. It interferes with the strict guidelines you've set yourselves. Isn't that so?'

'Well, I suppose I could argue, but I won't. So what happens now you've studied the Wolfman?'

'Oh, all I've done so far is scratch the surface.' Her hands were still on the index cards. 'There are other tests to be done, character analyses and so on. It'll take time.' She paused. 'What about you?'

'Well, we'll plod along, checking, examining, taking it –'

'Step by step,' she interrupted.

'That's right, step by step. Whether I'll be on the case

much longer or not I can't say. They may send me back to Edinburgh at the end of the week.'

'Why did they bring you to London in the first place?'

The waiter had come to clear away their dishes. Rebus sat back, wiping his lips with the serviette.

'Any coffees or liqueurs, sir?'

Rebus looked to Lisa. 'I think I'll have a Grand Marnier,' she said.

'Just coffee for me,' said Rebus. 'No, hold on, what the hell, I'll have the same.' The waiter bowed and moved off, his arms heavy with crockery.

'You didn't answer my question, John.'

'Oh, it's simple enough. They thought I might be able to help. I worked on a previous serial killing, up in Edinburgh.'

'Really?' She sat forward in her chair, the palms of her hands pressed to the tablecloth. 'Tell me.'

So he told her. It was a long story, and he didn't know exactly why he gave her as many details as he did – more details than she needed to know, and more, perhaps, than he should be telling to a psychologist. What would she make of him? Would she find a trace of psychosis or paranoia in his character? But he had her complete attention, so he spun the tale out in order to enjoy that attention the more.

It took them through two cups of coffee, the paying of the bill, and a balmy night-time walk through Leicester Square, across Charing Cross Road, up St Martin's Lane and along Long Acre towards Covent Garden. They walked around Covent Garden itself, Rebus still doing most of the talking. He stopped by a row of three telephone boxes, curious about the small white stickers covering every available inch of space on the inside of the booths: Stern corrective measures; French lessons; O and A specialist;

TV; Trudy, nymphet, Spank me; S/M chamber; Busty blonde – all of them accompanied by telephone numbers.

Lisa studied them, too. 'Every one a psychologist,' she said. Then: 'That's quite a story you've just told, John. Has anyone written it up?'

Rebus shrugged. 'A newspaper reporter wrote a couple of articles.' Jim Stevens. Christ, hadn't he moved to London, too? Rebus thought again of the newspaper story Lamb had shown him, the *unattributed* newspaper story.

'Yes,' Lisa was saying, 'but has anyone looked at it from your point of view?'

'No.' She looked thoughtful at this. 'You want to turn me into a case study?'

'Not necessarily,' she said. 'Ah, here we are.' She stopped. They were standing outside a shoe shop in a narrow, pedestrianised street. Above the rows of shops were two storeys of flats. 'This is where I live,' she said. 'Thank you for this evening. I've enjoyed it.'

'Thank you for the meal. It was great.'

'Not at all.' She fell silent. They were only two or three feet apart. Rebus shuffled his feet. 'Will you be able to find your way back?' she asked. 'Should I point you in the right direction?'

Rebus looked up and down the street. He was lost. He had not been keeping track of their meanderings. 'Oh, I'll be all right.' He smiled and she smiled back but did not speak. 'So this is it then,' he persisted. 'No offer of a coffee?'

She looked at him slyly. 'Do you really want a coffee?'

He returned the look. 'No,' he admitted, 'not really.'

She turned from him and opened the door to the side of the shoe shop. The shop claimed to specialise in handmade and non-leather shoes. Beside the door to the flats was an entryphone boasting six names. One of them read simply 'L Frazer'. No 'Dr', but then he supposed she wouldn't want to be disturbed by people needing a medical doctor, would she? There were times when a qualification was best kept under wraps.

Lisa drew the mortice key out of the lock. The stairwell was brightly lit, its plain stone painted cornflower blue. She turned back towards him.

'Well,' she said, 'since you don't want a coffee, you'd better come on up ...'

She later explained, running a hand over his chest as they lay together in bed, that she saw no point in the little games people played, the slow edging towards a moment when both would admit that what they really wanted was to make love.

So instead she led Rebus up to her first floor flat, took him into the darkened room, undressed and got into bed, sitting with her knees tucked up in front of her.

'Well?' she said. So he had undressed, too, and joined her. She lay now with her arms reaching behind her to grab at the bedposts, her body dusky in the light cast from a street lamp outside. Rebus ran his tongue back up along the inside of her leg, the inner thigh, her legs supple. She smelt of jasmine, tasted of flowers more pungent still. Rebus was self-conscious at first. His own body had become an embarrassment, while hers was in fine, toned condition. (Squash and swimming, she told him later, and a strict diet.) He ran his fingers over the ripples, the corrugations in her flesh. There was some sagging to the skin above her stomach, some creasing to the sides of her breasts and to her throat. He looked down and saw his own distended chest. There was still some muscle to his stomach, but there was also excessive fleshiness; not supple, tired and ageing. Squash and swimming: he would take up some exercise, join a health club. There were enough of them in Edinburgh.

He was eager to please. Her pleasure became his only goal, and he worked tirelessly. There was sweat in the room now. A lot of sweat. They were working well together, moving fluidly, each seeming to sense what the other was about to do. When he moved slightly too quickly and bumped his nose on her chin, they laughed quietly, rubbing foreheads. And when later he went in search of her fridge and cold liquid, she came too, popping an ice cube into her mouth before kissing him, the kiss extending downwards as she sank to her knees in front of him.

Back in bed, they drank chill white wine from the bottle and kissed some more, then began all over again.

The air between them had lost its nervous charge and they were able to enjoy themselves. She moved on top, rearing above him, her rhythm increasing until all he could do was lie back and watch with his eyes closed, imagining the room in diffuse light, a cold spray of water, a smoothness of skin.

Or a woman. The Wolfman could be a woman. The Wolfman was playing with the police, seemed to know the way they thought and worked. A woman? A woman officer? Cath Farraday came to mind, with her Teutonic face, that wide but angular jaw.

Jesus, here he was with Lisa, thinking of another woman! He felt a sudden pang of guilt, hitting him in the stomach a moment before a very different reaction arched his back and his neck, while her hands pressed down upon his chest, her knees clamped to his hips.

Or a woman. Why the teeth? Leaving not a single clue except those bites. Why? Why not a woman? Why not a policeman? Or … or …

'Yes, yes.' Her breath escaped with a hiss, the word losing all meaning as she repeated it ten, twenty, thirty times. Yes what?

'Yes, John, yes, John, yes …'
Yes.

* * *

It had been another busy day for her, a day spent pretending to be what she's not, but now she was out again, prowling. She is beginning to like the way she can move so smoothly through the two worlds. Earlier this evening she was the guest at a dinner party in Blackheath. Mock-Georgian elegance, stripped pine doors, talk of school fees and fax machines, of interest rates and foreign property – and the Wolfman. They asked for her opinion. Her opinion was reasoned, intelligent, liberal. There was chilled Chablis and an exquisite bottle of Chateau Montrose: the '82. She could not choose between the two, so enjoyed a glass of both.

One guest was late arriving, a journalist on one of the better dailies. He apologised. They asked for tidbits from the next day's news, and he supplied them generously. The sister paper to his own was a downmarket tabloid. He told them the next day's front page would have a headline reading SECRET LIFE OF GAY WOLFMAN. Of course, as the journalist knows, this is nothing more than a ruse, to try to bait the killer. And she knows too, naturally. They smile at one another across the table, as she lifts more pasta expertly with her fork. How stupid of them to run a story like that: gay Wolfman indeed! She chuckles into her oversized wine glass. The conversation turns to motorway traffic, wine acquisition, the state of Blackheath Common. Blackheath, of course, is where they buried the plague victims, piling the corpses high. Black Death. Black Heath. One letter separates the two. She smiles at this, too, discreetly.

The meal over, she took a taxi back across the river and got out at the beginning of her street. She intended to go straight home, but walked past her door and kept on walking. She shouldn't be doing this, shouldn't be out here, but it feels right. After all, the toy in the gallery must be lonely. It's always so cold in the gallery. So cold Jack Frost could bite off your nose.

Her mother must have told her that. Her mother. *Long nosehairs, Johnny, are so unbecoming in a gentleman.* Or her father, singing nonsense songs while she hid herself in the garden. 'Fuck art,' she hisses quietly to herself.

She knows where to go, too. Not far. The intersection of one road with a much larger one. There are many like it in London. Traffic lights, and a few women wandering back and forth, sometimes crossing at the lights so that the drivers can see them, can see their legs and their white bodies. If a car window is rolled down, a woman may lean down close to the driver so that they can discuss terms. Professional, but not very discreet. She knows that sometimes the police will make a rudimentary attempt to close down business, knows too that policemen are among the whores' best customers. That's why it's dangerous for her to come here. Dangerous but necessary: she has an itch, and women like these go missing all the time, don't they? No one gets suspicious. No one starts alarm bells ringing. Alarm bells are the last thing you need in this part of the city. Like with her first victim, by the time they got to her she was a meal for rats. Animal feed. She chuckles again, and makes to walk past one of these women, but stops.

'Hello, love,' says the woman. 'Anything you want?'

'How much for the night?'

'For you, love, a hundred.'

'Very well.' She turns and starts back towards her own street, her own house, so much safer there than out here. The woman follows noisily a yard or two behind, seeming to understand. She does not let the woman catch up until she is at the front door and the key is in the lock. The gallery beckons. Only it doesn't look like a gallery any more.

It looks like a butcher's block.

'Nice place you've got, love.'

She puts a finger to her lips. 'No talking.' The woman begins to look suspicious, looks as though she's thinking twice about being here. So she goes to her and grabs at a breast, planting a clumsy, smeared kiss across puffy lips. The prostitute looks startled for a second, then manages a rehearsed smile.

'Well, you're certainly not a gentleman,' she says.

She nods, pleased with this remark. The front door is locked now. And she goes to the door of the gallery, slips the key in, unlocks it.

'In here, love?' The woman is removing her coat as she walks across the threshold. The coat is down past her shoulders by the time she sees the room itself. But by then, of course, it's too late, far too late.

She moves in on her, like a trained worker on a production line. Hand over the mouth, good pressure on the knife and a quick backward arc before the thrust. She has often wondered if they see the knife, or are their eyes closed in terror by then? She imagines them with eyes bulging open, focussing on the knife as, point directed towards them, it swings back and then flies forward towards their face. She can find out, can't she? All she needs is a strategically placed wall-mirror. Must remember that for next time.

Gurgle, gurgle. The gallery is such a marvellous setting, poised between Apollo and Dionysus. The body slips to the floor. Time for the real work now. Her brain is humming – mummydaddymummydaddy mummydaddymummydaddy – as she crouches to her task.

'It's only a game,' she whispers, her voice a mere tremble at the back of her throat. 'Only a game.' She hears the woman's words again: *certainly not a gentleman*. No, certainly not. Her laughter is harsh and abrupt. Suddenly, she feels it again. No! Not already! *Next time*. The knife twitches. She hasn't even finished with this one. She can't possibly do another tonight! It would be madness. Sheer madness. But the craving is there, an absolute and unappeasable hunger. This time with a mirror. She covers her eyes with a bloodstained hand.

'Stop!' she cries. 'Stop it, daddy! Mummy! Make it stop! Please, make it stop!'

But that's the problem, as she knows only too well. Nobody *can* make it stop, nobody *will* make it stop. On it must go, night after night now. Night after night. No letting up, no pausing for breath.

Night after night after night.

Fibs

'You've got to be kidding!'

Rebus was too tired to be truly angry, but there was enough exasperation in his voice to worry the caller on the other end of the telephone, delegated to order Rebus to Glasgow.

'That case isn't supposed to be heard until the week after next.'

'They moved it,' says the voice.

Rebus groaned. He lay back on his hotel bed with the receiver pressed to his ear and checked his watch. Eight thirty. He'd slept soundly last night, waking at seven, dressed quietly so as not to disturb Lisa and had left her a note before making his exit. His nose had led him to the hotel with only a couple of wrong turnings along the way and now he had walked into this telephone call.

'They brought it forward,' the voice is saying. 'It starts today. They need your testimony, Inspector.'

As if Rebus didn't know. He knows that all he has to do is go into the witness box and say he saw Morris Gerald Cafferty (known in the protection game as 'Big Ger') accept one hundred pounds from the landlord of the City Arms pub in Grangemouth. It's as easy as that, but he needs to be there to say it. The case against Cafferty, boss of a thuggish protection and gaming racket, is not airtight. In fact, it's got more punctures than a blind dressmaker's thumb.

He resigns himself to it. Must it be? Yes, it must be. But there was still the problem of logistics.

'It's all been taken care of,' says the voice. 'We did try phoning you last night, but you were never there. Catch the first available shuttle from Heathrow. We'll have a car meet you and bring you into Glasgow. The prosecution reckons he'll call you about half past three, so there's time enough. With any luck, you can be back in London by tonight.'

'Gee, thanks,' says Rebus, voice so thick with irony the words hardly escape into the air.

'You're welcome,' says the voice.

He found that the Piccadilly Line went to Heathrow, and Piccadilly Circus tube was right outside the hotel. So things started well enough, though the tube ride itself was slow and stifling. At Heathrow, he picked up his ticket and had just enough time for a dash into the Skyshop. He picked up a *Glasgow Herald*, then saw the row of tabloids on another shelf: SECRET LIFE OF GAY WOLFMAN; SICK KILLER 'NEEDS HELP' SAY POLICE; CATCH THIS MADMAN.

Cath Farraday had done well. He bought a copy of all three papers as well as the *Herald* and made for the Departure Lounge. Now that his mind was working, he saw all around him people reading the same headlines and the stories below them. But would the Wolfman see the stories? And if so, would he or she make some kind of move? Hell, the whole thing might be about to crack open and here he was heading four hundred miles north. Damn the judicial system, the judges and advocates and solicitors and all. The Cafferty case had probably been brought forward so that it would not interfere with a golf game or a school sports day. Some spoilt child's involvement with an egg-and-spoon race might be behind this whole breathless journey. Rebus tried to calm down, sucking in gulps of air and releasing them slowly. He didn't like flying as it was. Never since his days in the SAS, when they had dropped him from a helicopter. Jesus! That was no way to calm yourself.

'Will passengers for British Airways Super Shuttle flight –'

The voice was cool and precise, triggering a mass movement. People rose to their feet, checked their baggage and made for the gate just mentioned. Which gate? He'd missed the announcement. Was it his flight? Maybe he should phone ahead so they would have the car waiting. He *hated* flying. That was why he had come down by train on Sunday. Sunday? And today was Wednesday. It felt like over a week had passed. In fact, he'd been in London only two full days.

Boarding. Oh, Christ. Where was his ticket? He'd no luggage, nothing to worry about there. The newspapers wriggled beneath his arm, trying to break free and fall in a mess on the floor. He pushed them back together again, squeezing them tightly with his elbow. He had to calm down, had to think about Cafferty, had to get everything straight in his mind, so that the defence could find no chink in his story. Keep to the facts, forget about the Wolfman, forget about Lisa, Rhona, Sammy, Kenny, Tommy Watkiss, George Flight ... Flight! He hadn't notified Flight. They would wonder where he was. He'd have to phone when he landed. He should phone now, but then he might miss the shuttle. Forget it. Concentrate on Cafferty. They would have his notes ready for him when he arrived, so he could go through them before he entered the witness box. There were only the two witnesses, weren't there? The frightened publican, whom they had more or less coerced into giving evidence, and Rebus himself. He had to be strong, confident and believable. He caught sight of himself in a full-length mirror as he made for the Departure Gate. He looked like he'd spent a night on the tiles. The memory of the night made him smile. Everything would be all right.

He should phone Lisa, too, just to say … what? Thank you, he supposed. Up the ramp now, the narrow doorway in front of him, flanked by smiling steward and stewardess.

'Good morning, sir.'

'Good morning.' He saw they were standing by a stack of complimentary newspapers. Christ, he could have saved himself a few bawbees.

The aisle was narrow too. He had to squeeze past businessmen who were stuffing coats, briefcases and bags into the luggage lockers above their seats. He found his own window seat and fell into it, wrestling with the seatbelt and securing it. Outside, the groundcrew were still working. A plane took off smoothly in the distance, the dull roar perceptible even from here. A plump middle-aged woman sat beside him, spread her newspaper out so that half of it fell onto Rebus's right leg, and began to read. She had offered no greeting, no acknowledgment of his existence.

FYT, madam, he thought to himself, still staring out of the window. But then she gave a loud 'tsk', prompting him to turn towards her. She was staring at him through thick-lensed spectacles, staring and at the same time rapping a finger against the newspaper.

'Nobody's safe these days,' she said, as Rebus examined the news story and saw that it was some fanciful piece about the Wolfman. 'Nobody. I won't let my daughter out these nights. A nine o'clock curfew I told her, until they catch him. Even then you can never be sure. I mean, he could be *anybody*.'

Her look told Rebus that he, too, was not beyond suspicion. He smiled reassuringly.

'I wasn't going to go,' she went on, 'but Frank – that's my husband – he said it was all booked so I should.'

'Visiting Glasgow, are you?'

'Not exactly visiting. My son lives there. He's an accountant in the oil industry. He paid for my ticket, so I could see how he's getting on. I worry about him, what with being so far away and everything. I mean, it's a rough place Glasgow, isn't it? You read about it in the papers. Anything could happen up there.'

Yes, thought Rebus, his smile fixed, so unlike London. There was a sound like an electronic doorbell, and the Fasten Seatbelts sign came on, next to where the No Smoking sign was already lit. Jesus, Rebus could kill for a cigarette. Was he in Smoking or No Smoking? He couldn't make out, and couldn't remember which he'd plumped for at the ticket desk. Was smoking allowed on airplanes these days anyway? If God had meant man to smoke at 20,000 feet, wouldn't he have given us all longer necks? The woman next to him looked to have no neck at all. Pity the poor serial killer who tried cutting his way through *that* throat.

That was a terrible thing to think, God, please forgive me. As penance, he began to concentrate on the woman's conversation, right up until take-off, when even she was forced to stop talking for a moment or two. Rebus, taking advantage of the situation, tucked his newspapers into the pocket on the back of the seat in front of him, leaned his head against the back of his own seat, and promptly fell asleep.

George Flight tried Rebus's hotel again from the Old Bailey, only to be told that Rebus had 'left in a hurry' earlier in the morning after asking how best to get to Heathrow.

'Looks like he's done a runner,' DC Lamb commented. 'Frightened off by our consummate professionalism, I shouldn't wonder.'

'Leave off, Lamb,' growled Flight. 'Mind you, it is a bit mysterious. Why would he leave without saying anything?'

'Because he's a Jock, with all due respect, sir. He was probably worried you were going to drop a bill into his lap.'

Flight smiled obligingly, but his thoughts were elsewhere. Last night Rebus had been seeing that psychologist, Dr Frazer, and now he was in a hurry to leave London. What had happened? Flight's nose twitched. He liked a good honest mystery.

He was in court to have a quiet word with Malcolm Chambers. Chambers was prosecuting counsel in a case involving one of Flight's snouts. The snout had been incredibly stupid, had been caught red-handed. Flight had told the man there was little he could do, but he would do what he could. The snout had given him a lot of very useful tips in the past year, helping put a few fairly nasty individuals behind bars. Flight guessed he owed the man a helping hand. So he would talk to Chambers, not to influence the prosecutor – that was unthinkable, naturally – but to fill in some details on the snout's useful contribution to police work and to society, a contribution which would come to a sad end should Chambers push for the maximum sentence.

Et cetera.

Dirty job, but someone had to do it and besides, Flight was proud of his network of informers. The idea of that network suddenly splintering was … well, best not to consider it. He wasn't looking forward to going to Chambers, begging bowl in hand. Especially not after the farce involving Tommy Watkiss. Watkiss was back out on the street, probably telling the story in pubs up and down the East End to a laughing chorus of hangers-on. All about how the arresting constable had said, 'Hello, Tommy, what's going on here?' Flight doubted Chambers would ever forget it, or let Flight forget it. What the hell, best get the begging over and done with.

'Hello there.' It was a female voice, close behind him. He

turned to face the cat-like eyes and bright red lips of Cath Farraday.

'Hello, Cath, what are you doing here?'

She explained that she was at the Old Bailey to meet with the influential crime reporter from one of the more upmarket dailies.

'He's halfway through covering a fraud case,' she explained, 'and never strays too far from the courtroom.'

Flight nodded, feeling awkward in her presence. From the corner of his eye he could see that Lamb was enjoying his discomfort, so he tried to be brave and steeled himself to meet the full force of her gaze.

'I saw the pieces you placed in today's press,' he said.

She folded her arms. 'I can't say I'm optimistic about their chances of success.'

'Do the reporters know we're spinning them a yarn?'

'One or two were a bit suspicious, but they've got a lot of hungry readers out there starving for want of another Wolfman story.' She unfolded her arms and reached into her shoulder-bag. 'Ergo, they've got a lot of hungry editors, too. I think they'll take any tidbit we throw them.' She had brought a pack of cigarettes from her bag, and, without offering them out, lit one, dropped the pack back into her bag and snapped the bag shut.

'Well, let's hope something comes of it.'

'You said this was all Inspector Rebus's idea?'

'That's right.'

'Then I'm doubtful. Having met him, I wouldn't say psychology was his strong point.'

'No?' Flight sounded surprised.

'He doesn't *have* a strong point,' broke in Lamb.

'I wouldn't go that far,' said Flight protectively. But Lamb merely gave that insolent grin of his. Flight was part-embarrassed, part-furious. He knew exactly what Lamb's

121

grin was saying: *don't think we don't know why you're sticking so close to him, why you two are so chummy.*

Cath had smiled at Lamb's interruption, but when she spoke her words were directed at Flight: she did not deign to consort with the lower ranks. 'Is Rebus still around?'

Flight shrugged. 'I wish I knew, Cath. I've heard he was last seen heading off towards Heathrow, but he didn't take any luggage with him.'

'Oh well.' She didn't sound disappointed. Flight suddenly shot a hand into the air, waving. Malcolm Chambers acknowledged the signal and came towards them, walking as though no effort whatsoever was involved.

Flight felt the need for introductions. 'Mr Chambers, this is Inspector Cath Farraday. She's the Press Liaison Officer on Wolfman.'

'Ah,' said Chambers, taking her hand momentarily in his. 'The woman responsible for this morning's lurid headlines?'

'Yes,' said Cath. Her voice had taken on a new, soft, feminine edge, an edge Flight couldn't recall having heard before. 'Sorry if they spoiled your breakfast.'

The impossible happened: Chambers's face cracked into a smile. Flight hadn't seen him smile outside of the courtroom in several years. This really was a morning for surprises. 'They did not spoil my breakfast,' Chambers was saying, 'I found them highly entertaining.' He turned to Flight, indicating by this that Cath was dismissed. 'Inspector Flight, I can give you ten minutes, then I'm due in court. Or would you prefer to meet for lunch?'

'Ten minutes should suffice.'

'Excellent. Then come with me.' He glanced towards Lamb, who was still feeling slightly snubbed by Cath. 'And bring your young man with you if you must.'

Then he was gone, striding on noisy leather soles across the floor of the concourse. Flight winked at Cath, then followed, Lamb silent and furious behind him. Cath grinned, enjoying Lamb's discomfort and the performance Chambers had just put on. She'd heard of him, of course. His courtroom speeches were reckoned to be just about the most persuasive going, and he had even collected what could only be described as 'groupies': people who would attend a trial, no matter how convoluted or boring, just to hear his closing remarks. Her own little coterie of news reporters seemed bland by comparison.

So Rebus had scuttled off home, had he? Good luck to him.

'Excuse me.' A short blurred figure stood before her. She narrowed her eyes until they were the merest slits and peered at a middle-aged woman in a black cloak. The woman was smiling. 'You're not on the jury for court eight by any chance?' Cath Farraday smiled and shook her head. 'Oh well,' sighed the usher, moving off again.

There was such a thing in law as a hung jury, but there were also ushers who would happily see some individual jurors, the rogue jurors, hung. Cath turned on her pointed heels and went off to fulfil her appointment. She wondered if Jim Stevens would remember he was meeting her? He was a good journalist, but his memory was like a sieve at times and seemed especially bad now he was to be a father.

Rebus had time to kill in Glasgow. Time to visit the Horseshoe Bar, or walk through Kelvinside, or even venture down to the Clyde. Time enough to look up an old friend, always supposing he'd had any. Glasgow was changing. Edinburgh had grown corpulent these past few years, during which time Glasgow had been busy getting fit. It had a toned, muscular look to it, a confident swagger rather than the drunken stagger which had been its public perception for so long.

It wasn't all good news. Some of the city's character had

seeped away. The shiny new shops and wine bars, the bright new office blocks, all had a homogenous quality to them. Go to any prosperous city in the world and you would find buildings just like them. A golden hue of uniformity. Not that Rebus was grieving; anything was better than the old swampland Glasgow had been in the 50s, 60s and early 70s. And the people were more or less the same: blunt, yet wonderfully dry in their humour. The pubs, too, had not changed very much, though their clientele might come more expensively and fashionably dressed and the menu might include chilli or lasagne along with the more traditional fare.

Rebus ate two pies in one pub, standing at the bar with his left foot resting on the polished brass rail. He was biding his time. The plane had landed on schedule, the car had been waiting, the journey into Glasgow had been fast. He arrived in the city centre at twenty minutes past twelve, and would not be called to give his evidence until around three.

Time to kill.

He left the pub and took what he hoped might be a shortcut (though he had no ready destination in mind) down a cobbled lane towards some railway arches, some crumbling warehouse buildings and a rubble-strewn waste-land. There were a lot of people milling about here, and he realised that what he had thought were piles of rubbish lying around on the damp ground were actually articles for sale. He had stumbled upon a flea market, and by the look of the customers it was where the down and outs did their shopping. Dank unclean clothes lay in bundles, thrown down anywhere. Near them stood the vendors, shuffling their feet, saying nothing, one or two stoking up a makeshift fire around which others clustered for warmth. The atmosphere was muted. People might cough and hack and wheeze, but they seldom spoke. A few punks, their resplendent mohicans as out of place as a handful of parrots in a cage of sparrows, milled around, not really looking like they meant to buy anything. The locals regarded them with suspicion. Tourists, the collective look said, just bloody tourists.

Beneath the arches themselves were narrow aisles lined with stalls and trestle tables. The smell in here was worse, but Rebus was curious. No out-of-town hypermarket could have provided such a range of wares: broken spectacles, old wireless sets (with this or that knob missing), lamps, hats, tarnished cutlery, purses and wallets, incomplete sets of dominoes and playing cards. One stall seemed to sell nothing but pieces of used soap, most of them looking as though they had come from public conveniences. Another sold false teeth. An old man, hands shaking almost uncontrollably, had found a bottom set he liked, but could not find a top set to match. Rebus wrinkled his face and turned away. The mohicans had opened a game of Cluedo.

'Hey, pal,' they called to the stall-holder, 'there's nae weapons here. Where's the dagger an' the gun an' that?'

The man looked at the open box. 'You could improvise,' he suggested.

Rebus smiled and moved on. London was different to all this. It felt more congested, things moved too quickly, there seemed pressure and stress everywhere. Driving a car from A to B, shopping for groceries, going out for the evening, all were turned into immensely tiring activities. Londoners appeared to him to be on very short fuses indeed. Here, the people were stoics. They used their humour as a barrier against everything Londoners had to take on the chin. Different worlds. Different civilisations. Glasgow had been the second city of the Empire. It had been the first city of Scotland all through the twentieth century.

'Got a fag, mister?'

It was one of the punks. Now, up close, Rebus saw she

was a girl. He'd assumed the group had been all male. They all looked so similar.

'No, sorry, I'm trying to give up –'

But she had already started to move away, in search of someone, anyone, who could immediately gratify. He looked at his watch. It was gone two, and it might take him half an hour to get from here to the court. The punks were still arguing about the missing Cluedo pieces.

'I mean, how can you play a game when there's bits missing? Know what I mean, pal? Like, where's Colonel Mustard? An' the board's nearly torn in half, by the way. How much d'ye want for it?'

The argumentative punk was tall and immensely thin, his size and shape accentuated by the black he wore from tip to toe. 'Twa ply o' reek,' Rebus's father would have called him. Was the Wolfman fat or thin? tall or short? young or old? did he have a job? a wife? a husband even? Did someone close to him know the truth, and were they keeping quiet? When would he strike next? And where? Lisa had been unable to answer any of these questions. Maybe Flight was right about psychology. So much of it was guesswork, like a game where some of the pieces are missing and nobody knows the rules. Sometimes you ended up playing a game completely different to the original, a game of your own devising.

That was what Rebus needed: a new set of rules in his game against the Wolfman. Rules which would be to his benefit. The newspaper stories were the start of it, but only if the Wolfman made the next move.

Maybe Cafferty would get off this time, but there'd always be another. The board was always prepared for a fresh start.

Rebus gave his evidence and was out of the court by four. He handed the file on the case back to his driver, a balding middle-aged detective sergeant, and settled into the passenger seat.

'Let me know what happens,' he said. The driver nodded.

'Straight back to the airport, Inspector?' Funny how a Glaswegian accent could be made to sound so sarcastic. The sergeant had managed somehow to make Rebus feel his inferior. Then again, there was little love lost between east and west coasts. There might have been a wall dividing the two, such was their own abiding cold war. The driver was repeating his question, a little louder now.

'That's right,' said Rebus, just as loudly. 'It's a jet-setting life in the Lothian and Borders Police.'

His head was fairly thrumming by the time he got back to the hotel in Piccadilly. He needed a quiet night, a night alone. He hadn't managed to contact Flight or Lisa, but they could wait until tomorrow. For now, he wanted nothing.

Nothing but silence and stillness, lying on the bed and staring at the ceiling, his mind nowhere.

It had been one hell of a week, and the week was only halfway through. He took two paracetamol from the bottle he had brought and washed them down with half a glass of tepid tap-water. The water tasted foul. Was it true that London water had passed through seven sets of kidneys before reaching the drinker? It had an oily quality in his mouth, not the sharp clear taste of the water in Edinburgh. Seven sets of kidneys. He looked at his cases, thinking of the amount of stuff he had brought with him, useless stuff, stuff he would never use. Even the bottle of malt sat more or less untouched.

There was a telephone ringing somewhere. His telephone, but he managed to ignore the fact for fully fifteen seconds. He growled and clawed at the wall with his hand, finally finding the receiver and dragging it to his ear.

'This had better be good.'

'Where the fuck have you been?' It was Flight's voice, anxious and angry.

'Good evening to you too, George.'

'There's been another killing.'

Rebus sat up and swung his legs off the bed. 'When?'

'The body was discovered an hour ago. There's something else.' He paused. 'We caught the killer.'

Now Rebus stood up.

'What?'

'We caught him as he was running off.'

Rebus's knees almost failed him, but he locked them. His voice was unnaturally quiet. 'Is it him?'

'Could be.'

'Where are you?'

'I'm at HQ. We've brought him here. The murder took place in a house off Brick Lane. Not too far from Wolf Street.'

'In a house?' That was a surprise. The other murders had all taken place out of doors. But then, as Lisa had said, the pattern kept changing.

'Yes,' said Flight. 'And that's not all. The killer was found with money on him stolen from the house, and some jewellery and a camera.'

Another break in the pattern. Rebus sat down on the bed again. 'I see what you're getting at,' he said. 'But the method – ?'

'Similar, to be sure. Philip Cousins is on his way. He was at a dinner somewhere.'

'I'm going to the scene, George. I'll come to see you afterwards.'

'Fine.' Flight sounded as though he had hoped for this. Rebus was scrabbling for paper and a pen.

'What's the address?'

'110 Copperplate Street.'

Rebus wrote the address on the back of his travel ticket from the trip to Glasgow.

'John?'

'Yes, George?'

'Don't go off again without telling me, okay?'

'Yes, George.' Rebus paused. 'Can I go now?'

'Go on then, bugger off. I'll see you here later.'

Rebus put down the telephone and felt an immense weariness take control of him, weighting his legs and arms and head. He took several deep breaths and rose to his feet, then walked to the sink and splashed water on his face, rubbing a wet hand around his neck and throat. He looked up, hardly recognising himself in the wall-mounted mirror, sighed and spread his hands either side of his face, the way he'd seen Roy Scheider do once in a film.

'It's showtime.'

Rebus's taxi driver was full of tales of the Krays, Richardson and Jack the Ripper. With Brick Lane their destination, he was especially vociferous on the subject of 'Old Jack'.

'Done his first prossie on Brick Lane. Richardson, though, he was evil. Used to torture people in a scrapyard. You knew when he was electrocuting some poor bastard, 'cos the bulb across the scrapyard gates kept flickering.' Then a low chuckle. A sideways flick of the head. 'Krays used to drink in that pub on the corner. My youngest used to drink in there. Got in some terrible punch-ups, so I banned him from going. He works in the City, courier sort of stuff, you know, motorbikes.'

Rebus, who had been slouching in the back seat, now gripped the headrest on the front passenger seat and yanked himself forward.

'Motorbike messenger?'

'Yeah, makes a bleeding packet. Twice what I take home a week, I'll tell you that. He's just bought himself a flat down in Docklands. Only they call them "riverside apartments" these days. That's a laugh. I know some of the guys who built them. Every bloody shortcut in the book. Hammering in screws instead of screwing them. Plasterboard so thin you can almost see your neighbours, never mind hear them.'

'A friend of my daughter works as a courier in the City.'

'Yeah? Maybe I know him. What's his name?'

'Kenny.'

'Kenny?' He shook his head. Rebus stared at where the silvery hairs on the driver's neck disappeared into his shirt collar. 'Nah, I don't know a Kenny. Kev, yes, and a couple of Chrisses, but not Kenny.'

Rebus sat back again. It struck him that he didn't know what Kenny's surname was. 'Are we nearly there?' he asked.

'Two minutes, guv. There's a lovely shortcut coming up should save us some time. Takes us right past where Richardson used to hang out.'

A crowd of reporters had gathered outside in the narrow street. Housefront, pavement, then road, where the crowd stood, held back by uniformed constables. Did nobody in London possess such a thing as a front garden? Rebus had yet to see a house with a garden, apart from the millionaire blocks in Kensington.

'John!' A female voice, escaping from the scrum of newsmen. She pushed her way towards him. He signalled for the line of uniforms to break momentarily, so as to let her through.

'What are you doing here?'

Lisa looked a little shaken. 'Heard a newsflash,' she gasped. 'Thought I'd come over.'

'I'm not sure that's such a good idea, Lisa.' Rebus was thinking of Jean Cooper's body. If this were similar ...

'Any comment to make?' yelled one of the newsmen. Rebus was aware of flashguns, of the bright homing lamps attached to video cameras. Other reporters were shouting now, desperate for a story that would reach the first editions.

'Come on then,' said Rebus, pulling Lisa Frazer towards the door of number 110.

Philip Cousins was still dressed in dark suit and tie, suitably funereal. Isobel Penny was in black, too, a full length dress with long, tight sleeves. She did not look funereal. She looked divine. She smiled at Rebus as he entered the cramped living-room, nodding in recognition.

'Inspector Rebus,' said Cousins, 'they said you might drop by.'

'Never one to miss a good corpse,' Rebus replied drily. Cousins, stooping over the body, looked up at him.

'Quite.'

The smell was there, clogging up Rebus's nostrils and lungs. Some people couldn't smell it, but he always could. It was strong and salty, rich, clotting, cloying. It smelt like nothing else on earth. And behind it lurked another smell, more bland, like tallow, candle-wax, cold water. The two contrasting smells of life and death. Rebus was willing to bet that Cousins could smell it, but he doubted Isobel Penny could.

A middle-aged woman lay on the floor, an ungainly twist of legs and arms. Her throat had been cut. There were signs of a struggle, ornaments shattered and knocked from their perches, bloody handprints smeared across one wall. Cousins stood up and sighed.

131

'Very clumsy,' he said. He glanced towards Isobel Penny, who was sketching on her notepad. 'Penny,' he said, 'you look quite delightful this evening. Have I told you?'

She smiled again, blushed, but said nothing. Cousins turned to Rebus, ignoring Lisa Frazer's silent presence. 'It's a copycat,' he said with another sigh, 'but a copycat of little wit or talent. He's obviously read the descriptions in the newspapers, which have been detailed but inaccurate. I'd say it was an interrupted burglary. He panicked, went for his knife, and realised that if he made it look like our friend the Wolfman then he might just get away with it.' He looked down at the corpse again. 'Not terribly clever. I suppose the vultures have gathered?'

Rebus nodded. 'When I came in there were about a dozen reporters outside. Probably double that by now. We know what they want to hear, don't we?'

'I fear they are going to be disappointed.' Cousins checked his watch. 'Not worth going back to dinner. We've probably missed the port and cheese. Damned fine table, too. Such a pity.' He waved his hand in the direction of the body. 'Anything you'd like to see? Or shall we wrap this one up, as it were?'

Rebus smiled. The humour was as dark as the suit, but any humour was welcome. The smell in the air had been distilled now to that of raw steak and brown sauce. He shook his head. There was nothing more to be done in here. But outside, outside he was about to create an outrage. Flight would hate him for it, in fact everybody would hate him for it. But hate was fine. Hate was an emotion, and without emotion, what else was left? Lisa had already staggered out into the tiny hallway, where a police officer was trying awkwardly to comfort her. As Rebus came out of the room, she shook her head and straightened up.

'I'm fine,' she said.

'The first one always hits you hard,' said Rebus. 'Come

on, I'm going to try out a spot of psychology on the Wolfman.'

The huddle of reporters and cameramen had become a sizeable crowd, now including the interested and the curious amateurs. The line of uniformed policemen had locked arms in a small but unbreakable chain. The questions began: Over here! Can we ask you who you are? You were at the canal, weren't you? A statement – Anything to say – Wolfman – Is it – The Wolfman? Is it – Just a few words if –

Rebus had walked to within a few inches of them, Lisa by his side. One of the reporters had leaned close to Lisa, asking for her name.

'Lisa, Lisa Frazer.'

'Are you working on the case, Lisa?'

'I'm a psychologist.'

Rebus cleared his throat noisily. The reporters were like mongrels in a dogs' home, calming quickly when they realised it was their turn at last for the feeding bowl. He raised his arms, and they fell quiet.

'A short statement, gentlemen,' said Rebus.

'Can we just ask who you are first?'

But Rebus shook his head. It didn't matter, did it? They would know soon enough. How many Scottish coppers were working on Wolfman? Flight would know, Cath Farraday would know and the journalists would find out. That didn't matter. Then one of them, unable to hold back, asked the question.

'Have you caught him?' Rebus tried to catch the man's eye, but every eye was silently asking the same thing. 'Is it the Wolfman?'

And this time Rebus nodded. 'Yes,' he said emphatically. 'It's the Wolfman. We've caught him.' Lisa looked at him in dumb surprise.

More questions, yelled now, screeched, but the chain in

front of them would not break and somehow they did not think simply to walk around it. Rebus had turned away and saw Cousins and Isobel Penny standing just outside the door of the house, rigid, unable to believe what they had just heard. He winked at them and walked with Lisa to where his cab still waited. The driver folded his evening paper and stuck it down the side of his seat.

'You fairly got them going, guv. What did you say?'

'Nothing much,' said Rebus, settling back in his seat and smiling towards Lisa Frazer. 'Just a few fibs.'

'Fibs!'

So this was what Flight looked like when he was angry. 'Fibs!'

He seemed unable to believe what he was hearing. 'You call that a few fibs? Cath Farraday's going apeshit trying to calm those bastards down. They're like fucking animals. Half of them are ready to go to print on this! And you call it "fibs"? You're off your trolley, Rebus.'

So it was back to 'Rebus', was it? Well then, so be it. Rebus remembered that they'd promised they'd have dinner together this evening, but somehow he doubted the invitation still stood.

George Flight had been interviewing the murderer. His cheeks were veined with blood, his tie unknotted and hanging loose around his half unbuttoned shirt. He paced what floor there was in the small office. Rebus knew that outside the closed door people were listening in a mixture of fear and amusement: fear at Flight's anger, amusement that Rebus was its sole recipient.

'You're the fucking limit.' Flight's anger had peaked; his voice had dropped by half a decibel. 'What gives you the right –'

Rebus slapped the desk with his hand. He'd had enough

of this. 'I'll tell you what gives me the right, George. The mere fact of the Wolfman gives me the right to do anything I think best.'

'Best!' Flight sounded freshly outraged. 'Now I've heard it all. Giving the papers a crock of shit like that is supposed to be "best"? By Christ, I'd hate to see your idea of "worst".'

Rebus's voice was every bit the equal of Flight's now, and rising. 'He's out there somewhere and he's laughing his head off at us. Because he seems to know how we'll play every round, he's knocking hell out of us.' Rebus grew quiet: Flight was listening now, and that was what he wanted. 'We need to get him riled, get him to lift his head over the trench he's hiding in so he can see what the fuck is going on. We need him angry, George. Not angry at the world. Angry at *us*. Because when he raises his head, we'll be ready to bite it off.

'We've already accused him of being everything from gay to a cannibal from Pluto. Now we're telling everyone he's been caught.' Rebus was reaching his point, his defence. He lowered his voice still further. 'I don't think he'll be able to take that, George. Really I don't. I think he'll have to make contact. Maybe with the papers, maybe directly with us. Just to let us know.'

'Or kill again,' countered Flight. '*That* would let us know.'

Rebus shook his head. 'If he kills again, we keep it quiet. Total media blackout. He gets no publicity. Everybody still thinks he's been caught. Sooner or later, he'll have to show himself.'

Rebus was completely calm now, and so was Flight. Flight rubbed both hands over his cheeks and down to his jaw. He was staring into space, thinking it over. Rebus did not doubt the plan would work. It might take time, but it would work. Basic SAS training: if you can't locate your

135

enemy, make the enemy come to you. Besides, it was the only plan they had.

'John, what if the publicity doesn't bother him? Publicity *or* the lack of it?'

Rebus shrugged. He had no answer to that. All he had were case histories and his own instincts.

Finally, Flight shook his head. 'Go back to Edinburgh, John,' he said tiredly. 'Just do it.' Rebus stared at him, not blinking, willing him to say something else. But George Flight simply walked to the door, opened it, and closed it behind him.

That was it then. Rebus released his breath in a long hiss. Go back to Edinburgh. Wasn't that what everyone had wanted all along? Laine? Lamb and the rest of them? Flight too, maybe. Even Rebus himself. He'd told himself he could do no good here. Well, he was doing no good, so why not go home?

The answer was simple: the case had grabbed him by the throat. There was no escaping it. The Wolfman, faceless, bodiless, had pressed a blade to Rebus's ear and was holding it there, ready to slice. And besides, there was London itself, full of its own stories. Rhona. Sammy. Sammy and Kenny. Rebus had to remind himself that he was still interested in Kenny.

And Lisa.

Above all there was Lisa. The taxi had dropped her off at her flat. She had been quite pale, but insisted she was all right, insisted he go on without her. He should ring her, check she really was okay. What? And tell her he was leaving? No, he had to confront Flight. He opened the door and went into the Murder Room. Flight was not there. The curious faces looked at him from their desks, their telephones, their wallcharts and photographs. He looked at no one, but especially not at Lamb, who was grinning from behind a manila file, his eyes peering over at Rebus.

Flight was in the hallway outside, deep in discussion with the Duty Sergeant, who nodded and moved off. Rebus saw Flight sag, leaning his back against the wall, rubbing his face again. He approached slowly, giving George Flight an extra moment or two of peace and quiet.

'George,' he said. Flight looked up, smiled weakly.

'You never give up, John, do you?'

'I'm sorry, George. I should have checked with you before I pulled a stunt like that. Block the story if you want.'

Flight gave a short humourless laugh. 'Too late. It's been on the local radio news already. The other stations can't just sit back. It'll be on every local news report by midnight. It's your snowball, John. You started it running down the hill. All we can do now is watch it getting bigger and bigger.' He stabbed a finger into Rebus's chest. 'Cath is going to be after your guts, lad. She's the one they'll blame, the one who'll have to apologise, who'll have the job of gaining their trust all over again.' Flight now wagged the finger backwards and forwards, then grinned. 'And if anyone can do it, Inspector Cath Farraday can.' He checked his watch. 'Right, I've let the bugger stew long enough. Time to get back to the interview room.'

'How's it going?'

Flight shrugged. 'Singing like Gracie Fields. We couldn't stop him if we wanted to. He thinks we're going to pin all the Wolfman killings on him, so he's telling us everything he knows, and some things he's probably making up besides.'

'Cousins said it was a copycat, done to disguise a cocked-up burglary.'

Flight nodded. 'I sometimes think Philip's in the wrong game. This guy's a petty thief, not the bloody Wolfman. But I'll tell you what is interesting. He's told us he sells the stuff on to a mutual friend.'

'Who?'

'Tommy Watkiss.'

'Well, well.'

'Coming?' Flight pointed along the corridor, towards the stairwell. Rebus shook his head.

'I want to make a couple of phone calls. I might catch you up later.'

'Suit yourself.'

Rebus watched Flight go. Sometimes it was only brute stubbornness that kept humans going, long after their limbs and intellect had told them to quit. Flight was like a footballer playing in extra time. Rebus hoped he could see the game out to its end.

They watched him as he walked back through the Murder Room. Lamb in particular seemed to peer at him from behind a report, eyes gleaming with amusement. There was a noise coming from his office, a strange tapping noise. He pushed open the door and saw on his desk a small toy, a grotesque plastic jaw atop two oversized feet. The jaw was bright red, the teeth gleaming white, and the feet walked to a clockwork whirr while the jaws snapped shut, then open, shut then open. Snap, snap, snap. Snap, snap, snap.

Rebus, furious at the joke, walked to the desk, lifted the contraption and pulled at it, his own teeth bright and gritted, until it snapped in two. But the feet kept on moving, stopping only when the spring had run down. Not that Rebus was noticing. He was staring at the two halves, the upper and lower jaws. Sometimes things weren't what they seemed. The punk at the Glasgow flea market had turned out to be a girl. And at the flea market they had been selling teeth, false plastic teeth. Like a supermarket pick'n'mix counter. Any size you liked. Christ, he should have seen it sooner!

Rebus walked quickly back through the Murder Room.

Lamb, doubtless responsible for the joke, seemed ready to say something until he saw the look on Rebus's face, an urgent, don't-mess-with-me look. He ran along the corridor and down the stairs, down towards the euphemism known as an Interview Room. 'A man is helping police with their enquiries.' Rebus loved those euphemisms. He knocked and entered. A detective was changing the tape in a recording machine. Flight was leaning across the table to offer a cigarette to a dishevelled young man, a young man with yellow bruising on his face and skinned knuckles.

'George?' Rebus tried to sound composed. 'Could I have a word?'

Flight pushed back his chair noisily, leaving the cigarette packet with the prisoner. Rebus held open the door, indicating for Flight to move outside. Then he thought of something, and caught the prisoner's eye.

'Do you know somebody called Kenny? he asked.

'Loads.'

'Rides a motorbike?'

The young man shrugged again and reached into the packet for a cigarette. There was no answer forthcoming, and Flight was outside waiting, so Rebus closed the door.

'What was that all about?' asked Flight.

'Maybe nothing,' said Rebus. 'Do you remember when we went to the Old Bailey, how someone shouted out when the case was stopped?'

'Someone in the public gallery.'

'That's right. Well, I recognised the voice. It's a teenager called Kenny. He's one of those motorcycle messengers.'

'So?'

'He's going out with my daughter.'

'Ah. And that bothers you?' Rebus nodded.

'Yes, a bit.'

'And that's what you want to see me about.'

Rebus managed a weak smile. 'No, no, nothing like that.'

'So what's on your mind?'

'I was in Glasgow today, giving evidence. I had a bit of free time and went to a flea market, the sort of place tramps go to do their messages –'

'Messages?'

'Their shopping,' Rebus explained.

'And?'

'And there was a stall selling false teeth. Odds and sods. Top sets and bottom sets, not necessarily matching.' He paused to let those final three words sink home. 'Is there someplace like that in London, George?'

Flight nodded. 'Brick Lane for one. There's a market there every Sunday. The main road sells fruit, veg, clothes. But there are streets off, where they sell anything they've got. Bric-a-brac, old rubbish. It makes for an interesting walk, but you wouldn't buy anything.'

'But you could buy false teeth there?'

'Yes,' said Flight after a moment's thought. 'I don't doubt it.'

'Then he's been cleverer than we thought, hasn't he?'

'You're saying the bite marks aren't real?'

'I'm saying they're not the Wolfman's teeth. The lower set smaller than the upper? You end up with a pretty strange jaw, as Doctor Morrison showed us, remember?'

'How can I forget? I was going to feed the pictures to the press.'

'Which is probably exactly what the Wolfman wanted. He goes to Brick Lane market, or at least to somewhere like it, and buys any upper and lower set. They don't match, but that doesn't matter. And he uses them to make those damned bite marks.'

Flight seemed dismissive, but Rebus knew the man was hooked. 'He can't be that clever.'

'Yes he can,' persisted Rebus. 'He's had everything

140

worked out from the start … from *before* the start! He's been playing with us like we were clockwork, George.'

'Then we have to wait until Sunday,' Flight said thoughtfully. 'Search every stall at every market, find the ones selling false teeth – there can't be many – and ask.'

'About the person who bought a set of teeth *without trying them for size*!' Rebus burst out laughing. It was ridiculous. It was absolutely mad. But he was sure it was true, and he was sure the stall-holder would remember, and would give a description. Surely most of the customers would try for size. It was the best lead they'd had so far, and it might just be the only one they'd need.

Flight was smiling too, shaking his head at the dark comic reality of it. Rebus held a closed fist in front of him, and Flight brought his open palm to rest beneath it. When Rebus opened his hand, the plastic chattering teeth fell into Flight's palm.

'Just like clockwork,' said Rebus. 'What's more, we've got Lamb to thank.' He thought about this. 'But I'd rather he didn't get to know.'

Flight nodded. 'Anything you say, John. Anything you say.'

Back at his desk, Rebus sat in front of a fresh sheet of paper. The Wolfman had been too clever. Too clever by half. He thought of Lisa, of her notion that the killer might have a criminal record. It was possible. Possible, too, that the Wolfman simply knew how the police worked. So, he might be a policeman. Or work in forensics. Or be a journalist. A civil rights campaigner. Work in the law. Or write bloody scripts for television. He might just have done his reading. There were plenty of case histories in libraries and bookshops, plenty of biographies of murderers, tracing how they were caught. By studying them, you could learn how *not* to get caught. However hard Rebus tried he just couldn't whittle away at the list of possibilities. The teeth might be yet another dead end. That was why they had to make the Wolfman come to *them*.

He threw down his pen and reached for the telephone, trying Lisa's number. But the phone just rang and rang and rang. Maybe she'd taken a couple of sleeping pills, or gone for a walk, or was a heavy sleeper.

'You stupid prick.'

He looked towards the open door. Cath Farraday was standing there, in her favourite position, against the jamb, arms folded. As if to let him know she'd been there for some time.

'You incredibly stupid little man.'

Rebus pinned a smile to his face. 'Good evening, Inspector. How can I help you?'

'Well,' she said, coming into the room, 'you can start by keeping your gob shut and your brain in gear. You never speak to the press. Never!' She was rearing over him now, looking ready to butt him in the face. He tried to avoid her eyes, eyes sharp enough to cut a man open, and found himself staring instead at her hair. It, too, looked dangerous.

'Do you understand me?'

'FYTP,' said Rebus, speaking without thinking.

'What?'

'Loud and clear,' he said. 'Yes, loud and clear.'

She nodded slowly, not seeming completely convinced, then threw a newspaper onto the desk. He hadn't noticed the paper till now, and glanced towards it. There was a photograph on the front, not large but large enough. It showed him talking to the reporters, Lisa standing nervously by his side. The headline was larger: WOLFMAN CAUGHT? Cath Farraday tapped the photograph.

'Who's the bimbo?'

Rebus felt his cheeks growing red. 'She's a psychologist. She's helping on the case.'

Cath Farraday looked at Rebus as though he were something more than merely stupid, then shook her head and turned to leave. 'Keep the paper,' she said. 'There are plenty more where it came from.'

* * *

She sits with the newspaper in front of her. There are several more piled on the floor. She has the scissors in her hand. One of the reports mentions who the policeman is: Inspector John Rebus. The report calls him an 'expert' on serial murders. And another report mentions that standing to his left is a 'police psychologist, Lisa Frazer'. She cuts around the photograph, then cuts another line, splitting Rebus from Frazer. Time and again she does this, until she has two new neat piles, one of John Rebus, one of Lisa Frazer. She takes one of the photographs of the psychologist and snips off her head. Then, smiling, she sits down to write a letter. A very difficult letter, but that doesn't matter. She has all the time in the world.

All the time.

Churchill

Rebus woke to his radio-alarm at seven, sat up in bed and rang Lisa. No reply. Maybe something was wrong.

Over breakfast, he skimmed the newspapers. Two of the quality titles carried bold front page stories recounting the capture of the Wolfman, but they were couched in speculative prose: Police are believed ... it is thought that ...; Police may have already captured the evil cut-throat killer. Only the tabloids carried pictures of Rebus at his little press conference. Even they, despite the shouting headlines, were being cagey; probably they didn't believe it themselves. That didn't matter. What mattered was that somewhere the Wolfman might be reading about his capture.

His. There was that word again. Rebus couldn't help but think of the Wolfman as a man, yet part of him was wary of narrowing the possible identity in this way. There was still nothing to indicate that it could not be a woman. He needed to keep an open mind. And did the sex of the beast really matter? Actually yes, probably it did. What was the use of women waiting hours just so that they could travel home from a pub or party in a mini-cab driven by another woman, if the killer they were so afraid of turned out to be a woman? All over London people were taking protective measures. Housing estates were patrolled by neighbour-hood vigilantes. One group had already beaten up a completely innocent stranger who'd wandered onto the estate because he was lost and needed directions. His crime? The estate was white, and the stranger was coloured. Flight had told Rebus how prevalent racism was in London, 'especially the south-east corner. Go into some of those estates with a tan and you'll end up being nutted.' Rebus had encountered it already, thanks to Lamb's own particular brand of xenophobia.

Of course, there wasn't nearly so much racism in Scotland. There was no need: the Scots had bigotry instead.

He finished the papers and went to HQ. It was early yet, a little after half past eight. A few of the murder team were busy at their desks, but the smaller offices were empty. The office Rebus had taken over was stuffy, and he opened the windows. The day was mild, a slight breeze wafting in. He could hear the distant sound of a computer printer, of telephones starting to ring. Outside, the traffic flowed in slow motion, a dull rumbling, nothing more. Without realising he was doing it, Rebus rested his head on his arms. This close to the desk, he could smell wood and varnish, mixed with pencil-lead. It reminded him of primary school.

A knock, echoing somewhere, jarred his sleep. Then a cough, not a necessary cough, a diplomatic cough.

'Excuse me, sir.'

Rebus lifted his head sharply from the desk. A WPC was standing, her head around the door, looking in at him. He had been sleeping with his mouth open. There was a trail of saliva on the side of his mouth, and a tiny pool of the stuff on the surface of the desk.

'Yes,' he said, still muzzy. 'What is it?'

A sympathetic smile. They weren't all like Lamb, he had to remember that. On a case like this, you became a team, came to feel as close to the others as you would to your best friend. Closer than that even, sometimes.

'Someone to see you, sir. Well, she wants to speak to

someone about the murders, and you're about the only one here.'

Rebus looked at his watch. Eight forty-five. He hadn't been asleep long then. Good. He felt he could confide in this WPC. 'How do I look?' he asked.

'Well,' she said, 'one side of your face is red from where you've been lying on it, but otherwise you'll do.' Then the smile again. A good deed in a naughty world.

'Thanks,' he said. 'Okay, send her in, please.'

'Right you are.' The head disappeared, but only momentarily. 'Can I get you a coffee or something?'

'Coffee would hit the spot,' said Rebus. 'Thanks.'

'Milk? Sugar?'

'Just milk.'

The head disappeared. The door closed. Rebus tried to look busy: it wasn't difficult. There was a mound of fresh paperwork to be gone through. Lab reports and the like. Results (negative) from door-to-door on the Jean Cooper murder from the interviews with everyone who'd been in the pub with her that Sunday night. He picked up the first sheet and held it in front of him. There was a knock on the door, so soft that he only just caught it.

'Come in,' he called.

The door opened slowly. A woman was standing there, looking around her as though her timidity might be about to turn to fright. She was in her late twenties, with closely cropped brown hair, but other than that she defied description. She was more a collection of 'nots' than anything else: not tall, but not exactly short; not slim, but by no means overweight, and her face lacked anything approaching a personality.

'Hello,' Rebus said, half-rising to his feet. He indicated a chair on the other side of the desk, and watched as, with breathtaking slowness, she closed the door, testing it afterwards to make sure it was going to stay shut. Only then did she turn to look at him – or at least towards him, for she had a way of focusing just to the side of his face, so that her eyes never met his.

'Hello,' she said. She seemed ready to stand throughout proceedings. Rebus, who had seated himself again, gestured once more with his hand.

'Please. Sit down.'

At last, she poised herself above the chair and lowered herself into it. Rebus had the feeling that he was the boss at some job interview, and that she wanted the job so much she'd worked herself into a good and proper state about it.

'You wanted to speak to someone,' he said, in what he hoped were soft and sympathetic tones.

'Yes,' she said.

Well, it was a start. 'My name is Inspector Rebus. And yours is …?'

'Jan Crawford.'

'Okay, Jan. Now, how can I help you?'

She swallowed, gazing at the window behind Rebus's left ear. 'It's the killings,' she said. 'They call him the Wolfman.'

Rebus was undecided. Maybe she was a crank, but she didn't seem like one. She just seemed jumpy. Perhaps she had good reason.

'That's right,' he cajoled. 'The papers call him that.'

'Yes, they do.' She had become suddenly excitable, the words spilling from her. 'And they said last night on the radio, this morning in the paper …' She pulled a newspaper clipping from her bag. It was the photograph of Rebus and Lisa Frazer. 'This is you, isn't it?'

Rebus nodded.

'Then you'll know. I mean, you must. The paper says he's done it again, they're saying you've caught him, or maybe you've caught him, nobody's sure.' She paused, breathing heavily. All the time her eyes were on the window. Rebus kept his mouth shut, letting her calm down. Her eyes were filling, becoming glossy with tears. As she spoke, one droplet squirmed out from the corner of an eye and crept down towards her lips, her chin. 'Nobody's sure whether you've caught him, but I could be sure. At least, I think I can be sure. I didn't get, I mean, I've been scared so long now, and I haven't said anything. I didn't want anybody to know, my mum and dad to know. I just wanted to shut it out, but that's stupid, isn't it?, when he could do it again if he's not caught. So I decided to, I mean, maybe I can ...' She made to stand up, thought better of it, and squeezed her hands together instead.

'Can what, Miss Crawford?'

'Identify him,' she said, her voice almost a whisper now. She searched in the sleeve of her blouse, found a tissue, and blew her nose. The tear dripped onto one knee. 'Identify him,' she repeated, 'if he's here, if you've caught him.'

Rebus was staring hard at her now, and at last his eyes found hers. Her brown eyes, covered with a film of liquid. He'd seen cranks before, plenty of them. Maybe she was, and maybe she wasn't.

'What do you mean, Jan?'

She sniffed again, turned her eyes to the window, swallowed. 'He almost got me,' she said. 'I was the first, before all the others. He almost got me. I was almost the first.'

And then she lifted her head. At first Rebus couldn't understand why. But then he saw. Under her right ear, running in a crescent shape towards her white throat, there was a dark pink scar, no more than an inch long.

The kind of scar you made with a knife.

The first intended kill of the Wolfman.

'What do you think?'

They faced one another across the desk. Four inches of

fresh paperwork had appeared in the in-tray, threatening to overbalance the pile and send it slewing down across the floor. Rebus was eating a cheese and onion sandwich from Gino's. Comfort food. One of the nice things about being a bachelor was that you could eat, without fear of regrets, onions, Branston pickle, huge sausage, egg and tomato sauce sandwiches, curried beans on toast and all the other delicacies favoured by the male.

'What do you think then?'

Flight sipped from a can of cola, giving slight closed-mouth burps between times. He had listened to Rebus's story and had met with Jan Crawford. She had now been taken to an interview room to be fed tea and sympathy by a WPC while a detective took her statement. Flight and Rebus both hoped she would not have to deal with Lamb.

'Well?'

Flight rubbed a knuckle against his right eye. 'I don't know, John. This case has gone ga-ga. You're off telling porkies to the press, your picture's all over the front pages, we've got our first – maybe not our last – copycat killing, then you come up with some idea of flea markets and false teeth. And now this.' He opened his arms wide, pleading for help to put his world back into some semblance of order. 'It's all a bit much.'

Rebus bit into the sandwich, chewing slowly. 'But it fits the pattern, doesn't it? From what I've read about serial killers, the first attempt is often botched. They're not quite ready, they haven't planned well enough. Somebody screams, they panic. He didn't have his technique honed. He didn't go for the mouth, so she was able to scream. Then he found that human skin and muscle is tougher than it looks. He'd probably seen too many horror films, thought it was like cutting through butter. So he scraped her, but not enough to do serious damage. Maybe the knife wasn't

149

sharp enough, who knows. The point is, he got scared and he ran.'

Flight merely shrugged. 'And she didn't come forward,' he said. 'That's what bothers me.'

'She's come forward now. Tell me this, George. How many rape victims do we actually *see*? I heard tell somebody reckons it's less than one in three. Jan Crawford is a timid little woman, scared half to death. All she wanted to do was forget about it, but she couldn't. Her conscience wouldn't let her. Her conscience brought her to us.'

'I still don't like it, John. Don't ask me why.'

Rebus finished the sandwich and made a show of wiping his hands together. 'Your copper's instinct?' he suggested, just a little sarcastically.

'Maybe,' said Flight, appearing to miss, or at least to ignore, Rebus's tone. 'There's just something about her.'

'Trust me. I've talked to her. I've been through it all with her. And, George, I believe her. I think it was him. Twelfth of December last year. That was his first time.'

'Maybe not,' said Flight. 'Maybe there are others who haven't come forward.'

'Maybe. What matters is, one did.'

'I still don't see what good this does us.' Flight picked up a sheet of paper from the desk and read the scribbled details. '"He was about six feet tall, white, and I think he had brown hair. He was running away with his back to me, so I couldn't see his face."' Flight put down the paper. 'That narrows things down nicely, doesn't it?'

Yes, Rebus wanted to say, it does. Because now I think I'm dealing with a man, and before this I wasn't sure. But he kept that particular thought to himself. He'd given George Flight enough grief in the past few days.

'That's still not the point,' he said instead.

'Then what in God's name *is* the point?' Flight had finished the can of cola and now tossed it into a metal wastepaper bin, where it rang against the side, the reverberation lasting for what seemed like an age.

When all was quiet again, Rebus spoke. 'The point is, the Wolfman doesn't know she didn't get a good look at him. We've got to persuade Miss Crawford to go public. Let the TV cameras feast on her. The One Who Got Away. Then we say that she's given us a good description. If that doesn't panic the bastard, nothing will.'

'Panic! Everything you do is designed to panic him. What good does that do? What if it simply frightens him off? What if he just stops killing and we never find him?'

'He's not the type,' Rebus said with authority. 'He'll go on killing because it's taken him over. Haven't you noticed how the murders are coming at shorter and shorter intervals? He may even have killed again since Lea Bridge, we just haven't found the body yet. He's possessed, George.' Flight looked at him as though seeking a joke, but Rebus was in deadly earnest. 'I mean it.'

Flight stood up and walked to the window. 'It might not even have been the Wolfman.'

'Maybe not,' Rebus conceded.

'What if she won't go public?'

'It doesn't matter. We still issue the news story. We still say we've got a good description.'

Flight turned from the window. 'You believe her? You don't think she's a crank?'

'It's possible, but I really don't think so. She's very plausible. She kept the details just vague enough to be convincing. It *was* three months ago. We can check on her if you like.'

'Yes, I'd like that very much.' The emotion had left Flight's voice. This case was draining him of every reserve he had. 'I want to know about her background, her present, her friends, her medical records, her family.'

'I could even get Lisa Frazer to give her some

151

psychological tests?' Rebus suggested, not altogether without tongue in cheek. Flight smiled faintly.

'No, just the checks I've mentioned. Get Lamb onto it. It'll keep him out of our hair.'

'You don't like him then?'

'Whatever gives you that idea?'

'Funny, he says you're like a father to him.'

The moment of tension was over. Rebus felt he had won another small victory. They both laughed, using their dislike of Lamb to strengthen the link between them.

'You're a good policeman, John,' Flight said. Rebus, despite himself, blushed.

'Sod off, you old fart,' he replied.

'That reminds me,' said Flight. 'I told you yesterday to go home. Have you any intention of doing so?'

'None at all,' said Rebus. There was a pause before Flight nodded.

'Good,' he said. 'That's good.' He walked to the door. 'For now.' He turned back towards Rebus. 'Just don't go rogue on me, John. This is my turf. I need to know where you are and what you're up to.' He tapped at his own head. 'I need to know what's going on up here. Okay?'

Rebus nodded. 'Fine, George. No problem.' But the fingers behind his back were crossed. He liked to work alone, and had the feeling Flight wanted to stick close to him for reasons other than traditional Cockney chumminess. Besides, if the Wolfman did turn out to be a policeman, nobody could be discounted, nobody at all.

Rebus tried Lisa again, but without success. At lunchtime, he was wandering around the station when he bumped into Joey Bennett, the constable who had stopped him on Shaftesbury Avenue that first night in London. Bennett was wary at first. Then he recognised Rebus. 'Oh, hello, sir. Was that your picture I saw in the papers?'

Rebus nodded. 'This isn't your patch, is it?' he asked.

'No, not exactly, sir. Just passing through, you might say. Dropping off a prisoner. That woman in the photo with you. She looked a bit of all –'

'Do you have your car with you?'

Bennett was wary again. 'Yes, sir.'

'And you're going back into town now?'

'To the West End, yes, sir.'

'Good. Then you won't mind giving me a lift, will you?'

'Er, no, sir. Of course not, sir.' Bennett broke into the least convincing smile Rebus had seen outside a synchronised swimming event. On their way out to the car, they passed Lamb.

'Teeth stopped chattering yet?' he asked, but Rebus was in no mood to respond. Lamb, undaunted, tried again. 'Going somewhere?' He managed even to make this simple question sound like a threat. Rebus stopped, turned and walked up to him, so that their faces were a couple of inches apart.

'If that's all right with you, Lamb, yes, I'm going somewhere.' Then he turned away again and followed Bennett. Lamb watched them go, half his teeth showing in a parody of a grin.

'Mind how you go!' he called. 'Shall I phone ahead and get the hotel to pack your bags?'

Rebus's reply was a two-fingered salute, a more determined stride, and a whispered 'FYTP'. Bennett heard him.

'Sorry, sir?'

'Nothing,' said Rebus. 'Nothing at all.'

It took them half an hour to reach Bloomsbury. Every second building seemed to sport a blue circular plaque commemorating some writer's having lived there. Rebus recognised few of the names. Finally, he found the building he was looking for, and waved Bennett goodbye. It was the

Psychology Department of University College in Gower Street. The secretary, who appeared to be the only living soul around at one o'clock, asked if she could help him.

'I hope so,' he said. 'I'm looking for Lisa Frazer.'

'Lisa?' The secretary seemed unsure. 'Oh, Lisa. Dear me, I don't think I can help. I haven't seen her in over a week. You might try the library. Or Dillon's.'

'Dillon's?'

'It's a bookshop, just around the corner. Lisa seems to spend a lot of her time in there. She loves bookshops. Or there's always the British Library. It's just possible she might be there.'

He left the building with a new puzzle. The secretary had seemed very distant, very fuzzy. Maybe it was just him. He was starting to read things into every situation. He found the bookshop and went inside. 'Shop' was something of an understatement. It was huge. He read on a wall that psychology books were to be found three floors up. So many books. One man could not hope to read them all in a lifetime. He tried to walk through the aisles without focusing. If he focused, he would become interested, and if he became interested he would buy. He already had over fifty books at home, piled beside his bed, waiting for that elusive weeklong break when he could concentrate on something other than police work. He collected books. It was just about his only hobby. Not that he was precious about it. He did not lust after first editions, signed copies and the like. Mostly, he bought paperbacks. And he was nothing if not catholic in his tastes: any subject matter would do.

So he tried to pretend he was wearing blinkers, pondered the essential difference between catholic and Catholic and finally reached the psychology section. It was a room joined onto other rooms as in a chain, but there was no sign of Lisa in any of the links. He did, however, find where some of her own library of books had no doubt originated. There was a shelf next to the cashier's desk, dedicated to crime and violence. One of the books she had loaned him was there. He picked it up and turned it over to look at the price. Then blinked twice in astonishment. So much money! And it wasn't even a hardback! Still, academic books always did carry steep price tickets. Strange really: weren't students, the intended readership after all, least able to afford these titles? It might take a psychologist to explain that one, or perhaps a shrewd economist.

Next to the criminology section were books on the occult and witchcraft, along with various packs of Tarot cards and the like. Rebus smiled at this curious marriage: police work and hocus-pocus. He picked up a book on rituals and flipped through it. A young, slender woman, in billowing satin dress and with long fiery hair, paused beside him to lift a Tarot set, which she took to the cash desk. Well, it took all sorts, didn't it? She looked serious enough, but then these were serious times.

Ritual. He wondered if there was an element of ritual to the Wolfman's particular spree. So far he had been seeking an explanation from the killer's psyche: what if the whole thing were some kind of rite? Slaughter and defilement of the innocent, that sort of thing. Charlie Manson and his swastika-tattooed forehead. Some said there was a Masonic element to Jack the Ripper's methods. Madness and evil. Sometimes you found a cause, and sometimes you just didn't.

Slash the throat.

Gouge the anus.

Bite the stomach.

The two ends of the human trunk, and something like the mid-point. Could there be a clue in that particular pattern?

There are clues everywhere.

The monster from his past, rearing up out of the dark deep waters of memory. That case had tied him up all right, but not half as much as this. He had thought the Wolfman might be a woman. Now a woman had conveniently appeared to tell him the Wolfman was a man. Very conveniently. George Flight was right to be wary. Perhaps Rebus could learn something from him. Flight did everything by the book, and in scrupulous detail. He didn't go running down the bloody hall with a pair of toy false teeth clutched in his sweaty hand. He was the type to sit down and think things through. That was what made him a good copper, better than Rebus, because he didn't snap at every red herring that came along. Better because he was methodical, and methodical people never let anything escape them.

Rebus left Dillon's Bookshop with his own little thundercloud hanging above his head and a plastic carrier-bag full of newly purchased books swinging from his right hand. He walked down Gower Street and Bloomsbury Street, took a fortuitous left at a set of traffic lights and found himself outside the British Museum, inside which, he knew from memory, was to be found the British Library. Unless, that was, they'd already moved it, as he'd read they were planning to.

But the British Library itself was off-limit to 'non-readers'. Rebus tried to explain that he was a reader, but apparently what this meant was that he had to be in possession of a reader's card. With hindsight, he supposed he could have flashed his ID and said he was on the trail of a maniac, but he didn't. He shook his head, shrugged his shoulders and went instead for a walk around the museum.

The place seemed full almost to bursting with tourists and school parties. He wondered if the children, their imaginations still open, were as thunderstruck as he was by the Ancient Egyptian and Assyrian rooms. Vast stone carvings, huge wooden gates, countless exhibits. But the real throng was around the Rosetta Stone. Rebus had heard of it, of course, but didn't really know what it was. Now he found out. The stone contained writing in three languages and thus helped scholars to work out for the first time what Egyptian hieroglyphics actually meant.

He was willing to bet they hadn't solved it overnight, or even over a weekend. Slow, painstaking graft, just like police work, toil as difficult as anything a bricklayer or miner could endure. And in the end it usually still came down to the Lucky Break. How many times had they interviewed the Yorkshire Ripper and let him go? That sort of thing happened more often than the public would ever be allowed to know.

He walked through more rooms, rooms airy and light and containing Greek vases and figurines, then, pushing open a glass double-door, he found himself confronted by the Sculptures of the Parthenon. (For some reason they had stopped advertising them as the Elgin Marbles.) Rebus walked around this large gallery, feeling almost as though he were in some modern-day place of worship. At one end, a gabble of school-kids squatted before some statues, trying to draw them, while their teacher walked around, trying to keep the grudging artists quiet. It was Rhona. Even at this distance he recognised her. Recognised her walk and the slant of her head and the way she held her hands behind her back whenever she was trying to make a point....

Rebus turned away, and found himself face to face with a horse's head. He could see the veins bulging from the marble neck, the open mouth with its teeth worn away to an indeterminate smoothness. No bite. Would Rhona thank him for walking over and interrupting her class, just to make smalltalk? No, she would not. But what if she spotted him? If he were to slink away, it would look like the action of a coward. Hell, he was a coward, wasn't he? Best to face facts and move back towards the doors. She might never spot him, and if she did she was hardly likely to announce the fact. But then he wanted to know about Kenny, didn't he? Who better to ask than Rhona? There was a simple answer: better to ask *anyone*. He'd ask Samantha. Yes, that's what he'd do. He'd ask Samantha.

He crept back to the doors and walked briskly towards the exit. Suddenly all the exquisite vases and statues had become ridiculous. What was the point in burying them behind glass for people to glance at in passing? Wasn't it better to look forward, forget about ancient history? Wouldn't it be better if he just took Lamb's ill-meant advice? There were too many ghosts in London. Way too many. Even the reporter Jim Stevens was down here somewhere. Rebus fairly flew across the museum courtyard only pausing when he reached the gates. The guards stared at him strangely, glancing towards his carrier-bag. They're just books, he wanted to say. But he knew you could hide anything in a book, just about anything. Knew from painful personal experience.

When feeling depressed, be rash. He stuck a hand out into the road and at the first attempt managed to stop an empty black cab. He couldn't remember the name of the street he wanted, but that didn't matter.

'Covent Garden,' he said to the driver. As the cab did what Rebus assumed was a fairly illegal u-turn, he dipped into his bag to claim the first prize.

He wandered around Covent Garden proper for twenty minutes, enjoying an open-air magic act and a nearby fire-eater before moving off in search of Lisa's flat. It wasn't too difficult to find. He surprised himself by recalling a kite shop and another shop which seemed to sell nothing but teapots. Took a left and a right and another right and found himself in her street, standing outside the shoe shop. The shop itself was busy. The clientele, like the serving staff, was very young, probably not yet out of teens. A jazz saxophone played. A tape perhaps, or someone busking in the distance. He looked up at the window to Lisa's flat, with its bright yellow roller blind. How old was she really? It was hard to tell.

And then, only then, he went to the door and pressed her buzzer. There was noise from the intercom, a crackle of movement. 'Hello?'

'It's me, John.'

'Hello? I can't hear you!'

'It's John,' he said loudly into the door frame, looking around him in embarrassment. But no one was interested. People glanced into the shop window as they passed, eating strange-looking snacks, vegetable-looking things.

'John?' As though she had forgotten him already. Then: 'Oh, John.' And the buzzer sounded beside him. 'Door's open. Come on up.'

The door to her flat was open, too, and he closed it behind him. Lisa was tidying the studio, as she called it. In Edinburgh it wouldn't have been called a studio. It would have been called a bedsit. He supposed Covent Garden didn't have such things as bedsits.

'I've been trying to get in touch,' he said.

'Me too.'

'Oh?'

She turned to him, noting the hint of disbelief in his voice. 'Didn't they tell you? I must've left half a dozen messages with, what was his name, Shepherd?'

'Lamb?'

'That's it.'

Rebus's hate for Lamb intensified.

'About an hour ago,' she went on, 'I called and they said you'd gone back to Scotland. I was a bit miffed at that. Thought you'd gone without saying goodbye.'

Bastards, thought Rebus. They really did hate his guts, didn't they? *Our expert from north of the border.*

Lisa had finished making a neat stack from the newspapers lying on the floor and the bed. She had straightened the duvet and the cover on the sofa. And now, a little out of breath, she was standing close to him. He slid his arm around her and pulled her to him.

'Hello,' he murmured, kissing her.

'Hello,' she said, returning the kiss.

She broke away from his hug and walked into the alcove which served as a kitchen. There was the sound of running tap-water, a kettle filling. 'I suppose you've seen the papers?' she called.

'Yes.'

Her head came out of the alcove. 'A friend called me up to tell me. I couldn't believe it. My picture on the front page!'

'Fame at last.'

'Infamy more like: a "police psychologist" indeed! They might have done their research. One paper even called me Liz Frazier!' She plugged the kettle in, switched it on, then came back into the room. Rebus was sitting on the arm of the sofa.

'So,' she asked, 'how goes the investigation?'

'A few interesting developments.'

'Oh?' She sat on the edge of the bed. 'Tell me.'

So he told her about Jan Crawford, and about his false teeth theory. Lisa suggested that Jan Crawford's memory might be helped by hypnosis. 'Lost memory' she called it. But Rebus knew this sort of thing was inadmissible as evidence. Besides, he'd experienced 'lost memory' for himself, and shivered now at the memory.

They drank Lapsang Souchong, which he said reminded him of bacon butties, and she put on some music, something soft and classical, and they ended up somehow sitting next to one another on the Indian carpet, their backs against the sofa, shoulders, arms and legs touching. She stroked his hair, the nape of his neck.

'What happened the other night between us,' she said, 'are you sorry?'

'You mean sorry it happened?'

She nodded.

'Christ, no,' said Rebus. 'Just the opposite.' He paused. 'What about you?'

She thought over her answer. 'It was nice,' she said, her eyebrows almost meeting as she concentrated on each word.

'I thought maybe you were avoiding me,' he said.

'And I thought you were avoiding me.'

'I went looking for you this morning at the university.'

She sat back, the better to study his face. 'Really?'

He nodded.

'What did they say?'

'I spoke to some secretary,' he explained. 'Glasses on a string around her neck, hair in a sort of a bun.'

'Millicent. But what did she tell you?'

'She just said you hadn't been around much.'

'What else?'

'That I might find you in the library, or in Dillon's.' He nodded over towards the door, where the carrier-bag stood propped against a wall. 'She said you liked bookshops. So I went looking there, too.'

She was still studying his face, then she laughed and pecked him on the cheek. 'Millicent's a treasure though, isn't she?'

'If you say so.' Why did her laugh have so much relief in it? Stop looking for puzzles, John. Just stop it right now. She was crawling away from him towards the bag.

'So what did you buy?'

He couldn't honestly remember, with the exception of the book he'd started reading in the taxi. *Hawksmoor*.

161

Instead, he watched her behind and her legs as she moved away from him. Spectacular ankles. Slim with a prominent hemisphere of bone.

'Well!' she said, lifting one of the paperbacks from the bag. 'Eysenck.'

'Do you approve?'

She thought this question over, too. 'Not entirely. Probably not at all, in fact. Genetic inheritance and all that. I'm not sure.' She lifted out another book, and shrieked. 'Skinner! The beast of behaviourism! But what made you –?'

He shrugged. 'I just recognised some names from those books you loaned me, so I thought I'd –'

Another book was lifted high for him to see. *King Ludd*. 'Have you read the first two?' she asked.

'Oh,' he said, disappointed, 'is it part of a trilogy? I just liked the title.'

She turned and gave him a quizzical look, then laughed. Rebus could feel himself going red at the neck. She was making a fool of him. He turned away from her and concentrated on the pattern of the rug, brushing the rough fibres with his hand.

'Oh dear,' she said, starting to crawl back. 'I'm sorry, I didn't mean to. I'm sorry.' And she placed a hand on either of his legs, kneeling in front of him, angling her head until his eyes were forced to meet hers. She was smiling apologetically. 'Sorry,' she mouthed. He managed a smile which said: 'that's okay'. She leaned across him and placed her lips on his, one of her hands sliding up his leg towards the thigh, and then a little higher still.

It was evening before he escaped, though 'escape' was perhaps putting it too harshly. The effort of easing himself from beneath Lisa's sleeping limbs was almost too much. Her body perfume, the sweet smell of her hair, the flawless warmth of her belly, her arms, her behind. She did not waken as he slid from the bed and tugged on his clothes. She did not waken as he wrote her another of his notes, picked up his carrier-bag of books, opened the door, cast a glance back towards the bed and then pulled the door shut after him.

He went to Covent Garden tube station, where he was offered a choice: the queue for the elevator, or the three hundred-odd spiralling stairs. He opted for the stairs. They seemed to go on forever, turning and turning in their gyre. His head became light as he thought of what it must have been like to descend this corkscrew during the war years. White tiled walls like those of public lavatories. Rumble from above. The dull echo of footsteps and voices.

He thought, too, of Edinburgh's Scott Monument, with its own tightly winding stairwell, much more constricted and unnerving than this. And then he was at the bottom, beating the elevator by a matter of seconds. The tube train was as crowded as he had come to expect. Next to a sign proclaiming 'Keep your personal stereo personal', a white youth wearing a green parka with matching teeth shared his musical taste with the rest of the carriage. His eyes had a distant, utterly vacant look and from time to time he swigged from a can of strong lager. Rebus toyed with the notion of saying something, but held back. He was only travelling one stop. If the glowering passengers were content to suffer silently, that was how it should be.

He prised himself out of the train at Holborn, only to squeeze into another compartment, this time on the Central Line. Again, someone was playing a Walkman at some dizzying level, but they were somewhere over towards the far end of the carriage, so all Rebus had to suffer was the Schhch-schch-schch of what he took to be drums. He was becoming a seasoned traveller now, setting his eyes so that they focused on space rather than on his fellow passengers, letting his mind empty for the duration of the journey.

God alone knew how these people could do it every day of their working lives.

He had already rung the doorbell before it struck him that he did not have a pretext for coming here. Think quickly, John.

The door was pulled open. 'Oh, it's you.' She sounded disappointed.

'Hello, Rhona.'

'To what do we owe the honour?' She was standing her ground, just inside the front door, keeping him on the doorstep. She was wearing a hint of make-up and her clothes were not after-work, relaxing-at-home clothes. She was going out somewhere. She was waiting for a gentleman.

'Nothing special,' he said. 'Just thought I'd pop round. We didn't get much of a chance to talk the other night.' Would he mention that he had seen her in the British Museum? No, he would not.

Besides, she was shaking her head. 'Yes we did, it was just that we had nothing to talk about.' Her voice wasn't bitter; she was simply stating a fact. Rebus looked at the doorstep.

'I've caught you at a bad time,' he said. 'Sorry.'

'No need to apologise.'

'Is Sammy in?'

'She's out with Kenny.'

Rebus nodded. 'Well,' he said, 'enjoy wherever it is you're going.' My God, he actually felt jealous. He couldn't believe it of himself after all these years. It was the make-up that did it. Rhona had seldom worn make-up. He half-turned to leave, then stopped. 'I couldn't use your loo, could I?'

She stared at him, seeking some trick or plan, but he

smiled back with his best impersonation of a crippled dog and she relented.

'Go on then,' she said. 'You know where it is.'

He left his carrier at the door, squeezed past her and began to climb the steep stairs. 'Thanks, Rhona,' he said.

She was lingering downstairs, waiting to let him out again. He walked across the landing to the bathroom, opened and closed the door loudly, then opened it again very quietly and crept back across the landing to where the telephone sat on a small and quite grotesque confection of brass, green glass and red hanging tassels. There were London phone books piled beneath this table, but Rebus went straight to the smaller 'Telephone & Addresses' book on the top of the table. Some of the entries were in Rhona's writing. Who, he wondered, were Tony, Tim, Ben and Graeme? But most were in Sammy's grander, more confident script. He flipped to the K section and found what he wanted.

'KENNY', printed in capitals with a seven figure number scribbled below the name, the whole enclosed by a loving ellipse. Rebus took pen and notepad from his pocket and copied down the number, then closed the book and tiptoed back to the bathroom, where he flushed the toilet, gave his hands a quick rinse and boldly started downstairs again. Rhona was looking along the street, no doubt anxious that her beau should not arrive and find him here.

'Bye,' he said, picking up the carrier, walking past her and setting off in the direction of the main road. He was nearly at the end of her street when a white Ford Escort turned off the main drag and moved slowly past him, driven by a canny-looking man with thin face and thick moustache. Rebus stopped at the corner to watch the man pull up outside Rhona's building. She had already locked the door and fairly skipped to the car. Rebus turned away before she could kiss or hug the man called Tony, Tim, Ben or Graeme.

In a large pub near the tube station, a barn of a place with walls painted torrid red, Rebus remembered that he had not tried the local brews since coming south. He'd gone for a drink with George Flight, but had stuck to whisky. He looked at the row of pumps, while the barman watched him, a proprietorial hand resting on one pump. Rebus nodded towards this resting hand.

'Is it any good?'

The man snorted. 'It's bloody Fuller's, mate, of course it's good.'

'A pint of that then, please.'

The stuff turned out to have a watery look, like cold tea, but it tasted smooth and malty. The barman was still watching him, so Rebus nodded approval, then took his glass to a distant corner where the public telephone stood. He dialled HQ and asked for Flight.

'He's left for the day,' he was told.

'Well then, put me through to anyone from CID, anyone who's helpful. I've got a telephone number I want tracing.' There were rules and regulations about this sort of thing, rules at one time ignored but of late enforced. Requests had to be made and were not always granted. Some forces could pull more weight than others when it came to number tracing. He reckoned the Met and the Yard ought to carry more weight than most, but just in case he added: 'It's to do with the Wolfman case. It might be a very good lead.'

He was told to repeat the number he wanted tracing. 'Call back in half an hour,' said the voice.

He sat at a table and drank his beer. It seemed silly, but it appeared to be going to his head already, with only half a pint missing from the glass. Someone had left a folded, smudged copy of the midday *Standard*. Rebus tried to concentrate on the sports pages and even had a stab at the concise crossword. Then he made the call and was put through to someone he didn't know, who passed him on to someone else he didn't know. A boisterous crowd, looking like a team of bricklayers, had entered the bar. One of them made for the jukebox, and suddenly Steppenwolf's *Born to be Wild* was booming from the walls, while the men urged the unwilling barman to 'wick it up a bit'.

'If you'll just hold a minute, Inspector Rebus, I believe Chief Inspector Laine wants a word.'

'But, Christ, I don't want –' Too late, the voice at the other end had gone. Rebus held the receiver away from him and scowled.

Eventually, Howard Laine came on the line. Rebus pushed a finger into one ear, pressing his other ear hard against the earpiece.

'Ah, Inspector Rebus. I wanted a quiet word. You're a hard man to catch. About that business last night.' Laine's was the voice of reasoned sanity. 'You're about a bollock-hair's breadth away from an official reprimand, understand? Pull a stunt like that again and I'll personally see to it that you're shipped back to Jockland in the boot of a National Express bus. Got that?'

Rebus was silent, listening closely. He could almost hear Cath Farraday sitting in Laine's office, smirking.

'I said, have you got that?'

'Yes, sir.'

'Good.' A rustling of paper. 'Now, you want an address I believe?'

'Yes, sir.'

'It's a lead, you say?'

'Yes, sir.' Rebus suddenly wondered if this would be worth it. He hoped so. If they found out he was abusing the system like this, they'd have him in the dole office with prospects roughly equivalent to those of a shoeshine boy on a nudist beach.

But Laine gave him the address and, as a bonus, supplied Kenny's surname.

'Watkiss,' said Laine. 'The address is Pedro Tower, Churchill Estate, E5. I think that's Hackney.'

'Thank you, sir,' said Rebus.

'Oh by the way,' said Laine, 'Inspector Rebus?'

'Yes, sir?'

'From what I've been told of Churchill Estate, if you're intending to visit, tell us first. We'll arrange for an SPG escort. All right?'

'Bit rough is it then, sir?'

'Rough doesn't begin to tell the story, son. We train the SAS in there, pretend it's a mock-up of Beirut.'

'Thanks for the advice, sir.' Rebus wanted to add that he'd been in the SAS and he doubted Pedro Tower could throw anything at him that the SAS HQ in Hereford hadn't. All the same, it paid to be cautious. The brickies were playing pool, their accents a mix of Irish and Cockney. *Born to be Wild* had finished. Rebus finished his pint and ordered another.

Kenny Watkiss. So there was a connection and rather a large one at that, between Tommy Watkiss and Samantha's boyfriend. How was it that in a city of ten million souls, Rebus had suddenly begun to feel an overwhelming sense of claustrophobia? He felt like someone had wrapped a muffler around his mouth and pulled a Balaclava down over his head.

'I'd be careful, mate,' said the barman as Rebus took delivery of his second pint. 'That stuff can kill you.'

'Not if I kill it first,' said Rebus, winking as he raised the glass to his lips.

The taxi driver wouldn't take him as far as the Churchill

Estate. 'I'll drop you off a couple of streets away and show you where to go, but there's no way I'm going in there.'

'Fair enough,' said Rebus.

So he took the taxi as far as the taxi would take him, then walked the remaining distance. It didn't look so bad. He'd seen worse on the outskirts of Edinburgh. A lot of dull concrete, nuggets of glass underfoot, boarded windows and spray-painted gang names on every wall. Jeez Posse seemed to be the main gang, though there were other names so fantastically contrived that he could not make them out. Young boys skateboarded through an arena constructed from milk-crates, wooden planks and bricks. You couldn't muzzle the creative mind. Rebus stopped to watch for a moment; it only took a moment to appreciate that these boys were masters of their craft.

Rebus came to the entrance of one of the estate's four high-rises. He was busy looking for an identifying mark when something went splat on the pavement beside him. He looked down. It was a sandwich, a salami sandwich by the look of it. He craned his neck to look up at the various levels of the tower block, just in time to catch sight of something large and dark growing larger and darker as it hurtled towards him.

'Jesus Christ!' He leapt into the safety of the block's entrance hall, just as the TV set landed, flattening itself with an explosion of plastic, metal and glass. From their arena, the boys cheered. Rebus moved outside again, but more warily now, and craned his neck. There was no one to be seen. He whistled under his breath. He was impressed, and a little scared. Despite the thunderous sound, nobody seemed curious or interested.

He wondered which television show had so angered the person somewhere above him. 'Everyone's a critic,' he said. And then: 'FYTP.'

He heard a lift opening. A young woman, greasy dyed-blonde hair, gold stud in her nose and three in each ear, spider-web tattoo across her throat. She wheeled a push-chair out onto the concrete. Seconds earlier she would have been beneath the television.

'Excuse me,' said Rebus above the noise of her wailing passenger.

'Yeah?'

'Is this Pedro Tower?'

'Over there,' she said, pointing a sharpened fingernail towards one of the remaining blocks.

'Thank you.'

She glanced towards where the television had landed. 'It's the kids,' she said. 'They break into a flat, and throw a sandwich out of the window. A dog comes to eat it, and they chuck a telly after it. Makes a helluva mess.' She sounded almost amused. Almost.

'Lucky I don't like salami,' Rebus said.

But she was already manoeuvring the pushchair past the fresh debris. 'If you don't shut up I'll fucking kill you!' she yelled at her child. Rebus walked on unsteady legs towards Pedro Tower.

Why was he here?

It had all seemed to make sense, had seemed logical. But now that he stood in the sour-smelling ground-floor hallway of Pedro Tower he found that he had no reason at all to be here. Rhona had said that Sammy was out with Kenny. The chances of them choosing to spend the evening in Pedro Tower must be slim, mustn't they?

Even supposing Kenny were here, how would Rebus locate the flat? The locals would sniff an enquiring copper from fifty paces. Questions would go unanswered, knocked doors would stay unopened. Was this what intellectuals called an impasse? He could always wait, of course. Kenny would be sure to return at some point. But wait where? In here? Too conspicuous, too unappealing. Outside? Too cold, too open, too many armchair critics high above him in the now-dark sky.

Which left him where precisely? Yes, this probably was an impasse. He walked from the block, his eyes on the windows above him, and was about to make off in the direction of the skateboarders when a scream split the air from the other side of Pedro Tower. He walked quickly towards the source of the sound and was in time to see the butt-end of a burning argument. The woman – no more than a girl really, seventeen, eighteen – hit the bedenimed man with a good right hand, sending him spinning. Then she stalked off as he, holding one side of his face, tried to hurl obscenities at her while at the same time feeling in his mouth for damaged teeth.

They did not interest Rebus particularly. He was looking past them to a low-built, dimly illuminated building, a prefabricated construction surrounded by grass and dirt. A weathered board, lit by a single bulb, proclaimed it The Fighting Cock. A pub? Here? That was no place for a policeman, no place for a *Scots* policeman. But what if …? No, it couldn't be so simple. Sammy and Kenny couldn't be in there, wouldn't be in there. His daughter deserved better. Deserved the best.

But then she reckoned Kenny Watkiss was the best. And maybe he was. Rebus stopped dead. Just what the hell was he doing? Okay, so he didn't like Kenny. And when he had seen Kenny cheering in the Old Bailey, he had put two and two together and come to the conclusion that Kenny was in deep with Tommy Watkiss. But now it turned out the two were related in some way and that would explain the cheer, wouldn't it?

The psychology books told him that coppers read the worst into every situation. It was true. He didn't like the fact that Kenny Watkiss was dating his daughter. If Kenny had been heir apparent to the throne, Rebus would still have been suspicious. She was his daughter. He'd hardly seen her since she had entered her teens. In his mind she was still a child, a thing to be cosseted, loved, and protected. But she was a big girl now, with ambition, drive, good looks and a grown-up body. She was grown-up, there was no escaping it, and it scared him. Scared him because she was Sammy, his Sammy. Scared him because he hadn't been there all these years to warn her, to tell her how to cope, what to do.

Scared because he was getting old.

There, it was out. He was growing old. He had a sixteen-year-old daughter and she was old enough to leave school and get a job, to have sex, to get married. Not old enough to go into pubs, but that wouldn't stop her. Not old enough for street-wise eighteen-year-olds like Kenny Watkiss. But grown-up all the same; grown-up without him, and now he too was old.

And by God he felt it.

He plunged his left hand deep into his pocket, his right hand still wrapped around the handle of the carrier-bag, and turned from the pub. There was a bus stop near where the taxi had dropped him. He'd go where the bus would take him. The skateboarders were coming along the path in front of him. One of them seemed very proficient, weaving without losing balance. As the boy approached, he suddenly flipped the board up so that it spun in the air in front of him. Both hands neatly grabbed the board by its running-tail and swung the board itself in a backward arc. Too late, Rebus saw the manoeuvre for what it was. He tried to duck but the heavy wooden board hit the side of his head with a sharp crack.

He staggered, dropped to his knees. They were on him immediately, seven or eight of them, hands gouging into his pockets.

'Fuckin' split my board, man. Lookatit. Fuckin' six inch split.'

A training shoe caught Rebus on the chin and sent him flying. He was concentrating on not losing consciousness, so much so that he forgot to fight or to scream or to defend himself. Then a loud voice:

'Oi! What the fuck d'you think you're up to?'

And they ran, rolling their boards until they had gained enough speed, the hard wheels crackling on the tarmac as they fled. Like a posse in an old western, Rebus thought with a smile. Like a posse.

'You all right, mate? Come on, let's get you up.'

The man helped Rebus to his feet. When his eyes regained their powers of focus, he saw blood on the man's lip, smeared across his chin. The man noticed him looking.

'My bird,' he said, his breath rich with alcohol. 'She fuckin' clocked me, didn't she? Got me a good one, too. Couple of loose teeth. Still, they was rotten anyway, probably saved me a fortune at the dentist's.' He laughed. 'Come on, let's get you into the Cock. A couple of brandies'll see you right.'

'Took my money,' Rebus said. He was clutching the carrier-bag to him like a shield.

'Never mind that,' said his Samaritan.

They were kind to him. They sat him down at a table, and every now and again a drink would appear, and someone would say 'That one's from Bill', or 'That one's from Tessa', or 'That one's from Jackie', or 'That one's from …'

They were kind to him. They collected a fiver so he could get a taxi back to his hotel. He explained that he was a tourist, down here for a bit of sightseeing. He'd managed to get lost, had jumped off a bus and ended up here. And they, kind souls, believed him.

They didn't bother phoning the police.

'Those bastards,' they spat. 'Waste of time. Wouldn't turn up till tomorrow morning and then they'd do nothing. It's the cops round here that are behind half the crimes, believe me.'

And he did. He did believe them. And another drink arrived, another brandy in a small schooner.

'All the best, eh?'

And they were playing cards and dominoes, a lively crowd, a regular crowd. The TV blared – a musical quiz show – and the jukebox sang and the one-armed bandit bleeped and buzzed and spat out an occasional win. He thanked God Sammy and Kenny weren't here. How would it have looked to them? He dreaded to think.

At one point he excused himself and went to the toilet. There was a jagged triangle of mirror nailed to one wall. The side of his head, jaw and ear, were red and would probably bruise. The jaw would ache for some time. Where the shoe had connected, there was already a red and purple welt. Nothing more. Nothing worse. No knives or razor blades. No massed assault. It had been a clean, professional hit. The way that kid had flipped the board, caught it and swung it. Professional. An absolute pro. If Rebus ever caught him, he would congratulate him on one of the sweetest moves he had ever seen.

Then he'd kick the little bastard's teeth so far down his throat they'd bite his small intestine.

He reached down the front of his trousers and drew out his wallet. The warning from Laine and the knowledge that he was on uncharted ground, had been enough to persuade Rebus that he should hide his wallet. Not to save him from muggers, no. So that no one would find his ID. It was bad enough being a stranger in this place, but being a copper.... So he had hidden the wallet, ID and all, down the front of his underpants, tucked into the elasticated waistband. He slipped it back there now. After all, he was not yet clear of

Churchill Estate. The night might turn out to be a long one.

He pulled open the door and headed back to his table. The brandy was working. His head was numb, his limbs pleasantly flexible.

'You all right there, Jock?'

He hates that name, absolutely loathes it, but he smiles nevertheless. 'I'm all right. Oh yes, I'm quite all right.'

'Great. By the way, this one's from Harry at the bar.'

* * *

After she has posted the letter, she feels a lot better. She does some work, but soon begins to twitch inside. It's like feeding a habit now. But it's also an art form. Art? Fuck art. So unbecoming in a man. So art unbecoming fuck in a man. So fuck a man in unbecoming art. They used to quarrel, squabble, argue all the time. No, that's not true. She remembers it that way but it wasn't that way. For a while it was, but then they just stopped communicating altogether. Her mother. Her father. Mother, strong, domineering, determined to be a great painter, a great watercolourist. Every day busy at an easel, ignoring her child who needed her, who would creep into the studio and sit quietly in a corner, crouched, trying not to be noticed. If noticed, she would be sent out of the room fiercely, red hot tears streaming down her face.

'I never wanted you!' her mother would screech. 'You were an accident! Why can't you be a *proper* little girl?'

Run, run, run. Out of the studio and down the stairs, through the morning room, and out of the doors. Father, quiet, innocuous, cultured, civilised father. Reading the newspapers in the back garden, one trousered leg crossed over the other as he reclined in his deckchair.

'And how's my little sweet this morning?'

175

'Mummy shouted at me.'

'Did she? I'm sure she didn't mean anything. She's a bit crochety when she's painting, isn't she? Come and sit here on my lap, you can help me read the news.'

Nobody visited, nobody came. No family, no friends. At first she went to school, but then they kept her at home, educating her themselves. It was all the rage with a certain section of a certain class. Her father had been left money by a great aunt. Enough money for a comfortable life, enough to keep the wolf from the door. He pretended to be a scholar. But then his painstakingly researched essays started to be rejected and he saw himself for what he was. The arguments grew worse. Grew physical.

'Just leave me alone will you? My art's what matters to me, not you.'

'Art? Fuck art!'

'How dare you!'

A dull, solid thump. A blow of some kind. From anywhere in the house she could hear them, anywhere but the attic. But she daren't go to the attic. That was where ... Well, she just couldn't.

'I'm a boy,' she whispered to herself, hiding beneath her bed. 'I'm a boy, I'm a boy, I'm a boy.'

'Sweetness, where are you?' His voice, all sugar and summery. Like a slide-projector show. Like an afternoon car-ride.

They said the Wolfman was homosexual. It wasn't true. They said they'd caught him. She almost whooped when she read it. Wrote them a letter and posted it. See what they'd make of that! Let them find her, she didn't care. He and she didn't care. But he cared that she was taking over his mind as well as his body.

Sweetness ... Oranges and lemons say the bells of ...

So unbecoming in a man. Long nosehairs, her mother had been talking about Daddy's nosehairs. Long nosehairs,

Johnny, are so unbecoming in a man. Why did she remember that utterance above all others? Long. Nose. Hairs. So. Unbecoming. In. A. Man. Johnny.

Daddy's name: Johnny.

Her father, who had sworn at her mother. Fuck art. Fuck was the dirtiest word there was. At school it had been whispered, a magic word, a word to conjure up demons and secrets.

And she's on the streets now, although she knows that really she should do something about the Butcher's Gallery. It needs cleaning badly. There are torn canvases everywhere. Torn and spattered. It doesn't matter: nobody visits. No family, no friends.

So she finds another one. This one's stupid. 'As long as you're not the Wolfman,' she says with a laugh. The Wolfman laughs too. He? She? It doesn't matter now. He and she are one and the same. The wound has healed. He feels whole, feels complete. It is not a good feeling. It is a bad feeling. But it can be forgotten for a moment.

Back in his house.

'Some gaff you've got here,' she says. He smiles, takes her coat and hangs it up. 'Bit of a smell though. You haven't got a gas leak, have you?'

No, not a gas leak. But a leak, yes. He slips his hand into his pocket, checks that the teeth are there. Of course they are, they're always there when he needs them. To bite with. The way he was bitten.

'Only a game, sweet.'

Only a game. Bitten in fun. On the stomach. Bitten. Not hard, more like blowing a raspberry. But that didn't stop it hurting. He touches his gut. It still hurts, even now.

'Where do you want me, love?'

'In here will do,' he says, taking out the key and beginning to unlock the door. The mirror was a bad idea. The last one had seen what was happening behind her, had

177

almost screamed. The mirror has been taken down. The door is unlocked.

'Keep it locked, do you? What you got in there, the crown jewels?'

And the Wolfman, showing teeth, smiles.

Know This, Womin

He woke up in his hotel room, which was something in itself, bearing in mind that he had no idea how he'd got there. He was lying on his bed, fully clothed, his hands pressed between his legs. Beside him lay the carrier-bag full of books. It was seven o'clock and by the quality of the light streaming in through the uncurtained window, it was morning rather than evening. So far so good. The bad news was that his head seared with two kinds of pain, bad when he opened his eyes, unbearable when he closed them. With eyes closed, the world spun at an awkward tilt. With eyes opened, it merely floated on a different plane.

He groaned, attempted to unglue his furred tongue from the roof of his mouth. Staggered to the sink and ran the cold tap for some moments, then splashed his face and cupped his hand, lapping water from it the way a mongrel might. The water was sweet, chlorinated. He tried not to think of kidneys ... seven sets of kidneys. Knelt by the toilet-pan and retched. The big white telephone receiver to God. What was the score? Seven brandies, six dark rums – he'd lost count after that. He squeezed an inch-long strip of toothpaste onto his brush and scrubbed at his teeth and gums. Then, only then, did he have the courage to examine himself in the wall-mirror.

There were two kinds of pain. One from the hangover, the other from the mugging. He'd lost twenty quid, maybe thirty. But the loss to his pride was above price. He held in his head a good description of a couple of the gang and especially the leader. This morning, he would give what he knew to the local station. His message would be clear: seek out and destroy. Who was he kidding? They'd rather protect their own villains than help an intruder from north of the border. *Our man from north of the border. Jockland. Jock.* But to let the gang get away with it was worse. What the hell.

He rubbed his jaw. It felt worse than it looked. There was a pale mustard bruise down one cheek and a graze on his chin. Good thing training shoes were all the rage. In the early 70s it would have been a steel-capped Airwear boot and he would not have been so chipper.

He was running out of clean clothes. Today, he would have either to buy some new bits and pieces or else find himself a laundrette. He had come to London intending to stay no more than two or three days. He'd thought that after that the Met would come to see that he could add nothing to the case. But instead here he was, coming up with possible leads, making himself useful, getting beaten up, turning into an over-protective father, having a holiday romance with a psychology lecturer.

He thought about Lisa, about the way the secretary at University College had acted. Something jarred about the whole incident. Lisa, who slept so soundly, the sleep of a clear conscience. What was that smell? That smell creeping into his room? The smell of cooking fat mingled with toast and coffee. The smell of breakfast. Somewhere downstairs they were busy perspiring over the griddles, breaking eggs to sizzle beside thick sausages and grey-pink bacon. The thought sent Rebus's stomach on a tiny rollercoaster ride. He was hungry, but the thought of fried food repelled him. He felt his just-cleaned mouth turning sour.

When had he last eaten? A sandwich on the way to Lisa's. Two packets of crisps in the Fighting Cock. Christ, yes, he was hungry. He dressed quickly, making a mental note of what needed buying – shirt, pants, socks – and headed down to the dining-room clutching three paracetamol tablets in his hand. A fistful of dullers.

They weren't quite ready to start serving, but when he announced that he needed only cereal and fruit juice, the waitress (a different face each day) relented and showed him to a table set for one.

He ate two small packets of cereal. A cereal killer. Smiled grimly and went to the trestle table to help himself to more juice. Lots more juice. It had a funny artificial smell to it, and a taste best described as 'wersh'. But it was cold and wet and the vitamin C would help his head. The waitress brought him two daily papers. Neither contained anything of interest. Flight had not yet used Rebus's idea of the detailed description. Maybe Flight had passed it on to Cath Farraday. Would she sit on it out of spite? After all, she hadn't been too happy about his last little stunt, had she? Maybe she was holding back on this one, just to show him that she could. Well, sod them. He didn't see anyone coming up with better ideas, with any ideas at all, come to that. Nobody wanted to make a mistake; they'd all rather sit on their hands than be seen to get it wrong. Jesus Christ.

When the first customer proper of the morning ordered bacon, eggs and tomatoes, Rebus finished his orange juice and left the restaurant.

In the Murder Room, he sat at one of the typewriters and prepared detailed descriptions of the gang members. His typing had never been proficient at the best of times, but today's hangover was compounded by an electronic typewriter of infernal complexity. He couldn't get the thing to set a reasonable line length, the tabs appeared not to work and every time he pressed a wrong key the thing bleeped at him.

'Bleep yourself,' he said, trying again to set it for single space typing.

Eventually, he had a typed description. It looked like the work of a ten-year-old, but it would have to do. He took the sheets of paper through to his office. There was a note from Flight on his desk.

'John, I wish you wouldn't keep disappearing. I've run a check on missing persons. Five women have been reported missing north of the river in the past forty-eight hours. Two of these could be explicable, but the other three look more serious. Maybe you're right, the Wolfman's getting hungrier. No feedback from the press stories yet though. See you when you've finished shagging the Prof.'

It was signed simply 'GF'. How did Flight know where he'd been yesterday afternoon? An inspired guess, or something more cunning and devious? It didn't really matter. What mattered were the missing women. If Rebus's hunch were true, then the Wolfman was losing some of his previous control and that meant that sometime soon he was bound to make a mistake. They need only goad him a little more. The Jan Crawford story might just do that particular trick. Rebus had to sell the idea to Flight – and to Farraday. They had to be made to see that it was the right move at the right time. Three missing women. That would bring the count to seven. Seven murders. There was no telling where it would stop. He rubbed at his head again. The hangover was returning with a steel-tipped vengeance.

'John?'

She was standing in the doorway, trembling, her eyes wide.

'Lisa?' He rose slowly to his feet. 'Lisa, what is it? What's wrong?'

She stumbled towards him. There were tears in her eyes and her hair was slick with sweat. 'Thank God,' she said, clinging to him. 'I thought I'd never ... I didn't know what to do, where to go. Your hotel said you'd already left. The Sergeant on the desk downstairs let me come up. He recognised me from the photo in the papers. My photo.' And then the tears came: hot, scalding, and loud. Rebus patted her on the back, trying to calm her, wanting to know just what the hell had happened.

'Lisa,' he said quietly, 'just tell me about it.' He manoeuvred her onto a chair, with his hand rubbing soothingly at her neck. Every bit of her seemed damp with perspiration.

She pulled her bag onto her lap, opened it, and drew from one of the three compartments a small envelope, which she handed silently to Rebus.

'What is it?' he asked.

'I got it this morning,' she said, 'addressed to me by name and sent to my home.'

Rebus examined the typed name and address, the first class stamp, and the postmark: London EC4. The frank stated that the letter had been posted the previous morning.

'He knows where I live, John. When I opened it this morning, I nearly died on the spot. I had to get out of the flat, but all the time I knew that maybe he was watching me.' Her eyes filled with water again, but she threw back her head so that the tears would not escape. She fished in her bag and came out with some paper tissues, peeling off one so that she could blow her nose. Rebus said nothing.

'It's a death threat,' she explained.

'A *death threat*?'

She nodded.

'Who from? Does it say?'

'Oh yes, it says all right. It's from the Wolfman, John. He says I'm going to be next.'

It was a rush job, but the lab, when they heard the circumstances, were happy to cooperate. Rebus stood with hands in pockets watching them at work. There was the crackle of paper in his pocket. He had folded the description of the gang members and tucked it away, perhaps for future use: for now, there were more important matters to attend to.

The story was straightforward enough. Lisa had been scared out of her wits by the letter, and more so by the fact that the Wolfman knew where she lived. She had tried contacting Rebus and when that failed had panicked, fleeing from her flat, aware that *he* might be watching her, might be about to pounce at any moment. The pity was, as the lab had already explained, she'd messed up the letter, gripping it in her hand as she fled, destroying any fingerprints or other evidence that there might have been on the envelope itself. Still, they'd do their best.

If the letter was from the Wolfman and not from some new and twisted crank, then there might well be clues to be had from the envelope and its contents: saliva (used to stick down both flap and stamp), fibres, fingerprints. These were the physical possibilities. Then there were more arcane elements: the typewriter itself might be traceable. Were there oddities of speech or misspellings which might yield a clue? And what about that postmark? The Wolfman had outwitted them in the past, so was the postal address another red herring?

The various processes involved would take time. The lab was efficient, but the chemical analyses could not be hurried. Lisa had come to the lab, too, as had George Flight. They were off in another part of the building drinking tea and going over the details for the fourth or fifth time, but Rebus liked to watch the lab boys at work. This was his idea of sleuthing. It also helped calm him to watch someone working in such painstaking detail. And he certainly needed calming.

His plan had worked. He had prodded and teased the

Wolfman into action. He should, though, have realised the danger Lisa might be in. After all, her photo had been in the papers, as had her name. They had even mistakenly termed her a police psychologist – the very people who, according to the earlier planted story, had come to the conclusion that the Wolfman might be gay, or transsexual, or any of the other barbs they had used. Lisa Frazer had become the Wolfman's enemy, and he, John Rebus, had led her into it by the nose. Stupid, John, oh so very stupid. What if the Wolfman had actually tracked her to her flat and ...? No, no, no: he couldn't bear to think of it.

But though Lisa's name had appeared in the newspapers, her address had not. So how had the Wolfman found out her address? That was much more problematic.

And much more chilling.

She was ex-directory, for a start. But as he knew only too well, this was no barrier to someone in authority, someone like a police officer. Jesus: was he *really* talking about another police officer? There had to be other candidates: staff and students at University College, other psychologists – they would know Lisa. Then there were those groups who could have linked an address to a name: civil servants, the local council, taxmen, gas and electricity boards, the postman, the guy next door, numerous computers and mailshot programmes, her local public library. Where could he start?

'Here you are, Inspector.'

One of the assistants handed him a photocopy of the typed letter.

'Thanks,' said Rebus.

'We're testing the original at the moment, scanning for traces of anything interesting. We'll let you know.'

'Right. What about the envelope?'

'The saliva tests will take a little longer. We should have something for you in the next couple of hours. There was also the photograph, of course, but it won't photocopy too well. We know which paper it was from, and that it was cut out with a pair of fairly sharp scissors, perhaps as small as manicure scissors judging from the length of each cut.'

Rebus nodded, staring at the photostat. 'Thanks again,' he said.

'No problem.'

No problem? That wasn't right; there were plenty of problems. He read through the letter. The typing seemed nice and even, as though the typewriter used was a new one, or a good quality model, something like the electronic machine he'd been using this morning. As for the content, well, that was something else again.

GET THIS, I'M NOT HOMOSEXUL, O.K.? WOLFMAN IS WHAT WOLFMAN DOES. WHAT WOLFMAN DOES NEXT IS THIS: HE KILLS YOU. DON'T WORRY, IT WON'T HURT. WOLFMAN DOES NOT HURT; JUST DOES WHAT WOLFMAN IS. KNOW THIS, WOMIN, WOLFMAN KNOWS YOU, WHERE YOU LIVE, WHAT YOU LOOK LIKE. JUST TELL THE TRUTH AND NO HARM CAN CUM TO YOU.

On a piece of plain A4-sized paper, folded in four to get it into the small white envelope. The Wolfman had cut a picture of Lisa from one of the newspapers. Then he had cut her head off and drawn a dark pencilled circle on her stomach. And this photograph of her trunk had accompanied the letter.

'Bastard,' Rebus hissed. 'Jesus, you bastard.'

He took the letter along the corridor and up the stairs to the room where Flight was sitting, rubbing at his face again.

'Where's Lisa?'

'Ladies' room.'

'Does she seem …?'

'She's upset, but she's coping. The doctor's given her some tranqs. What have you got there?' Rebus handed over the copy. Flight read through it quickly, intently. 'What the hell do you make of it?' he asked. Rebus sat himself down on a hard chair still warm from Lisa's presence. He reached out a hand and took the paper from Flight, then angled his chair so that both men could inspect the letter together.

'Well,' he said. 'I'm not sure. At first sight, it looks like the work of a near-illiterate.'

'Agreed.'

'But then again, there's something artful about it. Look at the punctuation, George. Absolutely correct, right down to every comma. And he uses colons and semi-colons. What sort of person could spell "woman" as "womin", yet know how to use a semi-colon?'

Flight studied the note intently, nodding. 'Go on.'

'Well, Rhona, my ex-wife, she's a teacher. I remember she used to tell me how frustrating it was that nowadays no one in schools bothered to teach basic grammar and punctuation. She said that kids were growing up now with no need for things like colons and semi-colons and no idea at all of how to use them. So I'd say we're dealing either with someone who has been well educated, or with someone in middle age, educated at a time when punctuation was still taught in every school.'

Flight gave a half-smile. 'Been reading your psychology books again I see, John.'

'It's not all black magic, George. Mostly it's just to do with common sense and how you interpret things. Do you want me to go on?'

'I'm all ears.'

'Well,' Rebus was running a finger down the letter again. 'There's something else here, something that tells me this

187

letter is genuinely from the killer, and not the work of some nutter somewhere.'

'Oh?'

'Go on, George, where's the clue?'

He held the paper out towards Flight. Flight grinned for a moment, then took it.

'I suppose,' he said, 'you're talking about the way the writer refers to the Wolfman in the third person?'

'You've just named the tune in one, George. That's exactly what I mean.'

Flight looked up. 'Incidentally, John, what the hell happened to you? Did you get in a fight or something? I thought the Scots gave up wearing woad a couple of years back?'

Rebus touched his bruised jaw. 'I'll tell you the story sometime. But look, in the first sentence, the writer refers to himself in the first person. He's taken our homosexual jibe personally. But in the rest of the letter, he speaks of the Wolfman in the third person. Standard practice with serial murderers.'

'What about the misspelling of homosexual?'

'Could be genuine, or it could be to throw us off the scent. "U" and "a" are at different ends of the keyboard. A two-fingered typist could miss the "a" if he was writing fast, if he was angry.' Rebus paused, remembering the list in his pocket. 'I speak from recent experience.'

'Fair enough.'

'Now look at what he actually says: "Wolfman is what Wolfman does". What the books say is that killers find their identity through killing. That's exactly what this sentence means.'

Flight exhaled noisily. 'Yes, but none of this gets us any closer, does it?' He offered a cigarette to Rebus. 'I mean, we can build up as clear a picture as we like of the bastard's personality, but it won't give us a name and address.'

Rebus sat forward in his chair. 'But all the time we're narrowing down the possible types, George. And eventually we'll narrow it down to a field of one. Look at this final sentence.'

"'Just tell the truth and no harm can cum to you,'" Flight recited.

'Skipping the pun, which is intriguing in itself, don't you think there's something very, I don't know, official sounding about that construction? Something very formal?'

'I don't see what you're getting at.'

'What I'm getting at is that it seems to me the sort of thing someone like you or me would say.'

'A copper?' Flight sat back in his chair. 'Oh, come on, John, what kind of crap is that?'

Rebus's voice grew quiet and persuasive. 'Someone who knows where Lisa Frazer lives, George. Think about it. Someone who knows that kind of information, or knows how to get it. We can't afford to rule out –'

Flight stood up. 'I'm sorry, John, but no. I simply can't entertain the notion that … that someone, some copper, could be behind all this. No, it's just not on.'

Rebus shrugged. 'Okay, George, whatever you say.' But Rebus knew that he had planted a seed now in George Flight's head, and that the seed would surely sprout.

Flight sat down again, confident that this time he had won a point from Rebus. 'Anything else?'

Rebus read the letter through yet again, sucking on his cigarette. He remembered how at school, in his English class, he had loved writing summaries and close interpretations of texts. 'Yes,' he said eventually. 'Actually there is. This letter seems to me more of a warning, a shot across the bows. He starts off by saying that he's going to kill her, but by the end of the letter he's tempered that line. He says nothing will happen if she tells the truth. I think he's looking for a retraction. I think he wants us to put out another story saying he's not gay.'

Flight checked his watch. 'He's in for another fright.'

'How do you mean?'

'The lunchtime edition will be hitting the streets. I believe Cath Farraday's put out the Jan Crawford story.'

'Really?' Rebus revised his idea of Farraday. Maybe she wasn't a vindictive old bat after all. 'So now we're saying we've got a living witness, and he must realise it's a fact. I think it might just be enough to blow what final fuses he's got up here.' Rebus tapped his head. 'To send him barking mad, as Lamb would put it.'

'You reckon?'

'I reckon, George. We need everybody at their most alert. He could try anything.'

'I dread to think.'

Rebus was staring at the letter. 'Something else, George. EC4: where's that exactly?'

Flight thought it over. 'The City, part of it anyway. Farringdon Street, Blackfriars Bridge, all around there. Ludgate, St Paul's.'

'Hmm. He's tricked us before, making us see patterns where none exist. The teeth for example, I'm sure I'm right about them. But now that we've got him rattled –'

'You think he lives in the City?'

'Lives there, works there, maybe just drives through there on his way to work.' Rebus shook his head. He didn't yet want to share with Flight the image which had just passed through his mind, the image of a motorcycle courier based in the City, a motorcyclist with easy access to every part of London. Like the man in leathers he'd seen on the bridge that first night down by the canal.

A man like Kenny Watkiss.

'Well,' he said instead, 'whatever, it's another piece of the jigsaw.'

'If you ask me,' said Flight, 'there are too many pieces. They won't all fit.'

'Agreed.' Rebus stubbed out the cigarette. Flight had already finished his own, and was about to light another. 'But as the picture emerges, we'll know better which bits we can discard, won't we?' He was still studying the letter. There was something else. What was it? Something at the back of his mind, lurking somewhere in memory.... Something stirred momentarily by the letter, but what? If he stopped thinking about it, maybe it would come to him, the way the names of forgotten actors in films did.

The door opened.

'Lisa, how are you?' Both men rose to offer her a seat, but she lifted a hand to show she preferred to stand. All three of them stood, a stiff triangle in the tiny box of a room.

'Just been sick again,' she said. Then she smiled. 'Can't be much more to bring up. I think I'm back to yesterday's breakfast already.' They smiled with her. She looked tired to Rebus, exhausted. Lucky she had slept so soundly yesterday. He doubted she'd get much sleep for the next night or ten, tranqs or not.

Flight spoke first. 'I've arranged for temporary accommodation, Dr Frazer. The less people who know where, the better. Don't worry, you'll be quite safe. We'll have a guard on you.'

'What about her flat?' asked Rebus.

Flight nodded. 'I've got two men there keeping an eye on the place. One inside the flat itself, the other outside, both of them hidden. If the Wolfman turns up, they'll cope with him, believe me.'

'Stop talking as though I'm not here,' Lisa snapped. 'This affects me too.'

There was a cold silence in the room.

'Sorry,' she said. She covered her eyes with her ringless

left hand. 'I just can't believe I was so *scared* back there. I feel –'

She tipped her head back again. The tears were too precious to be released. Flight placed a hand softly on her shoulder.

'It's all right, Dr Frazer. Really it is.' She gave a wry smile at this.

Flight kept on talking, feeding her with comforting words. But she wasn't listening. She was staring at Rebus, and he was staring back at her. Rebus knew what her eyes were telling him. They were telling him something of the utmost importance.

Catch the Wolfman, catch him quickly and destroy him utterly. Do it for me, John. But just do it.

She blinked, breaking the contact. Rebus nodded slowly, almost imperceptibly, but it was enough. She smiled at him, and suddenly her eyes were dry sparkling stones. Flight felt the change and lifted his hand away from her arm. He looked to Rebus for some explanation, but Rebus was studying the letter, concentrating on its opening sentence. What was it? There was something there, something just beyond his line of vision. Something he didn't get.

Yet.

Two detectives, one of them extraordinarily burly, like the prop-forward from a rugby team, the other tall and thin and silent, came to the labs to take Lisa away with them, away to a place of safety. Despite vigorous protests, Rebus wasn't allowed to know the destination. Flight was taking all of this very seriously indeed. But before Lisa could go, the lab people needed her fingerprints and to take samples of fibres from her clothes, all for the purpose of elimination. The two bodyguards went with her.

Rebus and Flight, exhausted, stood together at the drinks

machine in the long, brightly-lit hallway, feeding in coins for cups of powdery coffee and powdery tea.

'Are you married, George?'

Flight seemed surprised by the question, surprised perhaps that it should come only now. 'Yes,' he said. 'Have been the past twelve years. Marion. She's the second. The first was a disaster – my fault, not hers.'

Rebus nodded, taking hold of the hot plastic beaker by its rim.

'You said you'd been married, too,' Flight remarked. Rebus nodded again.

'That's right.'

'So what happened?'

'I'm not really sure any more. Rhona used to say it was like the continental drift: so slow we didn't notice until it was too late. Her on one island, me on another, and a great big bloody sea between us.'

Flight smiled. 'Well, you did say she was a teacher.'

'Yes, she still is actually. Lives in Mile End with my daughter.'

'Mile End? Bloody hell. Gentrified gangland, no place for any copper's daughter.'

Rebus smiled at the irony. It was time to confess. 'Actually, George, I've found out she's going out with someone called Kenny Watkiss.'

'Oh dear. Who is? Your missus or your daughter?'

'My daughter. Her name's Samantha.'

'And she's going out with Kenny Watkiss? How old is he?'

'Older than her. Eighteen, nineteen, something like that. He's a bike messenger in the City.'

Flight nodded, understanding now. 'He was the one who shouted from the public gallery?' Flight thought for a moment. 'Well, from what I know of the Watkiss family history, I'd say Kenny must be Tommy's nephew. Tommy's got a brother, Lenny, he's doing time just now. Lenny's a big softie, not like Tommy. He's in for fraud, tax evasion, clocking cars, naughty kites, I mean bad cheques. It's all fourth division stuff, but it mounts up, and when there's enough of it against you at any one sitting of the bench, well, it's odds on you'll go inside, isn't it?'

'It's no different in Scotland.'

'No, I don't suppose it is. So, do you want me to find out what I can about this bike messenger?'

'I already know where he stays. Churchill Estate, it's a housing estate in –'

Flight was chuckling. 'You don't have to tell any copper in Greater London where Churchill Estate is, John. They use that place to train the SAS.'

'Yes,' said Rebus, 'so Laine said.'

'Laine? What's he got to do with it?'

In for a penny, thought Rebus. 'I had Kenny's telephone number. I needed an address.'

'And Laine got it for you? What did you tell him it was for?'

'The Wolfman case.'

Flight flinched, his face creasing. 'You keep forgetting, John, you're our *guest* down here. You don't go pulling stunts like that. When Laine finds out –'

'If he finds out.'

But Flight was shaking his head. '*When* he finds out. There's no "if" about it, believe me. When he finds out, he won't bother with you. He won't even bother with who's directly above you. He'll go to your Chief Super back in Edinburgh and give him the most incredible verbals. I've seen him do it.'

Do a good job, John. Remember, you're representing our force down there.

Rebus blew on the coffee. The notion of anyone giving

'verbals' to Farmer Watson was almost amusing. 'I always did fancy getting back into uniform,' he said.

Flight stared at him. The fun was over. 'There are some rules, John. We can get away with breaking a few, but some are sacrosanct, carved into stone by God Almighty. And one of them states that you don't muck around with someone like Laine just to satisfy your own personal curiosity.' Flight was angry, and trying to make a point, but he was also whispering, not wanting anyone to hear.

Rebus, not really caring any more, was half-smiling as he whispered back. 'So what do I do? Tell him the truth? Oh hello there, Chief Inspector, my daughter's winching with someone I don't like. Can I have the young man's address, please, so I can go and belt him? Is that how I do it?'

Flight paused, then frowned. 'Winching?'

Now he too was smiling, though trying hard not to show it. Rebus laughed aloud.

'It means dating,' he said. 'Next you'll be telling me you don't know what hoolit means.'

'Try me,' said Flight, laughing too.

'Drunk,' explained Rebus.

They sipped their drinks in silence for a moment. Rebus thanked God for the linguistic barrier between them, for without it there would be no easy jokes, jokes which broke the tension. There were two ways to defuse tension: one was to laugh it away, the other was to resort to physical action. It was laugh or lash out. Once or twice now they had come near to trading punches, but had ended up trading grins instead.

Praise be for the gift of laughter.

'Anyway, I went to Hackney last night looking for Kenny Watkiss.'

'And you got those for your pains?' Flight was nodding towards the bruises. Rebus shrugged. 'Serves you right. Someone once told me hackney's French for a nag. Doesn't

195

sound French, does it? But I suppose it would explain the hackney carriage.'

Hackney. Nag. That horse in the British Museum, no bite. Rebus had to talk to Morrison about the bite marks.

Flight finished his drink first, draining the cup and tossing it into a bin beside the machine. He checked his watch.

'I better find a phone,' he said. 'See what's happening back at base. Maybe Lamb will have found something on that Crawford woman.'

'"That Crawford woman" is a victim, George. Stop making her sound like a criminal.'

'*Maybe* she's a victim,' said Flight. 'Let's get our facts straight before we go for the tea and sympathy routine. Besides, when did you join this little victim support group of yours? You know the way we have to play this sort of thing. It isn't nice necessarily, but it means we don't get it wrong.'

'That's quite a speech.'

Flight sighed and examined the tips of his shoes. 'Look, John, has it ever occurred to you that there might be another way?'

'The way of Zen perhaps?'

'I mean, a way other than your own. Or are the rest of us just thick, and you're the only policeman on the planet who knows how to solve a crime? I'd be interested to know.'

Rebus desperately did not want to blush, which is probably precisely why he did blush. He tried to think of a smart answer, but none came to mind right that second, so he kept silent. Flight nodded approval.

'Let's go find that phone,' he said. Now Rebus found the courage he needed.

'George,' he said. 'I need to know: who brought me here?'

Flight stared at him, wondering whether or not to

answer. He pursed his lips as he thought about it, and came up with an answer: what the hell.

'I did,' he said. 'It was my idea.'

'You?' Rebus seemed puzzled. Flight nodded confirmation.

'Yes, me. I suggested you to Laine and Pearson. A new head, fresh blood, that sort of thing.'

'But how in God's name did you know about me?'

'Well,' Flight was beginning to look sheepish. He made a play of examining the tips of his shoes again. 'Remember I showed you that file, the one with all the guesswork in it? On top of that I did some background reading on multiple murderers. Research, you could call it. And I came across that case of yours in some newspaper clippings from Scotland Yard. I was impressed.'

Rebus pointed a disbelieving finger. 'You were reading up on serial killers?'

Flight nodded.

'On the *psychology* of serial killers?'

Flight shrugged. 'And other aspects, yes.' Rebus's eyes had widened.

'And all this time you've been having a dig at *me* for going along with Lisa Frazer's – no, I don't believe it!'

Flight was laughing again. The apparently arch anti-psychologist revealed in his true light. 'I had to examine every angle,' he said, watching as Rebus, having finished his coffee, tossed the cup into a waste-bin. 'Now come on, we really should make that phone call.'

Rebus was still shaking his head as he followed Flight down the hall. But though he appeared to be in good humour, his brain was more active than ever. Flight had pulled the wool over his eyes with consummate ease. How far did the pretence actually stretch? Was he now seeing the real Flight, or yet another mask? Flight whistled as he walked and kicked at an imaginary football. No, not George Flight, Rebus decided in an instant: never George Flight.

There was a telephone in the admin offices. There was also, seated at a desk having a conversation with one of the senior staff, Philip Cousins, immaculate in grey suit and burgundy tie.

'Philip!'

'Hello there, George. How are things?' Cousins spotted Rebus. 'And Inspector Rebus, too. Still lending a Caledonian hand?'

'Trying,' said Rebus.

'Yes, very,' rejoined Flight. 'So what brings you here, Philip? Where's Isobel?'

'Penny's rather tied up, I'm afraid. She'll be sorry to have missed you, George. As for my presence here, I just wanted to double-check some facts on a murder case from last December. You might remember it, the man in the bathtub.'

'The one that looked like suicide?'

'That's right.' Philip Cousins's voice was as rich and slow as double cream. Rebus reckoned that the word 'urbane' had been invented with him in mind. 'I'm in court later today,' Cousins was saying. 'Trying to help Malcolm Chambers pin the deceased's wife for manslaughter at the very least.'

'Chambers?' Flight shook his head. 'I don't envy you that.'

'But surely,' Rebus interrupted, 'you'll be on the same side?'

'Ah yes, Inspector Rebus,' said Cousins, 'you are quite correct. But Chambers is such a scrupulous man. He'll want my evidence to be water-tight, and if it isn't, then he's as likely to undo me as is the defence counsel. More likely,

198

in fact. Malcolm Chambers is interested in the truth, not in verdicts.'

'Yes,' said Flight, 'I remember him having a right go at me once in the witness box, all because I couldn't recall offhand what kind of clock had been in the living-room. The case nearly crumbled there and then.' Flight and Cousins shared a comradely smile.

'I've just been hearing,' said Cousins, 'that there's fresh evidence on the Wolfman case. Do tell.'

'It's beginning to come together, Philip,' said Flight. 'It's definitely beginning to come together, due in no small part to my associate here.' Flight laid a momentary hand on Rebus's shoulder.

'I'm impressed,' said Cousins, sounding neither impressed nor unimpressed.

'It was luck,' said Rebus, as he felt he ought. Not that he believed what he was saying. Cousins's eyes on him were like packs of ice, so that the room temperature seemed to drop with every glance.

'So what do we have?'

'Well,' said Flight, 'we've got someone who claims she was attacked by the Wolfman but escaped from him.'

'Fortunate creature,' said Cousins.

'And,' continued Flight, 'one of the ... people helping us on the case this morning received a letter claiming to be from the Wolfman.'

'Good God.'

'We think it's kosher,' Flight concluded.

'Well,' said Cousins, 'this *is* something. Wait till I tell Penny. She'll be thrilled.'

'Philip, we don't want it getting out –'

'Not a word, George, not a word. You know it's all one-way traffic with me. But Penny should be told.'

'Oh, tell Isobel by all means,' said Flight, 'only warn her it's not to go any further.'

'Total secrecy,' said Cousins. 'I quite understand. Mum's the word. Who was it, by the way?' Flight appeared not to understand. 'To whom was this threatening letter addressed?'

Flight was about to speak, but Rebus beat him to it. 'Just someone on the case, as Inspector Flight says.' He smiled, trying to alleviate the brusqueness of his response. Oh yes, his mind was working now, working in a fever: nobody had told Cousins the letter was threatening, so how did he know it was? Okay, it was simple enough to work out that it wouldn't exactly have been fan mail, but all the same.

'Well then,' said Cousins, choosing not to press for details. 'And now, gentlemen,' he scooped up two manila files from the desk and tucked them under his arm, then stood, the joints of his knees cracking with the effort, 'if you'll excuse me, Court Eight awaits. Inspector Rebus,' Cousins held out his free hand, 'it sounds as though the case may be drawing towards its conclusion. Should we fail to meet again, give my regards to your delightful city.' He turned to Flight. 'See you soon, George. Bring Marion round for supper some evening. Give Penny a tinkle and we'll try to find one night in the calendar when all four of us are free. Goodbye.'

'Bye, Philip.'

'Goodbye.'

'Goodbye.'

'Oh.' Cousins had stopped in the doorway. 'There is just one thing.' He turned pleading eyes on Flight. 'You don't have a spare driver, do you, George? It's going to be hell getting a taxi at this time of day.'

'Well,' Flight thought hard, then had an idea, 'if you can hang on for a couple of minutes, Philip, I've got a couple of men here in the building.' He turned to Rebus, whose eyes had widened. 'Lisa won't mind, will she, John? I mean, if her car drops Philip off at the Old Bailey?'

Rebus could do little but shrug.

'Excellent!' said Cousins, clasping his hands together. 'Thank you so much.'

'I'll take you to them,' Flight said. 'But first I need to make a phone call.'

Cousins nodded towards the corridor. 'And I must visit the WC. Be back in a tick.'

They watched him leave. Flight was grinning, shaking his head in wonderment. 'Do you know,' he said, 'he's been like that ever since I met him? I mean, the sort of ambassadorial air, the aged aristocrat. Ever since I've known him.'

'He's a gentleman all right,' said Rebus.

'But that's just the thing,' said Flight. 'His background is every bit as ordinary as yours or mine.' He turned to the lab man. 'All right if I use your phone?'

He did not wait for an answer, but started dialling straight away. 'Hello?' he said into the receiver when he was finally connected. 'Who's that? Oh, hello, Deakin, is Lamb there? Yes, put him on, will you? Thanks.' While he was waiting, Flight picked invisible threads from his trousers. The trousers were shiny from too many wearings. Everything about Flight, Rebus noticed, seemed worn: his shirt collar had an edge of grime to it and the collar itself was too tight, constricting the loose flesh of the neck, pinching it into vertical folds. Rebus found himself transfixed by that neck, by the tufts of grey sprouting hair where the razor had failed in its duty. Signs of mortality, as final as a hand around a throat. When Flight got off the phone, Rebus would protest about sending Cousins off with Lisa. *Ambassadorial. Aristocrat.* One of the earlier mass killers had been an aristocrat, too.

'Hello, Lamb? What have you found on Miss Crawford?' Flight listened, his eyes on Rebus, ready to communicate anything of interest. 'Uh-huh, okay. Mm, I see. Yes.

Right.' All the time his eyes told Rebus that everything was checking out, that Jan Crawford was reliable, that she was telling the truth. Then Flight's eyes widened a little. 'What's that again?' And he listened more intently, moving his eyes from Rebus to study the telephone apparatus itself. 'Now that is interesting.'

Rebus shifted. What? What was interesting? But Flight had again resorted to monosyllables.

'Uh-hu. Mmm. Well, never mind. I know. Yes, I'm sure.' His voice sounded resigned to something. 'Okay. Thanks for letting me know. Yes. No, we'll be back in about, I don't know, maybe another hour. Right, catch you then.'

Flight held the receiver above the telephone, but did not immediately drop it back into its cradle. Instead, he let it hang there.

Rebus could contain his curiosity no longer. 'What?' he said. 'What is it? What's wrong?'

Flight seemed to come out of his daydream, and put down the receiver. 'Oh,' he said, 'it's Tommy Watkiss.'

'What about him?'

'Lamb has just heard that there isn't going to be a retrial. We don't know why yet. Maybe the judge didn't think the charges were worth all the aggro and told the CPS so.'

'Assault on a woman not worth the *aggro*?' All thought of Philip Cousins vanished from Rebus's mind.

Flight shrugged. 'Retrials are expensive. *Any* trial is expensive. We cocked it up first time round, so we lose a second chance. It happens, John, you know that.'

'Of course it happens. But the idea of a snake like Watkiss getting away with something like that –'

'Don't worry, he can't keep his nose clean for long. Breaking the law's in his blood. When he does something naughty, we'll have him, and I'll see to it there are no balls-ups, mark my words.'

Rebus sighed. Yes, it happened, you lost a few. More than a few. Incompetence or a soft judge, an unsympathetic jury or a rock-solid witness for the defence. And sometimes maybe the Procurator Fiscal thought a retrial not worth the money. You lost a few. They were like toothache.

'I bet Chambers is fuming,' Rebus said.

'Oh yes,' said Flight, smiling at the thought, 'I bet he's got steam coming out of his bloody shirt-cuffs.'

But one person would be happy at least, Rebus was thinking: Kenny Watkiss. He'd be over the moon.

'So,' said Rebus, 'what about Jan Crawford?'

Flight shrugged again. 'She seems straight as a die. No previous, no record of mental illness, lives quietly, but the neighbours seem to like her well enough. Like Lamb said, she's so clean it's frightening.'

Yes, the squeaky clean ones often were. Frightening to a policeman the way an unknown species might be to a jungle explorer: fear of the new, the different. You got to suspect that everyone had something to hide: the schoolteachers smuggled in porn videos from their holiday in Amsterdam; the solicitors took cocaine on their weekend parties; the happily married MP was sleeping with his secretary; the magistrate had a predilection for underage boys; the librarian kept a real skeleton hidden in the closet; the angelic looking children had set fire to a neighbour's cat.

And sometimes your suspicions were correct.

And other times they weren't. Cousins was standing at the door now, ready to leave. Flight laid a hand softly on his arm. Rebus recalled that he'd meant to say something to Flight, but how to phrase it? Would it do to say that Philip Cousins seemed almost too clean, with his surgeon's cold, manicured hands and his ambassadorial air? Rebus was wondering now, *seriously* wondering.

Since Flight had gone off with Philip Cousins to find Lisa

and her protectors, Rebus went back to the lab to hear the result of the first saliva test.

'Sorry,' said the white-coated scientist. He looked not yet to be out of his teens. Beneath his lab coat, there lurked a black T-shirt decorated with the name of a heavy metal band. 'I don't think we're going to have much luck. All we're finding so far is H_2O, tap-water. Whoever stuck the envelope down must have used a wet sponge or a pad or one of those old-fashioned roller things. No traces of saliva at all.'

The breath left Rebus's lungs. 'What about fingerprints?'

'Negative so far. All we've found are two sets which look like they're going to match Dr Frazer's. And we're not having any better luck with fibres or grease stains. I'd say the writer wore gloves. Nobody here has seen such a clean, speck-free job.'

He knows, Rebus was thinking. He knows everything we might try. So damned smart.

'Well, thanks anyway,' he said. The young man raised his eyebrows and spread his palms.

'I wish we could do more.'

You could start by getting a haircut, son, he thought to himself. You look too much like Kenny Watkiss. He sighed instead. 'Just do what you can,' he said. 'Just do what you can.'

Turning to walk away, Rebus felt a mixture of fresh rage and impotence, sudden savage frustration. The Wolfman was too good. He would stop killing before they could catch him; or he would simply go on killing again and again and again. No one would be safe. And most of all, it seemed, Lisa would not be safe.

Lisa.

She was being blamed by the Wolfman for the story Rebus had invented. It had nothing to do with Lisa. And if the Wolfman should somehow get to her it would be

Rebus's fault, wouldn't it? Where was Lisa going? Rebus didn't know. Flight thought it was safer that way. But Rebus couldn't shake off the idea that the Wolfman might well be a policeman. Might well be *any* policeman. Might be the brawny detective or the thin and silent detective. Lisa had gone off with them thinking them her protection. What if she had walked straight into the clutches of …? What if the Wolfman knew exactly …? What if Philip Cousins …?

A loudspeaker sounded from its recess in the ceiling.

'Telephone call for Inspector Rebus at reception. Telephone call for Inspector Rebus.'

Rebus walked quickly down the rest of the corridor and through the swing-door at the end. He didn't know if Flight was still in the building, didn't care. His mind was filling with horrors: Wolfman, Lisa, Rhona, Sammy. Little Sammy, his daughter. She'd seen enough terror in her life. He'd been responsible before. He didn't want her to be hurt ever again.

The receptionist lifted the receiver as he approached, holding it out to him. As he grabbed it, she pressed a button on the dial, connecting him to the caller.

'Hello?' he said, breathlessly.

'Daddy?' Oh Christ, it *was* Sammy.

'Sammy?' Nearly yelling now. 'What is it? What's wrong?'

'Oh, Daddy.' She was crying. The memory flashed in front of him, scalding his vision. Phone calls. Screams.

'What is it, Sammy? Tell me!'

'It's,' a sniff, 'it's Kenny.'

'Kenny?' He furrowed his brow. 'What's wrong with him? Has he been in a crash?'

'Oh no, Daddy. He's just … just *disappeared*.'

'Where are you, Sammy?'

'I'm in a call-box.'

'Okay, I'm going to give you the address of a police station. Meet me there. If you have to get a taxi, that's fine. I'll pay for it when you arrive. Understand?'

'Daddy.' She sniffed back tears. 'You've got to find him. I'm worried. Please find him, Daddy. Please. *Please!*'

By the time George Flight reached reception, Rebus had already left. The receptionist explained as best she could, while Flight rubbed his jaw, encountering stubble. He had argued with Lisa Frazer, but by Christ she'd been stubborn. Attractively stubborn, he had to admit. She'd told him she didn't mind bodyguards but that the idea of a 'safe location' was out of the question. She had, she said, an appointment at the Old Bailey, a couple of appointments actually, interviews she was doing in connection with some research.

'It's taken me weeks to set them up,' she said, 'there's no way I'm going to blow them out now!'

'But my dear,' Philip Cousins had drawled, 'that's just where we're headed.' He was, Flight knew, keen for a close to proceedings, glancing at his watch impatiently. And it seemed that Lisa and Cousins knew one another from the murder at Copperplate Street, that they had things in common, things they wanted to talk about. That they were keen to be going.

So Flight made a decision. What did it matter after all if she did visit the Bailey? There were few better protected spots in the whole city. It was several hours yet until the first of her interviews, but that didn't really bother her. She did not, she said, mind hanging around in the 'courthouse'. In fact, she rather enjoyed the idea. The two officers could accompany her, wait for her, then drive her on to whatever safe location Flight had in mind. This, at any rate, was Lisa Frazer's argument, an argument defended by Philip Cousins who could see 'no flaw in the reasoning, m'lud'. So, to smiles on their part and a shrug on Flight's, the course of action was decided. Flight watched the Ford Granada roll away from him – the two officers in the front, Philip and Lisa Frazer in the back. Safe as houses, he was thinking. Safe as bloody houses.

And now Rebus had buggered off. Oh well, he'd catch up with him no doubt. He didn't regret bringing Rebus down here, not a bit. But he knew it had been *his* decision, not one entirely endorsed by the upper echelons. Any balls-ups and it would be Flight's pension on the block. He knew that only too well, as did everyone else. Which was why he'd stuck so close to Rebus in the first few days, just to be sure of the man.

Was he sure of the man? It was a question he would rather not answer, even now, even to himself. Rebus was like the spring in a trap, likely to jump no matter what landed on the bait. He was also a Scot, and Flight had never trusted the Scots, not since the day they'd voted to stay part of the Union ...

'Daddy!'

And she runs into his arms. He hugs her to him, aware that he does not have to bend too far to accomplish this. Yes, she's grown, and yet she seems more childlike than ever. He kisses the top of her head, smells her clean hair. She is trembling. He can feel the vibrations darting through her chest and arms.

'Sshh,' he says. 'Ssshhh, pet, ssshhh.'

She pulls back and almost smiles, sniffs, then says, 'You always used to call me that. Your pet. Mum never called me pet. Only you.'

He smiles back and strokes her hair. 'Yes,' he says, 'your mum told me off for that. She said a pet was a possession and that you weren't a possession.' He is remembering now. 'She had some funny ideas, your mum.'

'She still does.' Then she remembers why she is here. The tears well up anew in her eyes.

'I know you don't like him,' she says.

'Nonsense, whatever gives you that –'

'But I love him, Daddy.' His heart spins once in his chest. 'And I don't want anything to happen to him.'

'What makes you think something's going to happen to him?'

'The way he's been acting lately, like he's keeping secrets from me. Mum's noticed it, too. I'm not just dreaming. But she said she thought maybe he was planning an engagement.' She sees his eyes widen, and shakes her head. 'I didn't believe it. I knew it was something else. I thought, I don't know, I just ...'

He notices for the first time that they have an audience. Until now they might have been in a sealed box for all the notice he has taken of their surroundings. Now, though, he sees a bemused desk sergeant, two WPCs clutching paperwork to their bosoms and watching the scene with a kind of maternal glow, two unshaven men slumped in seats against the wall, just waiting.

'Come on, Sammy,' he says. 'Let's go up to my office.'

They were halfway to the Murder Room before he remembered that it was not, perhaps, the most wholesome environment for a teenage girl. The photos on the walls were only the start of it. A sense of humour was needed on a case like the Wolfman, and that sense of humour had begun to manifest itself in cartoons, jokes and mock-ups of newspaper stories either pinned to the noticeboards or taped onto the sides of computer screens. The language could be choice, too, or someone might be overheard in conversation with someone from forensics.

'... torn ... ripped her right ... kitchen knife, they reckon ... slit from ear ... gouged ... anus ... nasty bastard ... makes some of them seem almost human.' Stories were swapped of serial killers past, of suicides scraped from railway lines, of police dogs playing ball with a severed head.

No, definitely not the place for his daughter. Besides, there was always the possibility that Lamb might be there.

Instead, he found a vacant interview room. It had been turned into a temporary cupboard while the investigation continued, filled with empty cardboard boxes, unneeded chairs, broken desk-lamps and computer keyboards, a heavy-looking manual typewriter. Eventually, the computers in the Murder Room would be packed back into the cardboard boxes, the files would be tidied away into dusty stacks somewhere.

For now, the room had a musty, barren feel, but it still boasted a lightbulb hanging from the ceiling, a table and two chairs. On the table sat a glass ashtray full of stubs and two plastic coffee cups containing a layer of green and black mould. On the floor lay a crushed cigarette packet. Rebus kicked the packet beneath some of the stacked chairs.

'It's not much,' he said, 'but it's home. Sit down. Do you want anything?'

She seemed not to understand the question. 'Like what?'

'I don't know, coffee, tea?'

'Diet Coke?'

Rebus shook his head.

'What about Irn-Bru?'

Now he laughed: she was joking with him. He couldn't bear to see her upset, especially over someone as undeserving as Kenny Watkiss.

'Sammy,' he asked, 'does Kenny have an uncle?'

'Uncle Tommy?'

Rebus nodded. 'That's the one.'

'What about him?'

'Well,' said Rebus, crossing his legs, 'what do you know about him?'

'About Kenny's Uncle Tommy? Not a lot.'

'What does he do for a living?'

'I think Kenny said he's got a stall somewhere, you know, in a market.'

Like Brick Lane market? Did he sell false teeth?

'Or maybe he just delivers to market stalls, I can't really remember.'

Delivers stolen goods? Goods given to him by thieves like the one they'd picked up, the one who had pretended to be the Wolfman?

'Anyway, he's got a few bob.'

'How do you know that?'

'Kenny told me. At least, I think he did. Otherwise how would I know?'

'Where does Kenny work, Sammy?'

'In the City.'

'Yes, but for which firm?'

'Firm?'

'He's a courier, isn't he? He must work for a company?'

But she shook her head. 'He went freelance when he had enough regular clients. I remember he said that his boss at the old place was pissed off –' She broke off suddenly and looked up at him, her face going red. She'd forgotten for a moment that she was talking to her father, and not just to some copper. 'Sorry, Dad,' she apologised. 'His boss was angry with him for taking away so much of the trade. Kenny was good, see, he knows all the shortcuts, knows which buildings are which. Some drivers get confused when they can't find some tiny alleyway, or when the numbers on a street don't seem to make sense.' Yes. Rebus had noticed that; how sometimes the street numbers seemed illogical, as though numbers had been skipped. 'But not Kenny. He knows London like the back of his hand.'

Knows London well, the roads, the shortcuts. On a motorbike, you could cut across London in a flash. Tow-paths, alleys – in a flash.

'What kind of bike does he have, Sammy?'

'I don't know. A Kawasaki something-or-other. He's got one that he uses for work, because it's not too heavy, and another he keeps for weekends, a really big bike.'

'Where does he keep them? There can't be too many safe places around the Churchill Estate?'

'There are some garages nearby. They get vandalised, but Kenny's put a reinforced door on. It's like Fort Knox. I keep kidding him about it. It's better guarded than his –' Her voice falls flat. 'How did you know he lives on Churchill?'

'What?'

Her voice is stronger now, curious. 'How did you know Kenny lives on Churchill?'

Rebus shrugged. 'I suppose he told me, that night I met him round at your place.'

She's thinking back, trying to recall the conversation. But there's nothing there, nothing she can latch onto. Rebus is thinking, too.

Like Fort Knox. A handy place to store stolen gear. Or a corpse.

'So,' he says, pulling his chair a little further in to the table. 'Tell me what *you* think has happened. What do you think he's been keeping from you?'

She stared at the table-top, shaking her head slowly, staring, shaking, until finally: 'I don't know.'

'Well, had you fallen out over anything? Maybe you'd been arguing?'

'No.'

'Maybe he was jealous?'

211

She gave a desperate laugh. 'No.'

'Maybe he had other girlfriends?'

'No!'

When her eyes caught his, Rebus felt a stirring of shame inside him. He couldn't forget that she was his daughter; nor could he forget that he needed to ask her these questions. Somehow he kept swerving between the two, careering into her.

'No,' she repeated softly. 'I'd have known if there was someone else.'

'Friends, then: did he have any close friends?'

'A few. Not many. I mean, he talked about them, but he never introduced me.'

'Have you tried calling them? Maybe one of them knows something.'

'I only know their first names. A couple of guys Kenny grew up with, Billy and Jim. Then there was someone called Arnold. He used to mention him. And one of the other bike messengers, I think his name was Roland or Ronald, something posh like that.'

'Hold on, let me jot these down.' Rebus took notebook and pen from his pocket. 'Right,' he said, 'so that was Billy, Jim. What was the other one?'

'Roland or Ronald or something.' She watched him writing. 'And Arnold.'

Rebus sat back in his chair. 'Arnold?'

'Yes.'

'Did you ever meet Arnold?'

'I don't think so.'

'What did Kenny say about him?'

She shrugged. 'He was just someone Kenny used to bump into. I think he worked the stalls, too. They went for a drink sometimes.'

It couldn't be the same Arnold, could it? Flight's bald sex-offender snitch? What were the chances? Going for a

212

drink? They seemed unlikely supping companions, always supposing it was the same Arnold.

'All right,' Rebus said, closing the notebook. 'Do you have a recent photo of Kenny? A good one, one that's nice and sharp.'

'I can get one. I've got some back at the house.'

'Okay, I'll get someone to drive you home. Give them the picture and they'll bring it back to me. Let's circulate Kenny's description, that's the first thing to do. Meanwhile I'll do some snooping, see what I can come up with.'

She smiled. 'It's not really your patch, is it?'

'No, it's not my patch at all. But sometimes if you look at something, or some place, for too long, you stop seeing what's there. Sometimes it takes a fresh pair of eyes to see what's staring you in the face.' He was thinking of Flight, of the reason Flight had brought him down here. He was thinking, too, of whether he, Rebus, could muster enough clout to organise a search for Kenny Watkiss. Maybe not without Flight to back him up. No, what was he thinking of? This was a missing person, for Christ's sake. It had to be investigated. Yes, but there were ways and ways of investigating, and he could count on no preferential treatment, no favours, when it came to the crunch. 'I don't suppose,' he asked now, 'you know whether or not his bikes are still in the garage?'

'I took a look. They're both still there. That was when I started to get worried.'

'Was there anything else in the garage?' But she wasn't listening to him.

'He hardly ever goes anywhere without a bike. He hates buses and stuff. He said he was going to name his big bike after … after me.'

The tears came again. This time he let her cry, though it hurt him more than he could say. Better out than in, wasn't that how the cliché went? She was blowing her nose when the door opened. Flight looked into the small room. His eyes said it all: *you might have taken her somewhere better than this.*

'Yes, George? What can I do for you?'

'After you left the lab,' the pause showed displeasure at not having been informed or left a message, 'they gave me a bit more gen on the letter itself.'

'I'll be with you in a minute.'

Flight nodded but directed his attention to Samantha. 'Are you okay, love?'

She sniffed. 'Fine, thanks.'

'Well,' he said archly, 'if you *do* want to register a complaint against Inspector Rebus, see the desk sergeant.'

'Ach, get away, George,' said Rebus.

Sammy was trying to giggle and blow her nose at the same time, and making a bit of a mess of both. Rebus winked towards Flight who, having done as much as he could (and for which Rebus was grateful), was now retreating.

'You're not all bad, are you?' said Samantha when Flight had gone.

'What do you mean?'

'Policemen. You're not all as bad as they say.'

'You're a copper's daughter, Sammy. Remember that. And you're a *straight* copper's daughter. Be sure to stick up for your old dad. Okay?'

She smiled again. 'You're not old, Dad.'

He smiled, too, but did not reply. In truth, he was basking in the compliment, whether it was mere flattery or no. What mattered was that Sammy, his daughter Sammy, had said it.

'Right,' he said at last, 'let's get you into a car. And don't worry, pet, we'll track down your missing beau.'

'You called me pet again.'

'Did I? Don't tell your mother.'

'I won't. And, Dad?'

'What?' He half-turned towards her just in time to receive her peck on the cheek.

'Thanks,' she said. 'Whatever happens, thanks.'

Flight was in the small office of the Murder Room. After the close confines of the interview cupboard, this space had suddenly taken on a new, much larger dimension. Rebus sat himself down and swung one leg over the other.

'So what's this about the Wolfman letter?' he said.

'So,' replied Flight, 'what's this about Kenny Watkiss disappearing?'

'You tell me yours and I'll tell you mine.'

Flight picked up a folder, opened it, took out three or four closely typed sheets of paper, and began to read.

'Typeface used is Helvetica. Unusual for personal correspondence, though used by newspapers and magazines.' Flight looked up meaningfully.

'A reporter?' Rebus said doubtfully.

'Well, think about it,' said Flight. 'Every crime reporter in England knows about Lisa Frazer by now. They could probably find out where she lives, too.'

Rebus considered this. 'Okay,' he said at last, 'go on.'

'Helvetica can be found on some electronic typewriters and electric golfball machines, but is more commonly found on computers and word processors.' Flight glanced up. 'This would correlate with density of type. The type itself is of very even quality ... blah, blah, blah. Also, the letters line up neatly, suggesting that a good quality printer has been used, probably a daisywheel, suggesting in turn the use of a high quality word processor or word-processing package. However,' Flight went on, 'the letter K becomes faint towards the tips of its stem.' Flight paused to turn the page. Rebus wasn't really paying a great deal of attention as yet, and neither was George Flight. Labs always came up with more information than was useful. So far, all Rebus had really been hearing was the chaff.

'This is more interesting,' Flight went on. 'Inside the envelope particles were found which appear to be flecks of paint, yellow, green and orange predominating. Perhaps an oil-based paint: tests are still continuing.'

'So we've got a crime reporter who fancies himself as Van Gogh?'

Flight wasn't rising to the bait. He read through the rest of the report quickly to himself. 'That's pretty much it,' he said. 'What's left is more to do with what they failed to find: no prints, no stains, no hair or fibres.'

'No personalised watermark?' Rebus asked. In detective novels, the personalised watermark would lead to a small family business run by an eccentric old man, who would recall selling the paper to someone called … And that would be it: crime solved. Neat, ingenious, but it seldom happened like that. He thought of Lisa again; of Cousins. No, not Cousins: it couldn't be Cousins. And besides, he wouldn't try anything with those two gorillas in attendance.

'No personalised watermark,' Flight was saying. 'Sorry.'

'Oh well,' Rebus offered, with a loud sigh, 'we're no further forward, are we?'

Flight was looking at the report, as though willing something, some clue, to grab his attention. Then: 'So what's all this about Kenny Watkiss?'

'He's scarpered under mysterious circumstances. Good riddance, I'd say, but it's left Sammy in a bit of a state. I said we'd do what we could.'

'You can't get involved, John. Leave it to us.'

'I don't want to get involved, George. This one's all yours.' The voice seemed ingenuous enough, but Flight was long past being fooled by John Rebus. He grinned and shook his head.

'What do you want?' he asked.

'Well,' said Rebus, leaning forward in his chair, 'Sammy did mention one of Kenny's associates. Someone called Arnold who worked on a market stall, at least she thinks he works in or around a market.'

'You think it's my Arnold?' Flight thought it over. 'It's possible.'

'Too much of a coincidence, you think?'

'Not in a city as small as this.' Flight saw the look on Rebus's face. 'I'm being serious, actually. The small-time crooks, they're like a little family. If this was Sicily, you could cram every small-timer in London into a village. Everybody knows everybody else. It's the big-timers we can't pin. They keep themselves too much to themselves, never go down the pub shooting their mouths off after a couple of Navy Rums.'

'Can we talk to Arnold?'

'What for?'

'Maybe he knows something about Kenny.'

'Even supposing he does, why should he tell us?'

'Because we're police officers, George. And he's a member of the public. We're here to uphold law and order, and it's his duty to help us in that onerous task.' Rebus was reflective. 'Plus I'll slip him twenty quid.'

Flight sounded incredulous. 'This is London, John. A score can hardly get a round of drinks. Arnold gives good gen, but he'll be looking for a pony at least.' Now he was playing with Rebus, and Rebus, realising it, smiled.

'If Arnold wants a pony,' he said, 'tell him I'll buy him one for Christmas. And a little girl to sit on it. Just so long as he tells me what he knows.'

'Fair enough,' said Flight. 'Come on then, let's go find ourselves a street market.'

The Gallery

Flight was struggling with half a dozen large brown-paper bags, the fruits – literally – of asking for Arnold at three or four market stalls so far. Rebus had refused the offers of free bananas, oranges, pears and grapes, though Flight had prodded him to accept.

'It's a local custom,' Flight said. 'They get annoyed if you don't accept. Like a Glaswegian offering you a drink. Would you turn it down? No, because then you'd offend him. Same with these guys.'

'What would I do with three pounds of bananas?'

'Eat them,' said Flight blandly. Then, cryptically: 'Unless you were Arnold, of course.'

He refused to explain the meaning of this, and Rebus refused to consider the various possibilities. They moved from stall to stall, passing most, stopping at only a few. In their way, they were like the women who crushed in all around them, feeling this or that mango or aubergine, checking prices at the various stalls, pausing only at a few to make their final purchases.

''Allo, George.'

'Blimey, George, where you been hiding yourself?'

'All right there, George? How's your love life?'

It seemed to Rebus that half the stall-holders and most of their box- and tray-carrying assistants knew Flight. At one point, Flight nodded behind one of the stalls, where a young man was disappearing rapidly along the street.

'Jim Jessop,' he said. 'He skipped bail a couple of weeks back.'

'Shouldn't we …?'

But Flight shook his head. 'Another time, eh, John? The little bugger was three-A's standard in the thousand metres. I don't feel like a run today, what about you?'

'Fair enough,' said Rebus, aware that here, in this place, on this 'patch', he was very much the bystander, the tourist. This was Flight's territory. The man moved confidently through the throng, spoke easily with the various vendors, was in every way quite at home. Eventually, after a chat with the man behind the fresh fish counter, Flight returned with a bag of mussels, another of scallops and information on where Arnold might be found. He led Rebus behind the market stalls onto the pavement and then into a narrow alleyway.

'Moules marinière,' he said, holding up one of the white polythene bags. 'Beautiful. Easy to cook, too. It's the preparation that takes up all the time.'

Rebus shook his head. 'You're full of surprises, George. I'd never have taken you for a cordon bleu.'

Flight just smiled, musing. 'And scallops,' he said, 'Marion loves those. I make a sauce with them and serve it with fresh trout. Again, it's all preparation. The cooking's the easy part.'

He enjoyed showing Rebus this other side of his personality, though he couldn't say why. Nor could he exactly say why he hadn't told John Rebus that Lisa had gone to the Old Bailey; had instead mumbled something about seeing her safely on her way. He thought probably his reasoning had to do with Rebus's spring-loaded emotions: if the Scotsman thought Lisa Frazer was *not* in Flight's place of safety, he'd probably go haring off after her, making a fool of himself 'neath blindfolded Justice herself. And Rebus was still Flight's responsibility, still the liability he always had been, if not more so.

They had come out of the alley onto a small-scale housing estate. The houses looked fairly new, but already the paint was flaking from the window sills. There were cries and squeals from just ahead. A kiddies' playground, concrete surrounded by concrete. A huge section of pipe had become a tunnel, a den, a hiding place. There were swings, too, and a see-saw. And a sand-pit which had become second home to the area's cats and dogs.

The children's imaginations knew few bounds: Pretend you're in hospital, and I'm the doctor; And then the spaceman's ship crashed on the planet; Cowboys don't *have* girlfriends; No, you're chasing *me*, because I'm the soldier and you're the guard; Pretend there isn't a pipe.

Pretend. There was no pretend about the energy they were expending. They couldn't stand still, couldn't pause for breath. They had to yell and jump and get involved. It made Rebus tired just to look at them.

'There he is,' said Flight. He was pointing towards a bench on the edge of the playground. Arnold was sitting there, his back very straight, hands clasping his knees. He had an intent look on his face, neither happy nor unhappy. The kind of look you sometimes saw at the zoo, when someone was peering into a particular cage or enclosure. It was best described as an interested look. Oh yes, Arnold was interested. It made Rebus's stomach queasy just to watch him. Flight seemed to take it all quite casually. He walked across to the bench and sat down beside Arnold, who turned, his eyes suddenly taking on a hunted, frightened look, his mouth creasing into an O. Then he exhaled noisily.

'It's you, Mister Flight. I didn't recognise you.' He gestured towards the bags. 'Been shopping? That's nice.'

The voice was flat, lacking emotion. Rebus had heard

addicts talk like that. Five percent of their brain was fixed on dealing with the external world, the remaining ninety-five concentrating on other things. Well, he supposed Arnold was a kind of addict too.

'Yes,' said Flight, 'just buying a few bits. You remember Inspector Rebus?'

Arnold followed Flight's eyes, staring up from his bench to where Rebus stood, his body purposely shielding Arnold from the children.

'Oh yes,' Arnold said blandly, 'he was in the car with you the other day, Mr Flight.'

'Well done, Arnold. Yes, that's right. You've got a good memory, haven't you?'

'It pays to have, Mr Flight. That's how I remember all the things I tell you.'

'Actually, Arnold,' Flight slid along the bench until his thigh was almost touching that of the other man. Arnold angled his own legs away from the policeman, his eyes intent on Flight's proximity to him. 'Speaking of memory, maybe you can help me. Maybe you can help Inspector Rebus, too.'

'Yes?' The word was stretched almost to breaking point.

'We were just wondering,' said Flight, 'whether you've seen Kenny lately. Only, he doesn't seem to have been around much, does he? I wondered whether he'd maybe gone on holiday?'

Arnold gazed up with milky, childlike eyes. 'Kenny who?'

Flight laughed. 'Kenny Watkiss, Arnold. Your mate Kenny.'

For a moment, Rebus held his breath. What if it was another Arnold? What if Sammy had got the name wrong? Then Arnold nodded slowly.

'Oh, that Kenny. He's not really a mate, Mr Flight. I mean, I see him now and again.' Arnold stopped, but Flight was nodding, saying nothing, expecting more. 'We have a drink together sometimes.'

'What do you talk about?'

The question was unexpected. 'What do you mean?'

'It's a simple enough question,' said Flight with a smile. 'What do you talk about? I wouldn't have thought the two of you would have much in common.'

'We just, we talk. I don't know.'

'Yes, but what do you talk about? Football?'

'Sometimes, yes.'

'What team does he support?'

'I don't know, Mr Flight.'

'You talk about football with him and yet you don't know what team he supports?'

'Maybe he told me and I forgot.'

Flight looked dubious. 'Maybe,' he agreed. Rebus knew his part in the drama now. Let Flight do the talking. Just keep quiet but look ominous, standing over Arnold like a thundercloud, staring down like an avenger onto that gleaming bald dome of a head. Flight knew exactly what he was doing. Arnold was growing nervous, his body jerking, unable to keep his head still, his right knee bobbing up and down.

'So what else do you talk about? He likes motorbikes, doesn't he?'

'Yes,' Arnold answered, guardedly now, for he knew what was happening to him.

'So do you talk about bikes?'

'I don't like bikes. Too noisy.'

'Too noisy? Yes, you've got a point there.' Flight nodded towards the play area. 'But this place is noisy, too, Arnold, isn't it? Yet you don't seem to mind the noise here. Why's that?'

Arnold turned on him, eyes burning. But Flight was ready with a smile, a smile more serious than any grimace.

'What I mean is,' he went on, 'you like some noises but not others. That's fair, isn't it? But you don't like motorbikes. So what else do you talk about with Kenny?'

'We just *talk*,' said Arnold, his face creased with anguish. 'Gossip, how the city's changing, the East End. This used to be all rows of cottages. There was a field and allotments. The families all used to have picnics on the field. They'd bring tomatoes or potatoes or a cabbage to your mum, saying they grew too much, and the kids would all play in the street. There weren't any Bangladeshis or what have you. Just proper East Enders. Kenny's mum and dad didn't live far from here. Two streets away from where I lived. Course, I was older than him. We never played together or anything.'

'And where did Uncle Tommy live?'

'He was over that way.' Arnold pointed with a finger. He had grown a little more confident now. Reminiscences couldn't do any harm, could they? And to talk freely came as such a relief after the careful duel he'd just gone through. So he opened up to them. The good old days. But between his words, Rebus could see a truer picture, a picture of how the other kids used to beat him up, play tricks on him, of how his father used to lock him in his room, starve him. The family breaking apart. Drifting into petty crime. Painfully shy, unable to form relationships.

'Do you ever see Tommy around?' Flight asked suddenly.

'Tommy Watkiss? Yes, I see him.' Arnold was still basking in the past.

'Does Kenny see him?'

'Of course he does. He works for him sometimes.'

'What? Deliveries, that sort of thing?'

'Deliveries, pick-ups –' Arnold halted, aware of what he was saying. This wasn't the past they were talking about any longer. This wasn't safe.

Flight leaned across so that his nose was almost touching Arnold's. All Arnold could do was lean back against the bench, its hard spars stopping him from escaping.

'Where is he, Arnold?'

'Who? Tommy?'

'You know bloody well who I mean! Kenny! Tell me where he is!'

Rebus half-turned, to see that the children had stopped playing and were watching this grown-up game.

'You going to fight, mister?' one of them called. Rebus shook his head and called back, 'Just pretending.'

Flight still had Arnold pinned to the bench. 'Arnold,' he hissed, 'you know me. I've always played fair by you.'

'I know that, Mr Flight.'

'But I'm *not* pretending. What I'm doing is losing my rag. Everything's going to hell in this city, Arnold, and I'm inclined to just shrug my shoulders and join in. Understand me? Why should I play fair when nobody else does, eh? So I'll tell you what I'm going to do, Arnold. I'm going to have to pull you in.'

'What for?' Arnold was terrified now. He didn't think Flight was playing a game. Rebus had the same feeling; either that or Flight was in line for an Oscar.

'For indecent exposure. You were going to expose yourself to those kids. I saw you getting ready. I saw your dick hanging out of your fly.'

'No, no.' Arnold was shaking his head. 'That's a lie.'

'Previous convictions don't lie, Arnold. Inspector Rebus saw you, too. He saw your prick waving in the air like a cocktail sausage. We both saw you, and that's what we'll tell the judge. Now who's he going to believe, eh? Think about that for a moment. Think about solitary. They'll have to hold you in solitary so the other prisoners don't kick the shit out of you. But that won't stop them pissing in your tea and gobbing in your food. You know the score, Arnold.

224

You've been there. And then one night, you'll hear your door being unlocked, and in they'll come. Maybe the screws, maybe the prisoners. They'll come in and they'll hold you down. One of them'll have a brush-handle, and one'll have a rusty old razor blade, won't they, Arnold? Won't they Arnold?'

But Arnold was trembling too violently to speak, trembling and babbling, bubbles of saliva bursting at either side of his mouth. Flight slid back along the bench away from him, then looked up at Rebus with sad eyes. Rebus nodded solemnly. This wasn't a nice business that they were in, not nice at all. Flight lit a cigarette. Rebus refused one. Two words were bouncing around the inside of John Rebus's skull.

Needs must.

And then Arnold started to talk. And when he had finished, Flight dug into a trouser pocket and drew out a pound coin, which he slapped down on the bench beside his shattered victim.

'There you go, Arnold. Get yourself a cup of tea or something. And stay away from playgrounds, all right?' Flight picked up his carrier-bags, picked out an apple from one, and tossed it into Arnold's lap, causing the man to flinch. Then he picked out another one and began to crunch on it, starting off back towards the market.

Needs must.

Back at HQ Rebus thought about Lisa. He felt the need for some human contact, for something clean and warm and separate from this other world he chose to inhabit, something to wash out his badly soiled mind.

Flight had warned him on the way back – 'no messing about this time, John. Leave it to us. You've got to stay out of it. It would look bad in court, copper with a grudge, that sort of line.'

'But,' Rebus had replied, 'I do have a grudge, George. This guy Kenny might have been shagging my daughter!'

Flight had glanced from the windscreen into Rebus's face, then had looked away.

'I said leave it to us, John. If you can't play it that way, I'll personally see that you go bouncing back down the ranks like a ball down a fucking stairwell. Got that?'

'Loud and clear.'

'It's not a threat, John. It's a promise.'

'And you always keep your promises, George, don't you? You seem to be forgetting something. It's your fault that I'm down here in the first place. You sent for me.'

Flight had nodded. 'And I can send you back just as quick. Is that what you want?'

Rebus had stayed silent, though he knew the answer. Flight knew it too, and smiled at this small triumph. They drove in silence after that, both men tainted by the memory of a playground and of a silent man, hands clasping his knees, staring ahead of him, his thoughts sweet with corruption.

Now Rebus was thinking of Lisa, thinking of how it would feel to take a shower with her, to scrub away a layer of London from them both. Maybe he would ask George again for the secret address. Maybe he could visit her. He remembered a conversation they'd had in bed. He'd asked if he could see her office in University College sometime.

'Sometime,' she'd said. 'Mind you, it's not a very nice room, nothing like those huge antique Oxbridge rooms you see in television dramas. It's a pokey little hole, to be honest. I hate it.'

'I'd still like you to show me around.'

'And I said okay.' She sounded on edge. Why was that? Why had she been so nervous of letting him see her room? Why had the secretary – Millicent, Lisa had called her – been so vague the day Rebus had visited? No, not just vague. Uncooperative. *Downright* uncooperative, now that he thought of it. What the hell was it they were keeping from him? He knew one way he could find out the answer, one sure and certain way. What the hell: Lisa was safe, and he'd been told to stay out of the Watkiss case, so what was stopping him from following up this latest mystery? He got to his feet. The answer was: nothing was stopping him, nothing at all.

'Where are you going?'

It was Flight, yelling at him from an open door as Rebus stalked down the hall.

'It's personal,' Rebus called back.

'I warned you, John! Don't get involved!'

'It's not what you think!' He stopped, turning to face George Flight.

'Well, what is it then?'

'Like I said, George, it's personal, okay?'

'No.'

'Look,' said Rebus, his emotions suddenly getting the better of him, all those thoughts he'd been keeping on a tight rein – Sammy, Kenny Watkiss, the Wolfman, the threat against Lisa – all boiling up. He swallowed, breathing hard. 'Look, George, you've got plenty to keep you busy, okay?' His finger stabbed at Flight's chest. 'Remember what I said: it could be a copper. Why don't you do some of your careful, precious, nit-picking investigation on *that*. The Wolfman could be here in this building. He could be working on the bloody case, hunting himself!' Rebus heard his voice growing hysterical and calmed quickly, regaining control over his vocal chords if nothing else.

'A sort of wolf in the fold, you mean?'

'I'm serious.' Rebus paused. 'He might even know where you've sent Lisa.'

'For Christ's sake, John, only three people know where Lisa's going. Me, and the two men I sent with her. Now you don't know those guys, but I do. We go back all the way to training college. I'd trust them with my life.' Flight paused. 'Will you trust me?'

Rebus said nothing. Flight's eyes narrowed disbelievingly, and he whistled. 'Well,' he said, 'that certainly answers my question.' He shook his head slowly. 'This case, John. I've been in the force God knows how many years, but this case, it's the worst. It's like every victim was somebody close to me.' He paused again, gathering strength. Now his finger jabbed at Rebus. 'So don't you *dare* think what I know you're thinking! It's the ultimate fucking insult!'

There was a long silence in the corridor. Typewriters chattered somewhere. Male voices were raised in laughter. A hummed tune floated down the hall towards and past them. It was as though the whole world were indifferent to this quarrel. And there they stood, not quite friends, not quite enemies, and not quite sure what to do any more.

Rebus studied the scuff marks on the linoleum. Then: 'Lecture over?'

Flight seemed pained by this response. 'It wasn't a lecture, it was just ... I want you to see my side of things.'

'But I do, George, I do.' Rebus patted Flight's arm and turned away from him again. He started to walk.

'I want you to stay here, John!' Walking. 'Do you hear me? I'm *ordering* you not to go.'

Rebus kept walking.

Flight shook his head. He'd had enough, absolutely up to his eyes, so that they stung now, stung as though he were in a smoky room. 'You're out on your ear, Rebus,' he called, knowing this to be the final warning. If Rebus kept walking now, Flight would be compelled to keep his word or else lose face, and he was damned if he'd lose face for a hard-headed Jock copper. 'Just keep walking!' he yelled. 'Keep walking and you're finished!'

Rebus walked. He didn't know exactly why, perhaps more out of pride than anything else. Stupid pride, pride he couldn't explain, but pride all the same. The same emotion that made grown men cry at football matches when *Flower of Scotland* was played as the Scots national anthem. All he knew was that he had something to do, and he would do it, like the Scots knew their job was to be footballers with more ambition than ability. Yes, that was him all right: more ambition than ability. They'd put it on his gravestone.

At the end of the corridor, he shoved open the swing doors. He didn't look back. Flight's voice followed him, trailing off as it grew in anger.

'Damn you, you stupid Jock bastard! You've bitten off more than you can chew this time, do you hear me? More than you can bloody well chew.'

FYTP.

Rebus was moving through the entrance hall when he came face to face with Lamb. He made to move past him, but Lamb placed a hand on Rebus's chest.

'Where's the fire?' he said. Rebus was trying to ignore him, was trying to make Lamb invisible. The last thing he needed now was this. His knuckles tingled with anticipation. Lamb was still talking, apparently oblivious to the danger he was in.

'She found you then, your daughter?'

'What?'

Lamb was smiling. 'She phoned here first, and they put her on to me. She sounded a bit upset, so I gave her the lab's number.'

'Oh.' Rebus could feel himself deflating. He managed a grudged 'thanks' and this time succeeded in moving around Lamb. But then Lamb spoke again.

'She sounded a bit tasty though. I like them young. How old is she again?'

Rebus's elbow shot back into Lamb's unprotected stomach, cutting off breath, doubling him over. Rebus studied his work; not bad for an old man. Not bad at all.

He walked.

Because he's on personal business, he stands outside the station and looks for a cab. One of the uniformed officers, who knows him from the scene of Sunday's murder, offers a lift in a patrol car, but Rebus shakes his head. The officer looks at him as if an insult has just been traded.

'Thanks anyway,' says Rebus, trying to sound conciliatory. But all he sounds is mad. Mad with Lamb, with himself, mad with the Wolfman case, mad with Kenny bloody Watkiss, mad with Flight, with Lisa (why did she have to be in Copperplate Street in the first place?) and, most of all, mad with London. Where are all the cabs, all the greedy black cabs, beetling like insects as they try to pick up fares? He's seen thousands of them this past week, but now that he needs one, they're all avoiding him. He waits anyway, eyes slightly unfocused. And as he waits, he thinks, and as he thinks he calms a little.

What the hell is he doing anyway? He's asking for trouble doing this. He's *begging* for it, like a black-clothed Calvinist pleading to be beaten for his sins. A lash across the back. Rebus had seen them all, all the available religions. He had tasted them and each one tasted bitter in its own particular way. Where was the religion for those who did not feel guilty, did not feel shame, did not regret getting angry or getting even, or, better yet, getting more than even? Where was the religion for a man who believed that good and bad must coexist, even within the individual? Where was the religion for a man who believed in God but not in God's religion?

And where were all the bloody taxis?

'Sod it then.' He walked up to the first patrol car he saw and tapped on the window, flashing his ID.

'Inspector Rebus,' he announced. 'Can you give me a lift to Gower Street?'

The building seemed as deserted as ever and Rebus feared that on this occasion perhaps even the secretary might have scarpered for an early start to the weekend. But no, she was there, like the retainer of some dusty mansion. He cleared his throat, and she looked up from her crochet.

'Yes?' she said. 'Can I help you?' She appeared not to remember him. Rebus brought out his ID and pushed it towards her.

'Detective Inspector Rebus,' he said, his voice stiff with authority. 'Scotland Yard. I want to ask you a few questions about Dr Frazer.'

The woman looked frightened. Rebus feared he had overdone the menace. He tried a don't-worry-it's-not-you-we're-interested-in sort of smile, a peaceable smile. But the woman looked no less afraid, and her fear flustered her.

'Oh, gracious,' she stammered. 'Oh my, oh my.' She looked up at him. 'Who did you say? Dr Frazer? But there's no Dr Frazer in the Department.'

Rebus described Lisa Frazer. The woman suddenly raised her head, recognising the description.

'Oh, Lisa? You mean Lisa? But there's some mistake. Lisa Frazer isn't a member of staff here. Gracious me, no. Though I believe she *may* have taken a tutorial or two, just filling in. Oh dear, Scotland Yard. What, I mean, surely she hasn't ... What has she done?'

'She doesn't work here?' Rebus needed to be certain. 'Then who is she?'

'Lisa? She's one of our research students.'

'A *student*? But she's –' He was about to say 'old'.

231

'A mature student,' the secretary explained. 'Oh dear, is she in trouble?'

'I came here before,' Rebus said. 'You didn't tell me any of this then. Why?'

'Came here before?' She studied his face. 'Yes, I remember. Well, Lisa made me promise not to tell anyone.'

'Why?'

'Her project, she said. She's doing a project on, now, what is it exactly?' She opened a drawer of her desk and pulled out a sheet of paper. 'Ah yes, "The Psychology of the Investigation of Serious Crime". She explained it to me. How she needed access to a police investigation. How she needed to gain trust. The courts, police and so on. She told me she was going to pretend to be a lecturer. I told her not to, I warned her, but she said it was the only way. The police wouldn't waste time with a mere student, would they?'

Rebus was stuck for an answer. The answer was no, they wouldn't. Why should they?

'So she got you to cover for her?'

The woman shrugged. 'Lisa is quite a persuasive young woman. She said probably I wouldn't have to tell lies. I could just say things like she's not here, she's not teaching today, that sort of thing. Always supposing anyone bothered to check up on her.'

'And has anybody checked up on her?'

'Oh yes. Why, only today I had a telephone call from someone she had arranged to interview. He wanted to be sure that she really was part of University College, and not just a journalist or a Nosey Parker.'

Today? An interview today. Well, that was one appointment she wouldn't be keeping.

'Who was this person?' Rebus asked. 'Do you remember?'

'I think I wrote it down,' she said. She lifted the thick

notepad beside her telephone and flipped through it. 'He did say who he was, but I can't remember. It was at the Old Bailey. Yes, that's right. She'd arranged to meet him at the Old Bailey. I usually write these things down as soon as someone mentions their name, just in case I forget later. No, there's no sign of it. That's funny.'

'Perhaps in the bin?' Rebus suggested.

'Well, perhaps.' But she sounded doubtful. Rebus lifted the small wicker paper-basket onto her desk and sifted through it. Pencil shavings and sweet-wrappers, an empty polystyrene coffee cup and crumpled bits of paper. Lots of bits of paper.

'Too big,' she would say as he started to uncrumple one, or: 'too small.' Until finally, he pulled out a sheet and spread it out on the desk. It was like some bizarre work of art, filled with doodles and hieroglyphs and little notes, phone numbers, names, addresses.

'Ah,' she said, sliding a finger over to one corner where something had been written in very faint, wavering pencil. 'Is that it?'

Rebus looked closer. Yes, that was it. That was most definitely it. 'Thank you,' he said.

'Oh dear,' said the secretary. 'Have I got her into trouble? Is Lisa in trouble? What has she done, Inspector?'

'She lied to us,' said Rebus. 'And because of that, she's ended up having to go into hiding.'

'Hiding? Gracious, she didn't mention anything about that.'

Rebus was beginning to suspect that the secretary was a couple of keys short of a typewriter. 'Well,' he said, 'she didn't know she was in trouble until today.'

The secretary was nodding. 'Yes, but she only phoned a little over an hour ago.'

Rebus's face creased into an all-over frown. 'What?'

'Yes, she said she was calling from the Old Bailey. She

wanted to know if there were any messages for her. She told me she had time to kill before her second appointment.'

Rebus didn't bother to ask. He dialled quickly, the receiver gripped in his hand like a weapon. 'I want to talk to George Flight.'

'Just a minute, please.' The ch–ch–ch–ch of a re-routing. Then: 'Murder Room, Detective Sergeant Walsh speaking.'

'It's Inspector Rebus here.'

'Oh yes?' The voice had become as rudimentary as a chisel.

'I need to speak to Flight. It's urgent.'

'He's in a meeting.'

'Then get him out! I told you, this is urgent.'

There was doubt, cynicism in the Sergeant's voice. Everyone knew that the Scotsman's 'urgent' wasn't worth its weight in breath. 'I can leave a message –'

'Don't fuck me around, Walsh! Either get him, or put me on to someone with a spare brain they're not sitting on!'

Ca-click. Brrrrr. The ultimate put-down. The secretary was staring at Rebus in horror. Perhaps psychologists never got angry. Rebus attempted a reassuring smile, but it came out like a clown's drunken greasepaint. He made a bowing motion before turning to leave, and was watched all the way out to the stairwell by a woman mortified almost to the core of her being.

Rebus's face was tingling with a newly stoked anger. Lisa Frazer had tricked him, played him like a fool. Christ, the things he'd told her. Thinking she wanted to help with the Wolfman case. Not realising he was merely part of her project. Christ, the things he had said. What had he said? Too much to recall. Had she been taping everything? Or simply jotting things down after he'd left? It didn't matter. What mattered was that he had seen in her something solid and believable amidst a sea of chaos. And she had been

Janus. Using him. Jesus Christ, she had even slept with him. Was that, too, part of the project, part of her little experiment? How could he ever be sure it wasn't? It had seemed genuine enough, but ... He had opened his mind to her, as she had opened her body to him. It was not a fair exchange.

'The bitch!' he exploded, stopping dead. 'The lying little bitch!'

Why hadn't she told him? Why hadn't she just explained everything? He would have helped her, he would have found time for her. No, he wouldn't. It was a lie. A research student? A project? He would have shown her the door. Instead he had listened to her, had believed her, had learned from her. Yes, it was true. He had learned a lot from her. About psychology, about the mind of the killer. Had learned from her books. Yes, but that wasn't the point. The point was that it had all become crass and diluted, now that he knew her for what she was.

'Bitch.' But his voice was softer, his throat tightening, as though a hand had slid around it and was slowly applying pressure. He swallowed hard, and began to take deep breaths. Calm down, John. What did it matter? What did any of it matter? It mattered, he answered himself, because he felt something for her. Or had felt something for her. No, still did feel something. Something he thought might have been returned.

'Who are you trying to kid?' Look at him, overweight and in his forties. Stuck at Inspector level and going nowhere except, if Flight carried out his promise, down. Divorced. A daughter distraught and mixing with darkness. Someone in London with a kitchen knife and a secret and a knowledge of Lisa. It was all wrong. He'd been clutching at Lisa the way drowning men reached out for a thin snap of straw. Stupid old man.

He stood at the main door to the building, not really sure

235

now. Should he confront her, or let it go, never see her again? Usually he relished confrontation, found it nourishing and exciting. But today, maybe not.

She was at the Old Bailey to interview Malcolm Chambers. He, too, was at this moment being tricked by her mock credentials, by that falsely prefixed 'Doctor'. Everyone admired Malcolm Chambers. He was smart, he was on the side of the law, and he made pots of money. Rebus had known coppers who were none of these; most could score only one out of three, a few managed two. Chambers would sweep Lisa Frazer off her feet. She would loathe him, until that loathing mingled with awe, and then she'd probably think that she loved him. Well, good luck to her.

He'd head back to the station, say his farewells, pack his bags, and head north. They could get along without him very well. The case was heading nowhere until the Wolfman bit again. Yet they had so much now, knew so much about him, had come so close to opening him up like a soft fat peach. Maybe he'd bite Lisa Frazer. What the hell was she doing at the Old Bailey when she should be in hiding? He needed to speak to Flight. What the hell was Flight up to anyway?

'Ach, to hell with the lot of you,' he muttered, plunging his hands into his pockets.

Two students, their voices loudly American, were heading towards him. They seemed excited, the way students always did, discussing this or that concept, ready to change the way the world thought. They wanted to get past, wanted to go into the building. He moved aside for them, but they didn't so much move past him as *through* him, as though he were insubstantial as exhaust fumes.

'Like, y'know, I think she likes me, but I'm not sure I'm ready for something like –'

So much for difficult concepts, thought Rebus. Why

236

should students be different from anyone else in the population? Why should they be thinking (and talking), about something other than sex?

'Yeah,' said the other one. Rebus wondered how comfortable he felt in his thick white T-shirt and thicker checked lumberjack shirt. The day was sticky. 'Yeah,' the American repeated. His accent reminded Rebus of Lisa's softer Canadian tones.

'But get this,' continued his companion, their voices fading as they moved deeper into the building, 'she *says* her mother hates Americans because one of them near raped her in the war.'

Get this. Where had Rebus heard that expression before? He fumbled in his jacket pocket and found a folded piece of paper. Unfolded it and began to read.

'GET THIS, I'M NOT HOMOSEXUL, O.K.?' It was the photocopy of the Wolfman's letter to Lisa.

Get this. It did have a transatlantic ring to it, didn't it? A curious way altogether of starting a letter. Get this. Be warned, watch out. There were several ways of starting a letter so that the reader knew he was to pay particular attention to it. But *get this*?

What did they know, or what did they suspect, about the Wolfman? He knew about police procedure (past offender, copper, both were possible). He was a he, if Jan Crawford were to be believed. He was quite tall, she thought. In the restaurant, Lisa Frazer had added her own ideas: he was conservative; most of the time he not only seemed normal, he was normal; he was, in her phrase, 'psychologically mature'. And he had posted a letter to Lisa from EC4. EC4, wasn't that where the Old Bailey was? He recalled his first and only visit to the building. The courtroom, and seeing Kenny Watkiss there. Then meeting Malcolm Chambers. What was it Chambers had said to George Flight?

Royally shafted. Own team. I don't like. Flight, I don't like being royally shafted ... own team ... get this. Get this, George.

Jesus Christ! Every ball on the table suddenly fell into a pocket until only the cue ball and the black were left. Every single ball.

'*Get this, George, I don't like being royally shafted by my own team.*'

Malcolm Chambers had studied in the USA for a while. Flight had told Rebus that. You tended to pick up mannerisms when you wanted to fit into a new and strange place. *Get this.* Rebus had tried to avoid the temptation in London, but it was strong. Studied in the USA. And now he was with Lisa Frazer. Lisa the student, Lisa the psychologist, Lisa with her photo in the newspapers. *Get this.* Oh, how the Wolfman must hate her. She was a psychologist after all and the psychologists had pronounced him gay, they had insights into what was wrong with him. He didn't think anything was wrong with him. But something was. Something that was slowly taking him over.

Old Bailey was in EC4. The Wolfman, rattled, had slipped up and posted his letter from EC4.

It was Malcolm Chambers, Malcolm Chambers was the Wolfman. Rebus couldn't explain it, couldn't exactly justify it, but he knew it all the same. It was like a dark polluted wave rolling over him, anointing him. Malcolm Chambers. Someone who knew about police procedure, someone above suspicion, someone so clean you had to scratch beneath the skin to find the filth.

Rebus was running. He was running along Gower Street in what he hoped was the right direction for the City. He was running and he was craning his neck to seek out a taxi. There was one ahead of him, at the corner beside the British Museum, but it was picking up a fare. Students or tourists. Japanese. Grins and cameras. Four of them, two men, two young women. Rebus stuck his head into the back of the cab, where two of them were already seated.

'Out!' he yelled, jerking a thumb towards the pavement.

'Oi, mate, what's your game?' The driver was so fat he could barely turn in his seat.

'I said out!' Rebus grabbed an arm and pulled. Either the young man was surprisingly light, or else Rebus had found hidden strength, for the body fairly flew from its seat, uttering a string of high-pitched comment as it went.

'And you.'

The girl followed obligingly and Rebus hurled himself into the cab, slamming shut the door.

'Drive!' he yelled.

'I'm not moving till I –'

Rebus shoved his ID against the window separating the back seats of the taxi from the front.

'Inspector Rebus!' he called. 'This is an emergency. I need to get to the Old Bailey. Break every traffic law you like, I'll sort it out later. But get your fucking skates on!'

The driver responded by switching his headlights on full beam before setting out into the traffic.

'Use your horn!' Rebus called. The driver did so. A surprising number of cars eased out of his way. Rebus was on the edge of his seat, gripping it with both hands to stop himself being thrown about. 'How long will it take?'

'This time of day? Ten or fifteen minutes. What's the matter, guv? Can't they start without you?'

Rebus smiled sourly. That was just the problem. Without him, the Wolfman could start whenever he liked. 'I need to use your radio,' he said. The driver slid his window further open.

'Be my guest,' he said, pulling the small microphone up towards Rebus. He'd worked on the cabs for twenty-odd years, but he'd never had a fare like this.

In fact, he was so excited, they were halfway there before he remembered to switch on the meter.

Rebus had told Flight as much as he could, trying not to sound hysterical. Flight sounded dubious about the whole thing, but agreed to send men to the Old Bailey. Rebus didn't blame George Flight for being wary. Hard to justify arresting a pillar of society on the strength of a gut feeling. Rebus remembered what else Lisa Frazer had said about serial killers: that they were products of their environments; that their ambitions had been thwarted, leading them to kill members of the social group above them. Well, that certainly wasn't true in Malcolm Chambers's case, was it? And what had she said about the Wolfman? His attacks were 'non-confrontational', so perhaps he was like that in his working life. Hah! So much for theory. But now Rebus began to doubt his own instincts. Jesus, what if he *was* wrong? What if the theory was right? He was going to look more than a little psychologically disturbed himself.

Then he recalled something George Flight had said. You could build up as neat a picture as you liked of the killer, but it wouldn't give you a name and address. Psychology was all well and good, but you couldn't beat a good old-fashioned hunch.

'Nearly there, guv.'

Rebus tried to keep his breathing regular. Be calm, John, be calm. However, there were no police cars waiting by the entrance to the Old Bailey. No sirens and armed officers, just people milling around, people finishing work for the day, people sharing a joke. Rebus left the cab driver unpaid and untipped – 'I'll settle later' – and pushed open the heavy glass door. Behind more bulletproof glass stood two security personnel. Rebus stuck his ID in front of their noses. One of them pointed towards the two vertical glass cylinders by which people were admitted to the building one at a time. Rebus went to one cylinder and waited. Nothing happened. Then he remembered, pushed the heel of his hand against the button and the cylinder door opened. He walked in, and waited for what seemed an eternity while the door slid shut behind him, before the door in front slid just as slowly open.

Another guard stood beside the metal detection equipment. Rebus, still holding open his ID, walked quickly past until he found himself behind the bulletproof glass of the reception area.

'Can I help?' said one of the security men.

'Malcolm Chambers,' said Rebus. 'He's a barrister. I need to see him urgently.'

'Mr Chambers? Hold on, I'll just check.'

'I don't want him to know I'm here,' Rebus warned. 'I just want to know where I can find him.'

'Just one moment.' The guard moved off, consulting with one of his companions, then slowly going through a sheet of paper attached to a clipboard. Rebus's heart was pounding. He felt like he was about to explode. He couldn't just stand here. He had to *do* something. Patience, John. Less haste, more speed, as his father had always said. But what the hell did that mean anyway? Surely haste was a kind of speed?

The guard was coming back.

'Yes, Inspector. Mr Chambers has a young lady with him at present. I'm told they're sitting together upstairs.'

Upstairs meant the concourse outside the courtrooms. Rebus flew up the imposing flight of steps two at a time. Marble. There was a lot of marble around him. And wood. And glass. The windows seemed huge. Bewigged counsels came down a spiral staircase, deep in conversation. A frayed-looking woman smoked a cheap cigarette as she waited for someone. It was a quiet pandemonium. People were moving past Rebus, moving in the opposite direction from him. Juries, finished for the day. Solicitors and guilty-looking clients. The woman rose to greet her son. The son's solicitor had a bored, drawn look. The concourse was emptying rapidly, the stairs taking people down to more glass cylinders and to the outside world.

About thirty yards from where Rebus stood, the two men were sitting, legs crossed, enjoying a cigarette. The two men Flight had sent with Lisa. Her bodyguards. Rebus ran to them.

'Where is she?'

They recognised him, seemed to realise immediately that something was wrong, and rose to their feet.

'She's interviewing some barrister –'

'Yes, but *where*?'

The man nodded towards one of the courtrooms. Court Eight! Of course: hadn't Cousins been due to give evidence in Court Eight? And wasn't Malcolm Chambers the prosecuting counsel?

Rebus pushed through the doors into the courtroom, but, cleaners apart, it was completely empty. There had to be another exit. Of course there was: the green padded door to the side of the jury-box. The door leading to the judges' rooms. He ran across the court and up the steps to the door, pulling it open, finding himself in a bright carpeted corridor. A window, flowers in a pot on a table. A narrow corridor, doors only on one side, the other wall a blank. Judges' names above the doors. The doors themselves locked. There was a tiny kitchenette, but it too was empty. One door eventually gave, and he peered into a jury room. Empty. Back into the corridor again, hissing now with frustration. A court usher, cradling a mug of tea, was coming towards him.

'No one's allowed –'

'Inspector Rebus,' he said. 'I'm looking for an advocate …

242

I mean, a barrister. Malcolm Chambers. He was here with a young woman.'

'They've just left.'

'Left?'

She gestured along towards the far end of the corridor. 'It leads to the underground car park. That's where they were headed.' Rebus made to squeeze past her. 'You won't catch them now,' she said. 'Not unless they're having trouble with the car.'

Rebus thought about it, gnawing at his bottom lip. There wasn't time. His first decision had to be the right one. Decision made, he turned from the usher and ran back towards the court, back across the court itself and out into the concourse.

'They've gone!' he yelled to the bodyguards. 'Tell Flight! Tell him they're in Chambers's car!' And then he was off again, down the steps towards the exit, pausing only to grab at a security man's sleeve. 'The car park exit, where is it?'

'Round the other side of the building.'

Rebus stuck a finger in the guard's face. 'Buzz down to the car park. Don't let Malcolm Chambers leave.' The guard stood there dumbly, staring at the finger. '*Do it!*'

And then he was off again, running, taking the stairs down three at a time, great leaps which almost sent him flying. He pushed his way to the front of the crowd waiting to leave.

'Police,' he said, 'emergency.' Nobody said anything. They were like cows, patiently waiting to be milked. Even so, it took a silent scream of an age for the cylinder to empty its cargo, close its doors, then open them again for Rebus.

'Come on, come on.' And then the door sucked itself open and he was out, out in the foyer, bursting through the main doors. He ran up to the corner, took a right, and ran again along the face of the building. Another right. He was on the other side of the building now. Where the car park exit was. A slope of road down into darkness. The car screeched as it came to the surface, hardly slowing as it climbed the hill to Newgate Street. It was a long gloss-black BMW. And in the passenger seat sat Lisa Frazer, looking relaxed, smiling, talking to the driver, not realising.

'Lisa!' But he was too far away, the traffic around him too loud. 'Lisa!' Before he could reach it, the car had turned into a flow of traffic and disappeared. Rebus cursed under his breath. Then looked around him for the first time and saw that he was standing next to a parked Jaguar, in the front of which sat a liveried chauffeur, staring out of the window at him. Rebus yanked at the doorhandle and threw open the door, reaching in with one hand to pull out the bemused driver. He was getting to be a dab hand at this: relieving people of their vehicles.

'Hoi! What the bleedin' 'ell –'

The man's cap rolled along the ground, given force by a gust of wind. For a moment, he knelt on the pavement, undecided whether to rescue the cap or the car. The moment was enough. Rebus gunned the engine and pulled away from the kerb, horns sounding behind him as he did so. At the top of the slight incline, he pressed his hand hard on the horn and careered left into the main road. A squeal of brakes. More horns. The pedestrians looking at him as though he were mad.

'Need lights,' he said to himself, glancing at the dashboard. Eventually, he found the headlamp switch and flipped them to full beam. Then took a hard right to bring himself into the middle of the road, passing the traffic, scraping the passenger side against an oncoming red bus, clipping a central bollard, uprooting the flimsy plastic construction and sending it flying into the path of the oncoming traffic.

244

They couldn't be too far ahead of him. Yes! He caught a glimpse of the BMW's tail-lights as it braked to turn a corner. He'd be damned if they'd lose him.

'Excuse me?'

Rebus flinched, startled, and nearly pulled the car onto the pavement. He looked in the rear-view mirror and saw an elderly gentleman sitting in the back seat, arms spread so as to keep himself upright. He appeared calm as he leaned forward towards Rebus.

'Would you kindly mind telling me what's going on? Am I being kidnapped?'

Rebus recognised the voice before he remembered the face. It was the judge from the Watkiss case. Jesus Christ, he'd run off with a judge!

'Only, if you are kidnapping me,' the judge went on, 'perhaps you'd allow me to call my wife. She'll burn the chops otherwise.'

Call! Rebus looked down again. Below the dashboard, between the driver's and front passenger seats, there was a neat black car-phone.

'Do you mind if I use your phone?' he asked, grinning with a face full of adrenalin.

'Be my guest.'

Rebus grabbed at the contraption and fiddled as he drove, his steering becoming more erratic than ever.

'Press the button marked TRS,' the judge suggested.

'Thank you, your honour.'

'You know who I am? I thought I recognised the face. Have I had you before me recently?'

But Rebus had dialled and was now waiting for the call to be answered. It seemed to take forever. And meantime, the BMW had nipped across an amber traffic light.

'Hold tight,' Rebus said, baring his teeth. The horn was a banshee wail as they pushed past the waiting traffic and flew across the intersection, traffic from left and right braking hard. One car dented the back of another. A motorcycle slewed on the greasy road. But they were across. The BMW was still in sight, less than half a dozen cars ahead now, yet still apparently unaware of the pursuing demon.

Finally, the call was answered.

'It's Rebus here.' Then, for his passenger's sake: 'Detective Inspector Rebus. I need to speak to Flight. Is he there?' There was a long pause. The connection crackled wildly, as though about to short out altogether. Rebus gripped the handset between hunched shoulder and angled cheek, driving with both hands to take first one bend and then another.

'John? Where are you?' Flight's voice sounded metallic and distant.

'I'm in a car,' said Rebus, 'a car I commandeered. I'm following Chambers. He's got Lisa Frazer with him. I don't think she knows he's the Wolfman.'

'But for Christ's sake, John, *is* he the Wolfman?'

'I'll ask him when I catch him. Did you send any cars to the Old Bailey?'

'I sent one, yes.'

'That was generous.' Rebus saw what was ahead. 'Oh shit!' He braked hard, but not hard enough. The old lady was shuffling slowly across the zebra crossing, her shopping trolley a step behind her like a pet poodle. Rebus swerved but couldn't avoid winging the trolley. It flew into the air as though fired from a cannon, dispensing groceries as it went: eggs, butter, flour, cornflakes raining down on the road. Rebus heard the woman screaming. At worst she'd have a broken arm. No, at worst the shock would kill her.

'Oh shit,' he said again.

The judge was staring out of the rear window. 'I think she's all right,' he said.

'John?' It was Flight's tin-can voice on the line. 'Who was that speaking?'

'Oh,' said Rebus. 'That was the judge. It's his Jaguar I've commandeered.' He had found the windscreen wiper switch and was letting them deal with the pancake mixture on the windscreen.

'You *what*?' So that was what a roar sounded like. The BMW was still in sight. But it had slowed a little, perhaps aware of the incident behind it.

'Never mind,' said Rebus. 'Look, just get some patrol cars up here. We're on …' He glanced out of windscreen and side window, but could see no street signs.

'High Holborn,' said the judge.

'Thanks,' said Rebus. 'We're on High Holborn, George.'

'Wait a second,' said Flight. There was a muffled exchange at his end of the line. Then he came back on again. He sounded tired. 'Please, John, tell me it isn't you behind these reports we're getting. The switchboards are lighting up like Christmas trees.'

'That's probably us, George. We took a bollard out a little way back, caused a couple of accidents and now we've just sent an old woman's messages flying everywhere. Yes, that's us.'

If Flight groaned, he did so quietly. Then: 'What if it's not him, John? What if you're wrong?'

'Then it's all a bit of a balls-up, George, and I'll probably get to see what the inside of a dole office looks like, if not a prison cell. Meanwhile, get those coppers down here!' Rebus looked at the handset. 'Judge, help me. How do I –'

'Just press Power.' Rebus did, and the illuminated digits faded.

'Thanks,' he said.

The traffic was slowing, a jam of lights up ahead. 'And,' the judge was saying, 'if you intend using the apparatus

247

again, I should probably inform you that it can be used in hands-free mode. Just dial and leave it in its little compartment there. You'll be able to hear the caller and they'll be able to hear you.' Rebus nodded his thanks. The judge's head was close to Rebus's ear, peering over his shoulder at the road ahead.

'So,' he said excitedly, 'you think Malcolm Chambers is behind all these killings?'

'That's right.'

'And what evidence do you have, Inspector?'

Rebus laughed, and tapped his head. 'Just this, your lordship, just this.'

'Remarkable,' said the judge. He seemed to be considering something. 'I always thought Malcolm was rather an odd young man. Fine in court, of course, very much the star prosecutor, playing to the gallery and what have you. But outside the courtroom, he seemed very different. Oh, very different indeed. Almost sullen, as though his mind were wandering.'

His mind had wandered all right, thought Rebus, wandered all the way over the edge.

'Would you like to speak to him?'

'You think I'm chasing him for a bet?'

The judge chuckled, pointing to the car-phone. 'I meant talk to him right now.'

Rebus went rigid. 'You mean you've got his number?'

'Oh yes.'

Rebus thought it over, but shook his head. 'No,' he said. 'He's got someone with him. An innocent woman. I don't want to panic him.'

'I see,' said the judge, settling back again. 'Yes, I suppose you're right. I hadn't thought of that.'

And then there was an electric purring inside the car. It was the phone, its display illuminated now and flashing. Rebus handed the set to the judge.

'Probably for you,' he said drily.

'No,' said the judge, 'just put it back and press Receive.' Rebus did so. Only then did the judge speak. 'Hello?'

The voice was clear, the reception signal strong. 'Edward? Is that you following me?'

It was Chambers's voice, sounding amused about something. The judge stared at Rebus, who could offer no suggestion for an answer.

'Malcolm?' said the judge, his composure intact. 'Is that you?'

'You should know. You're only about twenty yards behind me.'

'Am I? Which road are you on?'

The voice altered, taking on an edge of sudden viciousness. 'Don't fuck with me, Ted! Who's driving the fucking car? Can't be you, you haven't even got a licence. Who is it?'

The judge looked to Rebus again, seeking guidance. They listened together in silence and heard Lisa's faint voice.

'What's going on?' she was saying. 'What's happening?'

Then Chambers's voice. 'Shut up, bitch! You'll get yours.' The voice rose a chilling octave, sounding like a bad female impersonator, making the hairs on Rebus's neck bristle. 'You'll get yours.' Then it dropped again, speaking into the handset. 'Hello? Who's that? Who's there? I can hear you breathing, you little shit.' Rebus bit his lip. Was it better to let Chambers know, or to stay silent? He stayed silent.

'Oh well,' said Chambers with a sigh, as though resigned to this stalemate. 'Out she goes.'

Ahead, Rebus saw the BMW's passenger door swing open as the car veered onto the pavement.

'What are you doing!' screamed Lisa. 'No! No! Let me go!'

'Chambers!' Rebus yelled towards the handset. 'Leave her!' The BMW swerved back into the road, the door drifting shut. There was a pause.

'Hello,' said Chambers's voice. 'To whom am I speaking?'

'My name's Rebus. We met at –'

'John!' It was Lisa's voice, very afraid now, almost hysterical. The sound of the slap was a static crack in Rebus's ear.

'I said leave her!' Rebus yelled.

'I know you did,' said Chambers, 'but then you're hardly in a position to give orders. Anyway, now that I know you two know each other, that makes things interesting, doesn't it, Inspector?'

'You remember me?'

'I have an intimate knowledge of everyone on the Wolfman case. I've taken an interest in it from the start – for obvious reasons. There was always someone around willing to tell what they knew.'

'So you could keep one step ahead?'

'*One* step?' Chambers laughed. 'You flatter yourself. So tell me, Inspector, what do we do now? Do you stop your car – Edward's car, I should say – or do I kill your friend here? Do you know, she wanted to ask *me* about the psychology of court trials. She couldn't have picked better, could she, the little bitch?' Lisa was sobbing. Rebus could hear her, and every sound cut him a little deeper. 'Picture in the paper,' Chambers was cooing. 'Picture in the paper with the big tough detective.'

Rebus knew he had to keep Chambers talking. By keeping him talking, he was keeping Lisa alive. But the traffic had stalled. Red lights ahead. The BMW only a few cars in front, prevented from jumping the lights by another car directly in front of it. Could he …? Should he even be thinking of it? The judge was still gripping Rebus's headrest, staring out towards the gleaming black car, the car that was so close to them. So close ... and so stationary.

'Well?' It was Chambers's voice. 'Do you pull over, Inspector, or do I kill her?'

Rebus was staring hard at Chambers's car. He could see that Lisa was leaning away from Chambers, as though making to escape. But Chambers was gripping her with his left arm, his right presumably resting on the steering-wheel. So the man's attention would be focussed on the passenger side of the car, leaving the driver's side unguarded.

Rebus made up his mind and quietly opened his door, slipping out onto the reassuringly solid surface of the road. Horns were sounding around him. He paid them no heed. The lights were still at red. He began to move forward, crouching, but moving quickly. Chambers's driver's-side mirror! If Chambers looked into it, he'd have a clear view of Rebus's approach. Make it fast, John, make it.

Amber.

Shit!

Green.

He had reached the BMW, had gripped the doorhandle. Chambers looked out at him, a stunned expression on his face. And then the car in front moved off, and Chambers gunned the engine, the car accelerating forwards, tearing itself free of Rebus.

Shit! Car horns all around. Angry. Angry drivers rolling down their windows and yelling at him as he ran back to the Jaguar. Started the car, moved off. The judge's hand patted his shoulder.

'Good try, my boy. Good try.'

And Chambers's laughter on the car-phone. 'Hope I didn't hurt you, Inspector.' Rebus examined his hand, flexed it painfully. The fingers had nearly been pulled out of their joints. His little finger was swelling already. A break? Perhaps.

'So,' said Chambers, 'for the last time I make you an offer you can hardly refuse. Stop the car, or I kill Dr Frazer.'

'She's not a doctor, Chambers. She's just a student.' He swallowed: now Lisa knew that he knew. Not that it mattered one way or the other, not now. He took a deep breath. 'Kill her,' he said. Behind him, the judge gasped, but Rebus shook his head, reassuring him.

'What did you say?' asked Chambers.

'I said kill her. I'm not really bothered. She's led me a merry little dance this past week. It's her own fault she's in this deep. And after you've killed her, I'll take great pleasure in killing you, Mr Chambers.'

He heard Lisa's faint voice again. 'God, John, please no!' And then Chambers, seeming to grow calmer as Rebus grew more excited: 'As you wish, Inspector. As you wish.' The voice was as cold as a mortuary floor, any vestige of humanity gone. Perhaps partly it was Rebus's fault, taunting him with newspaper stories, with fabrications. But Chambers hadn't picked on Rebus: he had picked on Lisa. Had Rebus arrived a minute later at the Old Bailey, she would be on her way to certain death. As it was, nothing was certain.

Nothing but the fact of Malcolm Chambers's madness.

'He's turning onto Monmouth Street,' said the judge, his voice level. He had grasped the fact of Chambers's guilt, the horror of what had happened and what might still happen.

Rebus heard a flapping sound overhead, and glanced up towards where a helicopter was shadowing the chase. A police helicopter. He could hear sirens, too. So, it seemed, could Chambers. The BMW spurted ahead, slashing the side of another car as it squeezed into a space. The injured car stopped dead. Rebus braked, pulled on the steering-wheel, but still clipped it with his driver's-side bumper, the headlamp shattering.

'Sorry about that.'

'Never mind the car,' said the judge. 'Just don't let him get away.'

'He won't get away,' said Rebus, with sudden confidence. Now where the hell had that come from? The moment he thought about it, it disappeared again, leaving behind a quivering vapour.

They were on St Martin's Lane now. People mingling, pre-theatre or after work. The busy West End. Yet the traffic ahead had thinned for no apparent reason and the crowds gawped as first the BMW, then the Jaguar sped past.

As they approached Trafalgar Square Rebus saw, to right and left, police officers in luminous yellow jackets holding up the traffic in the side-streets. Now why would they do that? Unless ...

Road block! One entrance to the Square left open, all exits blocked, the Square itself kept empty for their arrival. In a moment they'd have him. God bless you, George Flight.

Rebus picked up the handset, his voice a snarl, specks of saliva dotting the windscreen as he spoke.

'Stop the car, Chambers. There's no place to go.'

Silence. They were skidding into Trafalgar Square now, traffic blaring in queues all around them, held back by the gloved, raised hand of authority. Rebus was buzzing again. The whole West End of London, brought to a standstill so that he might race a Jaguar against a BMW. He could think of friends who'd give whole limbs to be in his place. Yet he had a job to do. That was the bottom line. It was just another job to be cleared up. He might as well have been following teenage Cortina thieves through the streets of some Edinburgh housing-scheme.

But he wasn't.

They'd done one full circuit around Nelson's Column. Canada House, South Africa House and the National Gallery were just blurs. The judge was being thrown against the door behind Rebus.

'Hang on,' Rebus called.

'To what, pray?'

And Rebus laughed. He roared with laughter. Then he realised the line was still open to Chambers's BMW. He laughed even harder, picking up the handset, his knuckles white against the steering-wheel, left arm aching.

'Having fun, Chambers?' he yelled. 'Like the TV programme used to say, there's no hiding place!'

And then the BMW gave a jolt, and Rebus heard Chambers gasp.

'You bitch!' Another jolt, and sounds of a struggle. Lisa was retaliating, now that Chambers was intent on this speeding circuit without end.

'No!'

'Get off!'

'I'll –'

And a piercing scream, two piercing screams, both high-pitched, feminine in their intensity, and the black car didn't take the next bend, flew straight for the pavement, mounted it and bounced into a bus shelter, crumpling the metal structure and driving on into the walls of the National Gallery itself.

'Lisa!' Rebus cried. He brought the Jaguar to a sudden, pivoting stop. The driver's door of the BMW creaked open and Chambers stumbled out, slouching off in a half-run, clutching something in his right hand, one leg damaged. Rebus struggled with his own door, finally finding the handle. He ran to the BMW and peered in. Lisa was slumped in the passenger seat, a seatbelt passing in a diagonal across her body. She was groaning, but there were no signs of blood. Whiplash. Nothing more serious than whiplash. She opened her eyes.

'John?'

'You're going to be all right, Lisa. Just hang on. Somebody will be here.' Indeed, the police cars were closing in, uniforms running into the Square. Rebus looked up from the car, seeking Chambers.

'There!' The judge was out of the Jaguar and pointing with a rigid arm, pointing upwards. Rebus followed the line to the steps of the National Gallery. Chambers had reached the top step.

'Chambers!' Rebus yelled. 'Chambers!'

But the body disappeared from view. Rebus started towards the steps, finding his own legs to be less than solid. As though rubber instead of bone and cartilage were keeping him upright. He climbed the steps and entered the building by its nearest door – the exit door. A woman in a staff uniform was lying on the ground in the foyer, a man standing over her. The man gestured towards the gallery's interior.

'He ran inside!'

And where Malcolm Chambers went, Rebus would surely follow.

* * *

He ran and he ran and he ran.

The way he used to run from his father, running and climbing the steps to the attic, hoping to hide. But always caught in the end. Even if he hid all day and half of the night, eventually the hunger, the thirst, would force him back downstairs, to where they were waiting.

His leg hurts. And he's cut. His face is stinging. The

warm blood is trickling down his chin, down his neck. And he's running.

It wasn't all bad, his childhood. He remembers his mother delicately snipping away at his father's nosehairs. 'Long nosehairs are so unbecoming in a man.' It wasn't his fault, was it, any of it? It was theirs. They'd wanted a daughter; they'd never wanted a son. His mother had dressed him in pink, in girls' colours and girls' clothes. Then had painted him, painted him with long blonde curls, imagining him into her paintings, into her landscapes. A little girl running by a riverbank. Running with bows in her hair. Running.

Past one guard, past two. Lunging at them. The alarm is ringing somewhere. Maybe it's just his imagination. All these paintings. Where have all these paintings come from? Through one door, turn right, through another.

They kept him at home. The schools couldn't teach him the way they could. Home taught. Home made. His father, some nights, drunk, would knock over his mother's canvases and dance on them. 'Art! Fuck art!' He'd do his little dance with a chuckle in his throat and all the time his mother would sit with her face in her hands and cry, then run to her room and bolt shut the door. Those were the nights when his father would stumble through to *his* bedroom. Just for a cuddle. Sweet alcoholic breath. Just for a cuddle. And then more than a cuddle, so very much more. 'Open wide, just like the dentist tells you.' Christ, it hurt so much. A probing finger ... tongue ... the wrenching open ... And even worse was the noise, the dull grunting, the loud nasal breathing. And then the sham, pretending it had been just a game, that was all. And to prove it, his father would bend down and take a big soft bite out of his stomach, growling like a bear. Blowing a raspberry on the bare flesh. And then a laugh. 'You see, it was only a game, wasn't it?'

No, never a game. Never. Running. To the attic. To the garden, to squeeze behind the shed, where the stinging nettles were. Even their bite was not so bad as his father's. Had his mother known? Of course she had known. Once, when he had tried to tell her in a whispered moment, she had refused to listen. 'No, not your father, you're making it up, Malcolm.' But her paintings had grown more violent: the fields now were purple and black, the water blood-red. The figures on the riverbank had grown skeletal, painted stark white like ghosts.

He'd hidden it all so well for so long. But then she'd come back to him. And now he was mostly 'she', consumed by her, and by her need for … Not revenge, it couldn't really be called revenge. Something deeper than revenge, some huge and hungry need without a name, without a form. Only a function. Oh yes, a function.

This way and that. The people in the gallery make way for him. The alarm is ringing still. There's a hissing in his head like a child's rattle. Sss-sss-sss. Sss-sss-sss. These paintings he is running past, they're laughable. *Long nosehairs Johnny*. None mimicked real life, and less so the life beneath. None could ape the grim caveman thoughts of every human being on the planet. But then he pushes open another door and it's all so very different. A room of darkness and shadowplay, of skulls and frowning bloodless faces. Yes, this is how it is. Velázquez, El Greco, the Spanish painters. Skull and shadow. Ah, Velázquez.

Why couldn't his mother have painted like this? When they died. *(Together, in bed. A gas leak. The police said the child was lucky to be alive. Lucky his own bedroom window had been open a couple of inches.)* When they had died, all he'd taken with him from the house had been her paintings, every single one of them.

'Only a game.'

'Long nosehairs, Johnny.' Snipping with the scissors, his

257

father asleep. He'd pleaded with his eyes, pleaded with her to stick the point of the scissors into his father's fleshy noiseless throat. She'd been so gentle. Snip. So kind and gentle. Snip. *The child was lucky*.

What could they know?

* * *

Rebus walked up the stairs and through the bookshop. Other officers were close behind him. He motioned for them to spread out. There would be no escape. But he also warned them to keep their distance.

Malcolm Chambers was *his*.

The first gallery was large, with red walls. A guard pointed through the doorway on the right and Rebus strode towards it. By the side of the doorway, a painting showed a headless corpse, spouting blood. The painting mirrored Rebus's thoughts so well that he smiled grimly. There were spots of rust-coloured blood on the orange carpet. But even without these, he would have had no difficulty following Chambers's trail. The tourists and attendants stood back from him, pointing, showing him the way. The alarm bell was bright and sharp, focusing his mind. His legs had become solid once again and his heart pumped blood so loudly he wondered if others could hear it.

He took a right, from a small corner room into another large gallery, at the far end of which stood a set of hefty wooden and glass doors. Near them another attendant stood nursing a wounded arm. There was a bloody handprint on one door. Rebus stopped and looked through into the room itself.

In the furthest corner, slouched on the floor, sat the Wolfman. Directly above him on the wall was a painting of a monastic figure, the face cowled and in shadow. The figure looked to be praying to heaven. The figure was holding a skull. A smear of blood ran down and past the skull.

Rebus pushed open the door and walked into the room. Next to this painting was another, of the Virgin Mary with stars around what was left of her head. A large hole had been punched through her face. The figure beneath the paintings was still and silent. Rebus took a few paces forward. He glanced to his left and saw that on the opposite wall were portraits of unhappy looking noblemen. They had every right to be unhappy. Slashes in each canvas almost ripped their heads from their bodies. He was close now. Close enough to see that the painting next to Malcolm Chambers was a Velázquez, 'The Immaculate Conception'. Rebus smiled again. Immaculate indeed.

And then Malcolm Chambers's head jerked up. The eyes were cold, the face stippled with glass from the BMW's windscreen. The voice when it spoke was dull and tired.

'Inspector Rebus.'

Rebus nodded, though it had not been a question.

'I wonder,' Chambers said, 'why my mother never brought me here. I don't remember being taken anywhere, except perhaps Madame Tussaud's. Have you ever been to Madame Tussaud's, Inspector? I like the Chamber of Horrors. My mother wouldn't even come in with me.' He laughed, and leaned against the foot-rail behind him, ready to push himself to his feet. 'I shouldn't have torn those paintings, should I?' he was saying. 'They were probably priceless. Silly really. They're only paintings, after all. Why should paintings be priceless?'

Rebus had reached out a hand to help him up. At the same time, he saw the portraits again. Slashed. Not torn, *slashed*. Like the attendant's arm. Not by human hand, but with an instrument.

Too late. The small kitchen-knife in Chambers's hand was already pushing through Rebus's shirt. Chambers had leapt to his feet and was propelling Rebus backwards, back towards the portraits on the far wall. Chambers was infused with the strength of madness. Rebus felt his feet catch on the foot-rail behind him, his head fell back against one painting, thudding into the wall. He had his own right hand clasped around Chambers's knife-hand now, so that the tip of the knife was still gouging at his stomach but could go no deeper. He jerked a knee into Chambers's groin, at the same time jamming the heel of his left hand into Chambers's nose. There was a squeal as the pressure lessened on the knife. Rebus twisted Chambers's wrist, trying to shake free the knife, but Chambers's grip held fast.

Upright again, away from the wall now, they wrestled for control of the knife. Chambers was crying, howling. The sound chilled Rebus, even as he grappled with the man. It was like fighting with darkness itself. Unwanted thoughts sped through his mind: crammed tube trains, child molesters, beggars, blank faces, punks and pimps, as everything he'd seen and experienced in London washed over him in a final rolling wave. He dare not look into Chambers's face for fear that he would freeze. The paintings all around were blurs of blue, black and grey as he danced this macabre dance, feeling Chambers growing stronger and himself growing more tired. Tired and dizzy, the room spinning, a dullness coursing through his stomach towards the hole made by the knife.

The knife which is moving now, moving with new-found power, a power Rebus feels unable to counter with anything more than a grimace. He dares himself to look at Chambers. Does so, and sees the eyes staring at him like a bull's, the mouth set defiantly, the chin jutting. There is more than defiance there, more than madness, there is a resolution. Rebus feels it as the knife-hand turns. Turns one hundred and eighty degrees. And then he is being pushed backwards again. Chambers is rearing up, driving him on, powerful as an engine, until Rebus slams into another wall, followed by Chambers himself. It is almost an embrace. The bodies seemingly intimate in their contact. Chambers is heavy, a dead weight. His cheek rests against Rebus's. Until Rebus, recovering his breath, pushes the body away. Chambers staggers backwards into the room, the knife buried in his chest all the way up to the hilt. He angles his head to look down, dark blood dribbling from the corners of his mouth. He touches at the handle of the knife. Then looks up at Rebus and smiles, almost apologetically.

'So unbecoming ... in a man.' Then falls to his knees. Trunk falls forward. Head hits carpet. And stays like that. Rebus is breathing hard. He pushes himself up from the wall, walks to the centre of the room, and pushes at the body with the toe of his shoe, tipping Chambers sideways. The face looks peaceful, despite the welts of blood. Rebus touches two fingers to the front of his own shirt. They come away moist with blood. That didn't matter. What mattered was that the Wolfman had turned out to be human after all, human and mortal, mortal and dead. If he wanted to, Rebus knew he could take the credit. He didn't want the credit. He'd get them to take away the knife and check it for fingerprints. They would find only Chambers's. That didn't mean much, of course. The likes of Flight would still think Rebus had killed him. But Rebus hadn't killed the Wolfman, and he couldn't be sure exactly what had: cowardice? guilt? or something deeper, something never to be explained?

So unbecoming ... in a man. What kind of obituary was that?

'John?'

It was Flight's voice. Behind him stood two officers armed with pistols.

'No need for silver bullets, George,' said Rebus. He

stood there, surrounded by what he supposed would be millions of pounds' worth of damaged works of art, alarm bells ringing, while outside the traffic in central London would be backed up for miles until Trafalgar Square could be opened again.

'I told you it'd be easy,' he said.

Lisa Frazer was fine. Shock, a few bruises, whiplash. The hospital wanted to keep her in overnight, just to be sure. They wanted to keep Rebus in, too, but he refused. They gave him painkillers instead, and three stitches in his stomach. The cut, they said, was fairly superficial, but it was best to be safe. The thread they used was thick and black.

By the time he arrived at Chambers's huge two-storey flat in Islington, the place was crawling with police, forensics, photographers and the usual retinue. The reporters outside were desperate for a quote, some recognising him from the impromptu conference he had given outside the house on Copperplate Street. But he pushed past them and into the Wolfman's lair.

'John, how are you?' It was George Flight, looking bemused by the day's proceedings. He had placed a hand on Rebus's shoulder. Rebus smiled.

'I'm fine, George. What have you found?'

They were standing in the main hall. Flight glanced back into one of the rooms off this hall. 'You won't believe it,' he said. 'I'm still not sure I do.' There was a tang of whisky on Flight's breath. The celebrations had begun already.

Rebus walked to the door and into the room. This was where the photographers and forensics people were busiest. A tall man rose to his feet from behind a sofa and looked across to Rebus. It was Philip Cousins. He smiled and nodded. Near him stood Isobel Penny, sketchbook in hand. But Rebus noticed that she wasn't drawing, and her face

262

had lost all traces of liveliness. Even she, it seemed, could still be shocked.

The scene was certainly shocking. But worst of all was the smell, the smell and the buzzing of flies. One wall was covered in what had been paintings – very crudely done paintings, as even Rebus could tell. But now they had been slashed into tatters, some of which lay across the floor. And on the opposite wall was as much graffiti as would befit any tower block in Churchill Estate. Venomous stuff: FUCK ART. FEEL THE POOR. KILL PIGS. The stuff of madness.

There were two bodies thrown casually behind the sofa, and a third lying under a table, as though some rudimentary effort had been made to tidy them out of sight. Carpet and walls were stained with fine sprays of blood and the cloying smell told Rebus that at least one of the bodies had been here for several days. Easy to confront this now, now that it was at an end. Not so easy to work out the 'why?'. That was what worried Flight.

'I just can't find a motive, John. I mean, Chambers had everything. Why the hell did he need to …? I mean, why would he just …?' They were in the flat's living-room. No clues were being offered up. Chambers's private life seemed as tidy and innocuous as the rest of his home. Just that one room, that one secret corner. That apart, they might have been in any successful barrister's apartment, poring over his books, his desk, his correspondence, his computer files.

It didn't really bother Rebus. It wouldn't bother him supposing they never found out why. He shrugged.

'Wait till the biography's published, George,' said Rebus, 'maybe then you'll get your answer.' Or ask a psychologist, he thought to himself. He didn't doubt there would be plenty of theories.

But Flight was shaking his head, rubbing at his head, his face, his neck. He still couldn't believe it had come to an end. Rebus touched a hand to his arm. Their eyes met. Rebus nodded slowly, then winked.

'You should have been in that Jag, George. It was magic.'

Flight managed to pull a smile out of the air. 'Tell that to the judge,' he said. 'Tell that to the judge.'

Rebus ate that night at George Flight's home, a meal cooked by Marion. So at last they were having the promised dinner together, but it was a fairly sombre occasion, enlivened only by an interview with some art historian on the late-night news. He was talking about the damage to the paintings in the National Gallery's Spanish Room.

'Such pointless waste ... vandalism ... sheer, wanton ... priceless ... perhaps irreparable ... thousands of pounds ... heritage.'

'Blah, blah, blah,' said Flight sneeringly. 'At least you can patch up a bloody painting. These people talk half the time out of their arses.'

'George!'

'Sorry, Marion,' said Flight sheepishly. He glanced towards Rebus, who winked back at him.

Later, after she had gone to bed, the two men sat together drinking a final brandy.

'I've decided to retire,' said Flight. 'Marion's been nagging me for ages. My health's not what it was.'

'Not serious, I hope?'

Flight shook his head. 'No, nothing like that. But there's a security firm, they've offered to take me on. More money, nine till five. You know how it is.'

Rebus nodded. He'd seen some of the best of his elders drawn like moths to a lightbulb when security firms and the like came to call. He drained his glass.

'When will you be leaving?' Flight asked.

'I thought I'd go back tomorrow. I can come back down again when they need me to give evidence.'

Flight nodded. 'Next time you come, we've got a spare bedroom here.'

'Thanks, George.' Rebus rose to his feet.

'I'll drive you back,' said Flight. But Rebus shook his head.

'Call me a cab,' he insisted. 'I don't want you done for D and D. Think what it would do to your pension.'

Flight stared into his brandy glass. 'You've got a point,' he said. 'Okay then, a cab it is.' He slipped a hand into his pocket. 'By the way, I've got you a little present.'

He held the clenched fist out to Rebus, who placed his own open palm beneath it. A slip of paper dropped from Flight's hand into his. Rebus unfolded the note. It was an address. Rebus looked up at Flight and nodded his understanding.

'Thanks, George,' he said.

'No rough stuff, eh, John?'

'No rough stuff,' agreed Rebus.

Family

He slept deeply that night, but woke at six the next morning and sat up in bed immediately. His stomach hurt, a burning sensation as though he had just swallowed a measure of spirits. The doctors had told him not to drink alcohol. Last night he had drunk just the one glass of wine and two glasses of brandy. He rubbed the area around the wound, willing the ache to go away, then took two more painkillers with a glass of tap-water before dressing and putting on his shoes.

His taxi driver, though sleepy, was full of tales of yesterday's action.

'I was on Whitehall, wasn't I? An hour and a quarter in the cab before the traffic got moving again. Hour and a bleedin' quarter. Didn't see the chase either, but I heard the smash.'

Rebus sat back in silence, all the way to the block of flats in Bethnal Green. He paid the driver and looked again at the slip of paper Flight had given him. Number 46, fourth floor, flat six. The elevator smelled of vinegar. A crumpled paper package in one corner was oozing under-cooked chips and a tail-end of batter. Flight was right: it made all the difference having a good network of informers. It made for quick information. But what a good copper's network could get, so too could a good villain's. Rebus hoped he'd be in time.

He walked quickly across the small landing from the open lift to the door of one of the flats where two empty milk bottles stood to attention in a plastic holder. He picked up one bottle and hurried back to the lift just as its doors were shuddering to a close to place the milk bottle in the remaining gap. The doors stayed where they were. So did the lift.

You never knew when a quick getaway would be needed.

Then he walked along the narrow corridor to flat six, braced himself against the wall and kicked at the door-handle with the heel of his shoe. The door flew open and he walked into a stuffy hall. Another door, another kick and he was face to face with Kenny Watkiss.

Watkiss had been asleep on a mattress on the floor. He was standing now, clad only in underpants and shivering, against the furthest wall from the door. He pushed his hair back when he saw who it was.

'Jee-Jesus,' he stammered. 'What are you doing here?'

'Hello, Kenny,' said Rebus, stepping into the room. 'I thought we'd have a little chat.'

'What about?' You didn't get as frightened as Kenny Watkiss was by having your door kicked in at half past six in the morning. You only got that frightened by the idea of *who* was doing it and *why*.

'About Uncle Tommy.'

'Uncle Tommy?' Kenny Watkiss smiled unconvincingly. He moved back to the mattress and started pulling on a pair of torn denims. 'What about him?'

'What are you so scared of, Kenny? Why are you hiding?'

'Hiding?' That smile again. 'Who said I was hiding?'

Rebus shook his head, his own smile one of apparent sympathy. 'I feel sorry for you, Kenny, really I do. I see your kind a hundred times a week. All ambition and no brain. All talk but no guts. I've only been in London a week, and already I know how to find you when I want you.

Do you think Tommy *can't*? You think maybe he'll lay off? No, he's going to nail your head to the wall.'

'Don't talk daft.' Now that he was dressed, having pulled on a black T-shirt, Kenny's voice had lost some of its trembling. But he couldn't hide the look in his eyes, the haunted, hunted look. Rebus decided to make it easy for him. He reached into a pocket and brought out a packet of cigarettes, offered one to Kenny and lit it for him before taking one himself. He rubbed at his stomach. Jesus, it was hurting. He hoped the stitches were holding.

'You've been ripping him off,' Rebus said casually. 'He handled stolen goods, you were his courier, passing it down the chain. But you've been skimming a little off the top, haven't you? And with each job you'd take a little more than he knew about. Why? Saving for that Docklands flat? So you could start your own business? Maybe you got greedy, I don't know. But Tommy got suspicious. You were in court that day because you wanted to see him go down. It was the only thing that could have saved you. When he didn't, you still tried putting one over on him, yelling out from the public gallery. But by then it was only a matter of time. And when you heard that the case had been dropped altogether, well, you knew he'd come straight after you. So you ran. You didn't run far enough, Kenny.'

'What's it to you?' The words were angry. But it was the anger that came of fear. It wasn't directed at Rebus. He was merely the messenger.

'Just this,' Rebus said calmly: 'keep away from Sammy. Don't ever go near her again, don't even try to talk to her. In fact, your best bet right now is to get on a train or a bus or whatever and get the hell out of London. Don't worry, we'll pin Tommy for something sooner or later. Then maybe you can come back.' He had slipped a hand into his pocket again. It came out holding a fold of ten pound notes, four of which he peeled off and threw onto the mattress.

'I'm offering you a one-way ticket, and I'm suggesting you take it right now, this morning.'

The eyes and voice were wary. 'You're not going to take me in?'

'Why should I?'

The smile this time was more confident still. He looked at the money. 'It's just family, Rebus. That's all. I can take care of myself.'

'Can you?' Rebus nodded, taking in the room with its peeling wallpaper and boarded-up window, the mattress with its single rumpled sheet. 'Fair enough.' He turned to go.

'It wasn't just me, you know.'

Rebus stopped but didn't turn. 'What?' He tried not to sound interested.

'There was a copper, too. He was on a cut from the robberies.'

Rebus sucked in air. Did he need to know? Did he *want* to know? Kenny Watkiss didn't give him the choice.

'A detective called Lamb,' he said. Rebus exhaled silently, but, saying nothing, showing nothing, walked back out of the flat and, pulling open the lift doors, kicking away the milk bottle, pressed the button for the ground floor and waited for the slow descent.

Outside the block, he paused to stub out his cigarette. He rubbed at his stomach again. Stupid not to have brought the painkillers with him. From the corner of his eye, he could see the unmarked transit van in the car park. Six forty-five. There could be a perfectly rational explanation for it, for the fact that two men sat stonily in its front seats. They might be about to go to work, mightn't they?

In fact, Rebus knew damned fine that's what they were doing. And he had another choice now. He could let them go to work, or he could stop them. It took him another second or two to decide, but finally, with a picture of

Samantha's face in his head, he walked across nonchalantly to the van and, the men still ignoring his existence, thumped hard on the passenger-side window. The passenger looked at him with undisguised enmity, but, seeing that Rebus was undeterred, rolled down the window.

'Yeah?'

Rebus stuck his ID so far into the man's face that the plastic coating brushed against his nose.

'Police,' he snapped. 'Now get the fuck out of here. And tell Tommy Watkiss we've got his nephew under twenty-four hour watch. Anything happens, we'll know where to come and who to charge.' Rebus stood back and looked carefully at the man. 'Think you can remember all that, or do you want me to write it down?'

The passenger was growling audibly as he rolled the window back up. The driver was already starting the van. As it began to move off, Rebus gave its side a farewell kick. Maybe Kenny would leave and maybe he'd stay. It was up to him. Rebus had given him a chance. Whether the young man took it or not was out of Rebus's hands.

'Like Pontius Pilate,' he mumbled to himself as he made for the main road. Standing by a lamppost, waiting and praying for a black cab to come along, he saw Kenny Watkiss emerge from the flats, a duffel-bag slung across his shoulder, and, looking around him, start to jog towards the far end of the estate. Rebus nodded to himself. 'That's my boy,' he said, as, with protesting brakes, a cab slowed to a halt beside him.

'You're in luck, mate,' said the driver. 'I'm just starting my shift.' Rebus clambered in and gave the name of his hotel, then settled back, enjoying the city at this quiet hour. The driver, though, was in practice for the day ahead.

'Here,' he said, 'did you hear about that rumpus yesterday at Trafalgar Square? I was in a queue for an hour and a half. I mean, I'm all for law and order, but there must've been another way of going about it, mustn't there?'

John Rebus shook his head and laughed.

His suitcase sat closed on the bed beside the little-used briefcase and the bag of books. He was squeezing the last few items into his sports bag when there was a soft tapping at his door.

'Come in.'

She did. She was wearing a solid-foam neck-brace, but grinned it away.

'Isn't it stupid? They want me to wear it for the next few days, but I –' She saw the cases on the bed. 'You're not leaving already?'

Rebus nodded. 'I came here to help with the Wolfman case. The Wolfman case is finished.'

'But what about –'

He turned to her. 'What about us?' he guessed. She lowered her eyes. 'That's a good question, Lisa. You lied to me. You weren't trying to help. You were trying to get your bloody Ph.D.'

'I'm sorry,' she said.

'Me too. I mean, I can understand why you did it, why you think you *had* to do it. Really I can. But that doesn't make it any better.'

She straightened her back and nodded. 'Fair enough then,' she said. 'So, Inspector Rebus, if all I was doing was using you, why did I come here straight from the hospital?'

He zipped shut the bag. It was a good question. 'Because you got found out,' he said.

'No,' she said. 'That was bound to happen eventually. Try again.' He shrugged his shoulders. 'Oh,' she said, sounding disappointed. 'I was hoping you could tell me. I'm not really sure myself.'

He turned towards her again and saw that she was

smiling. She looked so stupid in the neck-brace that he had to return the smile eventually. And when she came towards him he returned her hug, too.

'Ouch!' she said. 'Not too hard, John.'

So he relaxed his muscles a little, and they kept on hugging. He was actually feeling mellow; the painkillers had seen to that.

'Anyway,' he said at last, 'you weren't much help.'

She pulled away from him. He was still smiling, but archly. 'What do you mean?'

'I mean all that stuff we talked about in the restaurant. All those index cards.' Rebus recited the list. 'Thwarted ambition. Victims from a social class above the killer. No confrontation ...' He scratched his chin. 'None of it fits Malcolm Chambers.'

'I wouldn't say that. We've still got to look at his home life, his background.' She sounded defiant rather than merely defensive. 'And I was right about the schizophrenia.'

'So you'll still do your project?'

She tried to nod; it wasn't easy. 'Of course,' she said. 'There's plenty of work to be done on Chambers, believe me. There must be clues there somewhere in his past. He must have left something.'

'Well, let me know what you find out.'

'John. Before he died, did he say anything?'

Rebus smiled. 'Nothing important,' he said. 'Nothing important.'

After she'd gone, after the promises of return trips and of weekends in Edinburgh, promises of postcards and phone calls, he took his luggage down to reception. George Flight was at the desk. Rebus put his key down next to where Flight was signing his name to several forms.

'Do you realise how much this hotel costs?' Flight said,

not looking up. 'Next time you visit, you really will have to bunk at my place.' Then he glanced towards Rebus. 'But I suppose you were worth it.' He finished with the forms and handed them to the receptionist, who checked them before nodding that everything was in order. 'You know the address to send them to,' Flight called back as the two men started towards the hotel's swing-doors.

'I really must get the lock on the boot fixed,' Flight said, shutting the car's back door on Rebus's luggage. Then: 'Where to? King's Cross?'

Rebus nodded. 'With one slight detour,' he said.

The detour, in Flight's words, turned out to be more than slight. They parked across from Rhona's flat in Gideon Park and Flight pulled on the handbrake.

'Going in?' he said. Rebus had been thinking about it, but shook his head. What could he tell Sammy? Nothing that would help. If he said he'd seen Kenny, she'd only accuse him of scaring him off. No, best leave it.

'George,' he said, 'could you maybe have someone drop in and tell her Kenny's left London. But stress that he's okay, that he's not in trouble. I don't want him lingering too long in her memory.'

Flight was nodding. 'I'll do it myself,' he said. 'Have you seen him yet?'

'I went this morning.'

'And?'

'And I was just in time. But I reckon he'll be all right.'

Flight studied the face next to him. 'I *think* I believe you,' he said.

'Just one thing.'

'Yes?'

'Kenny told me one of your men is involved. The baby-faced redneck.'

'Lamb?'

273

'That's the one. He's on Tommy Watkiss's payroll, according to Kenny.'

Flight pursed his lips and was silent for a moment. 'I think I believe that, too,' he said at last, very quietly. 'Don't worry, John. I'll deal with it.'

Rebus said nothing. He was still staring out at the windows of Rhona's flat, willing Sammy to come to one of them and see him. No, not see him, just so that *he* might see *her*. But there was no one at home. The ladies were out for the day with Tim or Tony or Graeme or Ben.

And it was none of Rebus's business anyway.

'Let's go,' he said.

So Flight drove him to King's Cross. Drove him through streets paved with nothing so very different from any other city. Streets ancient and modern, breathing with envy and excitement. And with evil. Not much evil, perhaps. But enough. Evil, after all, was pretty well a constant. He thanked God that it touched so few lives. He thanked God that his friends and family were safe. And he thanked God he was going home.

'What are you thinking about?' Flight asked as they idled at yet another set of traffic lights.

'Nothing,' said Rebus.

He was still thinking about nothing when he boarded the busy Inter City 125, and sat down with his newspapers and his magazines. As the train was about to move off, someone squeezed into the seat opposite him and deposited four large cans of strong lager on the table. The youth was tall and hard-looking with shorn hair. He glared at Rebus and turned up his personal cassette player. Tscchh-tscchh-tscchh it went, so loud Rebus could almost make out the words. The youth was grasping a ticket denoting Edinburgh as his destination. He put the ticket down and pulled on a ring-pull. Rebus shook his head wearily and smiled.

His own personal hell. As the train pulled away, he caught its rhythm and beat that rhythm out silently in his head.

FYTP
FYTP
FYTP
FYTP
FYTP
FYTP

All the way home.

Acknowledgements

Thanks for help with facts, figures, psychopaths and garden paths (*viz* leading the reader up the . . .) go to the following:

In London: Dr S. Adams, Ms Fiona Campbell, Chris Thomas, Mr Andrew Walker, the officers of Tottenham Police Station

In Newmarket: L. Rodgers

In Edinburgh: Professor J. Curt, Ms Alison Girdwood

In Fife: Mr & Mrs Colin Stevenson

In Glasgow: Alex Blair

In Canada: Mr Tiree Macgregor, Dr D. W. Nichol

In the USA: Dr David Martin, Ms Rebecca Hughes

Suggested further reading:

Elliott Leyton, *Hunting Humans* (Penguin)

Clive R. Hollin, *Psychology and Crime* (Routledge)

Professor Keith Simpson, *Forty Years of Murder* (Grafton)

Martin Fido, *Murder Guide to London* (Weidenfeld)

R. M. Holmes & J. DeBurger, *Serial Murder* (Sage)

R. H. C. Bull *et al.*, *Psychology for Police Officers* (Wiley)

David Canter, 'To Catch a Rapist', *New Society*, 4 March 1988

David Canter, 'Offender Profiles', *The Psychologist*, Vol 2, No 1, January 1989

StripJack

Acknowledgements

The first thing to acknowledge is that the constituency of North and South Esk is the author's creation. However, you don't need to be Mungo Park to work out that there must be some correlation between North and South Esk and the real world, Edinburgh being a real place, and 'south and east of Edinburgh' being a vaguely definable geographical area.

In fact, North and South Esk bears *some* resemblance to the Midlothian parliamentary constituency – prior to 1983's Boundary Commission changes – but also bites a small southernmost chunk out of the present Edinburgh Pentlands constituency and a westerly chunk out of East Lothian constituency.

Gregor Jack, too, is fiction, and bears no resemblance to any MP.

Thanks are due to the following for their inestimable help: Alex Eadie, who was until his retirement the MP for Midlothian; John Home Robertson MP; Professor Busuttil, Regius Professor of Forensic Medicine, University of Edinburgh; Lothian and Borders Police; City of Edinburgh Police; the staff of the Edinburgh Room, Edinburgh Central Library; the staff of the National Library of Scotland; staff and customers of Sandy Bell's, the Oxford Bar, Mather's (West End), Clark's Bar and the Green Tree.

Contents

To the only Jack I've ever stripped

He knows nothing; and he thinks he knows everything. That points clearly to a political career.

Shaw, *Major Barbara*

The habit of friendship is matured by constant intercourse.

Libianus, 4th century AD, quoted in *Edinburgh*, by Charles McKean

1
The Milking Shed

The wonder of it was that the neighbours hadn't complained, hadn't even – as many of them later told the newsmen – realized. Not until that night, the night their sleep was disturbed by sudden activity in the street. Cars, vans, policemen, the static chatter of radios. Not that the noise ever got out of hand. The whole operation was directed with such speed and, yes, even good humour that there were those who slept through the excitement.

'I want courtesy,' Chief Superintendent 'Farmer' Watson had explained to his men in the briefing room that evening. 'It may be a hoor-hoose, but it's on the right side of town, if you take my meaning. No telling who might be in there. We might even come across our own dear Chief Constable.'

Watson grinned, to let them know he was joking. But some of the officers in the room, knowing the CC better than Watson himself apparently did, exchanged glances and wry smiles.

'Right,' said Watson, 'let's go through the plan of attack one more time . . .'

Christ, he's loving this, thought Detective Inspector John Rebus. He's loving every minute. And why not? This was Watson's baby after all, and it was to be a home birth. Which was to say, Watson was going to be in charge all the way from immaculate conception to immaculate delivery.

Maybe it was a male menopause thing, this need to flex a bit of muscle. Most of the chief supers Rebus had known in his twenty years on the force had been content to push pens over paper and wait for retirement day. But not Watson. Watson was like Channel Four: full of independent programmes of minority interest. He didn't make waves exactly, but by Christ he splashed like hell.

And now he even seemed to have an informer, an invisible somebody who had whispered in his ear the word 'brothel'. Sin and debauchery! Watson's hard Presbyterian heart had been stirred to righteous indignation. He was the kind of Highland Christian who found sex within marriage just about acceptable – his son and daughter were proof – but who baulked at anything and everything else. If there was an active brothel in Edinburgh, Watson wanted it shut down with prejudice.

But then the informer had provided an address, and this caused a certain hesitation. The brothel was in one of the better streets of the New Town, quiet Georgian terraces, lined with trees and Saabs and Volvos, the houses filled with professional people: lawyers, surgeons, university professors. This was no seaman's bawdy-house, no series of damp, dark rooms above a dockside pub. This was, as Rebus himself had offered, an Establishment establishment. Watson hadn't seen the joke.

Watch had been kept for several days and nights, courtesy of unmarked cars and unremarkable plainclothes men. Until there could be little doubt: whatever was happening inside the shuttered rooms, it was happening after midnight and it was happening briskly. Interestingly, few of the many men arrived by car. But a watchful detective constable, taking a leak in the dead of night, discovered why. The men were parking their cars in side streets and walking the hundred yards or so to the front door of the four-storey house. Perhaps this was house policy: the slamming of after-hours car doors would arouse suspicion in the street. Or perhaps it was in the visitors' own interests not to leave their cars in broad street-light, where they might be recognized . . .

Registration numbers were taken and checked, as were photographs of visitors to the house. The owner of the house itself was traced. He owned half a French vineyard as well as several properties in Edinburgh, and lived in Bordeaux the year through. His solicitor had been responsible for letting the house to a Mrs Croft, a very genteel lady in her fifties. According to the solicitor, she paid her rent promptly and in cash. Was there any problem . . . ?

No problem, he was assured, but if he could keep the conversation to himself . . .

Meantime, the car owners had turned out to be businessmen, some local, but the majority visiting the city from south of the border. Heartened by this, Watson had started planning the raid. With his usual blend of wit and acumen, he chose to call it Operation Creeper.

'Brothel creepers, you see, John.'

'Yes sir,' Rebus answered. 'I used to own a pair myself. I've often wondered how they got the name.'

Watson shrugged. He was not a man to be sidetracked. 'Never mind the creepers,' he said. 'Let's just get the creeps.'

The house, it was reckoned, would be doing good business by midnight. One o'clock Saturday morning was chosen as the time of the raid. The warrants were ready. Every man in the team knew his place. And the solicitor had even come up with plans of the house, which had been memorized by the officers.

'It's a bloody warren,' Watson had said.

'No problem, sir, so long as we've got enough ferrets.'

In truth, Rebus wasn't looking forward to this evening's work. Brothels might be illegal, but they fulfilled a need and if they veered towards respectability, as this one certainly did, then what was the problem? He could see some of this doubt reflected in Watson's eyes. But Watson had been enthusiastic from the first, and to pull back now was unthinkable, would seem a sign of weakness. So, with nobody really keen for it, Operation Creeper went ahead. While other, meaner streets went unpatrolled. While domestic violence took its toll. While the Water of Leith drowning still remained to be solved . . .

'Okay, in we go.'

They left their cars and vans and marched towards the

3

front door. Knocked quietly. The door was opened from within, and then things began to move like a video on double-speed. Other doors were opened ... how many doors could a house have? Knock first, then open. Yes, they were being courteous.

'If you wouldn't mind getting dressed, please ...'

'If you could just come downstairs now ...'

'You can put your trousers on first, sir, if you like ...'

Then: 'Christ, sir, come and take a look at this.' Rebus followed the flushed, youthful face of the detective constable. 'Here we are, sir. Feast your peepers on this lot.'

Ah yes, the punishment room. Chains and thongs and whips. A couple of full-length mirrors, a wardrobe full of gear.

'There's more leather here than in a bloody milking shed.'

'You seem to know a lot about cows, son,' Rebus said. He was just thankful the room wasn't in use. But there were more surprises to come.

In parts, the house resembled nothing more lewd than a fancy-dress party – nurses and matrons, wimples and high heels. Except that most of the costumes revealed more than they hid. One young woman seemed to be wearing a rubber diving suit with the nipples and crotch cut away. Another looked like a cross between Heidi and Eva Braun. Watson watched the parade, righteous fury filling him. He had no doubts now: it was absolutely proper that this sort of place be closed down. Then he turned back to the conversation he was having with Mrs Croft, while Chief Inspector Lauderdale lingered only a short distance away. He had insisted on coming along, knowing his superior and fearing some almighty cock-up. Well, thought Rebus with a smile, no cock-ups in sight yet.

Mrs Croft spoke in a kind of gentrified Cockney, which became less gentrified as time went on and more couples spilled down the stairs and into the large, sofa-crammed living room. A room smelling of expensive perfume and proprietary whisky. Mrs Croft was denying everything. She was even denying that they were standing in a brothel at all.

4

I am not my brothel's keeper, thought Rebus. All the same, he had to admire her performance. She was a business-woman, she kept saying, a taxpayer, she had rights . . . and where was her solicitor?

'I thought it was her that was doing the soliciting,' Lauderdale muttered to Rebus: a rare moment of humour from one of the dourest buggers Rebus had ever worked with. And as such, it deserved a smile.

'What are you grinning at? I didn't know there was an interval. Get back to work.'

'Yes, sir.' Rebus waited till Lauderdale had turned away from him, the better to hear what Watson was saying, and then flicked a quick v-sign at him. Mrs Croft, though, caught the gesture and, perhaps thinking it intended at her, returned it. Lauderdale and Watson both turned towards where Rebus was standing, but by then he was already on his way . . .

Officers who had been posted in the back garden now marched a few pale-faced souls back into the house. One man had leapt from a first-floor window, and was hobbling as a result. But he was insistent, too, that no doctor was necess-ary, that no ambulance be called. The women seemed to find the whole thing amusing, and appeared especially taken by the looks on their clients' faces, looks ranging from the ashamed and embarrassed to the furious and embarrassed. There was some short-lived bravado of the I-know-my-rights variety. But in the main, everybody did as they were told: that is, they shut up and tried to be patient.

Some of the shame and embarrassment started to lift when one of the men recalled that it wasn't illegal to visit a brothel; it was only illegal to run one or work in one. And this was true, though it didn't mean the men present were going to escape into the anonymous night. Give them a scare first, then send them away. Starve the brothels of clients, and you'd have no brothels. That was the logic. So the officers were prepared with their usual stories, the ones they used with kerb-crawlers and the like.

'Just a quiet word, sir, between you and me, like. If I were you, I'd have myself checked over for AIDS. I'm serious. Most of these women could well be carrying the disease, even if it doesn't show. Mostly, it doesn't show till it's too late anyway. Are you married, sir? Any girlfriends? Best tell them to have a test, too. Otherwise, you never know, do you . . .?'

It was cruel stuff, but necessary; and as with most cruel words, there was a truth to it. Mrs Croft seemed to use a small back room as an office. A cash-box was found. So was a credit-card machine. A receipt-book was headed Crofter Guest House. As far as Rebus could tell, the cost of a single room was seventy-five pounds. Dear for a B&B, but how many company accountants would take the trouble to check? It wouldn't surprise Rebus if the place was VAT registered to boot . . .

'Sir?' It was Detective Sergeant Brian Holmes, newly promoted and bristling with efficiency. He was halfway up one of the flights of stairs, and calling down to Rebus. 'I think you better come up here . . .'

Rebus wasn't keen. Holmes looked to be a long way up, and Rebus, who lived on the second floor of a tenement, had a natural antipathy to stairs. Edinburgh, of course, was full of them, just as it was full of hills, biting winds, and people who liked to girn about things like hills and stairs and the wind . . .

'Coming.'

Outside a bedroom door, a detective constable stood in quiet discussion with Holmes. When Holmes saw Rebus reaching the landing, he dismissed the DC.

'Well, Sergeant?'

'Take a look, sir.'

'Anything you want to tell me first?'

Holmes shook his head. 'You've seen the male member before, sir, haven't you?'

Rebus opened the bedroom door. What was he expecting to find? A mock-up dungeon, with someone stretched out naked on the rack? A farmyard scene with a few chickens and sheep? The male member. Maybe Mrs Croft had a collection of them displayed on her bedroom wall. *And here's*

6

one I caught in '73. Put up a tough fight, but I had it in the end . . .

But no, it was worse than that. Much worse. It was an ordinary bedroom, albeit with red lightbulbs in its several lamps. And in an ordinary bed lay an ordinary enough looking woman, her elbow pressed into the pillow, head resting at an angle on her clenched fist. And on that bed, dressed and staring at the floor, sat someone Rebus recognized: the Member of Parliament for North and South Esk.

'Jesus Christ,' said Rebus. Holmes put his head round the door.

'I can't work in front of a fucking audience!' yelled the woman. Her accent, Rebus noted, was English. Holmes ignored her.

'This is a bit of a coincidence,' he said to Gregor Jack MP. 'Only, my girlfriend and me have just moved into your constituency.'

The MP raised his eyes more in sorrow than in anger.

'This is a mistake,' he said. 'A terrible mistake.'

'Just doing a bit of canvassing, eh, sir?'

The woman had begun to laugh, head still resting on her hand. The red lamplight seemed to fill her gaping mouth. Gregor Jack looked for a moment as though he might be about to throw a punch in her general direction. Instead he tried a slap with his open hand, but succeeded only in catching her arm, so that her head fell back on to the pillow. She was still laughing, almost girl-like. She lifted her legs high into the air, the bedcovers falling away. Her hands thumped the mattress with glee. Jack had risen to his feet and was scratching nervously at one finger.

'Jesus Christ,' Rebus said again. Then: 'Come on, let's get you downstairs.'

Not the Farmer. The Farmer might go to pieces. Lauderdale then. Rebus approached with as much humility as he could muster.

'Sir, we've got a bit of a problem.'

'I know. It must have been that bugger Watson. Wanted

7

his moment of glory captured. He's always been keen on publicity, you should know that.' Was that a sneer on Lauderdale's face? With his gaunt figure and bloodless face, he reminded Rebus of a painting he'd once seen of some Calvinists or Seceders ... some grim bunch like that. Ready to burn anyone who came to hand. Rebus kept his distance, all the time shaking his head.

'I'm not sure I – '

'The bloody papers are here,' hissed Lauderdale. 'Quick off the mark, eh? Even for our friends in the press. Bloody Watson must have tipped them off. He's out there now. I tried to stop him.'

Rebus went to one of the windows and peeped out. Sure enough, there were three or four reporters gathered at the bottom of the steps up to the front door. Watson had finished his spiel and was answering a couple of questions, at the same time retreating slowly back up the steps.

'Oh dear,' Rebus said, admiring his own sense of understatement. 'That only makes it worse.'

'Makes what worse?'

So Rebus told him. And was rewarded with the biggest smile he'd ever seen flit across Lauderdale's face.

'Well, well, who's been a naughty boy then? But I still don't see the problem.'

Rebus shrugged. 'Well, sir, it's just that it doesn't do anyone any good.' Outside, the vans were arriving. Two to take the women to the station, two to take the men. The men would be asked a few questions, names and addresses taken, then released. The women ... well, that was another thing entirely. There would be charges. Rebus's colleague Gill Templer would call it another sign of the phallocentric society, something like that. She'd never been the same since she'd got her hands on those psychology books ...

'Nonsense,' Lauderdale was saying. 'He's only got himself to blame. What do you want us to do? Sneak him out the back door with a blanket over his head?'

'No, sir, it's just – '

8

'He gets treated the same as the rest of them, Inspector. You know the score.'

'Yes, sir, but – '

'But what?'

But what? Well, that was the question. What? Why was Rebus feeling so uncomfortable? The answer was complicatedly simple: because it *was* Gregor Jack. Most MPs, Rebus wouldn't have given the time of day. But Gregor Jack was ... well, he was *Gregor Jack*.

'Vans are here, Inspector. Let's round 'em up and ship 'em out.'

Lauderdale's hand on his back was cold and firm.

'Yes, sir,' said Rebus.

So it was out into the cool dark night, lit by orange sodium lights, the glare of headlamps, and the dimmer light from open doors and twitching windows. The natives were restless. Some had come out on to their doorsteps, wrapped in paisley dressing gowns or wearing hastily found clothes, not quite hanging right.

Police, natives, and of course the reporters. Flash-guns. Christ, there were photographers too, of course. No camera crews, no video machines. That was something: Watson hadn't persuaded the TV companies to attend his little soirée.

'Into the van, quick as you can,' called Brian Holmes. Was that a new firmness, a new authority in his voice? Funny what promotion could do to the young. But by God they *were* quick. Not so much following Holmes' orders, Rebus knew, as keen to escape the cameras. One or two of the women posed, trying a lopsided glamour learned from page three, before being persuaded by WPCs that this was neither the time nor the place.

But the reporters were hanging back. Rebus wondered why. Indeed, he wondered what they were doing here at all. Was it such a big story? Would it provide Watson with useful publicity? One reporter even grabbed at a photographer's arm and seemed to warn him about shooting off too many pictures. But now they were keening, now they were shouting. And the flashbulbs were going off like flak. All because

9

they'd recognized a face. All because Gregor Jack was being escorted down the steps, across the narrow pavement, and into a van.

'Christ, it's Gregor Jack!'

'Mr Jack! A word!'

'Any comment to make?'

'What were you doing – '

'Any comment?'

The doors were closing. A thump with the constabulary hand on the side of the van, and it moved slowly away, the reporters jogging after it. Well, Rebus had to admit it: Jack had held his head high. No, that wasn't being accurate. He had, rather, held his head just low enough, suggesting penitence but not shame, humility but not embarrassment.

'Seven days he's been my MP,' Holmes was saying by Rebus's side. 'Seven days.'

'You must have been a bad influence on him, Brian.'

'Bit of a shock though, wasn't it?'

Rebus shrugged noncommittally. The woman from the bedroom was being brought out now, having pulled on jeans and a t-shirt. She saw the reporters and suddenly lifted the t-shirt high over her naked breasts.

'Get a load of this then!'

But the reporters were busy comparing notes, the photographers loading new film. They'd be off to the station next, ready to catch Gregor Jack as he left. Nobody paid her any attention, and eventually she let her t-shirt fall back down and climbed into the waiting van.

'He's not choosy, is he?' said Holmes.

'But then again, Brian,' answered Rebus, 'maybe he is.'

Watson was rubbing at his gleaming forehead. It was a lot of work for only one hand, since the forehead seemed to extend as far as Watson's crown.

'Mission accomplished,' he said. 'Well done.'

'Thank you, sir,' Holmes said smartly.

'No problems then?'

'Not at all, sir,' said Rebus casually. 'Unless you count Gregor Jack.'

Watson nodded, then frowned. 'Who?' he asked.

'Brian here can tell you all about him, sir,' said Rebus, patting Holmes' back. 'Brian's your man for anything smacking of politics.'

Watson, hovering now somewhere between elation and dread, turned to Holmes.

'Politics?' he asked. He was smiling. *Please be gentle with me.*

Holmes watched Rebus moving back inside the house. He felt like sobbing. Because, after all, that's what John Rebus was – an s.o.b.

2
Scratching the Surface

It is a truth universally acknowledged that some Members of Parliament have trouble keeping their trousers on. But Gregor Jack was not thought to be one of these. Indeed, he often eschewed troose altogether, opting for the kilt on election nights and at many a public function. In London, he took the jibes in good part, his responses matching the old questions with the accuracy of catechism.

'Tell us now, Gregor, what's worn beneath the kilt?'

'Oh nothing, nothing at all. It's all in perfect working order.'

Gregor Jack was not a member of the SNP, though he had flirted with the party in his youth. He *had* joined the Labour Party, but had resigned for never specified reasons. He was not a Liberal Democrat, nor was he that rare breed – a Scots Tory MP. Gregor Jack was an Independent, and as an Independent had held the seat of North and South Esk, south and east of Edinburgh, since his mildly surprising by-election win of 1985. 'Mild' was an adjective often used about Jack. So were 'honest', 'legal' and 'decent'.

All this John Rebus knew from memory, from old newspapers, magazines and radio interviews. There had to be something wrong with the man, some chink in his shining armour. Trust Operation Creeper to find the flaw. Rebus scanned the Saturday newsprint, seeking a story. He didn't find it. Curious that; the press had seemed keen enough last night. A story breaking at one thirty ... plenty of time, surely, to see it into print by the final morning edition. Unless, of course, the reporters hadn't been local. But they must have been, mustn't they? Having said which, he hadn't recognized any faces. Did Watson really have the front to get the London papers involved? Rebus smiled. The man had plenty of 'front' all right: his wife saw to that. Three meals a day, three courses each.

'Feed the body,' Watson was fond of saying, 'and you feed the spirit.' Something like that. Which was another thing: bible-basher or no, Watson was starting to put away a fair amount of spirits. A rosy glow to the cheeks and chins, and the unmistakable scent of extra-strong mints. When Lauderdale walked into his superior's room these days, he sniffed and sniffed, like a bloodhound. Only it wasn't blood he was sniffing, it was promotion.

Lose a Farmer, gain a Fart.

The nickname had perhaps been unavoidable. Word association. Lauderdale became Fort Lauderdale, and Fort quickly turned into Fart. Oh, but it was an apt name, too. For wherever Chief Inspector Lauderdale went, he left a bad smell. Take the Case of the Lifted Literature. Rebus had known the minute Lauderdale walked into his office that there would soon be a need to open the windows.

'I want you to stick close to this one, John. Professor Costello is highly thought of, an international figure in this field . . .'

'And?'

'And,' Lauderdale tried to look as though his next utterance meant nothing to him, 'he's a close personal friend of Chief Superintendent Watson.'

'Ah.'

'What is this – Monosyllable Week?'

'Monosyllable?' Rebus frowned. 'Sorry, sir, I'll have to ask DS Holmes what that means.'

'Don't try to be funny – '

'I'm not, sir, honest. It's just that DS Holmes has had the benefit of a university education. Well . . . five months' worth or thereabouts. He'd be the very man to coordinate the officers working on this highly sensitive case.'

13

Lauderdale stared at the seated figure for what seemed – to Rebus at least – a very long time. God, was the man really that stupid? Did no one appreciate irony these days?

'Look,' Lauderdale said at last, 'I need someone a bit more senior than a recently promoted DS. And I'm sorry to say that you, Inspector, God help us all, are that bit more senior.'

'You're flattering me, sir.'

A file landed with a dull thud on Rebus's desk. The chief inspector turned and left. Rebus rose from his chair and turned to his sash window, tugging at it with all his might. But the thing was stuck tight. There was no escape. With a sigh, he turned back and sat down at his desk. Then he opened the folder.

It was a straightforward case of theft. Professor James Aloysius Costello was Professor of Divinity at the University of Edinburgh. One day someone had walked into his office, then walked out again taking with them several rare books. Priceless, according to the Professor, though not to the city's various booksellers and auction rooms. The list seemed eclectic: an early edition of Knox's *Treatise on Predestination*, a couple of Sir Walter Scott first editions, Swedenborg's *Wisdom of Angels*, a signed early edition of *Tristram Shandy*, and editions of Montaigne and Voltaire.

None of which meant much to Rebus until he saw the estimates at auction, provided by one of the George Street auction houses. The question then was: what were they doing in an unlocked office in the first place?

'To be read,' answered Professor Costello blithely. 'To be enjoyed, admired. What good would they be locked up in a safe or in some old library display case?'

'Did anyone else know about them? I mean, about how valuable they are?'

The Professor shrugged. 'I had thought, Inspector, that I was amongst friends.'

He had a voice like a peat bog and eyes that gleamed like crystal. A Dublin education, but a life spent, as he put it, 'cloistered' in the likes of Cambridge, Oxford, St Andrews, and now Edinburgh. A life spent collecting books, too. Those left in his office – still kept unlocked – were worth at least as much as the stolen volumes, perhaps more.

'They say lightning never strikes twice,' he assured Rebus.

'Maybe not, but villains do. Try to lock your door when you step out, eh, sir? If nothing else.'

The Professor had shrugged. Was this, Rebus wondered, a kind of stoicism? He felt nervous sitting there in the office in Buccleuch Place. For one thing, he was a kind of Christian himself, and would have liked to be able to talk the subject through with this wise-seeming man. *Wise?* Well, perhaps not worldly-wise, not wise enough to know how snib locks and human minds worked, but wise in other ways. But Rebus was nervous, too, because he knew himself for a clever man who could have been cleverer, given the breaks. He had never gone to university, and never would. He wondered how different he would be if he had or could . . .

The Professor was staring out of his window, down on to the cobblestoned street. On one side of Buccleuch Place sat a row of neat tenements, owned by the university and used by various departments. The Professor called it Botany Bay. And across the road uglier shapes reared up, the modern stone mausoleums of the main university complex. If this side of the road was Botany Bay, Rebus was all for transportation.

He left the Professor to his muses and musings. Had the books been filched at random? Or was this designer theft, the thief stealing to order? There might well be unscrupulous collectors who would pay – no questions asked – for an early *Tristram Shandy*. Though the authors' names had rung bells, only that particular title had meant anything to Rebus. He owned a paperback copy of the book, bought at a car-boot sale on The Meadows for tenpence. Maybe the Professor would like to borrow it . . .

And so the Case of the Lifted Literature had, for Inspector John Rebus, begun. The ground had been covered before, as the case-notes showed, but it could be covered again. There were the auction houses, the bookshops, the private collectors . . . all to be talked to. And all to satisfy an unlikely friendship between a police chief superintendent and a professor of

Divinity. A waste of time, of course. The books had disappeared the previous Tuesday. It was now Saturday, and they would doubtless be under lock and key in some dark and secret corner.

What a way to spend a Saturday. Actually, if the time had been his own, this would have been a nice afternoon, which was perhaps why he hadn't balked at the task. Rebus collected books. Well, that was putting it strongly. He *bought* books. Bought more of them than he had time to read, attracted by this cover or that title or the fact that he'd heard good things about the author. No, on second thoughts it was just as well these were business calls he was making, otherwise he'd be bankrupting himself in record time.

In any case, he didn't have books on his mind. He kept thinking about a certain MP. Was Gregor Jack married? Rebus thought so. Hadn't there been some big society wedding several years previous? Well, married men were bread and butter to prostitutes. They just gobbled them up. Shame though, about Jack. Rebus had always respected the man – which was to say, now that he thought about it, that he'd been taken in by Jack's public image. But it wasn't all image, was it? Jack really had come from a working-class background, had clawed his way upwards, and *was* a good MP. North and South Esk was difficult territory, part mining villages, part country homes. Jack seemed to glide easily between the two hemispheres. He'd managed to get an ugly new road rerouted well away from his well-heeled constituents, but had also fought hard to bring new high-tech industry to the area, retraining the miners so that they could do the jobs.

Too good to be true. Too bloody good to be true . . .

Bookshops. He had to keep his mind on bookshops. There were only a few to check, the ones that had not been open earlier in the week. Footwork really, the stuff he should have been doling out to more junior men. But all that meant was that he'd feel bound to come round after them, double checking what they'd done. This way, he saved himself some grief.

Buccleuch Street was an odd mixture of grimy junk shops and bright vegetarian takeaways. Student turf. Not far from Rebus's own flat, yet he seldom ventured into this part of town. Only on business. Only ever on business.

Ah, this was it. Suey Books. And for once the shop looked to be open. Even in the spring sunshine there was a need for a light inside. It was a tiny shop, boasting an unenthusiastic window display of old hardbacks, mostly with a Scottish theme. An enormous black cat had made a home for itself in the centre of the display, and blinked slowly if malignly up at Rebus. The window itself needed washing. You couldn't make out the titles of the books without pressing your nose to the glass, and this was made difficult by the presence of an old black bicycle resting against the front of the shop. Rebus pushed open the door. If anything, the shop's interior was less pristine than its exterior. There was a bristle-mat just inside the door. Rebus made a note to wipe his feet before he went back into the street . . .

The shelves, a few of them glass-fronted, were crammed, and the smell was of old relatives' houses, of attics and the insides of school desks. The aisles were narrow. Hardly enough room to swing a . . . There was a thump somewhere behind him, and he feared one of the books had fallen, but when he turned he saw that it was the cat. It swerved past him and made for the desk situated to the rear of the shop, the desk with a bare lightbulb dangling above it.

'Anything in particular you're looking for?'

She was seated at the desk, a pile of books in front of her. She held a pencil in one hand and appeared to be writing prices on the inside leaves of the books. From a distance, it was a scene out of Dickens. Close up was a different story. Still in her teens, she had hennaed her short spiked hair. The eyes behind the circular tinted glasses were themselves round and dark, and she sported three earrings in either ear, with another curling from her left nostril. Rebus didn't doubt she'd have a pale boyfriend with lank dreadlocks and a whippet on a length of clothes-rope.

'I'm looking for the manager,' he said.

'He's not here. Can I help?'

Rebus shrugged, his eyes on the cat. It had leapt silently on to the desk and was now rubbing itself against the books. The girl held her pencil out towards it, and the cat brushed the tip with its jaw.

'Inspector Rebus,' said Rebus. 'I'm interested in some stolen books. I was wondering if anyone had been in trying to sell them.'

'Do you have a list?'

Rebus did. He drew it out of his pocket and handed it over. 'You can keep it,' he said. 'Just in case.'

She glanced down the typed list of titles and editions, her lips pursed.

'I don't think Ronald could afford them, even if he was tempted.'

'Ronald being the manager?'

'That's right. Where were they stolen from?'

'Round the corner in Buccleuch Place.'

'Round the corner? They'd hardly be likely to bring them here then, would they?'

Rebus smiled. 'True,' he said, 'but we have to check.'

'Well, I'll hang on to this anyway,' she said, folding the list. As she pushed it into a desk drawer, Rebus reached out a hand and stroked the cat. Like lightning, a paw flicked up and caught his wrist. He drew back his hand with a sharp intake of breath.

'Oh dear,' said the girl. 'Rasputin's not very good with strangers.'

'So I see.' Rebus studied his wrist. There were inch-long claw marks there, three of them. Whitened scratches, they were already rising, the skin swelling and breaking. Beads of blood appeared. 'Jesus,' he said, sucking on the damaged wrist. He glared at the cat. It glared back, then dropped from the desk and was gone.

'Are you all right?'

'Just about. You should keep that thing on a chain.'

She smiled. 'Do you know anything about that raid last night?'

Rebus blinked, still sucking. 'What raid?'

'I heard the police raided a brothel.'

'Oh?'

'I heard they caught an MP, Gregor Jack.'

'Oh?'

She smiled again. 'Word gets about.' Rebus thought, not for the first time, I don't live in a city, I live in a bloody village . . .

'I just wondered,' the girl was saying, 'if you knew anything about it. I mean, if it's true. I mean, if it is . . .' she sighed. 'Poor Beggar.'

Rebus frowned now.

'That's his nickname,' she explained. 'Beggar. That's what Ronald calls him.'

'Your boss knows Mr Jack then?'

'Oh yes, they were at school together. Beggar owns half of this.' She waved a hand around her, as though she were proprietress of some Princes Street department store. She saw that the policeman didn't seem impressed. 'We do a lot of business behind the scenes,' she said defensively. 'A lot of buying and selling. It might not look much, but this place is a goldmine.'

Rebus nodded. 'Actually,' he said, 'now that you mention it, it *does* look a bit like a mine.' His wrist was crackling now, as though stung by nettles. Bloody cat. 'Right, keep an eye out for those books, won't you?'

She didn't answer. Hurt, he didn't doubt, by the 'mine' jibe. She was opening a book, ready to pencil in a price. Rebus nodded to himself, walked to the door, and rubbed his feet noisily on the mat before leaving the shop. The cat was back in the window, licking its tail.

'Fuck you too, pal,' muttered Rebus. Pets, after all, were his pet hate.

Dr Patience Aitken had pets. Too many pets. Tiny tropical fish . . . a tame hedgehog in the back garden . . . two budgies in a cage in the living room . . . and, yes, a cat. A stray which, to Rebus's relief, still liked to spend much of its time on the prowl. It was a tortoiseshell and it was called Lucky. It liked Rebus.

'It's funny,' Patience had said, 'how they always seem to go for the people who don't like them, don't want them, or are allergic to them. Don't ask me why.'

As she said this, Lucky was climbing across Rebus's shoulders. He snarled and shrugged it off. It fell to the floor, landing on its feet.

'You've got to have patience, John.'

Yes, she was right. If he did not have patience, he might lose Patience. So he'd been trying. He'd been trying. Which was perhaps why he'd been tricked into trying to stroke Rasputin. *Rasputin*! Why was it pets always seemed to be called either Lucky, Goldie, Beauty, Flossie, Spot, or else Rasputin, Beelzebub, Fang, Nirvana, Bodhisattva? Blame the breed of owner.

Rebus was in the Rutherford, nursing a half of eight-shilling and watching the full-time scores on TV, when he remembered that he was expected at Brian Holmes' new house this evening, expected for a meal with Holmes and Nell Stapleton. He groaned. Then remembered that his only clean suit was at Patience Aitken's flat. It was a worrying fact. Was he *really* moving in with Patience? He seemed to be spending an awful lot of time there these days. Well, he liked her, even if she did treat him like yet another pet. And he liked her flat. He even liked the fact that it was underground.

Well, not quite underground. In some parts of town, it might once have been described as the 'basement' flat, but in Oxford Terrace, well-appointed Oxford Terrace, Stockbridge's Oxford Terrace, it was a *garden* flat. And sure enough it had a garden, a narrow isosceles triangle of land. But the flat itself was what interested Rebus. It was like a shelter, like a children's encampment. You could stand in either of the front bedrooms and stare up out of the window to where feet and legs moved along the pavement above you. People seldom looked down. Rebus, whose own flat was on the second floor of a Marchmont tenement, enjoyed this new perspective. While other men his age were moving out of the city and into bungalows, Rebus found a sort of amused thrill from walking *downstairs* to the front door instead of walking *up*. More than novelty, it was a reversal, a major shift, and his life felt full of promise as a result.

Patience, too, was full of promise. She was keen for him to move more of his things in, to 'make himself at home'. And she had given him a key. So, beer finished, and car persuaded to make the five-minute trip, he was able to let himself in. His suit, newly cleaned, was lying on the bed in the spare bedroom. So was Lucky. In fact, Lucky was lying on the suit, was rolling on it, plucking at it with his claws, was shedding on it and marking it. Rebus saw Rasputin in his mind's eye as he swiped the cat off the bed. Then he picked up the suit and took it to the bathroom, where he locked the door behind him before running a bath.

The parliamentary constituency of North and South Esk was large but not populous. The population, however, was growing. New housing estates grew in tight clusters on the outskirts of the mining towns and villages. Commuter belt. Yes, the region was changing. New roads, new railway stations even. New kinds of people doing new kinds of jobs. Brian Holmes and Nell Stapleton, however, had chosen to buy an old terraced house in the heart of one of the smallest of the villages, Eskwell. Actually, it was all about Edinburgh in the end. The city was growing, spreading out. It was the city that swallowed villages and spawned new estates. People weren't moving *into* Edinburgh; the city was moving into *them* . . .

But by the time Rebus reached Eskwell he was in no mood to contemplate the changing face of country living. He'd had trouble starting the car. He was *always* having trouble starting the car. But wearing a suit and shirt and tie had made it that bit more difficult to tinker beneath the bonnet. One fine weekend he'd strip the engine down. Of course he would. Then he'd give up and phone for a tow truck.

The house was easy to find, Eskwell boasting one main street and only a few back roads. Rebus walked up the garden path and stood on the doorstep, a bottle of wine gripped in one hand. He clenched his free fist and rapped on the door. It opened almost at once.

'You're late,' said Brian Holmes.

'Perogative of rank, Brian. I'm allowed to be late.'

Holmes ushered him into the hall. 'I did say informal, didn't I?'

Rebus puzzled for a moment, then saw that this was a comment on his suit. He noticed now that Holmes himself was dressed in open-necked shirt and denims, with a pair of moccasins covering his bare feet.

'Ah,' said Rebus.

'Never mind, I'll nip upstairs and change.'

'Not on my account. This is your house, Brian. You do as you please.'

Holmes nodded to himself, suddenly looking pleased. Rebus was right: this *was* his house. Well, the mortgage was his . . . *half* the mortgage. 'Go on through,' he said, gesturing to a door at the end of the hall.

'I think I'll nip upstairs myself first,' Rebus said, handing over the bottle. He spread his hands out palms upwards, then turned them over. Even Holmes could see the traces of oil and dirt.

'Car trouble,' he said, nodding. 'The bathroom's to the right of the landing.'

'Right.'

'And those are nasty scratches, too. I'd see a doctor about them.' Holmes' tone told Rebus that the young man assumed a certain doctor had been responsible for them in the first place.

'A cat,' Rebus explained. 'A cat with eight lives left.'

Upstairs, he felt particularly clumsy. He rinsed the wash-hand-basin after him, then had to rinse the muck off the soap, then rinsed the basin again. A towel was hanging over the bath, but when he started to dry his hands he found he was drying them not on a towel but on a foot-mat. The real towel was on a hook behind the door. Relax, John, he told himself. But he couldn't. Socializing was just one more skill he'd never really mastered.

He peered round the door downstairs.

'Come in, come in.'

Holmes was holding out a glass of whisky towards him. 'Here you go, cheers.'

'Cheers.'

They drank, and Rebus felt the better for it.

'I'll give you the tour of the house later,' Holmes said. 'Sit down.'

Rebus did so, and looked around him. 'A real Holmes from home,' he commented. There were good smells in the air, and cooking and clattering noises from the kitchen, which seemed to be through another door off the living room. The living room was almost cuboid, with a table in one corner set with three places for dinner, a chair in another corner, a TV in the third, and a standard lamp in the fourth.

'Very nice,' commented Rebus. Holmes was sitting on a two-person sofa against one wall. Behind him was a decent-sized window looking on to the back garden. He shrugged modestly.

'It'll do us,' he said.

'I'm sure it will.'

Now Nell Stapleton strode into the room. As imposing as ever, she seemed almost too tall for her surroundings, Alice after the 'Eat Me' cake. She was wiping her hands on a dishcloth, and smiled at Rebus.

'Hello there.'

Rebus had risen to his feet. She came over and pecked him on his cheek.

'Hello, Nell.'

Now she was standing over Holmes, and had lifted the glass out of his hand. There was sweat on her forehead, and she too was dressed casually. She took a swallow of whisky, exhaled noisily, and handed the glass back.

'Ready in five minutes,' she announced. 'Shame your doctor friend couldn't make it, John.'

He shrugged. 'Prior engagement. A medical dinner party. I was glad of an excuse to get out of it.'

She gave him rather too fixed a smile. 'Well,' she said, 'I'll leave you two to talk about whatever it is boys talk about.'

And then she was gone, the room seeming suddenly empty. Shit, what had he said? Rebus had tried to find words to describe Nell when speaking about her to Patience Aitken. But somehow the words never told the story. Bossy, stroppy, lively, canny, big, bright, a handful ... like another set of seven dwarves. Certainly, she didn't fit the stereotype of a university librarian. Which seemed to suit Brian Holmes just fine. He was smiling, studying what was left of his drink. He got up for a refill – Rebus refusing the offer – and came back with a manilla folder.

'Here,' he said.

Rebus accepted the folder. 'What is it?'

'Take a look.'

Newspaper cuttings mostly, magazine articles, press releases ... all concerning Gregor Jack MP.

'Where did you ...?'

Holmes shrugged. 'Innate curiosity. When I knew I was moving into his constituency, I thought I'd like to know more.'

'The papers seem to have kept quiet about last night.'

'Maybe they've been warned off.' Holmes sounded sceptical. 'Or maybe they're just biding their time.' Having just reseated himself, he now leapt up again. 'I'll see if Nell needs a hand.'

Leaving Rebus with little to do but read. There wasn't much he didn't already know. Working-class background. Comprehensive school in Fife, then Edinburgh University. Degree in Economics and Accounting. Chartered accountant. Married Elizabeth Ferrie. They'd met at university. She, the daughter of Sir Hugh Ferrie the businessman. She was his only daughter, his only child. He doted on her, could refuse her nothing, all, it was said, because she reminded him of his wife, dead these past twenty-three years. Sir Hugh's most recent 'companion' was an ex-model less than half his age. Maybe she, too, reminded him of his wife ...

Funny though. Elizabeth Jack was an attractive woman, beautiful even. Yet you never heard much about her. Since when was an attractive wife an asset not to be used by canny politicians? Maybe she wanted her own life. Skiing holidays and health resorts, rather than an MP's round of factory openings, tea parties, all that.

Rebus recalled now what it was that he liked about Gregor Jack. It was the background – so similar to his own. Born in Fife, and given a comprehensive education. Except that back then they'd been called secondary and high schools. Both Rebus and Gregor Jack had gone to a high school, Rebus because he passed his eleven-plus, the younger Jack because of good grades at his junior high. Rebus's school had been in Cowdenbeath, Jack's in Kirkcaldy. No distance at all, really.

The only muck that had ever been thrown at Jack seemed to be over the siting of a new electronics factory just inside his constituency. Rumours that his father-in-law had pulled a few strings ... It had all died down quickly enough. No evidence, and a whiff of writs for libel. How old was Jack? Rebus studied a recent newspaper photograph. He looked younger on paper than he did in real life. People in the media always did. Thirty-seven, thirty-eight, something like that. Beautiful wife, plenty of money.

And he ends up caught on a tart's bed during a brothel raid. Rebus shook his head. It was a cruel world. Then he smiled: serve the bugger right for not sticking to his wife.

Holmes was coming back in. He nodded towards the file. 'Makes you wonder, doesn't it?'

Rebus shrugged. 'Not really, Brian. Not really.'

'Well, finish your whisky and sit at the table. I'm informed by the management that dinner is about to be served.'

It was a good dinner, too. Rebus insisted on making three toasts: one to the couple's happiness, one to their new home, and one to Holmes' promotion. By then, they were on to their second bottle of wine and the evening's main course – roast

25

beef. After that there was cheese, and after the cheese, crannachan. And after all that there was coffee and Laphroaig and drowsiness in the armchair and on the sofa for all concerned. It hadn't taken long for Rebus to relax – the alcohol had seen to that. But it had been a nervous kind of relaxation, so that he felt he'd said too much, most of it rubbish.

There was some shop talk, of course, and Nell allowed it so long as it was interesting. She thought Farmer Watson's drinking habit was interesting. ('Maybe he doesn't drink at all. Maybe he's just addicted to strong mints.') She thought Chief Inspector Lauderdale's ambition was interesting. And she thought the brothel raid sounded interesting, too. She wanted to know where the fun was in being whipped, or dressed in nappies, or having sex with a scuba-diver. Rebus admitted he'd no answer. 'Suck it and see,' was Brian Holmes' contribution. It earned him a cushion over the head.

By quarter past eleven, Rebus knew two things. One was that he was too drunk to drive. The other was that even if he could drive (or be driven) he'd not know his destination – Oxford Terrace or his own flat in Marchmont? Where, these days, did he live? He imagined himself parking the car on Lothian Road, halfway between the two addresses, and kipping there. But the decision was made for him by Nell.

'The bed in the spare room's made up. We need someone to christen it so we can start calling it the guest bedroom. Might as well be you.'

Her quiet authority was not to be challenged. Rebus shrugged his acceptance. A little later, she went to bed herself. Holmes switched on the TV but found nothing there worth watching, so he turned on the hi-fi instead.

'I haven't got any jazz,' he admitted, knowing Rebus's tastes. 'But how about this . . .?'

It was *Sergeant Pepper*. Rebus nodded. 'If I can't get the Rolling Stones, I'll always settle for second best.'

So they argued 60s pop music, then talked football for a little while and shop for a bit longer still.

'How much more time do you think Doctor Curt will take?'

Holmes was referring to one of the pathologists regularly used by the police. A body had been fished out of the Water of Leith, just below Dean Bridge. Suicide, accident or murder? They were hoping Dr Curt's findings would point the way.

Rebus shrugged. 'Some of those tests take weeks, Brian. But actually, from what I hear, he won't be much longer. A day or two maybe.'

'And what will he say?'

'God knows.' They shared a smile; Curt was notorious for his fund of bad jokes and ill-timed levity.

'Should we stand by to repel puns?' asked Holmes. 'How about this: deceased was found near waterfall. However, study of eyes showed no signs of cataracts.'

Rebus laughed. 'That's not bad. Bit too clever maybe, but still not bad.'

They spent a quarter of an hour recalling some of Curt's true gems, before, somehow, turning the talk to politics. Rebus admitted that he'd voted only three times in his adult life.

'Once Labour, once SNP, and once Tory.'

Holmes seemed to find this funny. He asked what the chronological order had been, but Rebus couldn't remember. This, too, seemed worth a laugh.

'Maybe you should try an Independent next time.'

'Like Gregor Jack you mean?' Rebus shook his head. 'I don't think there's any such thing as an "Independent" in Scotland. It's like living in Ireland and trying not to take sides. Damned hard work. And speaking of work . . . some of us have been working today. If you don't mind, Brian, I think I'll join Nell . . .' More laughter. 'If you see what I mean.'

'Sure,' said Holmes, 'on you go. I don't feel so bad. I might watch a video or something. See you in the morning.'

'Mind you don't keep me awake,' said Rebus with a wink.

In fact, meltdown at the Torness reactor couldn't have kept him awake. His dreams were full of pastoral scenes, skin-divers, kittens, and last-minute goals. But when he opened his eyes there was a dark shadowy figure looming over him.

He pushed himself up on his elbows. It was Holmes, dressed and wearing a denim jacket. There was a jangle of car keys from one hand; the other hand held a selection of newspapers which he now threw down on to the bed.

'Sleep all right? Oh, by the way, I don't usually buy these rags but I thought you'd be interested. Breakfast'll be ready in ten minutes.'

Rebus managed to mumble a few syllables. He heaved himself upright and studied the front page of the tabloid in front of him. This was what he'd been waiting for, and he actually felt some of the tension leave his body and his brain. The headline was actually subtle – JACK THE LAD! – but the sub-head was blunt enough – MP NICKED IN SEX-DEN SWOOP. And there was the photograph, showing Gregor Jack on his way down the steps to the waiting van. More photos were promised inside. Rebus turned to the relevant pages. A pasty-faced Farmer Watson; a couple of the 'escorts' posing for the cameras; and another four shots of Jack, showing his progress all the way into the van. None from the cop-shop aftermath, so presumably he'd been spirited away. You couldn't hope to spirit this away though, photogenic or no. Ha! In the background of one of the photos Rebus could make out the cherubic features of Detective Sergeant Brian Holmes. One for the scrapbook and no mistake.

There were two more newspapers, both telling a similar tale graced by similar (sometimes even identical) photos. THE DISHONOURABLE MEMBER; MP'S VICE SHAME. Ah, the great British Sunday headline, coined by an elect of teetotal virgins boasting the combined wisdom of Solomon and the magnanimity of a zealot. Rebus could be as prurient as the next man, but this stuff was a class above. He prised himself out of bed and stood up. The alcohol inside him stood up too; then it began to pogostick its way around his head. Red wine and whisky. Bad news and a chaser. What was the phrase? Never mix the grain and the grape. Never mind, a couple of litres of orange juice would sort him out.

But first there was the little matter of the fry-up. Nell looked as though she'd spent all night in the kitchen. She had washed up the debris of the previous night, and now was providing a breakfast of hotel proportions. Cereal, toast, bacon, sausage and egg. With a pot of coffee taking pride of place on the dining table. Only one thing was missing.

'Any orange juice?' Rebus suggested.

'Sorry,' said Brian. 'I thought the paper shop would have some, but they'd run out. There's plenty of coffee though. Tuck in.' He was busy with another paper, a broadsheet this time. 'Didn't take them long to stick the knife in, did it?'

'You mean Gregor Jack? No, well, what can you expect?'

Holmes turned a page. 'Strange though,' he said, and let it lie at that, wondering whether Rebus would know . . .

'You mean,' Rebus replied, 'it's strange that the London Sunday's knew about Operation Creeper.'

Another page was turned. It didn't take long to read a newspaper these days, not unless you were interested in the adverts. Holmes folded the paper into four and laid it down on the table beside him.

'Yes,' he said, lifting a piece of toast. 'Like I say, it's strange.'

'Come on, Brian. Papers are always getting tip-offs to juicy stories. A copper looking for beer money, something like that. Chances are, you raid a posh brothel you're going to come out with some weel-kent faces.'

Hold on though . . . Even as he spoke, Rebus knew there was something more. That night, the reporters had been biding their time, hadn't they? Like they knew *exactly* who or what might be walking out of the door and down the steps. Holmes was staring at him now.

'What are you thinking?' Rebus asked.

'Nothing. No, nothing at all . . . yet. Not our business, is it? And besides, this is Sunday.'

'You're a sly bugger, Brian Holmes.'

'I've got a good tutor, haven't I?'

Nell came into the room carrying two plates, filled with glistening fried food. Rebus's stomach pleaded with its owner not to do anything rash, anything he would regret later on in the day.

'You're working too hard,' Rebus told Nell. 'Don't let him treat you like a skivvy.'

'Don't worry,' she said, 'I don't. But fair's fair. Brian did wash last night's dishes. And he'll wash this morning's too.'

Holmes groaned. Rebus opened one of the tabloids and tapped his finger against a photograph.

'Better not work him too hard, Nell, not now he's in pictures.'

Nell took the paper from him, studied it for a moment, then shrieked.

'My God, Brian! You look like something off the *Muppet Show*.'

Holmes was on his feet now, too, staring over her shoulder. 'And is that what Chief Superintendent Watson looks like? He could pass for an Aberdeen Angus.'

Rebus and Holmes shared a smile at that. He wasn't called Farmer for nothing . . .

Rebus wished the young couple well. They had made a commitment to living together. They had bought a house together and set up home. They seemed content. Yes, he wished them well with all his heart.

But his brain gave them two or three years at most.

A policeman's lot was not entirely a happy one. Striving towards inspectorship, Brian Holmes would find himself working still longer hours. If he could shut it all out when he got home of an evening or morning, fine. But Rebus doubted the young man would. Holmes was the type to get involved in a case, to let it rule his thinking hours whether on duty or off, and that was bad for a relationship.

Bad, and often terminal. Rebus knew more divorced and separated policemen (himself included) than happily married ones. It wasn't just the hours worked, it was the way police work itself gnawed into you like a worm, burrowing deep. Eating away from the inside. As protection against the worm, you wore armour plating – more of it, perhaps, than was necessary. And that armour set you apart from friends and family, from the 'civilians' . . .

Ach. Pleasant thoughts for a Sunday morning. After all, it wasn't *all* gloom. The car had started without a hitch (that is, without him having to hitch a ride to the nearest garage), and there was just enough blue in the sky to send hardy day-trippers off into the country. Rebus was going on a drive, too. An aimless tour, he told himself. A nice day for a drive. But he knew where he was headed. Knew where, if not exactly *why*.

Gregor Jack and his wife lived in a large, old, detached and walled residence on the outskirts of Rosebridge, a little further south than Eskwell, a little bit more rural. Gentry country. Fields and rolling hills and an apparent moratorium on new building work. Rebus had no excuse save curiosity for this detour, but he was not, it seemed, alone. The Jacks' house was recognizable by the half dozen cars parked outside its gates and by the posse of reporters who were lounging around, chatting to each other or instructing fed-up-looking photographers on how far they should go (morally rather than geographically) for that elusive picture. Clamber on to the wall? Climb that nearby tree? Try the back of the house? The photographers didn't seem keen. But just then something seemed to galvanize them.

By this time, Rebus had parked his own car further along the road. To one side of the road was a line of perhaps half a dozen houses, none of them spectacular in terms of design or size, but wonderfully isolated by those high walls, long driveways, and (doubtless) vast back gardens. The other side of the road was pasture. Bemused cows and fat-looking sheep. Some sizeable lambs, their voices not yet quite broken. The view ended at some steepish hills, three or so miles distant. It was nice. Even the troglodyte Rebus could appreciate that.

Which was perhaps why the reporters left a more bitter taste than usual beneath his tongue. He stood behind them, an observer. The house was dark-stoned, reddish from this distance. A two-storey construction, probably built in the early 1900s. Tacked on to it at one side was a large garage, and in front of the house at the top of the drive sat a white

Saab, one of the 9000 series. Sturdy and reliable, not cheap but not show-offish. Distinctive though: a car of distinction.

A youngish man, early thirties, a sneer creasing his face, was unlocking the gates just wide enough so that a younger woman, out of her teens but trying to look ten years older, could hand a silver tray to the reporters. She spoke louder than she needed to.

'Gregor thought you might like some tea. There may not be enough cups, you'll just have to share. There are biscuits in the tin. No ginger nuts, I'm afraid. We've run out.'

There were smiles at this, nods of appreciation. But throughout questions were being fired off.

'Any chance of a word with Mr Jack?'

'Can we expect a statement?'

'How's he taking it?'

'Is Mrs Jack in the house?'

'Any chance of a word?'

'Ian, is he going to be saying *anything*?'

This last question was directed at the sneering man, who now held up one hand for silence. He waited patiently, and the silence came. Then:

'No comment,' he said. And with that he began to close the gates. Rebus pushed through the good-natured crush until he was face to face with Mr Sneer.

'Inspector Rebus,' he said. 'Could I have a word with Mr Jack?'

Mr Sneer and Miss Teatray seemed highly suspicious, even when they accepted and examined Rebus's ID. Fair enough: he'd known of reporters who'd try a stunt just like this, fake ID and all. But eventually there was a curt nod, and the gates opened again wide enough to allow him to squeeze through. The gates were shut again, locked. With Rebus on the inside.

He had a sudden thought: What the hell am I doing? The answer was: He wasn't sure. Something about the scene at the gates had made him want to be on the other side of those gates. Well, here he was. Being led back up the gravel driveway, towards the large car, the larger house behind it, and the garage off to the side. Being led towards Gregor Jack MP, with whom, apparently, he wanted a word.

I believe you want a word, Inspector?

No, sir, just being nosey.

It wasn't much of an opening line, was it? Watson had warned him before about this ... this ... was it a character flaw? This need to push his way into the centre of things, to become involved, to find out for himself rather than accepting somebody's word, no matter who that somebody was.

Just passing, thought I'd pay my respects. Jesus, and Jack would recognize him, wouldn't he? From the brothel. Sitting on the bed, while the woman in the bed kicked up her legs, screeching with laughter. No, maybe not. He'd had other things on his mind after all.

'I'm Ian Urquhart, Gregor's constituency agent.' Now that he had his back to the reporters, the sneer had left Urquhart's face. What was left was a mixture of worry and bewilderment. 'We got word last night of what was coming. I've been here ever since.'

Rebus nodded. Urquhart was compact, a bunching of well-kept muscles inside a tailored suit. A bit smaller than the MP, and a bit less good-looking. In other words, just right for an agent. He also looked efficient, which Rebus would say was a bonus.

'This is Helen Greig, Gregor's secretary.' Urquhart was nodding towards the young woman. She gave a quick smile towards Rebus. 'Helen came over this morning to see if there was anything she could do.'

'The tea was my idea actually,' she said.

Urquhart glanced towards her. 'Gregor's idea, Helen,' he warned.

'Oh yes,' she said, reddening.

Efficient and faithful, thought Rebus. Rare qualities indeed. Helen Greig, like Urquhart himself, spoke in an educated Scots accent which did not really betray county of origin. He would hazard at east coast for both of them, but couldn't narrow things down any further. Helen looked either like she'd been to an early Kirk service, or was planning to attend one later on. She was wearing a pale woollen two-piece with plain white blouse offset by a simple gold chain around her neck. Sensible black shoes on her feet and thick black tights. She was Urquhart's height, five feet six or seven, and shared something of his build. You wouldn't call her beautiful: you'd call her handsome, in the way Nell Stapleton was handsome, though the two women were dissimilar in many ways.

They were passing the Saab now, Urquhart leading. 'Was there anything in particular, Inspector? Only, I'm sure you can appreciate that Gregor's hardly in a state . . .'

'It won't take long, Mr Urquhart.'

'Well, in you come then.' The front door opened, and Urquhart ushered both Rebus and Helen Greig into the house before him. Rebus was immediately surprised by how modern the interior was. Polished pine flooring, scatter rugs, Mackintosh-style chairs and low-slung Italian-looking tables. They passed through the hall and into a large room boasting more modern furnishings still. Pride of place went to a long angular sofa constructed from leather and chrome. On which sat, in much the same position as when Rebus had first met him, Gregor Jack. The MP was scratching absent-mindedly at a finger and staring at the floor. Urquhart cleared his throat.

'We have a visitor, Gregor.'

The effect was that of a talented actor changing roles – tragedy to comedy. Gregor Jack stood up and fixed a smile on to his face. His eyes now sparkled, looking interested, his whole face speaking sincerity. Rebus marvelled at the ease of the transformation.

'Detective Inspector Rebus,' he said, taking the proffered hand.

'Inspector, what can we do for you? Here, sit down.' Jack gestured towards a squat black chair, matching the sofa in design. It was like sinking into marshmallow. 'Something to drink?' Now Jack seemed to remember something and turned to Helen Greig. 'Helen, you took the tea out to our friends?'

She nodded.

'Excellent. Can't have the gentlemen of the press going without their elevenses.' He smiled towards Rebus, then lowered himself on to the edge of the sofa, arms resting on his knees so that the hands remained mobile. 'Now, Inspector, what's the problem?'

'Well, sir, it's really just that I happened to be passing, and saw that gang at the gates, so I stopped.'

'You know why they're here though?'

Rebus was obliged to nod. Urquhart cleared his throat again.

'We're going to prepare a statement for them over lunch,' he said. 'It probably won't be enough to see them off, but it might help.'

'You know, of course,' said Rebus, aware that he had to tread carefully, 'that you've done nothing wrong, sir. I mean, nothing illegal.'

Jack smiled again and shrugged. 'It doesn't need to be illegal, Inspector. It just has to be news.' His hands kept fluttering, as did his eyes and head. It was as though his mind were elsewhere. Then something seemed to click. 'You didn't say, Inspector,' he said, 'tea or coffee? Something stronger perhaps?'

Rebus shook his head slowly. His hangover was a dull presence now. No point swaddling it. Jack raised his soulful eyes to Helen Greig.

'I'd love a cup of tea, Helen. Inspector, you're sure you won't . . .?'

'No, thank you.'

'Ian?'

Urquhart nodded towards Helen Greig.

'Would you, Helen?' said Gregor Jack. What woman, Rebus wondered, would refuse? Which reminded him . . .

'Your wife's not here then, Mr Jack?'

'On holiday,' Jack said quickly. 'We've a cottage in the Highlands. Not much of a place, but we like it. She's probably there.'

'Probably? Then you don't know for sure?'

'She didn't make out an itinerary, Inspector.'

'So does she know . . .?'

Jack shrugged. 'I've no idea, Inspector. Maybe she does.

35

She's an insatiable reader of newsprint. There's a village nearby stocks the Sundays.'

'But she hasn't been in touch?'

Urquhart didn't bother clearing his throat this time before interrupting. 'There's no phone at the lodge.'

'That's what we like about it,' Jack explained. 'Cut off from the world.'

'But if she knew,' Rebus persisted, 'surely she'd get in touch?'

Jack sighed, and began scratching at his finger again. He caught himself doing it and stopped. 'Eczema,' he explained. 'Just on the one finger, but it's annoying all the same.' He paused. 'Liz . . . my wife . . . she's very much a law unto herself, Inspector. Maybe she'd get in touch, maybe she wouldn't. She's just as likely not to want to talk about it. Do you see what I mean?' Another smile, a weaker one, seeking the sympathy vote. Jack ran his fingers through his thick dark hair. Rebus wondered idly whether the perfect teeth were capped. Maybe the thatch was capped, too. The open-necked shirt didn't look like chain-store stuff . . .

Urquhart was still standing. Or, rather, was on his feet but in constant movement. Over to the window to peer through the net curtains. Over to a glass-topped table to examine some papers lying there. Over to a smaller table where the telephone sat, disconnected at the wall. So that even if Mrs Jack *did* try to call . . . Neither Urquhart nor Jack seemed to have thought of that. Curious. The room, the taste it displayed, seemed to Rebus not Jack's but his wife's. Jack looked like a man for older established pieces of furniture, safe comfy armchairs and a chesterfield sofa. A conservative taste. Look at the car he chose to drive . . .

Yes, Jack's car: now there was an idea, or rather an excuse, an excuse for Rebus's presence.

'Maybe if we could get that statement out *by* lunchtime, Gregor,' Urquhart was saying. 'Sooner we dampen things down the better, really.'

Not very subtle, thought Rebus. The message was: state your business and leave. Rebus knew the question he wanted to ask: Do you think you were set up? Wanted to ask, but daren't. He wasn't here officially, was a tourist merely.

'About your car, Mr Jack,' he began. 'Only, I noticed when I stopped that it's sitting there in the drive, on full view so as to speak. And there are photographers out there. If any pictures of your car get into the papers . . .'

'Everyone will recognize it in future?' Jack nodded. 'I see what you're getting at, Inspector. Yes, thank you. We hadn't thought of that, had we, Ian?' Better put it in the garage. We don't want everyone who reads a newspaper to know what kind of car I drive.'

'And its registration,' Rebus added. 'There are all sorts of people out there . . . terrorists . . . people with a grudge . . . plain nutters. Doesn't do any good.'

'Thank you, Inspector.' The door swung open and Helen Greig entered, carrying two large mugs of tea. A far cry from the silver salver routine at the gates. She handed one to Urquhart and one to Gregor Jack, then removed a slim box from where it had been held between her arm and her side. It was a fresh box of ginger nuts. Rebus smiled.

'Lovely, Helen, thanks,' said Gregor Jack. He eased two biscuits from the packet.

Rebus rose to his feet. 'Well,' he said. 'I'd better be going. Like I say, I only dropped in . . .'

'I do appreciate it, Inspector.' Jack had placed mug and biscuits on the floor and was now standing, too, hand held out again towards Rebus. A warm, strong and unflawed hand. 'I meant to ask, do you live in the constituency?'

Rebus shook his head. 'One of my colleagues does. I was staying with him last night.'

Jack raised his head slowly before nodding. The gesture could have meant anything. 'I'll open the gates for you,' Ian Urquhart was saying.

'Stay here and drink your tea,' Helen Greig said. 'I'll see the Inspector out.'

'If you like, Helen,' Urquhart said slowly. Was there a warning in his voice? If there was, Helen Greig seemed not to sense it. He fished in his pocket for the keys and handed them to her.

'Right then,' Rebus said. 'Goodbye, Mr Jack ... Mr Urquhart.' He took Urquhart's hand for a moment and squeezed it. But his attention was on the man's left hand. Wedding ring on one finger, and a signet ring on another. Gregor Jack's left hand sported just the one thick band of gold. Not, however, on his wedding finger, but on the finger next to it. The wedding finger was the one with the eczema ...

And Helen Greig? A few trinket rings on both hands, but she was neither married nor engaged.

'Goodbye.'

Helen Greig was first out of the house, but waited for him beside the car, jangling the keys in her right hand.

'Have you worked for Mr Jack long?'

'Long enough.'

'Hard work, being an MP, isn't it? I expect he needs to unwind from time to time – '

She stopped and glared at him. 'Not you too! You're as bad as that lot!' She gestured with the keys towards the gates and the figures beyond. 'I won't hear a word said against Gregor.' She started walking again, more briskly now.

'He's a good employer then?'

'He's not *like* an employer at all. My mother's been ill. He gave me a bonus in the autumn so I could take her for a wee holiday down the coast. *That's* the sort of man he is.' There were tears in her eyes, but she forced them back. The reporters were passing cups between them, complaining about sugar or the lack of it. They didn't seem to expect much from the approach of the two figures.

'Talk to us, Helen.'

'A word with Gregor and we can all go home. We've got families to think of, you know.'

'I'm missing communion,' joked one of them.

'Yes, communion with your lunchtime pint,' returned another.

One of the local reporters – by the accents, there weren't many of them present – had recognized Rebus.

'Inspector, anything to tell us?' A few ears pricked up at that 'Inspector'.

'Yes,' said Rebus, causing Helen Greig to stiffen. 'Bugger off.'

There were smiles at this and a few groans. The gates opened and were about to close, leaving Rebus on the outside again. But he pressed his weight against the gate and leaned towards the young woman, his mouth close to her ear.

'I forgot, I'll have to go back in.'

'What?'

'I forgot, or rather Mr Jack did. He wanted me to check on his wife, in case she was taking the news badly . . .'

He waited for the notion of this to sink in. Helen Greig puckered her lips in a silent O. The notion had sunk in.

'Only,' Rebus went on, 'I forgot to get the address . . .'

She stood on her toes and, so the newsmen wouldn't hear, whispered into his ear: 'Deer Lodge. It's between Knockandhu and Tomnavoulin.'

Rebus nodded, and allowed her to close and lock the gates. His curiosity was not exactly dispelled. In fact, he was more curious now than when he'd gone in. Knockandhu and Tomnavoulin: the names of a couple of malt whiskies. His head told him never to drink again. His heart told him differently . . .

Damn, he'd meant to phone Patience from Holmes' house, just to let her know he was on his way. Not that she kept him to an itinerary or anything . . . but all the same. He made for the reporter he recognized, the local lad, Chris Kemp.

'Hello, Chris. Got a phone in your car? Mind if I make a call . . .?'

'So,' said Dr Patience Aitken, 'how was your *ménage à trois?*'

'Not bad,' said Rebus, before kissing her loudly on the lips. 'How was your orgy?'

She rolled her eyes. 'Shop talk and overcooked lasagne.

39

You didn't manage home then?' Rebus looked blank. 'I tried phoning Marchmont, and you weren't there either. Your suit looks like you slept in it.'

'Blame the bloody cat.'

'Lucky?'

'He was doing the twist all over the jacket till I rescued it.'

'The *twist*? Nothing shows a man's true age more than his choice of dance step.'

Rebus was shedding the suit now. 'You haven't got any orange juice, have you?'

'Bit of a sore head? Time to stop the drinking, John.'

'Time to settle down, you mean.' He pulled off his trousers. 'All right if I take a bath?'

She was studying him. 'You know you don't have to ask.'

'No, but all the same, I like to ask.'

'Permission granted ... as always. Did Lucky do that, too?' She was pointing to the scratches on his wrist.

'He'd be in the microwave if he had.'

She smiled. 'I'll see about the orange juice.'

Rebus watched her make for the kitchen. He attempted a dry-mouthed wolf-whistle. From nearby, one of the budgies showed him how to do it properly. Patience turned towards the budgie and smiled.

He lay down in the foaming bath and closed his eyes, breathing deeply, the way his doctor had told him to. Relaxation technique, he'd called it. He wanted Rebus to relax a bit more. High blood pressure, nothing serious, but all the same ... Of course, there were pills he could take, beta-blockers. But the doctor was in favour of self-help. Deep relaxation. Self-hypnosis. Rebus had had half a mind to tell the doctor that his own father had been a hypnotist, that his brother still might be a professional hypnotist somewhere ...

Deep breathing ... emptying the mind ... relaxing the head, the forehead, the jaw, the neck muscles, the chest, the arms. Counting backwards down to zero ... no stress, no strain ...

At first, Rebus had accused the doctor of penny-pinching, of not wanting to give out costly drugs. But the damned thing seemed to work. He *could* help himself. He could help himself to Patience Aitken . . .

'Here you go,' she said, coming into the bathroom. She was holding a long thin glass of orange juice. 'As squeezed by Dr Aitken.'

Rebus slipped a sudsy arm around her buttocks. 'As squeezed by Inspector Rebus.'

She bent down and kissed him on his head. Then touched a finger to his hair. 'You need to start using a conditioner, John. All the life's going out of your follicles.'

'That's because it's headed somewhere else.'

She narrowed her eyes. 'Down, boy,' she said. Then, before he could make a grab for her again, she fled from the bathroom. Rebus, smiling, settled further into the bath.

Deep breathing . . . emptying the mind . . . *Had* Gregor Jack been set up. If so, who by? And to what purpose? A scandal, of course. A political scandal, a front-page scandal. But the atmosphere in the Jack household had been . . . well, *strange*. Strained, certainly, but also cold and edgy, as though the worst were still to happen.

The wife . . . Elizabeth . . . something didn't seem right there. Something seemed very odd indeed. Background, he needed more background. He needed to be *sure*. The lodge address was fixed in his mind, but from what he knew of Highland police stations little good would come of phoning on a Sunday. Background . . . He thought again of Chris Kemp, the reporter. Yes, why not? Wake up, arms, wake up, chest, neck and head. Sunday was no time to be resting. For some people, Sunday was a day of work.

Patience stuck her head round the door. 'Quiet night in this evening?' she suggested. 'I'll cook us a – '

'Quiet night be damned,' Rebus said, rising impressively from the water. 'Let's go out for a drink.'

'You know me, John. I don't *mind* a bit of sleaze, but this place is cheapskate sleaze. Don't you think I'm worth better?'

Rebus pecked Patience's cheek, placed their drinks on the table, and sat down beside her. 'I got you a double,' he said.

41

'So I see.' She picked up the glass. 'Not much room for the tonic, is there?'

They were seated in the back room of the Horsehair public house on Broughton Street. Through the doorway could be seen the bar itself, noisy as ever. People who wanted to have a conversation seemed to place themselves like duellists a good ten paces away from the person they wanted to talk with. The result was that a lot of shouting went on, producing much crossfire and more crossed wires. It was noisy, but it was fun. The back room was quieter. It was a U-shaped arrangement of squashy seating (around the walls) and rickety chairs. The narrow lozenge-shaped tables were fixed to the floor. Rumour had it that the squashy seating had been stuffed with horsehair in the 1920s and not restuffed since. Thus the Horsehair, whose real and prosaic name had long since been discarded.

Patience poured half a small bottle of tonic water into her gin, while Rebus supped on a pint of IPA.

'Cheers,' she said, without enthusiasm. Then: 'I know damned fine that there's got to be a reason for this. I mean, a reason why we're here. I *suppose* it's to do with your work?'

Rebus put down the glass. 'Yes,' he said.

She raised her eyes to the nicotine-coloured ceiling. 'Give me strength,' she said.

'It won't take long,' Rebus said. 'I thought afterwards we could go somewhere . . . a bit more your style.'

'Don't patronize me, you pig.'

Rebus stared into his drink, thinking about that statement's various meanings. Then he caught sight of a new customer in the bar, and waved through the doorway. A young man came forwards, smiling tiredly.

'Don't often see you in here, Inspector Rebus,' he said.

'Sit down,' said Rebus. 'It's my round. Patience, let me introduce you to one of Scotland's finest young reporters, Chris Kemp.'

Rebus got up and headed for the bar. Chris Kemp pulled over a chair and, having tested it first, eased himself on to it.

'He must want something,' he said to Patience, nodding towards the bar. 'He knows I'm a sucker for a bit of flattery.'

Not that it *was* flattery. Chris Kemp had won awards for his early work on an Aberdeen evening paper, and had then moved to Glasgow, there to be voted Young Journalist of the Year, before arriving in Edinburgh, where he had spent the past year and a half 'stirring it' (as he said himself). Everyone knew he'd one day head south. He knew it himself. It was inescapable. There didn't seem to be much left for him to stir in Scotland. The only problem was his student girlfriend, who wouldn't graduate for another year and wouldn't think of moving south before then, if ever . . .

By the time Rebus returned from the bar, Patience had been told all of this and more. There was a film over her eyes which Chris Kemp, for all his qualities, could not see. He talked, and as he talked she was thinking: Is John Rebus worth all this? Is he worth the effort I seem to have to make? She didn't love him: that was understood. 'Love' was something that had happened to her a few times in her teens and twenties and even, yes, in her thirties. Always with inconclusive or atrocious results. So that nowadays it seemed to her 'love' could as easily spell the end of a relationship as its beginning.

She saw it in her surgery. She saw men and women (but mostly women) made ill from love, from loving too much and not being loved enough in return. They were every bit as sick as the child with earache or the pensioner suffering angina. She had pity and words for them, but no medicines.

Time heals, she might say in an unguarded moment. Yes, heals into a callus over the wound, hard and protective. Just like she felt: hard and protective. But did John Rebus need her solidity, her protection?

'Here we are,' he said on his return. 'The barman's slow tonight, sorry.'

Chris Kemp accepted the drink with a thin smile. 'I've just been telling Patience . . .'

Oh God, Rebus thought as he sat down. She looks like a bucketful of ice. I shouldn't have brought her. But if I'd said I was popping out for the evening on my own ... well, she'd have been the same. Get this over and done with, maybe the night can be rescued.

'So, Chris,' he said, interrupting the young man, 'what's the dirt on Gregor Jack?'

Chris Kemp seemed to think there was plenty, and the introduction of Gregor Jack into the conversation perked Patience up a bit, so that she forgot for a time that she wasn't enjoying herself.

Rebus was interested mostly in Elizabeth Jack, but Kemp started with the MP himself, and what he had to say was interesting. Here was a different Jack, different from the public image, the received opinion, but different too from Rebus's own ideas having met with the man. He would not, for example, have taken Jack for a drinker.

'Terrible one for the whisky,' Kemp was saying. 'Probably more than half a bottle a day, more when he's in London by all accounts.'

'He never looks drunk.'

'That's because he doesn't *get* drunk. But he drinks all the same.'

'What else?'

There was more, plenty more. 'He's a smooth operator, but cunning. Deep down cunning. I wouldn't trust him further than I can spit. I know someone who knew him at university. Says Gregor Jack never did anything in his life that wasn't premeditated. And that goes for capturing *Mrs* Gregor Jack.'

'How do you mean?'

'Story is, they met at university, at a party. Gregor had seen her around before, but hadn't paid much attention. Once he knew she was *rich* though, that was another matter. He went at it full throttle, charmed the pants off her.' He turned to Patience. 'Sorry, poor choice of words.'

Patience, on her second g and t, merely bowed her head a little.

'He's calculating, you see. Remember, he was trained as

44

an accountant, and he's got an accountant's mind all right. What are you having?'

But Rebus was rising. 'No, Chris, let me get them.'

But Kemp wouldn't hear of it. 'Don't think I'm telling you all this for the price of a couple of beers, Inspector . . .'

And when the drinks had been bought and brought to the table, it was this train of thought which seemed to occupy Kemp.

'Why do you want to know anyway?'

Rebus shrugged.

'Is there a story?'

'Could be. Early days.'

They were talking now as professionals: the meaning was all in what was left unsaid.

'But there might be a story?'

'If there is, Chris, as far as I'm concerned it's yours.'

Kemp gulped at his beer. 'I was out there all day, you know. And all we got was a statement. Plain and simple. No further comment to make, et cetera. The story ties in with Jack?'

Rebus shrugged again. 'Early days. That was interesting, what you were saying about Mrs Jack . . .'

But Kemp's eyes were cool. 'I get the story first?'

Rebus massaged his neck. 'As far as I'm concerned.'

Kemp seemed to size the offer up. As Rebus himself knew, there was almost no offer *there* for the sizing. Then Kemp placed his glass on the table. He was ready to say a little more.

'What Jack didn't know about Liz Ferrie was that she ran with a *very* fast crowd. A rich fast crowd. People like her. It took Gregor quite a while before he was able to insinuate his way into the group. A working-class kid, remember. Still gangly and a bit awkward. But it happened, he had Liz hooked. Where he went, she would et cetera. And Jack had his own gang. Still does.'

'I don't follow.'

'Old schoolfriends mostly, a few people he met at university. His circle, you could call it.'

'One of them runs a bookshop, doesn't he?'

Kemp nodded. 'That's Ronald Steele. Known to the gang as Suey. That's why his shop's called Suey Books.'

'Funny nickname,' said Patience.

'I don't know how he came by it,' admitted Kemp. 'I'd *like* to know, but I don't.'

'Who else is there?' asked Rebus.

'I'm not sure how many there are altogether. The interesting ones are Rab Kinnoul and Andrew Macmillan.'

'Rab Kinnoul the actor?'

'The very same.'

'That's funny, I've got to talk to him. Or rather, to his wife.'

'Oh?'

Kemp was sniffing his story, but Rebus shook his head. 'Nothing to do with Jack. Some stolen books. Mrs Kinnoul is a bit of a collector.'

'Not Prof Costello's missing hoard?'

'That's it.'

Kemp was nothing if not a newsman. 'Any progress?'

Rebus shrugged.

'Don't tell me,' said Kemp, 'it's early days yet.'

And he laughed, and Patience laughed with him. But something had just struck Rebus.

'Not *the* Andrew Macmillan, surely?'

Kemp nodded. 'They were at school together.'

'Christ.' Rebus stared at the plastic-topped table. Kemp was explaining to Patience who Andrew Macmillan was.

'A very successful something-or-other. Went off his head one day. Toddled off home and sawed off his wife's head.'

Patience gasped. 'I remember that,' she said. 'They never found the head, did they?'

Kemp shook his own firmly fixed head. 'He'd have done his daughter in, too, but the kid ran for her life. She's a bit dotty now herself, and no wonder.'

'Whatever happened to him?' Rebus wondered aloud. It had been several years ago, and in Glasgow not Edinburgh. Not his territory.

'Oh,' said Kemp, 'he's in that new psychiatric place, the one they've just built.'

'You mean Duthil?' said Patience.

'That's it. Up in the Highlands. Near Grantown, isn't it?'

Well, thought Rebus, curiouser and curiouser. His geography wasn't brilliant, but he didn't think Grantown was *too* far from Deer Lodge. 'Is Jack still in touch with him?'

It was Kemp's turn to shrug. 'No idea.'

'And they were at school together?'

'That's the story. To be honest, I think Liz Jack is the more interesting character by far. Jack's sidekicks are scrupulous in keeping her out of the way.'

'Yes, why is that?'

'Because she's still the proverbial wild child. Still runs around with her old crowd. Jamie Kilpatrick, Matilda Merriman, all that sort. Parties, booze, drugs, orgies ... God knows. The press never gets a sniff.' He turned again to Patience. 'If you'll pardon the phrase. Not a sniff do we get. And anything we *do* get is blue pencilled with a fair amount of prejudice.'

'Oh?'

'Well, editors are nervous at the best of times, aren't they? And you've got to remember that Sir Hugh Ferrie is never slow with a libel suit where his family's concerned.'

'You mean that electronics factory?'

'Case in point.'

'So what about this "old crowd" of Mrs Jack's?'

'Aristos, mostly old money, some new money.'

'What about the lady herself?'

'Well, she certainly spurred Jack on in the early days. I think he always wanted to go into politics, and MPs can hardly afford not to be married. People start to suspect a shirt-lifting tendency. My guess is he looked for someone pretty, with money, and with a father of influence. Found her and wasn't going to let go. And it's been a successful marriage, so far as the public's concerned. Liz gets wheeled out for the photo opportunities and looks just right, then she disappears again. Completely different to Gregor, you see.

47

Fire and ice. She's the fire, he's the ice, usually with whisky added . . .'

Kemp was in a talkative mood tonight. There was more, but it was speculation. Still, it was interesting to be given a different perspective, wasn't it? Rebus considered this as he excused himself and visited the gents'. The Horsehair's trough-like urinal was brimful of liquid, as had always, to Rebus's knowledge, been the case. The condensation on the overhead cistern dripped unerringly on to the heads of those unwise enough to get too close, and the graffiti was mostly the work of a dyslexic bigot: REMEMBER 1960. There was some new stuff though, written in biro. 'The Drunk as a Lord's Prayer,' Rebus read. 'Our Father which are in heavy, Alloa'd be they name . . .'

Rebus reckoned that if he didn't have all he needed, he had all Chris Kemp was able to give. No reason to linger then. No reason at all. He came out of the gents' briskly, and saw that a young man had stopped at the table to chat with Patience. He was moving away now, back to the main bar, while Patience smiled a farewell in his direction.

'Who was that?' Rebus asked, not sitting down.

'He lives next door in Oxford Terrace,' Patience said casually. 'Works in Trading Standards. I'm surprised you haven't met him.'

Rebus murmured something, then tapped his watch with his finger.

'Chris,' he said, 'this is all your fault. You're too interesting by half. We were supposed to be at the restaurant twenty minutes ago. Kevin and Myra will kill us. Come on, Patience. Listen, Chris, I'll be in touch. Meantime . . .' he leaned closer to the reporter, lowering his voice. 'See if you can find who tipped off the papers about the brothel raid. *That* might be the start of the story.' He straightened up again. 'See you soon, eh? Cheers.'

'Cheerio, Chris,' said Patience, sliding out of her seat.

'Oh, right, bye then. See you.' And Chris Kemp found himself alone, wondering if it was something that he'd said.

Outside, Patience turned to Rebus. 'Kevin and Myra?' she said.

'Our oldest friends,' explained Rebus. 'And as good a get-out clause as anything. Besides, I *did* promise you dinner. You can tell me all about our next-door neighbour.'

He took her arm in his and they walked back to the car – her car. Patience had never seen John Rebus jealous before, so it was hard to tell, but she could have sworn he was jealous now. Well well, wonders would never cease . . .

3
Treacherous Steps

Springtime in Edinburgh. A freezing wind, and near-horizon-
tal rain. Ah, the Edinburgh wind, that joke of a wind, that
black farce of a wind. Making everyone walk like mime
artists, making eyes water and then drying the tears to a
crust on red-nipped cheeks. And throughout it all, that
slightly sour yeasty smell in the air, the smell of not-so-
distant breweries. There had been a frost overnight. Even the
prowling, fur-coated Lucky had yowled at the bedroom
window, demanding entry. The birds had been chirping as
Rebus let him in. He checked his watch: two thirty. Why the
hell were the birds singing so early? When he next awoke, at
six, they'd stopped. Maybe they were trying to avoid the rush
hour . . .

This sub-zero morning, it had taken him a full five minutes
to start his clown of a car. Maybe it was time to get one of
those red noses for the radiator grille. And the frost had
swollen the cracks in the steps up to Great London Road
police station, swollen and then fissured, so that Rebus
stepped warily over wafers of stone.

Treacherous steps. Nothing would be done about them.
The rumours were still rife anyway; rumours that Great
London Road was shagged out, wabbit, past its sell-by.
Rumours that it would be shut down. A prime site, after all.
Prime land for another hotel or office block. And the staff?
Split up, so the rumours went. With most of them being
transferred to St Leonard's, the Divisional HQ (Central). Much
closer to Rebus's flat in Marchmont; but much further from

Oxford Terrace and Dr Patience Aitken. Rebus had made himself a little pact, a sort of contract in his head: if, within the next month or two, the rumours became fact, then it was a message from on high, a message that he should not move in with Patience. But if Great London Road remained a going concern, or if they were moved to Fettes HQ (five minutes from Oxford Terrace) ... what then? What then? The fine print on the contract was still being decided.

'Morning, John.'

'Hello, Arthur. Any messages?'

The duty desk sergeant shook his head. Rebus rubbed his hands over his ears and face, thawing them out, and climbed the stairs towards his room, where treacherous linoleum replaced treacherous stone. And then there was the treacherous telephone ...

'Rebus here.'

'John?' It was the voice of Chief Superintendent Watson. 'Can you spare a minute?'

Rebus made noisy show of rustling some papers on his desk, hoping Watson would think he'd been in the office for hours, hard at work.

'Well, sir ...'

'Don't piss about, John. I tried you five minutes ago.'

Rebus stopped shuffling papers. 'I'll be right along, sir.'

'That's right, you will.' And with that the phone went dead. Rebus shrugged off his weatherproof jacket, the one which always let water in at the shoulders. He felt the shoulders of his suit-jacket. Sure enough, they were damp, matching his enthusiasm for a Monday-morning meeting with the Farmer. He took a deep breath and spread his hands in front of him like an old-time song and dance man.

'It's showtime,' he told himself. Only five working days till the weekend. Then he made a quick phone call to Dufftown Police Station and asked them to check on Deer Lodge.

'Is that d-e-a-r?' asked the voice.

'D-double e-r,' corrected Rebus, thinking: But it probably *was* dear enough when they bought it.

'Anything we're looking for in particular?'

An MP's wife ... leftovers from a sex orgy ... flour bags full of cocaine ... 'No,' said Rebus, 'nothing special. Just let me know what you find.'

'Right you are. It might take a while.'

'Soon as you can, eh?' And so saying, Rebus remembered that he should be elsewhere. 'Soon as you can.'

Chief Superintendent Watson was as blunt as a tramp's razor blade.

'What the hell were you doing at Gregor Jack's yesterday?'

Rebus was almost caught off guard. Almost. 'Who's been telling tales?'

'Never mind that. Just give me a bloody answer.' Pause. 'Coffee?'

'I wouldn't say no.'

Watson's wife had bought him the coffee-maker as a Christmas present. Maybe as a hint that he should cut down his consumption of Teacher's whisky. Maybe so that he'd stand a chance of being sober when he returned home of an evening. All it had done so far though was make Watson hyperactive of a morning. In the afternoon, however, after a few lunchtime nips, drowsiness would take over. Best, therefore, to avoid Watson in the mornings. Best to wait until afternoon to ask him about that leave you were thinking of taking or to tell him the news of the latest bodged operation. If you were lucky, you'd get off with a 'tut-tut'. But the mornings ... the mornings were different.

Rebus accepted the mug of strong coffee. Half a packet of espresso looked as though it had been tipped into the generous filter. Now, it tipped itself into Rebus's bloodstream.

'Sounds stupid, sir, but I was just passing.'

'You're right,' said Watson, settling down behind his desk, 'it *does* sound stupid. Even supposing you *were* just passing ...'

'Well, sir, to be honest, there was a little more to it than that.' Watson sat back in his chair, holding the mug in both hands, and waited for the story. Doubtless he was thinking: this'll be good. But Rebus had nothing to gain by lying. 'I like

52

Gregor Jack,' he said. 'I mean, I like him as an MP. He's always seemed to me to be a bloody good MP. I felt a bit . . . well, I thought it was bad timing, us happening to bust that brothel the same time he was there . . .' Bad timing? Did he really believe that was all there was to it? 'So, when I *did* happen to be passing – I'd stayed the night at Sergeant Holmes' new house . . . he lives in Jack's constituency – I thought I'd stop and take a look. There were a lot of reporters about the place. I don't know exactly why I stopped, but then I saw that Jack's car was sitting out on the drive in full view. I reckoned that was dangerous. I mean, if a photo of it got into the papers. Everybody'd know Jack's car, right down to its number plate. You can't be too safe, can you? So I went in and suggested the car be moved into the garage.'

Rebus stopped. That was all there was to it, wasn't it? Well, it was enough to be going on with. Watson was looking thoughtful. He took another injection of coffee before speaking.

'You're not alone, John. I feel guilty myself about Operation Creeper. Not that there's anything to feel guilty *about*, you understand, but all the same . . . and now the press are on to the story, they'll keep on it till the poor bugger's forced to resign.'

Rebus doubted this. Jack hadn't looked like a man ready or willing or about to resign.

'If we can help Jack . . .' Watson paused again, wanting to catch Rebus's eye. He was warning Rebus that this was all unofficial, all unwritten, but that it had already been *dis- cussed*, at some level far above Rebus himself. Perhaps, even, above Watson. Had the Chief Super been rapped over the knuckles by the high heidyins themselves? 'If we can help him,' he was saying, 'I'd like him to get that help. If you see what I mean, John.'

'I think so, sir.' Sir Hugh Ferrie had powerful friends. Rebus was beginning to wonder just *how* powerful . . .

'Right then.'

'Just the one thing, sir. Who gave you the info about the brothel?'

Watson was shaking his head even before Rebus had finished the question. 'Can't tell you that, John. I know what you're thinking. You're wondering if Jack was set up. Well, if he was, it had nothing to do with my informant. I can promise you that. No, if Jack *was* set up, the question that needs answering is why *he* was there in the first place, not why *we* were there.'

'But the papers knew, too. I mean, they knew about Operation Creeper.'

Watson was nodding now. 'Again, nothing to do with my informant. But yes, I've been thinking about that. It had to be one of us, hadn't it? Someone on the team.'

'So nobody else knew when it was planned for?'

Watson seemed to hold his breath for a moment, then shook his head. He was lying, of course. Rebus could see that. No point probing further, not yet at any rate. There would be a reason behind the lie, and that reason would come out in good time. Right now, and for no reason he could put his finger on, Rebus was more worried about *Mrs* Jack. Worried? Well, maybe not quite worried. Maybe not even *concerned*. Call it . . . call it *interested*. Yes, that was it. He was interested in her.

'Any progress on those missing books?'

What missing books? Oh, *those* missing books. He shrugged. 'We've talked to all the booksellers. The list is doing the rounds. We might even get a mention in the trade magazines. I shouldn't think any bookseller is going to touch them. Meantime . . . well, there are the private collectors still to be interviewed. One of them's the wife of Rab Kinnoul.'

'The actor?'

'The very same. Lives out towards South Queensferry. His wife collects first editions.'

'Better try to get out there yourself, John. Don't want to send a constable out to see Rab Kinnoul.'

'Right, sir.' It was the answer he'd wanted. He drained his mug. His nerves were already sizzling like bacon in a pan. 'Anything else?'

But Watson had finished with him, and was rising to

replenish his own mug. 'This stuff's addictive,' he was saying as Rebus left the office. 'But by God, it makes me feel full of beans.'

Rebus didn't know whether to laugh or cry . . .

Rab Kinnoul was a professional hit man.

He had made his name initially through a series of roles on television: the Scottish immigrant in a London sitcom, the young village doctor in a farming serial, with the occasional guest spot on more substantial fare such as *The Sweeney* (playing a Glasgow runaway) or the drama series *Knife Ledge*, where he played a hired killer.

It was this last part which swung things for Kinnoul. Noticed by a London-based casting director, he was approached and screen-tested for the part of the assassin in a low-budget British thriller, which went on to do surprising business, picking up good notices in the USA as well as in Europe. The film's director was soon persuaded to move to Hollywood, and he in turn persuaded his producers that Rab Kinnoul would be ideal for the part of the gangster in an Elmore Leonard adaptation.

So, Kinnoul went to Hollywood, played minor roles in a series of major and minor murder flicks, and was again a success. He possessed a face and eyes into which could be read anything, simply anything. If you thought he should be evil, he *was* evil; if you thought he should be psychotic, he *was* psychotic. He was cast in these roles and he fitted them, but if things had taken a different turning in his career he might just as easily have ended up as the romantic lead, the sympathetic friend, the hero of the piece.

Now he'd settled back in Scotland. There was talk that he was reading scripts, was about to set up his own film company, was retiring. Rebus couldn't quite imagine retiring at thirty-nine. At fifty, maybe, but not at thirty-nine. What would you do all day? Driving towards Kinnoul's home just outside South Queensferry, the answer came to him. You could spend all day every day painting the exterior of your house; supposing, that is, it was the size of Rab Kinnoul's house. Like the Forth Rail Bridge, by the time you'd finished painting it, the first bit would be dirty again.

Which was to say that it was a very large house, even from a distance. It sat on a hillside, its surroundings fairly bleak. Long grass and a few blasted trees. A river ran nearby, discharging into the Firth of Forth. Since there was no sign of a fence separating house from surroundings, Rebus reckoned Kinnoul must own the lot.

The house was modern, if the 1960s could still be considered 'modern', styled like a bungalow but about five times the scale. It reminded Rebus mostly of those Swiss chalets you saw on postcards, except that the chalets were always finished in wood, whereas this house was finished in harling.

'I've seen better council houses,' he whispered to himself as he parked on the pebbled driveway. Getting out of the car he did, however, begin to see one of the house's attractions. The view. Both spectacular Forth Bridges not too far away at all, the firth itself sparkling and calm, and the sun shining on green and pleasant Fife across the water. You couldn't see Rosyth, but over to the east could just about be made out the seaside town of Kirkcaldy, where Gregor Jack and, presumably, Rab Kinnoul, had been schooled.

'No,' said Mrs Kinnoul – Cath Kinnoul – as she walked, a little later, into the sitting room. 'People are always making that mistake.'

She had come to the door while Rebus was still staring.

'Admiring the view?'

He grinned back at her. 'Is that Kirkcaldy over there?'

'I think so, yes.'

Rebus turned and started up the steps towards the front door. There were rockeries and neat borders to either side of them. Mrs Kinnoul looked the type to enjoy gardening. She wore homely clothes and a homely smile. Her hair had been permed into waves, but pulled back and held with a clasp at the back. There was something of the 1950s about her. He didn't know what he'd been expecting – some Hollywood blonde, perhaps – but certainly he'd not been expecting this.

'I'm Cath Kinnoul.' She held out a hand. 'I'm sorry, I've forgotten your name.'

He'd phoned, of course, to warn of his visit, to make sure someone would be at home. 'Detective Inspector Rebus,' he said.

'That's right,' she said. 'Well, come in.'

Of course, the whole thing could have been done by telephone. The following rare books have been stolen . . . has anyone approached you . . .? If anyone should, please contact us immediately. But like any other policeman, Rebus liked to *see* who and what he was dealing with. People often gave something away when you were there in person. They were flustered, edgy. Not that Cath Kinnoul looked flustered. She came into the sitting room with a tray of tea things. Rebus had been staring out of the picture window, drinking in the scene.

'Your husband went to school in Kirkcaldy, didn't he?'

And then she'd said: 'No, people are always making that mistake. I think because of Gregor Jack. You know, the MP.' She placed the tray on a coffee table. Rebus had turned from the window and was studying the room. There were framed photographs of Rab Kinnoul on the walls, stills from his movies. There were also photos of actors and actresses Rebus supposed he should know. The photos were signed. The room seemed to be dominated by a thirty-eight-inch television, atop which sat a video recorder. To either side of the TV, piled high on the floor, were videotapes.

'Sit down, Inspector. Sugar?'

'Just milk, please. You were saying about your husband and Gregor Jack . . .?'

'Oh yes. Well, I suppose because they're both in the media, on television I mean, people tend to think they must know one another.'

'And don't they?'

She laughed. 'Oh yes, yes, they know one another. But only through me. People get their stories mixed up, I suppose, so it started to appear in the papers and magazines that Rab and Gregor went to school together, which is nonsense. Rab went to school in Dundee. It was *me* that went to school with Gregor. And we went to university together, too.'

So not even the cream of young Scottish reporters always got it right. Rebus accepted the china cup and saucer with a nod of thanks.

'I was plain Catherine Gow then, of course. I met Rab later, when he was already working in television. He was doing a play in Edinburgh. I bumped into him in the bar after a performance.'

She was stirring her tea absent-mindedly. 'I'm Cath Kinnoul now, Rab Kinnoul's wife. Hardly anyone calls me Gowk any more.'

'Gowk?' Rebus thought he'd misheard. She looked up at him.

'That was my nickname. We all had nicknames. Gregor was Beggar . . .'

'And Ronald Steele was Suey.'

She stopped stirring, and looked at him as though seeing him for the first time. 'That's right. But how . . . ?'

'It's what his shop's called,' Rebus explained, this being the truth.

'Oh yes,' she said. 'Well, anyway, about these books . . .'

Three things struck Rebus. One was that there seemed precious few books around, for someone who was supposedly a collector. The second was that he'd rather talk some more about Gregor Jack. The third was that Cath Kinnoul was on drugs, tranquillizers of some kind. It was taking a second too long for her lips to form each word, and her eyelids had a droop to them. Valium? Moggies even?

'Yes,' he said, 'the books.' Then he looked around him. Any actor would have known it for a cheap effect. 'Mr Kinnoul's not at home just now?'

She smiled. 'Most people just call him Rab. They think if they've seen him on television, they know him, and knowing him gives them the right to call him Rab. Mr Kinnoul . . . I can see you're a policeman.' She almost wagged a finger at him, but thought better of it and drank her tea instead. She held the delicate cup by its body rather than by the awkward handle, drained it absolutely dry, and exhaled.

'Thirsty this morning,' she said. 'I'm sorry, what were you saying?'

'You were telling me about Gregor Jack.'

She looked surprised. 'Was I?'

Rebus nodded.

'Yes, that's right, I read about it in the papers. Horrible things they were saying. About him and Liz.'

'Mrs Jack?'

'Liz, yes.'

'What's she like?'

Cath Kinnoul seemed to shiver. She got up slowly and placed her empty cup on the tray. 'More tea?' Rebus shook his head. She poured milk, lots of sugar, and then a trickle of tea into her cup. 'Thirsty,' she said, 'this morning.' She went to the window, holding the cup in both hands. 'Liz is her own woman. You've got to admire her for that. It can't be easy, living with a man who's in the public eye. He hardly sees her.'

'He's away a lot, you mean?'

'Well, yes. But she's away a lot, too. She has her own life, her own friends.'

'Do you know her well?'

'No, no, I wouldn't say that. You wouldn't believe what we got up to at school. Who'd have thought . . .' She touched the window. 'Do you like the house, Inspector?'

This was an unexpected turn in the conversation. 'It's . . . er, big, isn't it?' Rebus answered. 'Plenty of room.'

'Seven bedrooms,' she said. 'Rab bought it from some rock star. I don't think he'd have bothered if it hadn't been a *star's* home. What do we need seven bedrooms for? There's only the two of us . . . Oh, here's Rab now.'

Rebus came to the window. A Land-Rover was bumping up the driveway. There was a heavy figure in the front, hands clenching the wheel. The Land-Rover gave a squeal as it stopped.

'About these books,' said Rebus, suddenly an efficient official. 'You collect books, I believe?'

'Rare books, yes. First editions, mostly.' Cath Kinnoul, too, was starting to play another part, this time the woman who's helping police with their . . .

The front door opened and closed. 'Cath? Whose car's that in the drive?'

Rab Kinnoul came massively into the room. He was six feet two tall, and probably weighed fifteen stone. His chest was huge, a predominantly red tartan shirt stretched across it. He wore baggy brown corduroys tied at the waist with a thin, straining belt. He'd started growing a reddish beard, and his brown hair was longer than Rebus remembered, curling over his ears. He looked expectantly at Rebus, who came towards him.

'Inspector Rebus, sir.'

Kinnoul looked surprised, then relieved, then, Rebus thought, worried. The problem was those eyes; they didn't seem to change, did they? So that Rebus began to wonder whether the surprise, relief and worry were in Kinnoul's mind or in his own.

'Inspector, what's . . . I mean, is there something wrong?'

'No, no, sir. It's just that some books have been stolen, rare books, and we're going around talking to private collectors.'

'Oh.' Now Kinnoul broke into a grin. Rebus didn't think he'd seen him grin in any of his TV or film roles. He could see why. The grin changed Kinnoul from ominous heavy into overgrown teenager, lighting his face, making it innocent and benign. 'So it's Cath you want then?' He looked over Rebus's shoulder at his wife. 'All right, Cath?'

'Fine, Rab.'

Kinnoul looked at Rebus again. The grin had disappeared. 'Maybe you'd like to see the library, Inspector? Cath and you can have a chat in there.'

'Thank you, sir.'

Rebus took the back roads on his way into Edinburgh. They were nicer, certainly quieter. He'd learned very little in the

Kinnoul's library, except that Kinnoul felt protective towards his wife, so protective that he'd felt unable to leave Rebus alone with her. What was he afraid of? He had stalked the library, had pretended to browse, and sat down with a book, all the time listening as Rebus asked his simple questions and left the simple list and asked Cath Kinnoul to be on the lookout. And she'd nodded, fingering the xeroxed sheet of paper.

The 'library' in fact was an upper room of the house, probably intended at one time as a bedroom. Two walls had been fitted with shelves, most of them sheeted with sliding glass doors. And behind these sheets of glass sat a dull collection of books – dull to Rebus's eyes, but they seemed enough to bring Cath Kinnoul out of her daydreams. She pointed out some of the exhibits to Rebus.

'Fine first edition ... rebound in calfskin ... some pages still uncut. Just think, that book was printed in 1789, but if I cut open those pages I'd be the first person ever to read them. Oh, and that's a Creech edition of Burns ... first time Burns was published in Edinburgh. And I've some modern books, too. There's Muriel Spark ... *Midnight's Children* ... George Orwell ...'

'Have you read them all?'

She looked at Rebus as though he'd asked her about her sexual preferences. Kinnoul interrupted.

'Cath's a collector, Inspector.' He came over and put his arm around her. 'It could have been stamps or porcelain or old china dolls, couldn't it, love? But it's books. She collects books.' He gave her a squeeze. 'She doesn't read them. She collects them.'

Rebus shook his head now, tapping his fingers against the steering wheel. He'd shoved a Rolling Stones tape into the car's cassette player. An aid to constructive thought. On the one hand, you had Professor Costello, with his marvellous library, the books read and reread, worth a fortune but still there for the borrowing ... for the *reading*. And on the other hand there was Cath Kinnoul. He didn't quite know why he felt so sorry for her. It couldn't be easy being married to ...

well, she'd said it herself, hadn't she? Except that she'd been talking about Elizabeth Jack. Rebus was intrigued by Mrs Jack. More, he was becoming *fascinated* by her. He hoped he would meet her soon . . .

The call from Dufftown came just as he got into the office. On the stairs, he'd been told of another rumour. By the middle of next week, there would be official notification that Great London Road was to close. Then back I go to Marchmont, Rebus thought.

The telephone was ringing. It was always ringing either just as he was coming in, or else just as he was about to go out. He could sit in his chair for hours and never once . . .

'Hello, Rebus here.'

There was a pause, and enough snap-crackle over the line for the call to be trans-Siberian.

'Is that Inspector Rebus?'

Rebus sighed and fell into his chair. 'Speaking.'

'Hello, sir. This is a terrible line. It's Constable Moffat. You wanted someone to go to Deer Lodge.'

Rebus perked up. 'That's right.'

'Well, sir, I've just been over there and – ' And there was a noise like an excited geiger counter. Rebus held the receiver away from his ear. When the noise had stopped, the constable was still speaking. 'I don't know what more I can tell you, sir.'

'You can tell me the whole bloody lot again for a start,' Rebus said. 'The line went supernova for a minute there.'

Constable Moffat began again, articulating his words as though in conversation with a retard. 'I was saying, sir, that I went over to Deer Lodge, but there's no one at home. No car outside. I had a look through the windows. I'd say someone *had* been there at some time. Looked like there'd been a bit of a party. Wine bottles and glasses and stuff. But there's no one there at the minute.'

'Did you ask any of the neighbours . . .?' As he said it, Rebus knew this to be a stupid question. The constable was already laughing.

'There *aren't* any neighbours, sir. The nearest would be Mr and Mrs Kennoway, but they're a mile hike the other side of the hills.'

'I see. And there's nothing else you can tell me?'

'Not that I can think of. If there was anything in particular ...? I mean, I know the lodge is owned by that MP, and I saw in the papers ...'

'No,' Rebus was quick to say, 'nothing to do with that.' He didn't want *more* rumours being tossed around like so many cabers at a Highland games. 'Just wanted a word with Mrs Jack. We thought she might be up there.'

'Aye, she's up this way occasionally, so I hear.'

'Well, if you hear anything else, let me know, won't you?'

'Goes without saying, sir.' Which, Rebus supposed, it did. The constable sounded a bit hurt.

'And thanks for your help,' Rebus added, but received only a curt 'Aye' before the phone went dead.

'Fuck you too, pal,' he said to himself, before going off in search of Gregor Jack's home telephone number.

Of course, there was an almighty chance that the phone would still be unplugged. Still, it was worth a try. The number itself would be on computer, but Rebus reckoned he'd be quicker looking for it in the filing cabinet. And sure enough, he found a sheet of paper headed 'Parliamentary Constituencies in Edinburgh and Lothians' on which were given the home addresses and telephone numbers of the area's eleven MPs. He punched in the ten numbers, waited, and was rewarded with the ringing tone. Not that that meant –

'Hello?'

'Is that Mr Urquhart?'

'I'm sorry, Mr Urquhart's not here right at the moment – '

But of course by now Rebus recognized the voice. 'Is that you, Mr Jack? It's Inspector Rebus here. We met yester – '

'Why yes, hello, Inspector. You're in luck. We plugged the phone back in this morning, and Ian's spent all day taking calls. He's just taken a break. He thought we should unplug the thing again, but I plugged it back in myself when he'd gone. I hate to think I'm completely cut off. My constituents, after all, might need to get – '

'What about Miss Greig?'

'She's working. Work must go on, Inspector. There's an office to the back of the house where she does the typing and so on. Helen's really been a – '

'And Mrs Jack? Any news?'

Now the flow seemed to have dried up. There was a parched cough. Rebus could visualize a readjustment of facial features, maybe even a scratching of finger, a running of fingers through hair . . .

'Why . . . yes, funny you should mention it. She phoned this morning.'

'Oh?'

'Yes, poor love. Said she'd been trying for hours, but of course the phone was disconnected all day Sunday and busy most of today – '

'She's at your cottage then?'

'That's right, yes. Spending a week there. I told her to stay put. No point in her getting dragged into all this rubbish, is there? It'll soon blow over. My solicitor – '

'We've checked Deer Lodge, Mr Jack.'

Another pause. Then: 'Oh?'

'She doesn't seem to be there. No sign of life.'

There was sweat beneath the collar of Rebus's shirt. He could blame it on the heating of course. But he knew the heating wasn't *all* to blame. Where was this leading? What was he wandering into?

'Oh.' A statement this time, a deflated sound. 'I see.'

'Mr Jack, is there anything you'd like to tell me?'

'Yes, Inspector, there is, I suppose.'

Carefully: 'Would you like me to come over?'

'Yes.'

'All right, I'll be there as soon as I can. Just sit tight, all right?'

No answer.

'All right, Mr Jack?'

'Yes.'

But Gregor Jack didn't sound it.

Of course, Rebus's car wouldn't start. The sound it made was more and more like an emphysema patient's last hacking laugh. Herka-herka-her-ka-ka. Herka-herka-her.

'Having trouble?' This was yelled from across the car park by Brian Holmes, waving and about to get into his own car. Rebus slammed his car door shut and walked briskly over to where Holmes was just – with a first-time turn of the ignition – starting his Metro.

'Off home?'

'Yes.' A nod towards Rebus's doomed car. 'Doesn't sound as if you are. Want a lift?'

'As it happens, Brian, yes. And you can come along for the ride if you like.'

'I don't get it.'

Rebus was trying to open the passenger-side door, without success. Holmes hesitated a moment before unlocking it.

'It's my turn to cook tonight,' he said. 'Nell'll be up to high doh if I'm late . . .'

Rebus settled into the passenger seat and pulled the seatbelt down across his chest.

'I'll tell you all about it on the way.'

'The way where?'

'Not far from where you live. You won't be late, honest. I'll get a car to bring me back into town. But I'd quite like your attendance.'

Holmes wasn't slow; careful – yes, but never slow. 'You mean the male member,' he said. 'What's he done this time?'

'I shudder to think, Brian. Believe me, I shudder to think.'

There were no pressmen patrolling the gates, and the gates themselves were unlocked. The car had been put away in the garage, leaving the driveway clear. They left Holmes' car sitting on the main road outside.

'Quite a place,' Holmes commented.

'Wait till you see inside. It's like a film set, Ingmar Bergman or something.'

Holmes shook his head. 'I still can't believe it,' he said. 'You, coming out here yesterday, barging your way in – '

'Hardly barging, Brian. Now listen, I'm going to have a word with Jack. You sniff around, see if anything smells rotten.'

'You mean literally rotten?'

'I'm not expecting to find decomposing bodies in the flower beds, if that's what you're thinking. No, just keep your eyes open and your ears keen.'

'And my nose wet?'

'If you haven't got a handkerchief on you, yes.'

They separated, Rebus to the front door, Holmes around to the side of the house, towards the garage. Rebus rang the doorbell. It was nearly six. No doubt Helen Greig would be on her way home . . .

But it was Helen Greig who answered the door.

'Hello,' she said. 'Come in. Gregor's in the living room. You know the way.'

'Indeed I do. Keeping you busy, is he?' He laid a finger on the face of his wristwatch.

'Oh yes,' she said smiling, 'he's a real slavemaster.'

An unkind image came to Rebus then, of Jack in leather gear and Helen Greig on a leash . . . He blinked it away. 'Does he seem all right?'

'Who? Gregor?' She gave a quiet laugh. 'He seems fine, under the circumstances. Why?'

'Just wondering, that's all.'

She thought for a moment, seemed about to say something, then remembered her place. 'Can I get you anything?'

'No, thanks.'

'Right, see you later then.' And off she went, back past the curving staircase, back to her office to the rear of the house. Damn, he hadn't told Holmes about her. If Holmes peered in through the office window . . . Oh well. If he heard a scream, he'd know what had happened. He opened the living room door.

66

Gregor Jack was alone. Alone and listening to his hi-fi. The volume was low, but Rebus recognized the Rolling Stones. It was the album he'd been listening to earlier, *Let It Bleed*.

Jack rose from his leather sofa, a glass of whisky in one hand. 'Inspector, you didn't take long. You've caught me indulging in my secret vice. Well, we all have *one* secret vice, don't we?'

Rebus thought again of the scene at the brothel. And Jack seemed to read his mind, for he gave an embarrassed smile. Rebus shook the proffered hand. He noticed that a plaster had been stuck on the left hand's offending finger. One secret vice, and one tiny flaw . . .

Jack saw him noticing. 'Eczema,' he explained, and seemed about to say more.

'Yes, you said.'

'Did I?'

'Yesterday.'

'You'll have to forgive me, Inspector. I don't usually repeat myself. But what with yesterday and everything . . .'

'Understood.' Past Jack, Rebus noticed a card standing on the mantelpiece. It hadn't been there yesterday.

Jack realized he had a glass in his hand. 'Can I offer you a drink?'

'You can, sir, and I accept.'

'Whisky all right? I don't think there's much else . . .'

'Whatever you're having, Mr Jack.' And for some reason he added: 'I like the Rolling Stones myself, their earlier stuff.'

'Agreed,' said Jack. 'The music scene these days, it's all rubbish, isn't it?' He'd gone over to the wall to the left of the fireplace, where glass shelves held a series of bottles and glasses. As he poured, Rebus walked over to the table where yesterday Urquhart had been fussing with some papers. There were letters, waiting to be signed (all with the House of Commons portcullis at the head), and some notes relating to parliamentary business.

'This job,' Jack was saying, approaching with Rebus's drink, 'really is what you make of it. There are some MPs

67

who do the minimum necessary, and believe me that's still plenty. Cheers.'

'Cheers.' They both drank.

'Then there are those,' said Jack, 'who go for the maximum. They do their constituency work, and they become involved in the parliamentary process, the wider world. They debate, they write, they attend . . .'

'And which camp do you belong to, sir?' He talks too much, Rebus was thinking, and yet he says so little . . .

'Straight down the middle,' said Jack, steering a course with his flattened hand. 'Here, sit down.'

'Thank you, sir.' They both sat, Rebus on the chair, Jack on the sofa. Rebus had noticed straight away that the whisky was watered, and he wondered by whom? And did Jack know about it? 'Now then,' said Rebus, 'you said on the phone that there was something – '

Jack used a remote control to switch off the music. He aimed the remote at the wall, it seemed to Rebus. There was no hi-fi system in sight. 'I want to get things straight about my wife, Inspector,' he said. 'About Liz. I *am* worried about her, I admit it. I didn't want to say anything before . . .'

'Why not, sir?' So far, the speech sounded well prepared. But then he'd had over an hour in which to prepare it. Soon enough, it would run out. Rebus could be patient. He wondered where Urquhart was . . .

'Publicity, Inspector. Ian calls Liz my liability. I happen to think he's going a bit far, but Liz is . . . well, not quite temperamental . . .'

'You think she saw the newspapers?'

'Almost certainly. She always buys the tabloids. It's the gossip she likes.'

'But she hasn't been in touch?'

'No, no, she hasn't.'

'And that's a bit strange, wouldn't you say?'

Jack creased his face. 'Yes and no, Inspector. I mean, I don't know what to think. She's capable of just laughing the whole thing off. But then again . . .'

'You think she might harm herself, sir?'

'Harm herself?' Jack was slow to understand. 'You mean suicide? No, I don't think so, no, not that. But if she felt embarrassed, she might simply disappear. Or something could have happened to her, an accident ... God knows what. If she got angry enough ... it's just possible ...' He bowed his head again, elbows resting on his knees.

'Do you think it's police business, sir?'

Jack looked up with glinting eyes. 'That's the crux, isn't it? If I report her missing ... I mean report her *officially* ... and she's found, and it turns out she was simply keeping out of things ...'

'Does she seem the type who *would* stay out of things, sir?' Rebus's thoughts were spinning now. Someone had set Jack up ... but not his wife, surely? Sunday newspaper thoughts, but still they worried him.

Jack shrugged. 'Not really. It's hard to tell with Liz. She's changeable.'

'Well, sir, we could make a few discreet inquiries up north. Check hotels, guest houses – '

'It would have to be hotels, Inspector, where Liz is concerned. *Expensive* hotels.'

'Okay then, we check hotels, ask around. Any friends she might visit?'

'Not many.'

Rebus waited, wondering if Jack would change his mind. After all, there was always Andrew Macmillan, the murderer. Someone she probably knew, someone nearby. But Jack merely shrugged and repeated, 'Not many.'

'Well, a list would help, sir. You might even contact them yourself. You know, just phoning for a chat. If Mrs Jack was there, they'd be bound to tell you.'

'Unless she'd told them not to.'

Well, that was true.

'But then,' Jack was saying, 'if it turned out she'd been off to one of the islands and hadn't heard a thing ...'

Politics, it was all about politics in the end. Rebus was coming to respect Gregor Jack less, but, in a strange way, like him more. He rose and walked over towards the shelf unit, ostensibly to put his glass there. At the mantelpiece, he stopped by the card and picked it up. The front was a cartoon showing a young man in an open-topped sports car, champagne in an ice bucket on the passenger seat. The message above read GOOD LUCK! Inside was another message, written in felt pen: 'Never fear, The Pack is with you'. There were six signatures.

'Schoolfriends,' Jack was saying. He came over to stand beside Rebus. 'And a couple from university days. We've stuck pretty close over the years.'

A few of the names Rebus recognized, but he was happy to look puzzled and let Jack provide the information.

'Gowk, that's Cathy Gow. She's Cath Kinnoul now, Kinnoul as in Rab, the actor.' His finger drifted to the next signature. 'Tampon is Tom Pond. He's an architect in Edinburgh. Bilbo, that's Bill Fisher, works in London for some magazine. He was always daft on Tolkien.' Jack's voice had become soft with sentiment. Rebus was thinking of the schoolfriends *he'd* kept up with – a grand total of none. 'Suey is Ronnie Steele . . .'

'Why Suey?'

Jack smiled. 'I'm not sure I should tell you. Ronnie would kill me.' He considered for a moment, gave a mellow shrug. 'Well, we were on a school trip to Switzerland, and a girl went into Ronnie's room and found him . . . doing something. She went and told everyone about it, and Ronnie was so embarrassed that he ran outside and lay down in the road. He said he was going to kill himself, only no cars came past, so eventually he got up.'

'And suicide abbreviates to Suey?'

'That's right.' Jack studied the card again. 'Sexton, that's Alice Blake. Sexton Blake, you see. A detective like yourself.' Jack smiled. 'Alice works in London, too. Something to do with PR.'

'And what about . . .?' Rebus was pointing to the last secret name, Mack. Jack's face changed.

'Oh, that's . . . Andy Macmillan.'

70

'And what does Mr Macmillan do these days?' Mack, Rebus was thinking. As in Mack the Knife, grimly apt . . .

Jack was aloof. 'He's in prison, I believe. Tragic story, tragic.'

'In prison?' Rebus was keen to pursue the subject, but Jack had other ideas. He pointed to the names on the card.

'Notice anything, Inspector?'

Yes, Rebus had, though he hadn't been going to mention it. Now he did. 'The names are all written by the same person.'

Jack gave a quick smile. 'Bravo.'

'Well, Mr Macmillan's in prison, and Mr Fisher and Miss Blake could hardly have signed, could they, living in London? The story only broke yesterday . . .'

'Ah yes, good point.'

'So who . . .?'

'Cathy. She used to be an expert forger, though you might not think it to look at her. She used to have all our signatures off by heart.'

'But Mr Pond lives in Edinburgh . . . couldn't he have signed his own?'

'I think he's in the States on business.'

'And Mr Steele . . .?' Rebus tapped the 'Suey' scrawl.

'Well, Suey's a hard man to catch, Inspector.'

'Is that so,' mused Rebus, 'is that so.'

There was a knock at the door.

'Come in, Helen.'

Helen Greig put her head round the door. She was dressed in a raincoat, the belt of which she was tying. 'I'm just off, Gregor. Ian not back yet?'

'Not yet. Catching up on his sleep, I expect.'

Rebus was replacing the card on the mantelpiece. He was wondering, too, whether Gregor Jack was surrounded by friends or by something else entirely . . .

'Oh,' said Helen Greig, 'and there's another policeman here. He was at the back door . . .'

The door opened to its full extent, and Brian Holmes walked into the room. Awkwardly, it seemed to Rebus. It

71

struck him that Holmes was awkward in the presence of Gregor Jack MP.

'Thank you, Helen. See you tomorrow.'

'You're at Westminster tomorrow, Gregor.'

'God, so I am. Right, see you the day after.'

Helen Greig left, and Rebus introduced Jack to Brian Holmes. Holmes still seemed unnaturally awkward. What the hell was the matter? It couldn't just be Jack could it? Then Holmes cleared his throat. He was looking at his superior, avoiding eye contact with the MP altogether.

'Sir, er . . . there's something maybe you should see. Round the back. In the dustbin. I had some rubbish in my pockets and I thought I'd get rid of it, and I happened to lift the lid off the bin . . .'

Gregor Jack's face turned stark white.

'Right,' said Rebus briskly, 'lead the way, Brian.' He made a sweeping motion with his arm. 'After you, Mr Jack.'

The back of the house was well lit. Two sturdy black plastic bins sat beside a bushy rhododendron. Each bin had attached inside it a black plastic refuse bag. Holmes lifted the lid off the left-hand bin and held it open so that Rebus could peer inside. He was staring at a flattened cornflake packet and the wrapping from some biscuits.

'Beneath,' Holmes stated simply. Rebus lifted the cornflake packet. It had been concealing a little treasure chest. Two video cassettes, their casings broken, tape spewing from them . . . a packet of photographs . . . two small gold-coloured vibrators . . . two pairs of flimsy-looking handcuffs . . . and clothing, body-stockings, knickers with zips. Rebus couldn't help wondering what the hacks would have done if they'd found this lot first . . .

'I can explain,' said Jack brokenly.

'You don't have to, sir. It's none of our business.' Rebus said this in such a way that his meaning was clear: it might not be our business, but you'd better tell us anyway.

'I . . . I panicked. No, not really a panic. It's just, what with that story about the brothel, and now Liz is off somewhere

72

... and I knew you were on your way ... I just wanted rid of the lot of it.' He was perspiring. 'I mean, I know it must look strange, that's precisely why I wanted rid of it all. Not my stuff, you see, it's Liz's. Her friends ... the parties they have ... well, I didn't want you to get the wrong impression.'

Or the right impression, thought Rebus. He picked up the packet of photographs, which just happened to burst open. 'Sorry,' he said, making a show of gathering them up. They were polaroids, taken at a party it was true. Quite a party, by the look of it. And who was this?

Rebus held the photograph up so that Jack could see it. It showed Gregor Jack having his shirt removed by two women. Everyone's eyes were red.

'The first and last party I ever went to,' Jack stated.

'Yes, sir,' said Rebus.

'Look, Inspector, my wife's life is her *own*. What she chooses to get up to ... well, it's out of my hands.' Anger was replacing embarrassment. 'I might not *like* it, I might not like her *friends*, but it's *her* choice.'

'Right, sir.' Rebus threw the photographs back into the bin. 'Well, maybe your wife's ... friends will know where she is, eh? Meantime, I wouldn't leave that lot in there, not unless you want to see yourself on the front pages again. The bins are the first place some journalists look. It's not called "getting the dirt" for nothing. And as I say, Mr Jack, it's none of *our* business ... not yet.'

But it would be soon enough; Rebus felt it in his gut, which tumbled at the thought.

It would be soon enough.

Back inside the house, Rebus tried to concentrate on one thing at a time. Not easy, not at all easy. Jack wrote down the names and addresses of a few of his wife's friends. If not quite high society, they were certainly more than a few rungs above the Horsehair. Then Rebus asked about Liz Jack's car.

'A black BMW,' said Jack. 'The 3-series. My birthday present to her last year.'

Rebus thought of his own car. 'Very nice too, sir. And the

registration?' Jack reeled it off. Rebus looked a little surprised, but Jack smiled weakly.

'I'm an accountant by training,' he explained. 'I never forget figures.'

'Of course, sir. Well, we'd better be – '

There was a sound, the sound of the front door opening and closing. Voices in the hall. Had the prodigal wife returned? All three men turned towards the living room door, which now swung open.

'Gregor? Look who I found coming up the drive . . .'

Ian Urquhart saw that Gregor Jack had visitors. He paused, startled. Behind him, a tired-looking man was shuffling into the room. He was tall and skinny, with lank black hair and round NHS-style spectacles.

'Gregor,' the man said. He walked up to Gregor Jack and they shook hands. Then Jack placed a hand on the man's shoulder.

'Meant to look in before now,' the man was saying, 'but you know how it is.' He really did look exhausted, with dark-ringed eyes and a stoop to his posture. His speech and movements were slow. 'I think I've clinched a nice collection of Italian art books . . .'

He now seemed ready to acknowledge the visitors' presence. Rebus had been given Urquhart's hand and was shaking it. The visitor nodded towards Rebus's right hand.

'You,' he said, 'must be Inspector Rebus.'

'That's right.'

'How do you know that?' said Gregor Jack, suitably impressed.

'Scratch marks on the wrist,' the visitor explained. 'Vanessa told me an Inspector Rebus had been in, and that Rasputin had made his mark . . . his considerable mark, by the look of things.'

'You must be Mr Steele,' said Rebus, shaking hands.

'The very same,' said Steele. 'Sorry I wasn't in when you called. As Gregor here will tell you, I'm a hard man to – '

'Catch,' interrupted Jack. 'Yes, Ronnie, I've already told the Inspector.'

74

'No sign of those books then, sir?' Rebus asked Steele. He shrugged.

'Too hot to handle, Inspector. Do you have any idea how much that lot would fetch? My guess would be a private collector.'

'Stolen to order?'

'Maybe. A fairly broad range though ...' Steele seemed to tire quickly of the topic. He turned again to Gregor Jack and held his arms wide open, half shrugging. 'Gregor, what the hell are they trying to do to you?'

'Obviously,' said Urquhart, who was helping himself unasked to a drink, 'someone somewhere is looking for a resignation.'

'But what were you doing there in the first place?'

Steele had asked *the* question. He asked it into a silence which lasted for a very long time. Urquhart had poured him a drink, and handed it over, while Gregor Jack seemed to study the four men in the room, as though one of them might have the answer. Rebus noticed that Brian Holmes was studying a painting on one wall, seemingly oblivious to the whole conversation. At last, Jack made an exasperated sound and shook his head.

'I think,' Rebus said, into the general silence, 'we'd better be off.'

'Remember to empty your dustbin, sir,' was his final message to Jack, before he led Holmes down the driveway towards the main road. Holmes agreed to give him a lift into Bonnyrigg, from where Rebus could pick up a ride back into town, but otherwise reached, opened and started the car without comment. As he moved up into second gear, however, Holmes finally said: 'Nice guy. Do you think maybe he'd give us an invite to one of those parties?'

'Brian,' Rebus said warningly. Then: 'Not *his* parties, parties attended by his wife. It didn't look like their house in those photos.'

'Really? I didn't get that good a look. All I saw was my MP

75

being stripped by a couple of eager ladies.' Holmes gave a sudden chuckle.

'What?'

'Strip Jack Naked,' he said.

'Pardon?'

'It's a card game,' Holmes explained. 'Strip Jack Naked. You might know it as Beggar My Neighbour.'

'Really?' Rebus said, trying not to sound interested. But was that precisely what someone was trying to do, strip Jack of his constituency, his clean-cut image, perhaps even his marriage? Were they trying to beggar the man whose nickname also was Beggar?

Or was Jack not quite as innocent as he seemed? No, hell, be honest: he didn't *seem* all that innocent anyway. Fact: he had visited a brothel. Fact: he had tried to get rid of evidence that he himself had attended at least one fairly 'high-spirited' party. Fact: his wife hadn't been in touch. Big deal. Rebus's money was still on the man. In religion, he might be more Pessimisterian than Presbyterian, but in some things John Rebus still clung to faith.

Faith and hope. It was charity he usually lacked.

4
Tips

'We've got to keep this away from the papers,' said Chief Superintendent Watson. 'For as long as we can.'

'Right, sir,' said Lauderdale, while Rebus stayed silent. They were not talking about Gregor Jack, they were discussing a suspect in the Water of Leith drowning. He was in an interview room now with two officers and a tape recorder. He was helping with inquiries. Apparently, he was saying little.

'Could be nothing, after all.'

'Yes, sir.'

There was an afternoon smell of strong mints in the room, and perhaps this was why Chief Inspector Lauderdale sounded and looked more starched than ever. His nose twitched whenever Watson wasn't looking at him. Rebus all of a sudden felt sorry for his Chief Superintendent, in the way that he felt sorry for the Scotland squad whenever it was facing defeat at the hands of third-world part-timers. There but for the grace of complete inability go I . . .

'Just a bit of bragging, perhaps, overheard in a pub. The man was drunk. You know how it is.'

'Quite so, sir.'

'All the same . . .'

All the same, they had a man in the interview room, a man who had told anyone who'd listen in a packed Leith pub that he had dumped that body under Dean Bridge.

'It wis me! Eh? How 'bout that, eh? Me! Me! I did it. She deserved worse. They all do.'

And more of the same, all of it reported to the police by a fearful barmaid, nineteen next month and this was her first bar job.

Deserved worse, she did . . . they *all* do . . . Only when the police had come into the pub, he'd quietened down, gone all sulky in a corner, standing there with head bent under the weight of a cigarette. The pint glass seemed heavy, too, so that his wrist sagged beneath it, beer dripping down on to his shoes and the wooden floor.

'Now then, sir, what's all this you've been telling these people, eh? Mind telling us about it? Down at the station, eh? We've got seats down there. You can have a seat while you tell us all about it . . .'

He was sitting, but he wasn't telling. No name, no address, nobody in the pub seemed to know anything about him. Rebus had taken a look at him, as had most of the CID and uniformed men in the building, but the face meant nothing. A sad, weak example of the species. In his late thirties, his hair was already grey and thin, the face lined, bristly with stubble, and the knuckles had grazes and scabs on them.

'How did you get them then? Been in a fight? Hit her a few times before you chucked her in?'

Nothing. He looked scared, but he was resilient. Their chances of keeping him in were, to put it mildly, not good. He didn't need a solicitor; he knew he just had to keep his mouth shut.

'Been in trouble before, eh? You know the score, don't you? That's why you're keeping quiet. Much good will it do you, pal. Much good.'

Indeed. The pathologist, Dr Curt, was now being harried. They needed to know: accident, suicide, or murder? They desperately needed to know. But before any news arrived, the man began to talk.

'I was drunk,' he told them, 'didn't know what I was saying. I don't know what made me say it.' This was the story he stuck to, repeating it and refining it. They pressed for his name and address. 'I was drunk,' he said. 'That's all there is to it. I'm sober now, and I'd like to go. I'm sorry I said what I did. Can I go now?'

Nobody at the pub had been keen to press charges, not once the offending body was removed from the premises. Unpaid bouncers, thought Rebus, that's all we are. Was the man going to walk? Were they going to lose him? Not without a fight.

'We need a name and address before we can let you go.'

'I was drunk. Can I go now, please?'

'Your name!'

'Please, can I go?'

Curt still wasn't ready to pronounce. An hour or two. Some results he was waiting for . . .

'Just give us a name, eh? Stop pissing about.'

'My name's William Glass. I live at 48 Semple Street in Granton.'

There was silence, then sighs. 'Check that, will you?' one officer asked the other. Then: 'Now that wasn't so painful, was it, Mr Glass?'

The other officer grinned, then had to explain why. 'Painful . . . Glass . . . pane of glass, see?'

'Just do that check, eh?' said his colleague, rubbing at a headache which, these days, never seemed to leave him.

'They've let him go,' Holmes informed Rebus.

'About time. A wild haggis chase and no mistake.'

Holmes came into the office and made himself comfortable on the spare chair.

'Don't stand on ceremony,' said Rebus from his desk, 'just because I'm the senior officer. Why not take a seat, Sergeant?'

'Thank you, sir,' said Holmes from the chair. 'I don't mind if I do. He gave his address as Semple Street, Granton.'

'Off Granton Road?'

'That's the one.' Holmes looked around. 'It's like an oven in here. Can't you open a window?'

'Jammed shut, and the heating's – '

79

'I know, either on full blast or nothing. This place . . .' Holmes shook his head.

'Nothing a bit of maintenance wouldn't fix.'

'Funny,' said Holmes, 'I've never seen you as the sentimental sort . . .'

'Sentimental?'

'About this place. Give me St Leonard's or Fettes any day.'

Rebus wrinkled his nose. 'No character,' he said.

'Speaking of which, what news of the male member?'

'That joke's worn as thin as my hair, Brian. Why not part-ex it against a new one?' Rebus breathed out noisily through his nose and threw down the pen he'd been playing with. 'What you mean,' he said, 'is what news of *Mrs* Jack, and the answer is none, nada, zero. I've put out the description of her car, and all the posh hotels are being checked. But so far, nothing.'

'From which we infer . . .?'

'Same answer: nothing. She could still be off at some Iona spiritual retreat, or shacked up with a Gaelic crofter, or doing the Munros. She could be pissed-off at her hubby, or not know a thing about any of it.'

'And all that kit I found, the sex-shop stock clearance?'

'What about it?'

'Well . . .' Holmes seemed stuck for an answer. 'Nothing really.'

'And there you've put your finger on it, Sergeant. Nothing really. Meantime, I've got work enough to be getting on with.' Rebus laid a solemn hand on the pile of reports and case-notes in front of him. 'How about you?'

Holmes was out of his chair now. 'Oh, I've plenty keeping me busy, sir. Please, don't worry yourself about me.'

'It's natural for me to worry, Brian. You're like a son to me.'

'And you're like a father to me,' Holmes replied, heading for the door. 'The fa-ther I get from you, the easier my life seems to be.'

Rebus screwed a piece of paper into a ball, but the door closed before he had time to take aim. Ach, some days the job could be a laugh. Well, okay, a grin at least. If he forgot all about Gregor Jack, the load would be lighter still. Where would Jack be now? At the House of Commons? Sitting on some committee? Being fêted by businesses and lobbyists? It all seemed a long way from Rebus's office, and from his life.

William Glass . . . no, the name meant nothing to him. Bill Glass, Billy Glass, Willie Glass, Will Glass . . . nothing. Living at 48 Semple Street. Hold on . . . Semple Street in Granton. He went to his filing cabinet and pulled out the file. Yes, just last month. Stabbing incident in Granton. A serious wounding, but not fatal. The victim had lived at 48 Semple Street. Rebus remembered it now. Bedsits carved from a house, all of them rented. A rented bedsit. If William Glass was living at 48 Semple Street, then he was staying in a rented bedsit. Rebus reached for his telephone and called Lauderdale, to whom he told his story.

'Well, someone there vouched for him when the patrol car dropped him off. The officers were told to be sure he did live there, and apparently he does. Name's William Glass, like he said.'

'Yes, but those bedsits are short-let. Tenants get their social security cheque, hand half the cash over to the landlord, maybe more than half for all I know. What I'm saying is, it's not much of an address. He could disappear from there any time he liked.'

'Why so suspicious all of a sudden, John? I thought you were of the opinion we were wasting our time in the first place?'

Oh, but Lauderdale always knew the question to ask, the question to which, as a rule, Rebus did not have an answer.

'True, sir,' he said. 'Just thought I'd let you know.'

'I appreciate it, John. It's nice to be kept informed.' There was a slight pause there, an invitation for Rebus to join Lauderdale's 'camp'. And after the pause: 'Any progress on Professor Costello's books?'

Rebus sighed. 'No, sir.'

'Oh well. Mustn't keep you chatting then. Bye, John.'

'Goodbye, sir.' Rebus wiped his palm across his forehead. It *was* hot in here, like a dress rehearsal for the Calvinist hell.

The fan had been installed and turned on, and an hour or so later Doctor Curt provided the shit to toss at it.

'Murder, yes,' he said. 'Almost definitely murder. I've discussed my findings with my colleagues, and we're of a mind.' And he went on to explain about froth and unclenched hands and diatoms. About problems of differentiating immersion from drowning. The deceased, a woman in her late twenties or early thirties, had imbibed a good deal of drink prior to death. But she had been dead before she'd hit the water, and the cause of death was probably a blow to the back of the head, carried out by a right-handed attacker (the blow itself having come from the right of the head).

But who was she? They had a photograph of the dead woman's face, but it wasn't exactly breakfast-time viewing. And though her description and a description of her clothes had been given out, nobody had been able to identify her. No identification on the body, no handbag or purse, nothing in her pockets . . .

'Better search the area again, see if we can come up with a bag or a purse. She must have had *some*thing.'

'And search the river, sir?'

'A bit late for that probably, but yes, better give it a shot.'

'The alcohol,' Dr Curt was telling anyone who would listen, had 'muddied the water, you see', after which he smiled his slow smile. 'And the fish had eaten their fill: fish fingers, fish feet, fish stomach . . .'

'Yes, sir. I see, sir.'

All of which Rebus mercifully avoided. He had once made the mistake of making a sicker pun than Dr Curt, and as a result found himself in the doctor's favour. One day, he knew, Holmes would make a better pun yet, and then Curt would have himself a new pupil and confidant . . . So, skirting around the doctor, Rebus made for Lauderdale's office.

Lauderdale himself was just getting off the phone. When he saw Rebus, he turned stony. Rebus could guess why.

'I just sent someone round to Glass's bedsit.'

'And he's gone,' Rebus added.

'Yes,' Lauderdale said, his hand still on the receiver. 'Leaving little or nothing behind him.'

'Should be easy enough to pick him up, sir.'

'Get on to it, will you, John? He must still be in the city. What is it? – an hour since he left here. Probably somewhere in the Granton area.'

'We'll get out there right away, sir,' said Rebus, glad of this excuse for a little action.

'Oh, and John . . .?'

'Sir?'

'No need to look so smug, okay?'

So the day filled itself, evening coming upon him with surprising speed. But still they had not found William Glass. Not in Granton, Pilmuir, Newhaven, Inverleith, Canonmills, Leith, Davidson's Mains . . . Not on buses or in pubs, not by the shore, not in the Botanic Gardens, not in chip shops or wandering on playing fields. They had found no friends, no family, just bare details so far from the DHSS. And at the end of it all, Rebus knew, the man might be innocent. But for now he was their straw, to be clutched at. Not the most tasteful metaphor under the circumstances, but then, as Dr Curt himself might have said, it was all water under the bridge so far as the victim was concerned.

'Nothing, sir,' Rebus reported to Lauderdale at the end of play. It had been one of those days. Nothing was the sum total of Rebus's endeavours, yet he felt weary, bone and brain weary. So that he turned down Holmes' kindly offer of a drink, and didn't even debate over his destination. He headed for Oxford Terrace and the ministrations of Dr Patience Aitken, not forgetting Lucky the cat, the wolf-whistling budgies, the tropical fish, and the tame hedgehog he'd yet to see.

*

Rebus telephoned Gregor Jack's home first thing Wednesday morning. Jack sounded tired, having spent yesterday in Parliament and the evening at some 'grotesque function, and you can quote me on that'. There was a new and altogether fake heartiness about him, occasioned, Rebus didn't doubt, by the shared knowledge of the contents of that dustbin.

Well, Rebus was tired, too. The real difference between them was a question of pay scales . . .

'Have you heard anything from your wife yet, Mr Jack?'

'Nothing.'

There was that word again. Nothing.

'What about you, Inspector? Any news?'

'No, sir.'

'Well, no news is better than bad news, so they say. Speaking of which, I read this morning that that poor woman at Dean Bridge was murder.'

'I'm afraid so.'

'Puts my own troubles into perspective, doesn't it? Mind you, there's a constituency meeting this morning, so my troubles may just be starting. Let me know, won't you? If you hear anything, I mean.'

'Of course, Mr Jack.'

'Thank you, Inspector. Goodbye.'

'Goodbye, sir.'

All very formal and correct, as their relationship had to be. Not even room for a 'Good luck with the meeting'. He knew what the meeting would be about. People didn't like it when their MP got himself into a scandal. There would be questions. There would need to be answers . . .

Rebus opened his desk drawer and lifted out the list of Elizabeth Jack's friends, her 'circle'. Jamie Kilpatrick the antique dealer (and apparent black sheep of his titled family); the Hon. Matilda Merriman, notorious for her alleged night of non-stop rogering with a one-time cabinet member; Julian Kaymer, some sort of artist; Martin Inman, professional landowner; Louise Patterson-Scott, separated wife of the retail millionaire . . .

The 'names' just kept on coming, most of them, as Jack

himself had put it while making out the list, 'seasoned dissolutes and hangers-on'. Mainly old money, as Chris Kemp had said, and a long way away from Gregor Jack's own 'pack'. But there was one curio among them, one seeming exception. Even Rebus had recognized it as Gregor Jack scratched it on to the list.

'What? *The* Barney Byars? The original dirty trucker?'

'The haulier, yes.'

'A bit out of place in that sort of company, isn't he?'

Jack had owned up. 'Actually, Barney's an old school-pal of mine. But as time's gone on, he's grown friendlier with Liz. It happens sometimes.'

'Still, somehow I can't see him fitting in with that lot – '

'You'd be surprised, Inspector Rebus. Believe me, you would be surprised.' Jack gave each word equal weight, leaving Rebus in no doubt that he meant what he said. Still ... Byars was another fly Fifer, another famous son. While at school, he'd made his name as a hitchhiker, often claiming he'd spent the weekend in London without paying a penny to get there. After school, he made the news again by hitching his way across France, Italy, Germany, Spain. He'd fallen in love with the lorries themselves, with the whole business of them, so he'd saved, got his HGV licence, bought himself a lorry ... and now was the largest independent haulier that Rebus could think of. Even on last year's trip to London, Rebus had been confronted by a Byars Haulage artic trying to steer its way through Piccadilly Circus.

Well, it was Rebus's job to ask if anyone had seen hide or hair of Liz Jack. He'd gladly let others do the hard work with the likes of Jamie Kilpatrick and the grim-sounding Julian Kaymer; but he was keeping Barney Byars for himself. Another week or two of this, he thought, and I'll have to buy an autograph book.

As it happened, Byars was in Edinburgh, 'drumming up custom', as the girl in his office put it. Rebus gave her his telephone number, and an hour later Byars himself called back. He would be busy all afternoon, and he'd to go to dinner that evening 'with a few fat bastards', but he could see Rebus for a drink at six if that was convenient. Rebus wondered which luxury hotel would be the base for their drink, and was stunned, perhaps even disappointed, when Byars named the Sutherland Bar, one of Rebus's own watering holes.

'Right you are,' he said. 'Six o'clock.'

Which meant that the day stretched ahead of him. There was the Case of the Lifted Literature, of course. Well, he wasn't going to hold his breath waiting for a result there. They would turn up or they would not. His bet would be that by now they'd be on the other side of the Atlantic. Then there was William Glass, suspect in a murder inquiry, somewhere out there in a back close or a cobbled side street. Well, he'd turn up come giro day. If, that is, he was more stupid than so far he'd proved to be. No, maybe he was full of cunning. In which case he wouldn't go near a DHSS office or back to his digs. In which case he would have to get money from somewhere.

So – go talk to the tramps, the city's dispossessed. Glass would steal, or else he would resort to begging. And where he begged, there would be others begging, too. Put his description about, maybe with a tenner as a reward, and let others do your work for you. Yes, it was definitely worth mentioning to Lauderdale. Except that Rebus didn't want to do the Chief Inspector *too* many good turns, otherwise Lauderdale would think he was currying favour.

'I'd rather curry an alsatian,' he said to himself.

With a nice sense of timing, Brian Holmes came into the office carrying a white paper bag and a polystyrene beaker.

'What've you got there?' Rebus asked, suddenly hungry.

'You're the policeman, you tell me.' Holmes produced a sandwich from the bag and held it in front of Rebus.

'Corned chuck?' Rebus guessed.

'Wrong. Pastrami on rye bread.'

'What?'

'And decaffeinated filter coffee.' Holmes prised the lid from the beaker and sniffed the contents with a contented smile. 'From that new delicatessen next to the traffic lights.'

'Doesn't Nell make you up a sandwich?'

'Women have equal rights these days.'

Rebus believed it. He thought of Inspector Gill Templer and her psychology books and her feminism. He thought of the demanding Dr Patience Aitken. He even thought of the free-living Elizabeth Jack. Strong women to a man ... But then he remembered Cath Kinnoul. There were still casualties out there.

'What's it like?' he asked.

Holmes had taken a bite from the sandwich and was studying what was left. 'Okay,' he said. 'Interesting.'

Pastrami – now there was a sandwich filling that would be a long time coming to the Sutherland Bar.

Barney Byars, too, was a long time coming to the Sutherland. Rebus arrived at five minutes to six, Byars at twenty-five past. But he was well worth waiting for.

'Inspector, sorry I'm late. Some cunt was trying to knock me down five per cent on a four-grand contract, *and* he wanted sixty days to pay. Know what that does to a cash flow? I told him I ran a lorry firm, not fuckin' rickshaws.'

All of which was delivered in a thick Fife tongue and at a volume appreciably above that of the bar's early evening rumble of TV and conversation. Rebus was seated at one of the bar stools, but stood and suggested they take a table. Byars, however, was already making himself comfortable on the stool next to the policeman, laying his brawny arms along the bar-top and examining the array of taps. He pointed to Rebus's glass.

'That any good?'

'Not bad.'

'I'll have a pint of that then.' Whether from awe, fear, or just good management of his customers, the barman was on hand to pour the requested pint.

'Another yourself, Inspector?'

'I'm okay, thanks.'

'And a whisky, too,' ordered Byars. 'A double, mind, not the usual smear-test.'

Byars handed a fifty-pound note to the barman. 'Keep the change,' he said. Then he roared with laughter. 'Only joking, son, only joking.'

The barman was new and young. He held the note as though it were likely to ignite. 'Ehh ... you haven't got anything smaller on you?' His accent was effeminate west coast. Rebus wondered how long he'd last in the Sutherland.

Byars exasperated but rejecting Rebus's offer of help, dug into his pockets and found two crumpled one-pound notes and some change. He accepted his fifty back and pushed the coins towards the barman, then he winked at Rebus.

'I'll tell you a secret, Inspector, if I had to choose between having five tenners or one fifty, I'd go for the one fifty every time. Want to know why? Tenners in your pocket, people think nothing of it. But whip a fifty out, and they think you're Crœsus.' He turned to the barman, who was counting the coins out into the open till. 'Hey, son, got anything for eating?' The barman jerked round as though hit by a pellet.

'Ehh ... I think there's some Scotch broth left over from lunch.' His vowels turned broth into 'braw-wrath'. The braw wrath of the Scots, Rebus thought to himself. Byars was shaking his head. 'A pie or a sandwich,' he demanded.

The barman proffered the last lonely sandwich in the place. It looked unnervingly like pastrami, but turned out to be, as Byars put it, 'the guid roast beef'.

'One pound ten,' the barman said. Byars got out the fifty-pound note again, snorted, and produced a fiver instead. He turned back to Rebus and lifted his glass.

'Cheers.' Both men drank.

'Not bad at all,' Byars said of the beer.

Rebus gestured towards the sandwich. 'I thought you were going to dinner later on?'

'I am, but more importantly, *I'm* paying. This way, I won't eat as much and won't cost myself so much.' He winked again. 'Maybe I should write a book, eh? Business tips for sole traders, that sort of thing. Heh, speaking of tips, I once asked a waiter what "tips" meant. Know what he said?'

Rebus hazarded a wild guess. 'To insure prompt service?'

'No, to insure I don't piss in the soup!' Byars' voice was back to the level of megaphone diplomacy. He laughed, then took a bite of sandwich, still chortling as he chomped. He was not a tall man, five seven or thereabouts. And he was stocky. He wore newish denims and a black leather jacket, beneath which he sported a white polo-shirt. In a bar like this, you'd take him for ... well, just about anybody. Rebus could imagine him ruffling feathers in plush hotels and business bars. Image, he told himself. It's just another image: the hard man, the no-nonsense man, a man who worked hard and who expected others to work hard, too – always in his favour.

He had finished the sandwich, and was brushing crumbs from his lap. 'You're from Fife,' he said casually, sniffing the whisky.

'Yes,' Rebus admitted.

'I could tell. Gregor Jack's from Fife too, you know. You said you wanted to talk about him. Is it to do with that brothel story? I found that a bit hard to swallow.' He nodded towards the empty plate in front of him. 'Not as hard as that sandwich though.'

'No, it's not really to do with the ... with Mr Jack's ...no, it's more to do with Mrs Jack.'

'Lizzie? What about her?'

'We're not sure where she is. Any ideas?'

Byars looked blank. 'Knowing Lizzie, you'd better get Interpol on the case. She's as likely to be in Istanbul as Inverness.'

'What makes you say Inverness?'

Byars looked stuck for an answer. 'It was the first place that came to mind.' Then he nodded. 'I see what you mean though. You were thinking she might be at Deer Lodge, it being up that way. Have you looked?'

Rebus nodded. 'When did you last see Mrs Jack?'

'A couple of weeks ago. Maybe three weekends ago, I can

check. Funnily enough, it was at the lodge. A weekend party. The Pack mostly.' He looked up from his drink. 'I better explain that . . .'

'It's all right, I know who The Pack are. Three weekends ago, you say?'

'Aye, but I can check if you like.'

'A weekend party . . . you mean a party lasting the whole weekend?'

'Well, just a few friends . . . all very civilized.' A light came on behind his eyes. 'Ah-ha, I know what you're getting at. You know about Liz's parties then? No, no, this was tame stuff, dinner and a few drinks and a brisk country walk on the Sunday. Not really my mug of gin, but Liz had invited me, so . . .'

'You prefer her other kinds of party?'

Byars laughed. 'Of course! You're only young once, Inspector. I mean, it's all above board . . . isn't it?'

He seemed genuinely curious, not without reason. Why should a policeman know about 'those' parties? Who could have told him if not Gregor, and what exactly *would* Gregor have said?

'As far as I know, sir. So you don't know any reason why Mrs Jack might want to disappear?'

'I can think of a few.' Byars had finished both drinks, but didn't look like he was hanging around for another. He kept shifting on the stool, as if unable to get comfortable. 'That newspaper story for a start. I think I'd want to be well away from it, wouldn't you? I mean, I can see how it's bad for Gregor's image, not having his wife beside him, but at the same time . . .'

'Any other reasons?'

Byars was half standing now. 'A lover,' he suggested. 'Maybe he's whisked her off to Tenerife for a bit of pash under the sun.' He winked again, then his face became serious, as though he'd just remembered something. 'There were those phone calls,' he said.

'Phone calls?'

Now he was standing. 'Anonymous phone calls. Lizzie told

me about them. Not to her, to Gregor. Bound to happen, the game he's in. Caller would phone up and say he was Sir Somebody-Somebody or Lord This 'n' That, and Gregor would be fetched to the phone. Soon as he got to it, the line would go dead. That's what she told me.'

'Did these calls worry her?'

'Oh yes, you could see she was upset. She tried to hide it, but you could see. Gregor just laughed it off, of course. Can't afford to let something like that rattle him. She might even have mentioned letters. Something about Gregor getting these letters, but tearing them up before anyone could see them. But you'd have to ask Lizzie about that.' He paused. 'Or Gregor, of course.'

'Of course.'

'Right ...' Byars stuck out his hand. 'You've got my number if you need me, Inspector.'

'Yes.' Rebus shook hands. 'Thanks for your help, Mr Byars.'

'Any time, Inspector. Oh, and if you ever need a lift to London, I've got lorries make that trip four times a week. Won't cost you a penny, and you can still claim the journey on expenses.'

He gave another wink, smiled generally around the bar, and marched back out as noticeably as he'd marched in. The barman came to clear away plate and glass. Rebus saw that the tie the young man was wearing was a clip-on, standard issue in the Sutherland. If a punter tried to grab you, the tie came away in his hand ...

'Was he talking about me?'

Rebus blinked. 'Eh? What makes you think that?'

'I thought I heard him mention my name.'

Rebus poured the dregs from his glass into his mouth and swallowed. Don't say the kid was called Gregor ... Lizzie maybe ... 'What name is that then?'

'Lawrie.'

Rebus was more than halfway there before he realized he was headed not for Stockbridge comforts and Patience

Aitken, but for Marchmont and his own neglected flat. So be it. Inside the flat, the atmosphere managed to be both chill and stale. A coffee mug beside the telephone resembled Glasgow insofar as it, too, was a city of culture, an interesting green and white culture.

But if the living room was growing mould, surely the kitchen would be worse. Rebus sat himself down in his favourite chair, stretched for the answering machine, and settled to listen to his calls. There weren't many. Gill Templer, wondering where he was keeping himself these days . . . as if she didn't know. His daughter Samantha, phoning from her new flat in London, giving him her address and telephone number. Then a couple of calls where the speaker had decided not to say anything.

'Be like that then.' Rebus turned off the machine, drew a notebook from his pocket, and, reading the number from it, telephoned Gregor Jack. He wanted to know why Jack hadn't said anything about his own anonymous calls. Strip Jack . . . beggar my neighbour . . . Well, if someone *were* out to beggar Gregor Jack, Jack himself didn't seem overly concerned. He didn't exactly seem resigned, but he did seem unbothered. Unless he was playing a game with Rebus . . . And what about Rab Kinnoul, on-screen assassin? What was he up to all the time he was away from his wife? And Ronald Steele, too, a 'hard man to catch'. Were they *all* up to something? It wasn't that Rebus distrusted the human race . . . wasn't just that he was brought up a Pessimisterian. He was sure there was something happening here; he just didn't know what it was.

There was nobody home. Or nobody was answering. Or the apparatus had been unplugged. Or . . .

'Hello?'

Rebus glanced at his watch. Just after quarter past seven. 'Miss Greig?' he said. 'Inspector Rebus here. He does keep you working late, doesn't he?'

'You seem to work fairly late hours yourself, Inspector. What is it this time?'

Impatience in her voice. Perhaps Urquhart had warned her

against being friendly. Perhaps it had been discovered that she'd given Rebus the address of Deer Lodge . . .

'A word with Mr Jack, if possible.'

'Not possible, I'm afraid.' She didn't sound afraid; she sounded if anything a bit smug. 'He's speaking at a function this evening.'

'Oh. How did his meeting go this morning?'

'Meeting?'

'I thought he had some meeting in his constituency . . . ?'

'Oh, that. I think it went very well.'

'So he's not for the chop then?'

She attempted a laugh. 'North and South Esk would be mad to get rid of him.'

'All the same, he must be relieved.'

'I wouldn't know. He was on the golf course all afternoon.'

'Nice.'

'I *think* an MP is allowed one afternoon off a week, don't you, Inspector?'

'Oh yes, absolutely. That's what I meant.' Rebus paused. He had nothing to say, really; he was just hoping that if he kept her talking Helen Greig herself might tell him something, something he didn't know . . . 'Oh,' he said, 'about those telephone calls . . .'

'What calls?'

'The ones Mr Jack was getting. The anonymous ones.'

'I don't know what you're talking about. Sorry, I've got to go now. My mum's expecting me home at quarter to eight.'

'Right you are then, Miss Gr – ' But she had already put the phone down.

Golf? This afternoon? Jack must be keen. The rain had been falling steadily in Edinburgh since midday. He looked out of his unwashed window. It wasn't falling now, but the streets were glistening. The flat felt suddenly empty, and colder than ever. Rebus picked up the phone and made one more call. To Patience Aitken. To say he was on his way. She asked him where he was.

'I'm at home.'

'Oh? Picking up some more of your stuff?'

93

'That's right.'

'You could do with bringing a spare suit if you've got one.'

'Right.'

'And some of your precious books, since you don't seem to approve of my taste.'

'Romances were never my thing, Patience.' In fiction as in life, he thought to himself. On the floor around him were strewn some of his 'precious books'. He picked one up, tried to remember buying it, couldn't.

'Well, bring whatever you like, John, and as much as you like. You know how much room we've got here.'

We. We've got.

'Okay, Patience. See you later.' He replaced the receiver with a sigh and took a look around him. After all these years, there were *still* gaps on the wall-shelves from where his wife Rhona had removed her things. Still gaps in the kitchen, too, where the tumble-drier had sat, and her precious dishwasher. Still clean rectangular spaces on the walls where her posters and prints had been hung. The flat had last been redecorated–when?–in '81 or '82. Ach, it still didn't look too bad though. Who was he kidding? It looked like a squat.

'What have you done with your life, John Rebus?' The answer was: Not much. Gregor Jack was younger than him, and more successful. Barney Byars was younger than him, and more successful. Who did he know who was *older* than him and *less* successful? Not a single soul, discounting the beggars in the city centre, the ones he'd spent the afternoon with – without a result, but with a certain uncomfortable sense of belonging . . .

What was he thinking about? 'You're becoming a morbid old bugger.' Self-pity wasn't the answer. Moving in with Patience was the answer . . . so why didn't it feel like one? Why did it feel like just another problem?

He rested his head against the back of the chair. I'm caught, he thought, between a cushion and a soft place. He sat there for a long time, staring up at the ceiling. It was dark outside, and foggy, too, a haar drifting in across the city from the North Sea. In a haar, Edinburgh seemed to shift backwards through time. You half expected to see press-gangs on the streets of Leith, hear coaches clattering over cobblestones and cries of gardy-loo in the High Street.

If he sold the flat, he could buy himself a new car, send some money to Samantha. *If* he sold the flat . . . *if* he moved in with Patience . . .

'If shit was gold,' his father used to say, 'you'd have a tyke at yer erse.' The old bugger had never explained exactly what a tyke was . . .

Jesus, what made him think of that?

It was no good. He couldn't think straight, not here. Perhaps it was that his flat held too many memories, good and bad. Perhaps it was just the mood of the evening.

Or perhaps it was that the image of Gill Templer's face kept appearing unbidden (he told himself unbidden) in his mind . . .

5
Up the River

Burglary with violent assault: just the thing for a dreich Thursday morning. The victim was in hospital, head bandaged and face bruised. Rebus had been to talk with her, and was at the house in Jock's Lodge, overseeing the dusting for prints and the taking of statements, when word reached him from Great London Road. The call came from Brian Holmes.

'Yes, Brian?'

'There's been another drowning.'

'Drowning?'

'Another body in the river.'

'Oh Christ. Whereabouts this time?'

'Out of town, up towards Queensferry. Another woman. She was found this morning by someone out for a walk.' He paused while someone handed him something. Rebus heard a muted 'thanks' as the person moved away. 'It could be our Mr Glass, couldn't it?' Holmes said now, pausing again to slurp coffee. 'We expected him to stick around the city, but he could as easily have headed north. Queensferry's an easy walk, and mostly across open land, well away from roads where he might be spotted. If I was on the run, that's the way I'd do it . . .'

Yes, Rebus knew that country. Hadn't he been out there just the other day? Quiet back roads, no traffic, nobody to notice . . . Hang on, there was a stream – no, more a river – running past the Kinnouls' house.

'Brian . . .' he started.

'And that's another thing,' Holmes interrupted. 'The woman who found the body . . . guess who it was?'

'Cathy Gow,' Rebus said casually.

Holmes seemed puzzled, 'Who? Anyway, no, it was Rab Kinnoul's wife. You know, Rab Kinnoul . . . the actor. Who's this Cathy Gow . . . ?'

It was uphill from the Kinnoul house, and along the side of the hill, too. Not too far a walk, but the country grew if anything bleaker still. Fifty yards from the fast-flowing river there was a narrow road, leading eventually to a wider road which meandered down to the coast. For someone to get here, they either had to walk past the Kinnoul house, or else walk down from the road.

'No sign of a car?' Rebus asked Holmes. Both men had zippered their jackets against the snell wind and the occasional smirr.

'Any car in particular?' Holmes asked. 'The road's tarmac. I've had a look for myself. No tyre tracks.'

'Where does it lead?'

'It peters out into a farm track, then, surprise surprise, a farm.' Holmes was moving his weight from one foot to the other, trying in vain to keep warm.

'Better check at the farm and see – '

'Someone's up there doing precisely that.'

Rebus nodded. Holmes knew this routine well enough by now: he would do something, and Rebus would double check that it had been done.

'And Mrs Kinnoul?'

'She's in the house with a WPC, drinking sweet tea.'

'Don't let her take too many downers. We'll need a statement.'

Holmes was lost, until Rebus explained about his previous visit here. 'What about Mr Kinnoul?'

'He went off somewhere this morning early. That's why Mrs Kinnoul went for a walk. She said she always went for a walk in the morning when she was on her own.'

'Do we know where he's gone?'

Holmes shrugged. 'Just on business, that's all she could tell us. Couldn't say where or how long he'd be. But he should be back this evening, according to Mrs Kinnoul.'

Rebus nodded again. They were standing above the river, near the roadway. The others were down by the river itself. It was in spate after the recent rain. Just about wide enough and deep enough to be classed a river rather than a stream. The 'others' included police officers, dressed in waders and plunging their arms into the icy water, feeling for evidence which would long have been flushed away, forensics men, hovering above the body, the Identification Unit, similarly hovering but armed with cameras and video equipment, and Dr Curt, dressed in a long flapping raincoat, its collar turned up. He trudged towards Rebus and Holmes, reciting as he came.

'When shall we three meet again ... blasted heath et cetera. Good morning, Inspector.'

'Morning, Doctor Curt. What have you got for us?'

Curt removed his glasses and wiped spots of water from them. 'Double pneumonia, I shouldn't wonder,' he answered, replacing them.

'Accident, suicide, or murder?' asked Rebus.

Curt tut-tutted him, shaking his head sadly. 'You know I can't make snap decisions, Inspector. Granted, this poor woman hasn't been in the water as long as the previous one, but all the same ...'

'How long?'

'A day at most. But with the weight of water and all ... debris and so on ... she's taken a bit of a battering. Lucky she was found at all, really.'

'How do you mean?'

'Didn't the sergeant say? Her wrist caught in a dead branch. Otherwise, she'd almost certainly have been swept down into the river and out into the sea.'

Rebus thought about the direction the river would take, bypassing the only settlements ... yes, a body falling into the stream here might well have disappeared without trace ...

'Any idea who she is?'

'No identification on the body. Plenty of rings on her

fingers though, and she's wearing quite a nice dress, too. Care to take a look?'

'Why not, eh? Come on, Brian.'

But Holmes stood his ground. 'I had a look earlier, sir. Don't let me stop you though . . .'

So Rebus followed the pathologist down the slope. He was thinking: difficult to bring a body down here . . . but you could always roll it from the top . . . yes, roll it . . . hear the splash and assume it had fallen into the river . . . you might not know the wrist had caught in a branch. But to get a body up here in the first place – dead *or* alive – surely you'd need a car. Was William Glass capable of stealing a car? Why not, everyone else seemed to know how to do it these days. Kids in primary school could show you how to do it . . .

'Like I say,' Curt was saying, 'she's been bashed about a bit . . . can't tell yet whether post- or ante-mortem. Oh, about that other drowning at Dean Bridge . . .'

'Yes?'

'Recent sexual intercourse. Traces of semen in the vagina. We should be able to get a DNA profile. Ah, here we go . . .'

The body had been laid out on a plastic sheet. Yes, it was a nice dress, distinctive, summery, though torn now and smeared with mud. The face was muddy, too . . . and cut . . . and swollen . . . the hair drawn back and part of the skull exposed. Rebus swallowed hard. Had he been expecting this? He wasn't sure. But the photographs he'd seen made him sure in his mind.

'I know her,' he said.

'What?' Even the forensics men looked up at him in disbelief. The tableau must have alerted Brian Holmes, for he came stumbling down the slope to join them.

'I said I know her. At least, I think I do. No, I'm *sure* I do. Her name is Elizabeth Jack. Her friends call her Liz or Lizzie. She's . . . she *was* married to Gregor Jack MP.'

'Good God,' said Dr Curt. Rebus looked at Holmes, and Holmes stared back at him, and neither seemed to know what to say.

*

There was more to identification than that, of course. Much more. Death was certainly suspicious, but this had to be decided *officially* by the gentleman from the Procurator Fiscal's office, the gentleman who now stood talking with Dr Curt, nodding his head gravely while Curt made hand gestures which would not have disgraced an excited Italian. He was explaining – explaining tirelessly, explaining for the thousandth time – about the movement of diatoms within the body, while his listener grew paler still.

The Identification Unit was still busy shooting off photographs and some video film, wiping their camera lenses every thirty seconds or so. The rain had, if anything, grown heavier, the sky an unbroken shading of grey-black. An autopsy was needed, agreed the Procurator Fiscal. The body would be transported to the mortuary in Edinburgh's Cowgate, and there formal identification would take place, involving two people who knew the deceased in life, and two police officers who had known her in death. If it turned out *not* to be Elizabeth Jack, Rebus was in a dung-pile of trouble. Watching the body being taken away, Rebus allowed himself a muffled sneeze. Perhaps Dr Curt's diagnosis of pneumonia was right. He knew where he was headed: the Kinnoul house. With luck, he might find hot tea there. The forensics team squeezed wetly into their car and headed back to police headquarters at Fettes.

'Come on, Brian,' said Rebus, 'let's see how Mrs Kinnoul's getting on.'

Cath Kinnoul seemed in a state of shock. A doctor had been to the house, but had left by the time Rebus and Holmes reached the scene. They shed their sodden jackets in the hall, while Rebus had a quiet word with the WPC.

'No sign of the husband?'

'No, sir.'

'How is she?'

'Comfortably numb.'

Rebus tried to look bedraggled and pathetic. It wasn't difficult. The WPC read his mind and smiled.

'I'll make some tea, shall I?'

'Anything hot would hit the spot, believe me.'

Cath Kinnoul was sitting in one of the living room's huge armchairs. The chair itself looked like it was in the process of consuming her, while she looked about half the size and a quarter of the age she'd been when Rebus had last seen her.

'Hello again,' he said, mock-cheerily.

'Inspector . . . Rebus?'

'That's it. And this is Sergeant Holmes. No jokes, please, he's heard them all before, haven't you, Sergeant?'

Holmes saw that they were playing the comedy duo, trying to bring some life back into Mrs Kinnoul. He nodded encouragingly. In fact, he was glancing around wistfully, hoping to find a roaring log or coal fire. But there wasn't even a roaring gas fire for him to stand in front of. Instead, there was a one-bar electric job, just about glowing with warmth, and there were two radiators. He went and stood in front of one of these, separating his trousers from his legs. He pretended to be admiring the pictures on the wall in front of him. Rab Kinnoul with a TV actor . . . with a TV comedian . . . with a gameshow host . . .

'My husband,' Mrs Kinnoul explained. 'He works in television.'

Rebus spoke. 'No idea what he's up to today though, Mrs Kinnoul?'

'No,' she said quietly, 'no idea.'

Two witnesses who had known the deceased in life . . . Well, thought Rebus, you can scrub Cath Kinnoul. She'd fall apart if she *knew* it was Liz Jack out there, never mind having to identify the body. Even now, someone was trying to get in touch with Gregor Jack, and Jack would probably arrive at the mortuary with Ian Urquhart or Helen Greig, either of whom would do as the second nod of the head. No need to bother Cath Kinnoul

'You look soaked,' she was saying. 'Something to drink?'

'The WPC's making some tea . . .' But as he spoke, Rebus knew this was not what she was suggesting. 'A drop of the cratur wouldn't go amiss though, if it's not too much trouble.'

She nodded towards a sideboard. 'Right-hand cupboard,' she said. 'Please help yourself.'

Rebus thought of suggesting that she join them. But what pills had the doctor given her? And what pills had she taken of her own? He poured Glenmorangie into two long slim glasses and handed one to Holmes, who had taken up a canny position in front of a radiator.

'Mind you don't get steaming,' Rebus said in a murmur. Just then, the WPC appeared, carrying a tray of tea things. She saw the alcohol and almost frowned.

'Here's tae us,' said Rebus, downing the drink in one.

At the mortuary, Gregor Jack seemed hardly to recognize Rebus at all. Jack had been holding his weekly constituency surgery, Ian Urquhart explained to Rebus in a conspiratorial whisper. This was usually held on a Friday, but there was a Private Member's Bill in the Commons this Friday, and Gregor Jack wanted to be part of the debate. So, Gregor having been in the area on Wednesday anyway, they'd decided to hold the surgery on Thursday, leaving Friday free.

Listening to all this in silence, Rebus thought: Why are you telling me? But Urquhart was clearly nervous and felt the need to talk. Well, mortuaries could have that effect, never mind the fact that your employer was about to see scandal heaped upon scandal. Never mind the fact that your job was about to be made more difficult than ever.

'How did the golf game go?' Rebus asked back.

'What golf game?'

'Yesterday.'

'Oh.' Urquhart nodded. 'You mean Gregor's game. I don't know. I haven't asked him yet.'

So Urquhart himself hadn't been involved. He paused for so long that Rebus thought a dead end had been reached, but the need to speak was too great.

'That's a regular date,' Urquhart went on. 'Gregor and Ronnie Steele. Most Wednesday afternoons.'

Ah, Suey, Mr would-be teenage suicide . . .

Rebus tried to make his next question sound like a joke. 'Doesn't Gregor *ever* do any work?'

Urquhart looked stunned. 'He's always working. That game of golf . . . it's about the only free time I've ever known him have.'

'But he doesn't seem to be in London very often.'

'Ah well, the constituency comes first, that's Gregor's way.'

'Look after the folk who voted you in, and they'll look after you?'

'Something like that,' Urquhart allowed. There was no more time for talk. The identification was about to take place. And if Gregor Jack looked bad before he saw the body, he looked like a half-filled rag doll afterwards.

'Oh Christ, that dress . . .' He seemed about to collapse, but Ian Urquhart had a firm grip on him.

'If you'll look at the face,' someone was saying. 'We need to be definite . . .'

They all looked at the face. Yes, thought Rebus, that's the person I saw beside the stream.

'Yes,' said Gregor Jack, his voice wavering, 'that's my . . . that's Liz.'

Rebus actually breathed a sigh of relief.

What nobody had expected, what nobody had really considered, was Sir Hugh Ferrie.

'Let's just say,' said Chief Superintendent Watson, 'that a certain amount of . . . pressure . . . is being applied.'

As ever, Rebus couldn't hold his tongue. 'There's nothing to apply pressure *to*! What are we supposed to do that we're not already doing?'

'Sir Hugh considers that we should have caught William Glass by now.'

'But we don't even know – '

'Now, we all know Sir Hugh can be a bit hot-headed. But he's got a point . . .'

Meaning, thought Rebus, he's got friends in high places.

'He's got a point, and we can do without the media interest that's bound to erupt. All I'm saying is that we should give the investigation an extra *push* whenever and wherever we can. Let's get Glass in custody, let's make sure we keep everyone informed, and let's get that autopsy report as soon as humanly possible.'

'Not so easy with a drowning.'

'John, you know Dr Curt fairly well, don't you?'

'We're on second-name terms.'

'How about giving him that extra little nudge?'

'What happens if he nudges me back, sir?'

Watson looked like a kindly uncle suddenly tiring of a precocious nephew. 'Nudge him harder. I *know* he's busy. I *know* he's got lectures to give, university work to do, God knows what else. But the longer we have to wait, the more the media are going to fill the gaps with speculation. Go have a word, John, eh? Just make sure he gets the message.'

Message? What message? Dr Curt told Rebus what he'd always told him. I can't be rushed . . . delicate business, deciding an actual drowning from mere immersion . . . professional reputation . . . daren't make mistakes . . . more haste, less speed . . . patience is a virtue . . . many a mickle maks a muckle . . .

All of this delivered between appointments in the doctor's Teviot Place office. The Department of Pathology's Forensic Medicine Unit, divided in loyalties between the Faculty of Medicine and the Faculty of Law, had its offices within the University Medical School in Teviot Place. Which seemed, to Rebus, natural enough. You didn't want your Commercial Law students mixing with people who keened over cadavers . . .

'Diatoms . . .' Dr Curt was saying. 'Washerwoman's skin . . . blood-tinged froth . . . distended lungs . . .' Almost a litany now, and none of it got them any further. Tests on tissue . . . examination . . . diatoms . . . toxicology . . . fractures . . . diatoms. Curt really did have a thing about those tiny algae.

'Unicellular algae,' he corrected.

Rebus bowed his head to the correction. 'Well,' he said, rising to his feet, 'fast as you can, eh, Doctor? If you can't

104

catch me in the office, you can always try me by unicellular phone.'

'Fast as I can,' agreed Doctor Curt, chuckling. He too got to his feet. 'Oh, one thing I can tell you straight away.' He opened his office door for Rebus.

'Yes?'

'Mrs Jack was depilated. There'd be no getting *her* by the short-and-curlies . . .'

Because Teviot Place wasn't far from Buccleuch Street, Rebus thought he'd wander along to Suey Books. Not that he was expecting to catch Ronald Steele, for Ronald Steele was a hard man to catch. Busy behind the scenes, busy out of sight. The shop itself was open, the rickety bicycle chained up outside. Rebus pushed the door open warily.

'It's okay,' called a voice from the back of the shop. 'Rasputin's gone out for a wander.'

Rebus closed the door and approached the desk. The same girl was sitting there, and her duties still seemed to entail the pricing of books. There wasn't any room for any more books on the shelves. Rebus wondered where these new titles were headed . . .

'How did you know it was me?' he asked.

'That window.' She nodded towards the front-of-shop. 'It might look filthy from the outside, but you can see out of it all right. Like one of those two-way mirrors.'

Rebus looked. Yes, because the shop's interior was darker than the street, you could see out all right, you just couldn't see in.

'No sign of your books, if that's what you're wondering.'

Rebus nodded slowly. It was *not* what he was wondering . . .

'And Ronald's not here.' She checked the oversized face of her wristwatch. 'Should have been in half an hour ago. Must have got held up.'

Rebus kept on nodding. Steele had told him this girl's name. What was it again . . .? 'Was he in yesterday?'

She shook her head. 'We were shut. All day. I was a bit off

105

colour, couldn't come in. At the start of the university year, we do okay business on a Wednesday, Wednesday being a half-teaching day, but not just now . . .'

Rebus thought of Vaseline . . . vanishing cream . . . Vanessa! That was it.

'Well, thanks anyway. Keep an eye out for those books . . .'

'Oh! Here's Ronald now.'

Rebus turned round, just as the door rattled open. Ronald Steele closed it heavily behind him, started up the central aisle of books, but then almost lost balance and had to rest against a bookcase. His eyes caught a particular spine, and he levered the book out from the others around it.

'*Fish out of Water*,' he said. 'Out of water . . .' He threw the book as far as he could – a matter of a yard or so. It crashed into a bookcase and fell open on to the floor. Then he began picking books out at random and throwing them with force, his eyes red with tears.

Vanessa screamed at him and came round from her desk, making towards him, but Steele pushed past her and stumbled past Rebus, past the desk, and through a doorway at the very back of the shop. There was the sound of another door closing.

'What's back there?'

'The loo,' said Vanessa, stooping to recover a few of the books. 'What the hell's the matter with him?'

'Maybe he's had a bit of bad news,' Rebus speculated. He was helping her retrieve books. He stood up and examined the blurb on the back jacket of *Fish out of Water*. The front cover illustration showed a woman seated more or less demurely on a chaise longue, while a rugged suitor leant over her from behind, his lips just short of her bared shoulder. 'I think I might buy this,' he said. 'Looks like just my sort of thing.'

Vanessa accepted the book, then stared up from it to him, her disbelief not quite showing through the shock of the scene she'd just witnessed. 'Fifty pence,' she told him quietly.

'Fifty pence it is,' said Rebus.

*

And after the formal identification, while the autopsy took its defined and painstaking course, there were the questions. There were an awful lot of questions.

Cath Kinnoul had to be questioned. Gently questioned, with her husband by her side and a bloodstream dulled by tranqs. No, she hadn't really taken a close look at the body. She'd known from a good way off what it was. She could see the dress, could see that it *was* a dress. She'd run back to the house and telephoned for the police. Nine-nine-nine, the way they told you to in emergencies. No, she hadn't gone back out to the river. She doubted she'd ever go there again.

And, turning to Mr Kinnoul, where had *he* been this morning? Business meetings, he said. Meetings with potential partners and potential backers. He was trying to set up an independent television company, though he'd be grateful if the information went no further. And the previous evening? He'd spent it at home with his wife. And they hadn't seen or heard anything? Not a thing. They'd been watching TV all night, not current TV but old stuff kept on video, stuff featuring Mr Kinnoul himself . . . *Knife Ledge*. The on-screen assassin.

'You must have learned a few tricks of the trade in your time, Mr Kinnoul.'

'You mean acting?'

'No, I mean about how to kill . . .'

And then there was Gregor Jack . . . Rebus kept out of that altogether. He'd look at any notes and transcripts later. He didn't want to get involved. There was too much he already knew, too much prejudgement, which was another way of saying potential prejudice. He let other CID men deal with Mr Jack, and with Ian Urquhart, and with Helen Greig, and with *all* Elizabeth Jack's cronies and cohorts. For this wasn't merely a case of the lady vanishing; this was a matter of death. Jamie Kilpatrick, the Hon. Matilda Merriman, Julian Kaymer, Martin Inman, Louise Patterson-Scott, even Barney Byars. They'd all either been questioned, or were about to be. Perhaps they'd all be questioned again at a later date. There were missing days to be filled. Huge gaps in Liz Jack's life, the whole final week of her life. Where had she been? Who had she seen? When had she died? (Hurry up, please, Dr Curt. Chop-chop.) *How* had she died? (Ditto.) Where was her car?

But Rebus read all the transcripts, all the notes. He read through the interview with Gregor Jack, and the interview with Ronald Steele. A Detective Constable was sent to Braidwater Golf Course to check the story of the Wednesday afternoon game. The interview with Steele, Rebus read very carefully indeed. Asked about Elizabeth Jack, Steele admitted that 'she always accused me of not being enough fun. She was right, I suppose. I'm not exactly what you'd call a "party animal". And I never had enough money. She liked people with money to throw around, or who threw it around even if they couldn't afford it.'

A touch of bitterness there? Or just the bitter truth?

To all of which Rebus added one other question – had Elizabeth Jack ever left Edinburgh in the first place?

Then there was the separate hunt, the hunt for William Glass. If he *had* gone to Queensferry, where would he be next? West, towards Bathgate, Linlithgow, or Bo'ness? Or north, across the Forth to Fife? Police forces were mobilized. Descriptions were issued. *Had* Liz Jack spent any time at all at Deer Lodge? How could William Glass simply disappear? Was there any connection between Mrs Jack's death and her husband's 'night out' at an Edinburgh brothel?

This last line was the one pursued most eagerly by the newspapers. They seemed to be favouring a verdict of suicide in the case of Elizabeth Jack. Husband's shame . . . discovered after she's been on retreat . . . on her way home she decides she can't face things . . . sets off perhaps to visit her friend the actor Rab Kinnoul . . . but grows more desperate and, having read the details of the Dean Bridge murder, decides to end it all. Throws herself into the river above Rab Kinnoul's house. End of story.

Except that it wasn't the end of the story. As far as the papers were concerned, it was just the beginning. After all, this one had it all – a TV actor, an MP, a sex scandal, a death. The headline writers were boggled, trying to decide which order to put things in. Sex Scandal MP's Wife Drowns in TV Star's Stream? Or TV Star's Agony at MP Friend's Wife's Suicide Act? You could see the problem ... All those possessives ...

And the grieving husband? Kept well away from the media by protective friends and colleagues. But he was always available for interview by the police, when clarification of some point was required. While his father-in-law gave the media as many interviews as they needed, but kept his comments to the police succinct and scathing.

'What do you want to talk to me for? Find the bugger who did it, then you can talk all you want. I want the animal who did this put behind bars! Better make them bloody strong bars, too, otherwise I might just pull them apart and strangle the life out of the bugger myself!'

'We're doing what we can, believe me, Sir Hugh.'

'Is it enough though, that's what I want to know!'

'Everything we can ...'

Yes, everything. Leaving just the one final question: Did *any*one do it? Only Dr Curt could answer that.

6
Highland Games

Rebus packed an overnight bag. It was a large sports holdall, bought for him by Patience Aitken when she'd decided he should get fit. They'd enrolled together in a health club, bought all the gear, and had attended the club four or five times together. They'd played squash, been massaged, had saunas, encountered the plunge pool, gone swimming, survived the expensively equipped gymnasium, tried jogging . . . but ended up spending more and more time in the health club bar, which was stupid, the drinks being double the price they were at the pleasant-enough pub round the corner.

No longer a sports bag then, but these days an overnight bag. Not that Rebus was taking much this trip. He packed a change of shirt, socks and underwear, toothbrush, camera, notebook, a kagoul. Would he require a phrase book? Probably, but he doubted if one existed. Something to read though . . . bedtime reading. He found the copy of *Fish out of Water* and threw it in on top of everything else. The phone was ringing. But he was in Patience's flat, and she had her own answering machine. All the same . . .

He went through to the living room and listened as the message played. Then the caller's voice. 'This is Brian Holmes, trying to get in touch with -'

Rebus picked up the receiver. 'Brian, what's up?'

'Ah, caught you. Thought maybe you'd already headed for the hills.'

'I was just leaving.'

'Sure you don't want to drop by the station first?'

'Why should I?'
'Because Dr Curt is about to pronounce . . .'

The problem with drowning was that drowning and immersion were two entirely different things. A body (conscious or unconscious) might fall (or be pushed) into water and drown. Or an already dead body might be dumped into water as a means of concealment or to lead the police astray. Cause of death became problematical, as did time of death. Rigor mortis might or might not be present. Bruising on and damage to the body might be the result of rocks or other objects in the water itself.

However, froth from mouth and nose when the chest was pumped down on was a sign that the body was alive when it entered the water. So was the presence in the brain, marrow, kidney and so forth of diatoms. Diatoms, Dr Curt never tired of explaining, were micro-organisms which penetrated the lung membrane and would be pumped around the bloodstream by a still-beating heart.

But there were other signs, too. Silted matter in the bronchial tubes provided evidence of inhalation of water. A living person falling into water made attempts to grip something (a true-life 'clutching at straws') and so the hands of the corpse would be clenched. Washerwoman's skin, the shedding of nails and hair, the swelling of the body – all these could lead to an estimate of the amount of time the corpse had spent in the water.

As Curt pointed out, not all the relevant tests had been completed yet. It would be a few more days before the toxicology tests would yield results, so they couldn't be sure yet whether the deceased had taken any drink or drugs prior to death. No semen had been found in the vagina, but then the deceased's husband had provided information that the deceased 'had trouble' with the pill, and that her preferred method of contraception had always been the sheath . . .

Christ, thought Rebus, imagine poor old Jack being asked about that. Still, there might be even less pleasant questions to answer . . .

'What we have so far,' Curt said, while everyone begged him silently to get on with it, 'is a series of negatives. No froth from the mouth and nose ... no silted matter ... no clenched hands. What's more, rigor mortis would suggest that the body was dead prior to immersion, and that it had been kept in a confined space. You'll see from the photographs that the legs are bent quite unnaturally.'

At that moment, they knew ... but still he hadn't said it.

'I'd say the body was in the water not less than eight hours and not more than twenty-four. As to when death occurred, well, some time before that, obviously, but not too long, a matter of hours ...'

'And cause of death?'

Dr Curt smiled. 'The photographs of the skull show a clear fracture to the right-hand side of the head. She was hit very hard from behind, gentlemen. I'd say death was almost instantaneous ...'

There was more, but not much more. And much mumbling between officers. Rebus knew what they were thinking and saying: it was the same M.O. as the Dean Bridge killing. But it wasn't. The woman found at Dean Bridge had been murdered at that spot, not transported there, and she had been murdered on a riverside path in the middle of a city, not ... well, where *had* Liz Jack died? Anywhere. It could be anywhere. While people were muttering that William Glass had to be found, Rebus was thinking in a different direction: Mrs Jack's BMW had to be found, and found quickly. Well, he was already packed, and he'd okayed the trip with Lauderdale. Constable Moffat would be there to meet him, and Gregor Jack had provided the keys.

'So there it is, ladies and gentlemen.' Curt was saying. 'Murder would be my opinion. Yes, murder. The rest is down to your forensic scientists and yourselves.'

'Off are you?' Lauderdale commented, seeing Rebus toting his bag.

'That's right, sir.'

'Good hunting, Inspector.' Lauderdale paused. 'What's the name of the place again?'

'Where is it expensive to be a Mason, sir?'

'I don't follow . . . ah, right, a dear lodge.'

Rebus winked at his superior and made his way out towards his car.

It was very pleasing the way Scotland changed every thirty miles or so – changed in landscape, in character, and in dialect. Mind you, stick in a car and you'd hardly guess. The roads all seemed much the same. So did the roadside petrol stations. Even the towns, long, straight main streets with their supermarkets and shoe shops and wool shops and chip shops . . . even these seemed to blur one into the other. But it was possible to look beyond them; possible, too, to look further *into* them. A small country, thought Rebus, yet so various. At school, his geography teacher had taught that Scotland could be divided into three distinct regions: Southern Uplands, Lowlands, and Highlands . . . something like that. Geography didn't begin to tell the story. Well, maybe it did actually. He was heading due north, towards a people very different to those found in the southern cities or the coastal towns.

He stopped in Perth and bought some supplies – apples, chocolate, a half bottle of whisky, chewing gum, a box of dates, a pint of milk . . . You never knew what might not be available further north. It was all very well on the tourist trail, but if he stepped off that trail . . .

In Blairgowrie he stopped for fish and chips, which he ate at a Formica-topped table in the chip shop. Lashings of salt, vinegar and brown sauce on the chips. Two slices of white pan bread thinly spread with margarine. And a cup of dark-brown tea. The haddock was covered in batter, which Rebus picked off, eating it first before starting on the fish.

'You look as if you enjoyed that,' the frier's wife said, wiping down the table next to him. He had enjoyed it. All the more so since Patience wouldn't be smelling his breath this evening, checking for cholesterol and sodium and starch . . .

He looked at the list of delights printed above the counter. Red, white and black puddings, haggis, smoked sausage, sausage in batter, steak pie, mince pie, chicken ... with pickled onions or pickled eggs on the side. Rebus couldn't resist. He bought another bag of chips to eat while he drove ...

Today was Tuesday. Five days since Elizabeth Jack's body was found, probably six days since she died. Memories were short, Rebus knew. Her photograph had been in all the newspapers, had appeared on television and on several hundred police posters. And still no one had come forward with information. He'd worked through the weekend, seeing little of Patience, and he'd come up with this notion, this latest straw to be clutched at.

The scenery deepened around him, growing wilder and quieter. He was in Glenshee. In it and through it as quickly as he could. There was something sinister and empty about the place, a louring sense of dis-ease. The Devil's Elbow wasn't the treacherous spot it had seemed in his youth; the road had somehow been levelled, or the corner straightened. Braemar ... Balmoral ... turning off just before Ballater towards Cockbridge and Tomintoul, that stretch of road which always seemed to be the first of the winter to close for snow. Bleak? Yes, he'd call it bleak. But it was impressive, too. It just went on and on and on. Deep valleys hewn by glaciers, collections of scree. Rebus's geography teacher had been an enthusiast.

He was close now, close to his destination. He turned to the directions which he had scribbled down, an amalgam of notes from Sergeant Moffat and Gregor Jack. Gregor Jack ...

Jack had wanted to talk with him about something, but Rebus hadn't given him the chance. Too dangerous to get involved. Not that Rebus believed for one second that Jack had anything to hide. All the same ... The others though, the Rab Kinnouls and Ronald Steeles and Ian Urquharts ... there was definitely ... well, maybe not definitely ... but there was ... ach, no, he couldn't put it into words. He didn't really want to think about it even. Thinking about it, about all those permutations and possibilities, all those what ifs . . . well, they just made his head birl.

'Left and then right . . . along the track beside a fir plantation . . . up to the top of the rise . . . through a gateway. It's like *Treasure Hunt*.' The car was behaving impeccably (touch wood). Touch wood? He only had to stop the car and stretch his arm out of the window. No plantation now, but a wild wood. The track was heavily rutted, with grass growing high along a strip between the ruts. Some of the larger potholes had been filled in with gravel, and Rebus's speed was down to five miles an hour or less, but that didn't seem to stop his bones being shaken, his head snapped from side to side. It didn't seem possible that there could be a habitation ahead. Maybe he'd taken a wrong turning. But the tyre tracks he was following were fresh enough, and besides, he didn't fancy reversing all the way back along the trail, and there was no spot wide enough for a three-point turn.

At last, the surface improved, and he was driving on gravel. As he turned a long, high-cambered bend, he found himself suddenly in front of a house. On the grass outside was parked a police Mini Metro. A narrow stream trickled past the front entrance. There was no garden to speak of, just meadow and then forest, and a smell of wet pine in the air. In the distance, beyond the back of the house, the land climbed and climbed. Rebus got out of the car, feeling his nerves jangle back into position. The door of the Metro had already opened, and out stepped a farm labourer in police uniform.

It was like some sort of Guinness challenge: how large a man can you get in the front of a Mini Metro? He was also young, late teens or early twenties. He gave a big rubicund smile.

'Inspector Rebus? Constable Moffat.' The hand Rebus shook was as large as a coal shovel but surprisingly smooth, almost delicate. 'Detective Sergeant Knox was going to be here, but something came up. He sends his apologies and hopes I'll do instead, this being my neck of the woods, so to speak.'

Rebus, who was rubbing his neck at this point, smiled at the joke. Then he pressed a thumb either side of his spine and straightened up, exhaling noisily. Vertebrae clicked and crunched.

'Long drive, eh?' Constable Moffat commented. 'But you've made not bad time. I've only been here five minutes myself.'

'Have you had another look round?'

'Not yet, no. Thought I'd best wait.'

Rebus nodded. 'Let's start with the outside. Big place, isn't it? I mean, after that road up to it I was expecting something a bit more basic.'

'Well, the house was here first, that's the point. Used to have a fine garden, well-kept drive, and that forest was hardly there at all. Before my time, of course. I think the place was built in the 1920s. Part of the Kelman estate. The estate got sold off bit by bit. There used to be estate workers to keep the place in check. Not these days, and this is what happens.'

'Still, the house looks in good nick.'

'Oh, aye, but you'll see there's a few slates missing, and the gutters could do with patching up.'

Moffat spoke with the confidence of the DIYer. They were circling the house. It was a two-storey affair of solid-looking stone. To Rebus's mind, it wouldn't have been out of place on the outskirts of Edinburgh; it was just a bit odd to find it in a clearing in the wilderness. There was a back door, beside which sat a solitary dustbin.

'Do the bins get emptied around here?'

'They do if you can get them down to the roadside.'

Rebus lifted the lid. The smell was truly awful. A rotting side of salmon, by the shape of it, and some chicken or duck bones.

'I'm surprised the animals haven't been at those,' Moffat said. 'The deer or the wildcats . . .'

'Looks as though it's been in the bin long enough, doesn't it?'

'I wouldn't say they were last week's leavings, sir, if that's what you're getting at.'

Rebus looked at Moffat. 'That's what I'm getting at,' he agreed. 'The whole of last week, and for a few days before that, Mrs Jack was away from home. Driving a black BMW. Supposedly staying here.'

'Well, if she did, nobody I've spoken to saw her.'

Rebus held up a door key. 'Let's see if the inside of the house tells a different story, eh?' But first he returned to his car and produced two pairs of clear polythene gloves. He handed one pair to the constable. 'I'm not even sure these'll fit you,' he told him. But they did. 'Right, try not to touch anything, even though you're wearing gloves. It might be you could smear or wipe a fingerprint. Remember, this is murder we're talking about, not joyriding or cattle rustling. Okay?'

'Yes, sir.' Moffat sniffed the air. 'Did you enjoy your chips? I can smell the vinegar from here.'

Rebus slammed shut the car door. 'Let's go.'

The house smelt damp. At least, the narrow hallway did. The doors off this hallway were wide open, and Rebus stepped through the first, into a room which stretched from the front of the house to the back. The room had been decorated with comfort in mind. There were three sofas, a couple of arm-chairs, and beanbags and scatter cushions. There were TV and video, and a hi-fi system sitting on the floor, one of its speakers lying side on. There was also mess.

Mugs, cups and glasses for a start. Rebus sniffed one of the mugs. Wine. Well, the vinegary stuff left in it had once been wine. Empty bottles of burgundy, champagne, armagnac. And stains – on the carpet, on the scatter cushions, and on one wall, where a glass had landed with some force, shattering on impact. Ashtrays overflowed, and there was a small hand-mirror half hidden under one of the floor cushions. Rebus bent down over it. Traces of white powder around its rim. Cocaine. He left it where it was and approached the hi-fi, examining the choice of music. Cassettes, mostly. Fleet-wood Mac, Eric Clapton, Simple Minds ... and opera. *Don Giovanni* and *The Marriage of Figaro*.

'A party, sir?'

'Yes, but how recent?' Rebus got the feeling that this wasn't all the result of a single evening. A load of bottles looked to have been pushed to one side, making a little oasis of space on the floor, in the midst of which sat a solitary bottle – still upright – and two mugs, one with lipstick on its rim.

'And how many people, do you reckon?'

'Half a dozen, sir.'

'You could be right. A lot of booze for six people.'

'Maybe they don't bother clearing up between parties.'

Just what Rebus was thinking. 'Let's have a look around.'

Across the hall there was a front room which had probably once been dining room or lounge, but now served as a makeshift bedroom. A mattress took up half the floor space, sleeping bags covering the other half. There were a couple of empty bottles in here, too, but nothing to drink out of. A few art prints had been pinned to the walls. On the mattress sat a pair of shoes, men's, size nine, into one of which had been stuffed a blue sock.

The only room left was the kitchen. Pride of place seemed to go to a microwave oven, beside which sat empty tins, and packets of something called Microwave Popcorn. The tins had contained lobster bisque and venison stew. The double sink was filled with dishes and grey, speckled water. On a foldaway table sat unopened bottles of lemonade, packs of orange juice, and a bottle of cider. There was a larger pine breakfast table, its surface dotted with soup droppings but free from dishes and other detritus. On the floor around it, however, lay empty crisp packets, a knocked-over ashtray, bread-sticks, cutlery, a plastic apron and some serviettes.

'Quick way of clearing a table,' said Moffat.

'Yes,' said Rebus. 'Have you ever seen *The Postman Always Rings Twice?* The later version, with Jack Nicholson?'

Moffat shook his head. 'I saw him in *The Shining* though.'

'Not the same thing at all, Constable. Only, there's a bit in the film where . . . you must have heard about it . . . where

Jack Nicholson and the boss's wife clear the kitchen table so they can have a spot of you-know-what on it.'

Moffat looked at the table suspiciously. 'No,' he said. Clearly, this idea was new to him. 'What did you say the film was called . . .?'

'It's only an idea,' said Rebus.

Then there was upstairs. A bathroom, the cleanest room in the house. Beside the toilet sat a pile of magazines, but they were old, too old to yield any clue. And two more bedrooms, one a makeshift attempt like the one downstairs, the other altogether more serious, with a newish-looking wooden four-poster, wardrobe, chest of drawers and dressing table. Improbably, above the bed had been mounted the head of a Highland cow. Rebus stared at the stuff on the dressing table: powders, lipsticks, scents and paints. There were clothes in the wardrobe – mostly women's clothes, but also men's denims and cords. Gregor Jack could give no description of what clothing his wife had taken with her when she left. He couldn't even be sure that she'd taken any until he noticed that her small green suitcase was missing.

The green suitcase jutting out from beneath the bed. Rebus pulled it out and opened it. It was empty. So were most of the drawers.

'We keep a change of clothes up there,' Jack had told detectives. 'Enough for emergencies, that's all.'

Rebus stared at the bed. Its pillows had been fluffed up, and the duvet lay straight and smooth across it. A sign of recent habitation? God knows. This was it, the last room in the house. What had he learned at the end of his hundred-odd-mile drive? He'd learned that Mrs Jack's suitcase – the one Mr Jack *said* she'd taken with her – was here. Anything else? Nothing. He sat down on the bed. It crackled beneath him. He stood up again and pulled back the duvet. The bed was covered in newspapers, Sunday newspapers, all of them open at the same story.

MP Found in Sex Den Raid.

So she'd been here, and she knew. Knew about the raid,

about Operation Creeper. Unless someone else had been here and planted this stuff ... No, keep to the obvious. His eye caught something else. He moved aside one of the pillows. Tied to the post behind it was a pair of black tights. Another pair had been tied to the opposite post. Moffat was staring quizzically, but Rebus thought the young man had learned enough for one day. It was an interesting scenario all the same. Tied to her bed and left there. Moffat could have come, looked the house over, and gone, without ever being aware of her presence upstairs. But it wouldn't work. If you were *really* going to restrain someone, you wouldn't use tights. Too easy to escape. Tights were for sex-games. For restraint, you'd use something stronger, twine or handcuffs ... Like the handcuffs in Gregor Jack's dustbin?

At least now Rebus knew that she'd known. So why hadn't she got in touch with her husband? There was no telephone at the lodge.

'Where's the nearest call-box?' he asked Moffat, who still seemed interested in the tights.

'About a mile and a half away, on the road outside Cragstone Farm.'

Rebus checked his watch. It was four o'clock. 'Okay, I'd like to take a look at it, then we'll call it a day. But I want this place gone over for fingerprints. Christ knows, there should be enough of them. Then we need to check and double check the shops, petrol stations, pubs, hotels. Say, within a twenty-mile radius.'

Moffat looked doubtful. 'That's an awful lot of places.'

Rebus ignored him. 'A black BMW. I think some more handouts are being printed today. There's a photo of Mrs Jack, and the car description and registration. If she was up this way – and she *was* – *some*body must have seen her.'

'Well ... folk keep to themselves, you know.'

'Yes, but they're not blind, are they? And if we're lucky, they won't be suffering from amnesia either. Come on, sooner we look at that phone-box, the sooner I can get to my digs.'

*

Actually, Rebus's original plan had been to sleep in the car and claim the price of a B&B, pocketing the money. But the weather looked uninviting, and the thought of spending a night cramped in his car like a half-shut knife ... So, on the way to the phone-box, he signalled to a stop outside a roadside cottage advertising bed & breakfast and knocked on the door. The elderly woman seemed suspicious at first, but finally agreed that she had a vacancy. Rebus told her he'd be back in an hour, giving her time to 'air' the room. Then he returned to his car and followed Moffat's careful driving all the way to Cragstone Farm.

It wasn't much of a farm actually. A short track led from the main road to a cluster of buildings: house, byre, some sheds and a barn. The phone-box was by the side of the main road, fifty yards along from the farm and on the other side of the road, next to a lay-by big enough to allow them to park their two cars. It was one of the original red boxes.

'They daren't change it,' said Moffat. 'Mrs Corbie up at the farm would have a fit.' Rebus didn't understand this at first, but then he opened the door to the phone-box – and he understood. For one thing, it had a carpet – a good carpet, too, a thick-piled offcut. There was a smell of air freshener, and a posy of field flowers had been placed in a small glass jar on the shelf beside the apparatus.

'It's better kept than my flat,' Rebus said. 'When can I move in?'

'It's Mrs Corbie,' Moffat said with a grin. 'She reckons a dirty phone-box would reflect badly on her, seeing her house is closest. She's been keeping it spick and span since God knows when.'

A pity though. Rebus had been hoping for something, some hint or clue. But supposing there had been anything, it must certainly have been tidied away ...

'I'd like to talk to Mrs Corbie.'

'It's a Tuesday,' said Moffat. 'She's at her sister's on a Tuesday.' Rebus pointed back along the road to where a car was braking hard, signalling to pull into the farm's driveway. 'What about him?'

Moffat looked, then smiled coldly. 'Her son, Alec. A bit of a tearaway. He won't tell us anything.'

'Gets into trouble, does he?'

'Speeding mostly. He's one of the local boy racers. Can't say I blame him. There's not much to occupy the teenagers round here.'

'You can't be much more than a teenager yourself, Constable. *You* didn't get into trouble.'

'I had the Church, sir. Believe me, the fear of God is something to reckon with . . .'

Rebus's landlady, Mrs Wilkie, was something to reckon with, too. It started when he was changing in his bedroom. It was a nice bedroom, a bit overdone on the frills and finery, but with a comfortable bed and a twelve-inch black and white television. Mrs Wilkie had shown him the kitchen, and told him he should feel free to make himself tea and coffee whenever he felt like it. Then she had shown him the bathroom, and told him the water was hot if he felt like a bath. Then she had led him back to the kitchen and told him that he could make himself a cup of tea or coffee whenever he felt like it.

Rebus didn't have the heart to tell her he'd heard it all before. She was tiny, with a tiny voice. Between his first visit and his second, she had dressed in her best B&B-keeper's clothes and tied some pearls around her neck. He reckoned her to be in her late seventies. She was a widow, her husband Andrew having died in 1982, and she did the B&B 'as much for the company as the money'. She always seemed to get nice guests, interesting people like the German jam-buyer who had stayed for a few nights last autumn . . .

'And here's your bedroom. I've given it a bit of an airing and – '

'It's very nice, thank you.' Rebus put his bag on the bed, saw her ominous look, and shifted it off the bed and on to the floor.

'I made the bedspread myself,' she said with a smile. 'I was once advised to go professional, selling my bedspreads. But at my age ...' She gave a chuckle. 'It was a German gentleman told me that. He was in Scotland to buy jam. Would you credit it? He stayed here a few nights ...'

Eventually, she recalled her duties. She'd just go and make them a spot of supper. Supper. Rebus glanced at his watch. Unless it had stopped, it was not yet five thirty. But then, he'd booked bed and breakfast, and any hot meal tonight would be a bonus. Moffat had given him directions to the closest pub – 'tourist place, tourist prices' – before leaving him for the undoubted delights of Dufftown. The fear of God ...

He had just slipped off his trousers when the door opened and Mrs Wilkie stood there.

'Is that you, Andrew? I thought I heard a noise.' Her eyes had a glassy, faraway look. Rebus stood there, frozen, then swallowed.

'Go and make us some supper,' he said quietly.

'Oh yes,' Mrs Wilkie said. 'You must be hungry. You've been gone such a long time ...'

Then, the idea of a quick bath appealed. He looked into the kitchen first, and saw that Mrs Wilkie was busy at the stove, humming to herself. So he headed for the bathroom. There was no lock on the door. Or rather, there was a lock, but half of it was hanging loose. He looked around him, but saw nothing he could wedge against the door. He decided to take his chance and started both taps running. There was a furious pressure to the water, and the bath filled quickly and hotly. Rebus undressed and sank beneath the surface. His shoulders were stiff from the drive, and he massaged them as best he could. Then he lifted his knees so that his shoulders, neck and head slid into the water. Immersion. He thought of Dr Curt, of drowning and immersion. Skin wrinkling ... hair and nails shedding ... silt in the bronchial ...

A noise brought him to the surface. He cleared his eyes, blinked, and saw that Mrs Wilkie was staring down at him, a dish towel in her hands.

'Oh!' she said. 'Oh dear, I'm sorry.' And she retreated behind the door, calling through it: 'I quite forgot you were here! I was just going to ... well ... never mind, it can wait.'

Rebus screwed shut his eyes and sank beneath the waves . . .

The meal was, to his surprise, good, if a bit odd. Cheese pudding, boiled potatoes, and carrots. Followed by tinned steamed pudding and packet custard.

'So convenient,' as Mrs Wilkie commented. The shock of seeing a naked man in her bathtub seemed to have brought her into the here and now, and they talked about the weather, the tourists and the government until the meal was over. Rebus asked if he could wash the dishes, and was told he could not – much to his relief. Instead, he asked Mrs Wilkie for a front-door key, then set off, stomach full, clean of body and underwear, for the Heather Hoose.

Not a name he would have chosen for his own pub. He entered by the lounge door, but, the place being dead, pushed through another door into the public bar. Two men and a woman stood at the bar and shared a joke, while a barman studiously filled glasses from a whisky optic. The group looked round at Rebus as he came and stood not too far from them.

'Evening.'

They nodded back, almost without seeing him, and the barman returned the greeting, setting down three double measures of whisky on the bar.

'And one for yourself,' said one of the customers, handing across a ten-pound note.

'Thanks,' said the barman, 'I'll have a nip myself for later on.'

Behind the array of optics, bottles and glasses, the wall was mirrored, so Rebus was able to study the group without seeming to. The man who had spoken sounded English. There had been only two cars in the pub's courtyard, a beaten-up Renault 5 and a Daimler. Rebus reckoned he knew who owned which . . .

'Yes, sir?' asked the barman and Renault 5 owner.

'Pint of export, please.'

'Certainly.'

124

The wonder of it was that three well-off English tourists would drink in the public bar. Maybe they just hadn't noticed that the Heather Hoose possessed such an amenity as a lounge. All three looked a bit the worse for wear, mostly from drink. The woman had a formidable face, framed by dyed platinum hair. Her cheeks were too red and her eyelashes too black. When she sucked on her cigarette, she arched her head up to blow the smoke ceilingwards. Rebus tried counting the lines on her neck. Maybe it worked the way it did with tree-rings . . .

'There you are.' The pint glass was placed on a mat in front of him. He handed over a fiver.

'Quiet tonight.'

'Midweek and not quite the season,' recited the barman, who had obviously just said the same thing to the other group. 'It'll get busier later on.' Then he retreated to the till.

'Another round here when you're ready,' said the Englishman, the only one of the three to have finished his whisky. He was in his late thirties, younger than the woman. He looked fit, prosperous, but somehow faintly disreputable. It had something to do with the way he stood, slightly slouched and looming, as though he might be about either to fall down or else pounce. And his head swayed a little from side to side in time with his sleepy eyelids.

The third member of the group was younger still, mid-thirties. He was smoking French cigarettes and staring at the bottles above the bar. Either that, thought Rebus, or he's looking at *me* in the mirror, the way I'm looking at *him*. Certainly, it was a possibility. The man had an affected way of tapping the ash from his affected cigarette. Rebus noticed that he smoked without inhaling, holding the smoke in his mouth and releasing it in a single belch. While his companions stood, he rested on one of the high bar stools.

Rebus had to admit, he was intrigued. An unlikely little threesome. And about to become more unlikely still . . .

A couple of people had entered the lounge bar, and looked like staying there. The barman slipped through a doorway between rooms to serve these new customers, and this seemed to start off a conversation between the two men and the woman.

'God, the nerve. He hasn't served *us* yet.'

'Well, Jamie, we're not exactly gasping, are we?'

'Speak for yourself. I hardly felt that first one slip down. Should have asked for quadruples in the first place.'

'Have mine,' said the woman, 'if you're going to become ratty.'

'I am not becoming ratty,' said the slouching pouncer, becoming very ratty indeed.

'Well fuck you then.'

Rebus had to stifle a grin. The woman had said this as though it were part of any polite conversation.

'And fuck you, too, Louise.'

'Ssh,' the French-smoker warned. 'Remember, we're not alone.'

The other man and woman looked towards Rebus, who sat staring straight ahead, glass to lips.

'Yes we are,' said the man. 'We're all alone.'

This utterance seemed to signal the end of the conversation. The barman reappeared.

'Same again, barman, if you'll be so kind . . .'

The evening hotted up quickly. Three locals appeared and started to play dominoes at a nearby table. Rebus wondered if they were paid to come in and add the requisite local colour. There was probably more colour in a Meadowbank Thistle–Raith Rovers friendly. Two other drinkers appeared, wedging themselves in between Rebus and the threesome. They seemed to take it as an insult that there were other drinkers in the bar before them, and that some of those drinkers were standing next to *their* space at the bar. So they drank in dour silence, merely exchanging looks whenever the Englishman or his two friends said anything.

'Look,' said the woman, 'are we heading back tonight? If not, we'd better think about accommodation.'

'We could sleep at the lodge.'

Rebus put down his glass.

'Don't be so sick,' the woman retorted.

'I thought that was why we came.'

'I wouldn't be able to sleep.'

'Maybe that's why they call it a wake.'

The Englishman's laughter filled the silent bar, then died. A domino clacked on to a table. Another chapped. Rebus left his glass where it was and approached the group.

'Did I hear you mention a lodge?'

The Englishman blinked slowly. 'What's it to you?'

'I'm a police officer.' Rebus brought out his ID. The two dour regulars finished their drinks and left the bar. Funny how an ID had that effect sometimes . . .

'Detective Inspector Rebus. Which lodge did you mean?'

All three looked sober now. It was an act, but a good act, years in the learning.

'Well, officer,' said the Englishman, 'now what business is that of yours?'

'Depends which lodge you were talking about, sir. There's a nice police station at Dufftown if you'd prefer to go there . . .'

'Deer Lodge,' said the French-smoker. 'A friend of ours owns it.'

'Owned it,' corrected the woman.

'You were friends of Mrs Jack then?'

They were. Introductions were made. The Englishman was actually a Scot, Jamie Kilpatrick the antique dealer. The woman was Louise Patterson-Scott, wife (separated) of the retail tycoon. The other man was Julian Kaymer, the painter.

'I've already spoken with the police,' Julian Kaymer said. 'They telephoned me yesterday.'

Yes, they had *all* been questioned, asked if they knew Mrs Jack's movements. But they hadn't seen her for weeks.

'I spoke to her on the telephone,' Mrs Patterson-Scott announced, 'a few days before she went off on holiday. She didn't say where she was going, just that she fancied a few days away by herself.'

'So what are you all doing here?' Rebus asked.

'This is a wake,' said Kilpatrick. 'Our little token of

127

friendship, our time of mourning. So why don't you bugger off and let us get on with it.'

'Ignore him, Inspector,' said Julian Kaymer. 'He's a bit pissed.'

'What I am,' stated Kilpatrick, 'is a bit *upset*.'

'Emotional,' Rebus offered.

'Exactly, Inspector.'

Kaymer carried on the story. 'It was my idea. We'd all been on the phone to each other, none of us really able to take it in. Devastated. So I said why don't we take a run to the lodge? That was where we all met last.'

'At a party?' asked Rebus.

Kaymer nodded. 'A month back.'

'A great bloody big piss-up it was,' confirmed Kilpatrick.

'So,' said Kaymer, 'the plan was to drive here, have a few drinks in memory of Lizzie, and drive back. Not everybody could make it. Prior commitments and so on. But here we are.'

'Well,' said Rebus, 'I *would* like you to look inside the house. But there's no point going out there in the dark. What I *don't* want is the three of you going out there on your own. The place still has to be gone over for fingerprints.'

They looked a bit puzzled at this. 'You haven't heard?' Rebus said, recalling that Curt had only revealed his findings that morning. 'It's a murder hunt now. Mrs Jack was murdered.'

'Oh no!'

'Christ . . .'

'I'm going to be – '

And Louise Patterson-Scott, wife of the et cetera, threw up on to the carpeted floor. Julian Kaymer was weeping, and Jamie Kilpatrick was losing all the blood from his face. The barman stared in horror, while the domino players stopped their game. One of them had to restrain his dog from investigating further. It cowered under the table and licked its whiskery chops . . .

Local colour, as provided by John Rebus.

*

Finally, a hotel was found, not far out of Dufftown. It was arranged that the three would spend the night there. Rebus had considered asking Mrs Wilkie if she had any spare rooms, but thought better of it. They would stay at the hotel, and meet Rebus at the lodge in the morning. Bright and early: some of them had jobs to get back to.

When Rebus returned to the cottage, Mrs Wilkie was knitting by her gas fire and watching a film on the TV. He put his head round the living room door.

'I'll say goodnight, Mrs Wilkie.'

'Night-night, son. Mind, say your prayers. I'll be up to tuck you in a bit later on . . .'

Rebus made himself a mug of tea, went to his room, and wedged the chair against the door handle. He opened the window to let in some air, switched on his own little television, and fell on to the bed. There was something wrong with the picture on the TV, and he couldn't fix it. The vertical hold had gone. So he switched it off again and dug into his bag, coming up with *Fish out of Water*. Well, he'd nothing else to read, and he certainly didn't feel tired. He opened the book at chapter one.

Rebus woke up the next morning with a bad feeling. He half expected to turn and see Mrs Wilkie lying beside him, saying 'Come on, Andrew, time for the conjugals'. He turned. Mrs Wilkie was not lying beside him. She was outside his door and trying to get in.

'Mr Rebus, Mr Rebus.' A soft knock, then a hard. 'The door seems to be jammed, Mr Rebus! Are you awake? I've brought you a cup of tea.'

During which time Rebus was out of bed and half dressed. 'Coming, Mrs Wilkie.'

But the old lady was panicking. 'You're locked in, Mr Rebus. The door's stuck! Shall I call for a carpenter? Oh dear.'

'Hold on, Mrs Wilkie, I think I've got it.' His shirt still unbuttoned, Rebus put his weight to the door, keeping it shut, and at the same time lifted the chair away, stretching so as to place it nearer the bed. Then he made show of thumping the edges of the door before pulling it open.

'Are you all right, Mr Rebus? Oh dear, that's never happened before. Dear me no . . .'

Rebus lifted the cup and saucer from her hand and began pouring the tea back from saucer into cup. 'Thank you, Mrs Wilkie.' He made show of sniffing. 'Is something cooking?'

'Oh dear, yes. Breakast.' And off she toddled, back down the stairs. Rebus felt a bit guilty for having pulled the 'locked-door' stunt. He'd show her after breakfast that the door was all right really, that she didn't need to phone for cowboy carpenters to put it right. But for now he had to continue the process of waking up. It was seven thirty. The tea was cold but the day seemed unseasonally warm. He sat on the bed for a moment, collecting his thoughts. What day was it? It was Wednesday. What needed to be done today? What was the best order to do it in? He'd to return to the cottage with the Three Stooges. Then there was Mrs Corbie to speak to. And something else . . . something he'd been thinking about last night, in the melting moment between waking and sleep. Well, why not? He was in the area anyway. He'd telephone after breakfast. A fry-up by the smell of it, rather than Patience's usual choice of muesli or Bran Crunch. Ah, that was another thing. He'd meant to phone Patience last night. He'd do it today, just to say hello. He thought about her for a little while, Patience and her collection of pets. Then he finished dressing and made his way downstairs . . .

He was first to arrive at the lodge. He let himself in and wandered into the living room. Immediately, he knew something was different. The place was tidier. Tidier? Well, say then that there was less debris around than before. Half the bottles looked to have disappeared. He wondered what else had vanished. He lifted the scatter cushions, searching in vain for the hand-mirror. Damn. He fairly flew through to the kitchen. The back window was lying in shards in the sink and on the floor. Here, the mess was as bad as before. Except that the microwave had gone. He went upstairs . . . slowly.

The place seemed deserted, but you never could tell. The bathroom and small bedroom were as before. So was the main bedroom. No, hold on. The tights had been untied from their bedposts and were now lying innocently on the floor. Rebus crouched and picked one up. Then dropped it again. Thoughtfully, he made his way back downstairs.

A burglary, yes. Break in and steal the microwave. That was the way it was supposed to look. But no petty thief would take empty bottles and a mirror with him, no petty thief would have reason to untie pairs of tights from bedposts. That didn't matter though, did it? What mattered was that the evidence had to disappear. Now it would merely be Rebus's word.

'Yes, sir, I'm sure there was a mirror in the living room. Lying on the floor, a small mirror with traces of white powder on it . . .'

'And you're sure you're not merely *imagining* this, Inspector? You could be wrong, couldn't you?'

No, no, he couldn't. But it was too late for all that. Why take the bottles . . . and only some of them, not all? Obviously, because some bottles had certain prints on them. Why take the mirror? Maybe fingerprints again . . .

Should have thought of all this yesterday, John. Stupid, stupid, stupid.

'Stupid, stupid, stupid.'

And he'd done the damage himself. Hadn't he told the Three Stooges not to go near the lodge? Because it hadn't been fingerprinted. Then he'd let them wander off, with no guard left on the house. A constable should have been here all night.

'Stupid, stupid.'

It had to be one of them, didn't it? The woman, or one of the men. But why? Why had they done it? So it couldn't be proved they'd been there in the first place? Again, why? It didn't make much sense. Not much sense at all.

'Stupid.'

He heard a car approaching, pulling up outside, and went to meet it. It was the Daimler, Kilpatrick driving, Patterson-

Scott in the passenger seat, and Julian Kaymer emerging from the rear. Kilpatrick looked a lot breezier than before.

'Inspector, good morning to you.'

'Morning, sir. How was the hotel?'

'Fair, I'd say. Only fair.'

'Better than average,' added Kaymer.

Kilpatrick turned to him. 'Julian, when you're used to excellence as I am, you no longer recognize "average" and "better than".'

Kaymer stuck his tongue out.

'Children, children,' chided Louise Patterson-Scott. But they all seemed light of heart.

'You sound chirpy,' Rebus said.

'A decent night's sleep and a long breakfast,' said Kilpatrick, patting his stomach.

'You stayed at the hotel last night?'

They seemed not to understand his question.

'You didn't go for a drive or anything?'

'No,' Kilpatrick said, his tone wary.

'It's your car, isn't it, Mr Kilpatrick?'

'Yes . . .'

'And you kept the keys with you last night?'

'Look, Inspector . . .'

'Did you or didn't you?'

'I suppose I did. In my jacket pocket.'

'Hanging up in your bedroom?'

'Correct. Look, can we go ins – '

'Any visitors to your room?'

'Inspector,' interrupted Louise Patterson-Scott, 'perhaps if you'd tell us . . . ?'

'Someone broke into the lodge during the night, disturbing potential evidence. That's a serious crime, madam.'

'And you think one of us – ?'

'I don't think anything yet, madam. But whoever did it must have come by car. Mr Kilpatrick here has a car.'

'Both Julian and I are capable of driving, Inspector.'

'Yes,' said Kaymer, 'and besides, we all went to Jamie's room for a late-night brandy . . .'

'So any one of you could have taken the car?'

Kilpatrick shrugged mightily. 'I still don't see,' he said, 'why you think we should want – '

'As I say, Mr Kilpatrick, I don't think anything. All I know is that a murder inquiry is under way, Mrs Jack's last known whereabouts remain this lodge, and now someone's trying to tamper with evidence.' Rebus paused. 'That's all I know. You can come inside now, but, please, don't touch anything. I'd like to ask you all a few questions.'

Really, what he wanted to ask was: Is the house pretty much in the state you remember it from the last party here? But he was asking too much. Yes, they remembered drinking champagne and armagnac and a lot of wine. They remembered cooking popcorn in the microwave. Some people drove off – recklessly, no doubt – into the night, while others slept where they lay or staggered off into the various bedrooms. No, Gregor hadn't been present. He didn't enjoy parties. Not his wife's, at any rate.

'A bit of a bore, old Gregor,' commented Jamie Kilpatrick. 'At least, I thought he was till I saw that story about the brothel. Just goes to show . . .'

But there had been another party, hadn't there? A more recent party. Barney Byars had told Rebus about it that night in the pub. A party of Gregor's friends, of The Pack. Who else knew Rebus was on his way up here? Who else knew what he might find? Who else might want to stop him finding anything? Well, Gregor Jack knew. And what he knew, The Pack might know, too. Maybe not one of these three then; maybe someone entirely different.

'Seems funny,' said Louise Patterson-Scott, 'to think we won't be having parties here any more . . . to think Liz won't be here . . . to think she's gone . . .' She began to cry, loudly and tearfully. Jamie Kilpatrick put an arm around her, and she buried her face in his chest. She reached out a hand and found Julian Kaymer, pulling him to her so that he, too, could be embraced.

And that's pretty much how they were when Constable Moffat arrived . . .

Rebus, with a real sense of bolting the stable door, left Moffat to stand guard, much against the young man's will. But the forensics team would be arriving before lunchtime, and Detective Sergeant Knox with them.

'There are some magazines in the bathroom, if you need something to read,' Rebus told Moffat. 'Or, better still, here . . .' And he opened the car, reached into his bag, and took out *Fish out of Water*. 'Don't bother returning it. Think of it as a sort of present.'

Then, the Daimler having already left, Rebus got into his own car, waved back at Constable Moffat, and was off. He'd read *Fish out of Water* last night, every fraught sentence of it. It was a dreadful romantic tale of doomed love between a young Italian sculptor and a wealthy but bored married woman. The sculptor had come to England to work on a commission for the woman's husband. At first, she uses him like a plaything, but then falls in love. Meantime, the sculptor, bowled over by her at first, has moved his attentions to her niece. And so on.

It looked to Rebus as though the title alone had been what had made Ronald Steele pluck it from the shelf and throw it with such venom. Yes, just that title (the title, too, of the young sculptor's statue). The fish out of water was Liz Jack. But Rebus wondered whether she'd been out of water, or just out of her depth . . .

He drove to Cragstone Farm, parking in the yard to the rear of the farmhouse, scattering chickens and ducks before him. Mrs Corbie was at home, and took him into the kitchen, where there was a wondrous smell of baking. The large kitchen table was white with flour, but only a few globes of leftover pastry remained. Rebus couldn't help recalling that scene in *The Postman Always Rings Twice* . . .

'Sit yourself down,' she ordered. 'I've just made a pot . . .'

Rebus was given tea, and some of yesterday's batch of fruit scones, with fresh butter and thick strawberry jam.

'Ever thought about doing B&B, Mrs Corbie?'

'Me? I wouldn't have the patience.' She was wiping her hands on her white cotton apron. She seemed always to be wiping her hands. 'Mind you, it's not for shortage of space. My husband passed away last year, so now there's just Alec and me.'

'What? Running the whole farm?'

She made a face. 'Running it *down* would be more like it. Alec just isn't interested. It's a sin, but there you are. We've got a couple of workers, but when they see *he's* not interested, they can't see why *they* should be. We'd be as well selling up. That's what Alec would like. Maybe that's the only thing that stops me from doing it ...' She was looking at her hands. Then she slapped them against her thighs. 'Goodness, would you listen to me! Now, Inspector, what was it you wanted?'

After all his years on the force, Rebus reckoned that at last he was in the presence of someone with a genuinely clear conscience. It didn't usually take so long for people to ask what a policeman was after. When it *did* take so long, the person either knew already what was wanted, or else had absolutely nothing to fear or to hide. So Rebus asked his question.

'I notice you keep the telephone kiosk sparkling, Mrs Corbie. I was wondering if you'd noticed anything suspicious recently? I mean, anything up at the box?'

'Oh, well, let me think.' She placed the flat of one hand against her cheek. 'I can't say ... what sort of thing exactly, Inspector?'

Rebus couldn't look her in the eye – for he knew that she had started to lie to him.

'A woman perhaps. Making a telephone call. Something left in the box ... a note or a telephone number ... anything at all.'

'No, no, nothing in the box.'

His voice hardened a little. 'Well, outside the box then, Mrs

Corbie. I'm thinking specifically of a week ago, last Wednesday or maybe the Tuesday . . . ?'

She was shaking her head. 'Have another scone, Inspector.'

He did, and chewed slowly, in silence. Mrs Corbie looked to be doing some thinking. She got up and checked in her oven. Then she poured the last of the tea from the pot, and returned to her seat, studying her hands again, laying them against her lap for inspection.

But she didn't say anything. So Rebus did.

'You *were* here last Wednesday?'

She nodded. 'But not the Tuesday. I go to my sister's on a Tuesday. I was here all day Wednesday though.'

'What about your son?'

She shrugged. 'He might have been here. Or maybe he was in Dufftown. He spends a lot of time off gallivanting . . .'

'He's not here just now?'

'No, he's gone to town.'

'Which town?'

'He didn't say. Just said he was off . . .'

Rebus stood up and went to the kitchen window. It faced on to the yard, where chickens now pecked at Rebus's tyres. One of them was sitting on the bonnet of the car.

'Is it possible to see the kiosk from the house, Mrs Corbie?'

'Eh . . . yes, from the sitting room. But we don't spend much time in there. That is, I don't. I prefer here in the kitchen.'

'Could I take a look?'

Well, it was clear enough who *did* spend time in the living room. There was a direct line between sofa, coffee table and television set. The coffee table was marked with rings made by too many hot mugs. On the floor by the sofa there was an ashtray and the remains of a huge bag of crisps. Three empty beer cans lay on their sides beneath the coffee table. Mrs Corbie tut-tutted and went to work, lifting the cans. Rebus went to the window and peered out.

He could make out the kiosk in the distance, but only just. It was possible Alec Corbie might have seen something. Possible, but doubtful. Not worth sticking around for. He'd let DS Knox come and ask Corbie the questions.

'Well,' he said, 'thanks for your help, Mrs Corbie.'

'Oh.' Her relief was palpable. 'Right you are, Inspector. I'll see you out.'

But Rebus knew he had one last bet worth laying. He stood with Mrs Corbie in the yard and looked around him.

'I used to love farms when I was a lad. A pal of mine lived on one,' he glibly lied. 'I used to go up there every evening after tea. It was great.' He turned his wide-eyed nostalgic smile towards her. 'Mind if I take a wander round?'

'Oh.' No relief now; rather, sheer terror. Which didn't stop Rebus. No, it pushed him on. So that before she knew it, he was walking up to the hutches and sties, looking in, moving on. On past the chickens and the roused ducks, into the barn. Straw underfoot and a strong smell of cattle. Concrete cubicles, coiled hosepipes, and a leaking tap. There were pools of water underfoot. One sick-looking cow blinked slowly at him from its enclosure. But the livestock wasn't his concern. The tarpaulin in the corner was.

'What's under here, Mrs Corbie?'

'That's Alec's property!' she shrieked. 'Don't touch it! It's nothing to do with – '

But he'd already yanked the tarpaulin off. What was he expecting to find? Something . . . nothing. What he *did* find was a black BMW 3-series bearing Elizabeth Jack's registration. It was Rebus's turn to tut-tut, but only after he'd sucked in his breath and held back a whoop of delight.

'Dear me, Mrs Corbie,' he said. 'This is just the very car I've been looking for.'

But Mrs Corbie wasn't listening. 'He's a good laddie, he doesn't mean any harm. I don't know what I'd do without him.' And so on. While Rebus circled the car, looking but not touching. Lucky the forensics team was on its way. They'd be kept busy . . .

Wait, what was that? On the back seat. A huddled shape. He peered in through the tinted glass.

'Expect the unexpected, John,' he muttered to himself.

It was a microwave.

7
Duthil

Rebus telephoned Edinburgh to make his report and request an extra day's stay up north. Lauderdale sounded so impressed that the car had been found that Rebus forgot to tell him about the break-in at the lodge. Then, once Alec Corbie had arrived home (drunk and in charge of a vehicle – but let that pass), he'd been arrested and taken to Dufftown. Rebus seemed to be stretching the local police like they'd never been stretched before, so that Detective Sergeant Knox had to be diverted from the lodge and brought to the farm instead. He looked like an older brother of Constable Moffat, or perhaps a close cousin.

'I want forensics to go over that car,' Rebus told him. 'Priority, the lodge can wait.'

Knox rubbed his chin. 'It'll take a tow-truck.'

'A trailer would be better.'

'I'll see what I can do. Where will you want it taken?'

'Anywhere secure and with a roof.'

'The police garage?'

'It'll do.'

'What exactly are we looking for?'

'Christ knows.'

Rebus went back into the kitchen, where Mrs Corbie was sitting at the table studying an array of burnt cakes. He opened his mouth to speak, but kept his silence. She was an accessory, of course. She'd lied to him to protect her son. Well, they had the son now, and *he* was the one that mattered. As quietly as he could, Rebus left the farmhouse

138

and started his car, staring through the windscreen at his bonnet, where one of the chickens had left him a little gift . . .

He was able to avail himself of Dufftown police station for the interview with Alec Corbie.

'You're in keech up to your chin, son. Start at the beginning and leave nothing out.'

Rebus and Corbie, seated across the table from one another, were smoking, DS Knox, resting against the wall behind Rebus, was not. Corbie had prepared an extremely thin veneer of macho indifference, which Rebus was quick to wipe off.

'This is a murder investigation. The victim's car has been found in your barn. It'll be dusted for prints, and if we find yours I'm going to have to charge you with murder. Anything you think you know that might help your case, you'd better talk.'

Then, seeing the effect of these words: 'You're in keech up to your chin, son. Start at the beginning and leave nothing out.'

Corbie sang like his namesake: it didn't make for edifying listening, but it had an honest sound. First, though, he asked for some paracetamol.

'I've got a hell of a headache.'

'That's what daytime drinking does to you,' said Rebus, knowing it wasn't the drinking that was to blame – it was the stopping. The tablets were brought and swallowed, washed down with water. Corbie coughed a little, then lit another cigarette. Rebus had stubbed his out. He just couldn't deal with them any more.

'The car was in the lay-by,' Corbie began. 'It was there for hours, so I went and took a look. The keys were still in the ignition. I started her up and brought her back to the farm.'

'Why?'

He shrugged. 'Never refuse a gift horse.' He grinned. 'Or gift horse-power, eh?' The two detectives were not impressed. 'No, well, it was, you know, like with treasure. Finders keepers.'

'You didn't think the owner was coming back?'

He shrugged again. 'Never really thought about it. All I knew was that there were going to be some gey jealous looks if I turned up in town driving a BMW.'

'You planned to race it?' The question came from DS Knox.

'Sure.'

Knox explained to Rebus. 'They take cars out on to the back roads and race them one against one.'

Rebus remembered the phrase Moffat had used: boy racer. 'You didn't see the owner then?' he asked.

Corbie shrugged.

'What does that mean?'

'It means maybe. There was another car in the lay-by. Looked like a couple were in it, having an argument. I heard them from the yard.'

'What did you see?'

'Just that the BMW was parked, and this other car was in front of it.'

'You didn't get a look at the other car?'

'No. But I could hear the shouting, sounded like a man and a woman.'

'What were they arguing about?'

'No idea.'

'No?'

Corbie shook his head firmly.

'Okay,' said Rebus, 'and this was on . . .?'

'Wednesday. Wednesday morning. Maybe around lunchtime.'

Rebus nodded thoughtfully. Alibis would need re-checking . . . 'Where was your mother all this time?'

'In the kitchen, same as always.'

'Did you mention the argument to her?'

Corbie shook his head. 'No point.'

Rebus nodded again. Wednesday morning: Elizabeth Jack was killed that day. An argument in a lay-by . . .

'You're sure it was an argument?'

'I've been *in* enough in my time, it was an argument all right. The woman was screeching.'

'Anything else, Alec?'

Corbie seemed to relax at the use of his first name. Maybe he wouldn't be in trouble after all, so long as he told them . . .

'Well, the other car disappeared, but the BMW was still there. Couldn't tell if there was anyone in it, windows being tinted. But a radio was playing. Then in the afternoon – '

'So the car had been there all morning?'

'That's right. Then in the afternoon – '

'What time precisely?'

'No idea. I think there was horse-racing or something on the telly.'

'Go on.'

'Well, I looked out and there was *another* car had turned up. Or maybe it was the same one come back.'

'You still couldn't see?'

'I saw it better the second time. Don't know what make it was, but it was blue, light blue. I'm fairly sure of that.'

Cars would need checking . . . Jamie Kilpatrick's Daimler wasn't blue. Gregor Jack's Saab wasn't blue. Rab Kinnoul's Land-Rover wasn't blue.

'Anyway,' Corbie was saying, 'then there was *more* shouting the odds. I reckon it was coming from the BMW, because at one point the volume went right up on the radio.'

Rebus nodded appreciation of the observation.

'Then what?'

Corbie shrugged. 'It went quiet again. Next time I looked out, the other car was gone and the BMW was still there. Later on, I took a wander into the yard and through the field. Took a closer look. The passenger door was a bit open. Didn't look as though anyone was there, so I crossed the road. Keys were in the ignition . . .' He gave a final shrug. He had told his all.

And an interesting all it was. Two other cars? Or had the car from the morning returned in the afternoon? Who had Liz Jack been calling from the phone-box? What had she been arguing about? The volume rising on the radio . . . to mask an argument, or because, in the course of a struggle, the knob had been moved? His head was beginning to birl again. He suggested they have some coffee. Three plastic cups were brought, with sugar and a plate containing four digestive biscuits.

Corbie seemed relaxed in the hard-back chair, one leg slung over the other, and smoking yet another cigarette. So far Knox had eaten all the biscuits . . .

'Right,' said Rebus, 'now what about the microwave . . . ?'

The microwave was easy. The microwave was more treasure, again found by the side of the road.

'You don't expect us to believe that?' Knox sneered. But Rebus could believe it.

'It's the truth,' Corbie said easily, 'whether you believe it or not, Sergeant Knox. I was out in the car this morning, and saw it lying in a ditch. I couldn't believe it. Someone had just dumped it there. Well, it looked good enough, so I thought I'd take it home.'

'But why did you hide it?'

Corbie shifted in his seat. 'I knew my mum would think I'd nicked it. Well, anyway, she'd never believe I just *found* it. So I decided to keep it out of her way till I could come up with a story . . .'

'There was a break-in last night,' Rebus said, 'at Deer Lodge. Do you know it?'

'That MP owns it, the one from the brothel.'

'You know it then. I think that microwave was stolen during the break-in.'

'Not by me it wasn't.'

'Well, we'll know soon enough. The place is being dusted for prints.'

'Lot of dusting going on,' Corbie commented. 'You lot are worse than my mum.'

'Believe it,' Rebus said, rising to his feet. 'One last thing, Alec. The car, what did you tell your mum about *it*?'

'Nothing much. Said I was storing it for a friend.'

Not that she'd have believed it. But if she lost her son, she lost her farm, too.

'All right, Alec.' said Rebus, 'it's time to get it all down on paper. Just what you've told us. Sergeant Knox will help you.' He paused by the door. 'Then, if we're *still* not happy that you've told us the truth and nothing but, maybe it'll be time to talk about drunk driving, eh?'

It was a long drive back to Mrs Wilkie's, and Rebus regretted not having taken a room in Dufftown. Still, it gave him time to think. He had made a telephone call from the station, putting back a certain appointment until tomorrow morning. So the rest of today was free. Clouds had settled low over the hills. So much for the nice weather. This was how Rebus remembered the Highlands – louring and forbidding. Terrible things had happened here in the past, massacres and forced migrations, blood feuds as vicious as any. Cases of cannibalism, too, he seemed to recall. Terrible things.

Who had killed Liz Jack? And why? The husband was always the first to fall under suspicion. Well, others could do the suspecting. Rebus, for one, didn't believe it. Why not?

Why not?

Well, look at the evidence. That Wednesday morning, Jack had been at a constituency meeting, then a game of golf, and in the evening he'd attended some function . . . according to whom? According to Jack himself and to Helen Greig. Plus, his car was white. There could be no mistaking it for blue. Plus, someone was out to get Jack into terrible trouble. And *that* was the person Rebus needed to find . . . unless it had been Liz Jack herself. He'd thought about that, too. But then there were the anonymous phone calls . . . according to whom? Only Barney Byars. Helen Greig had been unable (or unwilling) to confirm their existence. Rebus realized now that he really did need to talk to Gregor Jack again. Did his wife have any lovers? Judging by what Rebus had learned of her, the question needed changing to: how many did she have? One? Two? More? Or was he guilty of judging what he did not know? After all, he knew next to nothing about Elizabeth Jack. He knew what her allies and her critics thought of her. But he knew nothing *of her*. Except that, judging by her tastes in friends and furnishings, she hadn't had much taste . . .

*

Thursday morning. A week since the body had been found.

He woke up early, but was in no hurry to rise, and this time he let Mrs Wilkie bring him his tea in bed. She'd had a good night, never once thinking him her long-dead husband or long-lost son, so he reckoned she deserved not to be kept out of the bedroom. Not only tea this morning, but ginger nuts, too. And the tea was hot. But the day was cool, still grey and drizzly. Well, never mind. He'd be heading back to civilization, just as soon as he'd paid his respects elsewhere.

He ate a hurried breakfast, and received a peck on the cheek from Mrs Wilkie before leaving.

'Come back again some time,' she called, waving to him from the door. 'And I hope the jam sells all right . . .'

The rain came on at its heaviest just as his windscreen wipers gave up. He stopped the car to study his map, then dashed outside to give the wipers a quick shake. It had happened before: they just stuck, and could be righted with a bit of force. Except this time they really had packed in. And not a garage in sight. So he drove slowly, and found after a while that the heavier the rain fell, the clearer his windscreen became. It was the slow fine rain that was the problem, blotting out all but the vaguest shapes and outlines. The heavy dollops of rain came and went so fast that they seemed to clear the windscreen rather than obscuring it.

Which was just as well, for the rain stayed heavy all the way to Duthil.

Duthil Special Hospital had been planned and built to act as a showpiece for treatment of the criminally insane. Like the other 'special hospitals' dotted around the British Isles, it was just that – a hospital. It wasn't a prison, and patients who arrived in its care were treated like patients, not prisoners. Treatment, not punishment, was its function, and with the brand new buildings came up-to-date methods and understandings.

All this the hospital's medical director, Dr Frank Forster, told Rebus in his pleasant but purposeful office. Rebus had spent a long time last night on the telephone with Patience, and she'd told him much the same thing. Fine, thought

Rebus. But it was still a place of detention. The people who came here came with no time limit attached, no 'sentence' that had to be served. The main gates were operated electronically and by guards, and everywhere Rebus had gone so far the doors had been locked again behind him. But now Dr Forster was talking about recreation facilities, staff/patient ratios, the weekly disco ... He was obviously proud. He was also obviously overdoing it. Rebus saw him for what he was: the front-man whose job it was to publicize the benefits of this particular special hospital, the caring attitude, the role of treatment. The likes of Broadmoor had come in for a lot of criticism in previous years. To avoid criticism, you needed good PR. And Dr Forster looked good PR. He was young for a start, a good few years younger than Rebus. And he had a healthy, scrupulous look to him, with a smile always just around the corner.

He reminded Rebus of Gregor Jack. That enthusiasm and energy, that public image. It used to be the sort of stuff Rebus associated with American presidential campaigns; now it was everywhere. Even in the asylums. The lunatics hadn't taken over; the image-men had.

'We have just over three hundred patients here,' Forster was saying, 'and we like the staff to get to know as many of them as possible. I don't just mean faces, I mean names. First names at that. This isn't Bedlam, Inspector Rebus. Those days are long past, thank God.'

'But you're a secure unit.'

'Yes.'

'You deal with the criminally insane.'

Forster smiled again. 'You wouldn't know it to look at most of our patients. Do you know, the majority of them – over sixty per cent, I believe – have above-average IQs? I think some of them are brighter than I am!' A laugh this time, then the serious face again, the caring face. 'A lot of our patients are confused, deluded. They're depressed, or schizophrenic. But they're not, I assure you, anything like the lunatics you see in the movies. Take Andrew Macmillan, for example.' The file had been on Forster's desk all along. He

145

now opened it. 'He's been with us since the hospital opened. Before that, he was in much less ... savoury surroundings. He was making no progress at all before he came here. Now, he's becoming more talkative, and he seems about ready to participate in some of the available activities. I believe he plays a very good game of chess.'

'But is he still dangerous?'

Forster chose not to answer. 'He suffers occasional panic attacks ... hyperventilation, but nothing like the frenzies he went into before.' He closed the file. 'I would say, Inspector, that Andrew Macmillan is on his way to a complete recovery. Now, why do you want to talk to him?'

So Rebus explained about The Pack, about the friendship between 'Mack' Macmillan and Gregor Jack, about Elizabeth Jack's murder and the fact that she had been staying not forty miles from Duthil.

'I just wondered if she'd visited.'

'Well, we can check that for you.' Forster was flipping through the file again. 'Interesting, there's nothing in here about Mr Macmillan knowing Mr Jack, or about his having that nickname. Mack, did you say?' He reached for a pencil. 'I'll just make a note ...' He did so, then flicked through the file again. 'Apparently, Mr Macmillan has written to several MPs in the past ... and to other public figures. Mr Jack is mentioned ...' He read a little more in silence, then closed the file and picked up the telephone. 'Audrey, can you bring me the records of recent visitors ... say in the last month? Thanks.'

Duthil wasn't exactly a tourist attraction, and, out of sight being out of mind, there were few enough entries in the book. So it was the work of minutes to find what Rebus was looking for. The visit took place on Saturday, the day after Operation Creeper, but before the story became public knowledge.

'"Eliza Ferrie,"' he read. '"Patient visited: Andrew Macmillan. Relation to patient: friend." Signed in at three o'clock and out again at four thirty.'

'Our regular visiting hours,' Forster explained. 'Patients

can have visitors in the main recreation room. But I've arranged for you to see Andrew in his ward.'

'His ward?'

'Just a large room, really. Four beds to a room. But we call them wards to enforce . . . perhaps enhance would be a better word . . . to enhance the hospital atmosphere. Andrew's in the Kinnoul Ward.'

Rebus started. 'Why Kinnoul?'

'Pardon?'

'Why call the ward Kinnoul?'

Forster smiled. 'After the actor. You must have heard of Rab Kinnoul? He and his wife are among the hospital's patrons.'

Rebus decided not to say anything about Cath Kinnoul being one of The Pack, about her having known Macmillan at school . . . It was no business of his. But the Kinnouls went up in his estimation; well, Cath did. She had not, it seemed, forgotten her one-time friend. *Nobody calls me Gowk any more.* And Liz Jack, too, had visited, albeit under her maiden name and with a twist to her Christian name to boot. He could understand that: the papers would have had a field day. MP's Wife's Visits to Crazed Killer. All those possessives. She couldn't have known that the papers were about to have their story anyway . . .

'Perhaps at the end of your visit,' Dr Forster said, 'you'd like to see some of our facilities? Pool, gym, workshops . . .'

'Workshops?'

'Simple mechanics. Car maintenance, that sort of thing.'

'You mean you give the patients spanners and screwdrivers?'

Forster laughed. 'And we count them in again at the end of the session.'

Rebus had thought of something. 'Did you say *car* mainten-ance? I don't suppose somebody could take a look at my windscreen wipers?'

Forster started to laugh again, but Rebus shook his head.

'I'm serious,' he said.

'Then I'll see what we can do.' Forster rose to his feet. 'Ready when you are, Inspector.'

'I'm ready,' said Rebus, not at all sure that he was.

There was much passing through corridors, and the nurse who was to show Rebus to Kinnoul Ward had to unlock and relock countless doors. A heavy chain of keys swung from his waistband. Rebus attempted conversation, but the nurse replied with short measures. There was just the one incident. They were passing along a corridor when from an open doorway a hand appeared, grabbing at Rebus. A small, elderly man was trying to say something, eyes shining, mouth making tiny movements.

'Back into your room, Homer,' said the nurse, prising the fingers from Rebus's jacket. The man scuttled back inside. Rebus waited a moment for his heart rate to ease, then asked: 'Why do you call him Homer?'

The nurse looked at him. 'Because that's his name.' They walked on in silence.

Forster had been right. There were few moans or groans or sudden curdling shrieks, and few enough signs of movement, never mind *violent* movement. They passed through a large room where people were watching TV. Forster had explained that actual television wasn't allowed, since it couldn't be pre-determined. Instead, there was a daily diet of specially chosen video titles. *The Sound of Music* seemed to be a particular favourite. The patients watched in mute fascination.

'Are they on drugs?' Rebus hazarded.

The nurse suddenly became talkative. 'As many as we can stick down their throats. Keeps them out of mischief.'

So much for the caring face . . .

'Nothing wrong with it,' the nurse was saying, 'giving them drugs. It's all in the MHA.'

'MHA?'

'Mental Health Act. Allows for sedation as part of the treatment process.'

Rebus got the feeling the nurse was reciting a little defence he'd prepared to deal with visitors who asked. He was a big bugger: not tall, but broad, with bulging arms.

'Do any weight training?' Rebus asked.

'Who? That lot?'

Rebus smiled. 'I meant you.'

'Oh.' A grin. 'Yeah, I push some weights. Most of these places, the patients get all the facilities and there's nothing for the staff. But we've got a pretty good gym. Yeah, pretty good. In here . . .'

Another door was unlocked, another corridor beckoned, but off this corridor a sign pointed through yet another door – unlocked – to the Kinnoul Ward. 'In there,' the guard commanded, pushing open the door. His voice became firm. 'Okay, walk to the wall.'

Rebus thought for a moment the nurse was talking to *him*, but he saw that the object of the command was a tall, thin man, who now rose from his bed and walked to the far wall, where he turned to face them.

'Hands against the wall,' the nurse commanded. Andrew Macmillan placed the palms of his hands against the wall behind him.

'Look,' began Rebus, 'is this really – ?'

Macmillan smiled wryly. 'Don't worry,' the nurse told Rebus. 'He won't bite. Not after what we've pumped into him. You can sit there.' He was pointing to a table on which a board had been set for chess. There were two chairs. Rebus sat on the one which faced Andrew Macmillan. There were four beds, but they were all empty. The room was light, its walls painted lemon. There were three narrow barred windows, through which some rare sunshine poured. The nurse looked to be staying, and took up position behind Rebus, so that he was reminded of the scene in Dufftown interview room, with himself and Corbie and Knox.

'Good morning,' Macmillan said quietly. He was balding, and looked to have been doing so for some years. He had a long face, but it was not gaunt. Rebus would have called the face 'kindly'.

'Good morning, Mr Macmillan. My name's Inspector Rebus.'

This news seemed to excite Macmillan. He took half a step forward.

'Against the wall,' said the nurse. Macmillan paused, then retreated.

'Are you an Inspector of Hospitals?' he asked.

'No, sir, I'm a police inspector.'

'Oh.' His face dulled a little. 'I thought maybe you'd come to ... they don't treat us well here, you know.' He paused. 'There, because I've told you that I'll probably be disciplined, maybe even put into solitary. Everything, any dissension, gets reported back. But I've got to keep telling people, or nothing will be done. I have some influential friends, Inspector.' Rebus thought this was for the nurse's ears more than his own. 'Friends in high places ...'

Well, Dr Forster knew that now, thanks to Rebus.

'... friends I can trust. People need to be told, you see. They censor our mail. They decide what we can read. They won't even let me read *Das Kapital*. And they give us drugs. The mentally ill, you know, by whom I mean those who have been *judged* to be mentally ill, we have less rights than the most hardened mass murderer ... hardened but *sane* mass murderer. Is that fair? Is that ... humane?'

Rebus had no ready answer. Besides, he didn't want to be sidetracked.

'You had a visit from Elizabeth Jack.'

Macmillan seemed to think back, then nodded. 'So I did. But when she visits me she's Ferrie, not Jack. It's our secret.'

'What did you talk about?'

'Why are you interested?'

Rebus decided that Macmillan did not know of Liz Jack's murder. How could he know? There was no access to news in this place. Rebus's fingers toyed with the chessmen.

'It's to do with an investigation ... to do with Mr Jack.'

'What has he done?'

Rebus shrugged. 'That's what I'm trying to find out, Mr Macmillan.'

Macmillan had turned his face towards the ray of sunshine. 'I miss the world,' he said, his voice dropping to a murmur. 'I had so many – friends.'

'Do you keep in touch with them?'

'Oh yes,' Macmillan said. 'They come and take me home with them for the weekend. We enjoy evenings out at the cinema, the theatre, drinking in bars. Oh, we have some wonderful times together.' He smiled ruefully, and tapped his head. 'But only in here.'

'Hands against the wall.'

'Why?' he spat. 'Why do I have to keep my hands against the wall? Why can't I just sit down and have a normal conversation like ... a ... normal ... person.' The angrier he got, the lower his voice dropped. There were flecks of saliva either side of his mouth, and a vein bulged above his right eye. He took a deep breath, then another, then bowed his head slightly. 'I'm sorry, Inspector. They give me drugs, you know. God knows what they are. They have this ... effect on me.'

'That's all right, Mr Macmillan,' Rebus said, but inside he was quivering. Was this madness or sanity? What happened to sanity when you chained it to a wall? Chained it, moreover, with chains that weren't real.

'You were asking,' Macmillan went on, breathless now, 'you were asking about ... Eliza ... Ferrie. You're right, she did come and visit. Quite a surprise. I know they have a home near here, yet they've never visited before. Lizzie ... Eliza ... did visit once, a long time ago. But Gregor ... Well, he's a busy man, isn't he? And she's a busy woman. I hear about these things ...'

From Cath Kinnoul, Rebus didn't doubt.

'Yes, she visited. A very pleasant hour we spent. We talked about the past, about ... friends. Friendship. Is their marriage in trouble?'

'Why do you say that?'

Another creased smile. 'She came alone, Inspector. She told me she was on holiday alone. Yet a man was waiting for

151

her outside. Either it was Gregor, and he didn't want to see me, or else it was one of her . . . friends.'

'How do you know?'

'Nursie here told me. If you don't want to sleep tonight, Inspector, get him to show you the punishment block. I bet Doc Forster didn't mention the punishment block. Maybe that's where they'll throw me for talking like this.'

'Shut it, Macmillan.'

Rebus turned to the nurse. 'Is it true?' he asked. 'Was someone waiting outside for Mrs Jack?'

'Yeah, there was somebody in the car. Some guy. I only saw him from one of the windows. He'd got out of the car to stretch his legs.'

'What did he look like?'

But the nurse was shaking his head. 'He was getting back in when I saw him. I just saw his back.'

'What kind of car was it?'

'Black 3-series, no mistake about that.'

'Oh, he's very good at noticing things, Inspector, except when it suits him.'

'Shut it, Macmillan.'

'Ask yourself this, Inspector. If this is a *hospital*, why are all the so-called "nurses" members of the Prison Officers' Association? This isn't a hospital, it's a warehouse, but full of headcases rather than packing cases. The twist is, the headcases are the ones *in charge*!'

He was moving away from the wall now, walking on slow, doped legs, but his energy was unmistakable. Every nerve was blazing.

'Against the wall – '

'Headcases! I took her head off! God knows, I did – '

'Macmillan!' The nurse was moving too.

'But it was so long ago . . . a different – '

'Warning you – '

'And I want so much . . . so much to – '

'Right, that's it.' The nurse had him by the arms.

' – touch the earth.'

In the end, Macmillan offered little resistance, as the straps were attached to his arms and legs. The guard laid him out on the floor. 'If I leave him on the bed,' he told Rebus, 'he just rolls off and injures himself.'

'And you wouldn't want that,' said Macmillan, sounding almost peaceful now that he'd been restrained. 'No, nurse, you wouldn't want that.'

Rebus opened the door, making to leave.

'Inspector!'

He turned. 'Yes, Mr Macmillan?'

Macmillan had twisted his head so it was facing the door. 'Touch the earth for me . . . please.'

Rebus left the hospital on shakier legs than he'd entered it. He didn't want the tour of the pool and the gym. Instead, he'd asked the nurse to show him the punishment block, but the nurse had refused.

'Look,' he'd said, 'you might not like what goes on here, I might not like some of what goes on, but you've seen how it is. They're supposed to be "patients", but you can't turn your back on them, you can't leave them alone. They'll swallow lightbulbs, they'll be shitting pens and pencils and crayons, they'll try to put their head through the television. I mean, they might *not*, but you just can't ever be sure . . . ever. Try to keep an open mind, Inspector. I know it's not easy, but try.'

And Rebus had wished the young man luck with his weight training before making his exit. Into the courtyard. He stooped by a flowerbed and plunged his fingers deep into it, rubbing the soil between forefinger and thumb. It felt good. It felt good to be outside. Funny the things he took for granted, like earth and fresh air and free movement.

He looked up at the hospital windows, but couldn't be sure which, if any, belonged to Macmillan's ward. There were no faces staring at him, no signs of life at all. He rose to his feet, went to his car and got in, staring out through the windscreen. The brief sunshine had vanished. There was drizzle again, obscuring the view. Rebus pressed the button . . . and the windscreen wipers came on, came on and stayed on, their blades moving smoothly. He smiled, hands resting on the steering wheel, and asked himself a question.

'What happens to sanity when you chain it to a wall?'

He took a detour on his way back south, coming off the dual carriageway at Kinross. He passed Loch Leven (scene of many a family picnic when Rebus had been a kid), took a right at the next junction, and headed towards the tired mining villages of Fife. He knew this territory well. He'd been born and brought up here. He knew the grey housing schemes and the corner shops and the utilitarian pubs. The people cautious with strangers, and almost as cautious with friends and neighbours. Street-corner dialogues like bare-knuckle fights. His parents had taken his brother and him away from it at weekends, travelling to Kirkcaldy for shopping on the Saturday, and Loch Leven for those long Sunday picnics, sitting cramped in the back of the car with salmon-paste sandwiches and orange juice, flasks of tea smelling of hot plastic.

And for summer holidays there had been a caravan in St Andrews, or bed and breakfast in Blackpool, where Michael would always get into trouble and have to be hauled out by his older brother.

'And a lot of bloody thanks I got for it.'

Rebus kept driving.

Byars Haulage was sited halfway up a steep hill in one of the villages. Across the road was a school. The kids were on their way home, swinging satchels at each other and swearing choicely. Some things never changed. The yard of Byars Haulage contained a neat row of artics, a couple of nondescript cars, and a Porsche Carrera. None of the cars was blue. The offices were actually Portakabins. He went to the one marked 'Main Office' (below which someone had crayoned 'The Boss') and knocked.

Inside a secretary looked up from her word-processor. The room was stifling, a calor-gas heater roaring away by the side of the desk. There was another door behind the secretary. Rebus could hear Byars talking fast and loud and uproariously behind the door. Since no one answered him back, Rebus reckoned it was a phone call.

'Well tell Shite-for-brains to get off his arse and get over here.' (Pause.) 'Sick? *Sick?* Sick means he's shagging that missus of his. Can't blame him, mind . . .'

'Yes?' the secretary said to Rebus. 'Can I help you?'

'Well never mind what he says,' came Byars' voice. 'I've got a load here that's got to be in Liverpool yesterday.'

'I'd like to see Mr Byars, please,' said Rebus.

'If you'll take a seat, I'll see whether Mr Byars is available. What's the name, please?'

'Rebus, Detective Inspector Rebus.'

At that moment, the door of Byars' office opened and Byars himself came out. He was holding a portable phone in one hand and a sheet of paper in the other. He handed the paper to his secretary.

'That's right, wee man, and there's a load coming up from London the day after.' Byars' voice was louder than ever. Rebus noticed that, unseen by her, Byars was staring at his secretary's legs. He wondered if this whole performance was for her benefit . . .

But now Byars had spotted Rebus. It took Byars a second to place him, then he nodded a greeting in Rebus's direction. 'Aye, you give him big licks, wee man,' he said into the telephone. 'If he's got a sick-note, fine, if not tell him I'm looking out his cards, okay?' He terminated the call and shot out a hand.

'Inspector Rebus, what the hell brings you to this blighted neck of the bings?'

'Well,' said Rebus, 'I was passing, and – '

'Passing my arse! Plenty of people pass through, but nobody stops unless they want something. Even then, I'd advise them to keep on going. But you come from round here, don't you? Into the office then, I can spare you five minutes.' He turned to the secretary and rested a hand on her shoulder. 'Sheena, hen, get on to tadger-breath in Liverpool and tell him tomorrow morning definite.'

'Will do, Mr Byars. Will I make a cup of coffee?'

'No, don't bother, Sheena. I know what the polis like to drink.' He gave Rebus a wink. 'In you go, Inspector. In you go.'

Byars' office was like the back room of a dirty bookshop, its walls apparently held together by nude calendars and centrefolds. The calendars all seemed to be gifts donated by garages and suppliers. Byars saw Rebus looking.

'Goes with the image,' he said. 'A hairy-arsed truck driver with tattoos on his neck comes in here, he thinks he knows the sort of man he's dealing with.'

'And what if a woman comes in?'

Byars clucked. '*She*'d think she knew, too. I'm not saying she'd be all wrong either.' Byars didn't keep his whisky in the filing cabinet. He kept it inside a wellington boot. From the other boot he produced two glasses, which he sniffed. 'Fresh as the morning dew,' he said, pouring the drinks.

'Thanks,' said Rebus. 'Nice car.'

'Eh? Oh, outside you mean? Aye, it's no' bad. Nary a dent in it either. You should see the insurance payments though. Talk about steep. They make this brae look like a billiard table. Good health.' He sank the measure in one gulp, then noisily exhaled.

Rebus, having taken a sip, examined the glass, then the bottle. Byars chuckled.

'Think I'd give Glenlivet to the ba'-heids I get in here? I'm a businessman, not the Samaritans. They look at the bottle, think they know what they're getting, and they're impressed. Image again, like the scuddy pics on the wall. But it's really just cheap stuff I pour into the bottle. Not many folk notice.'

Rebus thought this was meant as a compliment. Image, that's what Byars was, all surface and appearance. Was he so different from MPs and actors? Or policemen come to that. All of them hiding their ulterior motives behind a set of gimmicks.

'So what is it you want to see me about?'

That was easily explained. He wanted to ask Byars a little more about the party at Deer Lodge, seemingly the last party to be held there.

'Not many of us there,' Byars told him. 'A few cried off pretty late. I don't think Tom Pond was there, though he was expected. That's right, he was off to the States by then. Suey was there.'

'Ronald Steele?'

'That's the man. And Liz and Gregor, of course. And me. Cathy Kinnoul was there, but her husband wasn't. Let's see ... who else? Oh, a couple who worked for Gregor. Urquhart ...'

'Ian Urquhart?'

'Yes, and some young girl ...'

'Helen Greig?'

Byars laughed. 'Why bother to ask if you already know? I think that was about it.'

'You said a *couple* who worked for Gregor. Did you get the impression that they *were* a couple?'

'Christ, no. I think everybody *but* Urquhart tried to get the girl into the sack.'

'Did anyone succeed?'

'Not that I noticed, but after a couple of bottles of champagne I tend not to notice very much. It wasn't like one of Liz's parties. You know, not wild. I mean, everybody had plenty to drink, but that was all.'

'All?'

'Well, you know ... Liz's crowd was *wild*.' Byars stared towards one of the calendars, seemingly reminiscing. 'A real wild bunch and no mistake ...'

Rebus could imagine Barney Byars lapping it up, mixing with Patterson-Scott, Kilpatrick and the rest. And he could imagine them ... tolerating Byars, a bit of nouveau rough. No doubt Byars was the life and soul of the party, a laugh a minute. Only they were laughing *at* him rather than with him ...

'How was the lodge when you arrived?' Rebus asked.

Byars wrinkled his nose. 'Disgusting. It hadn't been cleaned since the last party a fortnight before. One of Liz's parties, not one of Gregor's. Gregor was going spare. Liz or somebody was supposed to have had it cleaned. It looked like a bloody

157

sixties squat or something.' He smiled. 'Actually, I probably shouldn't be telling you this, you being a member of the constabulary and all, but I didn't bother staying the night. Drove back about four in the morning. Absolutely guttered, but there was nobody about on the roads for me to be a menace to. Wait till you hear this though. I thought my feet were cold when I stopped the car. Got out to open the garage . . . and I didn't have any shoes on! Just the one sock and no fucking shoes! Christ knows how come I didn't notice . . .'

8
Spite and Malice

Did John Rebus receive a hero's welcome? He did not. There were some who felt he'd merely added to the chaos of the case. Perhaps he had. Chief Superintendent Watson, for example, still felt William Glass was the man they were looking for. He sat and listened to Rebus's report, while Chief Inspector Lauderdale rocked to and fro on another chair, sometimes staring ruminatively at the ceiling, sometimes studying the one immaculate crease down either trouser-leg. It was Friday morning. There was coffee in the air. There was coffee, too, coursing through Rebus's nervous system as he spoke. Watson interrupted from time to time, asking questions in a voice as thin as an after-dinner mint. And at the end of it all, he asked the obvious question.

'What do you make of it, John?'

And Rebus gave the obvious, if only mostly truthful, answer.

'I don't know, sir.'

'Let's get this straight,' said Lauderdale, raising his eyes from a trouser-crease. 'She's at a telephone box. She meets a man in a car. They're arguing. The man drives off. She hangs around for some time. Another car, maybe the same car, arrives. Another argument. The car goes off, leaving her car still in the lay-by. And next thing we know of her, she's turning up dumped in a river next to the house owned by a friend of her husband's.' Lauderdale paused, as though inviting Rebus to contradict him. 'We still don't know when or where she died, only that she managed to end up in

Queensferry. Now, you say this actor's wife is an old friend of Gregor Jack's?'

'Yes.'

'Any hint that they were a bit *more* than friends?'

Rebus shrugged. 'Not that I know of.'

'What about the actor, Rab Kinnoul? Maybe he and Mrs Jack . . .?'

'Maybe.'

'Convenient, isn't it?' said the Chief Superintendent, rising to pour himself another cup of black death. 'I mean, if Mr Kinnoul *did* ever want to dispose of a body, what better place than his own fast-flowing river, discharging into the sea, body turning up weeks later, or perhaps never at all. *And* he's always played killers on the TV and in films. Maybe it's all gone to his head . . .'

'Except,' said Lauderdale, 'that Kinnoul was in a series of meetings all day that Wednesday.'

'And Wednesday night?'

'At home with his wife.'

Watson nodded. 'We come back to Mrs Kinnoul again. Could she be lying?'

'She's certainly under his thumb,' said Rebus. 'And she's on all sorts of anti-depressants. I'd be surprised if she could tell Wednesday night at home in Queensferry from the twelfth of July in Londonderry.'

Watson smiled. 'Nicely put, John, but let's *try* to stick to facts.'

'What precious few there are,' said Lauderdale. 'I mean, we all *know* who the obvious candidate is: Mrs Jack's husband. She finds out he's been caught trousers-down in a brothel, they have a row, he may not mean to kill her but he strikes her. Next thing, she's dead.'

'He was caught trousers-up,' Rebus reminded his superior.

'Besides,' added Watson, 'Mr Jack, too, has his alibis.' He read from a sheet of paper. 'Constituency meeting in the morning. Round of golf in the afternoon – corroborated by his playing partner and checked by Detective Constable Broome. Then a dinner appointment where he made a speech to eighty or so fine upstanding members of the business community in Central Edinburgh.'

'And he drives a white Saab,' Rebus stated. 'We need to check car colours for everyone involved in the case, all Mrs Jack's friends and all Mr Jack's.'

'I've already put DS Holmes on to it,' said Lauderdale. 'And forensics say they'll have a report on the BMW ready by morning. I've another question though.' He turned to Rebus. 'Mrs Jack was, apparently, up north for anything up to a week. Did she stay all that time at Deer Lodge?'

Rebus had to give Lauderdale credit, the bugger had his thinking cap on today. Watson was nodding as though he'd been about to ask the selfsame thing, but of course he hadn't. Rebus *had* thought about it though.

'I don't think so,' he said. 'I *do* think she spent some time there, otherwise where did the Sunday papers and the green suitcase come from? But a whole week . . .? I doubt it. No signs of recent cooking. All the food and cartons and stuff I found were either from one party or another. There *had* been an attempt to clear a space on the living room floor, so one person or maybe two could sit and have a drink. But maybe that goes back to the last party, too. I suppose we could ask the guests while we're fingerprinting them . . .'

'Fingerprinting them?' asked Watson.

Lauderdale sounded like an exasperated parent. 'Purposes of elimination, sir. To see if any prints are left that can't be identified.'

'What would that tell us?' Watson said.

'The point is, sir,' commented Lauderdale, 'if Mrs Jack didn't stay at Deer Lodge, then *who* was she with and where *did* she stay? Was she even up north all that time?'

'Ah . . .' said Watson, nodding again as though understanding everything.

'She visited Andrew Macmillan on the Saturday,' added Rebus.

'Yes,' said Lauderdale, getting into his stride, 'but then she's next seen on the Wednesday by that yob at the farm. What about the days in between?'

'She was at Deer Lodge on the Sunday with her news-papers,' Rebus said. Then he realized the point Lauderdale was making. 'When she saw the story,' he continued, 'you think she may have headed south again?'

Lauderdale spread out his hands, examining the nails. 'It's a theory,' he said, merely.

'Well, we've plenty bloody theories,' said Watson, slapping one of his own much meatier hands down on the desk. 'We need something concrete. And let's not forget friend Glass. We still want to talk to him. About Dean Bridge if nothing else. Meanwhile . . .' he seemed to be trying to think of some path they might take, of some instructions or inspiration he might give. But he gave up and swigged back his coffee instead. 'Meanwhile,' he said at last, while Rebus and Lauder-dale waited for the imparted wisdom, 'let's be careful out there.'

The old man's really showing his age now, thought Rebus, as he waited to follow Lauderdale out of the office. *Hill Street Blues* was a long, long time ago. In the corridor, after the door was closed behind them, Lauderdale grasped Rebus's arm. His voice was an excited hiss.

'Looks like the Chief Super's on the way out, doesn't it? Can't be long before the high heidyins see what's going on and pension him off.' He was trying to control his glee. Yes, Rebus was thinking, one or two very public foul-ups, that's all it would take. And he wondered . . . he wondered if Lauderdale was capable of engineering a balls-up with this in mind. Someone had tipped off the papers about Operation Creeper. Christ, it seemed such a long time ago. But wasn't Chris Kemp supposed to be doing some digging into that? He'd have to remember to ask Kemp what he'd found. So much still needed to be done . . .

He was shrugging his arm free of Lauderdale when Wat-son's door opened again, and Watson stood there staring at the two of them. Rebus wondered if they looked as guilty and conspiratorial as he himself felt. Then Watson's eyes settled on him.

'John,' he said, 'telephone call. It's Mr Jack. He says he'd be grateful if you'd go and see him. Apparently, there's something he'd like to talk to you about . . .'

Rebus pressed the bell at the locked gate. The voice over the intercom was Urquhart's.

'Yes?'

'Inspector Rebus to see Mr Jack.'

'Yes, Inspector, be right with you.'

Rebus peered through the bars. The white Saab was parked outside the house. He shook his head slowly. Some people never learned. A reporter had been sent from one of the line of cars to ask who Rebus was. The other reporters and photographers took shelter in the cars themselves, listening to the radio, reading newspapers. Soup or coffee was poured from flasks. They were here for the duration. And they were bored. As he waited, the wind sliced against Rebus, squeezing through a gap between jacket and shirt collar, trickling down his neck like ice water. He watched Urquhart emerge from the house, apparently trying to sort out the tangle of keys in his hand. The reconnaissance reporter still stood beside Rebus, twitching, readying himself to ask Urquhart his questions.

'I shouldn't bother, son,' advised Rebus.

Urquhart was at the gate now.

'Mr Urquhart,' blurted the reporter, 'anything to add to your previous statement?'

'No,' said Urquhart coolly, opening the gate. 'But I'll repeat it for you if you like – bugger off!'

And with that, Rebus safely through the gate, he slammed it shut and locked it, giving the bars an extra shake to make sure they were secure. The reporter, smiling sourly, was heading back to one of the cars.

'You're under siege,' Rebus observed.

Urquhart looked like he'd done without sleep for a night or two too many. 'It's diabolical,' he confided as they walked towards the house. 'Day and night they're out there. God knows what they think they're going to get.'

'A confession?' Rebus hazarded. He was rewarded with a weak smile.

'That, Inspector, they'll never get.' The smile left his face. 'But I *am* worried about Gregor ... what all this is doing to him. He's ... well, you'll see for yourself.'

'Any idea what this meeting's all about?'

'He wouldn't say. Inspector ...' Urquhart had stopped. 'He's very fragile. I mean, he might say *any*thing. I just hope you can tell truth from fantasy.' Then he started to walk again.

'Are you still diluting his whisky?' Rebus asked.

Urquhart gave him an appraising look, then nodded. 'That's not the answer, Inspector. That's not what he needs. He needs friends.'

Andrew Macmillan, too, had gone on about friends. Rebus wanted to talk to Jack about Andrew Macmillan. But he wasn't in a hurry. He had paused beside the Saab, causing Urquhart to pause too.

'What is it?'

'You know,' said Rebus, 'I've always liked Saabs, but I've never had the money around to buy one. Do you think Mr Jack would mind if I just sat in the driver's seat for a minute?'

Urquhart looked at a loss for an answer. He ended up making a gesture somewhere between a shrug and a shake of the head. Rebus tried the driver's door. It was unlocked. He slid into the seat and rested his hands on the steering wheel, leaving the door itself open so Urquhart could stand there and watch.

'Very comfortable,' Rebus said.

'So I believe.'

'You've never driven it yourself then?'

'No.'

'Oh.' Rebus stared out of the windscreen, then at the passenger seat and the floor. 'Yes, well designed, comfortable. Plenty of room, eh?' And he turned in his seat, twisting his whole body round to examine the rear seat ... the rear floor. 'Heaps of room,' he commented. 'Lovely.'

'Maybe Gregor would let you take her for a spin?'

Rebus looked up keenly. 'Do you think so? I mean, when this has all blown over, of course.' He started to get out of the car. Urquhart snorted.

'Blown over? This sort of thing doesn't "blow over", not when you're an MP. The broth – . . . those allegations in the newspapers, they were bad enough, but now murder? No.' He shook his head. 'This won't just blow over, Inspector. It's not a raincloud, it's a mud bath, and mud sticks.'

Rebus closed the door. 'Nice solid clunk, too, when you shut it, isn't there? How well did you know Mrs Jack?'

'Pretty well. I used to see her most days.'

'But I believe Mr and Mrs Jack led fairly separate lives?'

'I wouldn't go that far. They *were* married.'

'And in love?'

Urquhart thought for a moment. 'I'd say so, yes.'

'Despite everything?' Rebus was walking around the car now, as though deciding whether or not to buy it.

'I'm not sure I understand.'

'Oh, you know, different sorts of friends, different lifestyles, separate holidays . . .'

'Gregor is an MP, Inspector. He can't always get away at the drop of a hat.'

'Whereas,' Rebus said, 'Mrs Jack was . . . what would you say? Spontaneous? Flighty, maybe even? The sort who'd say, let's just up and go?'

'Actually, yes, that's fairly accurate.'

Rebus nodded and tapped the boot. 'What about luggage room?'

Urquhart himself actually came forward and opened the boot.

'Goodness,' said Rebus, 'yes, there's plenty of room. Quite deep, isn't it?'

It was also immaculately clean. No mud or scuff marks, no crumbs of earth. It looked as though it had never been used. Inside were a small reserve petrol tank, a red warning triangle, and a half-set of golf clubs.

'He's keen on golf, isn't he?'

'Oh yes.'

Rebus closed the boot shut. 'I've never seen the attraction myself. The ball's too small and the pitch is too big. Shall we go in?'

Gregor Jack looked like he'd been to hell and back on an LRT bus. He'd probably combed his hair yesterday or the day before, and last changed his clothes then, too. He was shaven, but there were small patches of dark stubble the razor had missed. He didn't bother rising when Rebus entered the room. He just nodded a greeting and gestured with his glass to a vacant chair, one of the infamous marshmallow chairs. Rebus approached with care.

There was whisky in Jack's crystal tumbler, and a bottle of the stuff – three quarters empty – on the rug beside him. The room smelt unaired and unpolished. Jack took a gulp of liquid, then used the edge of the glass to scratch at his raw red finger.

'I want to talk to you, Inspector Rebus.'

Rebus sat down, sinking, sinking . . . 'Yes, sir?'

'I want to say a few things about me . . . and maybe about Liz, too, in a roundabout way.'

It was another prepared speech, another well-considered opening. There were just the two of them in the room. Urquhart had said he'd make a pot of coffee. Rebus, still jumpy from his meeting with Watson, had begged for tea. Helen Greig, it seemed, was at home, her mother having been taken ill – 'again', as Urquhart put it, before marching off kitchenwards. Faithful women: Helen Greig and Cath Kinnoul. Doggedly faithful. And Elizabeth Jack? Doggie-style faithful maybe . . . Christ, that was a terrible thing to think! And especially of the dead, especially of a woman he'd never met! A woman who liked to be tied to bedposts for a spot of . . .

'It's nothing to do with . . . well, I don't know, maybe it is.' Jack paused for thought. 'You see, Inspector, I can't help feeling that *if* Liz saw those stories about me, and *if* they upset her, then maybe she did something . . . or stayed away . . . and maybe . . .' He leapt to his feet and wandered over towards the window, looking out at nothing. 'What I'm trying to say is, what if I'm responsible?'

'Responsible, sir?'

'For Liz's ... murder. If we'd been together, if we'd been *here* together, it might never have happened. It *wouldn't* have happened. Do you see what I mean?'

'No good blaming yourself, sir – '

Jack whirled towards him. 'But that's just it, I *do* blame myself.'

'Why don't you sit down, Mr Jack – '

'Gregor, please.'

'All right ... Gregor. Now why don't you sit down and calm down.'

Jack did as he was told. Bereavement affected different people in different ways, the weak becoming strong and the strong becoming weak. Ronald Steele hurled books around, Gregor Jack became ... pathetic. He was scratching at the finger again. 'But it's all so ironic,' he spat.

'How's that?' Rebus wished the tea would hurry up. Maybe Jack would pull himself together in Urquhart's presence.

'That brothel,' Jack said, fixing Rebus's eyes with his own. 'That's what started it all. And the reason I was there ...'

Rebus sat forward. 'Why *were* you there, Gregor?'

Gregor Jack paused, swallowed, seemed to take a breath while he thought about whether to answer or not. Then he answered.

'To see my sister.'

There was silence in the room, so profound that Rebus could hear his watch ticking. Then the door flew open.

'Tea,' said Ian Urquhart, sidling into the room.

Rebus, who had been so eager for Urquhart's arrival, now couldn't wait for the man to leave. He rose from the chair and walked to the mantelpiece. The card from The Pack was still there, but it had been joined by over a dozen condolence cards – some from other MPs, some from family and friends, some from the public.

Urquhart seemed to sense the atmosphere in the room. He

left the tray on a table and, without a word, made his exit. The door had barely closed before Rebus said, 'What do you mean, your sister?'

'I mean just that. My sister was working in that brothel. Well, I suspected she was, I'd been *told* she was. I thought maybe it was a joke, a sick joke. Maybe a trap, to get me to a brothel. A trap and a trick. I thought long and hard before I went, but I still went. He'd sounded so confident.'

'Who had?'

'The caller. I'd been getting these calls ...' Ah yes, Rebus had meant to ask about those. 'By the time I got to the phone, the caller would have hung up. But one night, the caller got me straight away, and he told me: "Your sister's working in a brothel in the New Town." He gave me the address, and said if I went around midnight she'd just be starting her ... shift.' The words were like some food he didn't enjoy, but given him at a banquet so that he didn't dare spit it out, but had to go on chewing, trying hard not to swallow ... He swallowed. 'So along I went, and she *was* there. The caller had been telling the truth. I was trying to talk to her when the police came in. But it was a trap, too. The newsmen were there ...'

Rebus was remembering the woman in the bed, the way she kicked her legs in the air, the way she'd lifted her t-shirt for the photographers to see ...

'Why didn't you say anything at the time, Gregor?'

Jack laughed shrilly. 'It was bad enough as it was. Would it have been any better if I'd let everyone know my sister's a tart?'

'Well then, why tell me now?'

His voice was calm. 'It looks to me, Inspector, like I'm in deep water. I'm just jettisoning what I don't need.'

'You must know then, sir ... you must have known all along, that someone is setting you up to take a very big fall.'

Jack smiled. 'Oh yes.'

'Any idea who? I mean, any enemies?'

The smile again. 'I'm an MP, Inspector. The wonder is that I have any *friends*.'

'Ah yes, The Pack. Could one of them . . .?'

'Inspector, I've racked my brain and I'm no nearer finding out.' He looked up at Rebus. 'Honest.'

'You didn't recognize the caller's voice?'

'It was heavily muffled. Gruff. A man probably, but to be honest it could have been a woman.'

'Okay then, what about your sister? Tell me about her.'

It was soon told. She'd left home young, and never been heard of. Vague rumours of London and marriage had drifted north over the years, but that was all. Then the phone call . . .

'How could the caller know? How might they have found out?'

'Now *that*'s a mystery, because I've never told anybody about Gail.'

'But your schoolfriends would know of her?'

'Slightly, I suppose. I doubt any of them remember her. She was two years below us at school.'

'You think maybe she came back up here looking for revenge?'

Jack spread his palms. 'Revenge for what?'

'Well, jealousy then.'

'Why didn't she just get in touch?'

It was a point. Rebus made a mental note to get in touch with *her*, supposing she was still around. 'You haven't heard from her since?'

'Not before, not since.'

'Why *did* you want to see her, Gregor?'

'One, I really was interested.' He broke off.

'And two?'

'Two . . . I don't know, maybe to talk her out of what she was doing.'

'For her own good, or for yours?'

Jack smiled. 'You're right, of course, bad for the image having a sister on the game.'

'There are worse forms of prostitution than whoring.'

Jack nodded, impressed. 'Very deep, Inspector. Can I use that in one of my speeches? Not that I'll be making many of

169

those from now on. Whichever way you look at it, my career's down the Swanny.'

'Never give up, sir. Think of Robert the Bruce.'

'And the spider, you mean? I hate spiders. So does Liz.' He halted. '*Did* Liz.'

Rebus wanted to keep the conversation moving. The amount of whisky Jack had drunk, he might tip over any minute. 'Can I ask you about that last party up at Deer Lodge?'

'What about it?'

'For a start, who was present?'

Having to use his memory seemed to sober Jack up. Not that he could add much to what Barney Byars had already told Rebus. It was a boozy, sit-around-and-chat evening, followed by a morning hike up some nearby mountain, lunch – at the Heather Hoose – and then home. Jack's only regret was inviting Helen Greig to go.

'I'm not sure she saw any of us in a decent light. Barney Byars was doing elephant impressions, you know, where you pull out your trouser pockets and – '

'Yes, I know.'

'Well, Helen took it in good enough part, but all the same . . .'

'Nice girl, isn't she?'

'The sort my mum would have wanted me to marry.'

Mine too, thought Rebus. The whisky wasn't just loosening Jack's tongue, it was also loosening his accent. The polish was fading fast, leaving the raw wood of towns like Kirkcaldy, Leven, Methil.

'This party was a couple of weeks ago, wasn't it?'

'Three weeks ago. We were back here five days when Liz decided she needed a holiday. Packed a case and off she went. Never saw her again . . .' He raised a fist and punched the soft leather of the sofa, making hardly a sound and no discernible mark. 'Why are they doing this to me? I'm the best MP this constituency's ever had. Don't take my word for it. Go out and talk to them. Go to a mining village or a farm or a factory or a fucking afternoon tea party. They tell me

170

the same thing: well done, Gregor, keep up the good work.'
He was on his feet again now, feet holding their ground but
the rest of the body in motion. 'Keep up the good work, the
hard work. Hard work! It bloody is hard work, I can tell
you.' His voice was rising steadily. 'Worked my balls off for
them! Now somebody's trying to piss on my whole life from
a very high place. Why me? Why me? Liz and me . . . Liz . . .'

Urquhart tapped twice before putting his head round the
door. 'Everything all right?'

Jack put on a grotesque mask of a smile. 'Everything's fine,
Ian. Listening behind the door, are you? Good, wouldn't
want you to miss a word, would we?'

Urquhart glanced at Rebus. Rebus nodded: everything's
okay in here, really it is. Urquhart retreated and closed the
door. Gregor Jack collapsed into the sofa. 'I'm making such a
mess of everything,' he said, rubbing his face with his hand.
'Ian's such a good friend . . .'

Ah yes, friends.

'I believe,' said Rebus, 'that you haven't just been receiving
anonymous calls.'

'What?'

'Someone said something about letters, too.'

'Oh . . . oh yes, letters. Crank letters.'

'Do you still have them?'

Jack shook his head. 'Not worth keeping.'

'Did you let anyone see them?'

'Not worth reading.'

'What exactly was in them, Mr Jack?'

'Gregor,' Jack reminded him. 'Please, call me Gregor. What
was in them? Rubbish. Garbled nonsense. Ravings . . .'

'I don't think so.'

'What?'

'Someone told me you'd refuse to let anyone open them.
He thought they might be love letters.'

Jack hooted. 'Love letters!'

'I don't think they were either. But it strikes me, how could
Ian Urquhart or anyone else *know* which letters they were to
hand to you unopened? The handwriting? Difficult to tell

171

though, isn't it? No, it had to be the postmark. It had to be what was on the envelope. I'll tell you where those letters came from, Mr Jack. They came from Duthil. They came from your old friend Andrew Macmillan. And they weren't raving, were they? They weren't garbled or nonsense or rubbish. They were asking you to do something about the system in the special hospitals. Isn't that right?'

Jack sat and studied his glass, mouth set petulantly, a kid who's been caught out.

'Isn't that right?'

Jack gave a curt nod. Rebus nodded, too. Embarrassing to have a sister who's a prostitute. But how much *more* embarrassing to have an old friend who's a murderer? And mad, to boot. Gregor Jack had worked hard to form his public image, and harder still to preserve it. Rushing around with his vacuously sincere grin and strong-enough-for-the-occasion handshake. Working hard in his constituency, working hard in *public*. But his private life ... well, Rebus wouldn't have wanted to swop. It was a mess. And what made it so messy was that Jack had tried to hide it. He didn't have skeletons in his closet; he had a crematorium.

'Wanted me to start a campaign,' Jack was muttering. 'Couldn't do that. Why did you start this crusade, Mr Jack? To help an old friend. Which old friend is that, Mr Jack? The one who cut his wife's head off. Now, if you'll excuse me. Oh, and please remember to vote for me next time round ...' And he began a drunken, wailing laugh, near-manic, near-crying. Finally actually becoming crying, tears streaming down his cheeks, dripping into the glass he still held.

'Gregor,' Rebus said quietly. He repeated the name, and again, and again, always quietly. Jack sniffed back more tears and looked blurrily towards him. 'Gregor,' said Rebus, 'did you kill your wife?'

Jack wiped his eyes on his shirt-sleeve, sniffed, wiped again. He began to shake his head.

'No,' he said. 'No, I didn't kill my wife.'

*

No, because William Glass killed her. He killed the woman under Dean Bridge, and he killed Elizabeth Jack.

Rebus had missed all the excitement. He had driven back into town unaware of it. He had climbed the steps up to Great London Road station without knowing. And he had entered a place of jumpy, jittery clamour. Christ, what did it mean? Was the station definitely staying open? No move to St Leonard's? Which meant, if he remembered his bet, that he'd set up home with Patience Aitken. But no, it was nothing to do with the station staying open or being reduced to rubble. It was William Glass. A beat constable had come across him sleeping amidst the dustbins behind a supermarket in Barnton. He was in custody. He was talking. They were feeding him soup and giving him endless cups of tea and fresh cigarettes, and he was talking.

'But what's he saying?'

'He's saying he did them – both of them!'

'He's saying *what*?'

Rebus started calculating. Barnton ... not so far from Queensferry when you thought about it. They were thinking he'd have headed north or west, but in fact he'd started crawling back into town ... supposing he'd ever got as far as Queensferry in the first place.

'He's admitting both murders.'

'Who's with him?'

'Chief Inspector Lauderdale and Inspector Dick.'

Lauderdale! Christ, he'd be loving it. This would be the making of him, the final nail in the Chief Super's coffee-maker. But Rebus had other things to be doing. He wanted Jack's sister found, for a start. Gail Jack, but she wouldn't be calling herself that, would she? He went through the Operation Creeper case-notes. Gail Crawley. That was her. She'd been released, of course. And had given a London address. He found one of the officers who'd interviewed her.

'Yes, she said she was heading south. Couldn't keep her, could we? Didn't want to either. Just gave her a kick up the arse and told her not to come back up here again. Isn't it incredible? Catching Glass like that!'

'Incredible, yes,' said Rebus. He photocopied what notes there were, along with Gail Crawley's photograph, and scribbled some further notes of his own on to the copy. Then he telephoned an old friend, an old friend in London.

'Inspector Flight speaking.'

'Hello George. When's the retirement party then?'

There was laughter. 'You tell me, you were the one who persuaded me to stay on.'

'Can't afford to lose you.'

'Meaning you want a favour?'

'Official business, George, but speed is of the – '

'As usual. All right, what is it?'

'Give me your fax number and I'll send you the details. If she's at the address, I'd like you to talk to her. I've put down a couple of phone numbers. You can reach me anytime on one or the other.'

'Two numbers, eh? Got yourself in deep, have you?'

In deep . . . jettisoning what I don't need . . .

'You could say that, George.'

'What's she like?' By which he meant Patience, not Gail.

'She likes domesticity, George. Pets and nights in, candles and firelight.'

'Sounds perfect.' George Flight paused. 'I'll give it three months max.'

'Sod you,' said Rebus, grinning. Flight was laughing again.

'Four months then,' he said. 'But that's my final offer.'

That done, Rebus headed for the nerve centre, the one place he needed to station himself – the gents' toilets. Part of the ceiling had fallen down and had been replaced with a piece of brown cardboard on which some joker had drawn a huge eyeball. Rebus washed his hands, dried them, chatted to one of the other detectives, shared a cigarette. In a public toilet, he'd have been picked up for loitering. He *was* loitering, too, loitering with intent. The door opened. Bingo. It was Lauderdale, a frequent user of rest rooms when he was on an interrogation.

'All the time you're coming and going,' he'd told Rebus,

'the suspect's sweating that bit more, wondering what's up, what's happened that's new.'

'What's up?' Rebus asked now. Lauderdale smiled and went to splash water on his face, patting his temples and the back of his neck. He looked pleased with himself. More worrying, he didn't smell.

'Looks like our Chief Super may have got it right for once,' Lauderdale admitted. 'He said we should be concentrating on Glass.'

'He's confessed?'

'As good as. Looks as though he's sorting his defence out first.'

'What's that then?'

'The media,' said Lauderdale, drying himself. 'The media pushed him into doing it. I mean, killing again. He says it was *expected* of him.'

'Sounds to me like he's one domino shy of a set.'

'I'm not putting any words into his mouth, if that's what you're thinking. It's all on tape.'

Rebus shook his head. 'No, no, I mean, if he says he did it, then fair enough. That's fine. And by the way, it was me that shot JFK.'

Lauderdale was examining himself in the spattered mirror. He still looked triumphal, his neck rising from his shirt collar so that his head sat on it like a golf ball on its tee.

'A confession, John,' he was saying, 'it's a powerful thing is a confession.'

'Even when the guy's been sleeping rough for nights on end? Strung out on Brasso and hunted by Edinburgh's finest? Confession might be good for the soul, sir, but sometimes all it's worth is a bowl of soup and some hot tea.'

Lauderdale tidied himself, then turned towards Rebus. 'You're just a pessimist, John.'

'Think of all the questions Glass *can't* answer. Ask him some of them. How did Mrs Jack get to Queensferry? How come he dumped her *there*? Just ask him, sir. I'll be interested to read the transcript. I think you'll find the conversation's all one way.'

Exit the Inspector Rebus, leaving behind the Chief Inspector Lauderdale, brushing himself down like a statue examining itself for chips. He seems to find one, too, for he frowns suddenly, and spends longer in the washroom than intended . . .

'I need just a little bit more, John.'

They were lying in bed together, just the three of them: Rebus, Patience, and Lucky the cat. Rebus affected an American accent.

'I gave ya everything I got, baby.'

Patience smiled, but wasn't to be placated. She thumped her pillows and sat up, drawing her knees up to her chin. 'I mean,' she said, 'I need to know what you're going to do . . . what *we're* going to do. I can't decide whether you're moving in with me, or else moving out.'

'In and out,' he said, a final attempt at humour and escape. She punched him on the shoulder. Punched him hard. He sucked in his breath. 'I bruise easily,' he said.

'So do I!' There were almost tears in her eyes, but she wasn't going to give him the satisfaction. 'Is there anybody else?'

He looked surprised. 'No, what makes you think that?'

The cat had crawled up the bed to lie in Patience's lap, plucking at the duvet with its claws. As it settled, she started stroking its head. 'It's just that I keep thinking there's something you're about to tell me. You look as though you're gathering up the strength to say it, but then you never quite manage. I'd rather *know*, whatever it is.'

What was there to know? That he still hadn't made up his mind about moving in? That he still carried if not a flame then at least an unstruck Scottish Bluebell for Gill Templer? What was there to know?

'You know how it is, Patience. A policeman's lot is not a happy one, and all that.'

'Why do you have to get involved?'

'What?'

'In all these bloody cases, why do *you* have to get involved,

John? It's just a job like any other. I manage to forget about my patients for a few hours at a stretch, why can't you?'

He gave her just about his only honest answer of the evening. 'I don't know.'

The telephone rang. Patience picked the extension up off the floor and held it between them. 'Yours or mine?' she asked.

'Yours.'

She picked up the receiver. 'Hello? Yes, this is Doctor Aitken. Yes, hello, Mrs Laird. Is he now? Is that right? It isn't maybe just flu?'

Rebus checked his watch. Nine thirty. It was Patience's turn to do standby emergency for her group practice.

'A-ha,' she was saying, 'a-ha,' as the caller talked on. She held the receiver away from her for a second and hurled a silent scream towards the ceiling. 'Okay, Mrs Laird. No, just leave him be. I'll be there as soon as I can. What was your address again?'

At the end of the call, she stomped out of bed and started to dress. 'Mrs Laird's husband says he's on the way out this time,' she said. 'That's the third time in as many months, damn the man.'

'Do you want me to drive you?'

'No, it's all right, I'll go myself.' She paused, came over and pecked him on the cheek. 'But thanks for the offer.'

'You're welcome.' Lucky, disturbed from his rest, was now kneading Rebus's half of the duvet. Rebus made to stroke its head, but the cat shied away.

'See you later then,' said Patience, giving him another kiss. 'We'll have a talk, eh?'

'If you like.'

'I like.' And with that she was gone. He could hear her in the living room, getting together her stuff, then the front door opening and closing. The cat had left Rebus and was investigating the warm section of mattress from which Patience had lately risen. Rebus thought about getting up, then thought about not. The phone rang again. Another patient? Well, he wouldn't answer. It kept on ringing. He answered with a noncommittal 'Hello'.

'Took your time,' said George Flight. 'Haven't interrupted anything, have I?'

'What have you got, George?'

'Well, I've got the trots, since you ask. I blame it on that curry I had at Gunga's last night. I've also got the information you requested, Inspector.'

'Is that so, Inspector? Well would you mind passing it the hell on!'

Flight snorted. 'That's all the thanks I get, after a hard day's graft.'

'We all know the kind of graft the Met's interested in, George.'

Flight tut-tutted. 'Wires have ears, John. Anyway, the address was a no-show. Yes, a friend of Miss Crawley's lives there. But she hasn't seen her for weeks. Last she heard, Crawley was in Edinburgh.' He pronounced it head-in-burrow.

'Is that it?'

'I tried asking a couple of sleazebags connected with Croft.'

'Who's Croft?'

Flight sighed. 'The woman who ran the brothel.'

'Oh, right.'

'Only, we've had dealings with her before, you see. Maybe that's why she moved her operation north. So I talked to a couple of her "former associates".'

'And?'

'Nothing. Not even a trade discount on French with spanking.'

'Right. Well, thanks anyway, George.'

'Sorry, John. When are we going to see you down here?'

'When are we going to see you up *here*?'

'No offence, John, but it's all that square sausage and fizzy beer. It doesn't agree with me.'

'I'll let you get back to your smoked salmon and Scotch then. Night, George.'

He put the phone down, and considered for a moment.

Then he got out of bed and started to dress. The cat looked satisfied with this arrangement, and stretched himself out. Rebus searched for paper and a pen and scribbled a note to Patience. 'Lonely without you. Gone for a drive. John.' He thought about adding a few kisses. Yes, a few kisses were definitely in order.

'xxx'

Checking that he had car keys, flat keys and money, he let himself out, locking the door behind him.

If you didn't know, you wouldn't see.

It was a pleasant enough night for a drive, as it happened. The cloud cover kept the air mild, but there was no sign of rain or wind. It wasn't at all a bad night for a drive. Inverleith, then Granton, an easy descent to the coast. Past what had been William Glass's digs ... then Granton Road ... then Newhaven. The docks.

If you didn't know, you wouldn't see.

He was a lonely man, just out driving, just out driving slowly. They stepped out of shadowy doorways, or else crossed and recrossed at the traffic lights, like a sodium-lit fashion show. Crossed and recrossed. While drivers slowly drove, and slower yet, and slower. He saw nothing he wanted, so he took the car the length of Salamander Street, then turned it. Oh, he was a keen one. Shy, lonely, quiet and keen. Driving his beaten-up old car around the night-time streets, looking for ... well, maybe just looking *at*, unless he could be tempted ...

He stopped the car. She came walking smartly towards him. Not that her clothes were smart. Her clothes were cheap and cheerless, a pale raincoat, one size too big, and beneath it a bright red blouse and a mini-skirt. The mini-skirt, Rebus felt, was her big mistake, since her legs were bare and thinly unattractive. She looked cold; she looked as if she *had* a cold. But she tried him with a smile.

'Get in,' he said.

'Hand-job's fifteen, blow's twenty-five, thirty-five the other.'

Naïve. He could have arrested her on the spot. You never, *never* talked money till you were sure the punter was straight.

'Get in,' he repeated. She had a lot to learn. She got in. Rebus fished out his ID. 'Detective Inspector Rebus. I'd like a word, Gail.'

'You lot never give up, do you?' There was still Cockney in the accent, but she'd been back north long enough for her native Fife to start reasserting itself. A few more weeks, and that final 'you' would be a 'yiz': youse lot nivir gie up, dae yiz . . .?

She was a slow learner. 'How come you know my name?' she asked at last. 'Were you on that raid? After a freebie, are you, is that it?'

That wasn't it at all. 'I want to talk about Gregor.'

The colour drained from her face, leaving only eye make-up and slick red lipstick. 'Who's he when he's at home?'

'He's your brother. We can talk down the station, or we can talk at your flat, either suits me.' She made a perfunctory attempt at getting out of the car. It only needed a touch of his hand to restrain her.

'The flat then,' she said levelly. 'Just don't be all night about it, eh?'

It was a small room in a flat full of bed-sits. Rebus got the feeling she never brought men back here. There was too much of her about the place; it wasn't anonymous enough. For a start, there was a picture of a baby on the dressing table. Then there were newspaper cuttings pinned to the walls, all of them detailing the fall of Gregor Jack. He tried not to look at them, and instead picked up the photograph.

'Put that down!'

He did so. 'Who is it?'

'If you must know, it's me.' She was sitting on the bed, her two arms stretched out behind her, her mottled legs crossed. The room was cold, but there was no sign of any means of heating it. Clothes spilled from an open chest of drawers, and the floor was littered with bits and pieces of make-up. 'Get on with it then,' she said.

There being nowhere to sit, he stood, keeping his hands in his jacket pockets. 'You know that the only reason your brother was in that brothel was so he could talk to you?'

'Yeah?'

'And that if you'd told this to anyone – '

'Why should I?' she spat. 'Why the fuck should I? I don't owe him no favours!'

'Why not?'

'Why not? Because he's an oily git's why not. Always was. He's got it made, hasn't he? Mum and Dad always liked him better than me . . .' Her voice trailed off into silence.

'Is that why you left home?'

'None of your business why I left home.'

'Ever see any old friends?'

'I don't have any "old friends".'

'You came back north. You must have known there was a chance you'd bump into your brother.'

She snorted. 'We don't exactly move in the same circles.'

'No? I thought prostitutes always reckoned MPs and judges were their best clients?'

'They're just johns to me, that's all.'

'How long have you been on the game?'

She folded her arms tight. 'Just sod off, will you?' And there they were again, the not-quite-tears. Twice tonight he'd just failed to reduce a woman to tears. He wanted to go home and have a bath. But where was home?

'Just one more question, Gail.'

'Ms Crawley to you.'

'Just one more question, *Ms* Crawley.'

'Yeah?'

'Someone knew you were working in that brothel. Someone who then told your brother. Any idea who it might be?'

There was a moment's thought. 'Not a clue.'

She was lying, obviously. Rebus nodded towards the clippings. 'Still, you're interested in him, aren't you? You know he came to see you that night because he cares – '

'Don't give me that crap!'

Rebus shrugged. It *was* crap, too. But if he didn't get this woman on to Gregor Jack's side, then he might never find out who was behind this whole ugly thing.

'Suit yourself, Gail. Listen, if you want to talk, I'm at Great London Road police station.' He fished out a card with his name and phone number on it.

'That'll be the day.'

'Well . . .' He headed for the door, a matter of two and a half strides.

'The more trouble that piss-pot's in, the better I'll like it.' But her words had lost their force. It wasn't quite indecision, but perhaps it was a start . . .

9
Within Range

On Monday morning, first findings started filtering down from Dufftown, where the forensic tests of Elizabeth Jack's BMW were under way. Specks of blood found on the driver's-side carpet matched Mrs Jack's type, and there were signs of what might have been a struggle: marks on the dashboard, scuff-marks on the interiors of both front doors, and damage to the radio-cassette, as though it had been hit with the heel of a shoe.

Rebus read the notes in Chief Inspector Lauderdale's office, then handed them back across the desk.

'What do you think?' Lauderdale asked, stifling a Monday morning yawn.

'You know what I think,' said Rebus. 'I think Mrs Jack was murdered in that lay-by, inside her car or outside it. Maybe she tried to run away and was hit from behind. Or maybe her assailant knocked her unconscious first, *then* hit her from behind to make it look like the work of the Dean Bridge murderer. However it happened, I don't think William Glass did it.'

Lauderdale shrugged and rubbed his chin, checking the closeness of the shave. 'He still says he did. You can read the transcripts any time you like. He says he was lying low, knowing we were after him. He needed money for food. He came upon Mrs Jack and hit her over the head.'

'What with?'

'A rock.'

'And what did he do with all her stuff?'

'Threw it into the river.'

'Come on, sir . . .'

'She didn't have any money. That's what made him so angry.'

'He's making it up.'

'Sounds plausible to me – '

'No! With respect, sir, what it sounds like is a quick solution, one that'll please Sir Hugh Ferrie. Doesn't it matter to you that it isn't the truth?'

'Now look here . . .' Lauderdale's face was reddening with anger. 'Look here, Inspector, all I've had from you so far is . . . well, what is it? It's nothing really, is it? Nothing solid or concrete. Nothing you could hang a shirt on, never mind a case in a court of law. Nothing.'

'How did she get to Queensferry? Who drove her there? What sort of state was she in?'

'For Christ's sake, I *know* it's not cut and dried. There are still gaps – '

'Gaps! You could fit Hampden into them three times over!'

Lauderdale smiled. 'There you go again, John, exaggerating. Why can't you just accept there's less to this than meets your eye?'

'Look, sir . . . fine, charge Glass with the Dean Bridge murder, that's okay by me. But let's keep an open mind on Mrs Jack, eh? At least until forensics are finished with the car.'

Lauderdale thought about it.

'Just till they finish the car,' Rebus pressed. He wasn't about to give up: Monday mornings were hell for Lauderdale, and the man would agree to just about anything if it meant getting Rebus out of his office.

'All right, John,' Lauderdale said, 'have it your way. But don't get bogged down in it. Remember, *I'll* keep an open mind if *you* will. Okay?'

'Okay.'

Lauderdale seemed to relax a little. 'Have you seen the Chief Superintendent this morning?' Rebus had not. 'I'm not even sure he's in yet. Maybe he had a heavy weekend, eh?'

'None of our business really, sir.'

Lauderdale stared at him. 'Of course, none of our business. But if the Chief Super's *personal* problems start interfering with his – '

The phone rang. Lauderdale picked up the receiver. 'Yes?' He straightened suddenly in his chair. 'Yes, sir. Was I, sir?' He flipped open his desk diary. 'Oh yes, ten.' He checked his watch. 'Well, I'll be there right away. Yes, sir, sorry about that.' He had the good grace to blush as he put down the receiver.

'The Chief Super?' guessed Rebus. Lauderdale nodded.

'I was supposed to be in a meeting with him five minutes ago. Forgot all about the bloody thing.' Lauderdale got to his feet. 'Plenty to keep you occupied, John?'

'Plenty. I believe DS Holmes has some cars for me to look at.'

'Oh? Thinking of getting rid of that wreck of yours? About time, eh?'

And, this being his idea of wit, Lauderdale actually laughed.

Brian Holmes had cars for him, cars aplenty. Well actually, a Detective Constable seemed to have done the work. Holmes, it appeared, was already learning to delegate. A list of the cars owned and run by friends of the Jacks. Make, registration, and colour. Rebus glanced down it quickly. Oh great, the only possessor of a colour blue was Alice Blake (The Pack's Sexton Blake), but she lived and worked in London. There were whites, reds, blacks, and a green. Yes, Ronald Steele drove a green Citroën BX. Rebus had seen it parked outside Gregor Jack's house the night Holmes had gone through the bins . . . Green? Well, yes, green. He remembered it more as a greeny-blue, a bluey-green. *Keep an open mind.* Okay, it was green. But it was easier to mistake green for blue than, say, red for blue, or white, or black. Wasn't it?

Then there was the question of that particular Wednesday. Everyone had been asked: where were you that morning, that afternoon? Some of the answers were vaguer than

185

others. In fact, Gregor Jack's alibis were more watertight than most. Steele, for example, had been uncertain about the morning. His assistant, Vanessa, had been off work that day, and Steele himself couldn't recall whether or not he'd gone into the shop. There was nothing in his diary to help him remember either. Jamie Kilpatrick had been sleeping off a hangover all day – no visitors, no phone calls – while Julian Kaymer had been 'creating' in his studio. Rab Kinnoul, too, was hesitant; he recalled meetings, but not necessarily the people he'd met. He could check, but it would take time...

Time, the one thing Rebus didn't have. He, too, needed all the friends he could get. So far, he'd ruled out two suspects: Tom Pond, who was abroad, and Andrew Macmillan, who was in Duthil. Pond was a nuisance. He wasn't back from the States yet. He had been questioned by telephone of course, and he knew all about the tragedy, but he had yet to be fingerprinted.

Anyone who might have been at Deer Lodge had been, or was being, or would be, fingerprinted. Just, so they were reassured, for processes of elimination. Just in case there were any fingerprints left in the lodge, any that couldn't be accounted for. It was painstaking work, this collection and collation of tiny facts and tiny figures. But it was how murder cases worked. Mind you, they worked more easily when there was a distinct scene of crime, a locus. Rebus wasn't in much doubt that Elizabeth Jack had been killed, or as good as, in the lay-by. Had Alec Corbie seen something, something he was holding back? Was there something he might know, without knowing he knew? Maybe something he didn't think was important. What if Liz Jack had said something to Andrew Macmillan, something he didn't realize might be a clue? Christ, Macmillan still didn't know she was *dead*. How would he react were Rebus to tell him? Maybe it would jog his memory. Then again, maybe it would have an altogether different effect. And besides, could anything he said be trusted? Wasn't it possible that he held a grudge against Gregor Jack, the way Gail Crawley did? The way others might, too...

Who, really, was Gregor Jack? Was he merely a tarnished saint, or was he a bastard? He'd ignored Macmillan's letters; he'd tried to keep his sister from disgracing him; he was embarrassed by his wife. Were his friends really friends? Or were they truly a 'pack'? Wolves ran in packs. Hounds ran in packs. And so did newshounds. Rebus remembered that he'd still to track down Chris Kemp. Maybe he was clutching at straws, but it felt more as if they were clutching at *him* . . .

And speaking of clutch, that was something else to be added to his car's list of woes. There was a worrying whirring and grinding as he pushed the gear-shift from neutral into first. But the car wasn't behaving badly (windscreen wipers aside – they'd begun sticking again). It had taken him north and back without so much as a splutter. All of which worried Rebus even more. It was like a terminal patient's final rally, that last gleam of life before the support machines took over.

Maybe next time he'd take the bus. After all, Chris Kemp's flat was only a quarter of an hour from Great London Road. The harassed-sounding woman on the news desk had given him the address as soon as he asked for it. And he had asked for it only when told that Kemp was on his day off. She'd given him the reporter's home phone number first, and, recognizing the first three digits as designating a local code, Rebus had asked for the address.

'You could just as easily have looked in the book,' she'd said before ringing off.

'Thank you, too,' he answered to the dead connection.

It was a second-floor flat. He pressed the intercom button beside the main door of the tenement, and waited. And waited. Should have phoned first, John. But then a crackle, and after the crackle: 'Yeah?' The voice groggy. Rebus glanced at his watch. Quarter to two.

'Didn't wake you, did I, Chris?'

'Who is that?'

'John Rebus. Get your breeks on and I'll buy you a pie and a pint.'

A groan. 'What time is it?'

'Nearly two.'

'Christ . . . Never mind the alcohol, I need coffee. There's a shop at the corner. Fetch some milk, will you? I'll put the kettle on.'

'Back in two ticks.'

The intercom crackled into silence. Rebus went and fetched the milk, then buzzed the intercom again. There was a louder buzz from behind the door, and he pushed it open, entering the dim stairwell. By the time he reached the second floor, he was peching and remembering exactly why he liked living in Patience's basement. The door to Kemp's flat was ajar. Another name had been fixed to the door with Sellotape, just below Kemp's own. V. Christie. The girlfriend, Rebus supposed. A bicycle wheel, missing its tyre, rested against the hall wall. So did books, dozens of them, rickety, towering piles of them. He tiptoed past.

'Milkman!' he called.

'In here.'

The living room was at the end of the hall. It was large, but contained almost no space. Kemp, dressed in last week's t-shirt and the week before's denims, ran his fingers through his hair.

'Morning, Inspector. A timely alarm call. I'm supposed to be meeting someone at three o'clock.'

'Hint taken. I was just passing and – '

Kemp threw him a disbelieving glance, then busied himself at the sink, where he was trying his damnedest to get the stains off two mug-rims. The room served as living room and kitchen both. There was a fine old cooking range in the fireplace, but it had become a display case for pot plants and ornamental boxes. The actual cooker was a greasy-looking electrical device sited just next to the sink. On a dining table sat a word processor, boxes of paper, files, and next to the table stood a green metal filing cabinet, four drawers high, its bottom drawer open to show more files. Books, magazines, and newspapers were stacked on most of the available floor space, but there was room for a sofa, one armchair, TV and video, and a hi-fi.

'Cosy,' said Rebus. He actually thought he meant it. But Kemp looked around and made a face.

'I'm supposed to be cleaning this place up today.'

'Good luck.'

Coffee was spooned into the mugs, the milk splashed in after it. The kettle came to the boil and switched itself off, and Kemp poured.

'Sugar?'

'No thanks.' Rebus had settled on the arm of the sofa, as if to say: don't worry, I'm not about to linger. He accepted the mug with a nod. Kemp threw himself on to the armchair and gulped at the coffee, screwing up his face as it burned his mouth and throat.

'Christ,' he gasped.

'Heavy night?'

'Heavy week.'

Rebus wandered over in the direction of the dining table. 'It's a terrible thing, drink.'

'Maybe it is, but I was talking about *work*.'

'Oh. Sorry.' He turned from the table and headed over to the sink ... the cooker ... stopping beside the fridge. Kemp had left the carton of milk sitting on top of the fridge, next to the kettle. 'I'd better put this away,' he said, lifting the carton. He opened the fridge. 'Oh, look,' he said, pointing. 'There already *is* milk in the fridge. Looks fresh enough, doesn't it? I needn't have bothered going to the shop.'

He put the new carton of milk in beside the other, slammed shut the door, and returned to the arm of the sofa. Kemp was attempting something like a grin.

'You're sharp for a Monday.'

'But I can be blunt when I need to. What were you hiding from old Uncle Rebus, Chris? Or did you just need the time to check there was nothing *to* hide? A bit of blaw? That sort of thing. Or maybe something else, eh? Some story you're working on ... working on late into the night. Something *I* should know about. How about it?'

'Come on, Inspector. I'm the one who's doing *you* a favour, remember?'

'You'll have to refresh my memory.'

'You wanted me to see what I could find about the brothel story, about how the Sundays knew it was breaking.'

'But you never got back to me, Chris.'

'Well, I've been pressed for time.'

'You still are. Remember, you've got that meeting at three. Better tell me what you know, then I can be on my way.' Now Rebus slid off the arm and on to the sofa proper. He could feel the springs probing at him through what was left of the patterned covering.

'Well,' said Kemp, sitting forward in his chair, 'it looks like there was a kind of mass tip-off. All the papers thought they were getting an exclusive. Then, when they all turned up they knew they'd been had.'

'How do you mean?'

'Well, if there *was* a story, they had to publish. If they didn't, and their rivals did . . .'

'Editors would be asking questions about how come they got scooped?'

'Exactly. So whoever set the story up was guaranteed maximum exposure.'

'But who did set it up?'

Kemp shook his head. 'Nobody knows. It was anonymous. A telephone call on the Thursday to all the news desks. Police are going to raid a brothel in Edinburgh on Friday night . . . here's the address . . . if you're there around midnight, you're guaranteed to bag an MP.'

'The caller said that?'

'Apparently, his exact words were "at least one MP will be inside".'

'But he didn't name any names?'

'He didn't have to. Royalty, MPs, actors and singers – give those papers a sniff of any category and you've got them hooked. I'm probably mixing metaphors there, but you get the gist.'

'Oh yes, Chris, I get the gist. So what do you make of it?'

'Looks like Jack was set up to take a fall. But note, his name wasn't mentioned by the caller.'

'All the same . . .'

'Yes, all the same.'

Rebus was thinking furiously. If he hadn't been slouching on the sofa, he might have said he was thinking on his feet. Actually, he was debating with himself. About whether or not to do Gregor Jack a huge favour. Points against: he didn't owe Jack any favours; besides, he should try to remain objective – wasn't that what Lauderdale had been getting at? Points for: one really – he wouldn't just be doing Jack a favour, he might also flush out the rat who'd set Jack up. He made his decision.

'Chris, I want to tell you something . . .'

Kemp caught the whiff of a story. 'Attributable?'

But Rebus shook his head. 'Afraid not.'

'Accurate then?'

'Oh yes, I can guarantee it's accurate.'

'Go on, I'm listening.'

Last chance to bottle out. No, he wasn't going to bottle out. 'I can tell you why Gregor Jack was at that brothel.'

'Yes?'

'But I want to know something first – *are* you holding something back?'

Kemp shrugged. 'I don't think so.'

Rebus still didn't believe him. But then Kemp had no reason to tell Rebus anything. It wasn't as if Rebus was going to tell *him* anything that he didn't want him to know. They sat in silence for half a minute, neither friends nor enemies; more like trench soldiers on a Christmas Day kickabout. At any moment, the sirens might sound and shrapnel pierce the peace. Rebus recalled that he knew *one* thing Kemp wanted to know: how Ronald Steele got his nickname . . .

'So,' Kemp said, 'why *was* he there?'

'Because someone told him his sister was working there.'

Kemp pursed his lips.

'Working as a prostitute,' Rebus explained. 'Someone phoned him – anonymously – and told him. So he went along.'

'That was stupid.'

'Agreed.'

'And *was* she there?'

'Yes. She calls herself Gail Crawley.'

'How do you spell that?'

'C-r-a-w-l-e-y.'

'And you're sure of this?'

'I'm sure. I've spoken with her. She's still in Edinburgh, still working.'

Kemp kept his voice level, but his eyes were gleaming. 'You know this is a story?'

Rebus shrugged, saying nothing.

'You want me to place it?'

Another shrug.

'Why?'

Rebus stared at the empty mug in his hands. Why? Because once it was public knowledge, the caller would have failed, at least in his or her own terms. And, having failed, maybe they'd feel compelled to try something else. If they did, Rebus would be ready . . .

Kemp was nodding. 'Okay, thanks. I'll think it over.'

Rebus nodded too. He was already regretting the decision to tell Kemp. The man was a reporter, and one with a reputation to make. There was no way of knowing what he'd do with the story. It could be twisted to make Jack sound like samaritan or slime . . .

'Meantime,' Kemp was saying, rising from his chair, 'I better take a bath if I'm going to make that meeting . . .

'Right.' Rebus rose, too, and placed his mug in the sink. 'Thanks for the coffee.'

'Thanks for the milk.'

The bathroom was on the way to the front door. Rebus made show of looking at his watch. 'Go get into your bath,' he said. 'I'll let myself out.'

'Bye then.'

'See you, Chris.' He walked to the door, checking that his weight on the floorboards did not make them creak, then glanced round and saw that Kemp had disappeared into the bathroom. Water started splashing. Gently, Rebus turned the snib and locked it at the off position. Then he opened the door and slammed it noisily behind him. He stood in the stairwell, pulling the door by its handle so that it couldn't swing back open. There was a spy-hole, but he kept himself tucked in against the wall. Anyway, if Kemp came to the door he'd notice the snib was off ... A minute passed. Nobody came to the door. More fortuitously, perhaps, nobody came into the stairwell. He didn't fancy explaining what he was doing standing there holding on to a door handle ...

After two minutes, he crouched down and opened the letter box, peering in. The bathroom door was slightly ajar. The water was still running, but he could hear Kemp humming, then a-ha-hee-ha-ing as he got into the bath. The water continued to run, giving the noise-cover he needed. He opened the door quietly, slipped back indoors, and closed it, jamming it shut with a hardback book from the top of one of the stacks. The remaining books looked as though they might topple, but they steadied again. Rebus exhaled and crept along the corridor, past the door. Taps pouring ... Kemp still humming. This part was easy; getting back out would be the hard part, *if* he had nothing to show for the deception.

He crossed the living room and studied the desk. The files gave nothing away. No sign of the 'big story' Kemp was working on. The computer disks were marked numerically – no clues there. Nothing interesting in the open drawer of the filing cabinet. He turned back to the desk. No scribbled sheets of notes had been tucked beneath other, blank sheets. He flipped through the pile of LPs beside the stereo, but no sheets had been hidden there either. Under the sofa ... no. Cupboards ... drawers ... no. Bugger it. He went to the great iron range. Tucked away at the back, behind three or four pot plants, sat an ugly-looking trophy, Kemp's Young Journalist of the Year Prize. Along the front of the range sat the row of ornamental boxes. He opened one. It contained a CND badge and a pair of ANC earrings. In another box was a 'Free Nelson Mandela' badge and a ring which looked to be carved out of ivory. The girlfriend's stuff, obviously. And in the third box ... a tiny cellophane package of dope. He smiled. Hardly enough to run someone in for, half a quarter at most. Was this what Kemp had been so eager to conceal? Well, Rebus supposed a conviction wouldn't do the 'campaigning journalist' tag much good. Difficult to chastise public figures for their small vices when you'd been done for possession.

Bugger it. And on top of everything, he'd now to get out of the flat without being seen or heard. The taps had stopped running. No noise to cover his retreat ... He crouched by the range and considered. The bold as brass approach might be best. Just go marching past saying something about having left behind your keys ... Aye, sure, Kemp would fall for *that*. Might as well put five bar on Cowdenbeath for the league and cup double.

He found that, as he thought, he was staring at the range's small oven, or rather at the closed door of that oven. A spider-plant sat above it, with two of its fronds trapped in the door. Dear me, he couldn't have that, could he? So he pulled open the door, releasing the leaves. Sitting in the oven itself were some books. Old hardbacks. He lifted one and examined its spine.

John Knox on predestination. Well, wasn't *that* a coincidence.

The bathroom door flew in.

'Christ's sake!' Chris Kemp, who had been lying with his head floating on the surface of the water, now shot up. Rebus marched over to the toilet, lowered its lid, and made himself comfortable.

'Carry on, Chris. Don't mind me. Just thought I might borrow a few of your books.' He slapped the pile he was holding. They were resting on his knees, all seven of them. 'I like a good read.'

Kemp actually blushed. 'Where's your search warrant?'

Rebus looked stunned. 'Search warrant? Why should I need a search warrant? I'm just borrowing a few books, that's all. Thought I might show them to my old friend Professor Costello. You know Professor Costello, don't you?

194

Only this stuff's right up his street. No reason why you should mind me borrowing them ... is there? If you like, I'll go get that search warrant and – '

'Fuck off.'

'Language, son,' Rebus reprimanded. 'Don't forget, you're a journalist. You're the protector of our language. Don't go cheapening it. You just cheapen yourself.'

'I thought you wanted me to do you a favour?'

'What? You mean the story about Jack and his sister?' Rebus shrugged. 'I thought *I* was doing *you* a favour. I know keen young reporters who'd give their eye teeth for – '

'What do you want?'

Now Rebus sat forward. 'Where did you get them, Chris?'

'The books?' Kemp ran his hands down his sleek hair. 'They're my girlfriend's. As far as I know, she borrowed them from her university library ...'

Rebus nodded. 'It's a fair story. I doubt it would get you off the hook, but it's a fair story. For a start, it won't explain why you hid them when you knew I was on my way up to see you.'

'Hid them? I don't know what you're talking about.'

Rebus chuckled. 'Fine, Chris, fine. There I was, thinking I could do you a favour. *Another* favour, I should say ...'

'What favour?'

Rebus slapped the books again 'Seeing these get back to their rightful owner without anyone needing to know where they've been in the interim.'

Kemp considered this. 'In exchange for what?'

'Whatever it is you're keeping from me. I *know* you know something, or you think you do. I just want to help you do your duty.'

'My duty?'

'Helping the police. It *is* your duty, Chris.'

'Like it's *your* duty to go creeping around people's flats without their permission.'

Rebus didn't bother replying. He didn't need to reply: he just needed to bide his time. Now that he had the books, he had the reporter in his pocket, too. Safe and snug for future use . . .

Kemp sighed. 'The water's getting cold. Mind if I get out?'

'Any time you like. I'll go wait next door.'

Kemp came into the living room wearing a blue towelling robe and using a matching towel to rub at his hair.

'Tell me about your girlfriend,' Rebus said. Kemp filled the kettle again. He had used the minute's solitary time to do a little thinking, and he was ready now to talk.

'Vanessa?' he said. 'She's a student.'

'A divinity student? With access to Professor Costello's room?'

'*Everybody*'s got access to Prof Costello's room. He told you that himself.'

'But not everyone knows a rare book when they see it . . .'

'Vanessa also works part time in Suey Books.'

'Ah.' Rebus nodded. Pencilling in her prices. Earrings and a bicycle . . .

'Old Costello's a customer, so Vanessa knows him fairly well,' Kemp added.

'Well enough to steal from him, at any rate.'

Chris Kemp sighed. 'Don't ask me why she did it. Was she planning to sell them? I don't know. Did she want to keep them for herself? I don't know. I've asked her, believe me. Maybe she just had a . . . a brainstorm.'

'Yes, maybe.'

'Whatever, she reckoned Costello might not even miss them. Books are books to him. Maybe she thought he'd be as happy with the latest paperback editions . . .'

'But she, presumably, wouldn't be?'

'Look, just take them back, okay? Or keep them for yourself. Anything.'

The kettle clicked off. Rebus refused the offer of more coffee. 'So,' he said, as Kemp made himself a mug, 'what have you got to tell me, Chris?'

'It's just something Vanessa told me about her employer.'

'Ronald Steele?'

'Yes.'

'What about him?'

'He's having an affair with Mrs Rab Kinnoul.'

'Really?'

'Yes. Not your business, you see, Inspector. Nothing to do with law and order.'

'But a juicy story nevertheless, eh?' Rebus found it hard to talk. His head was birling again. New possibilities, new configurations. 'So how did she come to this conclusion?'

'It started a while back. Our entertainment correspondent on the paper had gone to interview *Mr* Kinnoul. But there'd been a cock-up over the dates. He turned up on a Wednesday afternoon when it should have been Thursday. Anyway, Kinnoul wasn't there, but Mrs Kinnoul was, and she had a friend with her, a friend introduced as Ronald Steele.'

'One friend visits another . . . I don't see – '

'But then Vanessa told me something. A couple of Wednesdays back, there was an emergency at the shop. Well, not exactly an *emergency*. Some old dear wanted to sell some of her deceased husband's books. She brought a list to the shop. Vanessa could see there were a few gems in there, but she needed to talk to the boss first. He doesn't trust her when it comes to the buying. Now, Wednesday afternoons are sacrosanct . . .'

'The weekly round of golf – '

'With Gregor Jack. Yes, precisely. But Vanessa thought, he'll kill me if this lot get away. So she rang the golf club, out at Braidwater.'

'I know it.'

'And they told her that Messrs Steele and Jack had cancelled.'

'Yes?'

'Well, I started to put two and two together. Steele's supposed to be playing golf every Wednesday, yet one Wednesday my colleague finds him out at the Kinnoul house, and another Wednesday there's no sign of him on the golf course. Rab Kinnoul's known to have a temper, Inspector.

He's known as a very *possessive* man. Do you think he knows that Steele's visiting his wife when he's not there?'

Rebus's heart was racing. 'You might have a point, Chris. You might have a point.'

'But like I say, it's hardly police business, is it?'

Hardly! It was *absolutely* police business. Two alibis chipped into the same bunker. Was Rebus nearer the end of the course than he'd suspected? Was he playing nine holes rather than eighteen? He got up from the sofa.

'Chris, I've got to be going.' Like spokes on a bicycle wheel, turning in his head: Liz Jack, Gregor Jack, Rab Kinnoul, Cath Kinnoul, Ronald Steele, Ian Urquhart, Helen Greig, Andrew Macmillan, Barney Byars, Louise Patterson-Scott, Julian Kaymer, Jamie Kilpatrick, William Glass. Like spokes on a bicycle wheel.

'Inspector Rebus?'

He paused by the door. 'What?'

Kemp pointed to the sofa. 'Don't forget to take your books with you.'

Rebus stared at them as though seeing them for the first time. 'Right,' he said, heading back towards the sofa. 'By the way,' he said, picking up the bundle, 'I *know* why Steele's called Suey.' Then he winked. 'Remind me to tell you about it some time, when this is all over . . .'

He returned to the station, intending to share some of what he knew with his superiors. But Brian Holmes stopped him outside the Chief Superintendent's door.

'I wouldn't do that.'

Rebus, his fist raised high, ready to knock, paused. 'Why not?' he asked, every bit as quietly as Holmes himself had spoken.

'Mrs Jack's father's in there.'

Sir Hugh Ferrie! Rebus lowered his hand carefully, then began backing away from the door. The last thing he wanted was to be dragged into a discussion with Ferrie. Why haven't you found . . . what are you doing about . . . when will you . . .? No, life was too short, and the hours too long.

'Thanks, Brian. I owe you one. Who else is in there?'

'Just the Farmer and the Fart.'

'Best leave them to it, eh?' They moved a safe distance from the door. 'That list of cars you made up was pretty comprehensive. Well done.'

'Thanks. Lauderdale never told me exactly what it was – '

'Anything else happening?'

'What? No, quiet as the grave. Oh, Nell thinks she might be pregnant.'

'What?'

Holmes gave a bemused smile. 'We're not sure yet . . .'

'Were you . . . you know, *expecting* it?'

The smiled stayed. 'Expect the unexpected, as they say.'

Rebus whistled. 'How does she feel about it?'

'I think she's holding back on the feelings till we know one way or the other.'

'What about you?'

'Me? If it's a boy he'll be called Stuart and grow up to be a doctor and a Scottish international.'

Rebus laughed. 'And if it's a girl?'

'Katherine, actress.'

'I'll keep my fingers crossed for you.'

'Thanks. Oh, and another bit of news – Pond's back.'

'Tom Pond?'

'The very one. Back from across the pond. We reached him this morning. I thought I'd go have a talk with him, unless you want to?'

Rebus shook his head. 'He's all yours, Brian, for what he's worth. Right now, he's about the only bugger I think is in the clear. Him and Macmillan and Mr Glass.'

'Have you seen the interview transcript?'

'No.'

'Well, I know you and Chief Inspector Lauderdale don't always get on, but I'll say this for him, he's sharp.'

'A Glass-cutter, you might say?'

Holmes sighed. 'I might, but you always seem to beat me to the pun.'

*

Edinburgh was surrounded by golf courses catering to every taste and presenting every possible degree of difficulty. There were links courses, where the wind was as likely to blow your ball backwards as forwards. And there were hilly courses, all slope and gully, with greens and flags positioned on this or that handkerchief-sized plateau. The Braidwater course belonged to the latter category. Players made the majority of their shots trusting either to instinct or fortune, since the flag would often be hidden from view behind a rise or the brow of a hill. A cruel course designer would have tucked sand traps just the other side of these obstacles, and indeed a cruel course designer had.

People who didn't know the course often started their round with high hopes of a spot of exercise and fresh air, but finished with high blood pressure and the dire need of a couple of drams. The club house comprised two contrasting sections. There was the original building, old and solid and grey, but to which had been added an oversized extension of breeze block and pebbledash. The old building housed committee rooms, offices and the like, but the bar was in the new building. The club secretary led Rebus into the bar, where he thought one of the committee members might be found.

The bar itself was on the first floor. One wall was all window, looking out over the eighteenth green and beyond to the rolling course itself. On another wall were framed photos, rolls of honour, mock-parchment scrolls and a pair of very old putters looking like emaciated crossbones. The club's trophies – the small trophies – were arrayed on a shelf above the bar. The larger, the more ancient, the more valuable trophies were kept in the committee room in the old building. Rebus knew this because some of them had been stolen three years before, and he'd been one of the investigating officers. They had been recovered, too, though utterly by accident, found lying in an open suitcase by officers called out to a domestic.

The club secretary remembered Rebus though. 'Can't recall the name,' he'd said, 'but I know the face.' He showed Rebus the new alarm system and the toughened glass case the trophies were kept in. Rebus hadn't the heart to tell him that even an amateur burglar could still be in and out of the place in two minutes flat.

'What will you have to drink, Inspector?'

'I'll have a small whisky, if it's no trouble.'

'No trouble at all.'

The bar wasn't exactly busy. A late-afternoon hiatus, as the secretary had explained. Those who played in the afternoon usually liked to get started before three, while those who came for an early evening round arrived around five thirty.

Two men in identical yellow V-neck pullovers sat at a table by the window and stared out in silence, sipping from time to time at identical bloody marys. Two more men sat at the bar, one with a flat-looking half pint of beer, the other with what looked suspiciously like a glass of milk. They were all in their forties, or slightly older; all my contemporaries, thought Rebus.

'Bill here could tell you a few stories, Inspector,' the club secretary said, nodding towards the barman. Bill nodded back, half in greeting, half in agreement. His own V-neck was cherry red, and did nothing to hide his bulging stomach. He didn't look like a professional barman, but took a slow, conspicuous pride in the job. Rebus reckoned him for just another member, doing his stint of duty.

Nobody had twitched at the secretary's mention of 'Inspector'. These men were law-abiding; or, if not, they were certainly law-*abetting*. They believed in law and order and that criminals should be punished. They just didn't think fiddling your tax was a criminal act. They looked ... secure. They thought of themselves as secure. But Rebus knew *he* held the skeleton keys.

'Water, Inspector?' The secretary pushed a jug towards him.

'Thank you.' Rebus adulterated the whisky. The secretary was looking around him, as though surrounded by bodies.

'Hector's not here. I thought he was.'

Bill the Barman chipped in: 'He'll be back in a sec.'

'Gone for the proverbial jimmy,' added the drinker of milk, while Rebus pondered which proverb he meant.

'Ah, here he comes.'

Rebus had imagined a large Hector, curly hair, distended gut, tangerine V-neck. But this man was small and had thinning, Brylcreemed black hair. He, too, was in his forties, and peered at the world through thick-lensed, thick-rimmed glasses. His mouth was set in a defiance at odds with his appearance, and he examined Rebus thoroughly while the introductions were made.

'How do you do?' he said, slipping a small, damp hand into Rebus's paw. It was like shaking hands with a well-brought-up child. His V-neck was camel-coloured but expensive-looking. Cashmere . . . ?

'Inspector Rebus,' the secretary said, 'is wondering about a particular round which was either played or was not played a couple of Wednesdays ago.'

'Yes.'

'I told him you're the brains of the set-up, Hector.'

'Yes.'

The secretary seemed to be struggling. 'We thought maybe you'd – '

But Hector now had enough information, and had digested it. 'First thing to do,' he said, 'is look at the bookings. They may not tell us the whole story, but they're the place to start. Who was playing?'

The question was directed at Rebus. 'Two players, sir,' he replied. 'A Mr Ronald Steele and a Mr Gregor Jack.'

Hector glanced behind Rebus to where the two drinkers sat at the bar. The room hadn't exactly grown quieter, but there was a palpable change of atmosphere. The drinker of milk spoke first.

'Those two!'

Rebus turned to him. 'Yes, sir, those two. How do you mean?'

But it was Hector's place to answer. 'Messrs Jack and Steele have a regular booking. Mr Jack was an MP, you know.'

'He still is, sir, so far as I know.'

202

'Not for much longer,' muttered the milk-drinker's companion.

'I'm not aware that Mr Jack has committed any crime.'

'I should think not,' snapped Hector.

'He's still a royal pain in the arse,' commented the milk-drinker.

'How's that, sir?'

'Books and never shows. Him and his cronies.' Rebus became aware that this was a long-festering sore, and that the man's words were directed more towards the club secretary and Hector than towards him. 'Gets away with it, too. Just because he's an MP.'

'Mr Jack has been warned,' Hector said.

'Reprimanded,' corrected the club secretary. The milk-drinker just screwed up his face.

'You kissed his bloody arse and you know it.'

'Now then, Colin,' said Bill and the Barman, 'no need to – '

'It's about time *some*body said it out loud!'

'Hear hear,' said the beer-drinker. 'Colin's right.'

An argument wasn't much use to Rebus. 'Do I take it,' he said, 'that Mr Jack and Mr Steele had a regular booking, but then wouldn't turn up?'

'You take it absolutely right,' said Colin.

'Let's not exaggerate or misrepresent,' said Hector quietly. 'Let us deal in facts.'

'Well, sir,' said Rebus, 'while we're dealing in facts, it's a fact that a colleague of mine, Detective Constable Broome, came out here last week to check on whether that particular round of golf had been played. I believe he dealt with *you*, seeing how the club secretary here was ill that day.'

'Remember, Hector,' the secretary interrupted nervously, 'one of my migraines.'

Hector nodded curtly. 'I remember.'

'You weren't exactly honest with DC Broome, were you, sir?' said Rebus. Colin was licking his lips, enjoying the confrontation.

'On the contrary, Inspector,' said Hector. 'I was *scrupulously* honest in answering the detective constable's questions. He just didn't ask the right ones. In fact, he was very sloppy indeed. Took one look at the bookings and seemed satisfied. I recall he was in a hurry . . . he had to meet his wife.'

Right, thought Rebus, Broome was for a carpeting then. Even so . . .

'Even so, sir, it was your duty – '

'I answered his questions, Inspector. I did not lie.'

'Well then, let's say that you were "economical with the truth".'

Colin snorted. Hector gave him a cold look, but his words were for Rebus. 'He wasn't thorough enough, Inspector. It's as simple as that. I don't expect my patients to help me if I'm not thorough enough in my treatment of them. *You* shouldn't expect *me* to do your work for you.'

'This is a serious criminal case, sir.'

'Then why are we arguing? Ask your questions.'

The barman interrupted. 'Hold on, before you start, *I've* got a question.' He looked at each of them in turn. 'What are you having?'

Bill the Barman poured the drinks. The round was on him, and he totted up the amount and scribbled it into a small notebook kept beside the till. The bloody marys from the window came over to join in. The beer-drinker was introduced to Rebus as David Cassidy – 'No jokes, please. How were my parents supposed to know?' – and the man called Colin was indeed drinking milk – 'ulcer, doctor's orders'.

Hector accepted a thin, delicate glass filled to the lip with dry sherry. He toasted 'our general health'.

'But not the National Health, eh, Hector?' added Colin, going on to explain to Rebus that Hector was a dentist.

'Private,' Cassidy added.

'Which,' Hector retorted, 'is what this club is supposed to be. Private. Members' private business should be none of our concern.'

'Which is why,' Rebus speculated, 'you've been acting as alibi for Jack and Steele?'

Hector merely sighed. '"Alibi" is rather strong, Inspector.

As club members, they are allowed to book *and* to cancel at short notice.'

'And that's what happened?'

'Sometimes, yes.'

'But not all the time?'

'They played occasionally.'

'How occasionally?'

'I'd have to check.'

'About once a month,' Barman Bill said. He held on to the glass-towel as if it were a talisman.

'So,' said Rebus, 'three weeks out of four they'd cancel? How did they cancel?'

'By telephone,' said Hector. 'Usually Mr Jack. Always very apologetic. Constituency business ... or Mr Steele was ill ... or, well, there were a number of reasons.'

'Excuses you mean,' Cassidy said.

'Mind you,' said Bill, 'sometimes Gregor'd turn up anyway, wouldn't he?'

Colin conceded that this was so. 'I went a round with him myself one Wednesday when Steele hadn't shown up.'

'So,' said Rebus, 'Mr Jack came to the club more often than Mr Steele?'

There were nods at this. Sometimes he'd cancel, then turn up. He wouldn't play, just sit in the bar. Never the other way round: Steele never turned up without Jack. And on the Wednesday in question, the Wednesday Rebus was interested in?

'It bucketed down,' Colin said. 'Hardly any bugger went out that day, never mind those two.'

'They cancelled then?'

Oh yes, they cancelled. And no, not even Mr Jack had turned up. Not that day, and not since.

The lull was over. Members were coming in, either for a quick one before starting out or for a quick one before heading home. They came over to the little group, shook hands, swopped stories, and the group itself started to fragment, until only Rebus and Hector were left. The dentist laid a hand on Rebus's arm.

'One more thing, Inspector,' he said.

'Yes?'

'I hope you won't think I'm being unsubtle . . .'

'Yes?'

'But you really should get your teeth seen to.'

'So I've been told, sir,' Rebus said. 'So I've been told. Incidentally, I hope you won't think *I'm* being unsubtle . . .?'

'Yes, Inspector?'

Rebus leaned close to the man, the better to hiss into his ear. 'I'm going to try my damnedest to see you on a charge for obstruction.' He placed his empty glass on the bar.

'Cheers then,' said Barman Bill. He took the glass and rinsed it in the machine, then placed it on the plastic dripmat. When he looked up, Hector was still standing where the policeman had left him, his sherry glass rigid in his hand.

'You told me on Friday,' Rebus said, 'that you were jettisoning what you didn't need.'

'Yes.'

'Then I take it you *did* feel you needed the alibi of your golf game?'

'What?'

'Your weekly round with your friend Ronald Steele.'

'What about it?'

'Funny isn't it? *I'm* making the statements and *you're* asking the questions. Should be the other way round.'

'Should it?'

Gregor Jack looked like a war casualty who could still hear and see the battle, no matter how far from the front he was dragged. The newsmen were still outside his gates, while Ian Urquhart and Helen Greig were still inside. The sounds of a printer doing its business came from the distant back office. Urquhart was ensconced in there with Helen. Another day, another press release.

'Do I need a solicitor?' Jack asked now, his eyes dark and sleepless.

'That's entirely up to you, sir. I just want to know why you've lied to us about this round of golf.'

206

Jack swallowed. There was an empty whisky bottle on the coffee table, and three empty coffee mugs. 'Friendship, Inspector,' he said, 'is . . . it's . . .'

'An excuse? You need more than excuses, sir. What *I* need right now are some facts.' He thought of Hector as he said the word. 'Facts,' he repeated.

But Jack was still mumbling something about friendship. Rebus rose awkwardly from his ill-fitting marshmallow-chair. He stood over the MP. MP? This wasn't an MP. This wasn't *the* Gregor Jack. Where was the confidence, the charisma? Where the voteworthy face and that clear, honest voice? He was like one of those sauces they make on cookery programmes – reduce and reduce and reduce . . .

Rebus reached down and grabbed him by his shoulders. He actually shook him. Jack looked up in surprise. Rebus's voice was cold and sharp like rain.

'Where were you that Wednesday?'

'I was . . . I . . . was . . . nowhere. Nowhere really. Everywhere.'

'Everywhere except where you were supposed to be.'

'I went for a drive.'

'Where?'

'Down the coast. I think I ended up in Eyemouth, one of those fishing villages, somewhere like that. It rained. I walked along the sea front. I walked a lot. Drove back inland. Everywhere and nowhere.' He began to sing. 'You're everywhere and nowhere, baby.' Rebus shook him again and he stopped.

'Did anyone see you? Did you speak to anyone?'

'I went into a pub . . . two pubs. One in Eyemouth, one somewhere else.'

'Why? Where was . . . Suey? What was he up to?'

'Suey.' Jack smiled at the name. 'Good old Suey. Friends, you see, Inspector. Where was he? He was where he always was – with some woman. I'm his cover. If anyone asks, we're out playing golf. And sometimes we are. But the rest of the time, I'm covering for him. Not that I mind. It's quite nice really, having that time to myself. I go off on my own, walking . . . thinking.'

'Who's the woman?'

'What? I don't know. I'm not even sure it's just the one . . .'

'You can't think of any candidates?'

'Who?' Jack blinked. 'You mean Liz? My Liz? No, Inspector, no.' He smiled briefly. 'No.'

'All right, what about Mrs Kinnoul?'

'Gowk?' Now he laughed. 'Gowk and Suey? Maybe when they were fifteen, Inspector, but not now. Have you seen Rab Kinnoul? He's like a mountain. Suey wouldn't dare.'

'Well, maybe Suey will be good enough to tell me.'

'You'll apologize, won't you? Tell him I *had* to tell you.'

'I'd be grateful,' Rebus said stonily, 'if you'd think back on that afternoon. Try to remember where you stopped, the names of the pubs, anyone who *might* remember seeing you. Write it all down.'

'Like a statement.'

'Just to help you remember. It often helps when you write things down.'

'That's true.'

'Meantime, I'm going to have to think about charging you with obstruction.'

'What?'

The door opened. It was Urquhart. He came in and closed it behind him. 'That's that done,' he said.

'Good,' Jack said casually. Urquhart, too, looked like he was just hanging on. His eyes were on Rebus, even when he was speaking to his employer.

'I told Helen to run off a hundred copies.'

'As many as that? Well, whatever you think, Ian.'

Now Urquhart looked towards Gregor Jack. He wants to shake him, too, Rebus thought. But he won't.

'You've got to be strong, Gregor. You've got to *look* strong.'

'You're right, Ian. Yes, look strong.'

Like wet tissue paper, Rebus thought. Like an infestation of woodworm. Like an old person's bones.

Ronald Steele was a hard man to catch. Rebus even went to his home, a bungalow on the edge of Morningside. No sign of life. Rebus went on trying the rest of the day. At the fourth ring of Steele's telephone, an answering machine came into play. At eight o'clock, he stopped trying. What he didn't want was Gregor Jack warning Steele that their story had come apart at its badly stitched seams. Given the means, he'd have kept Steele's answering machine busy all night. But instead his own telephone rang. He was in the Marchmont flat, slumped in his own chair, with nothing to eat or drink, and nothing to take his mind off the case.

He knew who it would be. It would be Patience. She would just be wondering if and when he intended making an appearance. She would just have been worried, that was all. They'd spent a rare weekend together: shopping on Saturday afternoon, a film at night. A drive to Cramond on Sunday, wine and backgammon on Sunday night. Rare . . . He picked up the receiver.

'Rebus.'

'Jesus, you're a hard man to catch.' It was a male voice. It was not Patience. It was Holmes.

'Hello, Brian.'

'I've been trying you for hours. Always engaged or else not answering. You should get an answering machine.'

'I've *got* an answering machine. I just sometimes forget to plug it in. What do you want anyway? Don't tell me, you're telephone-selling as a sideline? How's Nell?'

'As well as can be not expecting.'

'She's negative then?'

'I'm positive she is.'

'Maybe next time, eh?'

'Listen, thanks for the interest, but that's not why I'm calling. I thought you'd want to know, I had a very interesting chat with Mr Pond.'

A.k.a. Tampon, thought Rebus. 'Oh yes?' he said.

'You're not going to believe it . . .' said Brian Holmes. For once, he was right.

10
Brothel Creepers

The way Tom Pond explained it to Rebus, architects were either doomed to failure or else doomed to success. He had no doubt at all that he came into the latter category.

'I know architects my age, guys I went to college with, they've been on the dole for the past half dozen years. Or else they give up and go do something sensible like working on a building site or living on a kibbutz. Then there are some of us, for a time we can't put a foot wrong. This prize leads to that contract, and that contract gets noticed by an American corporation, and we start calling ourselves "international". Note, I say "for a time". It can all turn sour. You get in a rut, or the economic situation can't support your new ideas. I'll tell you, the best architectural designs are sitting locked away in drawers – nobody can afford to build the buildings, not yet anyway, maybe not ever. So I'm just enjoying my lucky break. That's all I'm doing.'

It was not *quite* all Tom Pond was doing. He was also crossing the Forth Road Bridge doing something in excess of one hundred miles an hour. Rebus daren't look at the speedo.

'After all,' Pond had explained, 'it's not every day I can go breaking the speed limit with a policeman in the car to explain it away if we get stopped.' And he laughed. Rebus didn't. Rebus didn't say much after they hit the ton.

Tom Pond owned a forty-grand Italian racing job that looked like a kit-car and sounded like a lawnmower. The last time Rebus had been sitting this close to ground level, he'd just slipped on some ice outside his flat.

'I've got three habits, Inspector: fast cars, fast women, and slow horses.' And he laughed again.

'If you don't slow down, son,' Rebus yelled above the engine's whine, 'I'm going to have to book you for speeding myself!'

Pond looked hurt, but eased back on the accelerator. And after all, he *was* doing them all a favour, wasn't he?

'Thank you,' Rebus conceded.

Holmes had told him he wouldn't believe it. Rebus was still trying. Pond had arrived back the previous day from the States, only to find a message waiting for him on his answering machine.

'It was Mrs Heggarty.'

'Mrs Heggarty being . . .?'

'She looks after my cottage. I've got a cottage up near Kingussie. Mrs Heggarty goes in now and again to give it a clean and check everything's okay.'

'And this time everything *wasn't?*'

'That's right. At first, she said there'd been a break-in, but then I called her back and from what she said they'd used my spare key to get in. I keep a key under a rock beside the front door. Hadn't made any mess or anything, not really. But Mrs Heggarty knew somebody'd been there and it hadn't been me. Anyway, I happened to mention it to the detective sergeant . . .'

The detective sergeant whose geography was better than fair. Kingussie wasn't far from Deer Lodge. It certainly wasn't far from Duthil. Holmes had asked the obvious question.

'Would Mrs Jack have known about the key?'

'Maybe. Beggar knew about it. I suppose *everybody* knew about it, really.'

All of which Holmes had relayed to Rebus. Rebus had gone to see Pond, their conversation lasting just over half an hour, at the end of which he had announced a wish to see the cottage.

'Be my guest,' Pond had said. And so Rebus was trapped in this narrow metal box, travelling so fast at times that his

211

eyeballs were aching. It was well after midnight, but Pond seemed neither to notice nor to mind.

'I'm still in New York,' he said. 'Brain and body still disconnected. You know, this all sounds incredible, all this stuff about Gregor and Liz and her being found by Gowk. Just incredible.'

Pond had been in the United States for a month; already he was hooked. He was testing out the language, the intonation, even some of the mannerisms. Rebus studied him. Thick, wavy blond hair (dyed? highlighted?) atop a beefy face, the face of someone who had been good-looking in youth. He wasn't tall, but he *seemed* taller than he was. A trick of posture; yes, to a certain extent, but he also had that confidence, that aura Gregor Jack had once possessed. He was firing on all cylinders.

'Can this car take a corner or what? Say what you like about the Italians, they build a mean ice cream and a meaner car.'

Rebus gritted his lower intestine. He was determined to talk seriously with Pond. It was too good a chance to miss, the two of them trapped like this. He tried to talk without his teeth knocking each other out of his mouth.

'So, you've known Mr Jack since school?'

'I know, I know, it's hard to believe, isn't it? I look so much younger than him. But yes, we only lived three streets apart. I think Bilbo lived in the same street as Beggar. Sexton and Mack lived in the same street, too. I mean, the same street as one another, not the same as Beggar and Bilbo. Suey and Gowk lived a bit further away, other side of the school from the rest of us.'

'So what drew you all together?'

'I don't know. Funny, I've never really thought about it. I mean, we were all pretty clever, I suppose. Down a gear for this corner . . . and . . . *like shit off a goddamned shovel*!'

Rebus felt as though his seat was trying to push its way through his body.

'More like a motorbike than a car. What do you think, Inspector?'

'Do you keep in touch with Mack?' Rebus asked at last.

'Oh, you know about Mack? Well ... no, not really. Beggar was the catalyst. I think it was only because I kept in touch with him that I kept in touch with everybody else. But after Mack ... well, when he went into the nuthouse ... no, I don't keep in touch. I think Gowk does. You know, she was the cleverest of the lot of us, and look what happened to her.'

'What did happen to her?'

'She married that spunk-head and started shovelling Valium because it was the only way she could cope.'

'Is her problem common knowledge then?'

He shrugged. 'I only know because I've seen it happen to other people ... other times.'

'Have you tried talking to her?'

'It's her life, Inspector. I've got enough trouble keeping myself together.'

The Pack. What did a pack do when one of its number grew lame or sick? They left it to die, the fittest trotting along at the head ...

Pond seemed to sense Rebus's thoughts. 'Sorry if that sounds callous. I was never one for tea and sympathy.'

'Who was?'

'Sexton was always ready with a willing ear. But then she buggered off south. Suey, too, I suppose. You could talk to him. He never had any answers, mind, but he was a good listener.'

Rebus hoped he'd be as good a talker. There were more and more questions to be answered. He decided – how would an American phrase it? – yes, to throw Pond a few curve-balls.

'If Elizabeth Jack had a lover, who would be your guess?'

Pond actually slowed down a little. He thought for a moment. 'Me,' he said at last. 'After all, she'd be stupid to plump for anybody else, wouldn't she?' And he grinned again.

'Second choice?'

'Well, there were rumours ... there were *always* rumours.'

'Yes?'

'Jesus, you want me to list them? Okay, Barney Byars for a start. Do you know him?'

'I know him.'

'Well, Barney's all right I suppose. Bit screwed up about class, but otherwise he's fine. The two of them were pretty close for a while . . .'

'Who else?'

'Jamie Kilpatrick . . . Julian Kaymer . . . I think that fat bastard Kinnoul even tried his luck. Then she was supposed to have had a fling with that grocer's ex.'

'You mean Louise Patterson-Scott?'

'Can you imagine it? Story was, the morning after a party they were found together in bed. But so what?'

'Anyone else?'

'Probably hundreds.'

'You never . . .?'

'Me?' Pond shrugged. 'We had a kiss and a cuddle a few times.' He smiled at the memory. 'It could have gone anywhere . . . but it didn't. The thing with Liz was . . . generosity.'

Pond nodded to himself, pleased that he had found the right word, the fitting epitaph.

Here lies Elizabeth Jack.
She gave.

'Can I use your telephone?' Rebus asked.

'Sure.'

He called Patience. He had tried twice before in the course of the evening – no reply. But there was a reply this time. This time, he got her out of bed.

'Where are you?' she asked.

'Heading north.'

'When will I see you?' Her voice had lost all emotion, all interest. Rebus wondered if it was merely a trick of the telephone.

'Tomorrow. Definitely tomorrow.'

'It can't keep on like this, John. Really, it can't.'

214

He sought for words which would reassure her while not embarrassing him in front of Pond. He sought too long.

'Bye, John.' And the receiver went dead.

They reached Kingussie well before dawn, having met little enough traffic and not a single patrol car. They had brought torches, though these weren't really necessary. The cottage was situated at the far corner of a village, a little off the main road but still receiving a good share of what street-lighting there was. Rebus was surprised to find that the 'cottage' was quite a modern bungalow, surrounded by a high hedge on all four sides, excepting the necessary gates which opened on to a short gravel drive leading up to the house itself.

'When Gregor and Liz got their place,' Pond explained, 'I thought what the hell, only I couldn't bear to rough it the way they do. I wanted something a bit more modern. Less charm, better amenities.'

'Nice neighbours?'

Pond shrugged. 'Hardly ever seen them. The place next door is a holiday home, too. Half the houses in the village are.' He shrugged again.

'What about Mrs Heggarty?'

'Lives the other side of the main drag.'

'So whoever's been living here . . .?'

'They could have come and gone without anyone noticing, no doubt about that.'

Pond left his headlights on while he opened the front door of the house. Suddenly, hallway and porch were illuminated. Rebus, freed from the cage, was stretching and trying to stop his knees from folding in on him.

'Is that the stone?'

'That's the one,' Pond said. It was a huge pebble-shaped piece of pinkish rock. He lifted it, showing that the spare key was still there. 'Nice of them to leave it when they went. Come on, I'll show you around.'

'Just a second, Mr Pond. Could you try not to touch anything? We might want to check for fingerprints later on.'

Pond smiled. 'Sure, but my prints'll be everywhere anyway.'

'Of course, but all the same . . .'

'Besides, if Mrs Heggarty's tidied up after our "guests", the place'll be polished and tidied from ceiling to floor.'

Rebus's heart sank as he followed Pond into the cottage. There was certainly a smell of furniture polish, mingling with air-freshener. In the living room, not a cushion or an executive toy looked to be out of place.

'Looks the same as when I left it,' Pond said.

'You're sure?'

'Pretty sure. I'm not like Liz and her crew, Inspector. I don't go in for parties. I don't mind other people's, but the last thing I want to have to do is clean salmon mousse off the ceiling or explain to the village that the woman with her arse hanging out of a Bentley back window is actually an Hon.'

'You wouldn't be thinking of the Hon. Matilda Merriman?'

'The same. Christ, you know them all, don't you?'

'I've yet to meet the Hon. Matilda actually.'

'Take my advice: defer the moment. Life's too short.'

And the hours too long, thought Rebus. Today's hours had certainly been way too long. The kitchen was neat. Glasses sat sparkling on the draining board.

'Shouldn't think you'll get many prints off them, Inspector.'

'Mrs Heggarty's very thorough, isn't she?'

'Not always so thorough upstairs. Come on, let's see.'

Well, someone had been thorough. The beds in both bedrooms had been made. There were no cups or glasses on display, no newspapers or magazines or unfinished books. Pond made show of sniffing the air.

'No,' he said, 'it's no good, I can't even smell her perfume.'

'Whose?'

'Liz's. She always wore the same brand, I forget what it was. She always smelt beautiful. Beautiful. Do you think she was here?'

'Someone was here. And we think she was in this area.'

'But who was she with – that's what you're wondering?'

Rebus nodded.

'Well, it wasn't me, more's the pity. I was having to make do with call girls. And get this – they want to check your medical certificate before they start.'

'AIDS?'

'AIDS. Okay, finished up here? Beginning to look like a wasted journey, isn't it?'

'Maybe. There's still the bathroom . . .'

Pond pushed open the bathroom door and ushered Rebus inside. 'Ah-ha,' he said, 'looks like Mrs Heggarty was running out of time.' He nodded towards where a towel lay in a heap on the floor. 'Usually, that would go straight in the laundry.' The shower curtain had been pulled across the bath. Rebus drew it back. The bath was drained, but one or two long hairs were sticking to the enamel. Rebus was thinking: We can check those. A hair's enough for an ID. Then he noticed the two glasses, sitting together on a corner of the bath. He leaned over and sniffed. White wine. Just a trickle of it left in one glass.

Two glasses! For two people. Two people in the bath and enjoying a drink. 'Your telephone's downstairs, isn't it?'

'That's right.'

'Come on then. This room's out of bounds until further notice. And I'm about to become a forensic scientist's nightmare.'

Sure enough, the person Rebus ended up speaking to on the telephone did not sound pleased.

'We've been working our bums off on that car and that other cottage.'

'I appreciate that, but this could be just as important. It could be *more* important.' Rebus was standing in the small dining room. He couldn't quite tie up these furnishings to Pond's personality. But then he saw a framed photograph of a couple young and in love, captured some time in the 1950s. Then he understood: Pond's parents. The furniture here had once belonged to them. Pond had probably inherited it but decided it didn't go with his fast women/slow horses lifestyle. Perfect, though, for filling the spaces in his holiday home.

217

Pond himself, who had been sitting on a dining chair, rose to his feet. Rebus placed a hand over the receiver.

'Where are you going?'

'For a pee. Don't panic, I'll go out the back.'

'Just don't go upstairs, okay?'

'Fine.'

The voice on the telephone was still complaining. Rebus shivered. He was cold. No, he was tired. Body temperature dropping. 'Look,' he said, 'bugger off back to bed then, but be here first thing in the morning. I'll give you the address. And I *mean* first thing. All right?'

'You're a generous man, Inspector.'

'They'll put it on my gravestone: he gave.'

Pond slept, with Rebus's envious blessing, in the master bedroom, while Rebus himself kept vigil outside the bathroom door. Once bitten . . . He didn't want a repetition of the Deer Lodge 'break-in'. This evidence, if evidence it was, would stay intact. So he sat in the upstairs hallway, his back against the bathroom door, a blanket wrapped around him, and dozed. Then he slid down the door, so that he was lying in front of it on the carpet, curled into a foetus. He dreamed that he was drunk . . . that he was being driven around in a Bentley. The chauffeur was managing to drive and at the same time stick his backside out of the window. There was a party in the back of the Bentley. Holmes and Nell were there, copulating discreetly and hoping for a boy. Gill Templer was there, and attempting to undo Rebus's zip, but he didn't want Patience to catch them . . . Lauderdale seemed to be there, too. Watching, just watching. Someone opened the drinks cabinet, but it was full of books. Rebus picked one out and started to read it. It was the best book he'd ever read. He couldn't put it down. It had everything . . .

In the morning, when he awoke, stiff and cold, he couldn't recall a line or a word of the book. He rose and stretched, twisting himself back into human shape. Then he opened the bathroom door and stepped inside, and looked towards where the glasses should be.

The glasses were still there. Rebus, despite his aches, almost smiled.

He stood in the shower for a long time, letting the water trampoline on his head, his chest and his shoulders. Where was he? He was in the Oxford Terrace flat. He should be at work by now, but that could be explained away. He felt rough, but not as rough as he'd feared. Amazingly, he'd been able to sleep on the journey back, a journey taken at a more sedate pace than that of the previous night.

'Clutch trouble,' Pond had said, only twenty miles out of Kingussie. He'd pulled into the side of the road and had a look under the bonnet. There was a lot of engine under the bonnet. 'I wouldn't know where to start looking,' he'd admitted. The trouble with these fancy cars was that capable mechanics were few and far between. In fact, he had to take the car to London for every service. So they'd ambled, an early-morning amble, having left the cottage under the stewardship of a bemused Detective Sergeant Knox and two overworked forensics people.

And Rebus had slept. Not enough, admittedly, which was why he'd resisted the temptation to run a bath and had opted for the shower instead. Difficult to nod off in a shower; all too easy in a hot morning bath. And he had chosen Patience's flat over his own – an easy choice, since Oxford Terrace was the right side of Edinburgh after the drive. They'd had a hellish crossing of the Forth Bridge: commuter traffic crawling citywards. Sales reps in Astras gave the Italian car the once-over, and comforted themselves with the thought that its crew looked like crooks of some kind, pimps or moneylenders . . .

He turned off the shower and towelled himself dry, changed into some clean clothes, and began the process of becoming a human being again. Shaving, brushing his teeth, then a mug of fresh-brewed coffee. Lucky pleaded at a window, and Rebus let the cat in. He even tipped some food into a bowl. The cat looked up at him, full of suspicion. This wasn't the Rebus he knew.

'Just be thankful while it lasts.'

What day was it? It was Tuesday. Over a fortnight since the brothel raid, nearly two weeks since Alec Corbie heard the lay-by argument and saw either two or three cars. There had been progress, most of it thanks to Rebus himself. If only he could shake his superiors' minds free of William Glass . . .

There was a note on the mantelpiece, propped up against the clock: 'Why don't we try meeting some time? Dinner tonight, or else – Patience.' No kisses: always a bad sign. No crosses meant she was cross. She had every right to be. He really had to make up his mind one way or the other. Move in or move out. Stop using the place as a public amenity, somewhere to have a shower, a shave, a shit, and, on occasions, a shag. Was he any better than Liz Jack and her mysterious companion, making use of Tom Pond's cottage? Hell, in some ways he was worse. Dinner tonight, or else. Meaning, or else I lose Patience. He took the biro out of his pocket and turned the note over.

'If not dinner, then just desserts,' he wrote. Utterly ambiguous, of course, but it sounded clever. He added his name and a row of kisses.

Chris Kemp had his scoop. A front-page scoop at that. The young reporter had worked hard after the visit from John Rebus. He'd tracked down Gail Crawley, a photographer in tow. She hadn't exactly been forthcoming, but there was a photograph of her alongside a slightly blurred picture of a teenage girl: Gail Jack, aged fourteen or so. The story itself was riddled with get-out clauses, just in case it proved to be false. The reader was left more or less to make up his or her own mind. MP's Visit to Mystery Prostitute – His Secret Sister? But the photos were the clincher. They were definitely of the same person, same nose, same eyes and chin. Definitely. The photo of Gail Jack in her youth was a stroke of genius, and Rebus didn't doubt that the genius behind it was Ian Urquhart. How else could Kemp have found, and so quickly found, the photograph he needed? A call to Urquhart, explaining that the story was worth his cooperation. Either

Urquhart himself searched out the picture, or else he persuaded Gregor Jack to find it.

It was in the morning edition. By tomorrow, the other papers would have their own versions; they could hardly afford not to. Rebus, having recovered his car from outside Pond's flat, idling at traffic lights had seen the paper-seller's board: Brothel MP Exclusive. He'd crossed the lights, and parked by the roadside, then jogged back to the newspaper booth. Returned to the car and read the story through twice, admiring it as a piece of work. Then he'd started the car again and continued towards his destination. I should have bought two copies, he thought to himself. He won't have seen it yet . . .

The green Citroën BX was in its drive, the garage doors open behind it. As Rebus brought his own car to a halt, blocking the end of the driveway, the garage doors were being pulled to. Rebus got out of the car, the folded newspaper in one hand.

'Looks like I just caught you,' he called.

Ronald Steele turned from the garage. 'What?' He saw the car parked across his driveway. 'Look, would you mind? I'm in a – ' Then he recognised Rebus. 'Oh, it's Inspector . . . ?'

'Rebus.'

'Rebus, yes. Rasputin's friend.'

Rebus turned his wrist towards Steele. 'Healing nicely,' he said.

'Look, Inspector . . .' Steele glanced at his wristwatch. 'Was it anything important? Only I'm meeting a customer and I've already overslept.'

'Nothing too important, sir,' Rebus said breezily. 'It's just that we've found out your alibi for the Wednesday Mrs Jack died is a pack of lies. Wondered if you'd anything to say to that?'

Steele's face, already long, grew longer. 'Oh.' He looked down at the toes of his well-scuffed shoes. 'I thought it was bound to come out.' He tried a smile. 'Not much you can keep hidden from a murder inquiry, eh?'

'Not much you *should* keep hidden, sir.'

'Do you want me to come down to the station?'

'Maybe later, sir. Just so we can get everything on record. But for the moment your living room would do.'

'Right.' Steele started to walk slowly back towards the bungalow.

'Nice area this,' commented Rebus.

'What? Oh, yes, yes it is.'

'Lived here long?' Rebus wasn't interested in Steele's answers. His only interest was in keeping the man talking. The more he talked, the less time he had in which to think, and the less time he had to think, the better the chances of him coming out with the truth.

'Three years. Before that I had a flat in the Grassmarket.'

'They used to hang people down there, did you know that?'

'Did they? Hard to imagine it these days.'

'Oh, I don't know . . .'

They were indoors now. Steele pointed to the hall phone. 'Do you mind if I call the customer? Make my apologies?'

'Whatever you like, sir. I'll wait in the living room, if that's all right.'

'Through there.'

'Fine.'

Rebus went into the room but left the door wide open. He heard Steele dialling. It was an old bakelite telephone, the kind with a little drawer in the bottom containing a notepad. People used to want rid of them; now they wanted them back, and were willing to pay. The conversation was short and innocent. An apology and a rescheduling of the meeting. Rebus opened his morning paper wide in front of him and made show of reading the inside pages. The receiver clattered back into its cradle.

'That's that,' said Steele, entering the room. Rebus read on for a moment, then lowered the paper and began to fold it.

'Good,' he said. Steele, as he had hoped, was staring at the paper.

'What's that about Gregor?' he said.

'Hm? Oh, you mean you haven't seen it yet?' Rebus

handed over the paper. Steele, still standing, devoured the story. 'What do you reckon, sir?'

He shrugged. 'Christ knows. I suppose it makes sense. I mean, none of us could think *what* Gregor was doing in a place like that. I can't think of a much better reason. The photos certainly look similar ... I don't remember Gail at all. Well, I mean, she was always *around*, but I never paid much attention. She never mixed with us.' He folded the paper. 'So Gregor's off the hook then?'

Rebus shrugged. Steele made to hand the paper back. 'No, no, you can keep it if you like. Now, Mr Steele, about this non-existent golfing fixture ...'

Steele sat down. It was a pleasant, book-lined room. In fact, it reminded Rebus strongly of another room, a room he'd been in recently ...

'Gregor would do anything for his friends,' Steele said candidly, 'including the odd telling of a lie. We made up the golf game. Well, that's not strictly true. At first, there *was* a weekly game. But then I started seeing a ... a lady. On Wednesdays. I explained it to Gregor. He didn't see why we shouldn't just go on telling everyone we were playing golf.' He looked up at Rebus for the first time. 'A jealous husband is involved, Inspector, and an alibi was always welcome.'

Rebus nodded. 'You're being very honest, Mr Steele.'

Steele shrugged. 'I don't want Gregor getting into trouble because of me.'

'And you were with this woman on the Wednesday afternoon in question? The afternoon Mrs Jack died?'

Steele nodded solemnly.

'And will she back you up?'

Steele smiled grimly. 'Not a hope in hell.'

'The husband again?'

'The husband,' Steele acknowledged.

'But he's bound to find out sooner or later, isn't he?' Rebus said. 'So many people seem to know already about you and Mrs Kinnoul.'

Steele twitched, as though a small electric shock had been administered to his shoulder blades. He stared down at the floor, willing it to become a pit he might jump into. Then he sat back.

'How did you . . .?'

'A guess, Mr Steele.'

'A bloody inspired guess. But you say other people . . .?'

'Other people are guessing too. You persuaded Mrs Kinnoul to take up an interest in rare books. It makes a good cover, after all, doesn't it? I mean, if you're ever found there with her. I even notice that she's modelled her library on your own room here.'

'It's not what you think, Inspector.'

'I don't think anything, sir.'

'Cathy just needs someone to listen to her. Rab never has time. The only time he has is for himself. Gowk was the cleverest of the lot of us.'

'Yes, so Mr Pond was telling me.'

'Tom? He's back from the States then?'

Rebus nodded. 'I was with him just this morning . . . at his cottage.'

Rebus waited for a reaction, but Steele's mind was still fixed on Cath Kinnoul. 'It breaks my heart to see her . . . to see what she's . . .'

'She's a friend,' Rebus stated.

'Yes, she is.'

'Well then, she's sure to back up your story; a friend in need and all that . . .?'

Steele was shaking his head. 'You don't understand, Inspector. Rab Kinnoul is . . . he *can* be . . . a violent man. Mental violence and physical violence. He terrifies her.'

Rebus sighed. 'Then we've only your own word for your whereabouts?'

Steele shrugged. He looked as though he might cry – tears of frustration rather than anything else. He took a deep breath. 'You think I killed Liz?'

'Did you?'

Steele shook his head. 'No.'

'Well then, you've nothing to worry about, have you, sir?'

224

Steele managed that grim smile again. 'Not a worry in the world,' he said.

Rebus rose to his feet. 'That's the spirit, Mr Steele.' But Ronald Steele looked like there was just about enough spirit left in him to fill a teaspoon. 'All the same, you're not making it easy for yourself . . .'

'Have you spoken to Gregor?' Steele asked.

Rebus nodded.

'Does *he* know about Cathy and me?'

'I couldn't say.' They were both heading for the front door now. 'Would it make any difference if he did?'

'Christ knows. No, maybe not.'

The day was turning sunny. Rebus waited while Steele closed and double locked the door.

'Just one more thing . . . ?'

'Yes, Inspector?'

'Would you mind if I took a look in the boot of your car?'

'What?' Steele stared at Rebus, but saw that the policeman was not about to explain. He sighed. 'Why not?' he said.

Steele unlocked the boot and Rebus peered inside, peered at a pair of mud-crusted wellingtons. There was muck on the floor, too.

'Tell you what, sir,' said Rebus, closing the boot. 'Maybe it'd be best if you came down to the station just now. Sooner we get everything cleared up the better, eh?'

Steele stood up very straight. Two women were walking past, gossiping. 'Am I under arrest, Inspector?'

'I just want to make sure we get *your* side of things, Mr Steele. That's all.'

But Rebus was wondering: Were there *any* forensics people left spare? Or had he tied each and every one of them up already? If so, Steele's car might have to wait. If not, well, here was another little job for them. It really was turning into *Guinness Book of Records* stuff, wasn't it? How many forensic scientists can one detective squeeze into a case?

'What case?'

'I've just told you, sir.'

Lauderdale looked unimpressed. 'You haven't told me *anything* about the murder of Mrs Jack. You've told me about mysterious lovers, alibis for assignations, a whole barrel-load of mixed-up yuppies but not a blind thing about *murder*.' He pointed to the floor. 'I've got someone downstairs who swears he committed both murders.'

'Yes sir,' Rebus said calmly, 'and you've also got a psychiatrist who says Glass could just as easily admit the murders of Gandhi or Rudolf Hess.'

'How do you know that?'

'What?'

'About the psychiatric report?'

'Call it an inspired guess, sir.'

Lauderdale began to look a little dispirited. He licked his lips thoughtfully. 'All right,' he said at last. 'Go through it one more time for me.'

So Rebus went through it one more time. It was like a giant collage to him now: different textures but the same theme. But it was also like a kind of artist's trick: the closer he moved towards it, the further away it seemed. He was just finishing, and Lauderdale was still looking sceptical, when the telephone rang. Lauderdale picked it up, listened and sighed.

'It's for you,' he said, holding the receiver towards Rebus.

'Yes?' Rebus said.

'Woman for you,' explained the switchboard operator. 'Says it's urgent.'

'Put her through.' He waited till the connection was made. 'Rebus here,' he said.

He could hear background noise, announcements. A railway station. Then: 'About bleedin' time. I'm at Waverley. My train goes in forty-five minutes. Get here before it leaves and I'll tell you something.' The line went dead. Short and sour, but intriguing for all that. Rebus checked his watch.

'I've got to go to Waverley Station,' he told Lauderdale. 'Why don't you talk to Steele yourself meantime, sir? See what you make of him?'

'Thank you,' said Lauderdale. 'Maybe I will . . .'

*

She was sitting on a bench in the concourse, conspicuous in sunglasses which were supposed to disguise her identity.

'That bastard,' she said, 'putting the papers on to me like that.' She was talking of her brother, Gregor Jack. Rebus didn't say anything. 'One yesterday,' she went on, 'then this morning, half a dozen of the bastards. Picture plastered all over the front pages . . .'

'Maybe it wasn't your brother,' Rebus said.

'What? Who else could it be?' Behind the dark lenses, Rebus could still make out Gail Crawley's tired eyes. She was dressed as though in a hurry – tight jeans, high heels, baggy t-shirt. Her luggage seemed to consist of a large suitcase and two carrier bags. In one hand she clutched her ticket to London, in the other she held a cigarette.

'Maybe,' Rebus suggested, 'it was the person who knew who you were, the person who told Gregor where to find you.'

She shivered. 'That's what I wanted to tell you about. God knows why. I don't owe the bastard any favours . . .'

Nor do I, thought Rebus, yet I always seem to be doing them for him.

'What about a drink?' she suggested.

'Sure,' said Rebus. He picked up her suitcase, while she clip-clopped along carrying the bags. Her shoes made a lot of noise, and attracted glances from some of the men lolling about. Rebus was quite relieved to reach the safety of the bar, where he bought a half of export for himself and a Bacardi and Coke for her. They found a corner not too near the gaming machine or the frazzled loudspeaker of the jukebox.

'Cheers,' she said, trying to drink and inhale at much the same time. She spluttered and swore, then stubbed out the cigarette, only seconds later to light another.

'Good health,' said Rebus, sipping his own drink. 'So, what was it you wanted to get off your chest?'

She snorted. 'I like that: get off your chest.' This time she remembered to swallow her mouthful of rum before drawing on the cigarette. 'Only,' she said, 'what you were saying, about how somebody might have known who I was . . .'

227

'Yes?'

'Well, I remembered. It was a night a while back. Like, a couple of months. Six weeks ... something like that. I hadn't been up here long. Anyway, the usual trio of pissed punters comes in. Funny how they usually come in threes ...' She paused, snorted. 'If you'll pardon the expression.'

'So three men came to the brothel?'

'Just said so, didn't I? Anyway, one of them liked the look of me, so off we went upstairs. I told him my name was Gail. I can't see the point of all those stupid names everybody else uses – Candy and Mandy and Claudette and Tina and Suzy and Jasmine and Roberta. I'd just forget who I was supposed to be.'

Rebus glanced at his watch. A little over ten minutes left ... She seemed to understand.

'So, anyway, I asked him if *he* had a name. And he laughed. He said, "You mean you don't recognize the face?" I shook my head, and he said, "Of course, you're a Londoner, aren't you? Well hen," he said, "I'm weel kent up here." Something stupid like that. Then he says, "I'm Gregor Jack." Well, I just started laughing, don't ask me why. He *did* ask me why. So I said, "No you're not. *I know* Gregor Jack." That seemed to put him off his stroke. In the end, he buggered off back to his pals. All the usual winks and slaps on the back, and I didn't say anything ...'

'What did he look like?'

'Big. Like a Highlander. One of the other girls said she thought she *had* seen him on the telly ...'

Rab Kinnoul. Rebus described him briefly.

'Sounds about right,' she conceded.

'What about the men who were with him?'

'Didn't pay much attention. One of them was the shy type, tall and skinny like a beanpole. The other was fat and had on a leather jacket.'

'You didn't catch their names?'

'No.'

Well, it didn't matter. Rebus would bet she could pick them out from a line-up. Ronald Steele and Barney Byars. A night out on the town. Byars, Steele, and Rab Kinnoul. A curious little assembly, and another incendiary he could toss in Steele's direction.

'Finish your drink, Gail,' he said. 'Then let's get you on to that train.'

But on the way, he extracted an address from her, the same one she had given before, the one he'd had George Flight check on.

'That's where I'll be,' she said. She took a final look around her. The train was idling, filling with people. Rebus lifted her suitcase in through one of the doors. She was still staring up at the glass roof of the station. Then she lowered her gaze to Rebus. 'I should never have left London, should I? Maybe nothing would have happened if I'd stayed where I was.'

Rebus tilted his head slightly. 'You're not to blame, Gail.' But all the same, he couldn't help feeling that she had a point. *If* she'd stayed away from Edinburgh, *if* she hadn't come out with that "*I know* Gregor Jack" . . . who could say? She stepped up on to the train, then turned back towards him.

'If you see Gregor . . .' she began. But there wasn't anything else. She shrugged and turned away, carrying her case and her bags with her. Rebus, never one for emotional farewells where prostitutes were concerned, turned briskly on his heels and headed back towards his car.

'You've what?'

'I've let him go.'

'You've let Steele go?' Rebus couldn't believe it. He paced what there was of Lauderdale's floor. 'Why?'

Now Lauderdale smiled coldly. 'What was the charge, John? Be realistic, for Christ's sake.'

'Did you talk to him?'

'Yes.'

'And?'

'He seems very plausible.'

'In other words, you believe him?'

'I think I do, yes.'

'What about his car boot?'

'You mean the mud? He told you himself, John, Mrs Kinnoul and he go for walks. That hillside's hardly what you'd call paved. You need wellies, and wellies get muddy. It's their *purpose*.'

'He admitted he was seeing Cath Kinnoul?'

'He admitted nothing of the sort. He just said there was a "woman".'

'That's all he'd say when *I* brought him in. But he admitted it back in his house.'

'I think it's quite noble of him, trying to protect her.'

'Or could it be that he knows she couldn't back up his story anyway?'

'You mean it's a pack of lies?'

Rebus sighed. 'No, I think *I* believe it, too.'

'Well then.' Lauderdale sounded – for Lauderdale – genuinely gentle. 'Sit down, John. You've had a hard twenty-four hours.'

Rebus sat down. 'I've had a hard twenty-four years.'

Lauderdale smiled. 'Tea?'

'I think some of the Chief Superintendent's coffee would be a better idea.'

Lauderdale laughed. 'Kill or cure, certainly. Now look, you've just admitted yourself that you believe Steele's story – '

'Up to a point.'

Lauderdale accepted the clause. 'But still, the man wanted to leave. How the hell was I going to hold him?'

'On suspicion. We're allowed to hang on to suspects a bit longer than ninety minutes.'

'Thank you, Inspector, I'm aware of that.'

'So now he toddles back home and gives the boot of his car a damned good clean.'

'You need more than mucky wellies for a conviction, John.'

'You'd be surprised what forensics can do . . .'

'Ah, now that's another thing. I hear you've been getting up people's noses faster than a Vick's inhaler.'

'Anybody in particular?'

'*Everybody* in the field of forensic science, it seems. Stop hassling them, John.'

'Yes, sir.'

'Take a break. Just for the afternoon, say. What about the Professor's missing tomes?'

'Back with their owner.'

'Oh?' Lauderdale waited for elucidation.

'A turn-up for the books, sir,' Rebus said instead. He stood up. 'Well, if there's nothing else – '

The telephone rang. 'Hold on,' Lauderdale ordered. 'The way things have been going, that'll probably be for you.' He picked up the receiver. 'Lauderdale.' Then he listened. 'I'll be right down,' he said at last, before replacing the receiver. 'Well, well, well. Take a guess who's downstairs.'

'The Dundonald and Dysart Pipe Band?'

'Close. Jeanette Oliphant.'

Rebus frowned. 'I know the name . . .'

'She's Sir Hugh Ferrie's solicitor. And also, it seems, Mr Jack's. They're both down there with her.' Lauderdale had risen from his chair and was straightening his jacket. 'Let's see what they want, eh?'

Gregor Jack wanted to make a statement, a statement regarding his movements on the day his wife was murdered. But the prime mover was Sir Hugh Ferrie; that much was obvious from the start.

'I saw that piece in the paper this morning,' he explained. 'Phoned Gregor to ask if it was true. He says it was. I felt a sight better for knowing it, though I told him he's a bloody fool for not telling anyone sooner.' He turned to Gregor Jack. 'A bloody fool.'

They were seated around a table in one of the conference rooms – Lauderdale's idea. No doubt an interview room wasn't good enough for Sir Hugh Ferrie. Gregor Jack had been smartened up for the occasion: crisp suit, tidied hair, sparkling eyes. Seated, however, between Sir Hugh and Jeanette Oliphant, he was always going to come home third in the projection stakes.

'The point is,' said Jeanette Oliphant, 'Mr Jack told Sir Hugh about something else he'd been keeping secret, namely that his Wednesday round of golf was a concoction.'

'Bloody fool – '

'And,' Oliphant went on, a little more loudly, 'Sir Hugh contacted me. We feel that the sooner Mr Jack makes a statement regarding his genuine actions on the day in question, the less doubt there will be.' Jeanette Oliphant was in her mid-fifties, a tall, elegant, but stern-faced woman. Her mouth was a thin slash of lipstick, her eyes piercing, missing nothing. Her ears stuck out ever so slightly from her short permed hair, as though ready to catch any nuance or ambiguity, any wrong word or overlong pause.

Sir Hugh, on the other hand, was stocky and pugnacious, a man more used to speaking than listening. His hands lay flat against the table top, as though they were attempting to push *through* it.

'Let's get everything sorted out,' he said.

'If that's what Mr Jack wants,' Lauderdale said quietly.

'It's what he wants,' replied Ferrie.

The door opened. It was Detective Sergeant Brian Holmes, carrying a tray of cups. Rebus looked up at him, but Holmes refused to meet his eyes. Not normally a DS's job, playing waiter, but Rebus could just see Holmes waylaying the *real* tea-boy. He wanted to know what was going on. So, it seemed, did Chief Superintendent Watson, who came into the room behind him. Ferrie actually half rose from his chair.

'Ah, Chief Superintendent.' They shook hands. Watson glanced from Lauderdale to Rebus and back, but there was nothing they could tell him, not yet. Holmes, having laid the tray on the table, was lingering.

'Thank you, Sergeant,' said Lauderdale, dismissing him from the room. In the general mêlée, Rebus saw that Gregor Jack was looking at him, looking with his sparkling eyes and his little boy's smile. Here we are again, he was saying. Here we are again.

Watson decided to stay. Another cup would be needed, but then Rebus declined the offer of tea, so there was a cup for

232

Watson after all. It was obvious from his face that he would have preferred coffee, his own coffee. But he accepted the cup from Rebus with a nodded thanks. Then Gregor Jack spoke.

'After Inspector Rebus's last visit, I did some thinking. I was able to recall the names of some of the places I went to that Wednesday . . .' He reached into his jacket's inside pocket and drew out a piece of paper. 'I looked in on a bar in Eyemouth itself, but it was packed. I didn't stay. I *did* have a tomato juice at a hotel outside the town, but again the bar there was packed, so I can't be sure anyone will remember me. And I bought chewing gum at a newsagent's in Dunbar on the way down. Apart from that, I'm afraid it's pretty vague.' He handed the list to the Chief Superintendent. 'A walk along the front at Eyemouth . . . a stop in a lay-by just north of Berwick . . . there was another car in the lay-by, a rep or something, but he seemed more interested in his maps than he did in me . . . That's about it.'

Watson nodded, studying the list as though it contained exam questions. Then he handed it on to Lauderdale.

'It's certainly a start,' said Watson.

'The thing is, Chief Superintendent,' said Sir Hugh, 'the boy knows he's in trouble, but it seems to me the only trouble he's in stems from trying to help other people.'

Watson nodded thoughtfully. Rebus stood up. 'If you'll excuse me a moment . . .' And he made for the door, closing it behind him with a real sense of escape. He had no intention of returning. There might be a slap on the wrist later from Lauderdale or Watson – bad manners that, John – but no way could he sit in that stifling room with all those stifling people. Holmes was loitering at the far end of the corridor.

'What's up?' he asked when Rebus approached.

'Nothing to get excited about.'

'Oh.' Holmes looked deflated. 'Only we all thought . . .'

'You all thought he was coming in to confess? Quite the opposite, Brian.'

'Is Glass going to end up going down for both murders then?'

Rebus shrugged. 'Nothing would surprise me,' he said. Despite his morning shower, he felt grimy and unhealthy.

'Makes it nice and neat, doesn't it?'

'We're the police, Brian, we're not meant to be char ladies.'

'Sorry I spoke.'

Rebus sighed. 'Sorry, Brian. I didn't mean to dust you off.' They stared at one another for a second, then laughed. It wasn't much, but it was better than nothing. 'Right, I'm off to Queensferry.'

'Autograph-hunting?'

'Something like that.'

'Need a chauffeur?'

'Why not. Come on then.'

A snap decision, Rebus was later to think, which probably saved his life.

11
Old School Ties

They managed not to speak about work on the way out to Queensferry. Instead, they spoke about women.

'What about the four of us going out some night?' Brian Holmes suggested at one point.

'I'm not sure Patience and Nell would get on,' Rebus mused.

'What, different personalities, you mean?'

'No, similar personalities. That's the problem.'

Rebus was thinking of tonight's dinner with Patience. Of trying to take time off from the Jack case. Of not making a Jack-ass of himself. Of jacking it all in . . .

'It was only a thought,' said Holmes. 'That's all, only a thought.'

The rain was starting as they neared the Kinnoul house. The sky had been darkening for the duration of the drive, until now, it seemed, evening had come early. Rab Kinnoul's Land-Rover was parked outside the front door. Curiously, the door to the house was open. Rain bounced off the car bonnet, becoming heavier by the second.

'Better make a run for it,' said Rebus. They opened their doors and ran. Rebus, however, was on the right side for the house, while Holmes had to skirt around the car first. So Rebus was first up the steps, and first through the doorway and into the hall. He shook his hair free of water, then opened his eyes.

And saw the carving knife swooping down on him.

And heard the shriek behind it.

'*Bastard!*'

Then someone pushed him sideways. It was Holmes, flying through the doorway. The knife fell into space and kept falling floorwards. Cath Kinnoul fell after it, her weight propelling her. Holmes was on her in an instant, pulling her wrist round, twisting it up against her back. He had his knee firmly on her spine, just below the shoulder blades.

'Christ almighty!' gasped Rebus. 'Jesus Christ almighty.'

Holmes was examining the sprawled figure. 'She took a knock when she fell,' he said. 'She's out cold.' He prised the knife from her grasp and released her arm. It flopped on to the carpet. Holmes stood up. He seemed wonderfully calm, but his face was unnaturally pale. Rebus, meantime, was shaking like a sick mongrel. He rested against the hallway wall and closed his eyes for a moment, breathing deeply. There was a noise at the door.

'Who the — ?' Rab Kinnoul saw them, then looked down at the unconscious figure of his wife. 'Oh hell,' he said. He knelt down beside her, dripping rainwater on to her back, her head. He was drenched.

'She's all right, Mr Kinnoul,' Holmes stated. 'Knocked herself out, that's all.'

Kinnoul saw the knife Holmes was holding. 'She had that?' he said, his eyes opening wide. 'Dear God, Cathy.' He touched a trembling hand to her head. 'Cathy, Cathy.'

Rebus had recovered a little. He swallowed. 'She didn't get those bruises from falling though.' Yes, there were bruises on her arms, fresh-looking. Kinnoul nodded.

'We had a bit of a row,' he said. 'She went for me, so I . . . I was just trying to push her away. But she was hysterical. I decided to go for a walk until she calmed down.'

Rebus had been looking at Kinnoul's shoes. They were caked with mud. There were splashes, too, on his trousers. Go for a walk? In *that* rain? No, he'd run for it, pure and simple. He'd turned tail and run . . .

'Doesn't look as though she calmed down,' Rebus said matter of factly. Matter of factly, she had almost murdered him, mistaking him for her husband, or so incensed by then

236

that any man – any victim – would do. 'Tell you what, Mr Kinnoul, I could do with a drink.'

'I'll see what there is,' said Kinnoul, rising to his feet.

Holmes phoned for the doctor. Cath Kinnoul was still unconscious. They'd left her lying in the hall, just to be on the safe side. It was best not to move fall victims anyway; and besides, this way they could keep an eye on her through the open door of the living room.

'She needs treatment,' Rebus said. He was sitting on the sofa, nursing a whisky and what were left of his nerves.

'What she needs,' Kinnoul said quietly, 'is to be away from me. We're useless together, Inspector, but then we're just as useless apart.' He was standing with his hands resting against the window sill, his head against the glass.

'What was the fight about?'

Kinnoul shook his head. 'It seems stupid now. They always start with something petty, and it just builds and builds . . .'

'And this time?'

Kinnoul turned from the window. 'The amount of time I'm spending away from home. She didn't believe there were any "projects". She thinks it's all just an excuse so I can get out of the house.'

'And is she right?'

'Partly, yes, I suppose. She's a shrewd one . . . a bit slow sometimes, but she gets there.'

'And what about evenings.'

'What about them?'

'You don't always spend *them* at home either, do you? Sometimes you have a night out with friends.'

'Do I?'

'Say, with Barney Byars . . . with Ronald Steele.'

Kinnoul stared at Rebus, appearing not to understand, then he snapped his fingers. 'Christ, you mean *that* night. Jesus, the night . . .' He shook his head. 'Who told you? Never mind, it must have been one or the other. What about it?'

'I just thought you made an unlikely trio.'

Kinnoul smiled. 'You're right there. I don't know Byars all

that well, hardly at all really. But that day he'd been in Edinburgh and he'd sewn up a deal ... a *big* deal. We bumped into each other at the Eyrie. I was in the bar having a drink, drowning my sorrows, and he was on his way up to the restaurant. Somehow I got roped in. Him and the firm he'd done the deal with. After a while ... well, it was good fun.'

'What about Steele?'

'Well ... Barney was planning on taking these guys to a brothel he knew about, but they weren't interested. They went their way, and Barney and me nipped into the Strawman for another drink. That's where we picked up Ronnie. He was a bit pissed, too. Something to do with the lady in his life ...' Kinnoul was thoughtful for a moment. 'Anyway, he's usually a bit of a boring fart, but that night he seemed all right.'

Rebus was wondering: Did Kinnoul know about Steele and Cathy? It didn't look like it, but then the man was an actor, a pro.

'And,' Kinnoul was saying, 'we all ended up going on to the ill-famed house.'

'Did you have a good time?'

Kinnoul seemed to think this an unusual question. 'I suppose so,' he said. 'I can't really remember too clearly.'

Oh, thought Rebus, you can remember clearly enough. You can remember, all right. But now Kinnoul was looking through the hallway at Cathy's still figure.

'You must think I'm a bit of a shite,' he said in a level tone. 'You're probably right. But, Christ ...' The actor had run out of words. He looked around the room, looked out of the window at what, weather willing, would have been the view, then looked towards the door again. He exhaled noisily, then shook his head.

'Did you tell the others what the prostitute told you?'

Now Kinnoul looked startled.

'I mean,' said Rebus, 'did you tell them what she said about Gregor Jack?'

'How the hell do you know about that?' Kinnoul fell onto one of the chairs.

'An inspired guess. Did you?'

'I suppose so.' He thought about it. 'Yes, definitely. Well, it was such a strange thing for her to say.'

'A strange thing for you to say, too, Mr Kinnoul.'

Kinnoul shrugged his huge shoulders. 'Just a laugh, Inspector. I was a bit pissed. I thought it would be funny to pretend to be Gregor. To be honest, I was a bit hurt that she didn't recognize Rab Kinnoul. Look at the photos on the wall. I've met all of them.' He was up on his feet again now, studying the pictures of himself, like he was in an art gallery and not seeing them for the thousandth, the ten thousandth time.

'Bob Wagner . . . Larry Hagman . . . I knew them all once.' The litany continued. 'Martin Scorsese . . . the top director, absolutely the top . . . John Hurt . . . Robbie Coltrane and Eric Idle . . .'

Holmes was motioning for Rebus to come into the hall. Cathy Kinnoul was coming round. Rab Kinnoul stood in front of his photographs, his mementoes, the list of names sloshing around in his mouth.

'Take it easy,' Holmes was telling Cathy Kinnoul. 'How do you feel?'

Her speech was slurred to incoherence.

'How many have you taken, Cathy?' Rebus asked. 'Tell us how many?'

She was trying to focus. 'I've checked all the rooms,' Holmes said. 'No sign of any empty bottles.'

'Well, she's taken something.'

'Maybe the doctor will know.'

'Yes, maybe.' Rebus leaned down close to Cathy Kinnoul, his mouth two inches from her ear. 'Gowk,' he said quietly, 'tell me about Suey.'

The names registered with her, but the question seemed not to.

'You and Suey,' Rebus went on. 'Have you been seeing Suey? Just the two of you, eh? Like the old days? Have you and Suey been seeing one another?'

239

She opened her mouth, paused, then closed it again, and slowly began to shake her head. She mumbled something.

'What was that, Gowk?'

Clearly this time: 'Rab mussn know.'

'He won't know, Gowk. Trust me, he won't know.'

She was sitting up now, holding her head in one hand while the other hand rested on the floor.

'So,' Rebus persisted, 'you and Suey have been seeing one another, eh? Gowk and Suey?'

She smiled drunkenly. 'Gow' an' Suey,' she said, enjoying the words. 'Gow' an' Suey.'

'Remember, Gowk, remember the day before you found the body? Remember that Wednesday, that Wednesday afternoon? Did Suey come and see you? Did he, Gowk? Did Suey pay a visit that Wednesday?'

'Wensay? Wensay?' She was shaking her head. 'Poor Lizzie ... poor, poor ...' Now she held her hand palm upwards. 'Gi' me th' knife,' she said. 'Rab'll never know. Gi' me th' knife.'

Rebus glanced at Holmes. 'We can't let you do that, Gowk. That would be murder.'

She nodded. 'Thas right, murder.' She said the final word very carefully, enunciating each letter, then repeated it. 'Cut off his head,' she said. 'An' they'll put me beside Mack.' She smiled again, the thought pleasing her. And all the time Rab Kinnoul's names were drifting from the other room ...

'... best, absolutely ... like to work with him again. Consummate professionalism ... and good old George Cole, too ... the old school ... yes, the old school ... the old school ...'

'Mack ...' Cathy Kinnoul was saying. 'Mack ... Suey ... Sexton ... Beggar ... Poor Beggar ...'

'The old school.'

Some school ties you just kept too long. Way after they should have been thrown out.

Rebus telephoned Barney Byars. The secretary put him through.

240

'Inspector,' came Byars' voice, all energy and business, 'I just can't shake you off, can I?'

'You're too easy to catch,' Rebus said.

Byars laughed. 'I've got to be,' he said, 'otherwise the clients can't catch me. I always like to make myself available. Now, what's your beef this time?'

'It's about an evening you spent not so long ago with Rab Kinnoul and Ronald Steele . . .'

Byars was able to substantiate the story in all but the most crucial details. Rebus explained about Kinnoul coming downstairs and repeating what Gail had said to him.

'I don't remember that,' Byars said. 'I was well on by then, mind. So well on I think I stumped up for the three of us.' He chuckled. 'Suey had his usual excuse of being flat broke, and Rab was carrying not more than ten bar by then.' Another chuckle. 'See, I always remember my sums, especially when it's money.'

'But you're sure you don't recall Mr Kinnoul telling you what the prostitute told him?'

'I'm not saying he *didn't* say it, mind, but no, I can't for the life of me remember it.'

Which made it Kinnoul's word against Byars' memory. The only thing for it was to talk to Steele again. Rebus could call in on the way to Patience's. It was a long way round for a shortcut, but it shouldn't take too long. Cathy Kinnoul was another problem. It didn't do to have knife-wielding pill-poppers running around at large. The family doctor, summoned by Holmes, had listened to their story and suggested that Mrs Kinnoul be admitted to a hospital on the outskirts of the city. Would there be any criminal charges . . .?

'Of course,' said Holmes testily. 'Attempted murder for starters.'

But Rebus was thinking. He was thinking of how badly Cath Kinnoul had been treated. Thinking, too, of all those obstruction charges he might be filing – Hector, Steele, Jack himself. And, most of all, thinking of Andrew Macmillan. He'd seen what 'special hospitals' did with the criminally insane. Cath Kinnoul would be treated anyway. So long as she underwent treatment, what was the point of pressing a charge of attempted murder on her?

So he shook his head – to Brian Holmes' astonishment. No, no charges, not if she was admitted straight away. The doctor checked that the paperwork would be a mere formality, and Kinnoul, who had come back to something like his senses by this time, agreed to the whole thing.

'In that case,' said the doctor, 'she can be admitted today.'

Rebus made one more call. To Chief Inspector Lauderdale.

'Where the hell did you disappear to?'

'It's a long story, sir.'

'It usually is.'

'How did the meeting go?'

'It went. Listen, John, we're formally charging William Glass.'

'What?'

'The Dean Bridge victim had had intercourse just before she died. Forensics tell me the DNA-test matches our man Glass.' Lauderdale paused, but Rebus said nothing. 'Don't worry, John, we'll start with the Dean Bridge murder. But really, just between us ... do you think you're getting anywhere?'

'Really, sir, just between us ... I don't know.'

'Well, you'd better get a move on, otherwise I'm going to charge Glass with Mrs Jack, too. Ferrie and that solicitor are going to start asking awkward questions any minute now. It's on a knife edge, John, understand?'

'Yes, sir, oh yes, I understand all about knife edges, believe me ...'

Rebus didn't walk up to Ronald Steele's front door – not straight away. First, he stood in front of the garage and peered in through a crack between the two doors. Steele's Citroën was at home, which presumably meant the man himself was at home. Rebus went to the door and pushed the bell. He could hear it sounding in the hall. Halls: he could write a book on them. My night sleeping in a hallway; the day I was almost stabbed in a hallway ... He rang again. It was a loud and unpleasant bell, not the kind you could easily ignore.

So he rang one more time. Then he tried the door. It was locked. He walked on to the little strip of grass running in front of the bungalow and pressed his face against the living room window. The room was empty. Maybe he'd just popped out for a pint of milk ... Rebus tried the gate to the side of the garage, the gate giving access to the back garden. It, too, was locked. He walked back to the front gate and stood beside it, looking up and down the silent street. Then he checked his watch. He could give it five minutes, ten at most. The last thing he felt like was sitting down to dinner with Patience. But he didn't want to lose her either ... Quarter of an hour to get back to Oxford Terrace ... twenty minutes to be on the safe side. Yes, he could still be there by seven thirty. Time enough. *Well, you'd better get a move on.* Why bother? Why not give Glass his moment of infamy, his second – his *famous* – victim?

Why bother with anything? Not for the praise of a pat on the back; not for the rightness of it; maybe, then, from sheer stubbornness. Yes, that would just about fit the bill. Someone was coming ... His car was pointing the wrong way, but he could see in his rearview. Not a man but a woman. Nice legs. Carrying two carrier bags of shopping. She walked well but she was tired. It couldn't be ...? What the ...?

He rolled down his window. 'Hello, Gill.'

Gill Templer stopped, stared, smiled. 'You know, I thought I recognized that heap of junk.'

'Ssh! Cars have feelings, too.' He patted the steering wheel. She put down her bags.

'What are you doing here?'

He nodded towards Steele's house. 'Waiting to talk to someone who isn't going to show.'

'Trust you.'

'What about you?'

'Me? I *live* here. Well, next street on the right to be honest. You *knew* I'd moved.'

He shrugged. 'I didn't realize it was round here.'

243

She gave him an unconvinced smile.

'No, honest,' he said. 'But now I *am* here, can I give you a lift?'

She laughed. 'It's only a hundred yards.'

'Please yourself.'

She looked down at her bags. 'Oh, go on then.'

He opened the door for her and she put the bags down on the floor, squeezing her feet in beside them. Rebus started the car. It spluttered, wheezed, died. He tried again, choke full out. The car gasped, whinnied, then got the general idea.

'Like I said, heap of junk.'

'*That's* why it's behaving like this,' Rebus warned. 'Temperamental, like a thoroughbred horse.'

But the field of an egg-and-spoon race could probably have beaten them over the distance. Finally, they reached the house unscathed. Rebus looked out.

'Nice,' he said. It was a double-fronted affair with bay windows either side of the front door. There were three floors all told, with a small and steep garden dissected by the stone steps which led from gate to doorway.

'I haven't got the whole house, of course. Just the ground floor.'

'Nice all the same.'

'Thanks.' She pushed open the door and manoeuvred her bags out on to the pavement. She gestured towards them. 'Vegetable stir-fry. Interested?'

It took him a moment's eternity to decide. 'Thanks, Gill. I'm tied up tonight.'

She had the grace to look disappointed. 'Maybe another time then.'

'Yes,' said Rebus, as she pushed the passenger door shut. 'Maybe another time.'

The car crawled back along her road. If it gives out on me, he thought, I'll go back and take her up on her offer. It'll be a sign. But the car actually began to sound healthier as it passed Steele's bungalow. There was still no sign of life, so Rebus kept going. He was thinking of a set of weighing scales. On one side sat Gill Templer, on the other Dr Patience Aitken.

The scales rose and fell, while Rebus did some hard thinking. Christ, it was hard too. He wished he had more time, but the traffic lights were with him most of the way, and he was back at Patience's by half past.

'I don't believe it,' she said as he walked into the kitchen. 'I really don't believe you actually kept a date.' She was standing beside the microwave. Inside, something was cooking. Rebus pulled her to him and gave her a wet kiss on the lips.

'Patience,' he said, 'I think I love you.'

She pulled back from him a little, the better to look at him. 'And there's not a drop of alcohol in the man either. What a night for surprises. Well, I think I should tell you that I've had a *foul* day and as a result I'm in a *foul* mood ... that's why we're eating chicken.' She smiled and kissed him. '"I think I love you,"' she mimicked. 'You should have seen the look on your face when you said that. A picture of sheer puzzlement. You're not exactly the last of the red-hot romantics, are you, John Rebus?'

'So teach me,' said Rebus, kissing her again.

'I think,' said Patience ... 'I think we'll have that chicken cold.'

He was up early next morning. More unusually, he was up before Patience herself, who lay with a satisfied, debauched look on her sleeping face and with her hair wild around her on the pillow. He let Lucky in and gave him a bigger than normal bowl of food, then made tea and toast for himself and Patience.

'Pinch me, I must be dreaming,' she said when he woke her up. She gulped at the tea, then took a small bite from one buttered triangle. Rebus half refilled his own cup, drained it, and got up from the bed.

'Right,' he said, 'I'm off.'

'What?' She looked at her clock. 'Night shift is it this week?'

'It's morning, Patience. And I've a lot on today.' He bent over her to peck her forehead, but she pulled at his tie, tugging him further down so that she could give him a salty, crumbly kiss on the mouth.

'See you later?' she asked.

'Count on it.'

'It would be nice to be able to.' But he was already on his way. Lucky came into the room and leapt on to the bed. The cat was licking his lips.

'Me too, Lucky,' said Patience. 'Me too.'

He drove straight to Ronald Steele's bungalow. The traffic was heavy coming into town, but Rebus was heading out. It wasn't yet quite eight. He didn't take Steele for an early riser. This was a grim anniversary: two weeks to the day since Liz Jack was murdered. Time to get things straight.

Steele's car was still in its garage. Rebus went to the front door and pressed the bell, attempting a jaunty rhythm of rings – a friend, or the postman ... someone you'd want to open your door to.

'Come on, Suey, chop-chop.'

But there was no answer. He peered through the letter box. Nothing. He looked in through the living room window. Exactly as it had been yesterday evening. The curtains hadn't even been pulled shut. No sign of life.

'I hope you haven't done a runner,' Rebus muttered. Though maybe it would be better if he *had*. At least it would be an action of some kind, a sign of fear or of something to hide. He could ask the neighbours if they'd seen anything, but a wall separated Steele's bungalow from theirs. He decided against it. It might only serve to alert Steele to Rebus's interest, an interest strong enough to bring him here at breakfast time. Instead, he got back into the car and drove to Suey Books. A hundred-to-one shot this. As he'd suspected, the shop was barred and meshed and padlocked. Rasputin lay asleep in the window. Rebus made a fist and pounded it against the glass. The cat's head shot up and it let out a sharp, shocked yowl.

'Remember me?' said Rebus, grinning.

Traffic was slower now, treacle through the sieve of the

road system. He slipped down on to the Cowgate to avoid the worst of it. If Steele couldn't be found, there was only one thing for it. He'd have to change Farmer Watson's mind. What's more, he'd have to do it this morning, while the old boy was bristling with caffeine. Now there was a thought . . . what time did that deli just off Leith Walk open . . . ?

'Well thank you, John.'

Rebus shrugged. 'We drink enough of *your* coffee, sir. I just thought it was time someone else did the buying for a change.'

Watson opened the bag and sniffed. 'Mmm, freshly ground.' He started to tip the dark powder into his filter. The machine was already full of water. 'What kind did you say?'

'Breakfast blend, sir, I think. Robustica and Arabica . . . something like that. I'm not exactly an expert . . .'

But Watson waved the apology aside. He put the jug in position and flipped the switch. 'Takes a couple of minutes,' he said, sitting down behind his desk. 'Right, John.' He put his hands together in front of him. 'What can I do for you?'

'Well, sir, it's about Gregor Jack.'

'Yes . . . ?'

'You know how you told me we'd to help Mr Jack if possible? How you felt he'd perhaps been set up?' Watson merely nodded. 'Well, sir, I'm close to proving not only that he was, but *who* did it.'

'Oh? Go on.'

So Rebus told his story, the story of a chance meeting in a red-lit bedroom. And of three men. 'What I was wondering was . . . I know you said you couldn't divulge your source, sir . . . but was it one of them?'

Watson shook his head. 'Way off, I'm afraid, John. Mmm, do you smell that?' The room was filling with the aroma. How could Rebus *not* smell it?

'Yes, sir, very nice. So it wasn't – ?'

'It wasn't anyone who *knows* Gregor Jack. If pro – ' He stuttered to a halt. 'Can't wait for that coffee,' he said, rather too eagerly.

'You were about to say, sir?' But what? What? Providence? Provost? Prodigal? Problem?

Provost? No, no. Not provost. Protestant? Proprietor? A name or a title.

'Nothing, John, nothing. I wonder if I've any clean cups . . .?'

A name or a title. Professor. *Professor!*

'You weren't about to mention a professor then?'

Watson's lips were sealed. But Rebus was thinking fast now.

'Professor Costello, for instance. He's a friend of yours, isn't he, sir? He doesn't know Mr Jack then?'

Watson's ears were turning red. Got you, thought Rebus. Got you, got you, got you. That coffee was worth every last penny.

'Interesting though,' mused Rebus, 'that the Professor would know about a brothel.'

Watson slapped the desk. 'Enough.' His light morning mood had vanished. His whole face was red now, except for two small white patches, one on either cheek. 'All right,' he said. 'You might as well know, it *was* Professor Costello who told me.'

'And how did the Professor know?'

'He said . . . he *said* he had a *friend* who'd visited the place one night, and now felt ashamed. Of course,' Watson lowered his voice to a hiss, 'there isn't any *friend*. It's the old chap himself. He just can't bring himself to admit it. Well,' his voice rising again, 'we're all tempted some time, aren't we?' Rebus thought of Gill Templer last night. Yes, tempted indeed. 'So I promised the Professor I'd have the place closed down.'

Rebus was thoughtful. 'And did you let him know when Operation Creeper was set for?'

It was Watson's turn to be thoughtful. Then he nodded. 'But he's . . . he's a *professor* . . . of *divinity*. He wouldn't have been the one to tip off the papers. And he doesn't *know* Gregor bloody Jack.'

'But you told him? Date *and* time?'

'More or less.'

'Why? Why did he need to know?'

'His "friend" ... The "friend" needed to know so he could warn anyone he knew from going there.'

Rebus leapt to his feet. 'Jesus Christ, sir!' He paused. 'With respect. But don't you see? There *was* a friend. There *was* someone who needed to be warned. But not so they could stop their friends being caught ... so they could *ensure* Gregor Jack walked straight into the trap. As soon as they knew when we were going in, all they had to do was phone Jack and tell him his sister was there. They knew he couldn't *not* go and check it out for himself.' He tugged open the door.

'Where are you off to?'

'To see Professor Costello. Not that I need to, not really, but I want to hear him say the name, I want to hear it for myself. Enjoy your coffee, sir.'

But Watson didn't. It tasted like charred wood. Too bitter, too strong. For some time now he'd been wavering; now he made the decision. He'd stop drinking coffee altogether. It would be his penance. Just like Inspector John Rebus was his comforter ...

'Good morning, Inspector.'

'Morning, sir. Not disturbing you?'

Professor Costello waved his arm airily around the empty room. 'Not a student in Edinburgh's awake at this – to them – ungodly hour. Not the divinity students at any rate. No, Inspector, you're not disturbing me.'

'You got the books all right, sir?'

Costello pointed towards his glass-fronted bookshelves. 'Safe and sound. The officer who delivered them said something about them being found abandoned ...?'

'Something like that, sir.' Rebus glanced back at the door. 'You haven't had a proper lock fitted yet.'

'*Mea culpa*, Inspector. Fear not, one's on its way.'

'Only I wouldn't like you to lose your books again ...'

'Point taken, Inspector. Sit down, won't you? Coffee?' The hand this time was directed towards an evil-looking percolator sitting smoking on a hotplate in a corner of the room.

'No thanks, sir. Bit early for me.'

Costello bowed his head slightly. He slid into the comfortable leather chair behind his comfortable oaken desk. Rebus sat on one of the modern, spindly metal-framed chairs the other side of it. 'So, Inspector, social niceties dispensed with . . . what can I do for you?'

'You gave some information to Chief Superintendent Watson, sir.'

Costello pursed his lips. 'Confidential information, Inspector.'

'At one time perhaps, but it may help us with a murder inquiry.'

'Surely not!'

Rebus nodded. 'So you see, sir, that changes things slightly. We need to know who your "friend" was, the one who told you about the . . . er . . .'

'I believe the phrase is "hoor-hoose". Almost poetic, much nicer at any rate than "brothel".' Costello almost squirmed in his chair. 'My friend, Inspector, I did promise him . . .'

'Murder, sir. I'd advise against withholding information.'

'Oh yes, agreed, agreed. But one's conscience . . .'

'Was it Ronald Steele?'

Costello's eyes opened wide. 'Then you already know.'

'Just an inspired guess, sir. You're a frequent customer in his shop, aren't you?'

'Well, I do like to browse . . .'

'And you were in his shop when he told you.'

'That's right. It was a lunchtime. Vanessa, his assistant, she was on her break. She's a student here, actually. Lovely girl . . .'

If only you knew, thought Rebus.

'Anyway, yes, Ronald told me his little guilty secret. He'd been taken to this hoor-hoose one night by some friends. He really was *very* embarrassed about it all.'

'Was he?'

'Oh, terribly. He knew I knew Superintendent Watson, and he wondered if I could pass word on about the establishment.'

'So we could close it down?'

'Yes.'

'But he needed to know the night?'

'He was *desperate* to know. His friends, you see, the ones who'd taken him. He wanted to warn them off.'

'You know Mr Steele is a friend of Gregor Jack's?'

'Who?'

'The MP.'

'I'm sorry, the name doesn't ... Gregor Jack?' Costello frowned, shook his head. 'No.'

'He's been in all the newspapers.'

'Really?'

Rebus sighed. The real world, it seemed, stopped at the door to Costello's office. This was a lighter realm altogether. He was almost startled by the sudden electronic twittering of the high-tech telephone. Costello apologized and picked up the receiver.

'Yes? Speaking. Yes, he is. Wait one moment, please.' He held the receiver out towards Rebus. 'It's for you, Inspector.' Somehow, Rebus wasn't surprised ...

'Hello?'

'The Chief Superintendent said I'd find you there.' It was Lauderdale.

'Good morning to you too, sir.'

'Cut the crap, John. I'm just in and already a bit of the ceiling's fallen off and missed my head by inches. I'm not in the mood for it okay?'

'Understood, sir.'

'I'm only phoning because I thought you'd be interested.'

'Yes, sir?'

'Forensics didn't take long with those two glasses you found in Mr Pond's bathroom.'

Of course they didn't. They had all the match-up prints they needed, taken so as to eliminate people from Deer Lodge.

'Guess who they belong to?' Lauderdale asked.

'One set will be Mrs Jack, the other set Ronald Steele.'

There was silence on the other end of the telephone.

'Was I close?' asked Rebus.

'How the hell did you know?'

251

'What if I told you it was an inspired guess?'
'I'd tell you you're a liar. Get back here. We need to talk.'
'Right you are, sir. Just one more thing . . .?'
'What?'
'Mr Glass . . . is he still on for the double?'
The line went dead.

12
Escort Service

The way Rebus saw it . . .

Well, it didn't take too much brain activity once the name had been established. The way he saw it, Ronald Steele and Elizabeth Jack had been lovers, probably for some time. (Christ, Sir Hugh was going to *love* this when it came out.) Maybe nobody knew. Maybe everybody but Gregor Jack knew. Anyway, Liz Jack decided to head north, and Steele joined her whenever he could. (Deer Lodge and back every day? A superhuman effort. No wonder Steele looked ready to drop all the time . . .) Deer Lodge itself though was a tip, a heap. So they moved into Pond's cottage, only using Deer Lodge itself for fetching changes of clothes. Maybe Liz Jack had been fetching clean clothes when she'd stopped and bought the Sunday rags . . . and found out all about her husband's apparently naughty night.

Steele, though, had plans way above the occasional legover scenario. He wanted Liz. He *wanted* her to himself. The quiet ones always got intense about that sort of thing, didn't they? He'd been making anonymous calls maybe. And sending letters. Anything to throw a spanner in the works of the marriage, anything to unsettle Gregor. Maybe that's why Liz had headed north, to get away from it all. Steele saw his chance. He'd already been to the brothel, and he'd already discovered just who Gail Crawley was. (All it took was a halfway decent memory, and maybe a question or two asked of the likes of Cathy Kinnoul.) Ah, Cathy . . . Yes, maybe Steele *was* seeing her too. But Rebus doubted it was for anything but conversation and counselling. There was that side to Steele, too.

Which didn't do anything to stop him trying to strip Gregor Jack, his lifelong friend, ally in his bookshop, all-round good guy, to strip him completely and utterly naked. The brothel plan was simple and knife-sharp. Find out the time of the planned raid . . . a call to Gregor Jack . . . and calls beforehand to the Docklands dirt-diggers.

The set-up. And Gregor Jack shed his first layer.

Did Steele try to keep it from Liz? Maybe, maybe not. He thought it would be the final screw in the marriage-coffin. It nearly was. But he couldn't be north with her all the time, telling her how great they could be together, what a shit Gregor was, et cetera, et cetera. And during the time she was alone, Liz Jack wavered, until finally she made up her mind not to leave Gregor but to leave Steele. Something like that. She was unpredictable after all. She was fire. And they argued. In his interview, he'd alluded to the argument itself: *She always accused me of not being enough fun . . . and I never had enough money either* . . . So they argued, and he stormed off, leaving her in the lay-by. Alec Corbie's blue car had been a green car, the green Citroën BX. Steele had sped off, only to return and continue the argument, an argument which became violent, violence which went a little too far . . .

The next bit was, to Rebus's mind, the cleverest, either that or the most fortuitous. Steele had to dump the body. The first thing to do was to get it away from the Highlands: there were too many clues up there to the fact that they'd spent time together. So he headed back towards Edinburgh with her in the boot. But what to do with her? Wait, there had been another killing, hadn't there? A body dumped in a river. He could make it look the same. Better still, he could send her body out to sea. So he headed for someplace he knew: the hill above the Kinnoul house. He'd walked up there with Cathy so many times. He knew the small road, a road never used. And he knew that even if the body *were* found, the first suspect would be the Dean Bridge killer. So, at some point, he gave her that blow to the head, the blow so like the one administered to the Dean Bridge victim.

And the beautiful irony was: his alibi for the afternoon was provided by Gregor Jack himself.

'And that's how you see it, is it?'

The meeting was in Watson's office: Watson, Lauderdale and Rebus. On the way in, Rebus had passed Brian Holmes.

'I hear there's a meeting in the Farmhouse.'

'You've got good hearing.'

'What's it about?'

'You mean you're not on the guest list, Brian?' Rebus winked. 'Too bad. I'll try to bring you a doggie-bag.'

'Big of you.'

Rebus turned. 'Look, Brian, the paint's hardly dry on your promotion as it is. Relax, take it easy. If you're looking for a quick road to Detective Inspector, go track down Lord Lucan. Meantime, I'm expected elsewhere, okay?'

'Okay.'

Too cocky by half, thought Rebus. But speaking of cocky, he was doing a bit of strutting himself, wasn't he? Sitting here in Watson's office, spouting forth, while Lauderdale looked worriedly towards his suddenly caffeine-free superior.

'And that's how you see it, is it?' The question was Watson's. Rebus merely shrugged.

'It sounds plausible,' said Lauderdale. Rebus raised half an eyebrow: having Lauderdale's support was a bit like locking yourself in with a starved alsatian . . .

'What about Mr Glass?' asked Watson.

'Well, sir,' said Lauderdale, shifting a little in his seat, 'psychiatric reports don't show him to be the most stable individual. He lives in a sort of fantasy world, you might say.'

'You mean he made it up?'

'Very probably.'

'Which brings us back to Mr Steele. I think we'd better have him in for a word, hadn't we. Did you say you brought him in yesterday, John?'

'That's right, sir. I thought we might give the boot of his

car a once-over. But Mr Lauderdale seemed convinced by Steele's story and let him go.'

The look on Lauderdale's face would remain long in Rebus's memory. Man bites alsatian.

'Is that so?' said Watson, also seeming to enjoy Lauderdale's discomfort.

'We'd no reason to hold him *then*, sir. It's only information received this morning which has allowed us – '

'All right, all right. So have we picked him up again?'

'He's not at home, sir,' said Rebus. 'I checked last night and then again this morning.'

Both men looked at him. Watson's look said: Very efficient. Lauderdale's look said: You bastard.

'Well,' said Watson, 'we'd better get a warrant out, hadn't we? I think there's quite enough that needs explaining by Mr Steele.'

'His car's still in its garage, sir. We could get forensics to take a look at it. Most probably he'll have cleaned it, but you never know . . .'

Forensics? They loved Rebus. He was their patron saint.

'Right you are, John,' said Watson. 'See to it, will you?' He turned to Lauderdale. 'Another cup of coffee? There's plenty in the pot, and you seem to be the only one drinking it . . .'

Strut, strut, strut. He was the little red rooster. He was the cock of the north. He'd felt it all along, of course: Ronald Steele. Suey, who had once tried to commit suicide when found by a girl masturbating in his hotel room.

'Bound to be a bit screwed up.' Who needed a psychology degree? What Rebus needed now was a combination of orienteering skills and old-fashioned man-hunting. His instincts told him that Steele would have headed south, leaving the car behind. (What use was it, after all? The police already had its description and licence number, and he'd known they were closing in. Or rather, he'd known *Rebus* was closing in.)

'Ain't nothing but a bloodhound,' he sang to himself. He'd just phoned the hospital where Cathy Kinnoul was now a patient. Early days, he'd been told, but she'd had a peaceful night. Rab Kinnoul, however, hadn't been near. Maybe this was understandable. It could be that she'd go for him with a broken water jug or try to strangle him with pyjama cord. All the same, Kinnoul was as shitty as the rest of them. Gregor Jack, too, risking all for a career in politics, a career he'd planned from birth, it seemed. Marrying Liz Ferrie not for herself but for her father. Completely unable to control her, so that he just stuffed her into a compartment, dusting her off for photo-shoots and the occasional public engagement. Yes, shitty. Only one person, to Rebus's mind, came out of this with anything like dignity intact, and that person was a burglar.

The forensics team had come up with a match for the prints on the microwave: Julian Kaymer. He'd swiped Jamie Kilpatrick's keys and driven to Deer Lodge in the dead of night, smashing the window to gain entry.

Why? To tidy away evidence of anything *too* scandalous. Which meant the cocaine-stained hand-mirror and two pairs of tights tied to a four-poster. Why? Simple: to protect what he could of a friend's reputation ... a dead friend's reputation. Pathetic, but noble, too, in a way. Stealing the microwave was outrageous really. PC Plod was supposed to put the whole thing down to kids, smashing their way into an empty house on the off-chance ... and making off not with the hi-fi (always a favourite), but with the microwave. He'd driven off with it, then thrown it away, only to have it found by the magpie himself, Alec Corbie.

Yes, Steele would be in London by now. His shop operated in the sphere of cash. There would have been some hidden somewhere; perhaps quite a lot. He might be on a flight out of Heathrow or Gatwick, a train to the coast and the boat over to France.

'Trains and boats and planes . . .'

'Somebody sounds happy.' It was Brian Holmes, standing in the doorway to Rebus's office. Rebus was seated at his desk, feet resting on the desk itself, hands behind his head.

'Mind if I come in, or do we need to reserve tickets to touch your hem?'

'You leave my hem out of this. Sit down.' Holmes was halfway to the chair when he tripped over a gash in the linoleum. He put his hands out to save himself, and found himself sprawled on Rebus's desktop, an inch from one of the shoes.

'Yes,' said Rebus, 'you may kiss them.'

Holmes managed something between a smile and a grimace. 'This place really should be condemned.' He slumped into the chair.

'Mind out for the shoogly leg,' warned Rebus. 'Any progress on Steele?'

'Not much.' Holmes paused. 'None at all, really. Why didn't he take his car?'

'We know it too well, remember? I thought *you* were responsible for putting together that list? Everybody in the world's car make, colour and registration number. Oh no, I forgot, you delegated the work to a detective constable.'

'What was it for anyway?' Rebus stared at him. 'Seriously. I'm just a *sergeant*, as you'll recall. Nobody tells me anything. Lauderdale was vaguer even than usual.'

'Mrs Jack's BMW was parked in a lay-by,' explained Rebus.

'That much I knew.'

'So was another car. An eye witness said it might be blue. It wasn't, it was green.'

'That reminds me,' said Holmes, 'I meant to ask you: what was she waiting around for?'

'Who?'

'Mrs Jack. At that lay-by, what was she hanging around there for?' While Rebus considered this, Holmes thought of another question. 'What about *Mr* Jack's car?'

Rebus sighed. 'What about it?'

'Well, I didn't get a good look at it that night you dragged me out there . . . I mean, it was in the garage, and there were lights to the front and back of the house, but not to the side. But you did say to have a snoop. The side door to the garage was open, so I wandered in. Too dark really, and I couldn't find the light switch . . .'

'Jesus Christ, Brian, get on with it!'

'Well, I was only going to ask: what about the car in Jack's garage? It was blue. At least, I *think* it was blue.'

This time, Rebus rubbed his temples. 'It's white,' he explained, slowly. 'It's a white Saab.'

But Holmes was shaking his head. 'Blue,' he said. 'It could never have been white, it was blue. And it was an Escort, *definitely* an Escort.'

Rebus stopped rubbing his temples. 'What?'

'There was some stuff on the passenger seat, too. I peered in through the side window. All that bumpf they give you with hire cars. That sort of thing. Yes, the more I think back on it, the clearer it comes. A blue Ford Escort. And whatever else was in that garage, there certainly wasn't room to swing a Saab . . .'

No rooster now, no strutting cock, no bloodhound. But rather cowed, sheepish, with his tail between his legs . . . Rebus took Holmes and his story to Watson first, and Watson called for Lauderdale.

'I thought,' Lauderdale said to Rebus, 'you told us Mr Jack's car was *white*?'

'It *is* white, sir.'

'You're sure it was a hire car?' Watson asked Holmes. Holmes thought again before nodding. This was serious. He was where he wanted to be, in the thick of things, but he was realizing, too, that here one mistake – one slightest error – could send him to limbo.

'We can check,' said Rebus.

'How?'

'Phone Gregor Jack's house and ask.'

'And warn him off?'

'We don't have to talk to *Jack*. Ian Urquhart or Helen Greig would know.'

'They could still tip him off.'

'Maybe. Of course, there's another possibility. The car Brian saw could have been Urquhart's or even Miss Greig's.'

'Miss Greig doesn't drive,' said Holmes. 'And Urquhart's car's nothing like the one I saw. Remember, they've all been checked.'

'Well, whatever,' said Watson, 'let's tread carefully, eh? Get on to the hire firms first.'

'What about Steele?' Rebus asked.

'Until we know what we're dealing with, we still want to talk to him.'

'Agreed,' said Lauderdale. He seemed aware that Watson was back in control, at least for now.

'Well,' said Watson, 'what are you all waiting for? Jump to it!'

They jumped.

There weren't that many hire firms in Edinburgh, and the third call brought a result. Yes, Mr Jack had hired a car for a few days. Yes, a blue Ford Escort. Did he give any reason for the hire? Yes, his own car was going in for a service.

And, thought Rebus, he needed a change of cars so he could escape the attentions of the press. Christ, hadn't Rebus put the idea into his head himself? Your car's out there ... being photographed ... everyone'll know what it looks like. So Jack had hired another car for a few days, just to help him get around incognito.

Rebus stared at the office wall. Stupid, stupid, stupid. He would have banged his head against the wall if he could have been sure it wouldn't fall down ...

It had been a devil of a job, the man from the hire firm said. The client had wanted his car-phone transferred from his own car to the hire car.

Of course: how else could Liz Jack have contacted him? He had been on the move all day, hadn't he?

Had the hire car been cleaned since its return? Naturally, a full valet service. What about the boot? The boot? The boot, had it been cleaned too? A bit of a wipe maybe ... Where was the car now? On hire again, a London business-man. A forty-eight-hour hire only, and due back by six o'clock. It was now a quarter to five. Two CID men would be waiting to drive it from the car-hire offices to the police pound. Were there any forensics people available at Fettes HQ . . .?

Stupid, stupid, stupid. Not the same car returning to the lay-by, but another car. Holmes had asked the question: what had Liz Jack been waiting for? She'd been waiting for her husband. She must have telephoned him from the box in the lay-by. She'd just had the argument with Steele. Too upset to drive herself home maybe. So he'd told her to wait there and he'd pick her up. He had a free afternoon anyway. He'd pick her up in the blue Escort. But when he'd arrived there had been another argument. About what? It could have been anything. What would it take to smash the ice that was Gregor Jack? The original newspaper story? The police finding evidence of his wife's lifestyle? Shame and embarrassment? The thought of further public scrutiny, of losing his precious constituency?

There was enough there to be going on with.

'Okay,' said Lauderdale, 'so we've got the car. Let's see if Jack's at home.' He turned to Rebus. 'You phone, John.'

Rebus phoned. Helen Greig answered.

'Hello, Miss Greig. It's Inspector Rebus.'

'He's not here,' she blurted out. 'I haven't seen him all day, or yesterday come to that.'

'But he's not in London?'

'We don't know where he is. He was with you yesterday morning, wasn't he?'

'He came into the station, yes.'

'Ian's going up the wall.'

'What about the Saab?'

'It's not here either. Hold on . . .' She placed her hand over the mouthpiece, but not very effectively. 'It's that Inspector Rebus,' he heard her say. Then a frantic hiss: 'Don't tell him anything!' And Helen again: 'Too late, Ian.' Followed by a sort of snarl. She removed her hand.

'Miss Greig,' said Rebus, 'how has Gregor seemed?'

'Same as you might expect of a man whose wife's been murdered.'

'And how's that?'

'Depressed. He's been sitting around in the living room, just staring into space, not saying much. Like he was thinking. Funny, the only time I got a conversation out of him was when he asked me about last year's holiday.'

'The one you went on with your mum?'

'Yes.'

'Remind me, where did you go again?'

'Down the coast,' she said. 'Eyemouth, round there.'

Yes, of course. Jack had uttered the name of the first town that had come to mind. Then he'd pumped Helen for details so he could prop up his rickety story . . .

He put down the receiver.

'Well?' asked Watson.

'His car's gone, and Gregor Jack with it. All that stuff he told us about Eyemouth . . . eye *wash* more like . . . he got it all from his secretary. She went there on holiday last year.'

The room was stuffy, the late afternoon outside preparing itself for thunder. Watson spoke first.

'What a mess.'

'Yes,' said Lauderdale.

Holmes nodded. He was a relieved man; more than that, inwardly he was rejoicing: the hire car had turned out to be fact. He'd proved his worth.

'What now?'

'I'm just thinking,' said Rebus, 'about that lay-by. Liz Jack has an argument with Steele. She tells him she's going back to her husband. Steele buggers off. What's the next he hears of her?'

'That she's dead,' answered Holmes.

Rebus nodded. Throwing all those books around the shop in his grief and his anger . . . 'Not only dead, but murdered. And the *last* he saw of her, she was waiting for Gregor.'

'So,' said Watson, 'he must know Jack did it? Is that what you're suggesting?'

'You think,' Lauderdale said, 'Steele's run off to *protect* Gregor Jack?'

'I don't think anything of the sort,' said Rebus. 'But *if* Gregor Jack is the murderer, then Ronald Steele has known for some time that he is. Why hasn't he done anything? Think about it: how could he come to the police? He was in way too deep himself. It would mean explaining everything, and explaining it would make him if anything a bigger suspect than Gregor Jack himself!'

'So what *would* he do?'

Rebus shrugged. 'He might try persuading Jack to come forward.'

'But that would mean admitting to Jack that –'

'Exactly, that *he* was Elizabeth Jack's lover. What would you do in Jack's position?'

Holmes dared to supply the answer. 'I'd kill him. I'd kill Ronald Steele.'

Rebus sat all that evening in Patience's living room, an arm around her as they both watched a video. A romantic comedy; only there wasn't much romance and precious little comedy. You knew from reel one that the secretary would go off with the bucktoothed student and not with her bloodsucking boss. But you kept on watching anyway. Not that he was taking much of it in. He was thinking about Gregor Jack, about the person he'd seemed to be and the person he really was. You peeled away layer after layer, stripped the man to the bone and beyond ... and never found the truth. Strip Jack Naked: a card game, also known as Beggar my Neighbour. Patience was a card game, too. He stroked her neck, her hair, her forehead.

'That's nice.'

Patience was a game easily won.

The film rolled past him. Another foil had entered the picture, a big-hearted con man. Rebus had yet to meet a con man in real life who was anything but the most predatory shark. What was the phrase? – they'd steal your false teeth and drink the water out of the glass. Well, maybe *this* con man was in with a chance. The secretary was interested, but she was loyal to her boss too, and *he* was doing everything short of whipping his sausage out and slapping it on her desk . . .

'A penny for them.'

'They're not worth it, Patience.' They'd find Steele, they'd find Jack. Why couldn't he relax? He kept thinking of a set of clothes and a note, left on a beach. Stonehouse. Lucan had done it, hadn't he, disappeared without trace? It wasn't easy, but all the same . . .

The next thing he knew, Patience was shaking him by the shoulder.

'Wake up, John. Time for bed.'

He'd been asleep for an hour. 'The con man or the student?' he asked.

'Neither,' she said. 'The boss changed his ways and gave her a partnership in the firm. Now come on, partner . . .' She held her hands out to help him up on to his feet. 'After all, tomorrow *is* another day . . .'

Another day, another dolour. Thursday. Two weeks since they'd found Elizabeth Jack's body. Now all they could do was wait . . . and hope no more bodies turned up. Rebus picked up his office phone. It was Lauderdale.

'The Chief Super's bitten the bullet,' he told Rebus. 'We're holding a press conference, putting out wanteds on both of them, Steele and Jack.'

'Does Sir Hugh know yet?'

'I wouldn't want to be the one who tells him. He marches in here with his son-in-law, not knowing the bugger killed his daughter? No, I wouldn't want to be the one who tells him.'

'Am I supposed to be there?'

'Of course, and bring Holmes, too. After all, *he's* the one who spotted the car . . .'

The line went dead. Rebus stared at the receiver. Alsatian bites man after all . . .

*

Spotted it *and* told Nell about it all last night. Repeating the story, adding missed details, hardly able to sit down. Until she'd screeched at him to stop or else she'd go off her head. That calmed him down a little, but not much.

'You see, Nell, if they'd told me earlier, if they'd let me in on the whole story of the car colours, of *why* they were needed, well, we'd have nailed him all the sooner, wouldn't we? I don't want to, but really I blame John. It was him who . . .'

'I thought you said it was Lauderdale who gave you the job in the first place?'

'Yes, true, but even so John should have – '

'Shut up! For God's sake, just shut up!'

'Mind you, you're right, Laud – '

'*Shut up!*'

He shut up.

And now here he was at the press conference, and there was Inspector Gill Templer, who had such a rapport with the press, handing out sheets of paper – the official release – and generally making sure that everyone knew what was going on. And Rebus, of course, looking the same as ever. Which was to say, tired and suspicious. Watson and Lauderdale hadn't made their entrance yet, but would do so soon.

'Well, Brian,' said Rebus quietly, 'reckon they'll promote you to Inspector for this?'

'No.'

'What then? You look like a kid who's about to get the school prize.'

'Come on, be fair. We all know you did most of the work.'

'Yes, but *you* stopped me haring after the wrong man.'

'So?'

'So now I owe you a favour.' Rebus grinned. 'I *hate* owing favours.'

'Ladies and gentlemen,' came Gill Templer's voice, 'if you'll find yourselves a seat we can start . . .'

A moment later Watson and Lauderdale entered the room. Watson was first to speak.

'I think you all know why we've called this conference.' He

paused. 'We're looking for two men we think may be able to help us with a certain inquiry, a murder inquiry. The names are Ronald Adam Steele and Gregor Gordon Jack . . .'

The local evening paper had it in by its lunchtime edition. The radio stations were broadcasting the names in their hourly news slots. The early evening TV news carried the story. The usual questions were being asked, to which the usual 'no comment's were being appended. But the phone call itself came only at half past six. The call was from Dr Frank Forster.

'I'd have known sooner, Inspector, only we don't like to let the patients listen to the news. It just upsets them. It's only when I was getting ready to go home that I turned on the radio in my office . . .'

Rebus was tired. Rebus was terribly, terribly tired. 'What is it, Dr Forster?'

'It's your man Jack, Gregor Jack. He was here this afternoon. He was visiting Andrew Macmillan.'

13
Hot-Head

It was nine that evening when Rebus reached Duthil Hospital. Andrew Macmillan was sitting in Forster's office, arms folded, waiting.

'Hello again,' he said.

'Hello, Mr Macmillan.'

There were five of them: two 'nurses', Dr Forster, Macmillan and Rebus. The nurses stood behind Macmillan's chair, their bodies less than two inches from his.

'We've sedated him,' Forster had explained to Rebus. 'He may not be as talkative as usual, but he should stay calm. I heard about what happened last time . . .'

'Nothing happened last time, Dr Forster. He just wanted to have a normal conversation. What's wrong with that?'

Macmillan looked on the verge of sleep. His eyes were heavy-lidded, his smile fixed. He unfolded his arms and rested the hands delicately on his knees, reminding Rebus at that moment of Mrs Corbie . . .

'Inspector Rebus wants to ask you about Mr Jack,' explained Forster.

'That's right,' said Rebus, resting against the edge of the desk. There was a chair for him, but he was stiff after the drive. 'I was wondering why he visited. It's unusual after all, isn't it?'

'It's a first,' corrected Macmillan. 'They should put up a plaque. When I saw him come in, I thought he must be here to open an extension or something. But no, he just walked right up to me . . .' His hands were moving now, carving air, his eyes held by the movements they made. 'Walked right up to *me*, and he said ... he said, "Hello, Mack." Just like that. Like we'd seen one another the day before, like we saw one another *every* day.'

'What did you talk about?'

'Old friends. Yes, old friends ... old friend*ships*. We'd always be friends, he told me. We couldn't *not* be friends. We went back *all the way*. Yes, all the way back ... All of us. Suey and Gowk, Beggar and me, Bilbo, Tampon, Sexton Blake ... Friends are important, that's what he said. I told him about Gowk, about how she visited sometimes ... about the money she gives this place ... He didn't know about any of that. He was interested. He works too hard though, you can see that. He doesn't look healthy any more. Not enough sunlight. Have you ever seen the House of Commons? Hardly any windows. They work away in there like moles ...'

'Did he say anything else?'

'I asked him why he never answered my letters. Do you know what he said? He said he *never even received them!* He said he'd take it up with the post office, but I know who it is.' He turned to Forster. 'It's you, Dr Forster. You're not letting out any of my mail. You're steaming off the stamps and using them for yourself! Well, be warned, Gregor Jack MP knows all about it now. Something'll be done now.' He remembered something and turned quickly to Rebus. 'Did you touch the earth for me?'

Rebus nodded. 'I touched the earth for you.'

Macmillan nodded too, satisfied. 'How did it feel, Inspector?'

'It felt fine. Funny, it's something I've always taken for granted – '

'Never take *anything* for granted, Inspector,' said Macmillan. He was calming a little. All the same, you could see him fighting against the soporifics in his bloodstream, fighting for the right to get angry, to get ... to get mad. 'I asked him about Liz,' he said. 'He told me she's the same as ever. But I didn't believe *that*. I'm sure their marriage is in trouble. In-com-pat-ible. My wife and I were just the same ...' His voice trailed off. He swallowed, laid his hands flat against his knees again and studied them. 'Liz was never one of The Pack. He should have married Gowk, only Kinnoul got to her first.' He looked up. 'Now *there's* a man who needs treatment. If Gowk knew what she was about, she'd have him see a psychiatrist. All those roles he's played . . . bound to have an effect, aren't they? I'll tell Gowk next time I see her. I haven't seen her for a while . . .'

Rebus shifted his weight a little. 'Did Beggar say anything else, Mack? Anything about where he was headed or why he was here?'

Macmillan shook his head. Then he sniggered. 'Headed, did you say? *Headed?*' He chuckled to himself for a few moments, then stopped as abruptly as he'd started. 'He just wanted to let me know we were friends.' He laughed quietly. 'As if I needed reminding. And one other thing. Guess what he wanted to know? Guess what he asked? After all these years . . .'

'What?'

'He wanted to know what I'd done with her head.'

Rebus swallowed. Forster was licking his lips. 'And what did you tell him, Mack?'

'I told him the truth. I told him I couldn't remember.' He brought the palms of his hands together as if in prayer and touched the fingertips to his lips. Then he closed his eyes. The eyes were still closed when he spoke. 'Is it true about Suey?'

'What about him, Mack?'

'That he's emigrated, that he might not be coming back?'

'Is that what Beggar told you?'

Macmillan nodded, opening his eyes to gaze at Rebus. 'He said Suey might not be coming back . . .'

The nurses had taken Macmillan back to his ward, and Forster was putting on his coat, getting ready to lock up and see Rebus out to the car park, when the telephone rang.

'At this time of night?'

'It might be for me,' said Rebus. He picked up the receiver. 'Hello?'

It was DS Knox from Dufftown. 'Inspector Rebus? I did as you said and had someone stake out Deer Lodge.'

'And?'

'A white Saab drove in through the gateway not ten minutes ago.'

There were two cars parked by the side of the road. One of them was blocking the entrance to Deer Lodge's long driveway. Rebus got out of his own car. DS Knox introduced him to Detective Constable Wright and Constable Moffat.

'We've already met,' Rebus said, shaking Moffat's hand.

'Oh yes,' said Knox. 'How could I forget, you've been keeping us so busy? So, what do you think, sir?'

Rebus thought it was cold. Cold and wet. It wasn't raining now, but any minute it might be on again. 'You've called for reinforcements?'

Knox nodded. 'As many as can be mustered.'

'Well, we could wait it out till they arrive.'

'Yes?'

Rebus was sizing Knox up. He didn't seem the kind of man who enjoyed waiting. 'Or,' he said, 'we could go in, three of us, one standing guard on the gate. After all, he's either got a corpse or a hostage in there. If Steele's alive, the sooner we go in, the better chance he's got.'

'So what are we waiting for?'

Rebus looked to DC Wright and Constable Moffat, who nodded approval of the plan.

'It's a long walk up to the house, mind,' Knox was saying.

'But if we take a car, he's bound to hear it.'

'We can take one up so far and walk the rest,' suggested Moffat. 'That way the exit road's good and blocked. I wouldn't fancy wandering up that bloody road in the dark only to have him come racing towards me in that car of his.'

'Okay, agreed, we'll take a car.' Rebus turned to DC Wright. 'You stay on the gate, son. Moffat here knows the layout of the house.' Wright looked snubbed, but Moffat perked up at the news. 'Right,' said Rebus, 'let's go.'

*

They took Knox's car, leaving Moffat's parked across the entrance. Knox had taken one look at Rebus's heap and then shaken his head.

'Best take mine, eh?'

He drove slowly, Rebus in the front beside him, Moffat in the back. The car had a nice quiet engine, but all the same . . . all around was silence. Any noise would travel. Rebus actually began to pray for a sudden storm, thunder and rain, for anything that would give them sound-cover.

'I enjoyed that book,' said Moffat, his head just behind Rebus's.

'What book?'

'*Fish Out of Water*.'

'Christ, I'd forgotten all about it.'

'Cracking story,' said Moffat.

'How much further?' asked Knox. 'I can't remember.'

'There's a bend to the left then another to the right,' said Moffat. 'We better stop after the second one. It's only another couple of hundred yards.'

They parked, opening the doors and leaving them open. Knox produced two large rubber torches from the glove compartment. 'I was a cub scout,' he explained. 'Be prepared and all that.' He handed one torch to Rebus and kept the other. 'Moffat here eats his carrots, he doesn't need one. Right, what's the plan now?'

'Let's see how things look at the house, then I'll tell you.'

'Fair enough.'

They set off in a line. After about fifty yards, Rebus turned off his torch. It was no longer necessary: all the lights in and around the lodge seemed to be burning. They stopped just before the clearing, peering through what cover there was. The Saab was parked outside the front door. Its boot was open. Rebus turned to Moffat.

'Remember, there's a back door? Circle around and cover it.'

'Right.' The constable moved off the road and into the forest, disappearing from sight.

'Meantime, let's check the car first, then take a look through the windows.'

Knox nodded. They left their cover and crept forwards. The boot itself was empty. Nothing on the car's back seat either. Lights were on in the living room and the front bedroom, but there was no sign of anyone. Knox pointed with his torch towards the door. He tried the handle. The door opened a crack. He pushed it a little further. The hall was empty. They waited a moment, listening. There was a sudden eruption of noise, drums and guitar chords. Knox jumped back. Rebus rested a calming hand on his shoulder, then retreated to look again through the living room window. The stereo. He could see its LEDs pulsing. The cassette player, probably on automatic replay. A tape had been winding back while they'd approached the house. Now it was playing.

Early Stones. 'Paint It Black'. Rebus nodded. 'He's in there,' he said to himself. *My secret vice, Inspector.* One of many. At any rate, it meant he might not have heard the car's approach, and now the music was on again he might not even hear them entering the house.

So they entered. Moffat was covering the kitchen, so Rebus headed directly upstairs, Knox behind him. There was fine white powder on the wooden banister, leftovers from the dusting the house had been given by forensics. Up the stairs . . . and on to the landing. What was that smell? *What was that smell?*

'Petrol,' whispered Knox.

Yes, petrol. The bedroom door was closed. The music seemed louder up here than downstairs. Thump-thump-thump of drum and bass. Clashing guitar and sitar. And those cheesegrater vocals.

Petrol.

Rebus leaned back and kicked in the door. It swung open and stayed open. Rebus took in the scene. Gregor Jack standing there, and against the wall a bound and gagged figure, its face puffy, forehead bloody. Ronald Steele. Gagged? No, not exactly a gag. Scraps of paper seemed to fill his mouth, scraps torn from the Sunday papers on the bed, all the stories which had started with his plotting. Well, Jack had made him eat his words.

Petrol.

The can lay empty on its side. The room was reeking. Steele looked to have been drenched in the stuff, or was it just sweat? And Gregor Jack standing there, his face at first full of mischief, but then turning, turning, softening, softening into shame. Shame and guilt. Guilt at being caught.

All of this Rebus took in in a second. But it took less time than that for Jack to strike the match and drop it.

The carpet caught immediately, and then Jack was flying forwards, knocking Rebus off balance, powering past Knox, heading for the stairs. The flames were moving too fast. Too fast to do anything. Rebus grabbed Steele by his feet and started to drag him towards the door. Dragging him of necessity *through* the fire itself. If Steele *was* soaked in petrol ... Well, no time to think about that. But it was sweat, that was all. The fire licked at him, but it didn't suddenly engulf the body.

Out into the hallway. Knox was already pounding down the stairs, following Jack. The bedroom was an inferno now, the bed like a kind of pyre in the centre of it. Rebus went back and glanced in. The mounted cow's head above the bed had caught and was crackling. He grabbed the door handle and dragged the door shut, thanking God he hadn't kicked it off its hinges in the first place ...

It was a struggle, but he managed to haul Steele to his feet. Blood was caked on the face, and one eye had swollen shut. The other eye had tears in it. Paper was spilling from his mouth as he tried to speak. Rebus made a perfunctory attempt at loosening the knots. It was baler twine, and tight as tight could be. Christ, his head was hurting. He couldn't think why. He hefted the taller man on to his shoulder and started down the stairs.

At some point, Steele disgorged the paper from his mouth. His first words were: 'Your hair's on fire!'

So it was, at the nape of the neck. Rebus patted his head with his free hand. The back of his head was crispy, like strands of breakfast cereal. And something else: it was hurting like blazes.

They were at the bottom of the stairs now. Rebus dumped Steele on to the floor then straightened up. There was a tidal sound in his ears, and his eyes fogged over for a moment. His heart was thumping in sympathy with the rock music. 'I'll get a knife from the kitchen,' he said. Entering the kitchen, he saw that the back door was wide open. There were noises from outside, shouts, but indistinct. Then a figure stumbled into view. It was Moffat. He was holding both hands to his nose, covering the nose like a protective mask. Blood was pouring down his wrists and chin. He lifted the mask away to speak.

'The bastard butted me!' Flecks of blood flew from his mouth and his nostrils. 'Butted me!' You could tell he thought it wasn't fair play.

'You'll live,' said Rebus.

'The sergeant's gone after him.'

Rebus pointed to the hall behind him. 'Steele's in there. Find a knife and cut him loose, then both of you get out.' He pushed past Moffat and out of the back door. Light from the kitchen flooded the immediate scene, but beyond that was darkness. He'd dropped his torch up in the bedroom, and now cursed the fact. Then, eyes adjusting to the changing light, he ran across the small clearing and into the forest beyond.

More haste, less speed. He moved carefully past trunks and bushes and saplings. Briars tugged at him, but they were a minor nuisance. His main worry was that he didn't know where he was heading. The ground was sloping upwards, that much he could tell. As long as he kept moving upwards with it, he wouldn't be chasing his own tail. His foot caught on something and he fell against a tree. The breath left him. His shirt was wringing wet, his eyes stinging from a mixture of recent smoke and present sweat. He paused. He listened.

'Jack! Don't be stupid! Jack!'

It was Knox. Up ahead. A good distance ahead, but not impossible. Rebus took a deep breath and started walking.

Miraculously, he came out of the forest and into a larger clearing. The slope seemed steeper here, the ground sprawling with bracken and gorse and other low spiky plants. He caught a sudden flash of light: Knox's torch. Way over to the right of him and slightly uphill. Rebus began jogging, lifting his legs high to avoid the worst of the undergrowth. All the same, something kept tearing at his trouser-legs and his ankles. Stinging and scratching. Then there were patches of short grass, areas where quicker progress was possible – or would have been possible if he'd been fitter and younger. Ahead of him, the torch moved in a circle. The meaning was clear: Knox had lost his quarry. Instead of continuing to head for the beam of light, Rebus swung away from it. If it were possible for only two men to fan out, then that's what Rebus was trying to ensure they did, widening the arc of the search.

He came to the top of the rise, and the ground levelled out. He got the feeling that in daytime it would make a bleak picture. There was nothing here but stunted wilderness, hardly fit for the hardiest sheep. Way ahead a shadow rose into the sky, some hill-range or other. The wind, which had dried his shirt but chilled him to the marrow, now dropped. Jesus, his head was hurting. Like sunburn but a hundred times worse. He stared up at the sky. The outlines of the clouds were visible. The weather was clearing. A sound had replaced the whistling of the wind in his ears.

The sound of running water.

It grew louder as he moved forwards. He had lost Knox's torchlight now, and was conscious of being alone; conscious, too, that if he strayed too far, he might not find his way back. A route wrongly taken could leave him heading towards nothing but hill and forest. He glanced back. The line of trees was still just about visible, though the house lights beyond were not.

'Jack! Jack!' Knox's voice seemed miles away. Rebus decided that he would skirt round towards it. If Gregor Jack was out there, let him freeze to death. The rescue services would find him tomorrow . . .

The running water was much closer now, and the ground beneath his feet was becoming rockier, the vegetation sparse. The water was somewhere below him. He stopped again. The shapes and shades in front of him . . . they didn't make sense. It was as if the land were folding in on itself. Just then, a huge chunk of cloud moved away from the moon, the large, nearly full moon. There was light now, and Rebus saw that he was standing not four feet from a sheer drop of five or six yards, a drop into a dark, twisting river. There was a noise to his right. He turned his head towards it. A figure was staggering forwards, bent over nearly double from exhaustion, its arms swinging loose and almost touching the ground. An ape, he thought at first. He looks just like an ape.

Gregor Jack was panting hoarsely, almost moaning from effort. He wasn't watching where he was going; all he knew was that he had to keep moving.

'Gregor.'

The figure wheezed, the head jerking up. It came to a stop. Gregor Jack rose to his full height, arching his head to the sky. He lifted his tired arms and rested his hands on his waist, for all the world like a runner at the end of his race. One hand went instinctively to his hair, tidying it back into place. Then he bent forwards and put his hands on his knees, and the hair flopped forwards again. But his breathing was becoming steadier. Eventually he straightened up again. Rebus saw that he was smiling, showing his perfect teeth. He began shaking his head and chuckling. Rebus had heard the sound before from people who'd lost: lost everything from their freedom to a big bet or a game of five-a-side. They were laughing at circumstance.

Gregor's laughter collapsed into a cough. He slapped at his chest, then looked at Rebus and smiled again.

Then sprang.

Rebus's instinct was to dodge, but Jack was moving away from him. And both of them knew precisely where he was headed. As his foot touched the last inch of earth, he leapt out into the air, jumping feet first. A couple of seconds later came the sound of his body hitting the water. Rebus toed his way to the edge of the rock and looked down, but the cloud was closing in again overhead. The moonlight was lost. There was nothing to see.

Making their way back to Deer Lodge, there was no need for Knox's torch. The flames lit up the surrounding countryside. Glowing ash landed on the trees as they made their way through the woods. Rebus ran his fingers over the back of his head. The skin was stinging. But he got the feeling shock might have set in: the pain wasn't quite so bad as before. His ankles stung too – thistles, probably. He'd run through what had turned out to be a field full of them. There was no one near the house. Moffat and Steele were waiting by Knox's car.

'How good a swimmer is he?' Rebus asked Steele.

'Beggar?' Steele was massaging his untethered arms. 'Can't swim a stroke. We all learned at school, but his mum used to give him a note excusing him.'

'Why?'

Steele shrugged. 'She was scared he'd catch verrucas. How's the head, Inspector?'

'I won't need a haircut for a while.'

'What about Jack?' Moffat asked.

'He won't be needing one either.'

They searched for Gregor Jack's body the following morning. Not that Rebus was there to participate. He was in hospital and feeling dirty and unshaven – except for his head.

'If you have a problem with baldness,' one senior doctor told him, 'you could always wear a toupee till it grows back. Or a hat. Your scalp will be sensitive, too, so try to keep out of the sun.'

'Sun? What sun?'

But there was sun, during his time off work there was plenty of it. He stayed indoors, stayed underground, reading book after book, emerging for brief forays to the Royal Infirmary to have his dressings changed.

'I could do that for you,' Patience had told him.

'Never mix business and pleasure,' was Rebus's enigmatic response. In fact, there was a nurse up at the infirmary who had taken a shine to him, and he to her . . . Ach, it wouldn't go anywhere; it was just a bit of flirting. He wouldn't hurt Patience for the world.

Holmes visited, always with a dozen cans of something gassy. 'Hiya, baldie,' was the perennial greeting, even when the skinhead had become a suedehead, the suedehead longer still.

'What's the news?' asked Rebus.

Apart from the fact that Gregor Jack's body had still not been recovered, the big news was that the Farmer was off the booze after having been 'visited by the Lord' at some revivalist Baptist meeting.

'It's communion wine only from now on,' said Holmes. 'Mind you – ' pointing to Rebus's head, 'for a while there I thought maybe *you* were going to go Buddhist on us.'

'I might yet,' said Rebus. 'I might yet.'

The media clung to the Jack story, clung to the idea that he might still be alive. Rebus wondered about that, too. More, he still wondered why Jack had killed Elizabeth. Ronald Steele could shed no light on the problem. Apparently, Jack had spoken hardly a word to him all the time he'd held him captive . . . Well, that was Steele's story. Whatever *had* been said, it wasn't going any further.

All of which left Rebus with scenarios, with guesswork. He played out the scene time after time in his head – Jack arriving at the lay-by, and arguing with Elizabeth. Maybe she'd told him she wanted a divorce. Maybe the argument was over the brothel story. Or maybe there'd been something else. All Steele would say was that when he'd left her, she'd been waiting for her husband.

'I thought about hanging around and confronting him . . .'

'But?'

Steele shrugged. 'Cowardice. It's not doing something "wrong" that's the problem, Inspector, it's getting caught. Wouldn't you agree?'

'But if you *had* stayed . . .?'

Steele nodded. 'I know. Maybe Liz would have told Gregor to bugger off and have stuck with me instead. Maybe they'd both still be alive.'

If Steele hadn't fled from the lay-by ... *if* Gail Jack hadn't come north in the first place ... What then? Rebus was in no doubt: it would have worked out some other way, not necessarily any less painful a way. Fire and ice and skeletons in the closet. He wished he could have met Elizabeth Jack, just once, even though he had the feeling they wouldn't have got on ...

There was one more news story. It started as another rumour, but the rumour turned out to be a leak, and the leak was followed by notification: Great London Road was to undergo a programme of repair and refurbishment.

Which means, thought Rebus, I move in with Patience. To all intents, he already had.

'You don't have to sell your flat,' she told him. 'You could always rent it.'

'Rent it?'

'To students. Your street's half full of them as it is.' This was true. You saw the migration in the morning, down towards The Meadows carrying their satchels and ring-binders and supermarket carriers; back in the late afternoon (or late night) laden with books and ideas. The notion appealed. If he rented out his flat, he could pay Patience something towards living here with her.

'You're on,' he said.

He was back at work one full day when Great London Road Police Station caught fire. The building was razed to the ground.

ALSO BY IAN RANKIN

The Black Book

'Rankin is a master of his craft' *Independent On Sunday*

When a close colleague is brutally attacked, Inspector John Rebus is drawn into a case involving a hotel fire, an unidentified body, and a long forgotten night of terror and murder. Pursued by dangerous ghosts and tormented by the coded secrets of his colleague's notebook, Rebus must piece together a jigsaw no one – perhaps not even he – wants completed.

'James Ellroy once called Rankin "the Scottish James Ellroy" in jest. They have the darkness in common, certainly, but Rankin has more elegance' *Time Out*

'No one captures the noirish edge of the city as well as Rankin' *Sunday Telegraph*

ALSO BY IAN RANKIN

Let It Bleed

'Britain's No. 1 crime writer' *Daily Mirror*

Struggling through another Edinburgh winter Rebus finds himself sucked into a web of intrigue that throws up more questions than answers. Was the Lord Provost's daughter kidnapped or just another runaway? Why is a city councillor shredding documents that should have been waste paper years ago? And why on earth is Rebus invited to a clay pigeon shoot at the home of the Scottish Office's Permanent Secretary?

Sucked into the machine that is modern Scotland, Rebus confronts the fact that some of his enemies may be beyond justice.

'A master in his field' *Scotland On Sunday*

'First rate crime fiction with a fierce realism' *Sunday Telegraph*

ALSO BY IAN RANKIN

Black & Blue

'Rankin excels himself . . . a first-rate and gripping novel'
Sunday Times

Rebus is juggling four cases trying to nail one killer – who
might just lead back to the infamous Bible John. And he's doing
it under the scrutiny of an internal inquiry led by a man he has
just accused of taking backhanders from Glasgow's Mr Big.

Added to that there are TV cameras on his back investigating
a miscarriage of justice, making Rebus a criminal in the eyes of
a million or more viewers. Just one mistake is likely to mean
an unpleasant and not particularly speedy death or, worse still,
losing his job.

'A powerfully complex crime novel that offers a panoramic
portrait of modern Scotland' *Mail On Sunday*

Also by Ian Rankin
Witch Hunt

Witch is a terrorist – one of the best – but this job is going to test even her to the very limit. This time her cold calculation may desert her just when she needs it most.

On her tail are three very different detectives – one woman, two men. Two at the beginning of their careers; one staking a lifetime's experience on tracking Witch down, following a hunch to the end.

Dominic Elder's hunch takes him from England to Europe and back, but the clues that solve the biggest crimes, dig out the deepest secrets, are often the smallest ones – ones that only the junior sleuths, fresh out of spy school, pick up. But will he listen?

'When reading Rankin, you know you're in good hands' *Irish Times*

'Rankin is a master of his craft' *Independent On Sunday*

All Orion/Phoenix titles are available at your local bookshop or from the following address:

> Mail Order Department
> Littlehampton Book Services
> FREEPOST BR535
> Worthing, West Sussex, BN13 3BR
> *telephone* 01903 828503, *facsimile* 01903 828802
> e-mail MailOrders@lbsltd.co.uk
> (Please ensure that you include full postal address details)

Payment can be made either by credit/debit card (Visa, Mastercard, Access and Switch accepted) or by sending a £ Sterling cheque or postal order made payable to *Littlehampton Book Services*.
DO NOT SEND CASH OR CURRENCY

Please add the following to cover postage and packing

UK and BFPO:
£1.50 for the first book, and 50p for each additional book to a maximum of £3.50

Overseas and Eire:
£2.50 for the first book plus £1.00 for the second book and 50p for each additional book ordered

---

BLOCK CAPITALS PLEASE

name of cardholder ....

address of cardholder ....

....

....

postcode ....

delivery address
(if different from cardholder)

....

....

....

postcode ....

☐ I enclose my remittance for £ ....

☐ please debit my Mastercard/Visa/Access/Switch (delete as appropriate)

card number ☐☐☐☐☐☐☐☐☐☐☐☐☐☐☐☐

expiry date ☐☐☐☐   Switch issue no. ☐☐

signature ....

prices and availability are subject to change without notice